OUT OF NOWHERE

DORIS MORTMAN

OUT OF NOWHERE

Kensington Books
http://www.kensingtonbooks.com

KENSINGTON BOOKS are published by

Kensington Publishing Corp.
850 Third Avenue
New York, NY 10022

Library of Congress Card Catalog Number: 97-075385
ISBN 1-57566-301-5

First Printing: July, 1998
10 9 8 7 6 5 4 3 2 1

Printed in the United States of America

For my son, Alex.
To know him is to love him.

Background information doesn't come out of nowhere. It comes from people who've been generous with their time, their expertise, their support, or simply their friendship. Those who helped me with this book were wonderful, I'm grateful to each and every one of them, but they're only responsible for speaking to me. Any mistakes are mine.

I thank them all, especially David Fox, who opened so many doors and graciously escorted me through them, and Dan Starer, of Research for Writers, who answered all my questions, and then some. Thanks also to Lt. Jack Hackett, Commanding Officer of the Crime Scene Unit for the New York Police Department; Inspector Philip Pulaski, Commanding Officer of the Forensic Investigations Division, New York Police Department, Police Officer Craig Copius, Firearms Instructor, Hempstead Police Department; Inspector Bill Dempsey, Public Affairs Officer of the United States Marshals Service, Arlington, Virginia; and Suzanne McCarthy, R.N., at the Massachusetts General Hospital.

Thanks also to Peter Lampack, Sally McCartin, Walter Zacharius, Ann LaFarge, and all my other friends at Kensington. Loving thanks to my daughter, Lisa, and my mother, Annette Langfelder, for being such thoughtful readers. And thanks to David, for loving me back.

PROLOGUE

Miami, 1978

The gleaming white Crown Victoria rolled past the crowds that had gathered around the courthouse for the last day of the trial. Two other Fords, one in front, one behind, also slowed. Local police ringed the building, forming a solid blue line of defense. Stationed on surrounding rooftops and armed with an impressive arsenal of automatic weapons, deputies from the Special Operations Group, the paramilitary arm of the United States Marshals Service, stood guard, as the customized sedan and its escorts came to a stop. A government helicopter hovered overhead.

Five inspectors, their eyes shaded by mirrored sunglasses, jumped out of the two support vehicles, took their positions, and pointed high-powered rifles into the crowd, hoping to dissuade anyone who might be tempted to rush the main car. The rear door of that car opened and United States Marshal Samuel Bates stepped out, automatically scanned the immediate vicinity, then reached inside to assist the woman at the center of this storm.

Cynthia Stanton's hand shook as her feet touched the pavement, but only Marshal Bates could know that. Her outward demeanor projected absolute calm. Cries of support greeted her. "Go get 'em!" seemed to be the unanimous sentiment. Others shouted, "We're with you!" and "You've got guts!" They clamored for a wave or a smile or even a brief nod, but she issued no response. Instead, she turned and started up the wide stone staircase. Her determined step faltered only once: when a lone voice rose above the throng.

"Say hi to Ken."

Cynthia stiffened, her face paled, but she continued her march.

"Are you all right?" Bates asked. He kept his eyes straight ahead, denying the vicious heckler the satisfaction of knowing they had heard him.

"No, I'm not," Cynthia whispered, her voice staggering over a lump of anger and grief and fear. "But I've waited too long and sacrificed too much to care about trash like him. Today, the only thing I care about is the verdict." Her eyes watered, but remained fixed. "I need it to be just," she said softly. "For Ken."

Ken, Cynthia's older brother, a senior DEA agent working undercover, had been killed several months before—shortly after Cynthia agreed to be the star witness in the government's case against a group suspected of laundering money for Colombian cocaine distributors. Her name was not published in any newspaper, broadcast over any station, nor casually bandied about any of the offices involved. Yet somehow, they found out who she was. Ken's murder was a warning.

Instead of being intimidated by his death, Cynthia became infuriated. Many, particularly her family, urged her not to testify, to let the government make their case without her. When two other DEA agents—one who had infiltrated the cocaine manufacturing plant in Cali, Colombia, the other, inside one of the distribution networks in New York—also turned up dead, the pressure to back away increased. But so did Cynthia's sense of outrage.

In the late seventies, south Florida was the epicenter of America's burgeoning drug trade. Since Miami was the primary entry point for Colombian narcotics, Dade County was where the government focused its enforcement efforts. Ken's undercover task force was only part of a massive operation being staged by the Treasury Department, the Drug Enforcement Agency, and the Federal Prosecutor's Office. Many lives were lost. Other lives were ruined.

As they often did with gangster sagas, the press romanticized the story. Operation Laundry Day dominated the news for months. In the process, Cynthia Stanton became a national heroine.

She also became a target.

When Cynthia married Lionel Baird, everyone thought they were a perfect match: bright, Ivy-educated, good-looking, feet firmly planted on the fast track. But they were not a happily-ever-after couple. After their daughter, Erica, was born, and their initial chemistry abated, their differences sharpened. Cynthia wanted to combine marriage, family, and work. For Lionel, work and ambition presented a constant conflict with marriage and family. Work always won. When Cynthia discovered he had begun to fill his off-hours with his boss's daughter, she sued for divorce and full custody of their four-year-old daughter. She left Nathanson & Spelling to assume a high-level position at the prestigious Hudson National Bank. When her mother became ill, Cynthia went back to court and petitioned for permission to take her daughter to Miami so she could be near her parents.

Lionel, who'd married Nan Nathanson, didn't contest when a judge decreed that Erica was better off in Florida with her mother. His new wife exhibited little interest in his child. He was granted generous visitation rights and in the beginning exercised them almost religiously. But as the demands of his career and Nan Nathanson Baird's social agenda began to devour his time, his visits grew sporadic. Though he spoke to Erica almost every day, more and more of their weekends were canceled. There were command-performance cocktail parties, client dinners, country-club dances and golf outings he simply couldn't miss. "You understand, don't you, sweetheart?" became his mantra.

Cynthia's position as vice president of the Installment Loan Department at the Miami branch of the Hudson National Bank enabled her to buy a small, but graciously appointed home in a young, northern Miami community less than an hour from her job and ten minutes from the condominium of the elder Stantons. Cynthia's mother had recovered from her bout with cancer, and, for the moment, both parents were healthy.

Erica had lots of friends, a good school, a nearby park where she could run with her dog, Checkers, and plenty of beach to play on. She saw her grandparents nearly every day and her uncle Ken, often. Nana and Poppy took her to museums and concerts in both Miami and Palm Beach, shell collecting on the beach and for dinner at Joe's Stone Crabs every other Sunday during season. Uncle Ken took her to the movies and once, when she asked to see where he worked, gave her a tour of the always-hectic Miami Metro police station, which he felt would be far more exciting than the more subdued offices of the DEA. Erica loved it and immediately declared that when she grew up, she intended to be a policeman like her uncle.

For three years, Cynthia's life maintained a comfortable rhythm, due in large part to the presence of Ken. While Cynthia and her brother made a joke of their current singleness, they were grateful for the opportunity to experience a sibling renaissance. Always close as children, they fell back into a familiar pattern of mutual involvement. Cynthia, who vacillated between panic about the dangers inherent in his work and fascination, pestered him to tell her everything he could about his work at the DEA. Ken was equally curious about what was happening at the bank.

Things were going well; Hudson National was positively flush with surplus cash. In fact, almost every south Florida bank was experiencing a sudden but steady influx of currency. While that should have been good news, Cynthia sensed a universal undercurrent of nervousness. At first, she attributed the anxiety to the old saw that after every boom, there's a bust.

Then an alarm sounded. During one of her periodic reviews, she discovered large volumes of currency going in and out of certain accounts on a regular basis. Cash—big amounts in small denominations—was being deposited and several days later, wire-transferred to banks in Panama or Switzerland. A further check revealed that the names on those accounts were fictitious.

Perhaps it was because Ken had heightened her awareness of the growing presence of narcotics traffickers in Miami, but she immediately concluded that drugs were the root of this financial florescence and embarked on a quiet, but thorough investigation.

She began by checking whether these overly active accounts were in compliance with the Bank Secrecy Act. Designed to help track money-laundering activity, the BSA mandated reporting any currency transactions over $10,000 by the same person on the same day. What Cynthia found startled her. Many of the fictitious accounts escaped notice because the deposits were limited to $9,000, allowing them to slide in just under the level of required reporting. Other accounts ate cash like omnivores, gobbling up bills brought to the bank in shoe boxes, paper bags, and suitcases. The two bank officials who regularly received this booty rarely seemed to remember to file CTRs.

In her own department, large-denomination cashier's checks were being issued to individuals without any supporting loan documents. Reams of stolen or counterfeit securities had been accepted as collateral.

From her years at Nathanson & Spelling, Cynthia knew that most insider thefts targeted the blank certificate. She also knew that stealing securities was easy. The insider only had to fold the securities into a newspaper or stuff them into a briefcase or slip them in a pocket and he could walk out without detection. When—and if—the certificates were found to be missing, the brokerage house included them on one of the "hot lists" of stolen securities maintained by the National Crime Information Center, Interpol, or the Securities Validation Systems. Unfortunately, by that time, most of them had been converted into cash and were untraceable.

Apparently, along with their other shortcomings, several of Cynthia's colleagues had neglected to check the "hot list," because listed as collateral for a series of questionable loans was a batch of securities valued at several hundreds of thousands of dollars. According to the NCIC, these particular certificates had been stolen from Nathanson & Spelling.

For several days, Cynthia debated her next course of action. Recognizing that she probably had unearthed something very dirty, she went to Ken.

"The only way to win this battle against the cartels," he told Cynthia, "is to put a choke hold on the flow of drug dollars out of the country. If we make the movement of drug money as risky as trafficking in the drugs themselves, we might actually achieve deterrence."

Before she brought the matter to the DEA, however, Cynthia insisted on vetting her suspicions. "I'm not going to ruin anyone's life on a guess."

Ken helped by initiating a confidential credit check on Nathanson & Spelling employees. Many securities thieves are people whose debts to bookies or loan sharks make them vulnerable to organized-crime families who frighten them into stealing securities in exchange for the elimination of their due bills. On the suspicious list were several clerks, an accountant, and an in-house attorney with negative credit ratings. Two of these men had houses in foreclosure, cars about to be repossessed, and daily threats of suits by collection agencies.

By cross-checking with New York City Police data banks, it was discovered that a small-time loan shark being detained by the NYPD had one man's name on his list of debtors: a hard-luck gambler whose addiction had gotten out of hand.

Cynthia didn't recognize the man's name as someone she had known when she worked at Nathanson & Spelling, but again, she was loath to accuse him without absolute proof. On impulse, she called Lionel and asked him if he knew anything about a specific group of Nathanson & Spelling certificates on the "hot list."

"Only that they were stolen and properly reported. Why?"

"Because they've turned up down here as collateral against some highly suspicious loans."

"So they've been fenced. What do you expect me to do about it?"

Cynthia didn't like Lionel's tone. It was snippy, bordering on defensive.

"I expect you to be concerned," she retorted. "Narcotics money is being laundered by the truckload. The government is beginning to investigate. When Nathanson & Spelling's name came up, I thought I was doing you a favor by telling you. Especially since rumor has it you're about to have your name added to the firm's."

Over the past several years, Lionel had brought an enormous amount of business to Nathanson & Spelling. So much so that his mentor and father-in-law, Maurice Nathanson, felt pressured not only to make Lionel chief operating officer, but also to add his name to the firm's. Cynthia recalled laughing when her source said that Lionel had insisted upon star billing. When she heard he got his wish, she realized just how influential he had become.

"I thank you for your concern," Lionel said, "but if someone steals from us, we can hardly be considered responsible."

"The government might see it differently," Cynthia replied. "Ignorance is not always an adequate defense against charges of complicity."

"What the hell are you suggesting?"

"The thief, or thieves, might be on staff."

Lionel exploded. "That's ridiculous!"

Cynthia grappled with her conscience about how much she could, and should, tell Lionel. "Sometimes, when people hit hard times, they get desperate and do things they'd never do ordinarily."

There was a long silence. When Lionel spoke, he sounded guarded. "I gather you have some names you want to run by me?"

"I do." Cynthia prayed that his ambition hadn't consumed all of his principles. Rather than ask about one man, she went down the entire list, and even added a few names. Her heart stopped when Lionel singled out that particular man to defend.

"How could you even think that about him?" Lionel demanded.

"I agree he's a nice man," she said, hoping Lionel wouldn't

remember that he started at Nathanson & Spelling after Cynthia had left. "But I heard he's fallen on hard times."

"That's simply not true," Lionel said, more emphatically than was needed. "The last time I spoke to him, he was planning to take his wife on a vacation to Europe. What the hell is this all about?"

Cautiously, she explained that it was possible that this man had stolen the securities in question and might be tied in with people connected to the Colombian drug cartels.

"Oh, for goodness sake, Cynthia. Has the Florida sun addled your brain? I'm beginning to think that everyone who lives in or near Miami thinks the entire world is tied in to the Colombians."

She decided to ignore his sarcasm. "I never thought of you as naive, Lionel, but here's something for you to consider. Nathanson & Spelling has relationships with a host of Swiss banks. Some of them are suspected of doing business with major traffickers. If I were you, I'd watch out for anyone accepting uncommonly large cash payments or cashier's checks for large blocks of securities."

"And if I were you, Cynthia, I wouldn't butt my nose in where it doesn't belong!"

He went on to accuse her of creating this entire scenario simply to harass and embarrass him. He ranted about her still being bitter about their divorce, jealous of his new wife, and choking on sour grapes over his being made a name partner. At that, Cynthia hung up.

When she reported what she had gleaned from her conversation with Lionel—editing his fictional ravings—Ken did another check on their suspect and found that the man was miraculously debt-free. Moreover, he had an impressive balance in his bank account and had indeed taken his wife on a second honeymoon—to Switzerland.

When Ken suggested that now was the time to turn over whatever information she had uncovered to the U. S. Attorney's Office, Cynthia hesitated.

"The minute I give them what I have, my career is finished," she told Ken. "Why would anyone want a whistleblower on staff?"

As an agent about to go undercover to ferret out some of those involved in the drug trade, Ken was not happy with Cynthia's decision. As a brother, he couldn't disagree. Instead, he urged a compromise: before he left on assignment, he would arrange DEA surveillance of the bank officers in question. She would keep her eyes and ears open.

"You might pick up something that would lead to an arrest," he said, handing her the name of someone she could contact in his stead. "If we can catch them in direct, personal contact with anyone related to the cartel, we might not need you or your files."

Three months later, purely by chance, Cynthia overheard a conversation about one of the officers meeting Jaime Bastido later that afternoon. According to her contact at the DEA, Bastido was the primary launderer for the Espinosa cartel. The surveillance team was alerted.

They followed the bank officer to a parking lot. There, he met with Bastido, who was accompanied by two of his couriers. A large red suitcase was moved from one car to another. The DEA made an immediate arrest. When they searched Bastido, they found $2,000 in cash in his pockets, $25,000 jammed under the front seat of his car, and $426,000 in cashier's checks stuffed in his briefcase. When they opened the suitcase, they expected to find more cash, and perhaps a cache of stolen securities. Instead, they found fifty kilos of cocaine.

It was then that Cynthia Stanton's life changed forever. The investigation she embarked on nearly a year before had placed her on a treadmill that allowed no turning back. The files she had put together on the three officers of the Hudson National Bank proved that these people had committed gross violations of the Bank Security Act by not filing appropriate CTRs, as well as in some instances filing false reports. They had received large payoffs in return for accepting large, illegal cash deposits and percentages of transactions involving the issuance of cashier's checks in fictitious names. And they had accepted stock certificates they knew were stolen and facilitated the wire transfer of millions of dollars to offshore banks. This was valuable evidence, to be sure, but, as the lead attorney told Cynthia, without her corroboration, their case wasn't nearly as solid as it could be.

Cynthia suddenly realized that she had been so caught up in the investigation, she had neglected to consider its aftermath. On some level, she believed she could hand this information over to the authorities and walk away. The attorneys were saying that wasn't going to happen. For weeks, she agonized about what to do, kicking herself for allowing her crusader instincts to override her common sense. Then she thought about Ken; she hadn't heard from him in months. He was doing his part, she reasoned. She had to do hers. And besides, the sooner this was over, the sooner Ken could come home and life could return to normal.

When she agreed to be a witness, she discovered that her presence was required for two trials, not one. The government had cast a large net. In Miami, she would be testifying directly against her coworkers at Hudson. Indirectly, she would be helping to verify the government's case against Bastido as well as his Colombian employers. In New York, she would be testifying against the staffer from Nathanson & Spelling, as well as several mobsters from the crime families distributing Colombian Gold. Again, as if to absolve themselves, the attorneys took great pains to warn her of the consequences. People hold grudges, they told her. And the angrier they are, the longer they hold on to them.

She thought she understood. Then her brother's bullet-riddled body washed up on a beach in the Keys, and she realized she didn't understand anything except that she had put her life—and the lives of everyone close to her—in danger.

The day of her brother's funeral, a strange man hovered at the edge of the crowd. For a moment, it crossed Cynthia's mind that he might be an emissary from the Espinosa cartel, but she quickly dismissed that frightening thought. There were too many police guarding the proceedings. Besides, the cropped haircut, sunglasses, and navy blue suit pegged him as government issue, probably one of Ken's colleagues from the DEA. Later, back at her house, when Dan Connor flashed his silver star and announced himself as an inspector from the United States Marshals Service, Cynthia was stunned and confused. Like so many others, she believed that marshals had gone the way of the frontier.

Connor, accustomed to this lack of civilian recognition, explained that the Marshals Service is responsible for the security of all federal judicial proceedings. "And has been for two hundred years."

Basically, he and his deputies were going to protect Cynthia, Erica, and the Stantons during the trial. They also would make certain that Cynthia got to and from the courthouses without incident.

"Here in Miami," he said, "district personnel will transport you in our own surface vehicles. When you have to testify in New York, you'll be escorted by a team of inspectors."

She nodded, but she was barely paying attention. Numb from the day's events, all she wanted was to hasten Marshal Connor's exit so that she could be alone with her grief. It was when he mentioned moving her and Erica out of their house and into a safe house that she snapped to attention.

"We have to move you out of the Danger Zone as quickly as possible," he said crisply.

"I'm not going anywhere, and neither is my daughter!"

"You're a government witness. An endangered witness, to be precise. You need to be protected. Your brother's death should have made that clear." He spoke without any apparent compassion.

"Maybe what my brother's death showed me was that I shouldn't be a government witness," Cynthia said.

He was unmoved. "It's too late for that. They know what you know. Whether or not you swear to it in open court is irrelevant."

The logic of his words and the matter-of-fact tone of his voice terrified Cynthia because what he said was true. She had made her choice awhile ago; now she had to deal with the consequences of that decision.

Over the next several weeks, Cynthia met with Marshal Connor frequently, sometimes with her parents, sometimes without. Their discussions—many of which were quite heated—centered around the best way to protect her and her family. Inevitably, the subject of permanent relocation was raised.

"The United States Marshals Service operates the federal Witness Security Program," he said, anticipating the negative response he received. He waited for Cynthia's tirade to subside before continuing. Instead of trying to convince her, he surprised her by reminding her how serious relocation is.

"While the Marshals Service takes every precaution necessary to protect an individual," he warned, "your security ultimately depends on your willingness to follow our guidelines. Simply put, we can only protect you if you want to be protected."

Cynthia was not a foolish woman. The last thing she wanted was for her daughter, her parents—or herself—to wind up lying next to Ken.

"I understand how precarious my situation is," she said, her inner struggle obvious, "but I'm having trouble wrapping my arms around the notion of simply disappearing off the face of the earth."

"I assure you, there's nothing simple about it, Ms. Stanton. Nonetheless, I urge you to allow the process to move forward. You have a big decision to make and not much time in which to make it."

Cynthia's breath snagged. She hated when he raised the matter of time. It made her feel as if a large clock swung precipitously over her head. As each second passed, the clock descended a notch, spreading its shadow over her like a dark stain, blotting out life as it was, obliterating her as she was.

"Okay," she whispered, barely able to say the words for fear that the very act of speaking them would evaporate her on the spot. "Let's get on with it."

The next day, a local FBI agent brought a psychologist to her home for the first of many visits. Over the next several weeks, she, Erica, and the Stantons were asked hundreds of questions. Some were extremely personal, ranging from Cynthia's sexual proclivities and needs to whether or not Erica wet her bed. The main focus, however, was on relationships: mother-daughter, granddaughter-grandparents, father-daughter.

Cynthia asked if her parents could enter the program with her. She feared what might happen if she and Erica were taken from them so soon after Ken. Marshal Connor wouldn't commit to that, but if the Stantons didn't go with them, she and Erica would be able to maintain contact through secure mail-forwarding channels. He also assured her that they could speak to each other through secure telephone hookups. For Cynthia, that was a comfort.

After all the questions were asked and the last iota of information was obtained, the pertinent data was evaluated by the Office of Enforcement Operations in the Criminal Division at the Department of Justice. Their decisions surprised Cynthia.

"Having gone over the mitigating circumstances as well as their psychological profiles, it's believed that your parents can be adequately protected right here," Connor said.

He expected Cynthia to be relieved that he wasn't suggesting uprooting her parents. She was anything but.

"Ken told me about the violence associated with drug-related cases. He told me that these bastards adhered to some sick code about not only destroying witnesses, but their families as well." She could barely hold back the torrent of emotion that threatened to drown her. "They've already killed Ken. I couldn't live with the burden of knowing I've killed my parents as well."

Dan Connor would hate that as well, but his job was to convince her to do what the Service had decided was best.

"Cynthia, we can and would relocate your parents. I want you to know that. I also want you to know that the psychologist didn't recommend it for precisely the reason you cited. Ken's death, coupled with your participation in this trial, has upset their emotional equilibrium. We don't feel they could make the move successfully. Adjusting to a new environment and new identity would be too hard for people of their age, particularly in their current state of mind."

"I'd help them," she pleaded, fighting back her tears, trying so hard to appear strong and capable. "Please. If anything happened to them because of me . . ."

"Our belief is that those who might look to exact revenge on you will leave your parents alone because," he said with an uncharacteristic flush of discomfort, "they're older, and while their deaths would upset you, they wouldn't destroy you. Your daughter's would."

Cynthia felt as if someone had just injected her with ice water. For a long time, she simply stared into space.

"If my parents are going to stay in Florida, I'll go alone. Ricki can move to New York and live with her father."

Dan Connor winced. Her pain was so keen and so powerful, it reached out and strangled his heart. He shook his head. He didn't trust himself to speak.

"Lionel loves her. He'd do anything to protect her."

"I'm sure he would try, Cynthia, but he's not equipped, either mentally or physically, to offer Erica the kind of security she needs."

Cynthia looked as if he had handed her a shovel and asked her to dig her daughter's grave.

"He's her father." Her voice was almost too low to hear. "I can't ask her to give him up." Tears dotted Cynthia's cheeks. "I can't punish her. She didn't do anything wrong."

Her sobs struck Dan like bullets. He had been a marshal for twenty years. In the eight years since the official establishment of the Witness Security Program—and for some time before—he had relocated hundreds of people. Most were criminals who testified to avoid their own imprisonment; it was rare that any of them inspired anything even approaching sympathy. Cynthia was different. She was innocent.

"Often, we arrange and monitor visitations between a child and a nonprogram parent," he said, offering a straw.

Cynthia wiped her eyes with the back of her hand and listened attentively. She knew him well enough by now to be able to distinguish between what he thought was a good idea and what was not. She sensed what he would advise; also that this decision was hers to make.

"What's the downside to that?" she asked.

"Erica's safety depends on the world believing that she's dead.

With all due respect, Lionel Baird strikes me as a hotshot. I'm worried that he couldn't keep his mouth shut."

For the first time in months, Cynthia laughed. "You've got that right!"

He allowed her to enjoy her brief amusement. "Then it's settled. You and Erica will enter the program alone."

Her smile was gone in an instant as the realization of what she was agreeing to struck home. "What is this going to do to my daughter?"

He admired her for not asking what it was doing to do to her, yet was concerned for the very same reason. "Why don't you talk with Dr. Felder? She's better equipped to help with those matters."

The psychologist was sympathetic, but honest. Entering WITSEC, she told Cynthia, was a cataclysmic psychological event. It was the equivalent of suffering a social death and subsequent rebirth.

"To maintain your physical safety," Dr. Felder said, "WITSEC removes you from everything that defines your emotional security. You have to sever your relationships with relatives and friends, give up whatever status you held in your community, whatever profession gave you satisfaction, and whatever income gave you comfort. You'll be moved to a completely new community and asked to fit in without drawing attention to yourself. Worst of all, you'll be stripped of your names and whatever possessions might endanger you by that attachment."

"Like a pet?" Cynthia asked, thinking of Erica's beloved cocker spaniel, Checkers.

"I'm afraid so."

In her five years working with the Marshals Service, Hannah Felder had counseled many potential protected witnesses. None had affected her as deeply as Cynthia Stanton. This was not some two-bit criminal eager to escape jail time. This was a woman agonizing about how she was going to teach her child to lie after nine years of preaching to her about the truth. About how she was going to tell that child to give up not only her friends, her grandparents, and her father, but also her name. Her identity. Her place in the only universe she had ever known. She was going to have to train a child who by nature was open, to be secretive, one who had been expressive, to be enigmatic, one who had been a natural friend, to become a constant stranger.

"I wish I had a prescription for handling a situation as complex as the one you're about to face, but there is no magic pill, Cynthia, and I have too much respect for you to lie. The best advice I can give you is that children take their cues from their parents. If you do well, so will Erica. She's a curious young girl, so she's going to demand lots of explanations. Be as truthful as you can, even if at times that truth hurts. There should be honesty between the two of you even if there can't be honesty between the two of you and the rest of your new world. Because without truth, you permit a sense of mystery and mistrust to gain strength."

Cynthia thought long and hard about what Dr. Felder said. She also thought a great deal about the doctor's view on how to deal with the problem of Lionel.

"I can't justify taking her away from her father because of a choice I made," Cynthia said.

"Neither can you put her in harm's way to assuage your guilt."

"He's rich and powerful and despite what our marital history might say about him, he loves Erica and would put his own life on the line to protect her."

"Maybe so, but would his wife?"

Nan. Nan Nathanson Baird suddenly went from being a nuisance to a key element in the decision about Erica's future. Cynthia couldn't imagine her intentionally jeopardizing a child's life, but Nan wasn't Erica's mother. She might not feel bound by the same rules of silence.

It took awhile to work out the details and to convince Cynthia that WITSEC was indeed her only realistic option, but in the end, she agreed with Connor: painful as it was to deny Erica the right to see her father, it was in the best interests of everyone involved. Having made the decision, Cynthia refused to look back. She signed the Memorandum of Understanding which stipulates the rights and obligations of those in the program: they can't jeopardize their security by returning to the "Danger Zone" where they were recruited, having direct contact with people from their past without specific authorization, or ever mentioning anything that would give rise to suspicion. If they do, it's grounds for termination.

"WITSEC moves you to someplace far from the Danger Zone where we know you'll be safe," Dan explained. "You'll surrender all outward forms of identification such as birth certificate, driver's license, social security card, et cetera. We'll provide you with all new documentation as well as constant supervision by one of our deputies. We'll help you find a job, a home, and, most important, a new identity."

"What happens to *me?*" Cynthia asked. "Who I am and everything I've worked so hard to achieve? What happens to my life?"

"In essence," he said, gently, "you're erased."

By the end of the day, three employees of the Hudson National Bank, the vice president of the Installment Loan Department, a loan officer, and the head teller, had been convicted of laundering more than $90 million. Jaime Bastido and two of his two henchman were also found guilty as charged. As with the mobsters and the Nathanson & Spelling employee on trial in New York, all would serve lengthy prison sentences. Cynthia had expected to feel triumphant, but as she and Marshal Bates exited the courtroom and ran into a wall of reporters, all she felt was fear. *What if one of them works for the cartel?* It was the same thought that had been running through her brain many times a day—every day—since the trial began. It was why she couldn't wait for this ordeal to be over.

After uttering "no comment" a dozen times and shielding herself from the insistent glare of popping flashbulbs, she allowed Sam Bates to take her arm and escort her down a darkened hall. They came out through a side door. The police had cordoned off a small area and actually had managed to keep the crowds at bay.

The Crown Victoria and its entourage pulled away from the courthouse. As it moved down the street, an anonymous-looking car pulled out of a nearby parking lot and fell in behind them. A reporter whose car was in the same lot and, therefore, happened on the scene, took notice because his eye had caught something odd: the dark-colored car had no license plate. Moving quickly, he and his cameraman jumped into their vehicle and gave chase.

The procession moved up the turnpike like an out-of-step funeral cortege, traveling in a slow-speed, wavy line to Cynthia's home in North Miami. There, on Palmetto Drive, the Crown Victoria stopped. The government's lead car turned the corner onto Ibis Lane and stopped on the side of the house. The backup car parked at an angle in the middle of the street, preventing anyone from entering the area. The unlicensed car hovered a block behind. The reporter pulled into a driveway, hoping to deflect any unwanted attention. Everyone's eyes were trained on the house.

Marshal Bates accompanied Cynthia to the door. He opened the door and called inside to someone. Seconds later, the marshal who had been guarding the premises ushered Bates and Cynthia inside. Several minutes passed. Bates appeared at the door, apparently to watch a pool-maintenance man walk to the curb from the back of the house, get into his truck, and drive away. When he was assured all was as it should be, Sam Bates returned to his car. The Crown Victoria pulled away, followed by the backup car. The third car remained parked on the side.

Suddenly, the car with no license plate screeched toward the house. A window opened and something that looked like a cannon poked its deadly nose outside. There was a loud bang followed by a horrendous explosion. Flames engulfed the house. The car moved, fired a bomb into the government sedan, then sped away, leaving death and destruction in its wake.

That evening, the reporter who had watched the entire conflagration spoke to the nation from the charred remains of the Stanton home.

". . . less than three hours after the conclusion of the trial at which her testimony led to the conviction of six people involved in money laundering for the Colombian drug cartels, Cynthia Stanton, her nine-year-old daughter Erica, and two United States marshals were murdered, bringing Operation Laundry Day to a horrific end.

"Investigators remain tight-lipped, but we've learned from a reliable source that the DEA believes this was a contract hit paid for by the Espinosa cartel. Local officials, reminding everyone that Ms. Stanton also testified at a trial in New York which put more than a dozen people away, blame the mob. According to our source, whoever is responsible will pay dearly. Cynthia Stanton was a good samaritan and a concerned citizen. She stood up for what was right and wound up paying for it with her life as well as the lives of her brother and her daughter."

Cynthia and Erica watched the news inside a private government hangar at the back end of Miami International Airport. Tears filled Cynthia's eyes as she watched her house burst into flames. Erica's eyes appeared vacant.

Dan Connor turned off the television. It was important that his charges saw the report. They had to know that the Marshals Service had kept its word: to most of the world, they were dead; though the Espinosa cartel and the Mafia each knew they hadn't ordered the hit, they couldn't be certain that the other one hadn't. Eager as he was to have Cynthia and Erica on their way, he didn't rush their exit. They needed a few more minutes on the ground, in the past.

"It was all make-believe," Cynthia said, trying to reassure her silent daughter. "No one was there, Ricki, honey. No one was hurt."

Erica nodded, but her eyes remained glued to the darkened screen. She was so wan, so void of all expression, Cynthia wondered if she was in shock.

"What about Checkers?" Her eyes were closed. Cynthia couldn't tell if she was revisiting the horrible images of a few minutes ago or more pleasant memories of times spent with her beloved cocker spaniel.

"He's safe. Remember we asked Aña to mind him?" Erica's lower lip quivered at the mention of Aña Colon . They were best friends and had been from the day Erica and Cynthia moved in across the street. "Aña will take good care of him, Ricki."

Sam Bates interrupted. "Sorry, but the plane is ready. We have to go." He opened a door and led them out onto the tarmac.

Dan Connor embraced Cynthia. "Good luck," he said, giving her a quick hug, keeping his arm around her as they watched Erica lumber up the steps alongside Sam and enter the plane. "She'll be okay. It'll take time, but believe me, she'll be fine."

"I hope so," Cynthia said.

"She will." He smiled at Cynthia. "She's got you."

"And who've I got?" Cynthia asked. For the first time, she looked scared. Really scared.

"You've got me," Dan said, escorting her to the steps where Sam Bates waited. "You've got your daughter. And you've got Sam."

After a last good-bye, Cynthia hurried up the steps, frightened that if she lingered another second, she would never leave. Once onboard, she put on her bravest face.

They were an hour into the flight when Erica spoke.

"Where are we going?" she asked.

Cynthia, Dan, and Sam Bates had already spent hours explaining the purpose of WITSEC and why Cynthia had decided that she and Erica had to disappear. Ken's murder had made their predicament extremely vivid. Though she hated bringing it up again and again, Dr. Felder had told Cynthia that the wrenching reality of his death made it easier for Erica to understand their need to hide. Added to that were the months of inspectors living in their house; that had been a compromise worked out by Dan and Cynthia. Rather than disrupt their lives by going to a safe house, inspectors guarded them on-site. As Dan had told his superiors, "They'll be leaving that house and those lives soon enough."

"To a small town in the middle of nowhere," Cynthia said quietly. "Someplace where we can be safe."

"Does Daddy know we're safe?"

Cynthia didn't think there was anything left of her heart to break. Obviously there was.

"Yes, sweetheart. Now, he knows we're safe."

"Did you send him the pictures? I don't want him to forget us."

Cynthia and Erica had packed up a box of their favorite snapshots. Dan had promised he would give them to Lionel at their memorial services; Cynthia's parents had refused to hold a funeral. He would tell him they had been in a metal box which was why they weren't burned.

"Your daddy could never forget you, Ricki. He loves you. You have to remember that."

Erica nodded, but slowly, lifelessly. "I'm going to miss him." Her voice was a whisper laden with sorrow.

For several minutes, a ponderous silence canopied the cabin.

"What are our new names going to be?" she asked, her voice showing the strain of trying to act like a big girl.

"I have to change both of my names, but Marshal Dan said you can keep your first name if you'd like. You can be Erica something or other." Cynthia smiled, trying to make this horrible renomination process seem like a game.

Erica considered her options for a few moments, then looked at her mother, her expression serious and thoughtful. "No," she said. "We're in this together, Mommy. We're a team, you and me. Remember? That's what you said." Cynthia nodded. She couldn't speak. "If you're changing your first name, so am I."

That decided, she returned her attention to the clouds outside the plane. Just then, they were brighter and easier to deal with than the darker clouds that hovered inside the cabin.

"Will we have to hide forever?" she asked after awhile.

Unable to respond, Cynthia looked to the marshal in charge to answer Erica.

Samuel Bates knew that in cases like this, although a number of people had been convicted and sent away, others who had been tangentially involved roamed free. Some would retreat into silent anonymity, happy that their participation—whether great or minimal—hadn't landed them in a federal prison. Some might remain anonymous, far from happy, and definitely not silent.

It could be years before the Service would deem it safe for Erica and Cynthia to leave the program, if ever. Cynthia was looking to him for hope. Since he also knew that at this moment, particularly with a young child, even the slightest equivocation on his part could cost them their lives, he offered her none.

He spoke bluntly and firmly. "Yes," he said to Erica. "You and your mother have to hide forever."

CHAPTER

ONE

New York City. Twenty years later.

A young woman lay at the foot of an unmade bed. Her body, naked and mutilated, sprawled immodestly, face up. Her legs were spread wide and open, but there was nothing inviting about the pose. Fresh blood formed a dark pool beneath her groin and stained her thighs. Dozens of deep, angry gashes from something sharp marred her flesh. Her long, blond hair had been hacked off and stuffed in her mouth like a gag. One breast listed to the left, the other had been savagely excised by a sadistic butcher. Blood tattooed the room, splattered in hideous patterns on walls, bed linens, furniture, and carpet. Broken lamps and overturned chairs told of a struggle. Every light in the apartment was on, and from speakers housed in a living-room cabinet, Wagner's *Die Walküre* screamed in obscene accompaniment.

The uniformed officers, who had protected the scene and, therefore, the integrity of the evidence, briefed the Homicide detectives from the Nineteenth Precinct, then moved out into the hall to calm the neighbors. When the team from the Crime Scene Unit arrived, they and the detectives from the One-Nine began their initial walk-through.

Hands stuffed in pockets or clasped behind their backs, the group surveyed the area, careful not to touch, smudge, or dislodge anything. Once everyone had an overview of the crime, the bureau detectives started to screen witnesses and gather information, the forensics team began the painstaking task of collecting evidence.

An investigator from the Medical Examiner's Office stood by as the assisting CSU detective started sketching the layout of the living room. The lead CSU detective, who caught the case, stood in the doorway of the bedroom and conducted a mental survey of the area before entering with a camera.

Tall and slim in her navy coveralls, her shiny auburn hair neatly restrained by a backward baseball cap, Amanda Maxwell worked quickly to preserve the essential history of the scene. She moved inside and began the overall photographs, looking at and away from the site of the event. These would provide the investigators, as well as the attorneys for both sides, eye-level views that would identify the relative location of evidence to be collected.

Overalls and eye-level orientation shots completed, she paused and determined a primary field of view. Once established, she set down a two-foot-square sheet of photo mat board that acted as a perspective grid. Making certain that the grid lay flat on the floor, she climbed atop a small stool that was part of her equipment bag, shifted the flash on her camera upward so the light would bounce off the ceiling, then, finally, looked at the victim.

Friends never understood how she could do this. They wondered why she never got sick or fainted or cried at the inhuman aftermath of violent human behavior. She tried to explain, but they couldn't understand: a lens created distance. She was there, but removed. The body—no matter what condition it was in—was the subject, the murder scene the background, her camera an instrument for collecting evidence. Difficult as it was for civilians to comprehend, police work advanced on intellect, instinct, objectivity, and dogged insistence. Emotion had no place at a crime scene; it distorted one's vision and blurred the facts.

While her colleagues watched, she photographed the victim and her surroundings. By elevating the camera, Amanda ensured the accuracy of grid measurements used by the lab to prepare a scale map. Having completed the basics, she began the tedious work of documenting the scene and the crime, frame by frame. First, she circled the body, moving from the head clockwise to the right arm, to the feet, then to the left arm, shooting up, down, and across. Then she moved in to record the wounds.

This was the most difficult part of her job. Confronting such callous and extreme violation was a grisly task that never got easier. Amanda thought that was because the technology of violence was advancing, and the purveyors of violence were becoming more creative. Every day, there were new weapons, new poisons, new and increasingly horrible ways to torture the flesh. Thankfully, most people rarely confronted death. Since memory was compassionate, over time the images associated with death, no matter how disturbing or painful, softened into fuzzy remembrances of a still and silent body, lying in a neat bed or a satin-lined coffin. Those who saw death every day knew it was far more complicated than that, and far uglier. Death smelled and offended. It demanded a brutish invasion of privacy that would have been unheard of and unconscionable before the cessation of life. And it stripped away any illusions one might have about the absolute, innate goodness of man; evil lurked inside the best of us.

Moving with a practiced step, Amanda hid behind her lens and clicked off shots from every conceivable angle, mapping every square inch, including minute details like dust on a nightstand, a torn dust ruffle, a dislodged telephone receiver. After each picture, she stopped to properly document it. Exposure 4, 325 E. 78th, Apt 20A. Bedroom from south wall. Victim, overhead. Exposure 17, 325 E. 78th, Apt. 20A. Close-up of victim's genital area. Exposure 45, 325 E. 78th, Apt. 20A. Victim's abdomen. Ultraviolet filter. Exposure 52, 325 E. 78th, Apt 20A. Bathroom off bedroom. Bloodstains: floor, toilet, sink, shower curtain. Wide-angle lens.

She worked quickly and thoroughly, changing perspective, making notes. Using a selection of lenses and filters, her photographs ranged from the buttons on the stereo to the food in the refrigerator, to the gaping hole where the woman's right breast had been cut away, to the breast itself, which they found tossed in the toilet, discarded as carelessly as a dirty tissue. When she had completed her routine, the medical examiner's team chalked an outline of the body, removed it, and Amanda began the procedure all over again. By repeating the same shots with the chalk image—without the chaos that always occurred when the body was still present—she was assured of having one good negative out of two shots of the same scene.

"Hey, Max!" Pete Doyle groused impatiently. He had sketched the rest of the apartment and taken measurements. He wanted to complete that part of his job in the bedroom and adjoining bathroom but couldn't start until she finished. "Anytime this century."

Amanda remained unhurried. She finished the roll, riffled through her notes, and took a quick look around to assure herself that she hadn't missed anything.

"The only thing you haven't photographed is me," Pete said. "And I'm growing a beard, for crissakes!"

"Good! It'll cover your face." As she passed him, she playfully pinched Pete's cheek.

He grabbed the bill of her NYPD baseball cap and turned it face front. "If you're gonna wear the cap, wear it right, dammit! You look like a Met fan!"

Amanda shook her head and looked at him pitifully. "Forget it, Pete. No amount of sweet talk is going to get me to go to bed with you."

The investigator from the ME's Office and a third detective from the CSU, who had come to replace Amanda, laughed. Pete's unabashed lusting was the joke of the CSU. Pete was approaching forty and fighting hard to maintain a self-promoted reputation as a ladies' man. Amanda was in her late twenties and had made it clear from the start that she didn't date where she worked.

"Max." Harry Benson, from CSU handed her a slip of paper with an address on it. "The lieutenant wants you to head over to the One-Seven. Cleland's over there. He's caught a multiple homicide and requested your camera on-site."

Although everyone in the CSU was qualified to photograph crime scenes, as well as collect other forms of forensic evidence, Amanda was known as the best "shooter" in the unit. It wasn't unusual for her to be called in on cases where the lead detective believed that photographs would not only help in the investigation of the crime, but also in the conviction of the perpetrator.

"Bye, guys!" she said as she packed up her equipment, slung one bulky bag over her shoulder, gripped another, and started for the door.

"See you back at the house, Max," Harry said, as he set to work bagging the victim's bloody underpants. "And don't worry, after we finish here, we'll mend Pete's broken heart with a couple of beers."

Amanda eyed Pete with a critical gaze. "Just what that body needs is a few more beers."

"Love ya, babe," Pete said, sucking in his gut as he saluted her.

Amanda laughed and blew him a kiss. "Yeh. Me too you."

Walter Clarke's office was a showcase for the anal retentive. There wasn't a speck of dust or a dulled pencil point or an errant paper clip—ever. The glass partition that separated the head of New York City's Crime Scene Unit from his detectives sparkled. His furniture always looked freshly polished. And it never moved. Even after large meetings, everything was in its designated place, as if Clarke had nailed it to the floor—which some members of his squad thought he had. He was a man who believed in the sanctity of order. "A well-ordered home breeds a well-ordered mind" was his favorite saying. Some believed it was precisely that philosophy that had greased his rise to the top and made him such a good lieutenant. Others thought it made him a pain in the neck.

As Amanda approached Clarke's office, she could see he was busy. The two precinct detectives who'd worked the case that morning were there as well as a private investigator she'd seen at several different precincts. It amused her to see someone with a stubble, a leather jacket, and an open shirt slouched in a chair in the *sanctum sanitorum,* as the lieutenant's crib was called. Usually, the instant one passed through that sanitized portal, postures automatically straightened, ties were knotted, attitudes were crisp and "at attention." Clarke spotted her and waved her inside.

"Got anything, Max?" he asked, eyeing the thick folder under her arm.

Amanda looked from the Chief to the man lounging in the chair. She didn't discuss police business in front of strangers.

"Jake Fowler," Walter said, correctly interpreting her silence. "He's a PI who was tailing the victim."

Jake Fowler curled his lip at Clarke's condescending tone. He understood that most detectives, forensic and precinct, preferred to work without outside interference and, on the whole, were not exactly fans of private investigators, but still.

"Vivian Wyland was a rich girl from North Carolina with a wild streak and a drinking problem," he said, directing his explanation exclusively to Amanda.

He had royal blue eyes that focused sharply on a target, then fixed and held. Though his overall manner was casual, Amanda sensed it was a calculated pose, meant to disarm. He was clearly taking her measure, just as she was taking his.

"Her parents had lost touch with her and were worried that something bad might happen. Turns out they were right."

"The preliminary tox reports attest to the drinking problem," Caleb Green, the lead detective, said. "Her blood alcohol was stratospheric."

"We've got witnesses who place her at some cowboy bar in the East Thirties. The kind of trashy joint that gets a gimmick and is suddenly chic." Green's partner, Mickey Moran rolled his eyes. He was a meat-and-potatoes guy who grew up in Queens, married his high school sweetheart, served in the Marines before joining the police force, visited his parents regularly, drank beer from a bottle, hung an American flag outside his home on national holidays, and took pride in being one of the good guys. He didn't understand chic—trashy or otherwise.

"Could be that her killer was a regular," Amanda said.

She opened her folder, extracted four enlarged photographs, and laid them out in front of Walter. The detectives moved around the desk so they could view them right side up. Fowler stayed where he was. His eyes traveled between the photographs and the woman who had taken them. It was difficult to tell which fascinated him more.

Amanda pointed to a faint rectangle in the center of what she described as abdominal flesh. "Since this case presented itself as a probable rape, I took a number of body shots with a UV filter. Often, it produces images of otherwise invisible materials or wounds. This," she said, tracing the outline of the rectangle, "appears to be the imprint of a belt buckle. With a Western motif," she added pointedly.

"He must've been banging away pretty heavy to leave a print like that," Caleb muttered.

Mickey snorted in agreement, opened his notebook, and flipped through his notes. "According to one of the witnesses, the girl left The Hitching Post at about 3 A.M. draped over some muscle-bound dude of about thirtysomething."

"What was this dude dressed like?" Jake asked. "Wall Street? Bridge and Tunnel?"

Mickey grunted. "Gimme a break, Fowler. What d'ya think he was wearing? A three-piece suit and a bowler? He was in jeans and boots. Just like the rest of the make-believe cowboys."

Amanda stifled a smile. Mickey barely tolerated PIs. The fact that he didn't come at Jake with his usual barrage of insults was a sign of respect, albeit grudging.

"Nice going, Max," Caleb said, still studying the photograph. "This baby stays under wraps."

The photograph was powerful evidence. Not only could it identify a killer, but it was certain to move a jury. The last thing this group wanted was for their suspect to read about this in the newspapers and toss the buckle.

"Do you want one, Walter?" Amanda asked, already returning the remaining photographs to her folder.

"Nope. Caleb and Mickey are working the case. You hold on to the others. The fewer who know about this the better."

"What about me?" Jake had his hand out.

Amanda looked to Walter, who shook his head, then leaned on his desk, bringing his face close to Jake's. His eyes narrowed, and his lips assumed a hard line.

"If I hear so much as a whisper about this on the street, Jake, I'll have your ass as well as your license. Got it?"

Jake pushed himself up and out of his chair, got to the door, and shrugged. "I'm only trying to help."

"Yeah, right!" Mickey snickered. "Don't call us, we'll call you."

"Anytime, big fella," Jake said as he closed the door behind him.

Walter watched him go with a smile that approached affectionate.

"Anyone want to fill me in?" Amanda asked, clearly confused.

"Jake's a cowboy," Caleb said, fully aware of the irony in that description. "He likes to ride into the middle of a problem, solve it single-handedly, kick up some dust, and get out of town."

"He's not what you'd call a team player," Mickey added.

"Jake's brilliant and talented, tenacious almost to a fault, unbelievably principled, and can be quite charming—when he wants to be," Walter said, summing up.

Amanda looked from one to the other, intrigued. "But?"

"The man never met a rule he didn't want to break," Caleb said.

A sly grin insinuated itself on Walter's face. "Which is what makes him one of the best PIs in the business!"

Amanda raced up the steps of the West Side brownstone where she lived, keys already jangling in her hand. She unlocked the front door, emptied her mailbox, and jogged up three flights to her apartment. It had been a long day. She would have loved a leisurely soak, but all time would allow was a quick shower. She pulled three pairs of panty hose off the shower rod where they had been drying, turned on the water, and began stripping off her clothes as she ran into the living room to check her messages.

In her bedroom, she opened the closet, studied its contents. Which of her three Little Black Dresses would she wear this evening? she wondered. This recent flurry of fancy dinners was beginning to point out major gaps in her wardrobe. Before, her social life didn't cry out for anything *Vogue;* she got by on the same clothes she used for work: slacks, sweaters, tee shirts, and blazers. The last several months had been different. She closed her eyes, snatched one at random, brought it into the bathroom, and hung it on the back of the door to steam out any possible wrinkles.

Amanda's shower was more than a luxury; at the end of every workday, she needed to scrub off the smell that insisted upon clinging to her. Perfume didn't work. Neither did simply soaping her body. The smell crept into the hollow center of her hair shafts and deep into her sinuses. For the sinuses, she kept strong peppermints in the darkroom and munched on them most of the day. For her hair, she used a lightly scented lemon shampoo.

Fortunately, her shoulder-length hair was sleek, straight, and well cut; it didn't demand endless blow-drying. She didn't like wearing a lot of makeup and there, too, she was lucky. Her skin was clear and creamy; foundation was more of a concession to convention than a requirement. She did use a light pink blush and, at night, lined, shadowed, and mascaraed her large, cocoa brown eyes. Her favorite feature was her mouth: Her lips were full, and though she enjoyed coloring them, she only owned four lipsticks—russet, wine red, pink/brown, and light mauve. Tonight felt wine red.

She slipped into her dress—black jersey, mandarin neck, long sleeves—added a pair of black suede shoes, pearl studs, and a gold watch that still looked strange on her wrist. Despite her protests, he had insisted upon giving it to her for her birthday; she only wore it when she saw him.

Downstairs, she walked to the corner of Eighty-ninth and Columbus and hailed a cab.

"The Pierre, please. Sixtieth and Fifth."

As they pulled away from the curb, she looked to see if anyone was watching her departure. Out of the corner of her eye, she thought she saw a man beneath a restaurant awning turn and follow the progress of the car. Quickly, she found her compact, flipped open the top and watched him watching her through the mirror. It was dark, and he was hidden in the shadows. He could have been waiting for a friend. Or a cab. He could have been taking refuge from the cold. Or stalking her.

The taxi stopped in front of the Pierre. She got out, walked quickly to the entrance, through the lobby to the elevators. Alone in the car, she pressed four and twelve. She got out at four and waited a few minutes before taking another elevator down to where she could exit on the Sixtieth Street side of the hotel. She waited inside while the doorman hailed her a cab, then rushed from the building into the car, her hand shielding her face from the wind.

"Tavern on the Green." Again, she scrutinized the street. This time, no one seemed to be paying attention.

In the parking lot of the famous tourist haven, she exited the taxi and was immediately spirited into a sleek, black limousine.

"Good evening, Miss Maxwell."

"Good evening, Thompson. Where to tonight?"

La Crémaillère was a charming country restaurant situated on the border of New York and Connecticut. They had been here before, so there was no need for Amanda to identify herself. Robert, the owner, greeted her effusively and immediately escorted her to a table in the front room, near the fireplace.

The gentleman she had come to see stood and watched her progress. He was a dignified-looking man with salt-and-pepper hair and that polished, well-tended look so prevalent among the very rich. A broad smile enlivened his face as she approached. He embraced her warmly. When she was seated, he fussed to make sure she was comfortable. A waiter poured her some wine.

She took a sip, nodded her satisfaction to the waiter, and tipped her glass toward her host. "Excellent! As always."

"You're sure you like it?"

"I'm sure."

"Did you have any trouble getting here?"

"None at all." She found his nervousness endearing. It was as if he still couldn't believe she was in his life.

"You look very beautiful this evening." His hand reached across the table, found hers, and squeezed it. "And thank you for wearing the watch. I know you hate it."

She laughed. "I don't hate it. It's just . . . well, not quite my style," she said.

"And what exactly is your style?"

Amanda glanced at his expensive Italian suit, his bespoke shirt, silk tie, thick gold cuff links and perfectly buffed nails. Almost reflexively, she looked at her own hands, unmanicured and bare except for the watch. Her dress, which had put a big dent in her paycheck, probably didn't cost as much as his cologne.

"Simple, unadorned, frugal and more often than not, police issue," she said without defense.

"You're far too special a woman to be unadorned."

"It's what I'm used to. Accessories make me uncomfortable."

"You could learn to love pretty things," he said gently, trying not to push.

"Maybe, but right now, my life doesn't exactly lend itself to furs and jewels."

"That could change, you know. All you have to do is think seriously about my offer to come into the business."

"I did think about it," she said.

"Seriously?"

She pursed her lips in concern. He had leaped to the conclusion that she was going to accept. That thought obviously pleased him. "I know it's hard for you to believe," she said, sorry to disappoint him, "but I like what I do."

"I'm not asking you to give up photography. Your work is really quite spectacular. It's the . . . police stuff ." He literally squirmed.

Amanda smiled in sympathy. She couldn't blame him for finding her job so distasteful. Why would anyone encourage spending one's life in the company of dead bodies. "I haven't dismissed the idea completely, though. I've been reading the material you gave me and studying the business section of the *Times.*"

"And?" he said eagerly.

"I'm interested, but," she cautioned, "not hooked."

"That just means I have to work harder at convincing you."

"Let's go slow with that, okay?" She leaned over and caressed his cheek. He held her hand there. "For now, I'd rather concentrate on us."

"Whatever you want," he said in a voice raspy with emotion.

If she needed time, he would give it to her; he was grateful to have it to give. And if, after time had passed she still felt the same way, he would accept her decision rather than doing what he usually did, which was to bulldoze over her concerns and/or personal wishes and dismiss them as irrelevant. Though he was accustomed to having people compliment him on his strengths, which he believed were many, he wasn't unaware of his faults. He knew he was arrogant, demanding, egotistical, often disrespectful and highly impatient. Also, like many men who had achieved his astonishing level of success, he believed most people's feelings and opinions were secondary to his.

But this lovely young woman wasn't most people. He was Lionel Baird. And Amanda was his daughter.

She had reentered his life six months before on a steamy Wednesday night in August. He was in the bar at the Four Seasons sipping a very cold vodka as he waited for his estranged wife, Pamela Richard-

son Baird. Their appointment was for six-thirty. It was nearly seven.
He decided to give her until the hour, then he intended to leave.
Suddenly, a young woman slid into the chair opposite him.

"I'm sorry, but I'm expecting someone," he said crisply.

"I know."

"Well, then, if you don't mind . . ."

"I'd like you to take a walk with me," she said softly.

He could see she was nervous, but determined. That made him
nervous. He was an extremely powerful, highly visible man. There
were a lot of kooks in this world. For all he knew, she was a member
of a cult or some militant do-good group that had selected him as
their villain of the month. Either that, or she was an uptown hooker
with a unique method of solicitation.

"If you don't get up and walk away from this table," he snarled,
"I'll signal my bodyguard, and he will escort you outside. I assure
you, it will not be a pleasant experience."

She didn't flinch. Instead, she placed a fresh, pink camellia in
front of him. His eyes narrowed. A few seconds later, a memory
gripped him. He had bought a pink camellia only once in his life:
for his daughter . . . the last time she was in New York.

"Who the hell are you? And what do you want?"

"I'll tell you who I am—outside."

"I don't go anywhere without my bodyguard."

She shrugged. "Fine. He can walk behind us or in front of us.
He can't walk with us."

Overwhelmed by curiosity—and impressed with the fact that she
wasn't at all cowed by him—Lionel paid the check, signaled for
Bruno to follow them, and did what the young woman asked. With
a vigilant, square-bodied Bruno trailing several paces behind, they
left the restaurant, turned right and then right again, onto Park
Avenue. She didn't look like a terrorist with her summery dress
clinging to her shapely body and her hair blowing in the gentle
evening breeze. But, he reminded himself, danger didn't always have
an ugly face.

"Let's get to the point, shall we? I have an appointment."

"No, you don't," she said. "I'm the one who called your house
and told your butler Mrs. Baird wanted to meet you."

Lionel stopped and looked at her. "Who are you?" he demanded
again.

"I'll let you figure that out," she said mysteriously. "But let's
keep walking. I don't want to attract an audience."

As they strolled up Park Avenue, she reminisced about things only his daughter could have known, because they were moments only he and his daughter shared: the day he took her to Yankee Stadium and they almost caught a foul ball; the day he taught her to skim rocks on the lake in Central Park; the day she brought him to school in Miami for show-and-tell.

"I wanted my friends to know I really did have a father," the young woman said softly.

Slowly, Lionel turned to her. He remained wary, but she had his full attention.

"You bought me that pink camellia because you said it matched the color of my dress. That was the day you took me to the ballet for the first time. We saw *Swan Lake*."

Lionel grabbed her arm. He was trembling with emotion. His eyes bored into hers. "How do you know these things?"

"I know because I was there," she said quietly. "I'm your daughter, Ricki."

Lionel shook his head in disbelief. Anger flooded his eyes. "What is this? Some kind of cruel joke! My daughter's dead!"

Hearing Lionel's voice, Bruno started for them. "Tell him to stay back," she insisted.

"How dare you tell me what to do!" Lionel glared at her. His face was flushed with bluster and defiance. Inside, however, he was frightened, and not because he believed she posed a threat. It was vague and fleeting, like a needle piercing skin, but deep inside a place that had been numb for twenty years, he felt an awakening.

"I'm not going to rob you or hurt you," she said. "Now tell him to back off!"

Lionel hesitated, then held up his hand, halting the beefy man's approach.

"Thank you," she said.

"Just get on with it," he ordered.

She reached into her handbag and pulled out a small toy which she handed to Lionel. It was a tiny caboose from a set of electric trains. Lionel gasped. He had bought this for his daughter at F.A.O. Schwarz. She was about four. They had been talking about names. He had told her she was named Erica after his mother, Frederica. When she asked after whom he was named, he had answered, "the trains." When she didn't understand, he took her into the huge toy store and showed her an enormous display of electric trains, all imprinted with the name Lionel. Then he let her select whichever car she wanted. She picked the little red caboose.

"I wasn't supposed to take anything with me," the woman claiming to be his Ricki said, "but I made Mom sew this into my pillow. It's been with me all along."

Lionel caressed the toy in his hand, unwilling to let his emotions spill out onto his face. When he looked at her again, he was ashen.

"I need a drink," he said gruffly. "And we need to talk."

They returned to the Four Seasons, where he arranged for a table in the far corner of the Pool room.

"Why?" he said after he had fortified himself with vodka. "Why did you let me believe that you were dead?"

"It was the only way Mom and I would be safe."

He was quiet, clearly trying to absorb the impact of her reappearance, as well as the knowledge that he had been excluded from this monumental decision to disappear.

"Did your mother think I didn't love you?" he asked. "That I wouldn't miss you? Or her?"

Amanda could see how hurt he was. And confused. She didn't blame him, but the decision hadn't been hers to make. And she was not about to second-guess her mother, not after all they'd been through.

"I was devastated when I heard that you and your mother had been killed," Lionel said plainly.

Actually, his grief had destroyed his second marriage. Nan couldn't understand the length of his mourning, because she couldn't fathom the enormity of his loss, particularly his grief over Cynthia. Despite their divorce, Lionel considered Cynthia and Erica his family. Cynthia was and would always be the love of his life; the divorce had been her choice, not his. Nan was, and always had been, a conduit for his ambition. It all seemed quite foolish now, but he supposed that then, he fantasized that once he had attained senior partner status at Nathanson & Spelling, Nan would evaporate, he would make things right with Cynthia, she and Erica would return to him, and life would be perfect. Then, suddenly, in a fiery instant that shook him to his core, his family—and his fantasy—were gone.

"I never got over it."

Lionel's daughter reached across the table and touched his hand. "I missed you too," she said. "Every day of my life."

★ ★ ★

In the months that followed, father and daughter met frequently. Lionel was obsessed with every facet of Amanda's life in hiding. She explained about WITSEC and how she and Cynthia eventually wound up in the Northwest, living as Beth and Amanda Maxwell. She told him their only contact with their past were letters to and from the Stantons. And she told him about the United States marshal she came to call Uncle Sam.

She wouldn't tell him Sam's last name, the names she and her mother had used or the towns they had lived in before Washington, what Cynthia was doing or where she was living now.

Lionel took that as a sign that she still didn't trust him and, once again, groused that he should have been told the truth, that Uncle Sam, whoever he was, was wrong, that he would have kept their secret no matter what pressure had been brought to bear.

Another time, gentle prodding elicited the news that over the years, Uncle Sam and Beth had fallen in love. Lionel felt oddly jealous.

He stifled his impulse to ask other questions, like how did Amanda feel about her mother and this marshal, had Beth ever been with anyone else or was Sam simply convenient, et cetera, and instead, inquired about Amanda's love life.

Amanda answered quite matter-of-factly: "I don't have one."

"Why not?"

"You have to trust someone before you can love them, and, as you can imagine, I'm not big on trusting."

With a humorless, ironic laugh, Lionel agreed. He had eliminated trust from his emotional repertoire twenty years ago when he watched a news report about a house in Miami bursting into flames that took the lives of a woman and a nine-year-old child he had been assured would be safe.

"Neither am I," he said. "Which is probably why I'm about to be divorced for the third time."

"Well, at least this time, you won't be alone," Amanda said, a warm smile burnishing her lips.

"Nope! I've got my Ricki back, and all's right with the world."

Instantly, the smile disappeared. In its place was stark annoyance.

"I've told you a dozen times to call me Amanda, not Ricki. I don't know whether it's an innocent mental block or some stubborn ego thing, but get over it. If you don't, you're going to get us both killed!" He started to dismiss her concerns as an overreaction, but she stopped him cold. "They're out there," she stated with unalterable conviction. "And they're still looking for us."

Suddenly, Lionel felt ashamed. And guilty. He couldn't accept the notion that danger had so completely defined his daughter's and his ex-wife's lives, because he couldn't imagine living that way. It made him uncomfortable on too many levels, which was why his subconscious insisted on clinging to the fairy tale that they had left Miami, gone to another town, and lived happily and safely ever after. Amanda insisted that was not the case.

"Why do you think I demand we keep our relationship a secret? And that we meet in out-of-the-way places? And take extraordinary precautions to make sure no one follows us? This is not a game, Lionel. They want us dead."

Her voice was low and chilling in its intensity.

"Have you and . . . Beth ever had any reason to believe that your cover was blown?" he asked.

Amanda paused. Lionel might have taken her hesitation as a slight, but he quickly realized it was a survival mechanism. It pained him to see how automatic it was.

"They killed Poppy Stanton."

"He died in an automobile accident," Lionel said gently. He didn't want to contradict her, but he had gone to the funeral. He had seen the police reports. He had comforted his former mother-in-law. "Nanny Stanton said he lost control of the car."

"They cut his brakes."

Lionel was shaken by her emotionless response. This wasn't grief or paranoia speaking, this was someone with an intimate knowledge of the facts.

"This so-called accident occurred two years after the trial. The Espinosa family wasn't sure we had really died in the explosion at the house. But if we were alive, they wanted to send us a message: This death was intentional."

"How'd a story like that stay out of the papers?"

"Nanny and Poppy had been under loose surveillance. When the local police chief was given the name of the victim, he impounded the car and contacted the Marshals Service immediately. The service had its own mechanics go over the vehicle." Amanda's eyes flamed with anger. "Those bastards didn't even make an attempt at subtlety. They simply slashed the lines." She gritted her teeth at their brazenness.

"The service came up with a sanitized mechanic's report that the chief passed on to the newspapers. The car was fine. Unfortunately, the driver was too old to be behind the wheel. His reflexes were slow. He lost control and slammed into a concrete divider. End of story. Remember, we're talking about south Florida. This kind of thing happens all the time."

"Did your grandmother know?"

Amanda shook her head. "It would have terrified her. She was frightened enough as it was." Suddenly, several disparate thoughts collided, and a truth became apparent. "You set her up in Arizona and supported her until she died, didn't you?"

"Eleanor was a terrific woman. I didn't want her to become a prisoner in her apartment, and that's what was happening. Charles was gone. So were you, your mother, and Ken. She had no one to care for and nothing to do. I simply gave her a fresh start in a new place."

"She liked it there," Amanda said, wistfully. "Thank you."

Lionel smiled. "You're welcome." It was nice to be appreciated for a good deed, and for Lionel, a rare one. "Did you attend Charles's funeral?" he asked, suddenly fearful that she and Beth had been present and he missed them.

"No. Uncle Sam thought it was too dangerous." Amanda's brow furrowed. "Besides, we had been relocated, again."

"I know how close Cynthia was to Charles," Lionel said, unable to squelch a certain bitterness about destiny—and Uncle Sam—denying him a similar closeness with his daughter. "It must have hurt your mother terribly not to say good-bye to her father."

"More than you know."

Amanda winced and slipped behind an impenetrable mask that was becoming more and more familiar. Once again, she appeared to be evaluating the wisdom of revealing something of her past.

"When Nanny Stanton died, Mom insisted that we be allowed to attend her funeral. Uncle Sam had several of his superiors visit us to try and dissuade her."

The situation wasn't funny, yet Lionel laughed at the image of a roomful of United States marshals trying to convince Cynthia that she was better served not going. The Cynthia Stanton he knew couldn't be budged off any point once she had decided she was right; when it concerned her family, she was as malleable as a block of concrete. Amanda, realizing why Lionel had laughed, smiled as well, but only for a moment.

"We flew into Miami the day before the funeral, just hours after

Nanny's body arrived from Phoenix. The service got us a car with South Carolina plates, some warm-weather tourist clothes, and directed us to a seedy motel outside of Fort Lauderdale. Uncle Sam came with us. Several of his Miami colleagues had gone on ahead to make sure the place was safe. We checked in and holed up until dark. Then we drove down to Miami to the funeral home where we were supposed to have a private half hour visit."

Her voice had dropped an octave, becoming low and ominous. Lionel ached as he watched her relive these moments.

"It was late. Everyone had gone. The alarm was off and the door was unlocked, as it was supposed to be. We had to use flashlights and it wasn't exactly the way Mom and I would have wanted it to be, but we had our visit with Nanny. Uncle Sam and another marshal stood guard.

"When we were ready to leave, Uncle Sam activated the alarm and locked the door behind us. The four of us were in the parking lot, maybe thirty feet from the car, when suddenly there was a loud noise and a burst of heat." Her eyes squeezed shut and she flinched. "It was a firebomb. The other marshal covered Mom. Uncle Sam threw himself on top of me. I hit the pavement so hard, I broke my nose and my jaw. The last thing I heard before I passed out was Uncle Sam yelling at us to stay down. When I woke up, I was in the recovery room of Jackson Memorial. A plastic surgeon had reconstructed my face."

Since Lionel hadn't seen her in twenty years, he never thought to scrutinize her features, but he did now. As a child, she had overwhelmingly favored her mother, his only genetic contribution a dimpled chin. He was pleased to note that the surgeon had preserved that particular resemblance. He also noted, with a start, that without surgery Amanda would have become a duplicate of Cynthia. Ironic, he thought, but the Espinosas' botched attempt to kill her protected her. "And Cynthia?" he asked, wondering if she too had undergone a physical change that would make her unrecognizable.

"She suffered some second-degree burns. As did Uncle Sam. They're both fine, though."

"Who threw the bomb?" Lionel demanded. "And how the hell did he know where you were going to be and when?"

"Whoever tossed it was gone by the time backup arrived. As to how he knew?" She shrugged. "No plan is foolproof."

"Did they catch the bomber and question him?"

"Yes and no. Two days after the event, a body was found along

I-70, burned beyond recognition. Forensics showed he had been killed with the same type of incendiary bomb as the one thrown at us."

"He didn't get the job done, so they did him," Lionel concluded.

"Correct." Amanda suddenly realized that for the first time in her life, she was confiding in someone other than her mother or Sam. It felt strange, but good. "We think Espinosa realized he had outfoxed himself with Poppy. Our absence at the funeral didn't necessarily mean we were dead. More likely, we knew about the brakes and stayed away. So they waited for Nanny to die. When she did, they had someone at the airport in Phoenix find out where her body was being sent. Then, they planted someone outside the place and waited. If we showed up, they were ready."

Lionel took her hand in his. It pained him to think of all the horrors she had endured in her young life. Worse, it wasn't over.

"They know you're alive," he said, his face paled by that realization.

Amanda nodded. "It's been thirteen years since that particular incident. We were relocated several times before settling in Washington. Uncle Sam was transferred to another region for several years. But yes, they know."

"Do they know where you and your mother live?"

"No," she said with an eerie calm. "If they did, we'd be dead."

"So what do we do?"

She looked at her father and wondered whether it had been cruel to reenter his life. Just then, his face was etched with fear. She wished she could press a button, exit, and return his life to whatever it had been before. But that wasn't possible.

"We do what they're doing, Lionel," she said. "We watch. And we wait."

CHAPTER

TWO

Amanda befriended the camera when she was thirteen. Like most things in her life, the alliance was born of necessity. She and Beth had been living in a small town outside Spokane, Washington, for over a year. It was the longest they had remained in one place since their escape from Miami, but they were hardly comfortable. Four years on the run had stripped them of any sense of safety. Whatever security the words home, family, and community used to convey was gone. It had been erased along with their true identities.

Before entering WITSEC, Amanda and Beth had been gregarious, sociable, and altruistic. Their travails forced them to draw inward, behind an invisible carapace that kept them separate and apart from anyone who might venture too near. While they were pleasant enough, and each had a coterie of acquaintances—Beth from her new position as a mathematics professor at a small college, Amanda from among her classmates—they never fully engaged anyone, never shared any private thoughts or personal anecdotes, never allowed themselves to move from the outside, in.

How could they, when even the most innocuous encounter provided an opportunity for disaster? In one city, Beth was in a hurry and, without thinking, signed a check using the name Cynthia. In another, something prompted Amanda to tell her fourth-grade class that she used to live in a place where it never snowed. In yet another, someone noticed a leftover claim check for a bicycle repair shop in Portland, their previous home. Each time, they were relocated and redocumented. After the deaths of the Stantons and the attempts on their lives, no one was taking any chances.

Beth still believed that her coming forward and testifying was the right thing to do, but she was nonetheless consumed with guilt for having done it. Thanks to her, her father was dead, and she and her daughter had been sentenced to a life of solitary confinement. They were deprived of anything that looked or felt familiar, forced to interact with people they could not really get to know. Every minute of every day, they pretended not to be who they were, while at the same time, pretending to be who they knew they were not.

It was hard enough for Beth to maintain the *façade du jour,* as she called it, but when she watched Amanda attempt to make her way without making waves, her heart ached. For a child to have to lie about her name, her family, and her history seemed unconscionable.

Life became a series of stressful complications, with even the most ordinary occurrences causing extraordinary consternation. Should Beth have the marshals run a check on someone who asks her out for dinner? Was teaching a large class risky? Should Amanda be allowed to join after-school clubs? Could she ask friends over? Were they giving themselves away if they bought a dog? There were a thousand questions like that. And no easy answers.

Everything demanded a discussion, even something as benign as an invitation to a slumber party. When Amanda was invited to Betsey Frye's birthday sleepover, her immediate reaction was to turn it down. Betsey had been very nice to Amanda, and they were cafeteria buddies, but Amanda shied away from most gatherings, particularly gabfests where everyone was expected to reveal their innermost secrets. After all, what could she say? Her whole life was a secret. While Beth understood, she just couldn't bear to think of her daughter spending yet another night at home alone while other girls her age were giggling and pigging out on junk food and mooning over some teen idol.

Determined to give Amanda at least a taste of normalcy, Beth told her to accept and convinced her that everything would be all right. On the two weekends preceding the party, Beth held slumber-party rehearsals designed to give Amanda confidence. Amidst a buffet of potato chips, cheese puffs, Tootsie Rolls, and other assorted snacks, they stayed up and talked until they were senseless with fatigue. They raised every subject imaginable and asked every question that could possibly be asked, the ruder and more intrusive, the better. Then, they concocted plausible stories about who they were, where they were from, and why Amanda had no father or grandparents or pets or photo albums.

Thinking about photo albums made Amanda nervous. "What if someone takes a picture of me?"

Beth nodded. That could be a problem. "What if you take the pictures?" she said, suddenly inspired. "That way you're the one in control. Plus, it puts you in the middle of things, yet . . ."

"Not really." Amanda's eyes widened, and her lips spread in a hopeful smile as she considered the possibility.

The next day, they went into Spokane and bought a small auto-focus camera. The salesman showed Amanda the basics, gave her a few pointers on taking candids, sold her a how-to book, several rolls of film, and told her to have fun. After the first hour or so, that's exactly what Amanda did. Not only was she a hit with the girls, especially after she gifted them with the developed prints, but she loved the process of capturing people on film.

Amanda Maxwell had finally found the perfect companion: If she was careful, the camera wouldn't betray her. And if she had to move again, she wouldn't have to leave it behind.

The art scene used to happen on Saturday in SoHo. Suddenly, it shifted to Chelsea. It started when Matthew Marks, a young art dealer with a thriving Madison Avenue gallery, decided he needed space that would allow him to show large canvases and heavy sculpture. Unable to find what he wanted in SoHo, he made the daring decision to renovate a derelict garage on West Twenty-second Street. He was told no one would come to Chelsea, that the area was too dicey, too heavily associated with leather bars and streetwalkers. He went ahead anyway, opening several months later with an Ellsworth Kelly show that drew a thousand people.

That particular Saturday, Amanda was headed to Chelsea for the opening of a Philip-Lorca DiCorcia exhibition. It was bitter cold, with a windchill that made the air feel arctic. Pulling her scarf up over her nose, she got out of the cab and detoured toward the water, intrigued by a string of ice floes dotting the mighty Hudson. Reaching inside her coat, she pulled out her camera and brought it up to her eye. She turned the lens slowly, bringing the central image closer while reducing the frame until the Jersey Palisades and the Chelsea wharf disappeared, automatically eliminating any markers that could identify a specific place. In her view was a patch of dark water supporting thick, glacierlike forms. It was an edgy contrast of black and white, placid, yet disturbing. Intrigued, she snapped a dozen pictures.

She was about to tuck her camera back inside her coat when, across the street, she noticed a makeshift cardboard shelter resting against a building. Protruding slightly was a pile of rags within which, Amanda guessed, lay one of New York City's homeless. An over-burdened shopping cart stood guard, packed with the belongings of someone who didn't belong anywhere or to anyone. Amanda felt drawn to the solitude and anonymity of the picture. Quietly, as if the click of her shutter might disturb the dweller's sleep, she recorded the moment.

Over the years, she had created a stunning collection of street-scapes—bleakscapes, as she called them—photographs of life's for-gotten souls that she had taken on various avenues and back alleys in an assortment of cities. She captured their images when they slept or begged or chatted on a park bench or lay in a darkened alleyway drinking away their misery. Mindful of their privacy, she kept her distance, using a long lens that wouldn't intrude or embarrass or frighten. They intrigued her because she felt she was one of them. Not as ragged or downtrodden, perhaps, but just as alienated.

By the time she entered the gallery, her body was chilled, and her mood was gray. She pulled off her earmuffs, stuffed them in the pocket of her coat along with her gloves and scarf, and walked inside. Usually, she enjoyed getting lost in a throng of art *aficionados,* eaves-dropping on the various off-the-cuff critiques, but just then, the crowd loomed like a threatening swarm. Retreating, she found a quiet corner where she could admire one of DiCorcia's photographs without too much disruption.

Amanda related to DiCorcia's work because he, too, found drama in ordinary moments. The photographs on display were of pedestrians idling along sidewalks in big cities, caught by a nosy lens. One showed a man in a black boater, smoking a cigarette as he ambled through a street in an unknown Italian city. His eyes looked at the camera as one would look at a stranger, curious and cautious, as if to say, "What are you looking at?" Amanda's bleakscapes were frank obser-vations of the human condition, externals that intimated an internal isolation, but retained a respectful distance between camera and soul. DiCorcia's candids were more confrontational, poking into private moments via a hidden lens. To Amanda's eye, the magic of his work was that each of his pictures felt like a frame in a documentary about life's ordinary moments.

She was musing about DiCorcia's lighting technique when Lloyd Franks, the owner of the gallery, caught her eye, waved, and, via hand signals, told her he wanted to meet with her later. She nodded and smiled, but inside her stomach knotted. Several months before, her friend, Annie, had encouraged Amanda to show her photographs to Lloyd. She had, and now Lloyd wanted to include several of them in a group show.

The whole thing had seemed harmless at the time, but now, she wondered: *Whatever had possessed me?* Money, for one. Annie had enticed her by reminding her how hot photography was and how much money she could make from the sale of her work. On Amanda's salary, it was hard to turn down a chance to earn a few extra dollars. There was ego, too. Amanda thought she did good work—as good as, or in some cases, better than many of those who already commanded a place in the photographic firmament.

Still, Amanda had spent most of her life hiding behind her camera, avoiding exposure. When Lloyd expressed interest, she was so flattered and flustered that she agreed without thinking the situation through. Once she did, she insisted on being billed as Anonymous; her affiliation with the police force was her excuse. She expected him to object to something so prima donna–ish, and turn her away with a thanks-but-no-thanks. Instead, Franks applauded her suggestion as a stroke of marketing genius.

"Something like that creates a buzz," he chortled. "It's like that political *roman à clef* about the '92 election. Who wrote it became the parlor game of the year."

Amanda smiled as she envisioned Annie's reaction to the news that she was actually going to exhibit her photographs. For sure, it would be loud and emphatic—Annie never heard of a whisper—and accompanied by a burst of exuberant gestures. Also, there would be a number of "I-told-you-so's" sprinkled among her congratulations. Annie's ego was one of the strongest Amanda had ever encountered, but she was never shy about reinforcing it.

Amanda had met Annie Hart at the morgue. Amanda was photographing an autopsy. Annie was doing research, or so she said just before her stomach heaved. When she was cleaned up and the color had returned to her face, she explained that she was a makeup artist on a soap opera and had come to the morgue to see what "a real-live dead person" looked like so she could replicate the look on her show. To thank Amanda for her kindness, Annie had insisted upon treating her to dinner—some other evening, of course. Amanda had demurred, but Annie Hart refused to be put off. She threatened to park herself on Amanda's doorstep or at the front desk of the Crime

Scene Unit offices on Jamaica Avenue in Queens, where Amanda worked. Dinner seemed easier. That had been nearly a year ago.

"*Bella signorina.* I didn't think it was possible, but you're as beautiful in the winter as you are in the summer."

Amanda's shoulders stiffened; she didn't like it when people came up behind her. But when she went to place the voice, the memory it aroused was warm and welcome.

"Tyler Grayson!" His name fell from her lips as her mouth spread in a smile of surprise and recognition. His sandy-colored hair wasn't as long, he was sporting a mustache and chin whiskers, and his clothes were definitely more city than *campagna,* but she would have known him anywhere.

"The very same." He leaned forward, held her arms gently, and kissed her on both cheeks. "I thought I recognized you when you walked in. I mean, who else wears a Nikon as a necklace?"

Amanda laughed self-consciously.

"You're still gorgeous," he continued, his pale gray eyes appraising her, "even if your taste in accessories hasn't improved much in five years."

Amanda flushed. "You haven't changed either. You're still way too charming to be believable."

"I should be insulted," he said with mock seriousness. "And maybe later I will be, but for now, it's nice to know you still find me charming."

"Always," Amanda said. "After all, if not for that irresistible charm of yours, I would've been tossed off the Pendolino and left to fend for myself in the wilds of Tuscany."

"Egads! A fate worse than death," he said, laughing along with her, both of them lost in a swirl of memories. "How'd you get here, by the way?" His eyes twinkled mischievously.

Amanda grinned. "I took a cab."

"Good move."

"See," she said. "I have learned a few things in five years."

They had met in Italy on a train headed from Rome to Florence. Amanda had intended to go to Florence, but in the rush at the station in Rome, she boarded a train headed in the opposite direction. When she discovered her error, about an hour outside of Naples, a sympathetic conductor checked his book of departure times and told her if she got off at the next stop, she could return to Rome in time to board the Pendolino, Italy's bullet train. He advised her just to get on and work out the difference in ticket prices later. It wasn't as easy as he made it sound.

She managed to get to Rome, find the correct track for the Pendolino and a car with an empty seat, but she quickly discovered that she was in first-class, which required reservations, and that not every conductor was as nice as Giancarlo. Since no one had claimed her seat, she thought there wouldn't be a problem. Then, the conductor asked to see her ticket. She tried to explain what had happened, but this was not a happy man who loved his work. Although she couldn't understand a word he was saying, it was clear that he didn't have any sympathy with her predicament. He wanted to walk through the cars, punch tickets, and be done with it.

Tyler, seated opposite Amanda, overheard the exchange and when it looked as if it might turn nasty, offered to referee. Amanda gratefully accepted. In perfect Italian, he mollified the conductor and negotiated an easy solution to the problem: the conductor would forget Amanda's unscheduled trip to and from Naples—"It was an honest mistake. Think of the international goodwill generosity like this creates"—and simply charge her the difference between the cost of the Pendolino first-class and her original, second-class ticket from Rome to Florence.

They spent the rest of the trip laughing about Amanda's endless journey, talking about the kindness of strangers, the perils of an American negotiating her way around Europe, and the infinite joy one could derive from Italian food and wine. When they arrived in Florence, Tyler asked if he could take Amanda to dinner that evening. She accepted, and for the next three weeks they were inseparable. To this day, it remained the most romantic interlude of Amanda's life.

"Have you had lunch?" he asked, interrupting her reverie.

"Not yet."

"The Empire Diner doesn't make *riboletta*," he warned. "And they don't serve red wine from a jug,"

Amanda pursed her lips and tapped her finger against her chin, pondering. "Is the soup hot?"

"Steaming."

"Is the bread fresh?"

"Baked this morning."

She nodded with great solemnity, then linked her arm through his and laughed. "Let's do it!"

* * *

Tyler Grayson and Amanda Maxwell had both gone to Italy that summer to escape and to heal. Tyler was recovering from a broken heart, as well as a shattered ego, and needed to clear his head before starting a big new job at Wolfe, Simons, a major New York brokerage firm. He had worked hard for this promotion—obsessively hard according to his ex-fiancée. He thought she understood the late nights and the weekends spent at the office instead of in the Hamptons. He thought she was as invested in his future as he was and was willing to make the necessary sacrifices. He thought wrong.

Amanda was suffering a meltdown from a job and a life that had simply gotten too much for her to handle. Her trip was meant to cleanse her mind, calm her soul, and mend her body.

When Amanda graduated from high school, she and Beth moved to Los Angeles so that she could commute to UCLA and Beth could be near Sam, who was now the head of Region XII. After only three semesters, Amanda left school and bounced from job to job, trying to find an occupation that fit her various inclinations. She started out at a film lab in a movie studio, but didn't like being a technician. She got a job as an assistant to one of LA's best-known fashion photographers, but got turned off by the incessant model-coddling. After several more months of aimlessness, she decided to do what she had wanted to do from the age of seven: she enrolled in the police academy.

Sam Bates thought Amanda was well suited for the profession. Beth was opposed. She knew that initially, Amanda's infatuation with police work had been tied up in feelings about her uncle Ken, feelings that became exaggerated after his death. Over the years, she supposed that Sam's presence probably had reinforced Amanda's view that law enforcement was a noble profession. But Beth had identified her brother's body. Beth had been squeezed by a government more interested in making its case than allowing her to live her life. Beth had to battle the Marshals Service to keep their promises about housing and employment. Beth had lost a brother, a parent, her career, the ability to have a husband and close friends and maybe even other children to law enforcement. She didn't want to lose her daughter.

Beth voiced her objections, and Amanda listened respectfully, but in the end said this was something she had to do.

"If I don't like it, or I'm not cut out for it, fine. But I've got to give it a chance."

She joined the LAPD as a recruit, her sights set on a detective's gold badge. On a sunny afternoon in South Central Los Angeles, however, her ambitions changed abruptly. She and her partner were on routine patrol when they came upon a massacre. Two cars had pulled up onto the lawn of a small house. Four men were standing outside, firing AK-47s indiscriminately into the house. Amanda's partner, Roger, blared cease and desist warnings over the megaphone. They knew these guys weren't going to listen, but it was procedure. Amanda called for backup, then blew out the tires of both their cars.

Within seconds, four black-and-whites screamed around the corner, screeched to a halt, and disgorged a troop of heavily armed police, who took off in pursuit of the gunmen. Amanda and Roger joined the chase. As Amanda passed the front of the house, she heard a baby screaming. She paused for only a moment, but in that moment, she lost sight of her quarry. One of the gang members must have ducked inside the house because suddenly, a gun barrel peered out a window. She heard Roger shouting at her to hit the ground. There was a flurry of explosive noises. Then there was silence.

Amanda spent eight hours in surgery. The doctors told Beth Amanda was lucky that her reflexes were so quick and that her partner had been able to get off a quick round before he, too, fell victim. Her recovery would take awhile—there was extensive internal bleeding—but Amanda would be fine. The puncture to her left lung would heal, leaving her with shortness of breath only after extreme exertion. No other vital organs had been permanently affected.

Roger lost an eye. A woman, her four children, ranging from three months to six years of age, and two teenage gang members lost their lives. Two others had been caught and would stand trial for murder. The remaining three were on the loose.

As she lay in her hospital bed, Amanda experienced a startling revelation: She had spent a lifetime looking over her shoulder and jumping at shadows, waiting for a hit man from the Espinosa cartel, or a mobster from New York to gun her down. The irony was that she had been gunned down, but her assailant didn't know or care who she was. The attack was serendipitous, but it impressed on Amanda, again, that disastrous things *could* happen and would happen, if she put herself out there.

When her physical wounds had healed enough to travel, Amanda announced that she was going on a photographic retreat.

"I need time to consider my options," she told her mother.

"Where are you going?"

Amanda shrugged. "Someplace where I can relax and figure out how I want to spend the rest of my life."

Italy was that place.

Amanda warmed her fingers by wrapping them around her soup bowl. Tyler rested his chin in his hands and smiled at her.

"What are you grinning at?" she asked.

"I can't believe that in a city of umpteen million people, we not only ran into each other, but you're not married with two kids."

"Not even close." She laughed, pleased by the relief that washed across his face. Tyler had been Amanda's first passionate affair; she hadn't been involved with anyone that intensely since. She wondered if he had remained similarly unentangled.

"Are you still a policewoman?" He still said the word gingerly, as if the act of speaking it was enough to provoke an arrest.

Amanda smiled. "I'm a detective with the Crime Scene Unit of the NYPD. My specialty is forensic photography."

Tyler held up his hands and shook his head as if she was going too fast for him to comprehend what she was saying. "What the hell is forensic photography? And when did you move to New York?" Unspoken was, "And why didn't you call me?"

Amanda heard the silent question, but just as he didn't speak it out loud, she didn't respond. Theirs had been a crossroads affair. They had loved each other fiercely, but they had met at one of life's junctions when each had far-reaching decisions to make and neither was emotionally prepared to commit to anything beyond the moment. Both had come to the romance damaged and shaken, but when they parted at the *stazione,* a sense of wholeness and surety had been restored to each, a reassurance that comes from the knowledge that they had shared something special.

"I moved here several years ago," she said. "But school kept me too busy to call anyone."

Actually, she had come to New York not too long after her return from Italy. She had thought about looking him up, but a serious romantic involvement was not part of her five-year plan. It would be much too distracting. She knew from watching her mother how difficult it was to establish a career and a foothold in a new community.

Complicating matters even more was the fact that New York was a Danger Zone, a place the Marshals Service preferred she avoid; Miami was the other city on their "you-can't-go-home-again" list.

By insisting on relocating to a Danger Zone, Amanda lost her right to WITSEC protection. It wasn't that she had abandoned her sense of caution. She had decided it was time for her to live her life where and how she pleased. As she told Beth and Marshal Bates, she would be careful. She wouldn't betray her mother or reveal anything she shouldn't. But she intended to do the work she had always wanted to do.

"I received my Bachelor of Science degree from the John Jay School of Criminal Justice and then went on to take a Master's in Forensic Science, with a concentration on photographic evidence."

Tyler laughed. "You are still the most incongruous woman I've ever met."

"I beg your pardon."

"Most women as good-looking as you spend their days working in elegant offices or shopping in elegant stores, and their nights dining in quaint bistros or posh restaurants. They never miss a manicure. They think a squad room and the morgue are settings for TV shows, and they rarely use the word *corpse* in casual conversation.

"You, on the other hand, are this stunning creature who's probably never been inside Bergdorf's, Bendel's, or Trixie's nail salon. Why bother, when you spend your days—and probably your nights— getting blood on your shoes and who knows what under your finger-nails snapping pictures of dead bodies. I don't get it."

"I love working with a camera," she said plainly, knowing that no amount of explaining could make her job palatable.

"Taking pictures of the Ponte Vecchio at sundown, I understand. A gunshot victim at dawn, I don't."

Amanda laughed, then grew mellow. "The sunsets in Florence were spectacular, weren't they?"

She closed her eyes for a moment, retrieving an image: the blazing yellow of midday light deepening to orange as evening settled on the terra-cotta roofs of that fifteenth-century city. Many an evening she and Tyler had witnessed day's end strolling along the Arno. She could almost feel the warmth of the sun on her face and the strength of his arm around her waist. When she opened her eyes it was clear that Tyler had also returned to *Firenze*.

"Everything about Florence was spectacular," he said quietly, his eyes fixed on hers.

Amanda twirled her spoon around in her soup. "I still have that necklace you bought me."

Tyler nodded. "I'm glad."

Again, a memory nestled between them. On their second night together, they wandered onto the Ponte Santa Trinita, looking down-river at the Ponte Vecchio, the only one of the antique Florentine bridges to have escaped the bombing of World War II.

"It's so beautiful," Amanda sighed as she reached for her camera.

"It was built in 1345, but the butchers, tanners, and blacksmiths who were the original occupants were evicted by Duke Something-or-other in the late fifteen hundreds because they made too much noise. Also, because they used the river as a garbage dump and the stench was foul. The workshops were rebuilt and rented to gold-smiths."

Amanda's eyes widened, prompting a laugh from Tyler. Few women could resist the allure of beautiful jewelry, even one wearing chinos, a tee shirt, and sporting a backpack. He took her arm and steered her toward the ancient span, where she ogled every window and every stall like a child at a magic show. She was especially drawn to the delicacy of the filigree necklaces.

"They look like golden spiderwebs," she said.

The night before they left to return to the States, he presented her with a thin chain of filigreed gold. He told her to think of him whenever she wore it. She did.

"Have you ever been back?" he asked.

"Without my private guide?" she said. "I wouldn't know where to go or what I was looking at. How about you?"

He shook his head. "It wouldn't be the same without you goading me to look beyond what I was seeing."

Tyler was a history buff and had generously shared his vast store of knowledge with Amanda. Whatever they saw, wherever they went, whether it was walking the streets Michelangelo once walked, feasting on the treasures inside the Uffizi Gallery, marveling at the statue of David or the architectural splendor of Brunelleschi's Dome, Tyler was able to recite facts and recount stories that injected an excitement that would have been missing otherwise. Her contribution was the keenness of her eye. She taught him how to look at beautiful things and how to find their essence, whether it was a building, a painting, a slash of sunlight on a river, or the colors in a glass of wine.

"Besides, my job doesn't afford me the luxury of time one needs to travel like that."

"You must be the king of Wall Street by now," she said.

He smiled. "Not yet. Right now, I'm working on being named the Crown Prince of Baird, Nathanson & Spelling."

Years of practice allowed Amanda to keep her surprise from showing on her face. "I thought you were going to work for Wolfe and something or other."

"I was and I did, but after a year there, no less than Lionel Baird himself asked me to join his firm as vice president."

"You have moved up in the world."

"Not high enough."

His voice had a familiar edge to it. In Italy, whenever Tyler described the atmosphere on Wall Street, it was in those same combative tones. When she pointed that out, he explained that the financial community was an arena in which gladiators battled to the death. When Amanda suggested that might be an exaggeration, Tyler disagreed. Ambition alone wasn't enough, he said. Neither was talent. One needed passion and dedication and a single-mindedness that overwhelmed all else. Amanda, who grew up believing that ambition could lead to discovery, found enslavement to a singular goal difficult to imagine.

"But," he said with a smile that wasn't duplicated in his eyes, "I'm working on it."

"On what?"

"Succeeding Lionel Baird."

"I gather Lionel Baird is the top dog."

Tyler nodded. "He's brilliant. There's no debating that. But, in case you're interested: Yes, his bark is as horrifying as his bite."

Amanda managed to look confused, but Lionel had told her his reputation as an ogre was well deserved.

"I suppose you don't get to be that rich and powerful by being a Boy Scout, but this guy enjoys pulling the wings off butterflies."

Amanda winced. Hearing her father described this way was painful.

"I've watched him chew up guys who've worked their hearts out for him." Tyler's eyes were tinged with a sadness she didn't understand. "Even if you give him everything you've got, it's not enough."

"Why stay?"

"Good question," he said, coming back from wherever he had been. "The answer is: Baird, Nathanson & Spelling is the best show in town. I'm one of the big brass there, and no matter how I feel about Lionel Baird, it makes no sense to leave. Especially since he'll probably retire in a few years."

"Are you in line to succeed him?"

"On paper, I'm one of several in a logical position to move into the vice chairman's seat. But that doesn't necessarily mean anything. Knowing Lionel, he'll make it into a contest between his vice presidents. The one who can bring the most money to Lionel's bottom line wins."

"Don't bite my head off," Amanda said, "but that doesn't sound unreasonable."

"It isn't really." Tyler looked at her, suddenly aware that he wasn't explaining himself very well. "Look. I don't believe in something for nothing. But honest merit should be rewarded, and I don't know if Lionel Baird can be trusted to do that."

"You don't like him," Amanda said.

"No. Not much."

"Why not?"

Tyler paused to weigh his words. "He doesn't think he's accountable to anyone for anything."

Over the past months, Lionel had gone out of his way to make up for his absence during those early years when he had allowed ambition to overwhelm his obligations as a father. But more than once in her life, Amanda had heard Lionel described in precisely the same way—by her mother.

"Does this mean you're going to back off and not make a run for it?"

Tyler's dark eyes glinted with determination. "Absolutely not! If I pull out of this race, I'll never get a second chance anywhere else. Everyone on the street is watching us. So whether I like it or not, I have to play Lionel's game."

Amanda shrugged. "Life isn't always about what you like or don't like. And it doesn't always give you a choice."

A slow, curious smile curled Tyler's lips. "That's very sage of you," he said, taking her hand and folding it into his. "How did you become so wise?"

"I didn't have a choice," she said quietly.

C H A P T E R

THREE

Pamela Richardson Baird studied the samples of personal stationery as if they were DNA slides. After intense deliberation, she decided on a simple, yet bold script, eminently more suitable to the wife of a United States senator than the block lettering that had symbolized her marriage to Lionel Baird, or the fussy French swirls and serifs from her first union. She made a note to call her saleswoman at Mrs. John L. Strong on Madison to order engraved note cards, letterheads, envelopes, and calling cards. After another moment of reflection, she decided to inquire about creating a personal logo by incorporating an eagle or some other bit of Americana.

She smiled. How delicious to have a personal logo of such import! Several friends had embraced symbols: a golf club for one woman who was obsessive about the game, a lily for a woman of the same name, a sewing needle with a swirl of thread for someone who had been a *couture* designer for an hour and a half. But they were trivialities, Pamela scoffed, not nearly as commanding as an American eagle or a flag.

While some women might find it embarrassing to be multimarried, Pamela was of another mind. As long as each marriage was an improvement over the last, it was cause for congratulations, not scorn. Certainly, her marriage to John Chisolm was a change for the better. Lionel Baird was wealthy, but so was John. Lionel was powerful, but his was an influence predominantly felt in financial circles. John was the senior senator from New York. His power was practically boundless. And John was social, definitely a plus over Lionel, who had to be dragged to charity functions and see-and-be-seen dinners. Pamela frowned briefly. Lionel was by far the better lover, but, she supposed, John compensated by being more gallant. And, John would probably be faithful, a concept that was completely alien to Lionel.

Her mood sobered suddenly as she wondered if perhaps ordering stationery was premature; not only hadn't she set a wedding date, she wasn't divorced yet. While it was true she didn't want to appear hasty, the quicker she attended to the dozens of details involved in establishing a new household, the more seamless the transition.

Pamela's attention to details had been one of the things that had attracted John to her. He needed a woman who was up to the task of tending to a man in the public eye, a woman who knew how to conduct their social life as if she were running a corporation, a woman who was willing to subordinate her ego to his. Pamela had been doing all of that for Lionel, without any thanks or credit for a job well-done. John not only appreciated her efforts, he encouraged them, always complimenting her on her exquisite taste and social acumen.

Pamela sighed. Men used to compliment her on her exquisite body and her sexual prowess. They used to wax poetic about her blond hair and green eyes and the way her lips felt against their skin. Now they praised the way she decorated a table and tied an Hermès scarf.

It was difficult growing older. Aside from the assortment of physical surprises associated with advancing age, it became harder to maintain a comely appearance without a staff of hairdressers, trainers, personal shoppers, and plastic surgeons. To focus so intensely on one's looks might seem shallow, but in her circle, attractiveness was paramount. Women in her set led lives keyed to four-star luncheons, designer labels, charity committee meetings, and networking. They weren't employed at chic auction houses or fashion concerns like those in the younger social set, but they worked hard nonetheless. Their jobs were to find, form, and maintain relationships with other women whose husbands were players—men who invested, or wielded power, or traded influence. The job was easy if the women liked each other, but Pamela had suffered through many a tedious lunch or endless bridge game rather than risk losing a card from Lionel's Rolodex.

She much preferred the afternoons she used to spend at the Mayfair Hotel, when she and Lionel were courting. He would dine at Le Cirque with his cronies, then work off his luncheon calories next door with her. Two, three, four times a week, they'd rendezvous in a luxurious suite, ravishing each other until they could barely stand. At night, at dinner with other couples, they restrained themselves to such an extent there were many who doubted they had ever been intimate. Pamela actually heard some wonder about the fact that they had never seen her and Lionel touch. If they had been at Pamela's apartment or Lionel's town house after dinner, they would have known otherwise.

They met at a cocktail party at his town house. She had come with a man who was looking to bring his company public and wanted Baird, Nathanson & Spelling to do the offering. When they were introduced, Lionel fixed his eyes on hers and stared until she thought she'd literally melt from the heat. His attention had been intense. While her escort made small talk, Lionel nodded and smiled, but his eyes never left hers. The two men briefly discussed business, but still, Lionel wouldn't let her out of his sight. They barely spoke and certainly no invitation was issued, yet when her date said it was time to leave, Pamela brushed him off, found her way to Lionel's bedroom, stripped off her clothes, and waited for him to join her. Ten minutes later, he did.

Few would have believed her, but Pamela hadn't pushed marriage. From the start, she had pegged Lionel as a man whose passions flamed hotter when he was unfettered. Instinctively, she understood that knowing he could leave was precisely the thing that kept him coming back. After several years, however, when she was convinced that nothing could diminish their passion, Pamela began dropping hints about it being time Lionel proposed. When he didn't, she issued an ultimatum: either they legitimized their affair, or she was moving on. He was honest. He admitted that she made him incredibly happy and that he couldn't imagine life without her. But he reminded her that he had failed at two marriages already; he didn't want to fail her.

"Some people aren't good risks," he told her. "We're better off the way we are."

She dismissed his concerns. She believed that after she had completely insinuated herself into his life, he would realize how perfectly suited they were. What a fool she had been!

Pamela's eyes pooled with tears of anger and regret. Lionel always said life was about choices and that one had to live with the consequences of one's decisions; that was his way of blaming her for whatever had gone wrong with them. But she refused to accept culpability. She was not the one who had grown distant and cold.

She was not the one who had vacated their bed. While Pamela would admit to several colossal screwups in her life, she placed the blame for the collapse of their marriage squarely on his philandering shoulders.

Her first husband had been a youthful mistake. She had married at twenty because Harrison Walton was rich, socially prominent, handsome in that blond, WASPish way, and because that's what young women with an eye on the Social Register did. Harrison Walton turned out to be a freak with a penchant for kinky sex and violent temper tantrums. A year and a half later, after he had beaten her so badly he not only precipitated a miscarriage but left her unable to bear children, they were divorced.

Her husband-to-be, John Chisolm was a middle-aged woman's calculated decision. He was a man of means and stature, one who wanted a physical relationship, but didn't place inordinate demands on her; in exchange, she didn't harbor extravagant expectations of him. They had a synergistic romance, one in which they functioned more as helpmates than lovers. She would give him a wife of impeccable taste and credentials. He would elevate her to the very peak of the social ladder. Together, after finishing the negotiations on an equitable prenuptial, they would form a seemingly perfect union.

But it was Lionel Baird who was the love of Pamela's life. There was no thought involved when she entered into a relationship with him, no intellectual reasoning about pluses and minuses. He generated in her emotions so strong and so overwhelming that the concept of choice was completely negated. He was the man she had dreamed of all her life, and dreamed of still. Lionel was the electricity that made her heart beat, and she had loved him to the point of madness. Which was why she hated him so thoroughly now.

He hadn't loved her back.

Pamela should have suggested a quiet dinner at home. When she and John dined out, it was impossible to string more than two sentences together before someone came over to their table to chat with the senator. And if those interruptions weren't enough to spoil her evening, each time she asked his opinion about something related to their upcoming nuptials, John snapped at her. When she asked how he'd feel about gold-eagle faucets for the powder room, he went berserk.

"I don't want to talk about towels or caterers or bathroom fixtures until your divorce is finalized! Do you understand me, Pamela?"

"You don't have to bite my head off," she hissed, wondering if anyone had heard him reprimand her. "And of course I understand. I've tried to get Lionel to sign the papers, but he's being . . . well, he's being Lionel!"

"I don't care what he's being. What I care about is being a senator, and, according to my pollsters, dating a married woman involved in a messy divorce isn't going to help me keep my job. So, do whatever you have to do to get it done!"

"There's nothing messy about my divorce, John, except perhaps that you and I have been screwing each other in your office, your apartment, the back of your limousine, and any other place you've decided you need to demonstrate your . . . power." Whatever Pamela's needs—and they were many—she refused to be spoken to like chattel. Those days were over. "I'm not going to relinquish my rights to stock in Baird, Nathanson & Spelling just to satisfy your pollsters. I need to secure my future."

"Your future is being the next Mrs. John Chisolm," he said, with a condescension that set Pamela's teeth on edge.

"Should I ask the last Mrs. John Chisolm how secure she feels?" Considering that Pamela had actively campaigned to replace Emily Chisolm in John's bed, that was probably unfair, but John had not been especially generous with his ex-wife. Pamela had no reason to expect that if they split—and her history proved nothing was certain—he would be generous with her. At her age, she couldn't afford to walk away from Lionel empty-handed.

Recognizing that they were on the brink of a serious argument, John moved quickly to mollify his fiancée. "I'm sorry, darling," he said, reaching across the table to clasp her hand. "I didn't mean to upset you. I'm simply distracted."

"Because?" Pamela wasn't completely assuaged, but there seemed to be no point in bringing this incident to a boil.

"I'm concerned about the election."

Election was the magic word, meant to remind Pamela how important his senatorial seat was; it was the power base both of them craved. If she wanted to feed off it, she had to work for it. And just then, both of them knew it loomed as an uphill battle. John's favorables were down. The people of New York didn't believe he was one of them. They didn't believe he understood or related to their problems. They viewed him as a well-heeled Brahmin more interested in retaining membership in that private, taxpayer-funded club known as the United States Senate than making sure New Yorkers were getting a fair shake from the federal government. To counter that impression, his advisors were doing focus groups and polls and tele-phone surveys in a frantic attempt to find a positive people-issue he could grab on to and use as his banner, before an opponent defined him by his negatives.

"They haven't come up with anything that's going to hit home with the voters," John groaned. "And with people taking to the airwaves beating their breasts in the name of morality, family values, and role models, I can't afford to allow our romance to take center stage. It's true that the country is no longer as intolerant of single or divorced officials as they once were, but that doesn't mean they like the notion of their senator dating a very visible, still-married woman." He smiled engagingly. "No matter how irresistible she is."

Pamela allowed the compliment, even though it had been offered as validation for his boorish behavior. She also allowed him to prattle on about the difficulties involved in trying to launch a meaningful campaign at a time when cynicism had turned most people off. They disliked politicians, distrusted government, and disbelieved the promises of anyone who said, "If elected . . ."

"Why not make drugs your central issue?" Pamela said quietly, not wishing to be overheard.

John's eyebrows narrowed. He didn't see her point immediately, but he was willing to listen. "Go on."

"This state has a number of large cities aside from the five bor-oughs of New York—Buffalo, Syracuse, Albany, Rochester. They're all being destroyed by drugs and the crime that comes with them, as are the surrounding suburban areas that never used to consider drugs their problem. For most people, this has become a quality-of-life issue. Climb on this bandwagon and you look like a crusader."

John shook his head. "It's been tried. Dole used it against Clinton and it never really resonated. People don't believe government can stop the flow of drugs onto the streets."

"That's because the government is too large a target and has always been the villain or the savior, depending on one's point of view. Try turning the heat on something smaller, more specific. Something the little guy can rail against."

"Like?"

Pamela leaned in close. "Banks and brokerage houses. The same people that refuse middle-class mortgages or small-business loans."

John stared at her, dumbstruck. She was right: John Q. Public hated banks and was highly suspicious of Wall Street.

"Drugs create big money," Pamela continued, "money that's

invested and laundered by this country's most respected financial institutions. They profit off it without blinking an eye about the immorality of where it came from. But when it's suggested that legalizing drugs would take a big chunk out of those profits, they scream the loudest about how that would put drugs into the hands of children. Well, guess what? Drugs are killing children, even as we speak."

John ruminated a bit. "Much of my support comes from the financial community," he said, thinking aloud. "They wouldn't like me making them the bad guys."

"They're used to being called bad guys." Pamela laughed. "I think they wear the title as a badge of honor. It sets them apart from the plebeians of this world."

"Still . . ."

"I'm not suggesting you blame the drug problem entirely on them, John. People wouldn't believe that. But they would believe that the banking industry has a powerful lobby that might be working overtime to prevent the government from taking any serious action against importing drugs." She let that sink in for a moment, then continued. "Your constituents know you're a rich man. For you to take on the very people who made you rich makes you look like a hero. And if Americans long for anything these days, it's a hero."

"You may have something here . . ." John couldn't hide his surprise that Pamela had given him what his highly paid staff couldn't seem to find: a viable issue on which to build a credible campaign.

Pamela saw his amazement. She resented it, but said nothing. She had goals other than John's approval.

"Besides," she said, "if you insinuate that Wall Street doesn't care if drugs are destroying Main Street, they'll be the first ones to contribute to your campaign."

"If for no other reason than to counter a negative image," John said, thinking he was following her lead.

Pamela hastened to correct him. "Because ridding the country of drugs is a winning issue and everyone wants to be on the side of a winner. Especially special-interest groups."

For the first time in her memory, John looked at her with honest respect. "You are a wonder, Pamela Richardson Baird. If I hadn't already asked you to marry me, I'd do it all over again," he said.

"Thank you, darling. That's sweet."

He lifted her hand to his lips and kissed it. "I need you by my side, Pamela. How do we get your divorce finalized?"

She shrugged delicately, as if she hadn't a clue. "I wish I knew. I've tried, but you know how stubborn Lionel is. It's hard to move him off a point."

"I'll move him," John said, his teeth bared. He and Lionel were longtime adversaries. It was easy for Pamela to press that button. "I'm the chairman of the Senate Banking Committee. We're currently reviewing several issues which are of interest to Lionel. Believe me, not only will he give you everything you want, but he'll do it quickly!"

Pamela caressed his cheek gratefully. Inside, she was cheering. This evening hadn't started out on a promising note, but it had certainly ended well. Not only was John going to confront Lionel, but it appeared as if he was going to make the financial community's ties to the business of drugs the centerpiece of his run for the senate. If he did, Pamela intended to make Lionel Baird the poster boy of that campaign.

What John didn't realize was that Pamela was waging a campaign of her own, one built solely on revenge.

John Chisolm detested Lionel Baird. For as long as he could remember, Lionel had served as a human roadblock, insinuating himself into the middle of whatever path John had chosen to take. When John was a young man starting out at Paine Webber, he and Lionel competed for customers. Then they competed for the hand of Nan Nathanson—and the attention of her powerful father, Maurice. When John decided to leave Wall Street and turn his sights to the House of Representatives, Lionel backed his opponent, who won. Two years later, John entered the fray better prepared and better armed and soundly defeated Lionel's man. The same scenario unfolded during each of John's senatorial campaigns. If Lionel wasn't backing John's opponent, he was challenging the efficacy of John's positions. Whenever Lionel was called before the Senate Banking Committee, his appearance heralded another performance of the Lionel and John show, each man landing his punches as close to the belt line as he dared. John didn't know when this animus between them began or why, but over the years, one thing was clear: These two men couldn't stand each other.

The senator marched down the wide hallway of Baird, Nathanson & Spelling flanked by his two aides, his stride purposeful, his features set in a do-not-disturb mask. He paused outside Lionel's office just long enough for Fredda MacDougall, Lionel's secretary, to announce his arrival. Then, without waiting for an invitation, he walked in, shut the door behind him, and approached Lionel's desk.

Lionel looked at his watch, then at his guest. "You've always been extremely punctual, Senator. It's one of your strengths."

On the drive over, John had tried to steel himself against just that type of barbed innuendo. Despite his best efforts, he clenched his fist and had to fight not to launch a roundhouse punch at Lionel's jaw. Instead, again without invitation, John seated himself.

Lionel laced his fingers together, rested his elbows on his massive leather-topped desk, and leaned forward, a bemused look on his face. "What can I do for you, Senator?" he said, as if John had come hat in hand to beg a favor.

"You can give Pamela her divorce."

Lionel shrugged innocently. "It's not up to me, John. For some reason, Pamela's stalling. Are you two having problems?"

"Cut the bullshit, Lionel! You're the one stringing it out. And probably just for the sheer joy of tormenting her."

"Quite the opposite. To put it bluntly, your bride-to-be is trying to shake me down for everything she can get."

John snorted his disgust. "Only you could define a reasonable settlement as a shakedown."

"Of course that settlement seems reasonable to you. You're not the one paying out!"

John threw up his hands in exasperation. "The woman was with you for nearly ten years, for goodness sakes. The settlement you and your lawyers laid out is not only insulting, it's unconscionable!"

"She didn't think so when she signed the prenuptial."

"Which she did without benefit of counsel." John pushed back his chair, rose from his seat, planted his hands on the desk, and hovered over Lionel. "She trusted you to do the right thing, and you fucked her!"

Lionel snickered. "I'd say we're both guilty of that. Wouldn't you?"

John reached across the desk and grabbed Lionel by the collar. "Don't you dare speak about Pamela that way." As he let go, he pushed Lionel back into his chair.

Lionel retreated, moving out from beneath the heat of John's anger. "Look, I did what any wealthy man, including you, Chisolm, would do," he insisted. "I protected my assets."

John shook his head and clucked his tongue in obvious disgust.

"You're acting like a lover scorned, Lionel, and the role doesn't become you."

John could see that his last remark scored; he knew it would. This was an area in which the two men were alike: It didn't matter how often Lionel cheated on Pamela, when she took up with another man, Lionel's manly pride was hurt.

"What's your interest in all this, John? I don't think you need her money for anything, so why the rush to get this divorce finalized?"

"It's quite simple, really. We'd like to be married. Is that so hard to believe?"

Lionel smirked. "What I believe doesn't matter to you. And what you would like doesn't concern me. I intend to see that Pamela abides by the agreement she signed. If that puts a crimp in your plans, well . . ."

John waited for a look of triumph to wash over Lionel's face before wiping it away.

"Speaking of putting a crimp in one's plans," he said, segueing smoothly, "I had another reason for visiting you this afternoon. Since we go way back, I thought I'd afford you the courtesy of telling you personally that the legislation you lobbied for—that bill to prevent large banks from selling stock or buying brokerage houses—has been put on hold."

Lionel's eyes blazed. "How dare you!" he seethed. "That's important legislation. You were a broker once. You know what's happening. Banks are getting too big, too powerful, and too greedy. If we're not careful, they could gobble up everything in sight and monopolize the finance industry."

"Spare me, Lionel. Since when do you give a damn about anyone but yourself?"

"You can't do this."

Chisolm laughed. "Ah, but I can. I'm the chairman of that committee. My party is in the majority. If I want it to go through, it will. If I want to table it, I can. And if I want to kill it," he said, rising from his chair, "it's as good as dead."

John turned and walked to the door, his demeanor one of confidence and dismissal.

"I don't believe this!" Lionel shouted. "You're threatening to stall an important bill simply to muscle me into giving your girlfriend a rich divorce?"

"I didn't threaten anything." John's voice was tauntingly calm.

"I simply asked how your negotiations were going and then filled you in on a matter of mutual interest."

"My colleagues aren't going to like this," Lionel warned.

The senator turned and glared at his nemesis. "What you or your friends on the Street like isn't my concern," he mocked. "What is important to me, is doing the right thing for the American public. If that doesn't square with you, that's just too damn bad!"

Fredda MacDougall ripped the white ribbon off the blue box and rummaged through the tissue in search of the booty that lay within. It wasn't every day she received something from Tiffany's, and Pamela had exquisite taste. When she opened the small blue sack, she found a charming red enamel-and-silver heart.

"Thank you sooo much," she enthused as she pinned the brooch to her dress. How wonderful of Pamela to remember that she had a collection of pins and that the heart was her favorite shape. "I adore it, but really, you shouldn't have."

"It was my pleasure," Pamela said, playing the game. They both knew that Pamela's gifts were payment for information Fredda supplied about Lionel, as were these elegant private luncheons in Pamela's Park Avenue apartment.

The maid served their lobster salad, refilled their wineglasses, and disappeared as quietly as she had appeared. Pamela would have preferred asking Fredda straight out what Lionel's reaction had been to John's visit, getting her answer, and ushering the bitter spinster out the door, but that was not the way their relationship worked.

Long ago, back when her affair with Lionel first began, Pamela sensed that the woman who guarded his gate might prove to be an invaluable asset. Although Lionel didn't see it, Pamela knew immediately that Fredda was in love with her employer. Aware that Fredda's feelings were unrequited, Pamela reached out and befriended her. Fredda was tall, with a large frame, chalky white skin, and curly dark hair that she kept way too short for a woman of her size. Aside from wonderful cornflower blue eyes, she could only be described as unattractive. She was single, in her late forties, an only child whose parents had passed on, with few friends and even fewer romantic memories to recall on lonely evenings. Pamela appealed to Fredda by pretending they were equals: two women who had foolishly fallen in love with the extremely difficult, yet wildly irresistible Lionel Baird.

Over the years, Pamela's emotional and financial investment paid off; Fredda proved herself a fount of information. In the beginning, the two women commiserated about Lionel's apparent determination to remain unattached, as if they were both in the running and may the best one win. After Pamela and Lionel were married, Fredda—wanting to appear gracious in defeat—became Pamela's eyes and ears, reporting in whenever she suspected Lionel was being unfaithful to her friend.

There was no question that Fredda felt empowered by her ability to have access to things Lionel's wife did not; it allowed her to believe that she, not Pamela, was the most important woman in Lionel's life. In a way, she was. Lionel trusted her with everything from stocking his favorite jelly beans to clearing his schedule whenever he needed to be at an "unscheduled business meeting." She knew his shoe size, what brand of golf ball he preferred, what his face looked like when he was about to lose his temper, and what his eyes looked like when he was telling a lie. She also knew from personal experience how heartless he could be, which was why she didn't feel guilty about sharing her intimate knowledge with another woman who loved him and suffered because of it.

"John said you looked lovely the other day," Pamela said, priming the pump.

Fredda flushed. "I didn't think the senator noticed," she said.

"He thought the blue of your dress made your eyes even prettier." Pamela had insisted that John pay attention to the color of Fredda's dress. "They are your best feature, you know." Pamela smiled and delicately sipped her wine.

Fredda imbibed as well. "The senator was in quite a mood," she confided.

"Was he really?"

"He stormed down the hall like Patton." Her blue eyes widened at the recollection. "He wasn't in with Mr. Baird very long either."

"How was he when he left?"

Fredda paused, tapping her index finger on her unrouged lips. "Quite relaxed, actually."

"And Lionel?"

"Mr. Baird was not a happy camper." Fredda shook her head and turned her attention to the remains of her lunch, pushing an errant piece of lettuce around on her plate. "Those two men are like a lighted match and kerosene. You can't put them together for even a second without someone blowing up."

Pamela nodded. Fredda had just confirmed John's opinion that he had indeed unnerved the usually unflappable Lionel Baird.

"I really think they hate each other."

"They're both rather volatile, that's true, but don't you think that's a common trait among powerful men?" Pamela said, as if the two women were indeed girlfriends.

"Oh, absolutely," Fredda said, dabbing at her mouth as she tried to hide her complete lack of experience behind a damask napkin.

While on the surface, toying with Fredda might appear cruel, Pamela viewed it as simply another aspect of their *quid pro quo* relationship. Fredda fed Pamela information. Pamela gave Fredda lovely gifts. Occasionally, Pamela said things that underscored Fredda's social ineptitude. Fredda enjoyed reporting on Lionel's misdeeds. Though her tales were always coated with compassion, as if it pained her to deliver such unpleasant tidings, her expression made it clear that hurting Pamela was fun.

"I don't know what they were arguing about," she said, the look of the spoiler on her face, "but I hope the senator didn't say anything incriminating."

Pamela eyed her quizzically.

"Lionel records his meetings."

Pamela struggled to remain impassive. John would not be happy about this turn of events. "Since when?"

"Since his first wife and his daughter were murdered," Fredda said with genuine emotion. Pamela looked confused. "Assuming that either the mob or the cartel was responsible, Mr. Baird believed it wasn't out of the realm of possibility that he, too, could become a target."

"That makes sense." Pamela hated herself for feeling sorry for Lionel.

"Over the years, he became so paranoid that in addition to having bodyguards and an obsession with security devices, he wired his office and his town house so he could tape—and film—most of his meetings and conversations."

"I didn't know that." Suddenly, Pamela wondered what else he had filmed. "What does he do with these tapes?"

"Most of them are either destroyed or simply get filed away."

"Knowing Lionel, I'd believe that he stays up nights replaying his greatest moments. He probably gives himself standing ovations." Pamela's voice was thick with sarcasm.

"He has other things to do at night," Fredda implied.

"Really?" Pamela's interest was keen. "Who is it this time?"

"You don't know her."

Pamela's relief was immediate. Several times, Lionel's *amour du jour* had been a woman in Pamela's circle. Even Fredda was appalled by his lack of discretion.

"Mr. Baird introduced her as a private art broker specializing in photography."

Pamela recalled that the last time she visited the town house, she noticed that Lionel had added some large photographs to his collection.

"She's young," Fredda said.

Pamela's eyebrows arched. "How young?"

"Late twenties. Early thirties."

"It would serve the old dog right if he had a heart attack *in flagrante*. How long has this been going on?"

"At least six months."

Traditionally, Lionel's flings were short-lived; variety seemed to be the spice of his life. Six months bordered on commitment.

"What does she look like?"

"I only saw her once—when he gave her a grand tour of the office. She's tall and slim, with reddish hair and brown eyes." She paused, considering her words. "What surprised me is how basic she is. Definitely not the type Mr. B. usually goes for. She's more L.L. Bean than Geoffrey Beene, but he doesn't seem to care. Since he hooked up with her, the man smiles all the time."

"What's her name?"

Fredda crinkled her brow. "He introduced her as Max. No last name. No real first name. Just Max."

Pamela tented her fingers, tapping them against each other. "Keep an eye on her, will you Fredda? There's something about this that worries me."

"You're right. Something must be terribly wrong," Fredda said, trying to squelch her sarcasm, not succeeding. "After all, why would a dynamic man like Mr. Baird want to get involved with a beautiful, brainy, young woman who makes him smile, when he could have two dried-up old matrons like us?"

Pamela cringed. Fredda simply laughed. Sometimes the truth hurt.

CHAPTER

FOUR

Amanda stared down the line as she pulled the trigger of her 9mm Glock. Again and again, she fired. Each time, she could hear her police-academy instructor counseling not to practice aiming a gun at a target.

"Condition yourself to respond to a threat."

Quickly, she reloaded, readjusted her sight, and fired off another magazine. Her hand trembled as she lowered her gun to her side and slipped the headset off her ears, letting it dangle around her neck like a scarf. She pressed the button that propelled the paper target forward and watched as a bullet-riddled outline approached. A smile of satisfaction appeared: All her shots had hit their mark.

"That poor bastard didn't stand a chance."

Amanda spun around, her finger ready to slide onto the trigger. Jake Fowler's hands flew up in a gesture of surrender.

"Whoa!" he said, backing up. "That was a compliment. Not an invitation to a duel."

Amanda held her pose for a moment before holstering her gun. "I don't like to be surprised."

"I'll remember that in case I ever get the urge to give you a birthday party."

Edgy, she turned away and began to pack up her gear.

"Speaking of cases, you were very persuasive the other day, Detective," Jake persisted. Amanda's face remained blank. "You nailed that sucker to the wall."

"And that made your day?"

"As a matter of fact, it did." His voice was light, but a shadow darkened his eyes. "There's nothing I like better than nailing someone who thought they'd gotten away with murder."

The case Jake was talking about had disturbed everyone in the Twentieth Precinct as well as the Crime Scene Unit. A young woman had disappeared three years ago after a fight with a boyfriend. She had come to New York from the Midwest a little over a year before and was working as a receptionist at a small advertising agency. According to her roommate, she had a few friends, no immediate family. The police were fairly certain that foul play was involved and that the boyfriend was probably responsible, but without a body they had no case.

Then, a man took his dog for a walk along a narrow strip of green between the West Side Highway and the Hudson River. The dog seemed to be playing when suddenly he dug up some bones the man didn't think had been buried by another dog. He called the police, who unearthed a skeleton. Although there was considerable evidence to suggest that this was the corpse of the missing woman, there was no available information on the woman's blood group, no dental records, and no X-rays. All they had were some photographs given to police by the woman's roommate. Amanda identified her by means of the electronic superimposition of images: Superimposing the image of the skull on the photographs of the victim's face showed a perfect match between the two. The same comparisons were carried out with the skull and photographs of forty other women of similar age and constitution. None made such a perfect match.

"Of course, had I been the defense attorney, I would've hammered away at the narrow scope of your corroborating survey."

"Oh, really?"

"Absolutely," he said with the swagger of one who believed few, if any, could challenge him and win. "Forty women hardly constitutes a numerically adequate sampling of women living in Manhattan, let alone the other four boroughs."

"Those women were not randomly selected," Amanda argued, equally certain of victory. "They represented every possible skull size and shape within the realm of possibility for the victim's age and physical characteristics."

Jake's eyes narrowed as he debated the wisdom of widening this war of words versus declaring a draw. "I spoke to the jury foreman afterward," he said, opting for a momentary cessation of hostilities. "According to him, your testimony was decisive."

"Lucky for us the jury wasn't privy to your reservations," she snapped.

Jake smirked and shook his head. "Hey! Don't go all defensive on me. I was speaking hypothetically."

Amanda thought she had recognized Jake in the rear of the courtroom when she was on the stand. She also recalled wondering what his connection to the trial was.

"What were you doing there, anyway?" she asked.

"I'd been called as a possible witness in a nasty divorce. Fortunately, the parties in question thought better of airing their dirty laundry in public and decided to settle. I had some time on my hands. I was in the building. I'd heard about this case, heard you were the expert witness, so I figured, what the hell? It beat going back to the office to do paperwork."

"I'm glad we made it worth your while," Amanda said as she prepared to leave.

"That you did." When she didn't pick up the conversation as he expected, he followed her to the locker room. "Look, it's late. How about we make peace over a cup of coffee or something?"

"I don't . . ."

"A glass of wine? A bottle of champagne? Some caviar, perhaps?"

As she went to open the door to the women's locker room, he blocked her way.

"The truth is I'm famished and little black fish eggs don't sound appealing to me either. How 'bout a Big Mac? A kosher dog with the works? Or maybe a pizza slice? How's that sound?"

His sky blue eyes twinkled with flirtatious tenacity. He was not going away.

"Pizza," she said, pushing past him into the locker room. "In twenty minutes."

"Fifteen," he said poking his head in. "I pick the place and the pie."

"Whatever!" She shoved him out, closed the door, and smiled all the way to the showers.

If someone asked Amanda to describe herself, she was certain *paranoid* would be the first word out of her mouth. Here she was, having a perfectly pleasant evening with a handsome, engaging— when he wanted to be—man whose cheeks dimpled seductively when he smiled, and instead of luxuriating in his attention, she was wondering why a busy PI would spend a free afternoon in a musty courtroom.

Also, whether or not it was mere coincidence that he was at the same shooting range, at the same time she was. WITSEC-syndrome had kicked in.

WITSEC-syndrome was the name she had given to the disease she assumed all protected witnesses have. Basically, it was a defense mechanism that compelled an otherwise normal person to barricade the place where she stored her feelings and completely isolate herself from even the remotest possibility of intimacy. No friends. No lovers. No worries. WITSEC-syndrome in a nutshell.

As she listened to Jake banter with their waiter, she recalled that recently, as he often did, Lionel had asked about her love life. She'd already told him she'd had a brief affair in Italy and confessed to several other short-lived romances. This time, when she said she was currently uninvolved, he groused about the foolishness of voluntary loneliness. Hoping to cork another lecture, she told him about WITSEC-syndrome. At first, he laughed. Then, he grew serious.

"You've been in New York and out of the program for nearly six years," he reminded her. "You've moved on in every other area of your life."

As she always did when she and her father discussed romance—or her lack of it—she claimed to be a victim of habit and raised the issue of trust. Most times, Lionel said he understood. This time, he said, "You've come to trust me because you can feel how much I love you." She nodded. There was no question about that. "If you open the door to the possibility, someday, someone else is going to love you."

Her father's words echoed in Amanda's brain as she studied the man seated across from her. She watched as he tasted the wine. When he sipped it and let it linger on his tongue before swallowing and declaring it suitable, it reminded her of Tyler and Italy, and again she mused about their serendipitous reunion. It would be nice to have someone love her, she conceded. Opening the door was the hardest part.

"I'm a big fan of the Upper West Side," Jake was saying. "You've got Central Park, Columbus Avenue, Lincoln Center down a few blocks. Sort of the best of all worlds, don't you think?" When Amanda didn't answer, Jake tapped the table in front of her with the bottom end of his fork. "Hello." Amanda snapped out of her reverie. "You do live in this neighborhood, right?"

"How do you know where I live?" Even to her ears, she sounded curt, but she couldn't help it. It was reflex.

Jake shook his head. When he looked at her, he laughed. "Man, this is gonna be tough."

"I beg your pardon!"

He moved so that his face was inches from hers. His eyes were soft, and those adorable dimples reappeared. "I'm a private eye, Detective Maxwell. I meet a babe with brains, I check it out. You have a problem with that?"

"Depends on what you dug up."

"Let's see," he said, leaning back and folding his arms across his chest. "You graduated from John Jay *summa cum laude*. In case that wasn't enough to wow the brass at the NYPD, you did the *summa* thing again with a Master's in Forensic Science."

"I'm a good student." Amanda shrugged. Jake laughed at the obvious understatement.

"You didn't bother going the uniform route. Nope. No riding patrol or passing out traffic tickets for you. Uh-uh. You went straight to anticrime and got shipped off to the roughest, nastiest precinct in the entire five boroughs." He looked to see who might be listening and spoke in an exaggerated stage whisper. "Don't tell anyone I said so, but you were probably sent up to the Three-Two because they wanted to test you."

"And why would they want to do that?"

Jake tapped his chin with his finger. "Hmmmm. Could it be that you were of the female gender and about as smart as they come?"

"Whatever." Amanda had passed the test, and they both knew it. Not only had she earned her Gold Shield in record time, but rumor had it she was already in line to become a second-grader.

"The way I heard it, you were one of the most aggressive cops on the beat. Relentless, in fact. Once you homed in on a suspect, you went after him with a vengeance. True?"

"The last I heard, tracking down criminals was a major part of the job description. True?"

He laughed, marveling at Amanda's sangfroid. "True, but don't be so modest. According to my sources, whenever you made a collar, there was enough solid evidence for an indictment and, if the DA didn't blow it, a conviction. No wonder Wally Clarke tapped you for the CSU. You're a real comer."

"And this is boring," Amanda said sharply. She didn't like being dissected. "Since you seem to be such a big fan of biographies, why don't you tell me how you became Dick Tracy?"

"Clarence Darrow's suits didn't fit."

"I take it that's code for 'I didn't like being a trial lawyer.' "

He clinked his glass with his knife. "Give this girl another slice of pizza."

"No more pizza," she said, pushing her plate away. "And no changing the subject."

His deep blue eyes fixed on hers, appraising and assessing. Amanda didn't flinch.

"I started out as a prosecutor in the Justice Department," he said, finally, "but I couldn't stand the bureaucracy."

"And after you left the law?"

"Pushy little devil, aren't you?"

"I'm a detective, too, remember?"

"Touché." He chuckled. She was a challenge. He liked that. "After my gig at Justice, I went to the *Times* as an investigative crime reporter."

"I take it that suit didn't fit either."

"Right again." He swirled his Chianti in his glass before finishing it. "Actually, it was probably me that didn't fit. I'm not big on rules."

"So I've heard."

The corner of his mouth lifted in a half smile. It pleased him to know that she had asked about him. It pleased him even more to see that she didn't care he knew she had asked.

"It took me awhile," he said, "but I finally figured out that if I became my own boss, I didn't have to wear suits."

"I noticed." She eyed his leather blazer, crewneck sweater, and well-worn jeans. "Does Boss Fowler have any rules?"

"Only for my staff." When Amanda's eyes widened, Jake smiled. "You pictured me doing the Philip Marlowe thing, didn't you? One-man shop. Beleaguered secretary. Ashtrays overflowing with unfiltered butts. Ratty office with a glass door, poor lighting, manual typewriters, a dial phone, and a bottle of scotch in the drawer of my desk." Amanda laughed. That was precisely the way she pictured him. "Well, my secretary is definitely beleaguered, but other than that, you're way off."

"So, tell me how it really is."

"Nice digs. Fifth Avenue, midtown. Six full-time investigators, a dozen or so part-timers, two secretaries, and a receptionist who doubles as the bookkeeper." He paused and again, Amanda felt she was being evaluated. "She's also my mother."

Amanda was stunned. Jake shrugged as if it was no big thing.

"She's one of the brightest, most capable women I know. She's the only one I trust to handle my money, and she won't bitch if we miss a paycheck."

The love and admiration Jake had for his mother spilled out of him. Amanda found it sweet and said so. He harrumphed and quickly moved on, but he didn't deny his feelings. Amanda gave him points for that.

"Fowler & Company handles mostly corporate stuff, the occasional divorce, missing persons, and my specialty, cases the police mark closed that someone wants reopened."

"Fowler & Company," Amanda repeated, absorbing all she had learned about her companion. "I definitely stand corrected. That is not a *shop.*"

"Don't get carried away," he said. "We're not exactly Pinkerton."

"You're not exactly Sam Spade either."

"I started out that way, but much to my chagrin, I discovered I couldn't do everything myself. Since I'm a do-everything kind of guy, I hired on an as-needed basis." He refilled both their wineglasses, took a swig, and grinned at her. "Don't be fooled by the midtown address or the business card. As I'm sure the boys with the badges would tell you, I'm still the obnoxious bulldog I was when I worked at Justice. I don't like bad guys, and if there's a way to nab 'em and drag their butts to jail, I'm on it!"

Amanda was intrigued by this man. Probably because she sensed that something other than mere ambition was driving him. Too, because he was as good at hiding the truth as she was. He was being free with the basics—the how, the where, the what—but he was definitely avoiding the why.

"Why'd you become a cop?" he said, changing the subject as if intuiting her thoughts.

"*Hill Street Blues,* puzzles, and photography," she said after appearing to muse.

"You win. I'm stumped."

"I was always fascinated by the solving of crimes because at their heart, each case is a puzzle, and I love puzzles." Like much of her biography, this answer had been carefully rehearsed. "Also, as you might have gathered, I love taking pictures. Forensic photography seemed a natural blend."

"I liked police shows, too," he said. "Even oldies but goodies like *Dragnet* and *Hawaii Five-O.* But my all-time favorite was *Magnum, P.I.*"

"Figures," Amanda said. "He never wore a suit either."

Jake gasped, as if she had just said something terribly profound. "I never thought of that, but you're right. No wonder Selleck was my idol. How are you on old movies?"

"Love 'em. Especially the ones starring Cary Grant." Jake groaned. "And Fred Astaire."

He gripped his heart. "Max! You're killing me."

"Sorry," she said, laughing. "I guess I'm drawn to elegant men."

"Is that your way of letting me down easy?"

"Well . . . elegant isn't exactly the way I'd describe you," she said playfully. "Then again, you did offer me champagne and caviar."

"Yes, I did," he said, looking smug. "You're the one who chose pizza."

"Mea culpa."

"I'll tell you what," he said, as he signaled for the check. "Next time, I'll wear a suit. You wear a skirt. And we'll do elegant."

Amanda arched an eyebrow. "We will?"

"Absolutely," he said as he took her arm and steered her toward the door. "We'll go to my place and order in. I'll put classical music on the stereo, candles and cloth napkins on the table, and instead of shoving the slices in our mouths, we'll use knives and forks. You can't get more elegant than that!"

"Pizza. Leather. And a sense of humor! I like the sound of this guy." Annie painted a delicate, almost invisible line on the upper lids of Amanda's eyes with a finely bristled artist's brush. When she finished, she whited out Amanda's real eyebrows, replacing each of them with a penciled half-moon curve. "So, what do you think? Are you going to see him again?"

"I don't know, and right now, I don't care."

"Okay, okay. Calm yourself. You're making my hand shake."

After she finished Amanda's eyes, she dipped a huge powder puff into a bowl of baking flour and coated Amanda's face with it. Then, she rouged Amanda's cheeks and brushed pearlescent powder in the deep cleavage formed by the bustier she was wearing. More white flour on Amanda's upper chest and neck, a swipe of pink lip gloss, and some shadowing along the side of her nose. Annie stood back to study the effect.

"I think we're there. Let's put on the wig and see what we've got."

Amanda fitted the white wig on her head, pulling several curls onto her forehead. Annie combed the remaining hair into a ponytail and twisted it into a fat curl that rested on Amanda's right shoulder, which was bare thanks to a scandalously low-cut peignoir tied under the breasts with an apricot-chiffon ribbon.

"Lounging up against those curtains and all those puffy cushions, Boucher himself wouldn't recognize you," Annie declared as Amanda adjusted the bustier, pushing her breasts up and out even further.

Amanda checked the lighting and her camera setting, then lay down on several sofa pillows that had been covered with a piece of celadon damask. Holding an ornate gold mirror in her hand, she reclined against an elegantly camouflaged chairback, lifted her chin, pursed her lips until they formed a moue that would have made Madame Pompadour envious, and then, when Annie nodded that everything looked right, pressed the shutter remote.

They were in the studio corner of Annie's SoHo loft, collaborating on the last photograph for Amanda's series of "Mirror Images": portraits of people—both present and past—studying themselves in the mirror. Some were historical, like the François Boucher–like subject of today's shoot. Others, like a portrait of Elvis Presley adjusting the belt on his famous white jumpsuit that Amanda and Annie had done two weeks before, depicted modern-day celebrities basking in their reflected glory.

Amanda had conceived the idea after she first met Annie and heard about her new friend's work in the theater. Amanda had been disguising and then photographing herself for years, but those black-and-white, eight-by-tens looked like photographs any family might have sitting on a piano or a mantel. They were anonymous strangers who looked strikingly familiar because they were everyone, yet no one in particular.

With Annie's help, Amanda moved on to full-color, large-scale re-creations of classic portraits by painters such as Boucher, Ingres, Reynolds and the like, as well as modern camera masters like Herb Ritts, Richard Avedon, Annie Leibovitz, and their colleagues. She'd select a portrait—male or female, it didn't matter—rent an appropriate costume, create a suitable background, then turn herself over to Annie and her box of putty and paints.

The results were astonishing. All looked authentic; some rated a double take they were so on point. Yet since every human has imperfections, every portrait was left with obvious flaws. In Amanda's version of the ubiquitous Madonna and child, Madonna, the entertainer, dressed in one of her *Evita* costumes, held her baby in the archetypal pose, but the breast the child was suckling was made of molded plastic. The sideburns of an eighteenth-century English nobleman fluffed out from a rubber forehead. And although the fedora and the smile were perfect, Amanda's Jimmy Durante had a nose that was an obvious concoction of putty and paste.

After the shoot was completed and they had cleaned up Annie's loft, Amanda showered and changed, and the two friends fixed an easy dinner—salad, bread, pasta, and wine—that they shared seated on cushions set around a large wooden cocktail table.

"In case I haven't told you lately, you are one fabulous makeup artist," Amanda said, lifting her wineglass and tilting it toward Annie in tribute.

Annie accepted the gesture of thanks with a quick nod and a broad sweep of her arm. "Thank you, my public," she said grandly. "One day, perhaps you'll be able to say you knew me when."

Amanda eyed Annie carefully, a hopeful smile creeping onto her lips. "Did you get a movie offer?"

"No, but . . ." she said dragging out the suspense, "I've been talking with some people about creating my own makeup line."

"What a great idea!" Amanda's enthusiasm was instant and sincere. "Tell me everything."

"There's not much to tell, really. I guess it started when the heroine on my soap turned delusional." She rolled her eyes and gestured as if she too had gone mad. "She has these fantasies about having lived in other times. Naturally, when we transport her back to wherever she lived last, I get to do my thing."

"Sort of like what we do on these shoots."

"Exactly. Well, that story boosted our ratings. The soap got hot. People began taking notice. My name got around and all of a sudden, stars from other soaps began calling to ask if I did private makeup consultations. I said yes, because, hey, what the hell!"

"Absolutely!" Amanda felt herself being swept up in Annie's excitement.

"But it didn't stop there. With all the films being shot in and around New York, my agent figured now was the time to push me for one of them. So, I worked one or two low-budget jobs, did some of the big guns at the Emmys, got a little publicity, a write-up in *W* and *Allure* and . . ."

"And now you're makeup artist to the stars!"

"Not exactly," Annie cautioned, "but the success of brands like Bobbie Brown, Nars, and Lorac has made it cool to have real makeup people develop cosmetics. I thought I'd call it, the Hart Line. What do you think?"

"I love it. So what have you done about getting it started?"

"I can't do anything until I get some money. I know what I'd like to put out there, and I know how it should be marketed, but I need a Sugar Daddy to bankroll the project."

"Banks?"

Annie shook her head. "Traditional lenders want all kinds of collateral. Look around you," she said, drawing Amanda's attention to her loft. "What've I got that a bank would consider collateral?"

"How about a large cosmetics company?"

"When you're willing to give them your name and your ideas for free, they don't want anything to do with you. When you begin to steal their customers and their profits, they're all over you, looking to buy you out. Go figure."

"I wish I could help," Amanda said.

"I know." Annie smiled warmly. "Just keep your fingers crossed and your eyes and ears open." She refilled Amanda's wineglass and topped off her own. "Speaking of keeping your eyes open," she said with a sly grin, "I say, if this Jake person asks, you go, girl."

"You know what I love most about you?" Amanda said, chuckling. "I thought we put an end to that particular conversation three hours ago."

"We did?" Annie's large espresso eyes grew even larger.

"You just don't let up, do you?"

"Hey! When you're on the other side of thirty, you can't afford to let guys like this get away."

Amanda's stomach lurched. She didn't remember discussing her age with Annie. "What makes you think I'm thirty?"

"Because we're the same age. Your birthday was in January. Mine's coming up in August."

Amanda searched her memory. She rarely told anyone her age and other than when she had a sweet-sixteen party so as not to appear conspicuous by its absence, never revealed the date of her real birthday. Could she have made that kind of mistake? Had she grown so comfortable with Annie that she would have let her guard down like that?

"If I thought hitting the big three-oh was so upsetting to you," Annie said, clearly concerned, "I never would have brought it up."

"It's not that," Amanda said, wanting to get off the subject.

"So what is it? You don't want to share about this new guy?"

Annie nudged Amanda under the table with her foot. "Afraid I might muscle in on your territory?"

Amanda forced herself to shake off her suspicions and laugh. Annie would be competition. About five-four, and very shapely, she had ivory skin and straight, licorice hair that she wore short, tucked behind her ears except for an errant piece she let droop onto her cheek. She had full lips that she liked to keep highly glossed and a wardrobe that was strictly downtown—head to toe black, broken only by touches of chocolate brown, midnight blue, and the occasional white tee shirt.

"I don't have any claims on Jake Fowler," Amanda insisted. "Territorial or otherwise. I don't even know if I like him. He's cocky, slightly arrogant, and nosy."

Annie laughed. "He pressed a button, didn't he?"

"Maybe," Amanda conceded. "But even if he did, he's not the only pebble on my beach."

Annie nodded as she finished chewing her pasta. "Right," she said, washing the food down with wine. "There's Mr. Three-Piece."

"His name is Tyler Grayson."

"Excuse me, Your Ladyship. I forgot."

"He's very nice, Annie."

"I know. You had a big thing with him once upon a time." She rested her back against her couch, stretched her legs, sipped her wine, and studied her friend. "And then, of course, there's that older man you've been sneaking around with."

Amanda felt the color drain from her face. She had never told Annie a thing about Lionel. She was certain of that. "What are you talking about?" Her heart was pounding.

"You've been seeing someone for months. If he was young and studly and you wanted me to simply writhe with jealousy, you would tell me his name, show me his picture, or introduce us.

"Instead, you're busy all the time with some anonymous dude who takes you places that require uptight little black dresses. Since I've been around the block a couple of times myself, I figure, one— Mr. Mysterious is taking you to expensive restaurants. Hence, the upscale wardrobe. Two—he's probably married and has a name I'd recognize. Hence, the secrecy. And three—only someone older who doesn't have to stay late in his office to impress his boss could take you out as often as this Romeo has. Exactly how far off base am I?"

"Not too far, actually." Amanda tried to keep her tone light, but it disturbed her that Annie had come so close to the truth. She and Lionel had to be more vigilant.

"You're not going to fill in the blanks, are you?" Annie looked her friend squarely in the eye and remained hopeful that perhaps this once, Amanda would open up. But Amanda had shut down, the way she always did when Annie ventured onto the property listed as Private.

"No," Amanda said with an implacability that had become all too familiar. "I'm not."

Annie pulled her knees up under her chin. The chill emanating from Amanda was palpable.

"How about if we change the subject?" she said.

"Good idea."

Annie raised her wineglass. "Here's to your upcoming show at the Lloyd Franks Gallery." She smiled warmly. "I'm proud of you, Max. You've come a long way."

Amanda clinked glasses and tried to appear upbeat, but inside, the WITSEC-syndrome burbled. As outlandish as it seemed—even to her—Amanda found herself suspecting Annie Hart of not being who she claimed to be. Suddenly, things Amanda had noticed but dismissed, loomed larger. Like finding issues of the *Miami Herald* in Annie's magazine basket. She said her soap was doing a shoot down there, and she wanted to soak up some local knowledge. But, Amanda thought, Annie was adopted. Her heritage was Latino. Did she come from Miami originally instead of being a native New Yorker as she claimed to be? Could she be related to someone from the Espinosa cartel? And what about their initial meeting? How odd was it to meet someone in a morgue and want to befriend her? Plus, Annie forced their second encounter, as well as their third and fourth. Amanda never took the lead in relationships. Maybe this was part of a plan and Annie was the setup. No, she told herself. She was simply being paranoid.

"I have to go." Amanda practically jumped to her feet. Minutes later, without any apology or explanation, she was gone.

Alone and upset, Annie stormed around her loft cleaning up and chiding herself for her carelessness. Teasing about the older man was one thing—trying to get Amanda to confirm Annie's suspicions was a reach—but mentioning her birthday was a serious slip-up. Whatever had prompted that lapse—wine, comfortable surroundings, a mistaken sense of invincibility—Annie couldn't let it happen again.

"Next thing you know," she said in a voice laced with disgust, "you'll call her Ricki!"

Someone was following her. Amanda sensed the tail shortly after she left Annie's apartment. Quickening her pace, she slipped her backpack off her left shoulder and shifted it so it rested on her back and left her arms free to go for her gun. Alert for any sudden changes in footstep patterns or the sound of an accomplice, she headed straight for the Houston Street station and prayed the platform wouldn't be empty. When the train arrived, she boarded swiftly, thankful that the seat she favored—the one near the door that connected the cars— was free. With her back covered and a full view, she was alert for anything that might give her stalker away, but whoever it was, was experienced enough to maintain a distance. At one point, she guessed he got off the train and reentered in another car. It was a long ride from Houston to Eighty-sixth Street. No one other than she had stayed in the same car for the entire journey.

Amanda was a detective, trained by the NYPD to defend herself against the ravages of all sorts of street crime. But if she was being tailed, it was not by a misguided youth bent on stealing her wallet or even some deviate hungry to assert his dominance over women by raping her. If she was a target, the shooter was a trained mob assassin. And that was a completely different kind of animal.

She exited the station on Broadway and turned uptown, going toward Eighty-ninth. Within seconds, she heard someone fall into line behind her, his footsteps patterning hers. Spotting a *bodega,* she walked in and pretended to peruse the shelves, her eyes trained on the door. When it was clear that no one had followed her inside, she bought a bottle of juice; if need be, she could smash the bottle and use the glass as a weapon. When she left the *bodega,* the footsteps were absent, but the feeling of a lurking presence remained.

Once inside her apartment, Amanda checked the locks on both windows and door. Though she kept her .38 tucked inside her belt, she removed her 9mm from its locked safebox and loaded it. Turning on a light in the bedroom, she retrieved a 12-gauge Remington short-barrel shotgun from a specially designed rack beneath her bed. She loaded that, locked it, carefully placed it in between her bed and a nightstand, then returned to her living room. Peering through a space between wooden blinds, she carefully surveyed the dimly lit street. For several minutes, she saw nothing. Then, a lone figure darted out of the shadows, walked briskly to the corner, and turned. Before he disappeared, the glow of the streetlamp caught him. The light touched his jacket and flashed back as if it had hit plastic. Or silk.

Or leather.

It was well past midnight, but Amanda was wide-awake. Fully dressed, she lay on her bed in the dark, staring at the ceiling as she waited for Sam Bates to return her call. The telephone rested on one side of her, her 9mm on the other. She had put away her .38, but her shotgun stood ready. She tried to be patient, but waiting for Sam to scout a public phone booth in downtown Los Angeles was difficult. Though she checked her apartment for bugs twice a day, Sam insisted that whenever they spoke, at least one of them be on an anonymous line.

She thought about calling Lionel, but rejected that idea. Hard as he tried, he really didn't understand. He would have Thompson pick her up and bring her to his town house. He would attempt to comfort her and probably would provide an intelligent ear for her conjecture. But he would perceive her speculation as encouragement to act, and that was not acceptable.

The ring of the telephone startled her.

"Uncle Sam?"

"The one and only."

She heard his voice and a Pavlovian calm sluiced over her. "Thanks for getting back to me so quickly," she said, suddenly wondering if perhaps this late-night cry for help was an overreaction. "I hope I didn't disturb you. I mean, this isn't an emergency or anything."

"What's the matter, Amanda? Has something happened?"

Amanda bolted upright and clicked on a light. The darkness no longer felt like an ally. While she had expected her call to surprise Sam, what she just heard wasn't surprise or Sam's habitual prudence. It was anxiety.

"My antennae are probably working overtime," she said, nerves prickling her skin, "but something's spooking me. Suddenly I'm suspicious of everyone and everything."

She relayed her qualms about Annie and her belief that tonight, she had been followed. "I can't be certain, but I don't think it's the first time."

"Your antennae are usually very accurate, Amanda. Be extra careful."

The voice that had calmed her only moments before became unsettling. In place of an assurance of safety, she heard alarm.

"What's happened that you don't want to tell me?" When he hesitated, she felt as if an arctic wind had rushed through her bedroom.
"Is Mom all right?"

"Yes. She's fine. But we're on alert. Jaime Bastido was released
from prison two weeks ago."

Amanda shivered. Her eyes automatically scanned her surroundings. Her fingers gripped the butt of her Glock. "Why didn't you
tell me?"

"We expected him to leave the country immediately. Like his
cohorts did."

"When were they released?" *Why hadn't anyone told her?*

"About five years ago." Sam heard the anger in her voice. He
pressed his ear against the telephone so he could assess Amanda's
level of distress, but it was difficult to do long-distance. "Both of
them returned home to Cali."

"And?"

"Word is they were killed the minute they hit Colombian soil."

"And Jaime?" Amanda asked, the pitch of her voice rising. "Did
he decide to take his chances and reembrace the motherland?"

Sam's silence terrified and infuriated Amanda.

"Jaime's disappeared."

"And neither you nor my mother thought to tell me about this!"
She was up and pacing, her body a tightly coiled spring of resentment.
"When exactly did you plan to clue me in? After Bastido gunned
me down? I'm out here, Sam," she said through gritted teeth. "In
plain sight. Did you forget that?"

Sam tried to respond, but Amanda was too enraged to hear him.

"I realize I forfeited my right to your protection by coming to
New York, but foolish me, I thought you cared. I thought I could
count on you."

"Hold on, Amanda." Sam's voice was stern. "We had a tail on
Bastido from the minute he left Joliet. He went to Miami, turned
up in San Diego a week later, then, two days ago, disappeared. We
think he might have sneaked into Mexico."

"Then, again, he might have hopped a train to New York."

"We checked the airports and train stations." That sounded lame
and ineffectual, and he knew it. He tried to recover by saying, "I'm
going to call the Service and put someone on you."

"Don't." Her voice was low and flinty. "I know how to take care
of myself."

"I don't want you to have to take care of yourself."

"Maybe not, but bottom line: That's the way it is."

It was rare that Amanda allowed emotions to surface, but the affection in Sam's voice—and her growing sense of peril—provoked an uninvited crowd of tears. Alone and threatened, she let them fall.

"Are you all right?" Sam asked.

"I'm fine." As she wiped her eyes, she hastened to slam the door on the soft spot that had produced this unguarded moment. It had taken years to achieve this level of self-control, but Amanda viewed it as a necessity. If her past had taught her anything, it was that thick skin served as protective armor. "Is there anything else I should know?"

"The Service and the Bureau are on nationwide alert. We're not certain he's crossed the border, but in case he has, we're also trying to get word to DEA agents working undercover in Mexico. Don't worry, sweetheart. When Bastido reappears, we'll know. And the minute we do, you'll know. I promise."

Amanda remained awake long after they said their good-byes. Why bother trying to sleep? She was already in the midst of a nightmare.

CHAPTER

FIVE

The captain announced they were third in line for takeoff and would be on their way to Chicago in a few minutes. Amanda checked her seat belt, clicked on the overhead light, and opened the *Morning Telegraph,* hoping to relax. Instead, her stomach somersaulted as if the plane had hit an air pocket: SENATOR ACCUSES MEXICAN DRUG CARTELS OF MONEY LAUNDERING. The article said Senator John Chisolm believed "Mexican drug cartels were taking a page out of the past and laundering money through American banks much as the Colombian cartels had during the seventies and eighties."

"Worse," he was quoted as saying, "they're getting loans from American banks to buy companies involved in cross-border businesses. It's outrageous to think that trucks paid for with American dollars are being used to transport heroin and cocaine across our borders and onto the streets of our cities."

The article went on to say that many members of Congress believed that the government of Mexico protected its narcotics dealers from prosecution, and for that deserved censure. The bylined reporter, a woman named Hallie Brendel, said that several of her sources—who insisted upon remaining anonymous—said it would be hypocritical for the American government to criticize the Mexicans when the same protection was being given by our government to the American financial community, which greatly profited from the sale of drugs.

"While most from the aforementioned community denied such charges," the piece continued, "Senator John Chisolm, Republican from New York, courageously broke ranks, stepped forward, and promised to launch a complete investigation.

Amanda skimmed the rest, but when she reached the last sentence, her gaze locked on the senator's words: "We'd better clean up our streets now, or we're going to have to do another mop-up, like we did after Operation Laundry Day. And believe me, we don't want that. The cost in dollars and human lives is more than any of us want to spend."

Amanda's eyes blurred. *Some of us have already spent more than our share,* she thought.

At another airport, Lionel Baird sat in the first-class lounge waiting to board a plane for Detroit. He, too, was fixed on Hallie Brendel's article, but his reaction wasn't nearly as visceral as Amanda's. Indeed, it was cynical. Lionel viewed this as the opening salvo in John Chisolm's reelection campaign.

"The bastard needed an issue," Lionel muttered to himself. "And just like the alligator he is, he's going to feed on his own."

"Excuse me, sir. Aren't you on Flight 555?"

Lionel looked up. He must have appeared befuddled because the woman repeated her question slowly, as if she thought he was a doddering fool who couldn't keep track of the time.

"The screen shows they've posted a final boarding call," she added, enunciating every word.

He wanted to tell her that the reason he wasn't raptly gazing at the televised departure schedule like every other trained poodle in this so-called lounge was that he wasn't accustomed to boarding calls, final or otherwise. On his private jet, the pilot took off at his say-so. He wanted to tell her that it had been at least fifteen years since he had flown a commercial airline, and he had not missed anything about the experience. But most of all, he wanted to tell her that even at his advanced age, he was able to maintain full control of his motor and intellectual skills and rarely, if ever, drooled. Instead, recalling Amanda's admonition against drawing attention to himself, he thanked her politely, retrieved his briefcase, and rushed toward the gate.

Once onboard, he set aside his pique and focused on the reason for this trip: Sam Bates had called and requested that Lionel join Amanda, Beth Maxwell, and himself at a safe site. According to the marshal, a situation had arisen that necessitated heightened security measures. Lionel agreed without hesitation, then pressed for specifics.

Reluctantly, Sam revealed that Jaime Bastido had gone underground. Although the FBI and the Marshals Service believed Jaime probably had gone to Mexico to offer his laundering expertise to the new kings of the trade, Sam assured Lionel that both agencies were committed to protecting Amanda and Beth. Also, he raised the possibility of assigning someone to Lionel.

"If Jaime and his friends know who Amanda is, they know who you are," the marshal said bluntly. "Your visibility, national name recognition, and media worthiness make you an extremely tempting target."

Lionel thanked Bates for his concern, but declined the offer of protection. He already had an intricate security system in place. Bates protested that perhaps Lionel was being too cavalier. "The Marshals Service doesn't send personnel to protect against breaking and entering. Our policy is only to make this offer if we believe someone's life is at stake."

Lionel thanked him, then patiently reminded him that thanks to Marshals Service policy, for twenty years he believed that his wife and daughter had been blown to bits.

"I'm sure my name is on several lists," he said dryly. "Money painted a bull's-eye on my chest years ago."

That night, hidden among the locals at Rudy's, a pizzeria in Closter, New Jersey, Lionel and Amanda discussed the call from Bates.

"Thank you for going along with this," she said, relieved that Lionel had assented to convene in Madison, Wisconsin. "And thank you for following Sam's instructions without an argument."

Lionel nodded as if compliance came naturally. They both knew it had taken enormous control to hold his tongue and not insist on having his way. Instead of flying with Amanda directly to Madison in Lionel's Gulfstream—which Lionel thought was safer and more efficient—Lionel would fly Northwest via Detroit. Amanda's flight was routed through Chicago. Bates and Beth would fly from Los Angeles to Milwaukee and drive over to meet them.

"I really don't care about trivial arrangements, Amanda," he said, his mouth puckering from the taste of his wine. Rudy's was known for its pizza, not its *Pino Grigio*. "Believe it or not, I am capable of being a regular guy."

He underlined his point by drawing her attention to the tables on either side of them, both of which held large families devouring pasta and pizza as if the FDA had just declared starch an elixir.

"What I do care about, however, is your safety, and, frankly, I'm not convinced the authorities are doing a proper job."

Lionel was furious that no one had thought to inform Amanda of Bastido's release. The fact that an agent had been surreptitiously assigned to protect her didn't quell his rage. He condemned Bates, the system, the Marshals Service, the police force, and any other organization that came to mind. When he announced that he intended to hire bodyguards for her, Amanda's reaction was swift and definite.

"Absolutely not! They already have the edge," she explained. "Don't make it sharper."

"What do you mean they have the edge?" Lionel squirmed. "What edge?"

"If whoever is looking for me has discovered my real identity, they know what I look like, where I live, where I work, and who my friends are." She paused, allowing the import of her words to sink in. "I, on the other hand, don't know who they are, how many there are, where they're coming from, or what they want." She shrugged helplessly and looked around the crowded restaurant. "Hell! They could be sitting next to me, and I wouldn't know until it was too late."

She was right. Assassins didn't wear signs advertising their presence. They skulked about in the gray, ambiguous world of the anonymous, watching and waiting for a moment when they could strike and escape, penalty-free. The thought made Lionel sweat.

"And don't think your bodyguards can't be bought, Lionel, because they can!" She saw the skepticism in his eyes and feared for him. Privilege created a bubble of false security, one that could be easily breached with the right promises or the proper amount of cash. To emphasize her point, she said, "I don't care how much you pay them. Loyalty comes with the paycheck. Someone offers to pay more, loyalty shifts, and you're left with your guard down."

Amanda was leaning across the table so that she could say what she had to say without anyone but Lionel hearing her. Her eyes were soft, but her tone was definite.

"I don't mean to frighten you, but I've led a different life, so I've learned different lessons. The main one is that there are very few people in this world you can trust unconditionally. I have two: you and Beth." He looked at her quizzically. She knew what he was thinking. "Uncle Sam is the one who taught me that unless someone's

life is inexorably linked to mine, they're not in the line of fire and, therefore, not to be trusted. And that includes him."

Lionel suddenly felt small and ignorant in the face of his daughter's courage. He brayed and pounded his fists and made grand pronouncements, but in the end, there was little he could do to help her or himself. Amanda was cool and matter-of-fact. There was no braggadocio in her assessment of her plight, no puffed-up bravado about how she intended to deal with it. Probably, Lionel supposed, because Amanda had lived most of her life with the knowledge that someday this scenario would play itself out.

"So, what do you do?" he asked, awed by her dispassion. "How do you protect yourself?"

"I make good use of the weapons I have: access to police files. My detective skills. And time."

Lionel was confused.

"For stalkers, the game is tormenting their victim, drip by drip by drip. What I have to do is analyze their method of torment for clues and use their play time to investigate them."

"What do you look for?"

The muscles in Amanda's face tightened. "Who would get the biggest thrill out of seeing Mom and me dead."

"Good Lord!" Lionel's agitation was escalating. Amanda might have soothed his nerves, but for his own safety, she believed he needed to grasp how very real the danger was.

"Mom's testimony changed a lot of lives," she said. "The Feds have zeroed in on Bastido as our biggest worry, but I'm not so sure. The cartel guys expect to be caught and put away. It's goes with the territory.

"But what about the Hudson National Bank officers. Or the man from Nathanson & Spelling. Or even the families of the mob mules. These weren't the kingpins raking in millions of dollars that they stashed in offshore banks for their old age. These were the big-risk, small-reward guys who lost everything when Mom fingered them. Which is why they make me nervous. They hate us. And they don't have anything left to lose."

Throughout his flight to Detroit, Lionel reran that conversation over and over in his head, mentally walking around it so he could view it from every conceivable angle. What troubled him most was the stink of uncertainty that surrounded this entire situation. There were no definite suspects, no particular plan, no clear-cut support

system, no bottom line. Just a lot of ifs and maybes, words that to him were anathema.

Alarmed, he struggled to find a sensible strategy. He considered the situation the way he would a business proposal. Divorcing his emotions from the process, he analyzed positives and negatives, outside influences, the law of probabilities as well as the existence of unpredictable possibilities. Aware that this type of circumstance exceeded his purview, he stretched his imagination as far as he could, and then again, pushing well beyond its usual borders.

But, he realized dismally as his plane landed, he was searching for a clean, quick, and efficient solution. There would be none because Amanda's gut was frighteningly on point: the most obvious threat was the least likely. And the least obvious suspect would surely be the hardest to find, the hardest to stop, and the one capable of the greatest harm.

In Wisconsin, spring played the reluctant debutante. It was early April, yet snow drew a frosty line around the two large lakes that centered this Midwestern capital. Blustery winds blew down from Canada and pushed temperatures well below the freezing mark, emptying the streets of all save a few warm-blooded citizens and hardy clusters of students on their way to the library, a dorm, The Union, or the Kollege Korner, a bar known more familiarly as the KK.

Lionel steered his rented car out the driveway of the Edgewater Hotel onto Wisconsin Avenue. He turned left onto East Gorham and headed north. The plan was for everyone to meet at a house Sam had borrowed on the shores of Lake Mendota; it was a weekend/summerhouse owned by a Chicago businessman who every now and then could be called upon to do a favor for the Marshals Service. Amanda was staying at a boardinghouse on the Lake Monona side of town and would arrive at about four o'clock. Lionel's instructions were to appear about five.

As Lionel wended his way around the road system that ringed this huge lake, his heart pumped faster than normal. He was nervous about a number of things: the plans the Marshals Service had come up with to protect Amanda, meeting Sam Bates, and, most especially, seeing the woman he still thought of as Cynthia Baird.

Vanity, and a rare pang of insecurity, prompted a quick look at his reflection in the rearview mirror. At sixty, he remained a good-looking man, he thought, even if the skin on his neck had gone a bit slack and the hair on his head had silvered and thinned. There were creases in his forehead and a puffiness to his cheeks that hadn't been there in his youth, but the distinctive, Kirk Douglas cleft in his chin—something Amanda had inherited, albeit delicately softened—still gave him a rakish aspect. His eyes, slightly hooded by age, were still bright and curious. His mind was still sharp, and his body still rewarded his passions.

He scowled. According to Amanda, his ex-wife and the marshal were lovers; that bothered Lionel more than he was willing to admit. His foot lifted off the accelerator to slow his progress and prioritize his emotions. Today was about personal safety, not petty jealousy, he reminded himself. No baggage could come through the door of that house. He wanted to comply fully and completely, yet jealous was how he felt.

Why, he wondered, did Beth's relationship with Marshal Bates disturb him so? After all, they had divorced twenty-five years before—because of him, although the decision was hers. Did he live in such a Lionel-centered world that he honestly expected women to carry a torch for him until the end of their days? Possibly. Was it because Beth Maxwell had reentered his life at a time when Pamela Baird was exiting? Unlikely. He had stopped caring about Pamela a long time ago and had never suffered from a lack of companionship.

Or was it because Cynthia Baird had excised Lionel from her life—and their daughter's—without so much as a phone call. Bates had been a stranger then, yet she had sought his counsel and acted on his advice. Lionel had been her husband. The father of her child. Why hadn't his feelings mattered?

It was getting dark. Behind him, a car turned on its headlights. Lionel snapped to attention. He had been careless and let his mind wander. How long had this car been following him? Was it a tail or an innocent driver on his way home from work? Lionel didn't know and believed he should have. Quickly, he switched his lights on. The car drew closer, narrowing the gap between them. Lionel sped up. As he did, he looked in his sideview mirror, noted the make of the car and that it bore Illinois plates. He dug into his suit pocket, took out a pen and started to jot down the numbers on the plate when the car turned off the main road. For the next quarter mile, Lionel held his breath, watching to see if it reappeared.

A mile or so later, just past Maple Bluff, the road curved. Lionel squinted as if to tighten his focus, both mentally and visually. He homed in on a point around the bend that jutted out into the lake. That headland was his mark. He was almost there.

Shaking off extraneous thoughts and readying himself for the unexpected, he followed the directions to a large white house that stood on a bluff overlooking Lake Mendota. As he drove around to a carport at the back where he had been told to park, he noted with grudging admiration that while the house appeared to be part of a community, it was set apart and somewhat isolated.

He walked around to the front, appreciating the Greek Revival style of the architecture as well as the landscaping, which took Madison's harsh winters into account, favoring hardy pines and evergreens. Beneath patches of snow that quilted the grounds, he spotted what appeared to be a small garden off to the right, facing west. From its location, he guessed it was a cutting bed. A larger garden faced south and probably produced a bounty of summer vegetables. Lionel might have spent most of his adult life in New York City, but he grew up in the suburbs of Connecticut with a mother who had a decidedly green thumb.

He rang the bell and waited, suspecting that his approach had been monitored. After several interminable minutes, during which Lionel actually entertained the thought that the man in the car with the Illinois plates was an assassin who somehow had beaten Lionel here, hidden in the shrubbery, and was about to gun him down, Amanda opened the door. He hoped his relief wasn't obvious.

"Welcome to Fort Maxwell," she gibed as she greeted him with an affectionate hug and escorted him into the living room.

It was a charming room with beautiful, white wooden window frames, moldings, and mantel. The pale yellow walls were refreshing in this gray winter's light; they must dazzle in summer. Tastefully furnished with area rugs, rustic wooden tables, and simple, white couches, the space exuded a welcome aided and abetted by accents of folk art and a cozy fire blazing away in the generous hearth. Here and there, Lionel noticed crockery vases filled with fresh flowers—Beth's touch.

When he first met her, she kept a small crockery vase of flowers on her desk. Each Monday, she brought in a new bouquet. One Monday morning, he left a bunch of lilies of the valley in a glass beaker. A card attached to a lilac ribbon said, "I hope these brighten your day. You could brighten mine by agreeing to join me for dinner." She always said that was the sweetest thing he ever did for her. In retrospect, it probably was.

"Hello, Lionel."

She was standing alongside the mantel, a tall, lean figure of a woman in gray-flannel slacks and a pale blue sweater set. Her hair was short now, the top falling softly onto her forehead, the sides swept loosely behind her ears. It was still a rich auburn, more red than brown, but, now he guessed that shade was more the work of a colorist than Mother Nature. She looked the same, yet different, older yet with a serenity he hadn't expected. He supposed he had anticipated a frightened bird in need of a strong arm and a comforting word. Perhaps that was what he wanted to find. Instead, the woman before him appeared comfortable with herself and in charge.

"Hello . . . Beth."

Amanda smiled. She knew he hated the fact that their names had been changed. Lionel noticed a brief, silent exchange between mother and daughter. Most likely Beth had wagered that he would stubbornly insist upon calling her Cynthia. Score one for his side.

"Thanks for coming," she said, gracefully striding toward him.

Suddenly, Lionel felt awkward and unsure about what to say or do. He couldn't respond "It's my pleasure to be here" because the reason for this visit had nothing to do with anything that would even remotely fall under the category of pleasant. Beth hadn't invited him to drop in for tea or come for dinner. In truth, she hadn't invited him at all. Bates had. And before they had parted those many years ago, they had been adversaries.

She must have sensed his discomfort because without waiting for a signal from him, she kissed his cheek and embraced him warmly. As they parted, she kept her hands on his arms and studied his face.

"You are still one of the most elegant men I know."

Amanda found herself intrigued by her mother's choice of adjectives. Elegant. That's what she had told Jake she was attracted to in a man. Now, she wondered if elegance topped her list of musts because that was how the man most noticeably absent from her life had always been described. And that was the blank she was looking to fill.

"And you, Beth Maxwell, are still the sexiest financial analyst I've ever met," Lionel said.

Amanda flinched. Hadn't Jake called her a "babe with brains"?

"And I am Marshal Samuel Bates."

Lionel and Beth seemed to freeze, like children who'd been caught doing something naughty. They turned to Sam, who stood in the doorway, his tall, sturdy frame creating a formidable presence.

As Beth traversed the room to physically draw Sam in, Lionel surveyed the man as if he were preparing for a joust. Sam's fitness,

Lionel decided, deserved respect, as did the no-nonsense look in his eyes. The starched white shirt, spit-shined black tie shoes, and midnight navy slacks fit the lawman image, but the red suspenders felt too out of character to be an accident. Maybe they were symbolic, Lionel thought, a sign of rank or part of a uniform. The Marines had the Red Berets. Perhaps the Service had a corps of super-marshals known as the Red Braces.

"Nice to meet you, Marshal," Lionel said, extending his hand.

The men shook hands, exchanged pleasantries, and carefully took each other's measure. Like the proverbial fly on the wall, Amanda stood back and observed as her mother, her father, and Uncle Sam danced with each other. While they were all exceedingly polite, begging each other's pardon, and avoiding stepping on each other's toes, their body language told a different story.

Beth, clearly torn between the two men, continuously shifted her weight from one leg to another. She was genuinely glad to see Lionel again and wanted to spend time reacquainting herself with her former husband, but she didn't want Sam to feel betrayed or cuckolded. It was as if she was timing her attentiveness, trying not to give one more than the other.

At first, Lionel ceded the center stage and played the role of the guest: listening, responding, taking his cue from someone else. It wasn't long before he tired of that and reverted to type, anointing himself chairman of the board and setting an agenda that catered exclusively to his needs, which at the present moment, were centered around reaffirming his connection to his—underline *his*—family.

Sam was ill at ease. This was difficult for him and not simply because the woman he loved was flirting with another man. Although this bore all the trappings of a friendly dinner party, the real purpose of this gathering was to assess the level of risk each of them might face in the coming months and define the parameters of a response. He was charged with the task of doing whatever was necessary to protect them. Just then, he wondered if he was up to the task.

When he was first alerted about Bastido's release, Sam had called Dan Connor, who was now head of the Marshals Service. He confessed his emotional involvement with Beth—and Amanda—and asked Dan whether he should take himself off the case. Sam was not the first marshal to become romantically attached to his charge, and he probably wouldn't be the last, but both Dan and Sam knew it was an issue that needed to be aired. In the end, Dan permitted Sam to stay on the case because he believed that Sam's attachment worked for them rather than against them.

Amanda suggested that everyone take a seat. To her surprise, her mother opted to take the place next to her father. Noting Sam's discomfort, Amanda suggested he pour everyone some wine while she went into the kitchen and brought out a tray of hors d'oeuvres.

When she was resettled on the couch, Beth asked about Annie. "How's she doing? Are you two still collaborating on your portraits?"

Funny that Annie's name should come up, Amanda thought. Over the past several days, questions about Annie and Jake had nagged at her. Had she misjudged them? Had she jumped to conclusions? Was that always-on-alert, often overactive radar system she and Beth had acquired working overtime? Amanda was too cautious to dismiss her suspicions out of hand, but Sam saying he had put her under surveillance explained a lot.

"She's great," Amanda said, hoping her enthusiasm didn't sound forced. "In fact, she's a woman on the verge."

Beth smiled. She had never met Annie, but Amanda spoke of her often and always in warm, caring tones. She was eager to hear more.

"She wants to produce a line of Annie Hart cosmetics. She's the makeup queen of the soaps and over the past several months, quite a few movie stars have called her when they come to New York for public appearances."

"I hope she can get this off the ground," Beth said. "From everything you've told me, Annie's talented and personable and quirky, which in that business is a plus."

"I agree."

"Isn't she the one who introduced you to Lloyd Franks?" Lionel asked.

Sam's eyes narrowed. He didn't like hearing about people whose names he didn't know. In his business, strangers could be aggressors in disguise. "Who's Lloyd Franks?"

Amanda explained about the art gallery and her upcoming exhibition.

"It's opening in two weeks. I wish you all could come."

"You're not using your name, are you?" Sam practically leaped off the couch. "Or showing anything that might reveal where Beth lives or you lived in the past or anything that . . ."

"No! No! No!" Amanda held up her hands, as if holding off a thundering herd. "He's listing the photographer as Anonymous. I'm not going to the opening. And," she said with great indignation, "I'm not an idiot! I know how to take care of myself!"

Sam swallowed whatever he was thinking.

Lionel noticed and, oddly, understood. He also noticed that Sam was nervously rubbing his fingers together. For the first time, he realized what a prickly situation this was for Marshal Bates. This man honestly and deeply cared about both Beth and Amanda. As a federal officer, he was sworn to protect them and had an entire agency at his disposal to do just that. But as a man, he felt the same way Lionel did: He'd kill anyone who tried to hurt these women with his bare hands!

"Who'd your friend get to back her?" he asked, changing the subject to take the heat off Bates.

"No one, yet." Amanda eyed Lionel. "Interested?"

He shrugged. "Maybe. Have her come see me and we'll talk."

Amanda grinned at the prospect. As she did, she realized how excited she was at the thought of helping her friend. And Annie was her friend, by any definition. Certainly, she had done more for Amanda in the short time they'd known each other than Amanda had done for her. Suddenly guilt-ridden, she remembered that Annie had called several times since that night at the loft; Amanda hadn't returned any of her calls. She hoped her persistent paranoia hadn't created an irreparable schism.

"I'll set it up first thing," Amanda said.

Sam's opposition was immediate and definite. "This is not the time to advertise your relationship with Lionel," he snapped sharply. "Until we know where Bastido and his cohorts are and what they're up to, the fewer people who know of your connection, the better."

Lurking beneath Sam's concern about security, Lionel suspected a deeper, more personal objection: Sam Bates didn't think Amanda should have made contact with her father in the first place. Did he think she should have allowed Lionel to believe his daughter was dead for safety reasons? Or was it because the honorable marshal had come to think of Amanda as his and was reluctant to share her? Inside, Lionel seethed, but he controlled his contrary impulses. Later, when all this was over, there would be plenty of time to deal with Marshal Bates.

"Only three people have to know: Annie, Lionel, and me." Amanda faced Sam squarely, adopting a pose that told him she had considered the consequences, analyzed the situation, and reached a conclusion. Moreover, she resented the implication that she was being capricious. "All I'm doing is making an introduction. Lionel is a sophisticated businessman, well-schooled in the art of discretion. And, in case you think I've lost my mind and/or I'm being horribly naive, run a check on Annie . . . if you haven't already."

Sam gritted his teeth so hard, Amanda could see the bones of his jaw. She had defied him. It wasn't the first time, but it was in front of a man she knew he considered a rival. Perhaps she was being foolish, but just then, she cared more about doing something nice for a friend than watching her back.

"Of course I'm going to have to explain how a lowly NYPD detective knows the mighty Lionel Baird," she said, turning away from the criticism she read in Sam's eyes toward the love she saw in Lionel's.

Lionel smiled. "Just tell her the truth: I'm one of your many admirers."

When they moved into the dining room for dinner, the conversation continued in the same schizophrenic vein: light and ordinary one minute, deep and ominous the next. If Beth and Lionel weren't reliving their past, or mother and daughter weren't catching up with each other, Lionel was interrogating Sam about Bastido, what was happening to the New York contingent of convicts related to the case, and what was being done to gather up the lot of them.

"We're doing the best we can," Sam said, unable to erase the irritation from his voice. He disliked being grilled, particularly by someone who not only wasn't providing a solution, but potentially could become part of the problem. "If you think it's beyond us, there's only one thing to do. Ask Beth to be relocated and have Amanda reenter WITSEC."

"No!" Both women responded quickly and hotly, glaring at Lionel as if he had actually made the request.

"I can't do it again," Beth declared, leaving no room for negotiation. "I don't have the strength to start over."

Amanda concurred. "Neither do I. I'd rather shoot it out than go through another identity change."

Lionel silently congratulated Bates. One word—WITSEC—and he was the hero, Lionel, the villain.

"You don't understand what it's like," Beth said, her eyes haunted. "Moving. Getting a job and a place to live. Trying to make your way in a new community. Finding those one or two people you think you can trust enough to see a movie with or invite over for dinner. Finding a way to be comfortable in your new skin."

"I'd have to give up police work." Amanda was staring at a spot on the wall. She appeared to be watching a play no one else could see, looking into a future no one could foretell. "Everything I've struggled to achieve over these past several years would be voided out. I'd be thirty years old with no résumé."

Loneliness infiltrated the room, taking a seat at the table like a familiar guest. Beth and Amanda didn't welcome the intruder, but neither did they flinch at its arrival. It had been a companion for so much of their lives, its presence felt normal; recognizing that affected Lionel more than anything they might have said.

Beth shook her head, disconsolate. "No," she said to no one, and everyone. "Not again."

Amanda and her mother looked at each other. Their gazes locked, leaving Lionel and Sam behind to enter a very private place where they stored their memories. No words were spoken, but a great deal was said about what they had been through, what it had taken to survive, what they would—and would not—be willing to endure.

"I'd have to leave New York," Amanda said. "Leave my friends. The few that I've made, that is." She turned to Lionel. "And I'd have to leave you."

"I didn't suggest that either of you move or change names or do anything you don't want to do." He resisted the impulse to glare at Bates; it wouldn't accomplish anything, and, without an alternative solution, he would come off looking petty. "I'm worried, that's all." He found Amanda's hand and held it. As he spoke, his eyes sought Beth's. He was desperate for her to understand the depth of his concern. "I just want you both to be safe."

"I know, Lionel," she said, "and I appreciate that. It's just . . . well, we've been there and . . ."

". . . we don't want to go back." Amanda completed her mother's sentence.

They both looked at Lionel.

"I don't want that either," he said.

Sam, sensing that the three of them could use a moment alone, excused himself. Before leaving the room, however, he said, "Technically, Beth is still in WITSEC and, therefore, under the protection of the Marshals Service." He looked directly at Lionel. "Despite what you might think, my personal feelings for Beth have never and will never compromise her safety. Not only is it my job, Lionel, but Beth is the love of my life. Trust me: No one is going to hurt her!"

As Sam left the room, Lionel's face displayed no emotion. Inside, however, jealousy again jousted with concern and fear.

"The last thing I want is for either of you to exit my life," Lionel said, breaking a nervous silence. "I've been there, and I couldn't deal with that again." Love and pain glistened in his eyes.

"I'm so sorry, Lionel." Beth's voice was a repentant whisper. It was difficult to look at him and realize that she had been responsible for that pain and blind to that love. "At the time, I felt I had no choice. I felt it was safer for us and . . ."

"In your place, I would have done the same thing." As he said it, he realized he meant it. "But let's leave the past in the past. We have the present to worry about and the future to plan."

Beth's smile said thank you. He returned the sentiment, then said, "I simply want to help."

"Your being here is a help."

Amanda started to agree, but Lionel wasn't listening. His expression had changed suddenly, shifting from nostalgia to machination. He looked from Beth to Amanda and then back to Beth.

"When Amanda was born, I opened two trust accounts: one for you and one for her. When you two . . . died . . . I didn't close them out. I couldn't." He swallowed hard. "I think in my heart, I wanted to believe that you were still alive, and if I kept them open, you'd come back." He tried to smile, but his emotions were too raw. "I guess it worked, because here you are."

Beth bit her lip and dabbed at her eyes, but she couldn't stem the tears that wet her cheeks. Over the years, she often wondered if Lionel thought of her. If he had grieved over her. If he ever missed her. Now, she knew.

"That money's yours, if and when you need it," Lionel said. His eyes fixed on Beth's. "There's enough in those trusts for both of you to live comfortably for the rest of your lives."

"That's sweet, Daddy." Amanda rose from her chair, came over to Lionel, and kissed his cheek. He couldn't bring himself to look at her, but his hand reached up and caressed her cheek. She never called him *Daddy*.

Beth grew thoughtful.

"What's the matter?" Lionel was afraid he had said or done something wrong. "I told you this . . ."

"In case. I know. But just in case, I have to ask you something. What names are the trusts in?"

"Cynthia Stanton Baird. And Erica Baird."

For the umpteenth time that evening, Beth and Amanda exchanged looks.

"We can't get to those trusts," Amanda said, rattling her father.

"Why not?"

"Because Cynthia and Erica Baird don't exist."

Beth explained. "We don't have birth certificates or driver's licenses or social security cards or anything else that a bank would require before turning those trusts over to us. We don't have any official documents in those names." She reached across the table and laid her hand on top of his. "Those two women are dead, Lionel."

"Then I'll put the trusts in the names of Beth and Amanda Maxwell," he said quickly, his voice ragged.

Amanda told him he couldn't do that either. "If you do, you strip us of our cover."

Lionel groaned and rubbed his temples. Frustration had given him a headache.

"Coffee, anyone?" Sam returned to the table with a pot of steaming coffee.

Beth and Amanda rose and cleared the table, giving Lionel time to digest what they had told him. When they returned, he was still cogitating.

"What if I turn both trusts over to an innocuous, practically untraceable corporation?" Lionel said, thinking aloud. "East Gorham Associates. Samuel Bates, president."

Sam was fascinated by Lionel's conjuring and flattered by this rare display of good faith, but said, "I can be traced to both Beth and Amanda."

Lionel was smiling. "I know," he said, wagging his finger in the air with a glint of pride. "I'm beginning to get the hang of this."

"The hang of what?"

"This protection thing. It's all about layers. Piling one on top of another to keep a comfortable distance between the good guys and the enemy." He tapped the cleft in his chin with his index finger. The others spoke, but he wasn't listening. He was noodling. When the idea was fully formed, he turned to Sam. "I'm assuming I can count on you to do the right thing."

"You can."

"I thought so," he said, offering Sam a verbal peace pipe. "Tomorrow morning, I'm going to call my personal lawyer, a man I would trust with my life and," he said, looking at Beth and Amanda, "yours. I'm going to instruct him to draw up incorporation papers for East Gorham Associates, listing Samuel Bates as president. Then, I'm going to have him redo the trusts with EGA as nominee for both. No names need appear on that paperwork."

Again, he shifted his focus onto Sam. "I'm also going to ask you to sign a separate document in which you acknowledge that you are acting on behalf of Beth and Amanda and have no claim to the funds in either trust. Although, if either Beth or Amanda needs money, as the nominee, you can withdraw the necessary amounts from the trusts. In the event of my death, you will turn the money over to Beth and Amanda. Naturally, you'll be compensated for your services, as any executor would be." He looked around the table. "Is this arrangement agreeable?"

"It's more than okay, Lionel," Beth said, humbled by her ex-husband's generosity.

He winked, grateful for her approval. "Does it adhere to the Marshals Service strict code of rules and regulations?"

"I'll have to run this by my superior, but I don't see a problem with it," Sam said.

"And you, Ricki," Lionel said, breaking the rules, but unable to stop himself. "Do you have any problems?"

Amanda looked as if she was about to scold him, but instead she laughed. "Do I have any problems with your plan to leave me a gazillion dollars? No. Do I have any problems with you?" He looked at her expectantly. "No. None whatsoever!"

Later that evening, Sam retired to his room, again allowing the Bairds their privacy. Around eleven, his cellular phone rang. He answered it immediately. Only two people had the number.

"Sam?"

He heard her voice and his heart sank. The other call would have been easier to handle because that would have been business. This was personal.

"I'm here, baby," he said, speaking softly so as not to be overheard. "What's going on?"

"Nothing good, that's for sure."

Her voice was weak and tremulous. He closed his eyes, visualizing her so that she didn't feel so far away, so disconnected.

"Talk to me."

"It's bad, Sam. I need you here. Now!"

"I can't do that," he said, hating himself. "Things are happening."

"Things are happening to me, too." Anger collided with a sob, making it sound as if she was choking on her words.

Sam's chest tightened. "I know. I want to be there for you." He paused, summoning the nerve to say what he had to say. "But I can't."

The silence that ensued was nuclear in its intensity.

"I love you," he insisted. "You know I'd do anything for you."

"But you can't," she sniped. "Don't worry about it, Sam. I understand. I've always understood. You're a United States marshal. Your work comes before anything. And anyone. Except for her, of course."

Had she been standing in front of him, firing bullets instead of insults, he would have taken every one. He deserved her wrath and her distrust. "I promised I'd always take care of you, and I will."

She laughed, but it was mirthless. That hurt him more than the sound of her tears. "I'll be out to see you in a couple of weeks," he vowed. "In the meantime, do what you have to do."

"Now it's my turn to say, I can't." He could almost see her face contort with the pain of having to ask him for what she didn't have. "I can't afford it."

Sam thought about Lionel and the trust funds. He thought about the woman on the other end of the phone, what she meant to him, what she needed, and what he owed her.

"You don't have to worry about money," he said, suddenly nervous.

"Since when?"

"That doesn't matter," he snapped. "What's important is that I've come into a minor fortune, and I intend to share it with you."

"And where, pray tell, did this fortune come from?"

Sam glanced over his shoulder, needing to reassure himself that no one was eavesdropping on his perfidy. "Let's just say that twenty years ago, I made an investment." He winced as he stepped over a line he had once believed was inviolate. He wanted to believe he had no choice. "Well, it's just paid off. Big-time!"

CHAPTER
SIX

Amanda returned from Wisconsin feeling oddly buoyant. Under the circumstances, she should have been guarded and on edge—part of her was—but being in the company of both her parents had been so unbelievably joyous, it overwhelmed all else. For two days, she had been part of a family. They shared kitchen-table conversations. They talked about ordinary, everyday things. They laughed and teased each other. Lionel even enlisted Beth's help in encouraging Amanda to go out more.

"I want our daughter to have what other daughters have," he declared in his best head-of-the-family voice, pontificating as if he and Beth had never divorced, let alone been separated for twenty years. "A husband. Children." His eyes widened and he chuckled at the thought. "Wouldn't you like to be a grandmother?" he asked Beth.

She agreed, "It would be wonderful."

Beth laughed with him, but behind her eyes she grew wistful. Lionel had drifted off into the land of what-might-be, which she knew to be a dangerous place. He was envisioning a grandchild as his chance to start over, to be the parent he had never been. Knowing him, he was already planning what toys to buy, which museums or ballparks to visit and when, probably even what college this Baird heir would attend. She didn't want to burst Lionel's bubble, but his fairy tale could never play out quite the way he imagined. WITSEC wasn't in the happily-ever-after business; they were only interested in alive-and-well. Lionel couldn't have a heart-to-heart with his future son-in-law or host his daughter's wedding or walk her down the aisle or brag about his grandchildren to his friends.

There's no need to bring him down, she thought. *If and when Amanda falls in love, there'll be plenty of time to work out the details.*

"Well, we're not going to have any grandbabies if that gorgeous young woman over there refuses to go out on dates," he was saying.

"I don't have a whole lot of time," Amanda protested.

"Make the time," Lionel commanded.

"Aye, aye," she said, saluting. "I understand my mission and shall attempt to fulfill it. Husband hunting shall commence the moment I return to base."

Lionel returned her salute with a jaunty snap. "See that it does," he said, basking in the moment. "Your mother may have found the secret to staving off the ravages of time, but I'm getting older by the minute. If you don't hurry, you're going to have to wheel me down the aisle."

A look passed between Amanda and Lionel that tweaked Beth's curiosity. She knew they were seeing a lot of each other—as long as Amanda remained vigilant, Beth supported the relationship—yet it felt odd to think that they had become close enough to have private jokes or that Lionel might know something she didn't.

"Is there anyone on the horizon?" Beth asked.

"She's met someone new, but she won't talk about him."

"Occupational hazard," Beth shrugged, defending her daughter's penchant for privacy.

"Right. I forgot." Lionel shook his head. "Every time I think I'm getting the hang of this, I screw up."

"It takes years to make this kind of duplicity second nature," Amanda said. Her tone was light, but she wasn't joking.

"You're avoiding the subject," Beth prodded.

"Okay! I met a guy through work. He's bright, good-looking, about thirty-five, and owns his own business. He's extremely arrogant," she said, pointedly eyeballing her father, "but he's nice to his mother."

"Sounds perfect," Lionel opined.

Sam, who had been discreetly hugging the background throughout the Baird family reunion, insinuated himself into the discussion. "What kind of business does he run?"

Amanda wriggled in her chair. "He's a PI."

Lionel wasn't thrilled and judging by the expressions on their faces, this information was not being well received by his companions, but he took his cue from Beth and left the interrogation to Sam. Let him be the bad guy.

"Does this PI have a name?" Sam asked.

"Jake Fowler."

Sam looked as if he had just entered that name into a computer. "How'd you meet him?"

"He was working a case I caught." Amanda wasn't happy. Jake was not the love of her life. She did not have designs on him. He was simply a man with whom she had gobbled pizza. She glowered at Lionel for raising the subject. "It was a coincidental meeting. Believe me, Lieutenant Clarke is neither a matchmaker nor a facilitator for Jaime Bastido. Can we drop this?"

Sam assented, but Lionel was certain that Jake Fowler was about to be investigated within an inch of his life, which was fine with him. Lionel was tempted to ask about the other gentleman Amanda mentioned, the one she had trysted with in Florence and subsequently run into in New York, but she was in a fit of pique as it was. Best to leave it alone for now.

"Now that you've declared the men in your life off-limits," he said, moving right along, "let's discuss the man in your mother's life." He folded his arms across his chest and turned to Sam. "So, Marshal Bates. Since I'm sure you know everything about me including what size shorts I wear, why not level the playing field by telling me a little about you!"

By the time everyone said their good-byes, a comfortable rapport had been established. Sam and Lionel weren't friends, but once they pushed their jealousy aside, they found room for mutual respect, trust, and even a modicum of admiration. Also, they had come to an agreement about the current crisis: Sam would captain plans for Beth's and Amanda's physical safety, Lionel, their financial security.

For Amanda, watching those two men interact had been an astounding experience, particularly when they jousted for Beth's attention. But nothing compared to the thrill of having both parents in the same place at the same time and on pretty much the same wavelength. It didn't happen immediately. They had to search to find a bridge over the chasm that separated them, but amazingly, they did. In fact, Beth and Lionel had reconnected in such a positive way, it allowed Amanda to indulge in a fantasy common to children of separated parents: that one day, Mom and Dad would get back together.

As for fulfilling their fantasies about a wedding and grandchildren,

Amanda had to put her husband hunting on hold. Upon her return to Manhattan, she went on double shift, working from two in the afternoon until eight the next morning, which made dating difficult, but not impossible.

Tyler Grayson was very understanding. When he called to ask her for dinner and Amanda explained the situation, he shifted his invitation to lunch.

"How about twelve o'clock at the Water Club?" When Amanda paused, he quickly amended the arrangements. "Better yet, how about eleven-thirty. That way, we'll be done in plenty of time for you to catch a cab and head to wherever it is you ghouls in blue call home."

He could hear the smile in Amanda's voice as she accepted. "Eleven-thirty is perfect. Is there a dress code or can I wear my black cape and pointy hat?"

"Whatever you show up in is fine with me," he said in a rich baritone that brought back some very sexy memories. "As long as you show up."

Amanda felt her cheeks flush. "See you then," she said.

As expected, the restaurant Tyler had selected was inspired. Abutting the river, sheltered from the bulk of Manhattan's intimidating crush of architecture by a nearby elevated highway, it occupied a unique berth. Isolated from the crowded city, it seemed to float on the waterway that separated one borough from another. The East River wasn't the Arno, and the lunch crowd in their expertly tailored business suits and perfectly coifed hair were a far cry from the tee shirt-and-sandal brigade that hunkered down for a bowl of *pasta e fagioli* in a Florentine trattoria, but Tyler's effort to re-create even a small part of the magic of that time did not go unnoticed. As Amanda was escorted to Mr. Grayson's table, tucked in a corner by a wall of windows, she smiled. Whatever else might have changed over the years, Tyler remained predictably surprising.

Part of her fascination with him was his unique ability always to know the right thing to do and say. Being consistently appropriate— without being rehearsed, which was how Amanda described her own carefully maintained decorousness—was a talent, one she assumed came from breeding and attending schools like Dartmouth and Wharton. Tyler seemed to substantiate that theory when she asked him how he managed to make everything appear so effortless. At first, he claimed it was all a facade and that nothing was effortless. Before she could comment, he quickly amended his response.

"Confessions of veneer aside, you're right about where I learned what. There's nothing like the Ivy League to pick up cues on socially correct behavior. And yes, Amanda, I am most definitely a product of my upbringing."

She recalled that while she had expected an expression that alluded to fond memories, his insouciant smile was recast into a tight line that spoke more of difficult times and hard lessons.

At the time, that had disturbed her, but when she thought about it later that evening, she realized it shouldn't have—nothing was ever one-dimensional with Tyler. Everything had layers. And everyone had secrets.

While she waited for Tyler to arrive, she watched the sun dance across the water, sparkling on the ripples created by a passing speedboat or the occasional barge. Befitting the onset of spring, the sun had shed the blue-gray cast that marked winter's light and re-dressed itself in a bright, buttercup yellow that looked as warm as it felt. A small bird swooped down and perched atop a nearby piling. Amanda created a frame with her fingers, brought the square to her eyes, and peered at the sparrow in repose.

Tyler approached the table quietly, not wishing to startle her. "Don't tell me you didn't bring your camera," he said as he bent down and brushed his lips against her cheek. His hands rested gently on her shoulders. She turned to face him. His gray eyes peered at her through long, sandy lashes. They were close enough to kiss.

"I can't tell you that because I don't go anywhere without it," she said, slightly unnerved by his presence and the way it made her feel. "But I left it up front, along with some other tools of the trade."

"Like a gun?" He looked horrified at the thought of handing the coat check girl a weapon.

Amanda laughed at the look on his face. "Uh-uh. That never leaves my side."

"I don't know if that's good or bad," he said, as he took his seat and spied the leather holster on her belt, the black butt of her weapon pressed against her side.

"It's neither," Amanda said, more relaxed now that there was some distance between them. "It simply is the way it is."

"So I should get used to it, is what you're telling me."

"Exactly."

"Okay," he said, blithely. "I can do that."

A waiter approached the table and asked if they cared for a cocktail. Tyler ordered a glass of white wine. Amanda was satisfied with water. The waiter nodded, presented them with menus, and went to fill Tyler's request.

Amanda, whom he assumed didn't frequent noon-hour watering holes, appeared intrigued. She glanced around the room, watching people buzz into each other's ears and exchange whispered asides. She appeared somewhat amused by the hivelike ambience.

Tyler took advantage of the pause in conversation to study her. For someone who claimed to have no affinity for expensive superficialities like fashion trends, he thought she looked remarkably stylish in her lightweight black-wool sweater, black pleated trousers, and navy jacket. Then again, when one was as tall and naturally beautiful as Amanda, labels didn't matter.

"Do you like this place?"

"I love it!" she replied. "I also love this day. Did you order blue skies and glorious sunshine?"

"I did," he confessed modestly. "But only because it's you. If I were dining with anyone else, I would've settled for the standard April fare: clouds, maybe some sun, and a possibility of rain."

Her lips, rouged in a brownish red that complemented the burnished tone of her hair, spread in an appreciative smile. "Well, thank you for going that one step beyond and making this so special. It takes me back to a time when things were wonderfully simple. And," she said, fixing her eyes on his, "simply wonderful."

"I could speak to you in Italian, if that would further the mood," he said, as he reached across the table and interlaced his fingers with hers.

"It's eleven-thirty," she reminded him. "We're here for lunch."

A slow smile lazed across his lips. "If I recall, lunch wasn't the only thing we did at eleven-thirty."

"Would you like to hear the specials?" the waiter asked. "Or do you need more time to . . . study the menu."

"I already know what's special," Tyler whispered, unabashed.

"I could use a minute." Amanda detached herself from his grasp and buried her face in the menu.

Over the years, Amanda had learned that the only way to triumph over the hand fate had dealt her was to work doubly hard at diminishing the impact WITSEC had on her life. Yes, she told herself, WITSEC was a colossal negative, but all children faced negatives. Parents divorced. Relatives died. Friends moved away. Stuff happened. Yet at moments like this, she wondered what kind of woman WITSEC had created. Growing up a protected witness had made her tough enough to be a top New York City detective and hard-boiled enough to accept humanity's seamier side without being permanently tainted. But she was unsteady on her feet romantically, unable to feel comfortable in the heat of a man's stare or safe when confronted with the rush of his passion. Even more damaging, she was never able to feel secure in the belief that someone could say, "I love you," and not have an ulterior motive.

Tyler, realizing that he had embarrassed her, called the waiter over, gave him their order, and moved to a less provocative topic. "I saw Lloyd Franks the other day. He's very excited about your participation in his upcoming exhibition. He says your portraits are sensational. Cindy Sherman without the angst."

Amanda beamed with delight. Cindy Sherman, a photographer who always used herself as a subject, was Amanda's inspiration. Amanda was fifteen when she first saw Sherman's work at the Seattle Art Museum. A series of black-and-white film stills, each photograph seemed vaguely familiar, yet wonderfully new. After a few minutes study, she realized that not only was every shot reminiscent of a scene in an old fifties movie, but the star of each photograph was the same person. And that person was the photographer.

For Amanda, it was like receiving a gift. She had been doing much the same thing—albeit for reasons other than artistic aesthetic. Yet seeing what Cindy Sherman had accomplished gave Amanda permission to continue experimenting with the genre without feeling she had to explain why she didn't use friends as subjects.

"That's quite a compliment," she said, modestly.

"Lloyd says you're talented." She flushed, and again Tyler marveled at the discrepancy between what she did and who she was. "Would it be too bold of me to ask if I could escort you to your opening?"

"I'd be honored," she said with honest regret, "but I can't go to the opening. I'm working."

Tyler shook his head. He knew that he was transposing his monstrous ambition onto her shoulders, but still . . . "Can't you change your shift?"

"I could, but right now, with all the recent budget cuts, the CSU is overworked and understaffed. Besides, I'm supposed to be Anonymous."

Ever since Sam had chastised her for allowing her photographs to be publicly displayed, the yellow caution light had blinked continuously inside her head. Contrary to what most artists with upcoming shows believed, Amanda felt the fewer who knew about this, the better. She refused to provide Franks with a mailing list of friends and colleagues, not that she had many of the former or thought it would interest many of the latter. And she declined Lloyd's invitation to make an appearance, giving him the same excuse she just gave Tyler: she was supposed to be Anonymous. And that's what she intended to be.

"Amanda Maxwell. Do you have any idea how difficult it is to court you?" Tyler said, exasperation pouring out of him.

Amanda smiled, flattered. "Are you courting me?"

Tyler threw his hands up, then reached for hers again. "I'm trying to!" He laughed, then grew serious. He fixed his eyes on hers and held her gaze, almost demanding that she not look away. When he spoke, his voice was gruff with emotion. "I never thought I'd see you again." He lowered his eyes and appeared to study the way their hands fit. "But like kismet, you've come back into my life. And just in time."

It seemed incongruous to see someone in a pin-striped power suit look so raw, but just then, Tyler's vulnerability was out there for the world to see.

"I've reached a critical crossroads," he said, speaking softly. "This is not easy for me to admit, but right now, I need someone I care about and someone I know I can trust to care about me, to hold my hand while I choose my path."

Amanda wanted to assure him of her constancy and willingness to help in whatever decisions he had to make, but, this was the worst possible time for him to reenter her life. She, too, was at a crossroads; not only couldn't she invite anyone to walk with her, she couldn't allow anyone to come close.

She mumbled something that seemed to satisfy Tyler, but before he could press her further, a conversation at a nearby table distracted them.

"Chisolm is going to regret this," one man declared, rather loudly.

"Who does he think is going to finance his campaign? The little people?"

A third man snorted. "I thought he understood the rules. You don't bite the hand that feeds you."

"John Chisolm only plays by the rules when he thinks the fix is in, and he's going to come out the winner." An eerily familiar voice pricked Amanda's skin. "My question isn't, did he bite us? He damn well did! What I want to know is do we bite back? Or do we sit back?"

Amanda wanted to ignore him, but that was impossible. Like a magnet, she turned in the direction of the voice. Lionel's eyes locked on hers for the briefest of moments and shifted quickly to her companion. Tyler, who also had been drawn to the familiar voice, nodded. Lionel acknowledged him, glanced again at Amanda, and returned his attention to those at his table. Amanda's palms were sweating.

"That," Tyler confided under his breath, "is the infamous Lionel Baird."

"Really." Amanda followed his lead and spoke in hushed tones. "He doesn't look particularly ferocious." But he did look powerful, she thought, seated at a table of six in the center of the room, presiding over a gathering of Wall Street puissants. "He does sound a bit intense."

Tyler laughed. "You have no idea!"

"Why are they in such an uproar?"

"You know who Senator Chisolm is, right?"

"Of course," Amanda nodded. "Wasn't he in the news recently?"

"Very much so." Judging by his expression, Tyler shared Lionel's low opinion of the senator. "In order to give his reelection campaign a boost, he's decided to launch a Senate investigation into ties between the financial community and drug traffickers."

"Is there such a thing?"

Tyler's eyebrows furrowed and his fingers tugged at his beard. "After foreign exchange and the oil industry, the laundering of dirty money is the world's third-largest business. And most of it comes from the illicit drug trade."

"I had no idea," she lied.

"Most people don't, but believe me, we're living in a narco-economy that's made drug traffickers the most influential special-interest group in the world. In fact, the money generated by traffickers has reached such monstrous proportions that there are Third World countries that literally would collapse if not for the money they make off drugs."

There was a keenness to Tyler's speech that bordered on zealotry. Amanda's interest was peaked.

"I don't like Chisolm's phony inquiry any more than they do," he said, tilting his head in the direction of Lionel's table, "but they have no right to cast any stones. Almost seventy percent of the proceeds from drug trafficking around the world gets laundered through the American and European banking system. To the tune of one hundred *billion* dollars a year. These guys make fortunes off drugs. They're only annoyed at Chisolm because he's spilling the beans."

"Why do you care so much, Tyler? After all, you work for Baird, Nathanson & Spelling. If they profit, you profit."

"But at what cost? Drugs have spawned a very nasty war that's claimed a lot of innocent people." He lowered his eyes and his voice. "Including some who were quite close to me." A moment passed before he allowed himself to meet her gaze again. "It's hard for me to look at this the way they do, as simply a bottom-line issue. For me, it's personal."

Amanda wanted to shout, "Me too. I lost an uncle, a father, grandparents, my freedom, my identity . . ." But before she could say anything, her beeper went off.

"I hate to do this, but I have to run," she said. "Something's gone down a couple of blocks from here." She rose to leave and was surprised when he joined her.

"I have an account here. They'll take care of the bill. I want to make sure you get a cab."

She kissed his cheek, charmed by his gallantry. She was rushing off to a gruesome crime scene and he was treating her as if she were a princess, too delicate to hail her own taxicab. She loved it. "You're the best."

"Yes," he said as he shepherded her through the maze of tables. "I am."

She was barely settled in the backseat of the taxi when her cellular phone rang.

"What were you doing with Tyler Grayson?" Lionel's bluntness was disquieting.

"Having lunch," she said, hoping he caught her annoyance. "I'd have thought you'd be delighted. He's perfect husband material. You should know. You picked him as one of the ones most likely to succeed you."

She expected an instant comeback. When it wasn't forthcoming, she wondered if they had been disconnected.

"I'm sorry, honey," he said finally. "I have no business telling you whom to see and what to do."

Regret and apology were so alien to the man she had come to

know that Amanda was unnerved. "What's wrong? Why are you so put out about me seeing him?"

"I don't know," he admitted. "I just am. Maybe because he is involved in B, N and S."

"If it helps, I met him years ago. Before he worked for you."

"In Italy? He's the one you met on the train?"

"The very same."

At Twenty-eighth Street, the taxi turned onto First Avenue. "Can we finish this some other time?" she asked as she paid the driver and opened the door. "I've got to run."

"Be careful," Lionel said. "I love you."

"Me too you." She smiled briefly as she tucked the phone in her bag and exited the cab. Yellow crime tape blocked off the sidewalk in front of a pharmacy, where a young boy, no more than thirteen, lay in a pool of his own blood. She ducked beneath the tape. "Amanda Maxwell," she said, flashing her badge to the uniform in charge. "CSU."

Cleland Jones greeted her at the door to the pharmacy. "I hope you're not coming from lunch. It's nasty in there."

"I ate light."

As they went inside and began their initial walk-through, Amanda reconnoitered the scene. It was a small store, one that probably prided itself on service that was far more personal than that of the supermarket drugstores that dominated these days. Wooden paneling framed the display cases against both walls and warmed the atmosphere. There were greeting cards and pretty travel items and along one wall, a pegboard display of doodads for the hair. Toward the middle of the store, the body of a woman who had been shot several times in the chest lay in the aisle stocked with body lotions and skin-care products. A jar of Alpha Hydroxy was still clutched in her hand. A second woman was spread out on the floor in front of the counter where the cash register was. Her face had been blown off. Next to her, swimming in a pool of blood, was a bag with a prescription for a child's antibiotic.

"Have we recovered the murder weapon?" Amanda asked, gulping down a wave of revulsion.

Cleland nodded. "Sawed-off shotgun. On the floor about ten feet from the counter. The perp probably dropped it when the owner plugged him with a handgun he kept on a shelf below the register."

"Where is the owner?"

"In surgery. He was shot up pretty bad."

Huge splashes of blood on what was left of the glass wall separating the pharmacist's workspace from the checkout counter seemed to confirm that. Ribbons of blood slithered down the remaining panes of glass onto the floor. Bloody handprints told a sad tale of a man trying to defend himself, searching for his gun while being ravaged by someone else's. Several of the freestanding shelves nearest that counter had been toppled, spewing plastic bottles of suntan lotion and hair conditioner onto the floor.

At the far right, Amanda noticed a set of bloody shoeprints leading away from the counter where the owner had been shot. Judging by the tread marks, they were a large size and rubber-soled. Probably sneakers.

"Did the owner say anything about a second gunman?" she asked, drawing Cleland's attention to the prints.

Cleland shook his head. Amanda turned to one of the Homicide guys.

"Any witnesses mention a second perp or a frightened customer running out the back?"

"We haven't completed our canvassing," he replied, acknowledging the shoeprints, "but we'll be sure to ask. Thanks, Max."

The two Homicide detectives left. Cleland went outside to confer with the team from the Medical Examiner's Office, which had just arrived. Amanda laid down her grid and set to work. She was in the midst of her overalls when near the shoeprints, her eye caught a dark smudge high up on the doorframe leading to the storeroom. Examining it more closely, Amanda guessed it had been made when someone grabbed on to the doorframe on the way out, probably for support. She looked down. Tiny drops of blood formed a dotted line that traced the man's exit. They were relatively fresh, an observation that caused Amanda to shudder.

While she and Tyler had been dining at the Water Club, flirting and laughing, someone had come into this store determined to rob it. The owner put up a fight. The weapons came out. And within minutes, a neighborhood pharmacy looked like an abattoir. A young boy barely in his teens lay dead on the sidewalk. His accomplice, another youngster who believed a gun made him invincible, was probably hiding in a nearby basement or alleyway, his life oozing from his body. Two housewives out to complete their list of errands had died in a callous assassination. And a man who had refused to hand his hard-earned money over to street thugs lay fighting for his life on a surgeon's table.

Amanda photographed the scene with her usual efficiency, but suddenly, the day wasn't as beautiful as it had seemed only an hour before.

Unless Amanda expected to be called to testify on behalf of the city or if some element of a case was unusual and might teach her something new, she didn't follow up on autopsy results. While some cities required their forensic photographer to work autopsies, New York City did not, and her case load prohibited leisurely learning. The two perpetrators in the pharmacy debacle interested her, however. They were very young—twelve and fourteen—but juvenile crime was a fact of life in New York. The evidence projected an image of complete disregard for human life on their part, but that, too, was not uncommon. She couldn't pinpoint why she was so interested, but something compelled her to ask for a copy of the coroner's findings.

As she suspected, the second shooter had been found later that same evening in an alley three blocks from the store. He had been shot, but not fatally, leading the ME to believe that his death had been caused by something else. The coroner performed an autopsy which proved inconclusive. The toxicology screens, however, told another story. Both boys had used cocaine shortly before their deaths. The younger boy, the one lying on the sidewalk, had inhaled only enough to get high; he died of a gunshot wound to the chest. His friend, however, had snorted a great deal of cocaine, prompting the logical conclusion that he was a regular user. This dose, however, had been mixed with PCP.

As Amanda read the report, goose bumps prickled her skin. This marked the tenth death of a teenager due to PCP-tainted cocaine over the past several months. According to the guys in the Narcotics Division, this was a new, highly potent strain of powder coming in from Mexico. It produced a good, quick high—making it desirable and, therefore, highly profitable—but it was fatal if used in large quantities.

Using the case as a cover, Amanda nosed about, asking friends in various precinct houses what they knew. Their answers chilled her blood. This was the hot drug on the street, especially popular with cocaine addicts whose increasing dependency demanded something with a bigger kick. Called Propaine by those who smoked it, this lethal mix turned its users violent, giving them delusions of supernatural powers. Worse, it produced an aura of invincibility, something that inevitably invited savagery.

As one of the undercover narcs put it: "Propaine's going to be the bane of our existence."

Not only was the department going to have to deal with crimes committed by desperate addicts, he said, but also vicious street wars being fought over distribution rights. The current combatants were several traditional mob families and a nasty Latino gang with roots in Los Angeles. The Latinos were demanding control over the market by claiming blood ties with the supplier—a large, well-organized, and formidable Mexican cartel.

"The Mexicans are the Colombians of the nineties," Amanda's friend told her. "They're the packagers and the shippers. They slip that killer shit in over the border any way they can and put it out on the street. While we run around picking up dead bodies, they sit back and rake in the bucks."

"Who's in charge?" Amanda held her breath.

He shrugged. "Right now the city is up for grabs. Two mob factions are playing king of the mountain, blowing each other away trying to gain control. In their spare time, they're going one-on-one with the *Blanca Muerte* boys."

"Who's running the show south of the border?"

"Rumor is the Mexis recruited a bunch of seasoned veterans to get them up to speed." He looked weary and somewhat resigned to being on the losing side of an age-old battle. The police, the Justice Department, the DEA, would fight the good fight, but everyone knew that while the players and the tactics had changed over the years, the basics remained the same: As long as there was demand, there would be supply. "Our sources in Juarez say they've got some Cali kingpins teaching a course in cocaine conglomerate management."

Amanda struggled to remain expressionless. She wasn't certain she succeeded. "Which Colombian lords are we talking about? There are so many to choose from."

"True, but they went for the top dog, everyone's favorite scumbags: the Espinosas."

"I thought they had been wiped out in the early eighties."

"So did the DEA. We all thought that when Raoul Espinosa was gunned down in his garden, we had seen the last of them, but evidently Raoul's little boys got bored being minor players in Colombia and decided to go where the action was. According to a couple of DEA snitches, they turned up in Juarez about five years ago.'' He threw his feet up on his desk, combed his hair with his fingers, and gritted his teeth in frustration. "As my man, Yogi Berra used to say, 'It's déjà vu all over again.' The Espinosas and the Savianos are spilling blood on the streets of New York.''

Amanda couldn't recall how their conversation had ended, what she did for the rest of the day, or how she got home. She unlocked the front door of her building, walked in, and immediately pressed her back up against the lobby wall, the sweat of an anxiety attack pouring off her body. Her breath was labored, her head was reeling. When the initial wave of panic subsided, she drew her pistol and climbed the stairs, hugging the wall as she went. Each landing loomed as a potential ambush. She proceeded slowly, quietly, listening for the merest of sounds—a flutter, a shuffle, a creaking floorboard— anything that might indicate the presence of an enemy. When she finally reached her apartment, she went inside, her gun cocked and ready. Assured that no one had invaded the premises, she bolted the locks on her door and closed her windows. She holstered her gun, went into her bathroom, and threw up.

An hour later, when the attack had passed and relative calm returned, she telephoned Uncle Sam in Los Angeles.

"We've got trouble," she said.

Jaime Bastido studied his face in the mirror. There was still some residual puffiness, particularly around his nose and chin, but nothing anyone would notice. He squinted and moved in for a closer look, examining his thinning gray hair and the soft folds of skin that still resided beneath his jaw. The plastic surgeon had wanted to eliminate those fleshy pleats, but Jaime said no: A smooth neck on a man his age would have given him away. Turning his back to the large mirror and holding a smaller mirror in his hand, he tilted his head to the right and then to the left, frowning at the faint white scars running along the line where his hair met his neck. The doctor had assured him these would disappear in a matter of months, but Jaime intended to reenter the United States in a few days. He combed his hair and looked again. The lines were practically invisible. Jaime smiled. Two neat rows of freshly capped teeth grinned back at him.

He stashed the mirror and checked his watch, his smile disappearing behind a nervous scowl. In less than an hour, he was to meet Pablo Contreras at Dos Amigos, a café overlooking Acapulco harbor.

Over lunch, he and Pablo would exchange packages: twenty-five thousand dollars for a United States passport, a New York driver's license, and an airline ticket for a flight leaving Acapulco that afternoon for Kennedy Airport, all in the name of Angel Rodriguez. But Jaime wasn't leaving Mexico that afternoon.

Though Contreras had a reputation for discretion, Jaime came from a place where sons didn't trust their mothers, let alone a supplier of false documentation. Immediately after they concluded their business, Jaime intended to take a taxi to the airport, but he was not flying anywhere. For the benefit of his tail—and there would be one—he would enter the main terminal, hang around until the tail had gone, then take a taxi to a rental-car agency. There, he intended to rent a car and take off for Mexico City. After an overnight stay, he would board a plane for Denver, where he would again stay overnight. The next morning, he would fly to Dallas, change planes, and take off for his final destination, Newark Airport. If the Espinosa brothers had hired an assassin—and that seemed like a sure bet— he was going to have to work hard to carry out his assignment.

Jaime was finished making life easier for those ingrates. He had gone to jail for their father, maintained his silence to protect the integrity of the cartel. He could have worked a deal with the government, but he refused. Again and again during his incarceration they came to him looking to bargain a reduced sentence for names and dates and evidence. Jaime gave them nothing. He was loyal to his patrons, because at the end of the day, he believed his fealty would be amply rewarded. What a fool he'd been!

After his release from jail, he had made his way to Juarez expecting the younger Espinosas to welcome him with open arms. After all, they had pleaded with him to join their new organization. They sent couriers and encoded messages to jail, begging him to come to Juarez and resume his role as financial advisor to the cartel. In exchange for his talent and expertise, they promised him a position of elevated status and a salary that seemed extravagant, even by their bloated standards.

Shortly after he arrived in Juarez, however, it was clear that they had lied. Instead of welcoming him, they treated him like their toady, demanding that he do this or take care of that without any thanks or displays of respect. The indignity of it all infuriated Bastido. Not even his salary, which was excessive, could quell his rage. He wasn't a CFO. He was an accountant, pure and simple. He had no say in management. His function was to keep the books, keep track of their bank accounts in Mexico, Colombia, Switzerland, Houston, and New York, and most important, to teach them how to wash money through legitimate institutions without being detected. The Mexicans, they said, were too inexperienced and too greedy to be able to handle the gargantuan profits that came with exporting drugs to America.

They told Jaime they knew they could trust him. They also made it clear that if ever he betrayed that trust, the consequences would be dire.

Maybe so, but after only a few weeks on the job, Jaime bucked. He was old and tired of being an errand boy for the Espinosas. In his mind, he deserved the respect due an elder statesman. When that was not forthcoming, he voiced his objections, loudly and often. In response, they threatened to turn him over to the American authorities; by crossing the border, and consorting with other known felons, Jaime had violated the terms of his parole.

Strong-arming might have worked with others in their employ, but Jaime was immune to their thunder. He had spent too many years in American prisons to be frightened by kids who thought they could rule an empire by cracking their father's whip. They were pretenders to the throne. If everyone else was too frightened to challenge their rule, Jaime wasn't.

Resentful of the fact that they had brought him to Juarez under false pretenses and treated him with such blatant disregard, Jaime turned vengeful. But he didn't act on his feelings right away. Instead, he went to work, completed his tasks, and paid obeisance to his masters, all the while thinking and plotting his revenge. Jaime had learned two things in prison: Often, people who shared the same enemy made the best allies, and that patience, particularly when concocting a battle plan, was indeed a virtue.

Ultimately, he conceded he was not equipped to launch an all-out war. The logistics required to pull off such an operation were simply too formidable. But Jaime had never thought of himself as a general. He was a businessman. For him, taking over the leadership of the cartel was far more appealing. And for the Espinosa scions, living with the humiliation of being deposed and disenfranchised by a lowly accountant would be far more devastating than taking a bullet.

Giving Jaime confidence was the knowledge that he had made some excellent contacts in the States: men who knew about pride and loyalty, men who understood that leadership wasn't something that was simply handed from father to son without appropriate tests and rites of passage. Jaime knew that he might have to prove himself, but he had no quarrel with that. He'd rather do a favor for a friend than work for those who had become foes.

And so, Jaime Bastido, armed with a new face, new name, and new purpose, boarded an Aero Mexico plane headed for the United States. As the plane lifted off, Jaime closed his eyes and slept. He needed to rest because he needed to be alert.

He had a lot of scores to settle.

CHAPTER

SEVEN

On January 10, 1977, in the middle of a raging snowstorm, Jake Fowler's father, Archie, left for work and never came home. His mother, Grace, notified the police, who searched for weeks without turning up a body or anything else that would explain his absence.

The first week in May, Archie's beloved beige, 1969 Dodge Dart convertible was found in a scrap yard in Hoboken, New Jersey. When the trunk was pried open, they found a badly crushed, badly decomposed body with a bullet hole in the skull that looked as if it had been made by a .22. Forensics said the corpse was a man whose vital statistics—height, weight, age—fit the same profile as Archie Fowler. They identified fibers taken from the floor of the trunk as ones that could have come from the same type of navy blue wool suit Archie had worn the day he disappeared. And they traced a pair of Johnston & Murphy shoes hidden underneath the front seat to a pair known to have been sold to the victim. No murder weapon was recovered, however. No fingerprints other than Archie's were found on the car. And since every single tooth had been extracted from the victim's mouth, there could be no comparison of dental records.

The family was stunned. Archie was an affable man who was well-known in the neighborhood. Always quick with a joke and a smile, fast to pick up a check or lend a helping hand, no one could imagine any reason why he might have been murdered, unless it was a robbery gone bad. Detectives worked another angle.

Archie was an accountant in private practice with his brother. Most of their clients were small business owners and professionals—doctors, lawyers, dentists—single practitioners who lived and worked in their Brooklyn neighborhood. When questioned, several of those recalled finding occasional discrepancies: an omission of a receivable here, a misplaced deposit there. Had any of them put two and two together, they surely would have come up with three. Archie might have been sued, but it probably wouldn't have gotten him murdered.

The police delved deeper and found that Archie had a side venture his brother and his wife knew nothing about: He kept the books for several businesses run by the Saviano crime family. And, according to a forensic accountant, had done enough skimming to accumulate a hefty bankroll. And establish a motive for murder.

While that seemed the most likely scenario, there was also the possibility that Archie had skipped town with the cash, leaving someone else to be buried in his place. To that end, the police questioned Jake's mother at length, searching the apartment for cash, pumping her about investments and possible hidden bank accounts. They asked about her marriage, their sex life, where Archie went on evenings he claimed he was working late, and with whom. They interrogated Archie's brother, Angus, who was furious about the humiliation he and his family were suffering and the damage all of this was doing to his reputation. They even questioned Jake and his younger sister, Jocelyn. In the end, no one knew anything beyond the obvious, no one could find any of the embezzled funds, and forensics couldn't state with absolute certainty that the body in the morgue was—or was not—Archie Fowler. It was painful to close the books on a mystery, but after months of digging into dark and private corners that yielded nothing, everyone seemed willing to let Archie Fowler rest in peace.

Everyone but Jake. He was fourteen years old. Not only couldn't he believe that his father was dead, but he wouldn't believe that his father had done anything to bring about his own demise. In his mind, there were simply too many pieces that didn't fit. How did Archie's car wind up in Hoboken and why did it take so long to locate? If all that money had been embezzled over all those years, where had he stashed it before running off? Why weren't there bankbooks or a key to a safety deposit box? Did he go alone? If not, why wasn't there any evidence of an affair? If that body wasn't Archie's, whose was it and how did it get in the trunk of that car? If that body was Archie's, who said it had to be the mob that killed him? Why not the periodontist he ripped off? Or the proctologist? Or Angus? He was the one who benefited the most from Archie's death. Aside from being able to take over Archie's clients and pocket one hundred percent of the profits, when they went into business together, the two brothers had taken out insurance policies on each other's lives. At Archie's death, Angus inherited $250,000.

"Angus is a climber," Jake groused. "Maybe he needed the insurance money to buy that silly wife of his a new Cadillac or another mink coat."

When Grace attempted to defend her brother-in-law, Jake reminded her that Archie had let his personal insurance policies lapse and that the only payoff was going to be one paid for by the business, to Angus.

"For all he knows, we're flat broke." Jake snorted in disgust. "Has he offered to help us out? I don't think so. Has he even asked if we were going to be okay? I don't think so. Do I ever want to see his fat face again?" he raged. "I don't think so!"

After awhile, Grace and Jocelyn turned a deaf ear to Jake's endless theorizing over what might have happened to Archie and at whose hand. Jocelyn was twelve and too busy struggling with the loss to wrestle with Jake over things that wouldn't bring her father back. As for Grace, she was grappling with larger issues. Instead of insurance policies or stock portfolios or a healthy bank account, Archie had left behind a stack of unpaid bills and a lifestyle she would have trouble maintaining on her teacher's salary. Without his income, things would be tight. When Jake pressed her about why she was so accepting of the police's version of events, it took all the self-control she possessed not to rail about her late husband's inadequacies—as a mate, a father, a brother, a partner, a friend.

Instead, she said she understood how difficult it was for Jake to accept that his father might have done what the police suggested. She claimed to share his shock and utter dismay at the thought of Archie stealing money from people who trusted him and worse, that he had been working for the Savianos. But the police had found ledgers that substantiated their accusations. A single .22 to the head was typical of gangland executions. And the Savianos had made a point of sending an enormous floral display to the funeral home.

"Like it or not," she told him, "it makes sense."

Jake felt that was taking the easy way out.

With uncharacteristic vehemence, Grace assured him, "There is nothing easy about your father's death, but if we're going to move on—and we are—we have to let go."

Jake never did, partly because he found an ally in his grandmother. Clara Fowler was another one who wasn't prepared to accept the notion that Archie had left this world prematurely and ignominiously. She felt Jake's misgivings had merit, mainly because she couldn't believe that her beloved Archie would leave a mother to mourn for her son or to explain away the terrible things he was accused of doing. By terrible, she didn't mean stealing from the Savianos—they were gangsters, they deserved whatever was done to them. She meant the stories about Archie having an affair or cheating his brother or his neighbors.

For years, Clara and Jake clung to the belief that everyone was wrong, except them. They'd go off into a corner and whisper about something they read or heard or thought might be possible. They tried to get others to go along, but Grace steadfastly refused even to listen, let alone validate any of their mental peregrinations. Once, however, they insisted.

Clara and three of her friends went on a cruise in the Caribbean. When their boat docked in Aruba, the women disembarked, planning to spend the day shopping. While wandering around the marketplace, Clara swore she saw Archie. She called out to him, he turned, and, for a long moment, the two stared at each other. Then, Clara claimed, he hurried down the street, ducked into an alley, and was gone by the time she got there. She went to the police, told them her tale, and begged them to help her find her son. They had her fill out a missing persons form, which Jake suspected they shredded the moment they heard the ship's horn leaving the harbor.

Over the years, Clara's sighting, as it came to be called, became part of the Fowler legend, mainly because Clara was not known for her imagination. She had always been a realist; most immigrants were. If anything, she was often accused of refusing to see beyond that which was directly in front of her. When Clara insisted that she had seen Archie on that island, some felt she was simply regurgitating her grandson's wishful thinking. Jake, they said, a young man obsessed with sanitizing his father's obituary, must have brainwashed the usually sensible Clara.

Others, knowing that Clara usually accepted things at face value, including human frailty, weren't so quick to dismiss her sighting as an old woman's mirage. Maybe her son was alive. Maybe he had his reasons for leaving. Maybe he was sick and had gone away to spare his family. Maybe his marriage wasn't as good as Grace said. Maybe . . . maybe . . . maybe.

Clara, who began to live on those maybes, went back to Aruba every year until she died.

In his eulogy, Jake said his grandmother died of a broken heart. Grace felt Clara was simply exhausted from chasing a chimera through an endless maze of one-way streets and dead ends.

Yet as she laid her mother-in-law to rest and looked upon that life-hardened face for the last time, Grace found herself wondering who had answered to Archie's name when Clara called. And why he ran.

It took almost three weeks for Jake to make good on his promise to treat Amanda to an elegant evening at his apartment, but not for lack of trying. When he called her after their first date, she was out of town. He left a message on her machine, and for several days they played phone tag. When at last he reached her and issued the invitation, she seemed receptive, but declined. That week, she was scheduled to work the 2:00 P.M. to 8:00 A.M. shift. At the beginning of the next week, she caught a case that required overtime. Another time, she was busy.

Finally, she called him. "How's tonight?"

"If your window's open, babe, I'm ready!" He was thrilled; he thought she had given him the brush. "How's seven?"

"Do I have to wear a dress?"

"Absolutely! I promised you an elegant evening, remember?"

"I know, but . . ."

"Besides," he said, as if confessing to a secret sin, "I'm a major leg man."

"And?"

"And while no one in his right mind would say you look anything less than spectacular in pants, there are some members of the male species who prefer women's stems to remain uncovered. Alas, I'm one of them."

Amanda found herself chuckling quietly. He had a way of doing that to her. "See you at seven," she said.

Jake's doorbell rang at six o'clock. "Did I get my signals crossed?" he said, expecting to see Amanda when he opened the door. His visitor turned out to be his former lover, Hallie Brendel.

Tall, blond, and exceedingly fit in black tights and a long, loose sweater, she laughed when she spied his apron.

"The Love Chef, I presume?" She strode past him into his apartment, her eyes canvassing for signs of a live-in.

"Won't you come in," Jake said sarcastically, his hand still on the door, his body still facing the hallway where she had stood only seconds before. "How nice of you to drop by." He shut the door, turned, and watched as Hallie made herself comfortable on his couch.

"You forgot, 'glad to see you.' " She draped her arm over the back of the couch and assumed a proprietary air that was not entirely unexpected, or unwarranted. She and Jake had been an item for more than three years. They had ceased to be an item two years ago. She was frustrated by Jake's refusal to commit and said so—frequently. Which prompted him to say good-bye.

"Some other time, perhaps." Jake made no attempt to hide his impatience.

"I suppose I should have called, but I thought our former . . . intimacy . . . entitled me to certain privileges."

"It did," he said ignoring the provocative pose she had affected. "When we were intimate. Now, if you don't mind . . ." He swept his arm in the direction of the door. It was her turn to ignore him.

"Actually, I'm here on business." Jake folded his arms across his chest and eyed her suspiciously. "I've recommended you to Senator Chisolm." Jake almost smiled at the triumphant ta-da in her voice.

"As what?"

"After our interview—I had an exclusive, you know—the senator and I were chatting and he happened to mention that he needs opposition research done on his opponent. I told him you did that sort of thing. He's interested. I thought you would be, too."

She shrugged delicately. A shock of silky blond hair fell onto her forehead. She combed it back with her fingers, slowly and sugges- tively, knowing that as her arm lifted, her sweater would pull against her breasts. It was a movement Jake was certain she had practiced dozens of times in front of a mirror, but he responded nonetheless, drinking in the physical panorama laid out before him: an alluring body, catlike green eyes, a wide, lush mouth. He had forgotten how sexy Hallie was. On television and in photographs, she came across much harder, as if her pale, ivory skin was made of marble instead of soft, creamy-toned flesh.

"Fowler & Company can always use new clients. Thanks for recommending us." He gave a slight, gracious bow of his head. He was grateful for referrals, but past experience signaled a secret agenda lurking beneath Hallie's generosity. "Is he going to call me? Or am I supposed to call him?"

"Actually," she said, making a show of uncrossing her legs,

adjusting her sweater, then crossing them again, "I told him I'd arrange a lunch." She smiled coyly. "I didn't think you'd mind."

Jake didn't like to interview prospective clients with outside parties present. Private investigations had a higher success rate if the details remained private. He frowned. "Who else is going to be at this lunch besides the senator and me?"

Hallie looked stung, but then she became, as Jake knew she would, defensive. For a woman who was indisputably gorgeous, undeniably intelligent, and firmly on the journalistic fast track, she had more insecurities than shoes—which ranked second on her list of passions, just below ambition.

"If you'd rather, I'll make the introductions and leave." She stood, clearly piqued. "I'd hate to befoul the atmosphere." She flung her designer backpack onto her shoulder and started for the door.

Jake reached for her arm. "I'm sorry, Hallie. I didn't mean that the way it sounded. It's just . . ."

"You're in a hurry to put the final touches on your dinner à deux. I understand. Pardon me for intruding." She continued her march to the door, her features frozen in a mask of controlled emotion.

Jake had seen that face a hundred times before—when he had forgotten to call or didn't compliment the way she looked or wasn't able to intuit her need to be comforted or praised or made love to. Hallie couldn't deal with any form of rejection or criticism, even if it was well intentioned. It was a flaw that undermined most of her personal relationships and had made her tenure at the *New York Times* difficult. Intellectually, she understood that it was an editor's job to critique someone's work. Emotionally, she viewed every blue-pencil mark as a slap. Ultimately, that over-the-top, narcissistic, me-first sensitivity got her fired. And drove Jake away.

"This dinner practically cooks itself," he said, softening his tone reflexively. Her self-centeredness was annoying, but her neediness never failed to evoke sympathy. He took her hand and led her back to the couch, which was precisely what she wanted him to do. He knew that and did it anyway. Jake Fowler was a nice guy. "It's been awhile. Catch me up."

Hallie pouted for a moment before speaking. "Well, as I'm sure you know, I'm at the *Morning Telegraph* now." Jake nodded. He had seen several of her articles. "It's such a relief to be at a newspaper that's willing to commit space to the stories behind the headlines."

Again, she stuck her nose in the air and sniffed, as if her tenure at the *Times* had been an exercise in tedium and the *Telegraph* was the road to a Pulitzer. It was a good daily newspaper with decent circulation figures and a growing reputation, but it was not the *New York Times.*

"What's the story behind Chisolm's investigation?" Jake asked. "Other than his pollster telling him that any story about drugs is a grabber?"

Hallie dismissed his cynicism with an arch of an eyebrow. "Don't be such a boor, Jake. The senator is genuinely concerned and is making a legitimate effort to stop the flow of drugs. He's going after the financial community because he believes they're the ones who've constructed the roadblocks that stand in the path of meaningful legislation."

She sounded rehearsed, as if she had swallowed one of Chisolm's stump speeches whole. Jake wondered what the senator had promised Hallie in return for this exclusive, bold-type coverage.

"Hey!" he said, looking to appease. "The guy may be onto something. *Cherchez les* bucks, I always say."

Hallie stood, her manner turning chilly. "You're always so flippant and critical. No one can ever measure up to your lofty standards, can they, Jake?"

He shook his head, exasperation washing his face. "I didn't say that, Hallie. Don't put words in my mouth. The guy's up for reelection. Half the crap these politicians throw out for our consumption is not altogether true, the other half is an outright lie. And you know it!"

Hallie had made her way to the door. Before facing him, she arranged her features in a calm, dignified mien. "You can judge the senator's level of sincerity for yourself when you meet him. I'll call you with the arrangements."

She was gone before he could protest—which they both knew he had no intention of doing.

Hallie was so consumed with self-righteous indignation that she didn't see the woman who was climbing the four flights until they collided with each other. It wasn't much more than a bump, but they paused for a second, sputtered excuse-me's, looked one another over in that quick but thorough way that women do, and continued as before. Hallie went down a few steps, stopped, and looked back up. Assuming this was Jake's dinner companion, Hallie wanted to take another minute to study the woman she now viewed as her competition.

She didn't like what she saw. It wasn't her looks that unsettled Hallie. They were both tall, well-built, women with good haircuts and a light hand with cosmetics. Hallie gave herself the edge when it came to chic, however; she would have bet that not one piece of the redhead's ensemble boasted a recognizable label. But Ms. No Name did have something Hallie didn't, something Hallie wanted desperately but couldn't seem to buy or borrow or learn: There was an air about the woman walking into Jake's apartment that said she knew who she was—and was comfortable with it.

Hallie disliked her immediately.

Jake's apartment surprised Amanda. It wasn't much larger than her own, but it was far more inviting. The living room was generous, with a working fireplace anchoring a handsome grouping of furniture at one end, a small kitchen tucked behind a half wall at the other. Two tall windows curtained in floor-length sheer whites defined the space in between. In front of the windows were simple, iron plant stands, each bearing a pot of fabulous white cymbidium orchids. She never would have imagined Jake Fowler being a fan of such fussy flowers; plus, they required a great deal of care. Then again, she wouldn't have imagined him being the kind to bother with candles or photographs, but there were plenty of both placed about the room.

"You cheated," Amanda scolded, pointing to Jake's black-silk shirt and black trousers. "You said I had to wear a skirt and you were going to wear a suit."

"I also said we were going to order in pizza." He grinned at her and his dimples flashed. "I lied."

She looked past him at the round, wooden table she assumed was for dining. There were chairs around the table and music playing softly in the background, but no place settings, no flowers, no sign of a meal about to be served. She wondered if they were going out. Suddenly, she became aware of a delicious scent filling the room.

"You're cooking?" she asked, unable to hide her astonishment.

"We're cooking," he corrected as he led her over to the stove where two enormous pots bubbled. "When I was in law school, I roomed with a guy whose parents owned a trattoria in Rome," he said as he handed Amanda a long-handled wooden spoon, pointed her in the direction of a large pot, and instructed her to stir. "This is the Saleppichi's specialty. I know you're going to want to make this at home, but," he said, holding out a hand as if to prevent her from throwing herself at him in an act of supplication, "the recipe is a secret I've vowed to take to my grave."

Amanda raised an eyebrow, accepting his challenge. "If this tastes as good as it smells," she insinuated, "that could be arranged."

Jake pursed his lips, considering the not-so-veiled threat. "I forgot I was sharing a kitchen with a woman who's packing!" Before she knew what was happening, he reached inside her jacket and patted her down, his hands following a line from her armpits to her thighs. He finished his inspection, stood tall, and, with a barely restrained grin, said, "Just checking."

"It's in my bag," she replied, without missing an orbit with her spoon or taking her eyes off him.

"Mine's in a drawer in my bedroom. Now that we've established the location of our respective weapons, would you like me to relieve you of your jacket?" He held out his hand.

Amanda laid the spoon down on the counter, slipped out of her jacket, and handed it to Jake, who whistled appreciatively. She was wearing one of her Little Black Dresses. This one-shouldered, black jersey was the most elegant—and the sexiest—one she owned. While she wouldn't admit it to a living soul, she had wanted to look her best this evening. Judging by Jake's expression, she had succeeded.

"You look positively scrumptious," he said, unabashed in his admiration. His eyes traveled downward. "And, as I suspected, Detective Max. You've got dynamite legs!"

"I could have told you that."

"Yes, I suppose you could have. But seeing is believing."

Amanda smiled as he lifted a pot lid and looked at its contents. He stirred something in a chunky red sauce. The pot she was tending held something thick, smooth, and yellow.

"Cornmeal." He poked at it with another spoon and declared that it would be awhile before it was done. "Keep stirring!"

She complied while he opened a bottle of wine. He poured some into a glass, looked at it in the light, and tasted it, letting it rest on his tongue before swallowing and allowing a pleased smile to illuminate his mouth. Satisfied with his selection, he handed her the crisp *chenin blanc* and invited her to drink. It was wonderful.

"I don't know, Fowler. A chef. A wine connoisseur. Orchids. Chopin. You're just filled with surprises tonight." Her face twisted into a grimace, as if she had looked into the future and seen something awful. "You're not going to break into song at any point, are you?"

"Only if you beg me."

She laughed. "Don't hold your breath."

While they stirred they talked. He asked about her life off-hours. She told him about her photography and, in a weak moment, about her upcoming exhibition. When he promised to attend and she explained that she would not be there, he dismissed that as an irrelevancy.

"I can go by myself," he said with feigned petulance.

Amanda smiled, at him and at the fleeting image of Jake Fowler and Tyler Grayson standing next to each other in front of one of her portraits. They were so opposite, so Shakesperean in the way their physical being and temperament contrasted. She wondered what it was about her that appealed to them. Was it something they had in common, or did she present herself differently to each of them? She must have been lost in her own musings, because Jake's voice startled her.

"Did you hypnotize yourself with all that stirring?" he asked, gently taking the spoon from her hand.

"I must have drifted off."

"Maybe I should burst into song."

Amanda recoiled, frightened and imperiled. "Oh, please. Anything but that," she pleaded.

"Stand back, woman."

Amanda obeyed, watching in stunned amusement as Jake lifted the pot she was stirring off the stove and walked toward the table. He tilted the pot down and began pouring the pastelike substance onto the table.

"What are you doing?" Amanda sputtered, aghast. She hadn't realized there was a special board covering the tabletop.

He smiled, but said nothing as he circled the table, laying down a line of golden meal that enlarged and spread and then, miraculously, stopped, about an inch from the edge. As she stood by like a dazed mannequin, he filled the hole he had left in the center with the contents of the second pot, a mix of beef and veal and lamb in a rich tomato sauce. Then, he set up a small snack table alongside each chair, upon which he placed a green salad, a wineglass, a napkin, and utensils.

He seated her, filled her wineglass with a Chianti Reserve and then proudly announced, "This, beautiful lady, is the way polenta is served in Italy. *Mangia*"

Amanda looked confused. "I would love to *mangia,* but I don't know how."

"You eat from the center out," he explained, taking a tablespoon and a fork in hand. "Grab some of the meat, add some of the polenta and enjoy, enjoy!"

Amanda felt like a three-year-old eating a new food for the first time. It took a few tries to get the hang of it, but once she did, she beamed with accomplishment. She couldn't remember having this much fun at a meal, and said as much to her host.

"I'm glad," he said, making no attempt to hide his desire for approval. "I wanted tonight to be special,"

"It is," she replied, trying to quell the storm of feeling inside her. "Very special."

The mood grew even more mellow as they sipped their wine and continued probing each other's inner selves. They found that their shared interests went far beyond TV police dramas and old movies. They both liked classical music, stand-up comics, the occasional off-Broadway play, mountains rather than beaches, a good bargain, and plain bagels. They both did yoga and were trained in the martial arts, Amanda a devotee of tae kwan do, Jake, of karate; both were black belts. Amanda favored baseball over Jake's passion, football, but both enjoyed basketball, particularly the Knicks. Jake enjoyed hitting the after-hours clubs every now and then. Amanda preferred hitting the slopes. His one experience with skiing was so humiliating he swore he'd never go near a ski slope, but he agreed to try again if she would go dancing with him.

When they finished eating, they cleared everything away and Jake suggested they retire to one of the couches. Before they did, he decided to build a small fire. Amanda excused herself and headed for the bathroom. In between the living room and the bedroom, there was a small gallery. Three walls were filled with pencil sketches. Some appeared to be deliberate caricatures, some were quickly drawn, others were serious portraits. She was certain that at least two of them had been done by police artists.

She intended to ask Jake about them, but when she returned to the living room, he was fussing with a hissing cappuccino machine and she became distracted by several old photographs on the mantel.

"Who are they?" she asked, pointing to one with two adults and two children mugging for the camera.

Jake didn't answer immediately. Instead, he busied himself with the contents of the tray he had brought from the kitchen. In the center of the cocktail table, he placed a plate of *biscotti*, a bottle of *vin santo* in which to dip the cookies, and two glasses. He set out

the two cups of cappuccino, sprinkled cinnamon and shaved chocolate over the frothy white caps, and handed Amanda a stirrer tipped
with rock sugar. Guessing that he was stalling, Amanda filled the
time by indulging in the ritual of the *biscotti*, letting the sweet mix
melt in her mouth as she waited for Jake to decide what he wanted
to tell her about that photograph, if anything.

"They were the Fowlers." His voice was tinged with bitterness.
He rose from his chair and brought the picture to the table. "This
was my father, Archie. This is my mother, Grace. This is my sister,
Jocelyn. And that handsome fella is me." He tried to keep things
light, but his smile was forced and his eyes had clouded.

She smiled with a gentleness that touched him. "You were adorable, no doubt about that." She looked at the photo again. He
couldn't possibly imagine how much she envied him mementos like
these. "Judging by this, you came from a fun family."

Jake nodded. "Yeah. We were. Once."

She guessed this was a difficult subject for him. She thought she
knew why. "Did your father pass away?"

Later, he decided it must have been the nearness of her or her
scent mingling with the wine and the warmth of the fire. Whatever
the reason, over the next several hours, he unburdened himself of
the story about his father, divulging everything about Archie van-
ishing, the body in the trunk of the car, and Grace's unwillingness
to disbelieve the police version of his disappearance.

"I don't believe people simply fall off the face of the earth,"
he said, confessing that the only thing substantiating his insistent
optimism was the ravings of his grandmother, who swore she saw
her son walking down a street on some Caribbean island.

Amanda found his story more credible than she could say. "Do
you think he's alive today?"

Jake shrugged and sipped at his cappuccino. His eyes fixed on
the fire, as if the flames were possibilities, there for the wise to
consider, or for the foolish to grab on to, regardless of the obvious
danger.

"Is there a connection between your father and the rogue's gallery
in that hallway?" she asked.

"You mean is that a branch of the Missing Persons' Bureau?"
His smile was brief. "Yes and no. One of those sketches was done
by a police artist in an attempt to locate witnesses who might have
seen my father." That didn't surprise Amanda. "The debate that
went on in my family over it was quite heated and sort of ridiculous

at the time, but years later, I realized that it was that debate that spawned my fascination with the notion of image and identity.

"I never thought the sketch was an exact likeness of my father. My mother thought it was an excellent approximation. My grandmother said it didn't do her Archie justice. Angus thought he looked too kind. My sister thought he looked evil." Jake chuckled, the way people do when they've realized something and they're waiting for the rest of the group to catch on. "It struck me that the sketch never varied. It was the way we saw Archie that made it different for each of us. That 'in the eye of the beholder' thing, I guess.

"Anyway, I became intrigued by the notion of how we see the people closest to us and started to collect drawings. Some are people I know. Others are celebrities. And some are missing persons I was hired to find."

"Did you?"

Jake nodded. "All except my father."

Amanda longed to commiserate with him. She had known her father was alive, yet when she was fourteen her hopes of seeing Lionel seemed just as far-fetched as Jake's chances of tracking down Archie.

As if he sensed that she had gone to visit a lonely place, she felt Jake's hand rest on her arm. He caressed her skin as he spoke about the hole in his heart where his father used to live.

"From the time I was fourteen years old, I've believed that Archie Fowler is alive and well, strutting around on some beach wearing a hideous turquoise-and-pink cabaña suit and drinking a piña colada."

He stared at her, unashamed of the emotion etched on his face. He was not a man who trusted easily, she knew that, yet at this moment, he was willing to let her see his fragility and trust her with his angst.

"At some point, I think I convinced myself that if I gave in to the notion that he was the man in the car, it was not only the ultimate act of disloyalty, but a form of filial desertion, a sin for which there is no penance. After all," he mumbled, almost to himself, "a good son never deserts his father."

Amanda felt tears pool in her eyes. *Does a good daughter desert her father? Does a good daughter let her father believe that she and her mother died in an explosion?*

Jake noticed her tears and immediately went to wipe them away. His fingers blotted them gently from her cheeks, then briefly touched her lips. Amanda held her breath, as if that would extend the pleasure of the moment. "I'm sorry, Max. I didn't mean to be such a downer. I hope I didn't spoil our evening."

Amanda almost laughed. This was one of the most intimate evenings she had ever spent with a man. "You couldn't possibly spoil tonight," she said. "On a scale of one to ten, this was an eleven. Truly. I had a wonderful time."

With remarkable ease, Jake took her face in his hands and kissed her. "I hope you don't think that you can sweet-talk me into giving you the recipe for that polenta, because it won't work. I'm a man of my word."

"Can't blame a girl for trying," she said as he kissed her again. His arms slid around her, and she knew she had a decision to make: Either she left or she slept with him. "I've got to go."

It was with extreme reluctance that she extricated herself from his embrace and rose from the couch.

"Come," he said, getting her jacket and her holster from the closet. "I'll walk you home."

"It's only a few blocks. It's not necessary," she protested, amazed at how she was reacting to the sensation of his hands on her as he helped her put on her jacket.

"Yes, it is." He threw on a coat, blew out the candles and opened the door. "If I walk you home, I get to kiss you good night." She laughed as they started down the stairs. "Hey!" he said. "Grace Fowler didn't raise a stupid child."

CHAPTER
EIGHT

Annie was so nervous she wanted to jump out of her skin. As she threw another pair of shoes back into the closet and rummaged about for a replacement, she wondered what had possessed her to raise the subject of a cosmetics company to Amanda. As usual, her mouth had worked before her brain and now, for better or worse, Lionel Baird was due to arrive at her apartment in twenty minutes.

Last week, when Amanda had called to say that Lionel might be interested in backing a cosmetics company, Annie was stunned. Not that her friend knew the omnipotent Mr. Baird—Annie had long suspected he was the older man in Amanda's life—but she never imagined that Amanda would speak to him about her cosmetics line or, even more astounding, that he would agree to meet with her.

The original plan called for the two women to go to Lionel's office together. Then Amanda got stuck doing an additional shift. Annie still would have preferred meeting the Great Man at his office, but early that morning, his secretary telephoned to say Mr. Baird wished to change the site of their meeting. He intended to come to her. That announcement had the same effect as a starting pistol—suddenly, Annie was off and running. Not only had she raced around trying to civilize her loft, but she had tried on a dozen different ensembles without success. Her ladylike, all-purpose black suit—the one she wore to expensive restaurants, business meetings, and funerals—would have been perfect for the offices of Baird, Nathanson & Spelling, but it was hardly something one wore at home.

Wriggling into the only unwrinkled item left in her wardrobe, she jumbled everything together, tossed it into the closet, jammed the door shut, tidied up as best she could, and ran to the bathroom for a last-minute makeup check. This was the business she was selling. She couldn't afford to look like she had slapped a face on!

When the buzzer sounded, for one mad moment she thought about pretending she wasn't home. Fortunately, sanity returned with her next breath. She pressed the button that allowed her visitor entry into the building and waited nervously for the elevator to stop at her floor.

She had seen Lionel Baird's picture in *Forbes* magazine, the *Times* and various weekly news journals, so she already knew what he looked like. When the door opened, however, she was taken aback, completely unprepared for the enormity of his presence. He loomed larger than life, taller, broader-shouldered, better-looking. Too, he exuded an aura so commanding, it momentarily immobilized her.

"May I come in?" he said quietly.

Annie's ivory face flushed pink, and she began to stammer like a peasant in the presence of the king. She hated hearing herself sound so utterly diminished, but she couldn't help it. "Oh, of course. I'm so sorry. Really. Forgive my manners. Come in. Sit down. Make yourself comfortable."

She walked briskly into the space she defined as a living room, trying to view it as a stranger might. She had never had anyone of his prominence visit before, so it was hard to find the proper perspective. Her friends were actors and artists and others who lived off paychecks that weren't always regular or large. Few lived uptown and when they did, it was in inexpensive, cookie-cutter apartments or west side walk-ups. She couldn't imagine the grandeur that was Lionel Baird's frame of reference.

Instead of politely following her lead, Lionel lingered at the entrance to the loft. He didn't look around so much as he sucked in the general atmosphere, trying to absorb the totality of what appeared before him. When finally he moved inside it was at a pace attuned to the observant prowl of his eyes. Rather than continuing with a generous sweep, his gaze settled now on particular vignettes and individual items: warehouse windows covered with feminine white sheers; a large, primitive wooden cocktail table that seemed to anchor the main seating area; two shabby-chic chairs balanced by a formal Biedermeier couch. Atop a faux-antique sideboard, more than two dozen different candlesticks were artfully arrayed in what he guessed was specific randomness, each bearing a candle at a different stage of meltdown.

One corner, where he assumed Amanda and Annie did her photography shoots, loomed as a ministage, replete with assorted props: a Florentine, three-panel screen; a huge Grecian urn; a potted palm; a Louis XIV chair with a gilded frame; a pile of enormous floor cushions in shiny damasks, lushly textured brocades, and thickly fringed velvets. Bolts of fabric, each with a swatch hanging loose as a tease, gathered like a bouquet against a wall.

Nearby, a dressmaker's dummy preened, garbed to excess in an abundance of fashionable remnants. On the opposite wall, hanging beneath an enormous mirror that looked as if it came from a saloon, was an equally gargantuan table festooned with wig stands. Each bore an elaborately coifed wig complemented by a fabulous face created from the plethora of jars and pots and tubes and brushes that blanketed the rest of the tabletop. In front of this cosmetic banquet stood two stools, where the subject's makeup was applied. Behind it, a Victorian-style wooden hat rack boasted *chapeaux* ranging from something richly plumed, à la Marie Antoinette, to a baseball cap bluntly embroidered, NOPE, NOT A CHANCE!

"Your home is charming," he said as he took the seat offered him.

That wasn't the adjective she would have chosen to describe her digs, but Annie thanked him anyway and offered him a drink: whiskey, wine, coffee, bottled water—carbonated or still—tea—hot or iced—diet soda, regular soda.

Lionel, noticing a bottle of wine chilling in a nearby cooler, abruptly halted her inventory by pointing. "May I open it?" he asked, fearing that if her trembling hands got hold of this bottle, tragedy would ensue.

"I passed nervous about an hour ago," she announced as she plunked down into the seat opposite him. "I think I'm approaching frantic. You'll let me know when I get there, won't you."

"Absolutely."

Lionel poured them each a glass and encouraged her to partake. As she did, he continued his visual survey of the young woman his daughter claimed to be her closest friend in New York. She was as attractive as Amanda said and, as Beth had described her, as quirky. She was clearly an avid collector, and although her pocketbook was limited, her taste was eclectic and surprisingly refined. And while she probably thought he turned up his nose at anything that didn't carry a designer label, he found her personal style quite appealing. Garbed in black spandex tights, black loafers, and a man's white dress shirt, cuffs and collar upturned, she conveyed not only confidence, but flair.

"So, how and why does one become a makeup artist?" he asked, noticing the quixotic assemblage of facial-feature paperweights that occupied a corner of the cocktail table: brass lips and eyes, marble mouths in different shapes, a nose or two, even a clay ear.

"That's easy. I started painting my face when I was five years old and never stopped." She laughed at the memory of that day. "I found my mother's makeup drawer and thought it was filled with magic. There were all these colorful sticks and tubes to play with, and so, I did. I smeared myself, the sink, a wall or two and the blanket on my bed. I thought everything looked beautiful. Unfortunately, my parents disagreed." She laughed again.

Lionel liked the sound of her laughter; it was sprightly and sincere, without any camouflage or restraint. If she were to influence his daughter in only one way, he hoped she would teach Amanda to laugh as freely. "I gather you were punished for this youthful burst of creativity."

"Let's just say their artistic sensibilities weren't as highly evolved as mine."

"Did you have any formal training, or did you hone your skills solely through trial and error?"

"Both," Annie said. "I got a Bachelor of Fine Arts in theatrical makeup. When I came to New York, I was lucky enough to work a few Broadway shows and apprentice with several masters of the craft. In my spare time, and I had plenty of it, I did makeovers at various cosmetics counters around town. Then, I got this soap job, which led to work on the Emmys, which led to some really fabulous publicity, which led to me thinking about capitalizing on my sudden fame." She smiled broadly. "That's the résumé. You ready for the pitch?"

"I'm not finished with the résumé." Lionel's tone was abrupt, truncating her running monologue. "That rather rapid recitation of your employment history was entertaining, but superficial. Amanda Maxwell's personal recommendation does carry significant weight, but we are discussing the possibility of financing a serious business venture."

Annie was unnerved, and it showed. "I didn't mean . . . I'm sorry if I sounded immature, but . . . well, I . . . ."

Lionel reached into his pocket and handed her an official-looking form. "Kindly fill this out."

She nodded dumbly. This was not the way she had wanted this interview to go. She lowered her eyes, escaping what she perceived as a critical gaze, and perused the endless list of inquiries. Where did she attend school? What was the name of her bank? Had she ever taken out any loans? If so, did any remain outstanding? Who were her previous employers? How long had she worked at each job? Had she ever owned her own business? If it was still operational, what were its profits and/or its losses? If it was not still operational, what happened to it? Whom should they call as business references? And what about character references? Were her parents living or dead?

Her heart drummed wildly in her chest. She'd made mistakes before, but this was a doozy. Whatever had she been thinking? That a man like Lionel Baird would simply walk in, love her lipstick shade, and hand her a check for three or four million dollars? That he wouldn't do due diligence on her background and financial situation? *I wasn't thinking,* a voice screamed inside her head.

"I'm a makeup artist, not a corporation, Mr. Baird," she said, trying to shift the focus of the conversation without sounding desperate or defeated. "I don't have things like collateral or a financial history or a 10Q. Hell, sometimes I wonder about my IQ!" she said, punctuating her sentence with a shaky smile. When he continued to stare at her expectantly, she took a deep breath, organized her thoughts, and plodded on.

"I don't have an impressive financial résumé, Mr. Baird, I know that. But I do have ideas, talent, and an intimate knowledge of my customer. That's the résumé you should be considering, the one that tells you how good I am at what I do. The one that tells you how hard I'd work to make my idea a reality and your investment profitable.

"You're a financial wizard. That's a fact. You know how to make a business grow better than most, but with all due respect, sir, you don't know my business at all. I do. I know I could produce a solid product, market it correctly and, ultimately, get women to buy it. Why? Because my line promotes a natural, youthful, look that makes women of all ages look pretty. And you know what, Mr. Baird? To most women, whether they're rich or poor, from the city or the suburbs, postadolescent or premenopausal, looking pretty is their bottom line."

She hoped he didn't notice that she was trembling. She also hoped he wouldn't laugh in her face. He didn't. But neither did he offer any encouragement. Instead, he returned to the issue of the financial form.

"I'm well aware of your qualifications, Miss Hart. If you weren't viable, I wouldn't have bothered to come here today. Now, despite your eloquent argument, I still must insist on some very basic information. Surely you know your social security number and the names and addresses of past employers." Annie would have preferred a kinder, gentler tone, but Lionel remained steely, focused, and on point. "I'm sure you understand, Miss Hart. I don't lend money to strangers." He pointed to the papers languishing in her hands. "Please. Complete this as best you can."

To Annie's ear, those words signaled termination. Lionel Baird was going to leave. He'd probably be polite and urge her to mail this back to him. Out of respect for her relationship with Amanda, he'd wait a reasonable amount of time, then call to say thanks, but no thanks. Annie began to rise so she could escort him to the door, but Lionel had leaned back in his chair and was leisurely sipping his wine. When she looked at him quizzically, he smiled.

"Since I assume this won't take very long," he said, pleasantly enough, "I'll wait."

That evening, Amanda planned to join Lionel at his town house for dinner. Since her shift ended at eight, she decided to go directly from the office. She showered in the locker room, changed into jeans, a tee shirt, a bulky sweater that camouflaged her more feminine attributes, and a leather coat that could belong to either gender. To further the androgynous illusion, once she was in a taxi, she stuffed her hair up under a baseball cap and hiked the collar of her coat. The cab dropped her off three blocks from Lionel's in front of a large apartment building on Third Avenue. In case she had a tail, she walked into the building and asked the doorman for directions to someplace innocuous. When she had stalled as long as she could, she headed for the town house, taking a ridiculously circuitous route. Once there, she rang the bell at the service entrance and waited for Thompson to allow her entry.

"Just once, I'd like to come through the front door," she said, grousing slightly, as Lionel greeted her.

"Soon, sweetheart." He hugged her close, speaking softly so that no one else could hear him. "Soon, Jaime Bastido and the others will be captured, this nightmare will be over, and we'll be free to be who we are: father and daughter."

As they separated, he caressed her cheek and then gently pinched her ear. It was a gesture from their past, reminding her that miracles did happen, that they had found each other again. If only she could believe that another miracle was in the cards.

They dined in the library, a space that felt far more intimate and, therefore, more comfortable than the formal dining room down the hall. Paneled in rich mahogany, lined with shelves of leather-bound books and furnished in deep tones of evergreen and wine, the room exuded an atmosphere of leisurely contemplation.

Amanda gratefully accepted Lionel's offer of wine. After sinking into one of the club chairs flanking the fireplace, she sipped the sauvignon blanc slowly, relishing its cold crispness on her tongue. Lionel smiled as he watched her rest her feet on an ottoman and visibly unwind. In the beginning, his world and his lifestyle had been so foreign to her, it was almost impossible for her to relax in his home or at some of his favorite haunts. He recalled how edgy and uptight she had seemed, rarely able to kick back and laugh without consciously wondering if it was proper to do so. Thankfully, she was adjusting.

"I'd ask how your day was, but I can't imagine it being anything but gruesome."

Amanda winced. One of her calls had been to a home where an infant had been brutalized by its mother's boyfriend. The man, high on Propaine, had beaten the three-month-old for crying while he was trying to have sex. When the baby's screams intensified due to the beating, he dropped it in a pot of boiling water. The mother, also whacked-out on drugs, panicked and ran from the apartment. A neighbor called the police. By the time help arrived, the boyfriend was gone and the baby was dead.

Amanda sought to anesthetize herself with the wine. "We never finished our conversation the other day about Tyler Grayson," she said, changing the subject. "Why were you so uptight about me having lunch with him?"

"I don't know," he admitted. "Maybe I was jealous." He smiled, but Amanda sensed he wasn't telling her everything. "Let's forget about yesterday's lunch and move on to tonight's dinner," he said, inviting her to join him at the table set up at the far end of the room. "Besides, I'm eager to tell you about my day. It wasn't as newsworthy as yours, I'm sure, but it was quite interesting."

Over a simple meal of grilled salmon and steamed vegetables, they discussed Lionel's meeting with Annie Hart.

"Frankly, I think your instincts are correct: Something's off," he said, reluctantly. "I'm glad Sam insisted we run a check on her."

Amanda pushed her food around on her plate. She had hoped Lionel was going to tell her she was wrong, that Annie Hart was on the level and that Amanda's WITSEC-syndrome was working overtime. Running Annie's vitals through FBI traces was a clear betrayal of their friendship, and that disturbed her. She didn't have many friends, so it bothered her to violate that bond. Yet self-protection had become a need that took precedence over everything else.

Lionel tried to be empathetic, but until it was firmly established that she didn't present any danger to his daughter, he didn't care about hurting Annie Hart's feelings. "She was extremely nervous."

"You're intimidating," Amanda retorted, defensively.

"True, but she didn't start shaking until I handed her the papers. Up to that point, she seemed unfazed by my so-called celebrity. She was loose and quite chatty." Lionel reviewed his impressions. "In fact, she came across as so savvy, her naïveté about anyone funding this project without doing a background check was glaring." Suddenly, he brightened. "Perhaps that's the good news."

"What do you mean?"

"An accomplished mole would have expected a thorough investigation and would have had a well-rehearsed cover story ready to go."

"What if I'm blowing everything out of proportion? What if Annie's simply a terrific girl with a lot of talent and a few dreams who got in over her head?"

"We'll both have egg on our faces, but we'll sleep easier." Lionel patted Amanda's hand, as if to remind her why this subterfuge was necessary. "And besides, if she's clean, I fully intend to set her up in business. Despite what she thinks, I do consider talent and drive valuable currency."

Amanda's throat tightened, and her eyes grew moist. "Thank you," she whispered.

"My pleasure." As he said it, he marveled at the enormity of that understatement. He doubted that Amanda could ever fully comprehend the pleasure she gave him.

From the moment she reentered his orbit, she had overwhelmed the galaxy that was his existence. Sometimes he believed it was impossible to take a breath without thinking about her, or visualizing her face, or wondering where she was and what she was doing. The joy she brought him was so intense, he practically bubbled with exultation. He longed to engulf her in the spoils of his wealth, and it required Herculean effort not to do so. Restraint was hardly a familiar companion, yet Lionel understood that to deluge her with luxuries would simply be indulging his need to give, not her desire to have. The only luxury she really longed for was peace, a feeling of being safe, of being free to conduct her life without being weighted down by the cumbersome armor of suspicion and fear. His problem was that peace couldn't be bought.

"Are you all right?" Amanda asked, concerned that Lionel had been quiet for so long and that his eyes were misted.

A slow smile displayed itself. "I'm fine," he assured her. "Really fine."

Amanda nodded, but like Lionel, she too had been thinking about their relationship. Unfortunately, her thoughts were darker than her father's.

"One of the reasons I became suspicious of Annie," she said, "was that without any solid facts, she seemed to know everything about you except your name. Whether she's connected to Bastido or one of the mob boys here in New York, or she simply made a hell of a guess, her on-target deduction told me we've gotten careless." She knew how much this was going to hurt him, so she hesitated for a second. "We can't see each other. Not until this is settled."

"No!" Lionel shook his head emphatically and slammed his fist down on the table. "I will not have my life defined by shadows."

Neither of them had noticed Thompson in the doorway. When Lionel spotted him he glowered, causing the older man to flush. "I'm sorry, sir. I thought you might like something else."

Amanda wondered how long he had been standing there and how much he had heard.

"When I need something, Thompson, I'll buzz." Lionel's agitation was obvious. Thompson exited swiftly.

"Should I be worried about him?" Amanda asked, her lips tight with concern.

Lionel rubbed his eyes, as if a headache had begun to pound. "No," he said. When he looked up, he appeared weary. "At least I don't think so."

"How long has he worked for you?"

"Twenty-three years." Lionel flipped through a mental checklist, evaluating his butler's long term of service. "He's as loyal as they come, Amanda. I know you think loyalty can be bought and that no one is an exception to that rule, but I believe Thompson comes close."

Amanda hoped he was right. "How many bodyguards do you have?" she asked, shifting focus.

"Three: Bruno Vitale, Al Heflin, and Tony Calandra. Bruno and Tony have been with me for five years, give or take. Al's relatively new, but he's a former cop and all his references checked out."

Amanda nodded. Lionel knew the three of them were going to be rechecked.

"I know this is difficult," she said, lowering her voice in case Thompson or someone else was loitering in the hallway, "but these people will buy or threaten anyone. You may not have been directly involved, Lionel, but you were married to Cynthia and you worked at Nathanson & Spelling. Don't forget that. Because they haven't."

Lionel looked away, unwilling to let Amanda see the guilt that was written in his eyes. He hadn't forgotten his marriage. Or what went on at Nathanson & Spelling. Or his involvement in the case.

"I bought a gun," he said quietly. Amanda didn't respond. She simply stared at him, waiting for a more complete explanation. "It's true, I usually rely upon my bodyguards for protection, but I decided to heed your advice and learn to defend myself."

"Have you? Learned to defend yourself, that is?"

"What do you mean?"

"Have you taken lessons in the proper way to discharge a weapon?"

With someone else, Lionel might have blustered around the issue, hoping to leave the impression that he was just shy of marksman status, but Amanda was too sophisticated, too knowledgeable about modern weaponry. He shook his head.

"What did you buy?" She tried to keep her tone neutral and nonjudgmental, but her body language screamed disapproval.

"A .22."

"A Saturday Night special?" Disbelief underlined her words and overwhelmed her face. "Do you know how close you have to be to an assailant to do any damage with a .22?"

"I know, I know. But let me tell you what my thinking was," Lionel said. "If a sneak attack came from one of my bodyguards, I could have a cannon in my pocket and it wouldn't matter. I'd be dead before I could put my hand on a gun. If my assailant's a stranger, all I'd have to do is get a single shot off and my bodyguards would take care of the rest."

He had a point, but Amanda continued to press the issue.

"I'd rather teach you how to use a Smith & Wesson Chief."

The Chief was a snub-nosed, .38 caliber gun popular with police as off-duty firepower. While most members of the NYPD, Amanda included, preferred their 9mm, semiautomatic police issue, the Chief was small, compact, and easily concealed. Amanda's was usually holstered in her belt, but the sight of it made Lionel uncomfortable. This evening she had left it in her purse, which lay on the couch behind her. She reached back and retrieved her gun, a shiny steel-barrel revolver with a smooth wooden butt.

"This is a bona fide weapon," she said, placing it on the table in front of Lionel. "It's small enough to be tucked away and powerful enough to save your life."

"Actually," he said, responding to a sudden remembrance, "I already own a .38." Amanda registered surprise. "It was given to me as a gift years ago. Since, as you can see, I have an aversion to pistols, I stored it away."

"May I see it?"

He rose and went to his desk. From a locked drawer, he extracted an old Smith & Wesson .38 revolver. When he brought it to the table and put it in front of her, her eyes widened with appreciation. It was a stunning piece, accented with gold inlay on the grip in place of the usual checkering. Viewed against modern-day weapons, like her on-duty semiautomatic for instance, it seemed to speak nostalgically of another time, when guns starred in Westerns and good-guy-bad-guy movies, not daily headlines.

"Who did this inlay work?" Amanda asked, turning the gun over, admiring its handiwork. Etched in gold on both sides of the grip, were Lionel's initials, surrounded by glorious flourishes on what appeared to be a coat of arms. It was a design worthy of Bat Masterson or Bill Hickok or any of the other heroes from America's pioneer past. It didn't seem appropriate for Lionel Baird, however.

"The man who gave it to me was a major gun aficionado. I handled an LBO that made him very, very rich. He wanted to reward me, so he gifted me with something he would regard as a treasure. Being a true son of Texas it was a gun. As for the inlay, it was done by the finest engraver in the country." Lionel eyed Amanda, eager to see her reaction. "A counterfeiter serving a fifteen-year jail sentence."

They both enjoyed a good laugh.

Amanda opened the pistol and spun the barrel. Someone kept it oiled and polished. Probably Thompson. She took it in her hand, feeling its heft. Her Glock had a grip made of plastic, so it was much lighter. Her .38 was a snub nose; this had a longer, more traditional barrel. She held the revolver up, pointed it away from Lionel, and squinted over its sight.

"Do you have ammunition for this?" she asked.

Lionel shrugged. "I wouldn't know what to buy," he confessed.

"Semi-wad cutters. One-hundred-fifty-eight-grain. I'll get them for you," she said, still studying the gun. "Here. Take it in your hand like this." She showed him how to receive a weapon. "Make sure the grip fits high into the curve between your thumb and your index finger. That puts your hand level with the barrel. It makes sighting easier." Lionel nodded, but seemed wary. "Don't put your finger on the trigger. Lay it along the side. That way you won't have any accidents."

She handed him the gun. He accepted it, but gingerly, grimacing as if he had just been presented with something quite distasteful.

"Do you take your gun with you everywhere you go?" he said, embarrassed by his ineptitude and unease around firearms.

"Yes. I'm required to carry a weapon even when I'm not working. There are one or two exceptions, but by and large, every member of the NYPD is armed, whether in uniform or not."

"You keep both of these at home?"

"Along with a 12-gauge Remington shotgun."

Lionel blanched. "Funny," he said, laying the pistol down next to Amanda's. "I thought handling a gun would be instinctual. That because I was a man, not only would I know immediately how to hold it, but I would feel exhilarated by the power and control inherent in such an object. In truth, I find it upsetting."

"It's good that you're nervous," Amanda said, returning the Chief to her bag. "Guns are capable of causing death at the flick of a finger. If you don't know how to use them, you could wind up killing someone by accident. Or hurting yourself. Which is why you and I are going to spend some time at a firing range. After all," she said, smiling encouragingly, "knowledge is power."

Lionel returned her smile, then sighed. "You've changed my life in many ways, my darling Amanda. All for the better. This, however, might be the one area in which change doesn't constitute an improvement."

"I understand your hesitancy, and I respect it. Every day I deal with the damage guns create. I'm not looking to turn you into some Wall Street Wyatt Earp, but if you own a gun, Lionel, you need to know what to do with it."

"Okay, but trust me," he said, his face still registering reservation. "I could spend a hundred hours on a firing range. I'm never going to feel comfortable with a gun in my hand."

CHAPTER

NINE

At six o'clock, Lloyd Franks feared that the four women hovering around the reception desk might be his only visitors. By eight, a sudden crush of the culturally curious had descended on Chelsea, and he feared he would run out of wine and floor space. Not only was the gallery swarming with New York notables who were actually talking about the art, but the show was almost sold out.

The photographs were exceptional—Lloyd did have an uncanny eye for talent—but it wasn't the quality of the pictures or the investment potential of particular artists that was providing the impetus to buy. There was a mesmeric aura pervading this show that had proved captivating. Each photograph focused on a single person who was defined by either costume or backdrop or preoccupation. Taken as a group, they constructed an intricate collage of social myths and personality traits that dared the viewer to probe his or her psyche, asking personal questions that only that particular individual could answer. And then, only in private.

On one side of the front bay, better-knowns like Sophie Calle, Nan Goldin, and Cindy Sherman established the "Who am I?" theme of the exhibition. On the opposite wall, three unknowns made their debut. As Lloyd had suspected, the four "Mirror Images" by Anonymous were creating the greatest buzz. Her photographs, like those of her more famous predecessors, were highly contrived self-portraits. The difference was that these had been shot through a wistful haze. They were not the stark, clean-edged History Portraits of Cindy Sherman, in which she playfully altered archival treasures and with tongue in cheek, challenged the authority of the old masters. Or the blunt, in-your-face perspectives of Nan Goldin, who dared you to criticize who she was or the life she led without examining yourself.

The woman in each of these Anonymous portraits stared into her mirror as if the reflection was that of a complete stranger. Since the faces were slightly blurred, it prompted the question: which was reflection, which was flesh? Which was reality, which was fantasy? The only definite was that in each, the subject, and probably the artist, clearly longed to be anyone but herself.

Jake was fascinated by Amanda's work, not only because of its artistry, but also in the way it explained her. In person, she projected an air of mystery, but he had filed that under occupational hazard. Most detectives were instinctively suspicious of others and excessively guarded about themselves. But these portraits showed a woman infected with a chronic case of mistrust, a woman determined to remain vague and ambiguous in a world that demanded clarity and candor. Yet while certainly, the camouflaging of self was the underlying motif of this entire exhibition, Jake guessed there was another reason Amanda's portraits were garnering the largest crowds.

Her subjects hailed from a time when women were traditionally categorized as delicate creatures. Yet despite the mythic fragility conveyed by their costumes and accoutrements, they didn't come off as damsels in distress. Instead, there was a subtle resoluteness about them that said they could take care of themselves. That they didn't need Lochinvar to ride in on his white charger and rescue them. That they would use camouflage, subterfuge, feminine wiles, or any other contrivance necessary to rescue themselves.

Jake wasn't surprised that so many women were entranced by these pictures. He guessed they sensed a kinship with Amanda's heroines. Most of them were women in charge, yet they, too, relied upon costume and makeup to create favorable impressions for themselves. They, too, survived by reinvention.

Jake could relate to the notion of hiding behind a self-crafted image. He did it every day. Presumably, so did most of the people in this room. Who they were was the image that stared back at them from the mirror, the image they wanted the public to see. Who they really were was probably the naked soul that only bared itself behind the safety of closed doors.

Jake presented himself as the cocky, self-assured private investigator who, on the face of it, feared little. What he did fear—being abandoned and unloved—was rarely, if ever revealed. Interesting, he thought. The night Amanda came over for dinner he told her far more than he had intended. She, on the other hand, had revealed nothing. They had discussed the past being prologue to the present, but only in the way it related to him and his father's disappearance. Somehow they never got to the person behind her badge or the history that had defined her as a woman.

His interest in Detective First Grade Maxwell increased when he went into the second gallery. On the center wall, confronting all who entered this bay, were half a dozen eighteen-by-twenty-four-inch matted photographs, appropriately called: Bleakscapes. Mounted without frames, they were exquisitely haunting studies of human isolation. It wasn't the place or the subject that engaged him, it was the condition of the place and the subject. Jake thought he understood what life on the streets was all about, but standing before these documentaries, he realized that his understanding was intellectual. Amanda's understanding was emotional.

An immense sadness gripped him. It was as if he was mourning for the lives these people had lost and, perhaps, for whatever contributions they might have made. As his eyes traveled from one to the other, his agitation grew, as did an unsettling sense of recognition. He made a career of tracking missing persons, but in each case, someone hired him to find those he sought. No one was looking for Amanda's people. They were the truly abandoned: unloved by their families, unwanted by their neighbors, discarded by society. They were faceless unknowns scraping out a meager existence in anonymous settings. What made these photographs so powerful was the painful truth that even if these people had been looking squarely into the camera, they still would have been faceless unknowns.

Jake shuddered at the sudden, unbidden thought that perhaps his father had become one of them. He bowed his head, engulfed in a moment of unexpected grief.

"I was beginning to think I'd never find you in this mob scene." Hallie Brendel planted herself next to him. Her arms were crossed in a pose of annoyance, a mood echoed in her voice. "Did it ever dawn on you to look for us?"

"Frankly, no," Jake said, irritated at the intrusion.

"Senator Chisolm is waiting in the other room," she said, as if he should have sensed their arrival.

"In a minute." He felt oddly linked to these images. He was loath to pull away.

"Must you be so difficult?" she said, straining to keep her voice low. "I tried to set this up for lunch, but you were too busy." Her eyes rolled in amazement. "As if a United States senator has nothing better to do than hang around waiting for Jake Fowler to free up his schedule. I asked you to join us for cocktails, but no, you *had* to come to this art thing. So I convinced the senator and Mrs. Baird to meet you here. Well, they've been here for twenty minutes. Where the hell have you been?" Hallie looked ready to stomp her foot.

"Okay. Okay." Resigned to his fate, Jake followed Hallie into the front room, snaking his way through the throng.

Standing in the absolute center of the gallery were John Chisolm and Pamela Baird, shaking hands and chatting amiably with passers-by. As he approached them, Jake assessed the couple. The senator was a man whose ego was always on display and in need of gratification, yet he exuded an air of confidence that Jake could only assume came from a long familiarity with wealth and power. Mrs. Baird, on the other hand, seemed less comfortable, less certain of her right to be in the center of things. The desire was there, and Jake guessed that she would fight to hold her ground, but the way her eyes flitted about made him think that inside she fretted that her grip on the good life was not as firm as she would have liked.

"Excuse me," Hallie said, practically shoving people out of her path. "Senator Chisolm, Mrs. Baird, this is Jake Fowler."

The gentlemen shook hands and a flurry of small talk ensued. When it became apparent that there was no way to avoid interruption, the senator and Jake moved their conversation outside. Hallie was eager to tag along, but felt she couldn't leave Pamela Baird standing alone. Unfortunately, her sense of protocol was not reciprocated. Just as the two women entered the second bay, Pamela spotted Lionel and, with only an offhanded apology, left Hallie to her own devices.

"What do you want, Pamela?" Lionel didn't even bother to turn around. He had recognized her perfume.

"I want to know when you're going to sign those papers."

"These photographs are incredible."

Lionel couldn't take his eyes off Amanda's pictures. One in particular—a young girl napping on a mattress in a filthy alleyway—held him in thrall. He couldn't imagine how it felt to be so completely at the mercy of the elements, both human and natural. Obviously Amanda could, and that made his heart ache.

"They are rather provocative," Pamela admitted, looking at them for the first time. Something about them looked familiar, but she didn't have time to search her memory as to where she might have seen them before. "I asked you a question, Lionel, one that needs to be answered."

He turned and faced her, his eyes so cold they froze the air around them. "I'll sign those papers when they read the way I want them to read."

"You're being cruel, Lionel."

"And you're being greedy. You signed a perfectly valid prenuptial agreement. The fact that you've decided you made a bad deal for yourself and want to renegotiate it doesn't negate the validity of the original document. As far as I'm concerned, and as far as the court is concerned, you were in your right mind, such as it is, at the time you signed the agreement, and, therefore, it stands as it was written."

Pamela flushed with indignation. She started to argue, but Lionel silenced her with an expression of complete intolerance.

"I'm not the one in a rush to remarry," he reminded her. "Think about that the next time you feel the urge to have your lawyer harass me with groundless claims."

He turned away from her with such brute finality, she knew she could scream in his ear and he would not respond. Stung by his rejection, she gathered what was left of her dignity, tossed back her head in a show of nonchalance, and strode away.

When she spotted Hallie Brendel, a smile sneaked across Pamela's lips. She might not be able to beat Lionel in a court of law, but she sure as hell could get even with him in the court of public opinion.

Annie watched the action from the sidelines. She had debated attending the opening—and risking a face-to-face with Lionel Baird—but in the end had decided she couldn't stay away. She had helped arrange this evening. Too, it was her friend's work that was being exhibited and that friend had tried to do something wonderful for her. It wasn't Amanda's fault that Annie hadn't thought things through. She and Amanda had spoken several times since Lionel's disastrous visit to her loft, but after the initial, "How did it go?" and "What did you think of him?" the two young women reached an unspoken accord: they would drop the subject until there was something concrete to discuss. That was ten days ago. There had been no word from Lionel Baird, concrete or otherwise.

When she spotted Lionel in the crowd, she buried herself in the midst of a group she knew would never catch his eye. He was too uptown-uptight to let his gaze linger on a bevy of black-garbed young people abounding in pierced body parts and tattoos. Safely concealed by this errant cluster, she observed him as he stood before each of Amanda's photographs, humble and adoring in their presence, as if they were religious icons rather than photographic commentaries on the ravages of loneliness.

While she had found him daunting, she was happy that Amanda had Lionel in her life. Not only could his wealth fulfill dreams, but, she conjectured, it might even be able to erase some of her nightmares. And judging by Amanda's erratic behavior of late, she was having plenty of those. For her part, Annie realized that despite the awkwardness of their initial encounter and the likelihood of him rejecting her request for backing, she would like to get to know Lionel Baird. Other, deeper reasons aside, he was so unlike anyone she had ever met before that she was intrigued and enthralled.

Her background was so modest, she had to assume that her imaginings about how someone on that rung of the ladder conducted his life were probably steeped in stereotypes. Given the chance, she'd like to know whether he went to the movies or only attended cultural events. Whether he watched sitcoms or only turned on the small screen for business reports and stock-market updates. Whether he was passionate or careful when he made love, honest or dishonest when stating his feelings.

Not for the first time, Annie rued her own dishonesty, and considered making a full confession. There would be a price to pay, she knew, but she couldn't feel any worse than she did now. And perhaps, she thought hopefully, the truth really would set them free.

The problem was she'd never know unless she tried.

Lionel saw Annie the minute she entered the gallery and Lloyd Franks swooped her up in an extravagant greeting. He saw her survey the crowd, probably looking for him, and lose herself amidst a gaggle of Village people. He knew she thought she blended in, but her compatriots presented an aspect of studied boredom. His impression of Annie Hart was that she didn't know the meaning of the word boring, which was precisely what he had liked about her: her blatant enthusiasm, her insatiable curiosity, and her rapacious need to surround herself with the people and things that made her happy.

What he didn't like was the undeniable sense that she was lying about something. While he should have felt somewhat relieved that the information they needed soon would be forthcoming, the thought that Amanda's only friend might be an enemy in disguise greatly disturbed Lionel. He had tangled with many wolves-in-sheep's-clothing during his lifetime, but those charlatans had been out to rob him of his position and his assets. They wanted him humbled and poor, but not necessarily dead. Suddenly, Lionel couldn't be in the same room with Annie Hart.

He turned and started for the second bay when Tyler Grayson approached him.

"Lionel," he said, extending his hand, "I didn't expect to see you here."

Lionel accepted the greeting, and, remembering that his daughter cared about Grayson, smiled. "I like doing the unexpected. Besides, over the past several years, I've become a big fan of photography. How about yourself?"

"When it's as good as this, it's hard not to be a fan," Tyler said. He pointed to Amanda's "Mirror Images." "These are spectacular, don't you think?"

Lionel nodded, swallowing his desire to gloat about the obvious talent of the photographer. He encouraged Tyler to chat about how he felt these pictures compared to Cindy Sherman's so he could study the young man. Being a father was still new to Lionel, which meant that he had to work harder at things that probably came instinctively to men whose relationships with their daughters had not been interrupted. But because he loved Amanda so fiercely, nothing was too difficult or tedious.

Though Lionel had several preconceived notions about Tyler Grayson, he tried to cast aside assumptions taken from their business relationship and view him as a father might view a potential suitor. Admittedly, Tyler Grayson was good-looking, dressed well, comported himself like a gentleman, boasted an impressive résumé and though somewhat lacking in the humor department, was possessed of a certain restrained charm that could be deemed attractive. If he were to vote on those qualities alone, Tyler would be more than acceptable.

But Lionel did know another side of the eligible Mr. Grayson. He knew him to be hugely ambitious and singularly focused. From experience, he counted that as a negative. He also knew that Tyler often displayed pigheaded inflexibility and took criticism as a personal affront—another negative mark in Lionel's book. He was bright, Lionel would give him that, but superior intelligence didn't guarantee a life without challenge. Now and then, someone was going to disagree with you about something, and they might be right. Even Lionel, who wouldn't waste his breath defending against the oft-lobbed charge of intractability, acceded to the possibility that, occasionally, he was fallible.

Once or twice in the beginning of their association, Lionel had taken Tyler to lunch. He thought if he could get to know him better, they might establish a greater rapport and, therefore, a more efficient working relationship. But Tyler proved to be intensely private. He seemed uncomfortable discussing anything other than office matters. Lionel tried, but family, friends, social life, and most extracurricular activities were off-limits. Eventually, Lionel concluded he was wasting his time. Tyler Grayson was an employee, not a prospective friend or investment partner. If he was hiding a past indiscretion, ashamed of an embarrassing family connection, or trying to prove something to a disapproving parent, a disinterested paramour, or the world in general, that was his business and his problem. If it spilled over to his job and began affecting his performance, then and only then would it become Lionel's business.

"By the way, who was your luncheon companion at the Water Club?" Lionel asked, hoping it sounded like a relatively innocent inquiry. "She was lovely."

Tyler hesitated. Lionel guessed his sense of privacy was wrestling with his need to promote himself to his employer. At the moment, he couldn't decide which side he wanted to win.

"Actually," Tyler began slowly, "she's the woman responsible for these amazing photographs. Unfortunately, she wants to remain anonymous, so I can't tell you who she is."

"Really?" Lionel feigned surprise. Also, he congratulated Grayson on finding a way to promote himself without betraying a confidence. "Well, next time you see her, please tell her she's gained a new admirer."

"I'll do that." Tyler nodded, hiding his pleasure.

"If you'll excuse me, I think I'll take in the rest of the exhibit. See you tomorrow."

Several minutes later, Lionel noticed that Tyler had gone.

The chink-chink of a cash register was ringing so loudly in Lloyd Franks's head, he was afraid it could be heard clear across the gallery. Every photograph had been sold. Three of them had been purchased by Lionel Baird. Since the eminent Mr. Baird had never graced Lloyd's gallery with his presence before, Lloyd was about to find him and fawn. Wealthy patrons were not, so to speak, a dime a dozen.

"I forgot to ask, Mr. Baird. Is there any special time you'd like these delivered?" Anytime between nine and five was fine with Lionel. "Just to be certain everything goes smoothly, I intend to install them personally," Lloyd continued. Ogling at fabulous residences was one of his favorite hobbies. He'd heard about Lionel's town house and couldn't wait to see it.

Lionel detested kowtowing, but he liked Franks, so he resisted the impulse to retort. Instead, he pointed to one of Amanda's bleakscapes.

"Has that one actually been sold, or is it on reserve?"

It was a poignant picture of a homeless man with his back to the camera. His head was bowed from the weight of his circumstances. Dressed in a tattered overcoat and crushed fedora, he carried a leather attaché case and was wending his way around a maze of garbage cans and alcohol-sodden street people looking like the businessman he once was. He was down on his luck and probably beyond the point of return, yet there was a sad dignity about him that commanded respect. There but for the grace of God, the photograph said.

"It's sold," said a strange voice.

Lionel turned and found himself looking into the face of a tall man garbed in the ubiquitous Chelsea uniform of black on black. In his case, leather and wool.

Lloyd Franks swiveled his head nervously from one to the other, trying to gauge Lionel's level of annoyance. He quickly made the introductions.

"Mr. Baird, this is Jake Fowler, a good friend of the gallery and the gentleman who purchased that particular bleakscape. Jake, this is Lionel Baird."

Both men recognized the other's name. Both tried to conceal that fact.

"Jake's a private investigator who's done some work for me," Lloyd explained. "Excellent work, as a matter of fact."

"Deadbeat patrol," Jake offered as a way of clarifying his assignments.

Lionel's mouth curled in a half smile. He could see how this guy might appeal to Amanda. Fowler was brash, but without contrivance.

"Does that mean I could wake up one morning and find you lurking in the bushes outside my house?"

"Only if you don't pay in full."

"Are you a collector, Mr. Fowler?"

Jake laughed. "Hardly," he said, making absolutely no attempt to impress Lionel.

"So what prompted you to buy this photograph, if you don't mind my asking?" Lionel was curious to see whether Jake would mention his acquaintance with Amanda.

As Tyler had done, Jake hesitated, but for completely different reasons. He was attempting to condense a magnum of emotion into a brief sentiment.

"Let's say it resonated with me."

"Fair enough," Lionel said, noting the shadow that dimmed the light in his eyes and the way he bit the inside of his lip. "This photographer has a heightened sensitivity, don't you think?"

Jake scanned the bleakscapes slowly. "He or she has been there," he said. "That's a special kind of solitude. Raw and cruel. And I don't know how you'd recognize it if you hadn't experienced it."

Jake visibly retreated. Lionel thought he knew where Fowler had gone and was sorry he had directed him there.

Fortunately, Jake was distracted by someone waving at him. Unfortunately, the hand doing the wave belonged to a pretty blonde who was standing with Pamela Baird and John Chisolm. Lionel thought Jake's smile seemed forced. Chisolm nodded in their direction. Pamela's face was devoid of expression. Lionel wanted to know who the woman was and what she was doing with his ex-wife and the senator, but he was not about to question Fowler, particularly in front of Lloyd Franks.

When the blonde began communicating with Jake via hand signals, Lionel removed himself from whatever exchange was taking place by asking Franks, "How long does this show run?" Lloyd responded, and for the next several minutes Lionel busied himself with the details of his sale. When the blonde, Pamela, and Chisolm had gone, he turned to Jake. "It's been a pleasure, Mr. Fowler. Enjoy your photograph."

"Likewise, Mr. Baird," Jake said, shaking Lionel's hand. As he watched Lionel's departure, Jake admired the man's cool. He had expected him to ask how Jake was acquainted with Pamela Baird, why he was bidding Senator Chisolm a good evening, and who their blond companion was. He must have been slightly curious about Jake's connection to them. Usually, men like Lionel Baird don't leave their curiosity unsatisfied. If they want to know, they ask and expect to be answered. He didn't.

And that made Jake curious.

* * *

Amanda's shift ended at two in the morning. It had been a bad night. It always was when the victims were children. Tonight, she had worked three different homicide sites. A gang dispute in one of the projects led to an accidental death when a stray bullet ripped through a window and killed a baby asleep in his crib. There was a murder/suicide where a man, distraught at the breakup of his marriage and his wife's new romance, broke into their apartment with a sawed-off shotgun and mowed down his ex-wife, her new lover, and three children, ages six months to four years. He then turned the gun on himself.

The worst was the last: four teens high on Propaine had performed a satanic ritual on the body of a six-year-old. After they had gang-raped and sodomized the boy, they drugged him, laid him out on a urine-stained cot in the basement of a vacant building in the East Village, gouged out his eyes, drew a pentagram in his chest with a razor and dripped candle wax and the blood of a chicken onto his mutilated body. The ME would verify the actual cause of death, but with blood dried around his nostrils and what appeared to be foam in his mouth, Amanda suspected the child had overdosed on the Propaine they had fed him before he felt the slash of the blade. It made her sick to think that she actually prayed that was the case.

Pete Doyle had teamed with her tonight. Neither of them spoke as they exited the elevator at CSU headquarters. They had already spent enough time venting their rage at a society that produced the kind of children who could do such evil things to other children. For Pete, nights like this were particularly difficult. He was divorced and admittedly randy, but everyone knew his two children were the light of his life. Amanda asked how a devoted father could stomach a scene like the one they just confronted.

"Our job is to find the evidence that will convict the scumbuckets who did this," he said, with uncharacteristic solemnity. "If we do our job really well, they're gonna be off the streets and locked up in a cage where they belong." He looked at her, his eyes those of a guard dog, watchful and uncompromising. "Which means they'll never get the chance to do this to my kids."

As they walked off the elevator their sober mood mirrored the dim, gloomy light of the lobby. In the stillness, their footsteps created a hollow echo. Amanda was so lost in her own thoughts she barely heard her name. It was only when Pete nudged her that she noticed Tyler standing alongside the door, waiting.

"I thought you might like a ride home," he said, speaking directly to Amanda, nodding politely at her partner.

"That would be nice."

Her tone was so flat Tyler wondered whether this was a good idea. She didn't seem as delighted by his sudden appearance as he had hoped, although she did look extremely drawn and pale.

"Rough night?" he asked.

She and Pete exchanged glances. "You might say that." Pete's laconic response made Tyler even more uncertain about his decision.

"I didn't mean to intrude."

Amanda stepped into the awkwardness, a warm smile illuminating her face. "Pete, this is a good friend of mine, Tyler Grayson." Tyler returned her smile and allowed himself to relax. "Tyler, this is my favorite teammate, Pete Doyle."

Pete reached out to shake Tyler's hand, then leered at Amanda. "I always knew you were crazy about me, Max." He turned to Tyler and issued a conspiratorial, guy-to-guy aside. "She denies it, but in my heart"—he thumped his chest for emphasis—"I knew."

"You're a lucky man," Tyler said, chuckling at the man's affectionate sense of drama.

The three of them walked outside, exchanged a few pleasantries, then separated. Pete headed for the parking lot, Tyler led Amanda to a black BMW parked at the curb.

"See you tomorrow, Max." Pete winked as he waved good night. "Nice meeting you, Tyler."

She heard the way Pete underscored the pronunciation of Tyler's name. It was way too Social Register for Doyle who preferred single syllable handles like Bob or Phil or Tom . . . or Max. "You've just sentenced me to weeks of incessant ribbing," she said as Tyler opened the door for her.

"He seems harmless enough."

Unless you're one of the skels he believed should be scratched off humanity's list, she thought. She could still see his face when he caught sight of that little boy lying on that filthy mattress. "We're going to catch the bastards who did this," he had muttered to Amanda, "and they're going to fry."

As she settled into Tyler's car, she watched Pete maneuver his eight-year-old Subaru onto the street. As he drove by them, he looked at her ride, raised his eyebrows, pursed his lips, elevated his chin, and gave her one of his well-fancy-that looks. She laughed. She was going to hear about the BMW, too.

As Tyler started the engine, he turned and looked at her. "Would you like to go straight home? Would you like a cup of coffee or a glass of wine? Or would you like to spend the night with me?" His gaze was soft and inviting. "One of the above? All of the above perhaps?"

"I don't want to go straight home," she said. "But a glass of wine sounds delicious." She paused, not to tease, but because she didn't commit easily to intimacy. Tonight, however, she needed something that would reaffirm the joy of life, something that would assure her that the world she inhabited was not all ugliness and violence and murder. "So does spending the night with you," she said.

He kissed her softly. His beard felt fuzzy on her face. "Your place or mine?"

"Yours." She answered quickly, instinctively. Amanda rarely allowed anyone inside her home. She had learned that as a child. A neighbor or a friend might feel free to poke around and look too closely at pictures and souvenirs and other things that could give her away.

"Are you sure?" Tyler thought he noted a trace of equivocation in her eyes, if not her voice.

"Absolutely."

He smiled, as if she had conferred a compliment on him, and somehow that made her sad. She wished it was as simple as "My place or yours," but it wasn't. She wished she could tell him the truth, but she couldn't. How could she say, I want to go to your apartment because it's safer. Because I'm being stalked by hired killers and I don't want them to see you or know your name or know that I care about you. Because everyone close to me is in danger.

Instead, she forced herself to brighten, and said instead, "I have a change of clothes in my bag. And somehow I think your selection of wine is a lot better than mine."

He laughed. "My place it is!"

Tyler's apartment was a co-op on East End Avenue with a view overlooking the river. Though he insisted it was basic and boring 1960's architecture updated with a few designer touches, Amanda thought it was wonderful. She envied him the luxury of space; her digs defined the word compact. While it was true that the L-shaped layout screamed "box," Tyler had opened it up by converting the smaller area into a study that took its design cues from the living room.

"I don't have dinner parties at home," he said, explaining why he had eliminated a dining room. "My entertaining is strictly expense-account."

The color scheme, a soothing pale taupe and black, set the overall mood. Comfortable, clean-lined sofas were softened with suede throw pillows—precisely placed, Amanda noted. A pair of beechwood-and-cane fauteuils upholstered in black leather held court in the living room, while two club chairs beckoned in the study. Here and there, striking antique pieces punctuated the decor, as did an occasional piece of sculpture. As befit Tyler's personal mantra of everything-under-control, there were no extraneous accessories or soft fabrics that might lose their shape or forget to fold.

Tyler ushered her into the kitchen, which shared the rest of the apartment's theme of understatement. Built into a lower cabinet was a small refrigerator that housed about three dozen bottles of wine.

"My one indulgence," he said as he took a bottle from the top rack. "Since cold air drops, the whites go on the bottom, the reds on top." He showed her his selection—a Brunello di Montelcino—knowing it would please her.

It did. Her smile was spontaneous, but conditional. "I cannot put that glorious grape to my lips until I take a shower," Amanda said. "Do you mind?"

"Hardly," he said, wrapping his arm around her and steering her toward the bedroom. "Is there anything you need? Soap? Shampoo? Someone to rub your back?"

"A long tee shirt or a bathrobe would be helpful."

"Your every wish is my command." He extracted a silk robe from his closet, gathered some fresh towels and a pair of flip-flops. Then, he allowed her some privacy.

When she came out of the bathroom, he was stripped down to a tee shirt and silk pajama bottoms, camped out on his bed. The lights were low. On a table next to the bed was the bottle of wine, two balloon-shaped goblets, and a plate of what looked like prosciutto.

"You look incredible," he whispered, truly awed by the sight of her.

Her hair was damp and unstyled, artlessly combed behind her ears. Her face was bare and glistening as was the slice of flesh he could see beneath the paisley robe that covered her nakedness. For a second, he was transported back in time to their first morning in Florence. She had come to him from the shower then, too, but she hadn't toweled off; she had left that to him. He felt aroused just thinking about it.

She must have sensed his response because she tightened the silk robe around her before joining him on the bed. He fluffed a stack of pillows and encouraged her to relax against them. Then he poured the wine, handed her a goblet, and raised his glass for a toast.

"To reunions," he said.

She clicked her glass with his and smiled before letting the velvety wine slither across her tongue and down her throat. He handed her a finger of prosciutto-wrapped melon. She bit into it, relishing the combined tastes of ham and ripe, sweet cantaloupe. Her murmur of ecstasy was almost sensual.

"This is not fair," she protested. "You know I can't resist a man who lavishes me with wine and prosciutto."

"Actually, I was counting on it," he said, leaning toward her and kissing her gently. They both smiled and sipped their wine, reliving their history, anticipating their future.

"I went to Lloyd's gallery tonight," Tyler said. Amanda nodded. She was more interested in feeding him an hors d'oeuvre. "Your pictures are amazing," he continued, trying to concentrate. "And I wasn't the only one who thought so."

"Really?"

"Every last one of the Anonymous photographs was sold. Within the first hour, I might add."

"I'm impressed with me, I think."

"You should be." Tyler unwrapped a piece of the thinly sliced ham and handed it to her. She chewed it slowly, washed it down with some wine, then licked her lips, savoring the pleasure. "Even Lionel Baird bought some of your work."

"He was there?" She expected he would be, but it felt so good to know that he had.

"As was his ex-wife and her new boyfriend, Senator John Chisolm. Believe me it was a Kodak moment when they spotted each other."

Amanda laughed at the image of Lionel and Chisolm squared off in the middle of an art gallery. Pamela must have been in her glory. From everything Lionel had told her about their marriage and its breakup, Amanda didn't think Pamela was going to be happily divorced, despite her public avowals of love for the senator. If Lionel so much as twitched a finger in her direction, she'd probably break all records getting back to him.

"Anyone else I might know?" When she realized she was thinking about Jake Fowler, she squirmed. She was practically naked in one man's bed. How could she be thinking about another?

"Lloyd introduced me to Annie Hart." Tyler shook his head. The memory had painted a wry smile on his lips. "She's your biggest fan, or so she says."

"She's a good friend." Amanda hoped that when Sam got the results of his check, that would still be true. "In fact, she's the one who introduced me to Lloyd."

"So they both told me."

As he sipped his wine, he drank in the sight of the woman next to him. Just then, she seemed the picture of contentment: damp hair, clean, glowing skin, her eyes half-closed. Earlier in the evening, he had seen another side of her. Her bleakscapes were about being friendless and forlorn, about feeling adrift and disconnected. He related because he, too, had spent time on that island of isolation.

"I have to agree with them about one thing," he said allowing himself to be enveloped by the voluptuous sensation of falling in love. "You're very talented, Amanda Maxwell. I only wish you had been there tonight so you could have felt the waves of admiration and appreciation that flowed through that gallery."

"I feel it from you, and that's enough." With her mouth still moist from the wine, she kissed him. "Thank you," she whispered. "I needed this tonight."

He couldn't speak, but his need was obvious. He placed her wineglass on the table and took her in his arms, licking the wine from her lips and tasting it on her tongue.

His embrace gripped Amanda with a familiarity she found intensely erotic. She had been with this man before. She had felt his hands on her body, his mouth on her flesh, his manhood inside her. He was a known commodity, not a stranger to be scrutinized or analyzed or guarded against. Tyler kissed her, and she kissed him back without hesitation. He slipped his hands inside the silken folds of her robe and she undid the sash, granting him access. He slid the silk off her shoulders and she offered him her breasts.

He went to them, hungrily and feasted like a starveling. She moaned softly as she felt herself respond to the pinch of his teeth, the brush of his lips, the gentle scratching of his beard. It had been so long since anyone had caressed her like this. Selfishly, she luxuriated in the symphony of sensation he evoked, her responses heightened by the enormity of her deprivation. The mere touch of his fingers or his tongue or his lips roused her entire being, as if thousands of individual nerve endings had been wired together: excite one, electrify all.

His mouth traveled upward, finding her lips and ravishing them. At the same time, his hands journeyed in another direction, drawn to the heat that was growing in her loins. Her hands followed a similar map, furrowing inside his pants, seeking confirmation of his attraction. He was pulsing with desire and she sighed as she felt the power of his wanting.

He groaned, shedding his clothing quickly. "God, I've missed you," he whispered just before his lips closed against hers.

Amanda knew she should tell him how good she felt, how magnificent he was as a lover, how wonderful it was to be with him again, but she didn't dare speak. She felt too vulnerable to risk saying even a single word. One might lead to another and while she felt freer with Tyler than with any man she had encountered since, that sense of liberation extended only to her body. She could give him that, but no more.

As he lay on top of her, she laced her arms around his neck and raised her hips, pressing her passion against his, sparking an urgency that threatened to consume them. Again, Amanda felt the blessing of past experience. Fully conversant in the language of each other's ardor, they moved in concert, allowing the crescendo to build at a tempo pleasing to both. As she felt him enter, her mind emptied of all thought and she surrendered to her own carnality, taking, being taken, riding out the lusty storm of human coupling.

When it was over, she felt exhausted, yet oddly refreshed. She had forgotten what it was like to behave like a woman. Tyler helped her remember, and for that she was grateful. She leaned over and kissed him. He smiled.

"This was perfect," she said.

With the tips of his fingers, he stroked her cheek. "You're perfect."

"Far from it. That's simply testosterone speaking." Amanda laughed, but inside, she felt guilty. Intimacy required a certain honesty. Her passion might have been guileless and aboveboard, but she was not.

"Maybe so." Tyler raised himself onto his elbow. As his eyes fixed on hers, his expression suddenly grew intense. "I agree that no one's perfect, but life is short. We have to cherish nights like this, because we don't know when, or if, we'll get another."

He leaned down and kissed her, but it felt different somehow, as if a door had been opened and a candle had blown out. Amanda knew that feeling: a ghost had entered the room. The question was, from out of whose past had the ghost come? His. Or hers?

Amanda arrived home at seven that morning. She entered her apartment, checked for bugs and possible intrusions, then punched the message button on her answering machine.

"Whatever you didn't tell me about yourself, your photographs did. They showed me your soul, and it's beautiful. Speak to you soon. Jake."

Amanda smiled almost giddily as a girlish blush tinted her cheeks.

As she headed for her bedroom, she passed a mirror and stopped. The woman looking back at her was a stranger. She was happy, radiant with the glow that only affection can evince. Amanda smiled at the woman admiringly. This person was lucky, she thought. She was young, pretty, single, living and working in New York. An exhibition of her photographs had been greeted with critical acclaim. And two very appealing gentlemen were interested in her. One had just made glorious, boundless, immensely satisfying love to her. The other, she believed, would like that same opportunity.

Again, Amanda studied the face in the mirror. What distinguished her from the woman in the hall was that that woman seemed so . . . normal. Envy sluiced over her as she closed her eyes and desperately tried to hold on to that feeling of being ordinary and well-adjusted and happy. In the end, she knew it was hopeless. Tyler had been right. She had to cherish whatever she had felt last night. Because it wouldn't last. It couldn't.

Because life wasn't perfect. And she wasn't normal.

CHAPTER
TEN

CHISOLM GOES TO WAR AGAINST WALL STREET
By Hallie Brendel

In a speech to community leaders on Long Island, Senator John Chisolm pledged to initiate an all-out battle against those who are responsible for bringing drugs into New York State, "whether they're in street clothes or three-piece suits!" Speaking over the cheers of the crowd, he challenged the financial community to "come clean about its role in the proliferation of these powdery killers of kids." According to the senator, the reason the Drug War has been such a disaster is "the government's failure to put its muscle where its mouth is." He places the blame for the consistent lack of significant drug legislation, in part, on the power and influence of the banking lobby.

"Drug traffickers don't count their money, they weigh it," he said, hoping to alert the public to the kind of money being laundered through the financial community. "It's time someone exposed those who favor personal profit over sane public policy. It's time someone said 'no' to Wall Street and 'yes' to our children!"

To put this in perspective, the senator reminded his audience that twenty years ago, a major, interagency task force, "Operation Laundry Day," was established with the objective of ferreting out those who laundered money for drug traffickers. This was during a time when drugs from Colombia were flowing like tap water into Miami and the number of drug-related deaths had skyrocketed nationwide. There had been an enormous public outcry to protect our borders and punish anyone and everyone involved.

As a way of answering that outcry—and to prove that "Operation Laundry Day" had been a success—the government showcased two trials, one in Miami and one in New York. Altogether, nineteen people were convicted; eighteen are currently serving or have completed their sentences. In addition, four people were killed in a violent explosion following the conclusion of the Miami trial: two United States marshals, the government's key witness, Cynthia Stanton Baird, and her nine-year-old daughter, Erica Baird.

The irony, according to a reliable source who insists on remaining anonymous, is that in his original deposition, Douglas Welch, the Nathanson & Spelling employee convicted of stealing stock certificates on behalf of the Saviano crime family, accused Lionel Baird, the ex-husband of the government's prime witness, of being in the thick of the money laundering that occurred during that period. He maintained that Mr. Baird knew about his dealings with the mob, but looked aside. Mr. Welch assumed that in exchange for that kindness, he was expected to keep silent about Mr. Baird's activities.

According to Welch's deposition, Lionel Baird knowingly allowed himself to be used as a laundryman for heroin traffickers. He was approached because Nathanson & Spelling had access to international transfer facilities and Mr. Baird was the senior officer in charge of executing large orders for clients dealing with Swiss banks. Welch explained the way the scheme worked: a Swiss bank placed an order for a block of securities worth about $100,000, an amount of money large enough to be considered suspicious, and promised that a courier would pay on the settlement date. On that date, a bank courier handed Mr. Baird a bag filled with cash. Rather than refuse the cash, and report the transaction to the authorities, Mr. Baird sent the stock certificates to Switzerland in care of a specified bank account registered to a dummy foreign company.

When Lionel Baird was questioned about this transaction, he maintained he never thought twice about it because he had done business with the man who had contacted him, a vice president of the Swiss bank in question, many times. None of their prior dealings had been suspect. He told the Justice Department it was obvious he had been duped. And since there seemed to be no concrete evidence to contradict that statement, other than the word of Douglas Welch, an admitted thief who, Lionel Baird contended, was simply bartering for a lighter sentence, no case was brought against Mr. Baird.

Mr. Welch was convicted but never went to prison. He committed suicide the day of his sentencing.

The reaction to the front page of the *Morning Telegraph* was seismic. Wall Street executives, particularly those who had been around during the trials, hid behind thick office doors, refusing to speak to the media. Attorneys in the Justice Department were unavailable for comment. No one who had been involved, even peripherally, would speak on the record. Except, of course, the senator. John Chisolm was all over the airways, denying that he fed Hallie Brendel any of the information about Lionel Baird, but, he said, "If he was duped, let's hope he's wiser from the experience."

"Are you accusing Lionel Baird of laundering money today?" one reporter asked, sniffing another, juicier angle to an otherwise ordinary political story.

"I'm not singling anyone out," Chisolm hedged. "What I'm saying is that in the absence of any serious money-laundering laws, sinks abound. As we speak, several Wall Street firms are under investigation. Baird, Nathanson & Spelling is only one of them."

Lionel Baird barricaded himself inside his town house and fumed. If Hallie Brendel had been anywhere near him, he would have strangled her without a second thought. What he would have done to John Chisolm wasn't fit to print.

He had to admit, this attack had been cleverly staged. Chisolm's statement had enough truth in it to make it difficult for Lionel to refute. In 1992, a task force known as "Operation Eldorado" was created to poke around in the securities and commodities markets to find out whether brokers were deliberately investing dirty money. Lionel assumed by Chisolm's comment that Eldorado was still functioning. Several years before, it had flushed out a handful of guilty brokers, two of whom were working out of a branch office in Panama. They were not however, as Chisolm had tried to imply, from Baird, Nathanson & Spelling.

Though furious about his reputation being sacrificed on the altar of his enemy's reelection campaign, there were far more important issues at stake. Resurrecting this case at this time was beyond irresponsible. If this so-called reporter wanted to tout the depth of her research, why hadn't she checked with the Justice Department or the local police or the DEA before penning this tripe? Unless she was completely daft, she had to know that if there were stings in progress, shining a spotlight on them was counterproductive at best, murderous at worst.

Every time he looked at the twenty-year-old picture of Cynthia and Erica that accompanied the piece, the image of their house bursting into flames flashed before his eye, and he relived the horror of that moment. The fact that they had not been in that house when it exploded didn't salve his anguish. They were in as much danger now as they had been then, more so thanks to this article.

He stormed around his bedroom like a bear with an arrow in his gut, snarling, flailing his arms, bumping into furniture and walls as if the physical contact would stem his rage. Where had this Brendel woman gotten her information about Welch and that stock transfer? Who had given her that picture of Cynthia and Erica? During his brief instances of reason, Lionel realized that transcripts of the trial were public record and newspapers all over the country had run pictures of Cynthia and Erica. She could have pulled them from any paper's morgue. But why drag them into this? Why bring Welch back from the dead? Certainly, there were enough drugs on the street for Chisolm to make his point without rehashing old news like "Operation Laundry Day." Why didn't he run his campaign in the here and now and leave the past alone?

He desperately wanted to call Amanda—for all he knew, she hadn't even seen this—but he had sworn he would never call her from this phone. And with a horde of reporters camped outside his door, he couldn't leave his house to find a pay phone without being bombarded. Suddenly, he remembered that Sam Bates had given him a number to use in case of emergencies. As far as Lionel was concerned, this more than qualified.

When Bates answered, Lionel read him the article—he couldn't fax it without leaving a trail—and was assured he had done the right thing. Sam would increase Amanda's protection and Beth's.

"I want to put a man on you," he told Lionel. "He'll keep his distance, and he'll be discreet."

"I already have bodyguards. But thanks." Lionel paused. "It might not seem so, Bates, but I do appreciate your concern, especially for Beth and Amanda. I know it goes beyond whatever duty might require, and I'm grateful."

"I told you in Wisconsin," Sam said after a moment of embarrassed silence. "I love those two women. I would do anything to protect them. And those they care about."

They talked for a few minutes about Bastido—the government

was fairly certain he was with the Espinosa brothers in Mexico—
and the men from Hudson National Bank. They had been released
from prison years before, but still, Lionel wondered whether their
thirst for revenge would ever be sated.

"We had them under surveillance for a long time after their release.
Nothing we've seen would lead us to believe they pose a threat, but
in light of recent events, we've assigned agents to watch them. So
far, they still look clean."

"That's a relief."

"Don't get too comfortable, Lionel. We still have the Savianos
to worry about."

"I thought Ray Saviano was doing life in Joliet," Lionel said,
dredging his memory. "Beth's testimony sent some of his lieutenants
away, but she wasn't responsible for his conviction."

"True, but there are some in the organization, Ray's son being
one of them, who believe that the Laundry Day trial weakened the
family by putting the fear of the law into the underlings."

"The ones who ratted on Saviano."

"Correct."

Lionel groaned. "You think Ray Junior has it in for Beth?"

"Could be. The problem is, the mobs are always into so much
stuff, it's hard to isolate which vendetta has priority."

"Any news about Annie Hart?" Lionel's voice was leaden.

"I'm sorry. That shouldn't be taking this long." Sam sounded
distracted.

"Is everything all right? Is Beth okay? Are you not telling me
something?"

"Beth's fine. I've told you everything."

"Something's bothering you, Bates. I can hear it in your voice."

"My sister's been diagnosed with ovarian cancer."

Sam's tone was inscrutable, as usual, but strained. Lionel was
moved by the other man's obvious effort to muffle his emotions.

"Is there anything I can do to help?" Lionel asked with genuine
concern. "I'm on the board of several highly regarded hospitals both
here and in Chicago. I can make sure she has the finest doctors in
the field."

"The doctor who performed the surgery enjoys a pretty good
reputation."

"And the hospital?"

"Supposedly the best in Seattle."

"Have they discussed postoperative treatment?"

"At least six months of chemo."

Lionel paused, wondering how best to say this. "Sam, if you need any financial assistance, it's not a problem. Understand?"

It took a minute for Sam to respond. When he did, his voice sounded odd, hurried, as if suddenly, he couldn't wait to end this conversation.. "That's awfully generous, but I've already taken care of it."

In quick order, he hastened to assure Lionel that his report on Annie Hart would be delivered within the next day or so, that he would give Beth Lionel's regards, and that they would be in touch again, soon.

Long after he returned the receiver to its cradle, Lionel thought about the abrupt way their call had ended. He wanted to assign Bates's impatience to angst about his sister's illness or embarrassment about Lionel feeling he needed charity. But Lionel had heard something other than anxiety in the marshal's voice. Whether it was false bravado or injured pride or something completely unrelated, he didn't know.

But it didn't sit right.

Pamela Baird hadn't felt so good since she started taking hormone replacements. Seeing Lionel's picture on the front page of the *Morning Telegraph,* reading the bald insinuations about his role in a scandalous money-laundering scam, knowing that at this very moment he was probably on the phone with his lawyers scrambling to craft a statement denying his participation—then and now—was simply too delicious.

She sipped her coffee with a broad smile on her face. Only a few minutes before, John had called. After lavishing her with praise, he expressed his surprise that she hadn't forewarned him.

"I thought it best. After all," she cooed, "your enmity toward Lionel is hardly a secret, darling. It was much better that you were truly surprised. If it appeared that you had planted the story, the press would simply dismiss the charge as either campaign rhetoric or a testosterone contest."

She said she leaked this information to Hallie to gain positive exposure for him and provide context to his message. He accepted that, as she knew he would, because his ego demanded that he believe her devotion was absolute. The truth was: this was a major offensive in her war against Lionel Baird. Whatever bounce John got from this was simply a by-product.

She could hardly wait to move in for the kill.

★ ★ ★

Fredda MacDougall was not having a good day. The telephones had not stopped ringing since seven, when she arrived at the office. If she hadn't thought to arrange for extra security in the lobby before leaving her apartment, she was certain she would have been greeted by an army of microphones aimed at her face like rifles.

Always an efficient field general, Fredda recruited two secretaries from the pool to screen Lionel's calls, stationed four extra bodyguards at various stations on the thirty-eighth floor and planted herself squarely in front of Lionel's office, her defense mechanisms on high alert. By the time Lionel marched down the hall and strode past her desk, the sound of a footstep was enough to get her growling like a rottweiler.

"How did you manage to sneak into the building without being seen?" she asked, following him into his office.

"I'm a master of disguise," he replied, handing her his coat.

Actually, he had exited the town house through a secret passageway that enabled him to get into his car without being seen. By ducking down in the back, it appeared as if his chauffeur was leaving the house alone. They'd driven to a Rolls Royce dealership on the East Side and entered the service garage. His chauffeur stayed behind to wait for the minor repair. While the gaggle of reporters swooped down on the poor man, Lionel walked out of the showroom and headed for a nearby subway.

"I walked out of the station and into the building without anyone even noticing me. They weren't looking for a commuter," he said, gloating like a child playing hide-and-seek.

"This is not a game, Lionel." Fredda glared at him with disapproval. "These people are vultures, and they're not going to leave you alone until they get what they want."

Her fear was genuine, as was her concern for his safety. Guiltily, Lionel realized his glibness was inappropriate.

"I'm sorry, Fredda. You're right. This is definitely not a game. Thanks to Chisolm, that harridan reporter is on a witch-hunt, and I'm the one in the pointy black hat."

"What are we going to do?"

Lionel lowered himself into the chair behind his desk, leaned back, and grinned at her. "We're going to have a press conference."

"What!"

"When one is on a runaway horse, one must grab the reins or risk getting thrown."

Fredda paused, reflected on his idea and, as always, stood in awe of her employer. "You're absolutely right," she said, chuckling because once again she was on the winning team. "Who do you think fed all this nonsense to the overzealous Miss Brendel?"

Lionel leaned forward and fixed his gaze on her face. "We both know that her reliable, but anonymous source is none other than your friend and my reluctant ex-wife."

Fredda shifted her considerable weight from one foot to the other.

"I know you two have a relationship of sorts," he said, refusing to unlock his visual hold on her. "I expect Pamela to be disloyal. She's a woman scorned. I don't expect that from you, Fredda."

"We have lunch occasionally," she confessed meekly. "And it's true, she asks about you from time to time, but," she hastened to add, "I think it's because she still loves you."

"What do you tell her?"

"Nothing she couldn't find out from reading the gossip columns." His expression hadn't changed since this conversation had started. Her inability to divine his mood was unsettling. "I would never discuss business with her. Or anything related to Baird, Nathanson & Spelling. I hope you know that, sir." She hadn't called him "sir" in years. Somehow, this seemed like a good time to revert to old habits.

"What about Douglas Welch? Have you ever discussed him outside the office?"

Fredda flushed. She'd forgotten Lionel knew about her brief affair with the late Mr. Welch. It was an office romance that had started at a Christmas party and was over well before the July outing. She'd known Welch was married, but he said his wife didn't understand him. Fredda was too inexperienced—and too needy—to recognize the world's oldest line. She was also too awed by Lionel Baird to have attached any significance to the fact that she was plucked from the steno pool and elevated to the vaunted position of executive secretary right around the time of the Laundry Day investigation. After Douglas's conviction and subsequent suicide, she wondered about that coincidence, but she wasn't dismissed or demoted, so she decided she had been promoted on merit, not as a bribe.

"Certainly not!" she said with indignation. "I can't believe you would even think such a thing."

"My good name has been attacked, Fredda, which has made me think of a lot of things." He continued to stare at her, but his eyes had gone vacant. When he spoke, his voice reverberated, as if echoing up from a deep, dark hollow. "Including the possibility that in a moment of extreme weakness, I might have told Pamela what transpired during that gruesome period of my life.''

He ground his teeth together as he fought to restrain the cascade of feelings that were surfacing.

"Foolishly, I assumed that everything surrounding the death of my wife and daughter was sacrosanct." Again, he stared at Fredda. This time, his eyes were full, but with an anger that blazed. "Obviously, I was wrong. Nothing is sacred."

Fredda felt the heat of his ire reach across the room and engulf her like the backdraft of a fire. Lionel's temper was legendary, and she had witnessed its devastation firsthand on more than one occasion, but usually it was triggered by sloppy thinking, a lazy, let-them-come-to-me sales approach, an analyst's inability to interpret trends, or some other fatal business flaw that might have caused Baird, Nathanson & Spelling to lose an account to another house. Rarely had Fredda seen it initiated by a newspaper article, even one that impugned his reputation; over the years, he had been slandered far worse than this and hadn't responded with such ferocity.

As she left his office and set about arranging the press conference, she pondered whether his outrage was born of the hostile rivalry with Senator Chisolm, his unresolved feelings for Pamela, or something deeper. It bothered her most of the morning, because knowing Lionel as she did, only something to do with Cynthia Stanton and Erica Baird could inspire such stunning wrath. And they had been dead for twenty years.

Hadn't they?

The auditorium on the seventh floor was packed to overflowing. More than one hundred correspondents representing every media outlet from the supermarket tabloids to the three major networks sat shoulder to shoulder, notepads and tape recorders at the ready. Backstage, Lionel watched Hallie Brendel enter the room and parade down the aisle as if accompanied by heralding trumpets. Tossing her hair in a gesture of studied nonchalance, she retrieved the front row center seat being saved for her by a *Telegraph* lackey, situated herself between reporters from the *New York Times* and the *Washington Post* as if she were their equal and this prime position was her due, then greeted those around her like a hostess, clearly enjoying her celebrity. There was no doubt that she felt inflated by the belief that she had been the force that had compelled Goliath to enter the arena.

She was right, Lionel thought begrudgingly. If not for her column, there would be no need for a press conference. He debated pricking her balloon by ignoring her, but decided that could boomerang. Petulance might come across as acknowledgment that what she alleged was, indeed, credible. His purpose was to squash future stories relating to Operation Laundry Day and its fallout. With that in mind, he signaled for the doors to be closed. Without any introduction, he strode onto the stage. A barrage of strobes greeted him as he took his place behind a wooden podium. Television cameras stared expectantly. His unblinking composure was enviable.

After the photographers had snapped their initial shots, he began. His eyes panned the crowd slowly. His gaze stopped and turned to steel as it fixed on Hallie Brendel.

"I called this press conference because I refuse to be fodder for anyone's mill," he stated without equivocation. "I will not allow myself to become the poster boy for Senator Chisolm's reelection campaign or the step stool for anyone's career ambitions."

Many who knew Hallie strained to see her reaction. She remained eyes front, shoulders square, head high, but her face had flushed brilliant pink.

"In this morning's *Telegraph*, Hallie Brendel insinuated that two decades ago, I committed a crime and went to great lengths to cover my felonious behavior. She also implied that those efforts inadvertently caused the death of a valued employee. Neither of those creative suppositions is correct.

"I will repeat what I testified to at the time: I believed the transaction in question was legitimate. I'd dealt with that particular Swiss banker on numerous occasions, none of which had produced any legal or SEC consequences. None even hinted at any impropriety. I had no reason to believe that particular deal was any different from those that preceded it. And since I knew of no crime, it follows that I did not plot, plan, or carry out a cover-up."

Each time he paused, so many camera shutters clicked it sounded like an invasion of insects. Lionel, who was extremely media savvy, allowed the photographers time to take their pictures; in return, when he began to speak again, they refrained from shooting.

"Douglas Welch did commit a crime." Lionel's voice was confident, certain that what he was saying was the absolute, unalterable gospel. "He stole hundreds of thousands of dollars in securities from Nathanson & Spelling and handed them over to representatives of the Saviano crime family in order to pay off his gambling debts. He admitted as much on the stand, under oath. According to Ms. Brendel, I knew of Mr. Welch's indebtedness, knew of his association with organized crime, and knew how he intended to clear up his obligations. None of that is even close to the truth."

He looked down at her, allowing a look of disgust to wash his face.

"Douglas Welch worked as a back-office clerk at Nathanson & Spelling. Inasmuch as he and I were not colleagues who conversed on a daily basis, I would've had no way of knowing those details. We had a passing acquaintance. As far as I knew, he was a decent family man who put in an honest day's work. I had no knowledge of his addiction and, therefore, would not have been privy to his problems with the Savianos. I didn't keep quiet about his dealings because I wasn't aware of them. I didn't ask him to keep quiet about my dealings, because I wasn't aware I was doing anything I needed to keep quiet about."

An acrid bitterness soured his voice. His body, nearly overpowered by temper, pitched slightly forward.

"As heinous as those statements were in their inaccuracy, what I found most despicable was Ms. Brendel's brazen, misguided, self-serving insinuation that today, I sanction, and in fact encourage, money laundering for drug traffickers. It was embarrassing in its falseness and downright criminal in its heartlessness."

Lionel's hands gripped the sides of the lectern, and he looked out at the crowd, demanding their full attention. His voice rumbled throughout the small amphitheater.

"Twenty years ago, my former wife felt compelled to come forward and testify on behalf of the government about just such practices. It was an act of extraordinary courage. She did it because drug traffickers had murdered her brother. In the end, they murdered her and my nine-year-old-daughter."

For a second, the room was completely noiseless, as if someone had pressed a mute button that silenced every voice, every camera, every pencil, every intake of breath. All eyes were on Lionel, who stood before them unashamed at his emotional display.

"I didn't wash money for pushers then, and I don't do it now." He glowered at Hallie. "Drug money isn't dirty, Ms. Brendel. It's filthy because it always has innocent blood on it." His lip curled with distaste. "You and John Chisolm should be ashamed of yourselves!"

With that, he turned and walked offstage. The press conference was over.

* ★ ★

Ray Saviano never thought he'd see the day that he agreed with anything Lionel Baird had to say, yet when he watched a replay of Baird's news conference, Ray almost cheered. That silver-tongued devil was right: Hallie Brendel had mucked around in something she shouldn't have. Not only had she dredged up unpleasant history, but she had shined an unwanted spotlight on a Saviano business venture that was best left in the shadows.

Ray didn't like spotlights. He liked headlines like these even less; tales of crime families getting rich by killing children with drugs aggravated even the most blasé segment of the populace. It made them think the fuzz wasn't doing its job, which made them feel unsafe, which riled them up and got them to demand that the government take away badges, or worse, pensions. Actions like that forced the Feds to go out and do their hero thing. They'd plant undercover agents, set up stings, muscle informants, stop the flow of product. They'd sell immunity to wise guys who knew enough to nail down indictments, and offer permanent protection to triggers who were willing to snitch on their bosses. One way or the other, someone was going to make them look good by going to jail. Ray should know. That's how he wound up in Joliet.

He was in his sixth year of a life sentence and except for two hours a day when he was allowed to exercise—alone—in the yard, he was confined to a cell in a solitary block. He was permitted TV, as many newspapers as he wanted, use of the telephone, and monitored visits. Which was good, because despite his incarceration, he continued to keep his hand in the Family's business.

He made the larger, long-range decisions. His son, Little Ray, ran the day-to-day and was doing a decent job, considering the limits of his intelligence. True, he had stepped on a lot of toes with his *braggadocio* ways and was currently embroiled in a management crisis, but what CEO hadn't faced a crisis while building an empire? Surely Lionel Baird had faced down a number of foes in his day. They probably didn't wrap their heads in bandannas or sport gold earrings and tattoos. Nor did they brandish machetes and Uzis like the *Blanca Muerte* boys, but different strokes for different folks.

Like Baird, Nathanson & Spelling, the Savianos was an organization, one that often came up against financial and territorial challenges. Lionel solved his problems by issuing stock and gobbling up his competitors. In the past, Big Ray's methods had been harsher, but, despite contradictory evidence presented at his trial, he and the other dons had toned down their murderous ways. They had learned to diversify and specialize and compete. Assassination became a last resort rather than a first step.

Then gangs moved into the city and threatened the status quo. Gangs were different from Families. Breaking the law was one thing— it was necessary in the course of business—but gangs operated without any sense of history or code of behavior amongst themselves. They'd shoot their enemies in front of their mothers. They'd steal from their neighbors. They'd lie to their friends. And they recruited anyone and everyone into their ranks.

Unfortunately, gangs weren't the Savianos' only problem. The mob's once-lucrative farm system—the garbage-hauling business, the concrete business, the Garment District, the Fulton Fish Market, the Javits Center—which provided both money and entry-level jobs for potential soldiers, were no longer under their control. Many of their other traditional sources of income—pornography, prostitution, numbers—were also drying up thanks to a "Cleanup Campaign" on the part of an overzealous, but surprisingly effective mayor. Having given the police free rein to do whatever was necessary to close down so many of the standard operations, profit opportunities were few and far between. The Mafia was being downsized.

Contributing to that shrinkage was the problem of age. At fifty-seven, Ray was one of the youngest of the godfathers. His contemporaries were, on average, in their late sixties. The leadership of New York's major crime syndicates were either sick and dying, imprisoned, or working for the government. Their replacements were, in Ray's mind, unworthy. They didn't share the same old-world values as their fathers. They lacked the loyalty that Ray's Cosa Nostra prided itself on. And they seemed to favor violence over management.

Ray spent his two-hour airing agitating about the long-term fallout from Lionel's press conference. Newscasters on every channel were predicting another spate of gang wars. What morons they were! The wars had begun months ago, but they were being fought on side streets and in back alleys. If the media thought that publicity like this would stop the combatants from killing each other, they were as naive as ever. If anything, this kind of news coverage was going to inspire copycats as well as accelerating the number of engagements. This relatively private war was about to burst out onto the avenues and boulevards where civilians lived. And once the body count included innocents, the police would mount an offensive that would make it difficult to do anything except back out or fight to the death.

The Savianos couldn't afford to do either; their coffers were at an all-time low. Which was why Ray had instructed his son to get involved with those damn Chicanos in the first place. He didn't like dealing with people who weren't his kind, but drugs were one of the few remaining cash cows; dominance of the Propaine market would infuse his operation with immediate and abundant cash. He was not about to let his plan be derailed by some small-time reporter who thought she could get where she wanted to be by pimping a dried-up politician. Big Ray had to neutralize whatever impact these stories were having on the public and their servants. He had to strike fast and hit hard because tomorrow something new could come along, and Propaine would become yesterday's high.

Before going back to his cell, he bribed the guard and placed a call to Little Ray to get a sense of what was happening. Nothing good, was the answer. The Espinosas were pumping Propaine into the States faster than oil through a pipeline. They wanted it sold quickly, for top dollar and without government interference. If the Savianos couldn't handle it, the Espinosas would either hook up with another Family or give their *compadres* an exclusive.

Back in his cell, Ray paced as he considered possible solutions. One option was to keep his hands clean and let Lionel Baird take care of this Brendel nuisance. Baird had humiliated her in front of her peers and a national audience, after all. But Brenda Starr wouldn't leave the limelight voluntarily. Women like that thrived on notoriety: Say anything, but spell my name right and make sure you photograph my best side.

Saviano snorted with disgust. In the old days, those articles would have ceased by now because their author would have been silenced, one way or the other. Granted, a hit would be messy—Baird had made her too visible to be taken out without huge consequences— but in-depth research might produce previous mistakes or indiscretions. If by some miracle she was clean, surely there was someone she cared about who had a naughty secret they wouldn't want revealed.

Unfortunately, the matter of what to do about Hallie Brendel was in Little Ray's hands, and there was no telling how he would handle it. Little Ray was part of a new, egocentric generation that only cared about money and power. They discounted things like loyalty, respect, and tradition, dismissing them as relics of another era that had nothing to do with them. Big Ray shuddered, imagining what his mentors would say. They'd had it too good, these kids. They'd been raised with fancy cars and ready cash. They dined in the finest restaurants and slept with upscale women. These young studs hadn't been tested the way Ray had, shooting it out *mano a mano,* following orders even if it meant doing some time. Yet they thought they were invincible. And why not? Seeing themselves glamorized on TV and in movies made it easy to believe that the public was entranced with the notion of the Mobster. That they were protected from arrest and harm by virtue of their celebrity. That even the government dicks thought they were cool. They thought that what they saw on the screen was how life was.

Big Ray knew differently. Real life was a hot bullet ripping through flesh. Real life was lying in the street staring up at the sky while blood gushed from a hole in your head. Real life was instant death.

Or worse, the slow decay that took place behind the walls of a prison.

Little Ray loved the idea that the press was onto this story; Big Ray had heard it in his voice. What could be more exciting than going up against the likes of Lionel Baird and a United States senator? It beat the hell out of wrestling with a bunch of spies from LA. Little Ray thought his star was on the rise. He believed that the more articles the *Telegraph* ran, the wider his swath, the more the public feared the mob squabbles spilling over into their precious neighborhoods, the quicker his name would go into the annals of Mafia warfare. As he gleefully reminded his father, he was already being called the poster boy for the Generation X mobsters.

He was a putz! He was so busy listening to his own press that he was deaf to the fact that Hallie Brendel had just sounded the trumpet that would bring the NYPD, the FBI, and every other government agency into the war he had started. Which would make it harder for everyone to launder their profits. Which would bankrupt the Savianos and piss off the Espinosas. Little Ray was known for swaggering down the streets of Little Italy shooting off his mouth, but when push came to shove, he didn't have the vaguest idea about how to conduct a war. If the Espinosas brought out the heavy artillery, Little Ray would be outmanned, outgunned and outmaneuvered. Also, he'd probably be killed.

Big Ray sat down on his cot and buried his face in his hands. In between blasts of empty bravura, he had heard something else in his son's voice, something even more upsetting than his baseless crowing—disrespect. He had expected it, but had hoped it would be later rather than sooner. He was in prison without any possibility of parole. His enemies knew that. His son knew that. It was a fact of life that didn't foster obedience. While he was still referred to as the "Dashing Don" and still treated with great deference by the old-timers, the younger generation had little use for a man whose kingdom was defined by bars.

Nonetheless, Big Ray had no intention of seeing his life's work destroyed and his Family name dishonored. One way or another, he intended to save his son's sorry butt. He'd plant a few seeds to shift the focus of Brendel's articles and move the spotlight somewhere else. He'd call in a few favors. He'd contact a couple of his peers and try to convince them that by uniting forces they could neutralize the opposition without a bloodbath.

But first he had to figure a few things out. Hallie Brendel had tossed out this line because she was fronting for John Chisolm. That was clear and reasonable. She expected to goose her own reputation by affixing it to a can't-miss cause. But why would Lionel Baird take the bait? For whom or what was he fronting?

No matter, Ray thought, honing step one of his game plan. *If you open your mouth near a dangling hook, one thing's certain: you're gonna get caught.*

CHAPTER

ELEVEN

At four o'clock in the morning, a man returning home after the late shift at a hospital in Queens turned the corner on 118th Street and Lexington Avenue and noticed a car with its lights on and a door open. He paused. There didn't seem to be anyone in the car. Still, he remained cautious. It could be a prostitute servicing a john. A drug deal going down. A couple having a fight. Some kids having sex. Truthfully, he didn't care. Whatever it was, he was tired. He didn't want to get involved or hassled.

He crossed the street and moved swiftly down the block, hugging the buildings, staying out of the light. As he passed the car, his gait slowed. A body was slumped over, partially hanging off the front seat. He was an orderly and could perform CPR, but even from where he stood, it was clear the driver was dead. Taking a few steps closer, he noticed someone in the backseat, also lifeless. He ran back to Lexington Avenue and called the police.

By the time the CSU arrived, the entire block had been cordoned off. Lights from the blue-and-whites were flashing, shattering the stillness that should accompany the last hours of night, but rarely did in a city this size. The ME's van was parked alongside the victims' car, body bags and gurneys waiting to receive their cargo. Officers from the Two-Five were already canvassing. As Amanda and Pete Doyle began their preliminary inspection of the scene, one of the detectives who'd caught the case concluded it was a routine gangland execution. At first glance, he appeared to be correct.

The driver's upper torso was bent over and slightly contorted. His head was level with the floor, his eyes and mouth permanently frozen in mid-scream. He looked as if he was still stunned that something like this could happen to him. Judging by the grease wipe around the entrance wound, the killer had been standing less than ten inches from his victim. Somehow Amanda didn't imagine that they'd carried on a long conversation.

In the backseat, a second man lay crumpled in the right corner. If not for the hole in his forehead, he could have been napping. As with the driver, there was no exit wound, which seemed to confirm the detective's theory. Mob hits with a .22 caliber handgun were common; the .22 lacks the velocity to penetrate the skull a second time. Instead, it ricochets around inside the skull, causing considerable brain damage and internal bleeding. This man had been shot through the right-side window and from a greater distance than his companion, but he was no less dead.

Before she photographed the victims, Amanda cleared the area surrounding the car so she and Pete could scan for evidence. They searched for bullet casings, cast-off blood, clothing tears, something that might have fallen from a pocket or that the perpetrators might have left behind. The site was annoyingly clean, save a shoeprint Amanda spotted next to the driver's door that had been made in a thin layer of dirt. It was fragile and far from perfect, but everything at a crime scene was significant until proven otherwise.

She placed her camera on a tripod and tilted it down. From her equipment bag, she retrieved a clear acetate ruler which she placed alongside the print to provide scale. She clicked off several pictures from that height, then removed the camera from the tripod and took a series of close-ups. That done, she sprayed the print with black primer; sprayed at an oblique angle it created shadows that helped distinguish grooves and patterns. Once she had recorded the painted shoeprint from a variety of ranges and angles, she circled the car slowly, searching for another print. Doyle took an impression of the shoeprint for additional analysis.

When Amanda signaled that she had completed phase one of her photographs, the ME team removed the bodies. Preliminary on-site identification by one of the detectives pegged the passenger as Vito Albanese, a *capo* during Big Ray Saviano's reign. The driver remained unknown.

Amanda took her second round of photographs, then joined Pete in the painstaking task of collecting trace evidence. Other than blood samples, there was very little. Amanda did find a tiny piece of fabric that had been snagged by the chrome near the driver's door handle.

The victim might have pushed open the door with the intention of fighting with his assailant or fleeing. The door probably hit the assailant, who quickly pulled away so that he could take aim and murder the man in the car. She was dropping the tiny swatch into an evidence envelope when a familiar voice intruded on her concentration.

"What's a nice girl like you doing in a place like this?"

Amanda turned, as did her partner, who was inside the car dusting for fingerprints.

"You talkin' to me, Fowler?" Pete called out.

"Hardly." Jake leaned into the car, and ogled. "You're pretty, Doyle, but not my type."

"Aw shucks. And I thought I looked particularly adorable tonight."

Jake shook his head. "There are a lot of ways to describe you, my man, but adorable is not one of them." He pointed to Amanda and grinned. "Now *this* is adorable."

"And this," Amanda said, fighting a blush, "is a crime scene." She looked at her watch, then back at Jake. "It's five o'clock in the morning. This isn't even close to where you live or work. So what, may I ask, are you doing here?"

"I have a friend on the Organized Crime Task Force. He clues me in whenever something goes down with the Saviano clan."

Amanda had forgotten about Archie Fowler's involvement with the Savianos. How perverse, she thought: she and Jake had a crime family in common. She wondered how *Cosmopolitan* would score that on one of their "How Compatible Are You?" quizzes.

"He said it looked like a run-of-the-mill hit."

Amanda wasn't so sure. While it was true the signs pointed to an execution: single gunshot wounds to the head, no murder weapon or casings found at the scene, no prints, hair strands, or other easily traceable evidence. But most Mafia hit men wore smooth, leather-soled shoes. The shoeprint she had photographed displayed a tread consistent with the lug-soled boots favored by the hip-hop crowd. Also, that fabric sample looked like one of those shiny synthetics found in the silky bomber jackets so popular with street gangs.

"What'd you get out of your prelim? Is this simply Mafia spring cleaning? Or have the Latinos joined the fun?"

"You know I'm not allowed to speculate," Amanda said.

"Uh-huh." Jake examined the scene, studying the parked car, the open door. "They knew their killers," he speculated, pointing out how neatly the car was parked against the curb. "This car stopped voluntarily."

Amanda and Pete had come to the same conclusion.

"My guess is they were waiting for someone. When that someone arrived, the driver opened his door to hand over merchandise or collect a bag of bucks."

Amanda hadn't thought about that, but it made sense.

"So who was the newly deceased expecting to meet? Some Mr. Big from another Family? Or a representative from the Savianos' newest business partners?" His jaw tightened and his voice sounded strained, as if he was struggling to dam a torrent of conjecture. "What difference," he said, too blithely, Amanda thought. "Either way, that's one less slimeball the city has to worry about."

"If it doesn't make any difference," she said, probing gently, "why climb out of bed at this ungodly hour to come to a crime scene? What're you looking for, Jake? What do you hope to find?"

"I don't know." He breathed deeply and shrugged, unable to come up with a rational response. "Maybe it's some weird and morbid compulsion, a subconscious fascination with gangland murders. Or maybe it's a distorted sense of vengeance. You know, an eye for an eye. A thousand of them for my father." His eyes turned vacant, as if he were traveling back in time, seeing other faces, other murders. "Any ID?" he asked when he returned to the present.

"They think the one in the back is Vito Albanese."

The muscles in Jake's jaw flexed, and his blue eyes narrowed. As he turned away from Amanda and looked into the car where Albanese's blood stained the seat, she was sure she heard him mutter, "Good!"

She stood by quietly and watched as he stuffed his hands in his pockets and studied the pavement, his right foot tapping with furious agitation.

"Albanese was the shooter," he said finally, spitting out the words as if they burned his tongue. "He did whoever we found in Archie's car."

"I thought you said they never found the shooter. That your father's case remained unsolved."

"Officially, that's true. I got this a couple of years ago from snitches within the organization," Jake explained. "It seems the Dodge Dart murder, as it's euphemistically known, was the one that 'made' Vito."

Amanda noticed he kept clenching and opening his fists, like a boxer loosening his hands before a fight.

"Can you imagine? That fucking lowlife bragged about it! About what a big man he was. About how easy it was to perform that sick, mob initiation ritual.'' His mouth pursed as if he had tasted something very bitter. "What could be easier? You just whack someone in cold blood, stuff them in the trunk of a car, leave them to rot at the bottom of a junk pile. And bingo! You're a member in good standing."

Amanda took his hand. "Jake," she said softly, but in a manner that demanded his attention. "Albanese is dead. Your father's been missing for twenty years. It's time to close the book on it."

Jake recoiled as if she had shot him. He shook off her hand, leaned in close, and glowered. "Dead or alive, those people took my father from me. So you can be damn sure I'm never going to forgive. I'm never going to forget. And I'm never, ever going to close the book on what happened to Archie Fowler!"

Furious, he stormed away, needing space and time to calm himself. Amanda regretted what she had said. Not only had her comment been tactless, it had been disingenuous. She hadn't closed the book on the Savianos. Nor would she. How dare she ask Jake to do what she refused to do?

Pete climbed out of the car and began to gather up his equipment.

"I think we've done whatever there is to do, sweet cakes," he said. "After I stow this gear, I'm going to call in to the house and see what's happening. Who knows. Maybe we'll get lucky."

Amanda nodded. They had three hours left on this shift. It had been a grueling night, and she was beat, but just then she was too distracted to think about her fatigue. She needed to apologize to Jake for her insensitivity.

"I'm sorry," she said, coming up behind him. "I was out of line."

"Yeah," he said without facing her. "Me too."

"I had no right to say what I did. Especially since I'd feel the same way if I were in your shoes."

"No, you wouldn't." When he turned around, she expected to see anger. Instead, his expression was nondescript, the laugh lines around his eyes were crinkled. "You'd feel wobbly in my shoes. And," he said looking at her feet, then his, then hers again, "probably a little foolish."

She surprised herself by laughing. She hadn't thought she had the energy.

"When do they free you from the asylum?" Jake asked, continuing his abrupt mood shift.

"Eight. And not a second sooner."

"Eight o'clock. Okay." He seemed to be talking to himself, but his eyes remained fixed on Amanda. "What're you doing this afternoon?"

"Sleeping, hopefully."

"You only need a few hours."

"That may work for rugged guys like you," Amanda said, holding her eyes open with her fingers, "but a girl needs her beauty sleep."

"For you, an hour and a half. Tops." Jake dismissed the notion as if sleep was as inconsequential to her looks as dry skin cream. "Now that we've cleared that up, what are your plans for this afternoon?"

She laughed at his dogged insistence. Whenever she was near this man, her head fizzed as if he carbonated the air. He energized her and exhausted her at the same time. "I don't know. But I take it you have something in mind."

"Indeed I do! I'll pick you up at noon." She groaned, and her head swayed from side to side like a weary metronome. "You know, you look gorgeous when you're trying to look pathetic," he said, offering only minimal sympathy for her fatigue. She groaned again. "Oh, all right. Twelve-thirty. But that's the absolute latest."

"For what?"

"The what doesn't matter because the who is me." He grinned, flashing those dimples of his. "And no fussing. This is a jeans and tee shirt kind of date."

"Yeah. Yeah. Last time you said suit and tie and lied."

He thought about that. "So I did. Well, this time I'm telling the truth." He crossed his heart, then held up his hand like a Boy Scout taking an oath. As he did, he took an inventory of her current ensemble, sneakers to ponytail. "This look works. Of course, I'd kill the latex gloves and the CSU jacket, but otherwise, come as you are."

"May I shower, *sahib?*"

He leaned close, sniffing the air around her. "I will admit, I'm not particularly fond of this scent."

"You don't like Eau de Morgue?" she said, astonished at his lack of taste. "I'll have to try something else."

An easy smile drifted onto his lips, as if they were sharing something intimate. "Now *you're* lying. You don't wear perfume."

She returned his smile, intrigued that he had noticed. She didn't even own a bottle of cologne. In her line of work, perfume was counterproductive. It could mask other scents that might lead to the discovery of evidence. Besides, the smell of death was all-pervasive. Nothing could compete with it, overpower it, or eliminate it.

"Say good-bye, Fowler." Pete wrapped his arm around Amanda's shoulder and turned her toward their car. "Me and my gal have to motor. We've got another homicide across town. Some guy must've thought the wife snored too loud, 'cause he smashed her head in with a baseball bat."

"Lovely." Amanda grimaced as she hoisted her bag onto her shoulder.

"Twelve-thirty," Jake reminded her.

As they drove away, Pete chuckled. "First there's Ty-ler. And now Fow-ler. So, Max-ie, which one makes you go hummmm?"

Amanda didn't have to look at him to see the lascivious grin on his face. "I'm not sure. Tyler," she said, emphasizing the correct pronunciation of his name, as opposed to the nursery-rhyme cadence Doyle seemed to favor, "is elegant and witty and very suave. Three cultivated characteristics which, for you, would be listed under alien concepts."

"And Jake?" Pete pressed, ignoring her gibe.

"Jake's got those nonstop dimples."

At the next red light, Pete turned to her, his face a portrait of injured male ego. "I have dimples," he said, plaintively.

Amanda bussed him on the cheek. As she did, she whispered, "I'll bet you do, but they're not on your face."

At precisely twelve-thirty, the downstairs buzzer rang.

"I'll be right down," Amanda said after Jake identified himself.

As promised, she was wearing almost precisely the same thing Jake had seen her in hours before—a white tee shirt and worn blue jeans. She had replaced the sneakers with loafers, the CSU jacket with a blazer, and her equipment bag with a leather knapsack. Also, she added a little makeup.

"Where to?" she asked, glad to see that this time he had been true to his word and had worn jeans, a denim shirt, and a navy sweatshirt tied around his waist.

"The Bronx."

Without any further explanation, he steered her toward the Eighty-sixth Street subway station. They caught an uptown C train and exited at 161st Street, right in front of Yankee Stadium.

"How could you miss the season's opener against Boston and call yourself a New Yorker?" Jake was so pleased with himself he practically glowed.

"I guess I couldn't," Amanda said.

"Exactly!"

As he took her arm and guided her through the throng, Amanda felt that delicious fizz beginning to bubble inside her. They followed the dim corridor past souvenir shops and food counters and rest rooms until they came to a wide portal through which Amanda could see sunlight and a huge baseball diamond. Their seats were down front, along the third-base line.

"Guard these with your life," he said, plunking her backpack down on his seat like a marker. "I'll be back in a couple of minutes. I'm going to get provisions."

Amanda saluted gravely and giggled as he loped up the steps and disappeared. She filled the time by admiring "the House That Ruth Built." It was enormous, large enough to hold nearly sixty thousand fans. While Amanda was indeed a fan of the sport, it surprised her to realize this was the first time she had ever attended a game in person.

She and Beth hadn't lived near a major-league stadium in Washington. When they moved to Los Angeles, Dodger stadium felt too open, too exposed. Beth particularly feared any situation which didn't provide protective cover and an instantly accessible exit. She also had a natural apprehension about crowds. When Amanda moved to New York, watching games on television became a warm-weather habit she indulged whenever she had the time. She never thought about going to a ballpark. Sitting in one now, however, she understood why so many people did.

It was a spectacular day to be outdoors. The sun sat high in the cerulean April sky, warming those who had gathered within the spacious coliseum. The grass was new and verdant, cut in a crosshatch pattern that seemed remarkably precise. The dirt that delineated the baselines was freshly raked. The bases marked the corners, each of them puffed and clean. It felt like a large picnic site, which in a way it was. Men in boldly striped shirts hawked everything from beer to peanuts to gourmet hot dogs, promoting their wares with a loud, distinctive Bronx accent. All around her, people shouted to the vendors, jumping up from their seats and grabbing their purchases, hoarding supplies in readiness for a long afternoon. People who didn't know each other exchanged predictions and encouragement about the season's prospects, fretted about a pitcher's arm or a slugger's batting average. They groused about the owner's interference or the manager's last press conference or a sportscaster's negative comment. Diehard fan loyalty was a form of camaraderie that crossed age, race, and economic lines. Amanda loved it.

Being one of very few women on her job, Amanda was surrounded by rabid sports enthusiasts. She didn't share their love of football or hockey—to her, if one had to pad nearly every inch of body surface, protect one's head with a helmet and one's face with a mask, it wasn't a sport, it was organized violence, and she saw enough of that at work. But she did love the NBA playoffs and America's national pastime.

She supposed those two sports attracted her because even though a team effort brought about the ultimate results, the contribution of each individual was vital and visible. There were no masks to hide a pitcher's embarrassment when he couldn't find the strike zone or a player's humiliation when he struck out or missed a fly ball. There were no pads to shield a leg from the cut of a cleat coming off a slide or protect a limb from an errant throw. Just like on the basketball courts, where nothing cushioned the pounding of a fall on a hardwood floor. One's character was on display all the time. Amanda found that courageous.

"Here you go," Jake said as he returned to his seat and slipped a brand-new Yankee cap on Amanda's head. He leaned in close, placing both hands on the brim of her cap, gently bending it until he had achieved the perfect curve. His head was already capped, his brim already properly curved. By keeping his hands on the front of the cap, he shielded Amanda's face from everyone but him. Smiling, he ducked beneath her hat and kissed her. "Let the game begin!" he declared, his eyes locked on hers.

Amanda smiled back at him, hoping he couldn't hear the fizz that had developed into a roar.

A fellow directly behind Amanda with a too-large belly hanging over too-tight jeans echoed Jake's words, but his sentiments were directed toward those unseen officials who were in charge.

"Let's play ball!" he shouted, exhorting his section mates to take up the chant. They did so eagerly and loudly. Within minutes, as if the higher-ups were actually responding to fan demands, the organ blared, and over the loudspeaker came the announcement of the day's lineups. The Yankees took the field. After the national anthem, Boston's leadoff batter came to the plate. And the battle was joined.

Amanda couldn't remember the last time she'd had this much fun. She cheered and booed, yelled at the umpires, argued with Jake about whether the third-base coach should have held a runner or waved him in, and chatted like buddies with people she'd never seen before. She sang hokey songs, did the wave, clapped raucously, and stomped her feet with the excited abandon of a child. She disregarded all the rules of good nutrition and stuffed herself with cholesterol, fat, sugar, salt, chemical additives, and food colorings. The only thing she said "no" to was beer.

"I hate it," she said bluntly during the seventh-inning stretch.

Jake shook his head and clucked his tongue. "I'm going to be up front about this," he said, his face wreathed in honest disclosure. "I'm looking to ply you with booze so that after the game, I can score. You catch my drift?"

"Your drift is hard to miss," Amanda replied, swallowing a grin.

He scowled, as if he actually believed his flirting had been subtle. "So what're my chances?"

"Plying me with beer? Slim and none." His disappointment was obvious. "With a bottle of good wine?" He looked hopeful. "Not bad," she said.

He slid his arm around her waist and drew her close enough to kiss. Instead, he simply said, "I can't wait."

Amanda stunned herself by responding, "Neither can I."

Back at Jake's apartment they fell into each other's arms the minute he closed the door, grabbing at each other in a burst of mutual ardor. Their lips touched and it was as if a torch had seared Amanda's nerve endings, amplifying every sensation to its extreme. There was no foreplay to this engagement. This passion was instant and cataclysmic. His tongue found hers and her body quaked with pleasure. Her hands raked through his hair and he pressed against her, allowing her to feel the fullness of his delight. As her arms laced around his neck, his hands clasped her waist, drawing her so close there was barely room for either of them to breathe.

Fully entwined, Jake moved them in the direction of his bedroom, his mouth ravishing hers as he groped for light switches and doorknobs. Along the way, she unbuttoned his shirt and pushed it down off his arms. He stripped her of her blazer, undid her belt, and unzipped her jeans. Clothes and shoes littered the hallway. He started to remove her tee shirt, but his lips refused to separate from hers. They clung to each other desperately, as if this was the first, the last, the only time they would ever experience this level of excitation, as if they were afraid it would disappear if they moved apart for even a moment.

When they reached the bedroom Jake reluctantly broke their embrace. Though he looked at her with unconcealed hunger, still, he hesitated, silently asking if she was sure. She didn't know if she fell in love with him in that instant, but she came close. He had divined that she didn't give herself easily, because she didn't trust easily. Before their lovemaking went any further, he needed her to know it was, indeed, lovemaking. He also needed her to know that he wanted her body. But more than that, he wanted her trust.

Without pause, she lifted her tee shirt over her head, letting it drop onto a nearby chair. With her eyes soldered to his, she unhooked her bra, liberating her breasts. Her flesh was smooth and ivory-toned, full and firm. Jake started for her, but she stopped him. Undressing herself was more than an erotic dance, it was a display of certitude. Slowly, she stepped out of her jeans and removed her panties. She pulled the band from her hair, tossed her auburn mane and let it fall onto her shoulders. When she was completely naked, shorn of all cover and disguise, she presented herself to him.

He approached her with the reverence and adoration a supplicant would offer a goddess. His hands touched her shoulders, then ran down her arms. She shivered, and her nipples tightened. He cupped her breasts and kissed them, one at a time. Amanda's head tilted backward, inviting him to continue his journey. His lips traveled up to her neck, onto her mouth, over to her ear. They got lost in the sweet skin beneath her chin, but his hands found her breasts and feasted, fondling her in a way that made her ache with need.

Her hands trembled as she undid his jeans, slid them down off his hips and gently outlined his manhood. Jake moaned at the feel of her hands on him. Quickly, he kicked off his clothes and lifted her into his arms. He held her for a moment, gazed down at the femininity before him and smiled.

"You're magnificent," he whispered.

Amanda returned his smile, reached up, and brought his mouth down to hers as he carried her to his bed and laid her down. She expected him to take her immediately, to gobble her up in a burst of blind passion, yet instead, she found herself luxuriating on a cushion of tenderness.

The room was dusky, illuminated only by the light from the hall. The window was opened slightly and the curtains were drawn, but Amanda had no wish to look beyond the confines of this bed. For now, this was all of the world she wanted to experience, Jake's body, the only territory she wanted to explore. At this particular moment, this particular man defined the boundaries of her existence.

As she lay against a fluff of pillows, Jake's sandalwood scent filling her nose, she felt as if she was in an ancient seraglio rather than a modern bachelor's apartment. His sheets felt cool against her back as he delicately traced the shadows that had formed on her body. His fingers flickered across her skin like the tips of a feathered plume, drawing dotted lines from one breast to another, from her temple to her chest, her navel to her groin. He didn't go near the places that screamed for him, yet she felt tight and moist and unbelievably hot. Their lips didn't touch, yet their eyes devoured each other. So arresting was their attraction that simply the nearness of him made her pulse with need.

As their desire accelerated, so did the pace. He moved onto her, an arm sliding beneath her, raising her hips until they brushed against his. Breathless, she felt herself undulating, swaying to an internal chant that required no words. Jake danced with her, their bodies moving in heated concert. Suddenly, he pulled away, but only slightly, leaving room for them to pleasure each other until their excitation bordered on pain. Sensing they could no longer stand being apart, he sheathed himself and brought them together in an explosion of feeling, both of them exulting in the glorious burst that came with sensual union.

Spent, but satisfied, they lay side by side, neither one feeling the need for cover. Jake clasped her hand in his, lacing their fingers together. Amanda nestled her head against him, purring softly.

"I'm a happy man," he said simply.

Amanda smiled. She had been a happy camper at Yankee Stadium. Once they walked into this apartment, she had catapulted so far beyond happy that she lost her ability to describe how she felt. Which was probably just as well: personal revelation was completely against her nature.

Jake lifted himself onto an elbow and gazed down at her. "You're being awfully quiet. Despite my reputation as a world-class swordsman, I'm a regular guy, which means I'm way too insecure to deal with quiet at a time like this."

Amanda caressed his cheek. He caught her hand, brought it to his lips, and kissed all five fingers. "Please tell me I wasn't alone in Wonderland."

"It was terrific," she said, reassuring him.

"I hear a but. I hate buts."

"Once again, you lied."

He looked confused, but only for a minute. "You're absolutely right. *Mea culpa.*"

He climbed out of bed and disappeared down the hall. When he returned, he was carrying a bottle of wine and two glasses. He had wrapped himself in a large towel and had another one draped over his arm which he tossed to her when his hands were free.

Instead of pouring the wine right away, he climbed back into bed. "The St. Emilion needs a few moments to breathe," he said, licking the crevice between her breasts. "Frankly, so do I."

Amanda had to bite her lip to keep a moan from escaping. She was not a woman with an encyclopedia of past lovers, yet neither was she inexperienced. She had felt desire and passion and satisfaction with other men, but Jake Fowler aroused something more, something different. It was an odd sensation and, for Amanda, difficult to place. Especially when he was this near and they were unclothed and she could feel her blood getting intoxicated once again by his presence.

"You were adorable at the game this afternoon," he said, nibbling on her earlobe. "Somehow I knew that beneath that starched NYPD uniform, there was a wild Yankee fan just dying to get out."

"How clever of you," Amanda murmured, wriggling as his hand crept beneath her towel.

"I thought so." As his lips grazed hers, she felt him smile. "How about some wine to celebrate?"

"When we left the score was tied," she reminded him as she took the glass he handed her.

"I wasn't talking about celebrating a Yankee win," he said, his expression turning serious. "I want to celebrate us."

The sweetness of that sentiment overwhelmed Amanda, rendering her speechless. Jake didn't seem to mind her silence. He filled it by sipping the robust red and licking his lips with honest relish. He watched as Amanda tasted her wine and struggled with her emotions. When he felt enough time had passed, he took her chin in his hand, turned her face toward him and looked her squarely in the eye.

"You're an incredible woman, Amanda Maxwell, and I think I'm falling for you." He saw her eyes pool and that slow smile she adored began to waltz across his lips. "I know that's not the suave thing to say, but I'm in a business that makes me real conscious of time." His smile faded as he too wrestled with feelings of love and loss and limits. "I don't want to waste a minute of any hour I can be with you, Max."

Tears dribbled onto Amanda's cheeks, but she made no attempt to wipe them away. She wasn't embarrassed by them, she was delighted.

They were the result of an emotion expressed, received, and reciprocated.

"Then don't," she said, stunned by her sudden abandon.

As Jake took her in his arms, along with the explosion of passion that his touch ignited, there was a resurgence of that other sensation, the one Amanda couldn't define. She reached for it, because often it seemed close enough to grab, but like a thought that skimmed one's consciousness, then disappeared yet was never completely gone, it continued to tease and elude her.

As evening became morning, their lovemaking was interspersed with sleep and talk and quiet companionship. But it was in the kitchen, where they were making breakfast and vigorously debating the wisdom of putting juvenile first offenders into boot camps or detention center, that she experienced an epiphany: that indefinable feeling, that odd sensation that came over her when she was with Jake, yet had never felt with anyone else was indeed something rare and special—it was one of connection.

C H A P T E R
TWELVE

When Amanda walked into her apartment, she felt as if she had been away for weeks instead of hours. Part of her wished it had been weeks; her time with Jake had been that exceptional. Unfortunately, reality had a way of intruding on even the most perfect idyll. Jake had to go to his office. When she mentioned this was her day off, he offered to play hooky, but she discouraged him. This was the only time she had to run errands, she told him. Either she did laundry or she'd have to get comfortable with the notion of going without underwear. It didn't surprise her that Jake liked that idea.

Since she never left her windows open when she was gone, the air in the apartment was stale. Quickly, she pulled back the drapes, lifted the blinds, cracked the windows, and allowed the golden light of a springtime sun to pour into the living room.

As she watched colors change and textures become enlivened under the influence of sunlight, she wondered what Jake would think of her apartment. He'd probably feel right at home in her living room because it was traditional in flavor. Though most of her furniture had come from secondhand stores, slipcovers, inexpensive reuphol-stery, and throw pillows worked decorative magic. Nothing matched in the conventional sense, but she supposed that's what gave the place its charm. Fat, cushy armchairs in serious bottle green velvet kept company with a love seat emblazoned with a boisterous butter-cup yellow print of huge flowers and ribbons. Tables and lamps performed functions. If they replicated particular periods or fit with other pieces, it was purely accidental. Odd bits of porcelain dotted tabletops and the mantel of her fireplace. Now and then, when she thought of it—usually after she had spoken to her mother—she filled the vases with fresh flowers. More often than not, they stood empty.

Down the hall in her bedroom, she opened the shutters and chuckled, imagining Jake in this effulgent garden. She guessed his expectation would be to find her living in a bare-walled cave, all dark colors and no-nonsense furnishings. Instead, he'd find a cozy, floral extravaganza created as a sanctuary.

Everywhere one looked—walls, curtains, bed skirt, comforter, easy chair—one was greeted by the same pink geranium chintz. Pale carpeting communed with the creamy wainscoting and ceiling moldings. Contrast was provided by the dark wood of her dresser and a variety of tables. Needlepoint pillows, a small needlepoint rug, and several decoupage lamps picked up at downtown auctions added to the Victorian feel of the room. It was fussy and flouncy and feminine, exactly the opposite of the image Detective Amanda Maxwell projected. But this room wasn't designed for a first-grade detective. This was Amanda's childhood fantasy fulfilled: a place in which a carefree little girl with solid roots and community ties might live, a little girl who had the same friends from kindergarten through high school, the same room in the same house in the same town.

This was also a place where a woman coming from a transient childhood could fool herself into thinking she'd actually set down roots. Here, she could accumulate too many magazines and complain about too little closet space. She could retreat behind the covers of a novel, or feel secure beneath a favorite afghan. And, she could live alone without feeling completely estranged, because mixed in with her anonymous bibelots were treasures that she and her mother had accumulated over the course of their travels.

They were the booty from a game Beth had initiated after their first few relocations. Amanda had been understandably distraught leaving Miami. When they had to move again within a month, and then again two months after that, Beth feared for her child's mental health. Amanda had withdrawn almost to the point of catatonia. No matter what Beth said or did or suggested as a way of helping her adapt, Amanda's response was, "What's the point?" She refused to refer to their living quarters as home, or the town in which they lived by its name. It was always the house in Nowhereland.

In order to pull Amanda out of the morass and give her a sense of belonging, Beth created The Quest. Ostensibly, the object of the game was to find knickknacks without detectable provenance. Beth's real objective was to create portable memories for herself and her daughter, to instill the feeling that home was wherever they were, not in which building they lived. More important, she wanted Amanda to feel as if she still had some modicum of control over her existence, that not everything they did or owned needed to be approved by the United States Marshals Service.

They reserved their hunting for weekends, combing flea markets or county fairs or shops that used the term "antique" loosely. It was a mother-daughter time that satisfied a normal desire to acquire, yet didn't break WITSEC's rules. Beth's rules demanded that they buy only things they really liked. Taste was a way of defining one's self, she told Amanda. By indulging those stylish instincts, Beth believed that no matter where they lived or what they called themselves, their purchases would stand as constant reminders of who they were—inside. Over the years, they evolved into totems of triumph over the faceless enemy that had condemned them to their solitary life in Nowhereland.

Most of The Quest collection remained in California with Beth, but when Amanda moved into this apartment, she appropriated whatever she thought she could use. Above her dresser was a large oval mirror in a carved wooden frame they had bought at a garage sale in Spokane. Flanking it were two candlesticks, one of plain brass that Beth found during their brief stay in Aberdeen, South Dakota, the other a Delft knockoff Amanda had fallen in love with at a county fair outside of Norfolk, Nebraska. There was a toile flowerpot they bought on a trip to Portland, Oregon, that Amanda filled with a cyclamen plant and kept on her windowsill, a crockery vase from a craft gallery in Rapid City, South Dakota, and Amanda's favorite, a series of monkey drawings Beth had bought as a birthday present for her on an excursion to Seattle.

Amanda lingered at the door of her retreat for a moment, then smiled as she returned to the living room and nestled into the welcoming arms of one of her chairs. Looking around, she realized that this apartment was not only fiercely personal, but intensely singular. Amanda never pictured anyone here with her. Those she cared about—Beth, Uncle Sam, Lionel—wouldn't take the risk; those she didn't never got an invitation. Annie had been here once or twice, but even she knew not to drop by unannounced.

Yet suddenly, Amanda had an overpowering urge to bring Jake here—to cook dinner for him and fill her apartment with fresh flowers and fragrant candles and music. She wanted to make love to Jake in her pink-and-white bower and see his dark hair resting against her

"Sweet Dreams" pillow. She wanted to serve him breakfast in bed on a white-wicker tray, watch a baseball game on TV, or sit quietly by the fire drinking wine. What amazed her was the realization that if her mind had opened to that possibility, if she was actually willing to admit him entrance to her haven, it meant that she believed she could do all of that without worrying about being unmasked or having her true identity discovered. Perhaps Lionel's admonition about allowing herself to trust and be loved in return was having an effect.

Thinking about Lionel, she grabbed the newspaper, curious as to whether Hallie Brendel had authored another hatchet job on her father's reputation. Amanda was dismayed to see that she had. Again, Lionel's name screamed across the front page:

BAIRD WASHED $8 MILLION: CHISOLM'S GOT THE PAPERS TO PROVE IT!

Amanda felt as if she had been tackled by the entire NFL. According to the article, someone had delivered a stack of stock certificates to Senator Chisolm that showed eight million dollars flowing through a single account at a small commodities house called Spairson, McShane & Partners. The name on the account was Alberto Della Robbia who claimed to be a certified representative of Unitex, a Swiss company dealing in raw materials. He was in fact a member of the Sicilian branch of the Saviano Family, known for his charm and finesse at money laundering. Della Robbia opened the account in December 1992. During the first four months of 1993, he washed over five million dollars. During the last three months of the year, he washed an additional three million. Government agents attempted to speak to Mr. Della Robbia, but he had conveniently disappeared. Spairson, McShane & Partners was listed as a subsidiary of Baird, Nathanson & Spelling. The executive named as the one in charge of the account was Lionel Baird.

Amanda's jaw tightened. She detested this campaign to vilify her father, but her biggest fear was that if Hallie Brendel dug deep enough, she'd unearth the truth about what happened—or didn't happen—twenty years ago. Furious, and more than a little concerned, she threw down the paper and went to call Lionel. As she reached for the phone, she noticed the blinking message light on her answering machine. She had three messages.

"If you're free this evening, let's have dinner." Lionel tried to sound casual, but she picked up an undertone that disturbed her.

He had been wonderful about obeying the rules she and Uncle Sam had set for him, but he was showing signs of stress. She worried that if he got too nervous, he might make a mistake that could cost them all.

The second message was from Annie. She, too, sounded slightly on edge.

"Hey, Max, it's me, Annie. Look, we have to talk. It's not an emergency. Okay, maybe it is. I don't know. I just need to speak to you. Call me. Soon."

Amanda didn't have time to process that before the final message played. "Miss Maxwell, this is Columbus Avenue Florist calling. We have an order we'd like to deliver. If you could give us a call at your convenience—555-8932."

Who'd be sending her flowers? Her hand trembled slightly as she dialed the number of the florist. The instant they picked up, she began timing the call. If it sounded suspicious, she wanted to be able to hang up before they could complete a trace. After identifying herself, the voice on her answering machine repeated his desire to deliver a bouquet of flowers. She asked who the sender was. "Tyler Grayson," the man responded. An unbidden smile tickled Amanda's lips.

"I have to do some errands," she said, scolding herself for being so paranoid. "I'll pick them up on my way home."

He protested that the arrangement was quite large and might be too cumbersome for her to handle, but she remained adamant. She didn't allow deliveries.

She returned Annie's call, but got her machine instead. Amanda left a message saying she'd get back to her. Then, she called Lionel on his cell phone. He didn't answer either. Tired of playing telephone tag, she decided to get on with her chores. She grabbed her laundry and a bag of dry cleaning. She was about to walk out the door when her phone rang.

"By the way, the Yankees won."

It was as if Jake's voice had reached through the phone and caressed her in places most often described as private. Her face flushed.

"Yay, team," she said, looking around as if someone was actually witness to her utter lack of composure.

"Hard to believe they could pull it off after their coach left." The gentle tease in his voice was seductive.

"Where are you?" she asked, curling up in a corner of her couch and hugging a pillow like a swooning adolescent.

"At the office. I'd invite you over so you could ravish my body, but my mother's here. We're close, but not that close."

"You're terrible!"

"I know. It's one of my most endearing qualities." A moment of silence ensued, a moment so fraught with anticipation it was almost sensuous. "Yesterday, last night, and this morning were truly incredible, Max. At the risk of sounding trite, I hope it was the same for you."

"It was." She wanted to say more. She wanted to tell him how remarkable she had felt being loved by him, how delicious she felt even now, but affectionate banter didn't come easily to her.

Jake sensed that, but he wasn't the type to let her off the hook.

"That's it?" he said with exaggerated incredulity. "*It was.* You know what, Maxwell, when it comes to laconic responses, you give Jack Webb a run for his money. Just the facts, is that it? No ruffles and flourishes. No, what a fabulous lover you are Jake Fowler. I've never, ever met a man as sensational as you. Where have you been all my life?"

"Nope." It was easier for her to deal with their intimacy humorously. She guessed he knew that. "No fancy adjectives. Just the facts. It was wonderful. You were wonderful. Ten-four."

He laughed. She could almost see his eyes crinkling and those dimples framing his mouth like parentheses.

"Okay," he said. "Play hard to get. See if I care." He paused, as if he was giving a quiz and she had thirty seconds to give the correct response.

"I care," she admitted.

"Good." His voice wrapped around her like a hug. "When can I see you again? Is tonight too soon."

She ached with disappointment. "I can't make it tonight. Or any other night this week. I've got the late shift."

"Well, fortunately for you, my middle name isn't Dracula. I'm able to function during daylight hours. How about brunch tomorrow morning?"

"Sounds good."

"At my mother's."

"That sounds even better. I'd love to meet your mother."

"Can't believe anyone would actually claim me as their own, eh?"

"Something like that."

"How's eleven? Grace starts serving at noon, whether anyone's at the table or not."

"See you then."

She sighed as she hung up the phone, her arms still embracing the pillow.

What are you doing? Her heart pounded as WITSEC-syndrome set in. She was behaving like a silly schoolgirl, mooning and spooning and giving her hormones free rein. Too much was happening, little of it good. This was not the time to let her guard down. She needed to keep a clear head and a sharp focus.

That might be difficult now that Jake Fowler had insinuated himself into her life. Actually, he had captivated her, drawing her into his orbit like a magnetic field. It wasn't just the sex, although that did register high on the Richter scale, it was the sense that what heightened their carnal satisfaction was an exchange of intimacy that felt very, very rare. The intelligent way in which he discussed her photographs and her work, pointing out how she revealed herself in each. Their mutual lack of shyness. The easy way in which he peeled back the layers of his life. The gentle manner he used trying to explore hers. He was arrogant and conceited and operated according to his own code of honor and justice, but there was an emotional directness about him Amanda found immensely appealing. How could she not? He had ventured into the thicket of secrets in which she lived quite boldly, undaunted by the dense tangle of reticence that surrounded her. Other men were intimidated by that deep and silent forest. Jake seemed undeterred.

Her eye caught the address of the florist, and she flushed.

"Speaking of other men," she muttered to herself, amazed that suddenly her social life demanded use of the plural.

Jake was brash and exciting and certainly, it felt as if he had captured the lion's share of her heart, but this was the morning after the night before. She had experienced a certain amount of afterglow the morning after her night with Tyler. That had faded. What was to say that this euphoria wouldn't fade?

Suddenly, Amanda felt as if she was pulling the petals off a daisy: she loves him, she loves him not, she loves him, no, she loves *him*. She laughed. Soon, she'd be scribbling her name with Mrs. before it to see which way it would look better: Mrs. Tyler Grayson or Mrs. Jake Fowler. She chided herself for bathing her ego this way, but debating about which of these sensational men was more appealing felt like such a luxury, she indulged a bit longer.

She had a strong physical attraction to both; admittedly, her response to Tyler was not quite as galvanic as her reaction to Jake. Intellectually, Tyler seduced her with his knowledge of history and politics, as well as his strong affinity for cultural pursuits. Jake was hardly an ignorant boor. It was his approach to the arts that separated him from Tyler and his interpretation of events. Tyler viewed creativity and opinion within a larger context, one based on historical perspectives and artistic ancestry. Jake looked at almost everything from the inside out: What made that person do what he or she did. Whether it was societal influences or an Oedipus complex, to Jake it was all about motivation, all about the past being prologue.

Emotionally, Amanda felt an attachment to Tyler. Jake electrified her, but like a split wire spitting sparks, it could either explode or fizzle. She had known Tyler longer. She felt she knew him better. She could trust him. Could she trust Jake?

On the surface, he should inspire the most trust. He had been open and forthright about his past, about his feelings concerning what happened to his father. Tyler was buttoned up and far more secretive. Amanda knew that his father had died when he was in high school. He mentioned that his mother died a little over a year ago. But he never provided any details. Tyler wasn't a man who felt comfortable revealing bits and pieces of his life. He was respectful of other people's silence. He expected them to be respectful of his.

Amanda understood that all too well. Experience had taught her that often it was better to leave certain things unsaid, better for the bearer of the secret, as well as for the curious. One couldn't unlearn a secret, and since the acquisition of any new knowledge provoked change, one had to exercise caution. Change wasn't always predictable or pleasant. Tyler never probed too deeply. He respected boundaries and never tried to trespass, a quality more akin to her own personality than the up-front, out-there, over-the-top manner of Jake Fowler. Sooner or later, a man like Jake would succumb to the tug of his curiosity and look to scale the fences she had erected around herself. After all, he would reason, he was open with her. Why couldn't she be open with him?

She stared at the pillow in her lap and an ironic laugh caught in her throat. A month ago, Lionel practically demanded that she find a boyfriend. Now, she had two. Of course, thanks to an attack of WITSEC-syndrome, instead of accepting that as a blessing, she viewed it as a vexing dilemma.

Again, her telephone rang. This time, it was Beth.

"Hi, sweetheart. I just wanted to see how you were doing."

They chatted for a few minutes about everything and nothing. As usual, Beth was calling from a secure phone at Sam's office. Amanda had checked her phones for bugs, so she felt free to unburden herself. She told her mother about the new men in her life. As she expected, Beth had the same dual response Amanda had: It was both wonderful and worrisome.

Amanda explained who Tyler was, how she had known him before, what she thought of him now. "He's sexy and charming and fun and flattering. And," she said, weighing her words, "safe, I guess."

"And Jake?"

Amanda giggled at the mention of his name. "Deliciously dangerous," she confessed, unable to expunge the delight from her voice. "I don't know what it is, but he arouses a sense of abandon in me, Mom. The man makes me tingle from the tips of my toes to the roots of my hair." She heard what she was saying, listened to what it implied and paused. "It's a feeling I'm not sure I can afford to have. Especially now."

Beth's heart broke. She wondered if there would ever be a time when she wouldn't feel as if she had ruined her daughter's life. When Amanda was younger, it was easier to compensate because they were together and happiness could be achieved with a movie or rides at an amusement park or a day playing The Quest. Once Amanda reached womanhood and moved away, Beth's ability to gift her daughter with good times and warm experiences diminished. The least she could do for her now was encourage her to grab a chance at love. As always, the question that nagged was: at what cost?

"How'd you know you were in love with Uncle Sam?" Amanda asked, feeling embarrassingly teenaged.

"It crept up on me, I think," Beth said, allowing herself to reminisce. "Sam was caring and protective, and I needed that."

"Did you ever have a romance with anyone else? Other than Lionel, of course."

"No. I couldn't afford to fall in love with a stranger," she said flat out, smothering whatever regrets she had about the limits placed on her.

"Did he sweep you off your feet?" Amanda asked, saddened by the sudden realization of how lonely her mother's life must have been. "Did he make you giddy with passion?"

"No." She was silent, clearly remembering another time, another man. "But I'd had that before."

Amanda blushed. Beth was referring to Lionel. "So how do you know you love him?"

"Love has many guises, Amanda. It's never the same. Even if you only love one man, the characteristics of the emotion change with time and circumstance."

Amanda couldn't see Beth running a fingertip over an old photograph of Lionel or the wistful look on her face.

"It's different with Sam," Beth said. "Because I'm different. My needs are different. Sam makes me feel safe and secure. He knows things about me no one else does, which means I can be intimate with him, both physically and verbally.

"I don't know if in another life Sam would be my choice for a mate," Beth said, "but in this life, he is."

Long after she hung up, Amanda thought about their conversation. Beth didn't come out and say as much, but Amanda sensed she was steering her in Tyler's direction. Better the devil you know, and all that. Actually, Amanda suspected if Beth really spoke her mind, she'd have told her not to be with anyone until Bastido was caught and Sam could assure them that the danger had passed. Certainly, there was merit in that advice. Anyone could become an innocent traitor. But Amanda had been alone for so long, and feeling connected to someone felt so good.

Amanda heard Beth's unspoken counsel, Sam's very vocal warnings, even the small voice in her head that warned against surrendering to her feelings. But inside, she was churning. Why must she continue to put her life on hold?

This is the wrong time, the voice said, echoing her mother.

It's always the wrong time, her heart said, mimicking her father.

Maybe it was because she hadn't gotten enough sleep and her senses were dulled. Maybe it was because Jake had taken her to a baseball game, and no one had ever done that before. Maybe it was because she was tired of coming back to her apartment alone and reacting with suspicion when a gentleman admirer sent her a bouquet of flowers. Whatever it was that prompted the decision, Amanda chose to listen to her heart.

The one thing she had learned sitting on the sidelines watching others enjoy relationships, was that love didn't follow rules or adhere to time schedules or wait for the world to be free of peril. If you wanted love in your life, you had to take it or leave it.

But know that if you left it, it might never come again.

★   ★   ★

When Amanda reached Lionel, he sounded particularly grumpy. Instead of agreeing to exercise their usual precautions, he insisted they eat at her apartment.

"I want to see where you live," he said, his tone slightly petulant. "And frankly, I'm too tired and uptight to try and elude whatever lunatics might be lurking outside my door. They don't deserve the attention we're giving them!"

When Amanda protested, he promised he wouldn't have Thompson drive him across town in the limousine. "I won't be obvious," he said, trying to reassure her.

His sentiments struck her as reckless. She argued with him about the wisdom of throwing caution to the winds and offered a dozen suggestions that would require minimal effort on his part, but in the end, he wore her down. The only point she won was that rather than eating takeout, she'd cook. He'd bring the wine. By the time they hung up, Amanda was looking forward to the evening.

Ten minutes before he arrived, however, she was a wreck. Her dinner guest may have been her father, but he was also the fabulously wealthy Lionel Baird. Suddenly, she second-guessed everything from the menu—salad, roast chicken, steamed broccoli, and garlic mashed potatoes—to her black gabardine slacks and short-sleeved white cashmere sweater.

She couldn't dust anything any more than she already had, nor could she Windex the mirrored squares on the door between the living room and the kitchen again. They were already so clean they shimmered. So she fluffed pillows until they begged for mercy. She fussed with a spray of tulips she had put in a vase next to the couch, as well as the assortment of roses she had bought to fill a cachepot that decorated another tabletop. Tyler's lush bouquet of spring flowers held court in the center of the table that separated her easy chairs. His sweet note—"I miss you, Tyler"—was tucked away in her nightstand drawer. She lit the candles on the cocktail table as well as a delicately scented candle that sat on the mantel. She stacked and restacked the art books she kept on an upholstered piano stool in front of the fireplace and fretted about whether Lionel would mind eating at the small round table she used for dining.

Within the first five minutes after admitting him to her home, Amanda forgot about all that. He was a wonderful guest, and she was glad to have his company. He brought her wine for dinner, pink camellias, which she put next to her bed, and a fresh gardenia corsage.

"It's as soft and lovely as your complexion," he said as he pinned it to her sweater.

He had dressed casually, with a sports jacket over black slacks and an ivory-collared cashmere sweater. They both chuckled at the coincidence.

As she gave him a brief tour, he oozed compliments, but without a hint of condescension or snobbery. Instead, he lauded her on her ability to do so much with so little.

"You have incredible taste," he said, raising his arms, looking around, including every last inch of her apartment in his appraisal. "Imagine what you could do with a larger budget."

"Yeah. Imagine," she said, laughing off his not-so-subtle attempt to raise, yet again, the subject of her joining him at Baird, Nathanson & Spelling.

Despite her offhand tone, she was grinning with pride as she invited him to take a seat. While she poured them each a glass of chilled Chardonnay, he reiterated how easily she would fit into his firm and how certain he was that she'd love the world of finance if only she would give it a try. She nodded on cue, agreed when expected to, but ultimately declined his offer. Since he hadn't expected her to do otherwise, he shrugged, toasted her good health, sipped his wine, and remained the picture of contentment.

Arrayed on the cocktail table in front of him was a basket filled with flat breads and a sliced baguette, a crock filled with a dark, gritty paste she called tapenade, and a marble slab displaying various Dutch cheeses. Lionel slathered the olive, anchovy, and caper spread on a slice of the crusty French bread and moaned with delight as its flavor crossed his tongue.

"By the way," he said, "I tried to call you all yesterday afternoon, last night, this morning. Where were you? I thought it was your day off."

Amanda blushed. Lionel leaned back against the couch, eyed her suspiciously, then smiled.

"Were you with the guy who sent those?" he asked, nodding toward Tyler's bouquet.

"No," she said, wondering how he knew the flowers had been a gift. "Someone else."

"Okay, let me guess who's the flowers. And who's the someone else." He thought she looked so adorably uncomfortable just then, he wanted to cry with happiness at being able to offer her some fatherly succor. "We have two contenders . . . that I know of: Tyler Grayson and the PI. What was his name?"

"Jake Fowler."

Lionel didn't have to work very hard. It was written all over her face. "My guess is Grayson sent the flowers. They're elegant and expensive and the proper way for a gentleman to court a lady."

Whenever he spoke of Tyler, his voice carried a tinge of disapproval. Tonight, she intended to find out why.

"But Fowler was the one you spent the day and the night and the morning with." He smiled conspiratorially. "I met your gumshoe at Lloyd Franks's gallery. He's good-looking, if you like tall, dark, and dimpled."

Amanda sighed and shook her head with mock exasperation, surrendering to the peculiarity of the moment. Her father was teasing her about a boyfriend. It was a slice of life that screamed adolescence redux, but since she had missed spending those years with him, she found the experience achingly pleasant.

"Did you speak to him?" she asked, sipping her wine and staring at him over the rim of her glass.

"I did."

He was tormenting her with his drip, drip, drip reenactment, but she found it endearing, so she followed his script.

"Did he make any sort of impression on you?"

"Actually, he did." Lionel took his time spreading the tapenade on another slice of bread. He chewed it slowly, savoring both the hors d'oeuvre and the moment. When he was finished with that activity, he leaned forward and rested his arms on his thighs. "I found him to be bright and insightful. He was, as you had described, a bit arrogant, but to me, that's a positive." Amanda tilted her wineglass at him: Touché. "Also rather spunky."

"I take it he didn't genuflect before you."

"Hardly." Lionel laughed. "There wasn't so much as a crease in the fellow's knees."

Amanda was pleased.

"I wasn't particularly impressed with his choice of friends, however." Lionel's visage had turned pensive. "While he was standing with me, he waved to a departing trio: John Chisolm, Pamela, and a blonde I didn't recognize at the time."

"And now you know her to be . . . ?"

"Hallie Brendel."

Amanda dismissed his concerns with a wave of her hand. "Jake used to be an investigative reporter. His Rolodex is probably filled with masthead names."

"He bought one of your bleakscapes, by the way," Lionel said, returning the conversation to a more pleasant level. "He said it 'resonated' with him."

Jake had raved about all her photographs, but that one, he said, had touched him deep in his soul.

"His father disappeared when he was a young boy. He's presumed dead."

"By everyone except the son."

"Yes."

"Good for him." Jake's attitude resonated with Lionel, who readily related to someone who refused to accept the early death of a loved one. "May I venture a guess that you're ever so slightly infatuated with this Fowler?"

Amanda nodded, trying to bite back a smile, but failing. "He does ring my chimes," she admitted.

"How about Grayson?"

"A few bells."

"Go with the chimes," Lionel advised.

Amanda didn't know whether she was about to step over a line, but she said, "Mom didn't say so directly, but she implied that she favored the bells. She thought they were safer than chimes."

Lionel appeared visibly stung. Amanda found his reaction instructional: Even after so many years, he wanted Beth to love him. Obviously, chimes lasted a lot longer than bells.

"She's probably right." He didn't sound convinced. Amanda's guess was that he didn't want to contradict Beth. She was the better parent. "It's probably better to be safe than sorry."

Amanda went over to him, bent down, and kissed his cheek. "Do you really believe that?"

"Not for a minute," he brayed, delighted that she wanted his honest opinion. "I don't ever want you to settle for someone simply because he feels safe. I want you to experience love in all its passionate glory." He caressed her cheek and pinched her ear. "But don't tell your mother I said so."

"I don't have to. She knows exactly how your mind works. Remember?"

Lionel helped her clear away the hors d'oeurves and bring the dinner dishes to the table. He uncorked the Pinot Noir he had brought, poured it into two big-bellied goblets, and brought those to the table as well. When they were settled, Amanda raised the subject of Hallie Brendel and Senator Chisolm's latest accusations.

"They're true," Lionel said, "to a point."

He explained that Spairson, McShane & Partners was the name of a company Baird, Nathanson & Spelling had bought out ten years before. It functioned as a separate, yet integrated entity.

"The commodities market is very volatile and loaded with risk. It lends itself to enormous profits and quick turnovers, particularly because it's not as tightly regulated as the other markets."

"Didn't you suspect anything?" Amanda asked, concerned about Lionel's increased agitation.

He shrugged in frustration. "I never saw the account."

"But your name's on it as the account supervisor."

"My name would appear on any account trading numbers that large. It doesn't mean I oversaw the actual conduct of business or had any significant input into the portfolio strategy. The man in charge of Spairson, McShane is Roscoe Harding."

"Do you think he laundered that money?"

Lionel shrugged and knitted his eyebrows. "As you know, there's this competition going on among my division heads to be named as my successor. I don't think Harding knew Della Robbia was one of the boys, but there's a lot of pressure on the men. Who knows what one of them, or all of them, wouldn't do to move up."

"Would he send those certificates to the senator?"

Lionel shook his head. "That would be cutting off his nose to spite his face. Besides, Roscoe and I had a rather lengthy conversation about the matter." His tone implied that *inquisition* might be a better way to describe their session. "Either he's become a pathological liar overnight or his explanation is correct. He thinks someone in the Saviano organization wanted those papers leaked to the press."

"But why? What purpose does it serve?"

"It makes me and my Wall Street cronies the bad guys and takes the heat off Little Ray and his merry band of thugs." Lionel tapped his finger nervously on the table. "It may also be Big Ray's idea of payback."

Amanda's radar went on alert.

"Despite what Ms. Brendel is reporting in her rag. B, N & S runs a pretty tight ship when it comes to money laundering. We know it's done all over the Street. We know there are probably names on our client roster which are false fronts for the mob or the cartels. But we police it as best we can. Better than most, I'd say." He looked at her. "My vice presidents know they'd be fired in a heartbeat if I discovered anyone on their staffs was washing. And that includes everyone from the highest-ranking executive down to the lowliest clerk."

The shadow of past mistakes clouded his eyes.

"After the government made laundering a priority and instituted instruments of control, we went through our files and terminated all suspicious accounts. We didn't want to go through the agony and humiliation of another trial, so we cleaned house. Big Ray lost a lot of money, which didn't exactly make him happy." The finger tapping became more rapid. "And let's not forget, he blames your mother for the problems that beset his Family and ultimately sent him away."

As it often did, Amanda felt unnerved by the knowledge that even after all these years, Operation Laundry Day continued to generate aftershocks.

"One of his lieutenants was gunned down the other night," she confided. "It was supposed to look like a typical gangland execution, but I think the Latinos are stirring the pot. They want the Families to wipe each other out so they can take control of New York's narcotics distribution."

"That makes what Roscoe told me sound even more logical."

"I agree. So why isn't the press hot on that story?"

"Because this seems fresher and more in tune with the times." Lionel grunted with disgust. "The continuous glut of gangster movies has anesthetized the public to the point where they almost don't care. Their senses are dulled when it comes to organized crime. Not only are mobs boring, but they don't appear to have any relevance to their everyday lives."

He held up his wine goblet. He tilted the glass back and forth, lost in the ebb and flow of the burgundy liquid.

"Catching white-collar criminals is a much better story," he said, somewhat wearily. "Suddenly, we're the guys everyone wants to nail. It fits in much better with the anger everyone has with corporate America. Get the big guns and bring them down. Make them pay for the problems their greed created. They earn too much. They fire too many. They're nothing but thieves in three-piece suits."

It was a powerful argument.

"How far do you think Chisolm will take this?"

The veins in Lionel's neck tightened. "As far as he can. Remember, he's riding a campaign train. They need tracks to run on."

"Would it help to speak to Hallie Brendel?"

"She interviewed me at the town house this afternoon, and, frankly, it was a colossal waste of time. Not only can't she see the forest for the trees, but she refuses to even look in the direction of the truth."

"I thought she was this crackerjack investigative reporter."

"In her own mind, perhaps." He shook his head. "The reality is she's being used. If she knows, she doesn't care because every head-line about me carries her byline."

"Is she getting all her information from Chisolm?"

"Most of it. But some of it's coming directly from my, you'll pardon the expression, wife."

"I forgot about Pamela," Amanda said.

"I wish I could forget about her," he said, with a sardonic laugh.

"So what are you supposed to do? Just sit back and let the senator and the *Telegraph* drag you through the mud?"

Lionel leaned across the table and patted her hand. "I'm today's news, sweetheart, but this will pass. Tomorrow, or the next day, something will knock me off the front page. Defending myself against every one of these charges will only drag this out."

"I can't imagine they're going to let this drop," she said.

"Not right away. First, they're going to look to extract a pound of flesh. Which is why Roscoe is going to have to come forward and explain that he had no idea Mr. Della Robbia was a Mafia thug in executive clothes."

Amanda played with the food on her plate. "Was Roscoe a leading candidate for associate CEO?"

"He was."

"Is he still?"

"Ray Saviano just eliminated poor Harding from the race." Lionel smirked. "Is this your not-so-subtle way of asking me if Mr. Floral Arrangement has moved up in the standings?"

"Well, has he?" she asked, unembarrassed by the flush that she knew was pinking her cheeks.

Lionel appeared to be going down a mental checklist. "Okay," he said, "here's the deal on Tyler Grayson. He's one of the brightest young men at B, N & S. He's an excellent manager, an intuitive trader, and a major rainmaker. He's responsible for millions of dollars on our bottom line."

"So what is it about him that makes you so uncomfortable?"

Lionel's expression said he didn't understand his response to Tyler any more than she did. "I can't put my finger on it. I guess the simplest answer is that his people skills don't measure up to his business skills. And frankly, as associate CEO of a major brokerage house, you need both."

"Would you deny him the position . . ."

"Just because he makes me itch?" he finished her sentence. "Probably not. We're in a bottom-line business, after all. But," he said, smiling slyly, "don't ask me how I'd feel about him as a son-in-law."

"Oh, please!" Amanda sprang to her feet and busied herself with the dishes.

Lionel followed her into the kitchen. When she looked at him, he seemed sad.

"Will I ever be able to acknowledge my son-in-law?" he asked.

Amanda swallowed the surge of emotion that threatened to erupt and forced herself to respond with a smile, albeit wobbly. "By the time I get married, you'll not only be able to grill your future son-in-law about his intentions, but you'll be able to walk me down the aisle. Because everyone who was ever involved in Operation Laundry Day will either be dead or too old to cause any trouble."

"From your lips," he said as he kissed her cheek.

"Would you mind getting the rest of the dishes while I start the coffee?" She was eager to change the subject. He knew it and complied with her wishes.

She closed the door to the dishwasher, turned around, and was greeted by a camera strobe going off in her face.

"What're you doing?" she practically screamed at him. "You know better than that."

"Whoa!" He took a step back and held up his hands. "Amanda, please. I didn't mean to upset you."

"But it does upset me. And you know why."

He acknowledged his error, looking like a little boy who had been caught licking frosting off a freshly baked cake.

"These articles don't help."

"I know. I just . . . well, I just want a picture of you. Is that so terrible?" Amanda's expression didn't change. He pressed on. "I'll have the film developed in New Jersey, near my club. I won't put it in my library or next to my bed. And I won't use it for my Christmas card. How's that?"

For the second time in one day, Amanda made a decision she hoped she wouldn't regret. Suddenly, she was exhausted from having to weigh the consequences of things normal people simply did.

"Okay," she said, clearly exasperated. "Just please, be careful."

Lionel put his arm around her and led her into the living room. "If it frightens you that much, I'll throw the entire roll out."

The entire roll. "What else is on it?"

Lionel looked sheepish. "The pictures I took of you and your mother when we were in Wisconsin. Remember?"

How could she forget? She thought Sam was going to explode when he saw Lionel with a camera.

"I thought Sam took that roll from you and dumped it."

He shrugged. "I employed a little sleight of hand."

"Meaning?"

"I switched cartridges. The one Sam destroyed was a roll of film I'd shot elsewhere."

Amanda glared at him, clearly horrified. "You can't do things like that, Lionel. Sam was looking to protect us, because we need protection. I thought you understood that."

"I know." He raised his hands, pleading guilty. "It's selfish and probably very stupid, but please. I've adhered to all your rules, followed all your guidelines. Can't you grant an old man one small favor? Let me have a picture of my wife and my daughter. You two are the only family I have."

He had aimed his argument at her heart and chosen his weapons well: *Family. Daughter.* Two powerful words, two devastating bullets that fired holes in her defenses. Her need to have a family, to be his daughter, overwhelmed all control. Connection became more powerful than fear, making it impossible to deny his request.

Even though that small voice inside her head shrieked that was precisely what she should do.

CHAPTER
THIRTEEN

Throughout the subway ride to Brooklyn, Amanda badgered Jake to tell her everything she needed to know about everyone who was going to be at this brunch. He remained frustratingly coy, providing the briefest of sketches, insisting that she had nothing to worry about from the people she was going to meet. His mother Grace, his sister, Jocelyn, her husband, Brad, and their two children, Barry and Brenda, eight and six respectively, were not people who hid behind manufactured personas. They were all very straightforward and easy to read. Besides, he told her, he wanted her to form her own impressions.

They got off the subway at Seventh Avenue in the heart of Park Slope and walked the two blocks to Grace's brownstone. Amanda loved this section of Brooklyn. To her, it felt like a unique pocket of urbanity, one that achieved its singular status by combining the intelligence and sophistication of big-city life with the communal blending of suburbia. On the street, there were young parents pushing strollers and holding on to toddlers as they headed to Prospect Park to take advantage of this delightful burst of spring. Also headed for the park were seniors, happily taking their daily constitutional, waving to friends, nodding to strangers. Inside the various coffee shops that dotted the avenue, tables were filled with people laughing and chatting amiably over a cup of coffee and a bagel. It was easy to understand why Grace never moved into Manhattan. And why Jake kept returning.

From the time Amanda entered Grace's brownstone apartment, she felt at home. Painted the palest of yellows and defined by an enormous, antique rug, the living room seemed reminiscent of what used to be called a parlor. There were high ceilings and tall windows that looked out on a tree-lined street and summoned a flood of daylight. Coral drapes hung from thick rods with ball finials. There were plaster moldings and chair rails and a carved marble fireplace, alongside of which sat a bouquet of logs in a large copper cauldron, patiently waiting for winter's return. The furniture, all covered in different, yet compatible florals invited relaxed, convivial conversation. All about the room, there were family photographs and hand-sewn needlepoint pillows, some faded with age. Amanda noticed that most of the pictures were of the grandchildren, but tucked in and around were a few snapshots of Jake and Jocelyn as children, and Grace and Archie in better days.

After introductions were made, the family moved into the dining room, where everyone seemed to have designated places at the round table cluttered with dishes and glassware and platters of food. Amanda took what appeared to be the one unassigned seat, in between Jocelyn and Jake. He was right, there was no pretension here. She might have been a guest, but that didn't relieve her of her share of kitchen duty. Grace didn't think twice about asking her to please pour the decaffeinated coffee and to pass the eggs. Nor did anyone try to stop Brenda from insisting that "Manda" was the only one who could spread cream cheese on her bagel.

She couldn't remember the last time she was in that kind of setting, if ever she was. Three generations of a family gathered around a table in what was clearly a regular ritual of renewal. Aside from devouring huge quantities of food, this was a time when they caught up on everyone's comings and goings. They had lost Archie. Grace wasn't going to allow them to lose contact with each other.

The children wandered in and out, creating their own special noise and disturbance. The grown-ups exchanged news and ideas, sometimes lapsing into loving, but heated debates about everything from whether Barry should be allowed to wear sneakers to school to current events. They were polite enough to ask about Amanda's job, but not about anything too personal. If they were assessing her qualifications for membership in the Fowler clan, they weren't obvious or obnoxious about it.

Jake was fabulous with his niece and nephew. He was their ally, their protector, and their advocate in any and all battles with the enemy—their parents. Jocelyn and Brad accepted his role as champion-in-residence with benign tolerance.

Jocelyn explained, "Children need a buddy. Jake needs to be their hero until he becomes someone's father." She made it sound simple. Amanda, whose frame of reference was so skewed when it came to how a family was supposed to function, admired this young woman's ability to be so inclusive and her husband's willingness to be so accommodating.

The kids were the best. Their acceptance was instantaneous. Of course, that might have had something to do with the fact that when Amanda went to the bakery to buy a coffee cake for Grace, she picked up some clown cupcakes as well. Also, she brought a disposable camera and, reverting back to her own childhood, made friends by snapping off two dozen pictures: individually, together, with each of their parents, both their parents, their grandmother, their uncle, *en famille*. Despite their squealing entreaties, there were no pictures taken with her.

Another pleasant surprise was how easily the Fowlers absorbed her into their ritual. Grace greeted her as if Amanda's presence at the table was usual. Jocelyn and Brad were a bit more curious, but they, too, were warm and welcoming. At one point, Amanda wondered whether it was because Jake brought a different woman each time and they were used to having strangers invade their brunch, or because "a friend of Jake's" was a rarity to be handled with kid gloves.

The only time things got dicey was when Brad mentioned that earlier he had watched an interview with Lionel Baird. Amanda wriggled in her chair. Lionel had neglected to mention that his interview was taped. He must not have wanted her to watch. According to Brad, Hallie Brendel began with the expected: had Lionel called for Roscoe Harding's resignation? No. Harding resigned on his own. Would he be brought up on charges? That was for the government to decide. Did Lionel know Della Robbia's real identity? Obviously not. How could he not? Wasn't he the head of Baird, Nathanson & Spelling and, therefore, responsible for all business conducted beneath its banner?

"I thought he was going to punch her," Brad reported.

"He probably should have," Jocelyn muttered, sounding to Amanda as if, at one time or another, she too had wanted to punch Hallie Brendel. Amanda wondered why and how the two women knew each other.

"Isn't he responsible?" Grace asked. "I mean, ultimately?"

"Theoretically, perhaps," Jake said. "But it's a multibillion-dollar-a-year business. There's no way he's going to keep an eye on every account. It was a dumb question."

He seemed uncomfortable, impatient. His eyes kept darting from Brad to Jocelyn to Grace, as if telegraphing the message that he wanted to end this conversation. They paid no attention.

"He accused Chisolm of being a Mafia pawn," Brad said, arching his eyebrows as if the audacity of the charge astonished him all over again.

In spite of his apparent disquiet, Jake laughed. "Chisolm must've loved that!"

Amanda noted that he sounded as if he had some insight as to what tickled the senator's funny bone. Then she remembered Lionel saying that Chisolm and Pamela had been at the Franks Gallery. Jake had waved to a blonde standing with them, later identified as Hallie Brendel. She had fluffed off Lionel's intimations of conspiracy. Now she wondered how well Jake knew Ms. Brendel. Also, when he had met the senator and Pamela Baird and what they had talked about. Suddenly, she regretted not being at her own opening. Clearly, it was much more of a happening than she ever imagined.

"Not likely," Brad said with muted authority. "Chisolm's ego needs constant stroking. He doesn't take insults lightly."

Brad was an attorney who specialized in environmental law. As a partner at a high-powered firm with offices in New York and Washington, political activism was part and parcel of his daily life. Either he was representing watchdog groups against environmentally abusive corporations, or he was lobbying for appropriate legislation. His knowledge of many politicians was firsthand. Being a New Yorker, it could be assumed that he had more than a passing acquaintance with Senator Chisolm.

"Did Baird back up his claim with anything substantive?" Grace asked as she brought a fresh pot of coffee to the table.

Brad took a minute to reconstruct the sequence of comments. "He cited Chisolm's statement that the incriminating documents were delivered to him. He didn't know by whom."

"Then it's possible they came from a mob informant." Amanda was loath to insinuate herself into this discussion, but she couldn't help herself. "Did the senator, or Ms. Brendel, attempt to verify any of the facts?"

Jake smiled. "Spoken like a real Gold Shield."

She shot him a look, then returned her attention to Brad.

"She kind of glossed over that," he said.

"Glossing is what Hallie does best," Jocelyn interjected. Jake shot her a look.

"What else did Baird throw at her?" Jake surrendered to the will of the majority. He couldn't fight them, so he decided to jump right in.

"He attacked the *Telegraph* for not reporting some gangland execution. According to Baird, it happened Friday night, and there wasn't word one about it in the Saturday afternoon edition. He says the mob fed this story about him to Chisolm and Brendel to keep the media heat off the really big story, which is the proliferation of drugs and the war that's going on over its distribution."

Jake looked at Amanda. No one missed the knowing glances they exchanged.

"Okay, what's up?" Brad asked. "Does Baird have a point?"

"I'd say so." Amanda remained cool. "I caught that case, and, yes, I believe it's part of a turf war."

"Between who and whom?" Grace's interest was piqued.

Amanda waited for Jake to tell her, but he had ceded the floor to her. "The Savianos and a Latino gang with roots in LA"

Mentioning the Saviano name around this table was as sacrilegious as inviting the Devil to sing in the choir. Grace and Jocelyn vibrated animus. Brad shook his head as if to say oh-no-not-them-again. Only Jake, who lived with this issue every single minute of every day, didn't change expression. His hostility toward the Savianos was as constant and unique as one's individual body scent.

"Look at the timing," Amanda continued quickly, hoping to redirect their attention. "Hallie Brendel begins her series of articles attacking Wall Street on behalf of Senator Chisolm. Mr. Baird counters with a news conference that makes her look irresponsible at best, self-serving at worst. It also doesn't do a lot for her relationship with the senator. Suddenly, out of nowhere, someone sends her an envelope stuffed with reporter catnip. Without verifying her facts, she attacks Lionel Baird while pushers are gunning each other down for the privilege of selling kids Propaine."

"If I were Lionel Baird," Jake said, admiringly, "I'd hire you to do my PR."

"She happens to be on the money." Brad's brow was furrowed. "Other than Chisolm and Brendel, whose motives are obvious, who else benefits from this attack on Baird?"

"The Savianos." Their name stumbled out of Grace's mouth as if it couldn't pass over her tongue without leaving a bitter aftertaste.

While Brad, Grace, and Jocelyn spewed invective about the hoodlums they believed killed Archie, Jake retreated to a place Amanda was beginning to recognize as his mental aerie. Something new had occurred to him, something he needed a few minutes to sort out. She watched as he organized thoughts and rearranged facts, creating new combinations that presented new possibilities.

"So," she asked quietly, leaning close to him so as not to disrupt the others. "What's wrong with this picture?"

"There's no question that the Savianos are priming this pump," he said, thinking out loud. "But which Ray is issuing the orders? Little Ray has never done anything clever in his entire life. He can't even pronounce the word subtle. He's a slam, bam, media ham kinda guy. Murder, mayhem, crushing a few skulls—he'll do whatever it takes to get his mug on the evening news. As you pointed out, the timing of these disclosures is well planned and well aimed. That's Big Ray's style."

"You think he's trying to regain control over his troops?" Brad overheard and wanted in on the discussion.

"Why not?" Jake shrugged. "It can't be easy sitting in the Big House watching your idiot son flush a lifetime's work down the toilet."

"He's been there awhile, and he's not getting out," Amanda reminded him. "Loyalties shift."

"True, but Big Ray amassed a lot of favors during his reign."

"Those Della Robbia papers didn't appear by accident," Brad said, following his brother-in-law's train of thought.

"Nor did Della Robbia disappear by coincidence." Jocelyn was also onboard. "That was a favor being called in."

"Give the little girl a cookie!" Jake smiled at his sister.

She laughed, almost triumphantly. "I guess that means Lionel Baird is right. Hallie Brendel is a tool of the mob. You gotta love it!"

Jake glowered at her. Did he think she was being irreverent? Or was his discontent related to her taking yet another snipe at Hallie Brendel? Why would he care?

Just then, Amanda recalled the curvaceous blonde on the stairway of Jake's building. Now she knew why Hallie Brendel's face had seemed vaguely familiar when she saw her at Lionel's news conference. Putting Jocelyn's caustic remarks together with Jake's agitation, the serendipitous meeting on the staircase, the waves at Lloyd's gallery: Amanda felt safe in assuming that Jake and the ubiquitious

Ms. Brendel had more than a passing acquaintance. Suddenly, Amanda felt out of place. Jake must have sensed something had changed because within a few minutes he suggested they leave.

Once on the street, Jake confronted the issue. "Yes. Once upon a time, Hallie and I were an item. As you may have already guessed, she didn't exactly win the Fowler seal of approval. Everyone was quite delighted when we had our unhappily ever after. Particularly, my sister." He grinned at the unbidden look of relief that washed over Amanda's face. "But they liked you."

"I liked them," Amanda said, as Jake took her hand and they headed for the subway.

"How could you not?" he exclaimed, pleased that Hallie hadn't become a wedge. "They're terrific!"

Amanda couldn't disagree. In fact, throughout the day, she was so taken with the way they interacted with each other, she couldn't help projecting, seeing herself married, with children, enjoying a Sunday meal with Beth, Sam, Lionel and whomever he was married to at the moment. Like a new coat, she kept trying it on, seeing if it fit, seeing how it felt. Not once during the day did she allow herself to worry about the cost.

Actually, she was elated to see how easily she blended in with another family. Most of the time, she felt as if she was trapped inside a Tina Barney photograph which typically displayed emotional disconnection and familial disease, two characteristics she felt she and Barney's subjects had in common. On the other hand, spending the day with the Fowlers was depressing because she didn't see how any of this was possible for her. Anyone she married would be immediately at risk, as would their relatives. And how, in good conscience, could she ever have children; no child should have to live her life.

Still, she thought, wasn't she entitled to some of what she had tasted today? Had she really been sentenced to an eternity of pressing her nose against the window of life?

As she and Jake headed for the subway, she realized that one of the reasons she was drawn to him was that he made her feel as if everything was possible. Probably because he continued to believe so devoutly in the impossible. He didn't care if he was the only one who believed Archie was alive. Until he had unalterable proof to the contrary, he would maintain his course and sail directly into the wind. He didn't care if others remained burdened by *couldn't* and paralyzed by *can't*. To him, each morning was a new start. And if evening brought disappointment, he remained bolstered by the knowledge that there was going to be another morning.

Another reason was that when Amanda was with him, she felt as if she, too, could live that way, as if she, too, could dare to hope for things that had previously seemed hopeless.

On the train into Manhattan, Jake got beeped. He had to go into the office. Amanda was fine with that. She was on duty that night and could use the time to read the papers. He got off at his stop, she continued on to the West Side.

As she came up out of the Eighty-sixth Street station, she went into a phone booth and called Uncle Sam. She had been treated so wonderfully by the Fowlers that she had decided to try and do them a favor, if at all possible.

"United States Marshals Service."

"Sam Bates, please. Amanda Maxwell calling."

"Marshal Bates is out of town, Miss Maxwell. This is Deputy Marshal Steinmetz. Can I help you?"

Amanda had spoken to Carl Steinmetz enough times to feel comfortable with him. He was young and friendly and, according to Uncle Sam, exceptionally talented.

"I have a project, Carl. A missing persons case that's been dormant for nearly twenty years."

"Nothing I like better than a hunt," Steinmetz said. She could almost see him salivating. "Who's the mp?"

"A guy named Archie Fowler. He was an accountant who lived in Brooklyn and listed the Saviano boys among his clients. From what the police on the case dug up, he'd been dipping his hand into their pot. Then one day, Archie went missing. Weeks later, a body turned up in the trunk of his car that was never positively ID'd. Forensics were pretty certain it was Archie. Some family members disagreed. A few years after the discovery, his mother claimed she saw him on a street in Aruba. There's never been another sighting, but his son, who's a PI here in the city, also cleaves to the notion that Archie Fowler is alive and well. They're nice people. I'd like to be able to put their minds at rest. One way or the other."

"Well, I'm intrigued," Carl said. "Give me the details, and I'll get right on it."

Amanda answered his questions as best she could. When she hung up, she wondered if she had done the right thing. What if Archie turned up dead? Or worse, turned up living another life with another woman and another family? She'd cross that bridge when she came to it, she told herself as she headed home.

On the corner of Eighty-ninth, she stopped at a newsstand and bought the Sunday *New York Times*. As she picked her copy off the pile, she was assaulted by the headline:

BAIRD CRIES FOUL. CALLS CHISOLM A PAWN, WELCH A COWARD.

All the other newspapers carried similar banners. Quickly, she scanned the *Times*.

In a television interview aired this morning and conducted by Hallie Brendel, Lionel Baird accused Senator John Chisolm of allowing himself to be used by the mob. He claimed that the documents given to the senator, and subsequently passed on to the Telegraph, *were part of an elaborate setup to take media attention off the bloody gang wars that are taking place on our city's streets.*

"Instead of going after the real story," he said, clearly accusing Ms. Brendel of being biased, "you're giving voice to a man who is not only being used as a pawn by the mob, but is so hell-bent on winning an election, and destroying my good name in the process, that he will do or say anything!"

As proof, he questioned the fact that the Telegraph *had made no mention of a gangland-style execution that took place late Friday night in East Harlem and was reported in this newspaper as well as other New York dailies. According to someone he called a reliable source, this was not an intra-Mafia war, but one in which several of the Families were being challenged by local factions of ruthless Latino gangs from Los Angeles. The goal, according to this unnamed source, is control of the lucrative New York drug market and distribution rights for the city's newest killer drug, Propaine, a deadly mix of cocaine and PCP.*

When Ms. Brendel asked if history wasn't repeating itself, Mr. Baird denounced her and the Telegraph *for being "willing to compromise common journalistic standards for an increase in circulation." When pressed to compare Douglas Welch's previous testimony about Mr. Baird laundering drug lords' money in the late seventies, and the claims being made today by Senator Chisolm's informant about similar activities, Mr. Baird responded by saying that Douglas Welch and John Chisolm indeed had something in common: they were both liars. The difference, he claimed, was that Senator Chisolm was accustomed to prevarication and, therefore, comfortable with it.*

"Douglas Welch was a low-level clerk with a gambling addiction who lied to save himself from prosecution. When no one believed his allegations and he was found guilty in a court of law, he took the coward's way out and killed himself."

Upstairs, in her apartment, she clicked on the television and surfed the channels for news. In between golf, basketball, and baseball, she found the same story being rehashed again and again. Each time, the commentator put a different spin on it and tacked on a new insight, but the bottom line was the same as the headline in the *Times:* Lionel had called Chisolm a liar and the late Douglas Welch a coward.

One interview did capture her full attention, however, because it was with that paragon of loyalty and discretion: Fredda MacDougall. When asked about Lionel's negative assessment of his former employee, she verified the fact that Douglas Welch was an inveterate gambler who had amassed a fortune in debts.

"How would you know that?" the interviewer asked.

Fredda could barely contain herself. "I was intimately acquainted with Mr. Welch at the time, so I was privy to things unknown to anyone else."

This femme-fatale act was pitiful. Amanda closed her eyes. She couldn't bear to watch.

"Was Mr. Baird involved in any way with the theft of those stock certificates as Mr. Welch claimed at his trial?"

Fredda pursed her lips and inhaled so deeply, her nostrils stuck together. "Absolutely not! Poor Douglas was simply looking for a way out of a terrible predicament. He had done something wrong and knew the penalty for his actions was going to be stiff. He couldn't reveal the names of those who had ordered him to steal those stocks, so he lashed out at Mr. Baird."

Fredda bit her lip, sighed, and gave a slight toss of her head. Amanda was certain she was imitating something she had seen in a Bette Davis movie.

"Mr. Baird might get angry, but he would never kill anyone. Douglas knew that."

"Why didn't you come forward before this?"

Good question, Amanda thought.

"I was protecting Douglas's family." She demurred; Susan Hayward in *Back Street*. "He had a wife and a son who loved him. They had to deal with his trial and his untimely death. I didn't want to cause them any more grief by making our affair public."

Amanda groaned. She was making a fool of herself. Maybe even a target.

The telephone rang. Amanda was trying to listen to the end of the interview, but Annie's voice was insistent.

"I'm coming over. I have to see you before our dinner this evening."

"What dinner?" Annie had managed to steal Amanda's attention.

"Didn't you check your machine?"

"I just got in," Amanda said, noticing the blinking red light for the first time.

"Well, Lionel Baird called. He wants to meet us for dinner. Amanda, he's doing the deal!"

That meant Sam's trace had come back clean. Amanda heaved a sigh of relief. "That's fabulous! But," she said, looking at her watch, "I go on shift at twelve."

"Okay. Fine. Whatever. Really, we have to talk. I'll be right over."

She hung up before Amanda could object. As she waited for her friend, she listened to Lionel's message. As usual, it was cryptic without any names mentioned—in case someone broke into her apartment. She called, but he was busy. He said he'd meet them at seven-thirty at a restaurant a couple of blocks from the town house. He'd reserved a private room.

As Amanda cleared out her dishwasher and put away the dishes from last night's dinner, she thought about Annie. She should have been flying high. Instead, she sounded stressed. Probably nervous about making such a big commitment. Who could blame her? Running one's own company was a huge responsibility and, if Amanda were honest, she wouldn't want to have to report profits and losses to Lionel.

Her buzzer rang. She let Annie in and waited until she could see her through the peephole. When she opened the door, she was rattled by Annie's appearance. Her eyes were dark and shadowed. Her pallor was gray. This was not the look of a woman on the brink of megasuccess.

"What's up?" Amanda asked, watching as Annie strode headlong into the living room and plunked herself down on a chair. Her fingers were laced, but not still. Amanda sat opposite her on the couch and waited. She felt as if Annie was ticking and that any second, a bomb would go off.

"I have something to tell you, and I have to do it now." She looked positively ragged.

"Okay. Unburden." Amanda tried to keep her tone light, but inside, she was churning.

Annie looked directly at Amanda. Her fingers stopped knitting. Every part of her seemed to freeze. "I know who you are," she whispered.

The bomb exploded inside Amanda's chest. Her heart began pounding at a dangerous rate, but she managed to keep her face void of expression. "What are you talking about?"

"I know who you are. You're Erica Baird." Amanda simply shook her head. She was unable to speak. She was barely breathing. "I know because I'm Aña. Aña Colon."

The pounding had moved to her head, thumping so loudly Amanda was certain she didn't hear Annie correctly.

"You gave me your dog, Checkers," this stranger who claimed to be a friend continued. "I took care of him, Ricki, because you loved him. And I loved you."

Amanda responded with a blank stare. Her insides were roiling, but her mouth remained still and mute.

"Do you remember the day we were walking through Washington Square Park and saw that black lab with the white ear. I pointed him out and mentioned that I used to have a dog like that. You got all misty. When I asked you why, you gave me some half-assed explanation about having a speck of dirt in your eye."

She extended her hand. Amanda pulled away.

"Okay, I know that's hardly decisive, but there were other clues that only someone who'd been really close to you would ever pick up. Like the way you spread your fingers, fit them together like a puzzle, and slide them up and down when you're nervous. Or the way your nostrils flare when you're angry. Or the way you hum along with everything, radio tunes, movie scores, TV themes, commercials."

Amanda narrowed her eyes and sat back on the couch, arms folded, her body language one of utter skepticism.

Annie forged ahead. "And let's not forget, my old friend, I'm a makeup artist. My specialty is faces, and I've made yours up dozens of times. It's been a lot of years, but your right eye still has that orange fleck in it. And despite the surgery you had, that little cleft still sits right at the tip of your chin."

Out of reflex, Amanda pulled her hair over the barely visible scars she felt had betrayed her. She felt sick. And scared. How did she know this woman wasn't a plant? That she hadn't been fed all this information by a traitor from the Marshals Service or someone else who'd managed to compile these bits and pieces over years of trailing Amanda and Beth. *Beth! Was she all right? She had to call Uncle Sam. She had to know if her mother was okay. But Uncle Sam was out of town.* Suddenly, she realized Lionel hadn't mentioned getting Sam's report. She had simply assumed that he had. *Why had she let this woman into her apartment? Why wasn't she wearing her gun?*

"You're delusional," she said, finding her voice at last. "Erica Baird's been dead for twenty years. I don't know what you hope to gain by concocting a story like this, but you're way off base. Thousands of people have clefts in their chins and orange flecks in their eyes."

"Thousands of people don't have a mole smack in the middle of their cleavage," she said, pointing to a spot on her own chest that was centered between her breasts. "Erica Baird did." Amanda's facial muscles didn't move, but her eyes had widened, making her look frightened. Annie hurried to dispel her alarm. "When you and I hooked up and hit it off so quickly, I thought it was one of those fabulous accidents. When we became friends and these things began to add up, I decided it was providence. We'd been best friends when we were kids. We became friends again as adults. Doesn't that tell you something, Amanda?"

Annie refused to look away, despite the hostility glaring back at her. "I don't think it was a constant, conscious thing, but I feel as if I've been looking for you forever. So, no matter what kind of sour puss you put on, I'm not going to be put off. I know that Erica Baird is alive and well and sitting across from me," she exclaimed, without any equivocation.

"Spare me the melodrama," Amanda said, her voice dripping condescension. "I don't mean to hurt your feelings, Annie, but you've been working on soap operas too long."

"Long enough to know a happy ending when I see one," Annie countered, refusing to budge.

Amanda also remained stubborn and quiet.

"If you'll let me," Annie said, softly, "I'll tell you how I know what I've said is true. When I'm finished, you'll see that you can trust me."

Amanda scowled, but she didn't throw Annie out or stop her from explaining.

"On that awful, awful day, Mom and I were watching your house, waiting for your mother to come home from the courthouse. Three cars drove up. One stopped on Palmetto Drive in front of your house, another right behind it. The third car turned the corner and parked on Ibis Lane at sort of an angle, blocking the street. We saw your mom and the marshal go into the house. A couple of minutes later, a pool guy came out, got into his truck, and drove away. At the same time, another man sneaked out the back of the house and got into a car that was sitting in the Parkers' driveway, next door." Annie's eyes widened as the scene replayed itself. "Then, all of a sudden, there was this horrific noise and your house disappeared inside an angry, orange ball."

She trembled and hugged herself as she must have done when she was nine and her best friend's house exploded before her eyes.

"We were stunned and frightened. We didn't know what to do. Should we call the police? Run over to the house? Rally the neighbors? We were panicking, yet I remember seeing this guy sort of fall out of that oddly parked car." She kneaded her forehead, encouraging the images to focus better. "Later, I realized he had positioned the car so that the passenger side faced away from the front of your house. That way, anyone standing on Palmetto who was watching the house or your mother or the marshals would have missed it. But Mom and I were at our kitchen window, the one that faces Ibis Lane." She tilted her head to the side and narrowed her eyes, watching the past slide before her. "We were too crazed to see him climb into the car parked at the Parkers', but I think Mom said she heard the door slam. Half a second later, the car that had led your mother's caravan into the neighborhood and blocked traffic on Ibis exploded as well." She swallowed hard. "I don't know when we looked back at the Parkers', but whenever it was, the car that had been standing in their driveway was gone. Everything was gone."

Tears trickled down Amanda's cheeks. Annie's face was dry, but pale with revisited shock.

"The newspapers said they had recovered the bodies of Erica and Cynthia Stanton. My parents and I went to your memorial service. I cried with Nanny and Poppy as we looked at the graves where you were supposedly laid to rest. But I don't think I ever really believed you were dead. Mainly, because of Checkers."

She looked as puzzled as she must have felt then.

"The night before the last day of the trial, you came over and said your mom was going to let you go to the courthouse with her. You asked me to take care of Checkers. I said okay. I loved Checkers and certainly didn't mind the idea of spending the day with him, but I remember thinking it was odd. You'd be home in the afternoon. Why not leave Checkers at the house the way you always did when you went out? He was a good dog. He didn't eat furniture or push over plants or anything like that.

"I was twelve years old when I saw a movie that talked about the witness protection program. Suddenly, everything made sense. You and your mom didn't die in that fire. You went into hiding. They wouldn't let you take Checkers with you, so you gave him to me to take care of."

"Did you? Take care of him, I mean?" Amanda asked, her heart aching with an ancient pain.

"You know I did," Annie said quietly. She retreated then, as a thought became an image and then a realization. "The two men who sped away were marshals. So were the guys who fired a bazooka into the house and that third car," she said, fitting the final pieces together. "You and your mother were nowhere near the house when the shit hit the fan."

"I left with my mother that morning, but stayed at a safe house until we met up at the airport." Amanda paused out of habit, but her doubts about Annie Hart's identity had evaporated. She could afford to be honest. "The pool-maintenance man was my mother."

"And Lionel Baird, the man I thought for a while was your lover, is your father."

Amanda nodded helplessly as she looked at the woman who had been her only friend for over a year and saw, clearly, the little girl who had been her best friend so many years before. It amazed her that someone with her eye for detail could have missed the fact that this was Aña: eyes big and round and dark as espresso, hair straight and black as licorice, skin white as a shell. But really, the distinguishing feature then and now were those lips: full and wide, with a slight beesting swell. The same lips that were smiling at her now.

"It really is you, isn't it?" Amanda said.

"Could there possibly be more than one of me?" Annie replied, jumping out of the chair and hugging Amanda fiercely.

Tears fell, embraces were exchanged, and for a few minutes they giggled and played catch-up. Abruptly, Annie halted their reunion.

"It's getting late. We're supposed to meet Lionel," she said. "Before we do, we need to talk."

"Okay. Talk."

"Listen, Max, sooner or later I was going to fess up about all this. I couldn't stand you not knowing who I was. But I did it tonight because we can't allow this deal to go through."

"Why not?"

"If Lionel's doing due diligence on me, and I can't imagine he isn't, he's bound to turn up the fact that I'm Aña Colon, Erica Baird's best friend and Miami neighbor. If he can put that together, so can the people you've been hiding from all these years. It's just too close for comfort."

Amanda sprawled against the couch, flattened by the reappearance of a familiar enemy—reality. "You're absolutely right," she groaned.

Uncle Sam probably had compiled a dossier on Annie that would make her head spin. Interesting, Amanda thought, that he hadn't called to interrogate her about Annie. She would have thought he'd have been on the phone the minute he made the connection, chiding her for her carelessness, grilling her about what she did or did not say. Then again, she hadn't heard from Sam in a couple of weeks. Carl had said he was away. Where was he? Did his absence have anything to do with Bastido? Or the Savianos? Or Annie? She controlled her rising sense of panic by telling herself he was communicating with Lionel and that she would hear the results of their dialogue tonight.

"But we're still going to meet with Lionel and talk this through," Amanda said, dusting off whatever negatives had landed on her shoulders. "I refuse to let the ridiculousness of my life ruin what could be a fantastic opportunity for you."

Annie vehemently disagreed. "No way, girlfriend. It took me twenty years to hook up with you again. If you think I'd let the notion of my name in lights and a gazillion dollars in profit take precedence over our rediscovered friendship, you are daft!"

Amanda laughed. Annie—and Aña—had always been able to make her laugh.

"Look," she said, "Lionel's a pretty clever fellow. He'll figure out a way to make this work." She was thinking of the trust funds he had set up, the way he arranged for Sam to take over the ownership and shield her and Beth.

"I know you may not want to tell me this, but is your mom okay?" Annie asked.

"She's fine, but don't ask me anything more about her." Annie agreed. Amanda eyed her carefully. "I had to change my name. Why'd you change yours?"

Annie could feel the sadness that had suddenly enveloped the room like a thick, gray fog. This was not an idle question.

"In junior high, some of the kids decided they didn't like Aña, too Cuban, I guess, so they called me Annie. I didn't object, so it stuck. I picked up Hart because, well, I was married for about a minute and a half."

"You were what?"

"Married. You know, do you take this man to be your awfully wedded husband . . ." She held her stomach as if the memory made her ill. "His name was Jack Hart. He was Mr. Smooth. Big car. Big muscles." She arched her eyebrows. "Big . . . everywhere. Hey! I was in love. We got drunk one night, ran off, and wound up in Maryland. When the hangover was gone, so was he."

Amanda laughed. "Not exactly a 'til death do us part type of guy."

"Not exactly. Anyway, I headed for New York with a few bucks in my pocket and a new name. It sounded Big Apple like, so I kept it."

Amanda's smile faded. "It didn't bother you, changing your name?"

"No. As you said before, I had a choice." She paused, pondering the matter more fully. "Besides, as an adopted child, I shied away from attaching my entire identity to the name Aña Colon because that's not who I am by birth. It's who my adoptive parents told me I was. I love them like crazy. They're the only parents I've ever known and the only ones I'll ever acknowledge, but bottom line: I'm someone else's baby, and until they show up to claim me, I'll never know who I really am."

When they were kids, Amanda and Annie never discussed her adoption. It didn't seem important. Over the years, it had obviously gained in importance.

"My name was my identity," Amanda said. "Erica Stanton Baird. It said where I came from, whom I belonged to and who I was. Suddenly, I couldn't be that person anymore. I had to be someone else." When she looked at Annie, her eyes were moist. "I changed my name six times before I was fifteen."

"How'd you do it?"

"You keep to yourself. And you learn how to keep a secret."

At nine years old, Annie hated being by herself for too long, and she was incapable of keeping a secret for more than a day, if that. The need to share and feel part of someone else was simply too strong. "It must have been lonely," she said.

Amanda's lip quivered. "You have no idea."

Annie realized that was true. She had grown up in a house that constantly overflowed with relatives and friends. Her parents had been childless for so long, they went overboard trying to enrich Annie's life. Wherever they took her—museums, concerts, movies, vacations—they took a friend or two or three. There were innumerable sleepovers, lavish birthday parties and celebrations. She couldn't recall a weekend without extra places at the dinner table. There was no way she could fathom Amanda's solitary existence.

"It must have been wonderful to be reunited with your father," Annie ventured, unsure about how much Amanda would, or could discuss.

"It took me almost five years to screw up the courage to confront him." Amanda smiled as she recalled that night at the Four Seasons, and all the nights since then. "But boy, am I glad I did." She thought about the pink camellias sitting in a bedside vase and how nice it was to have him here for dinner. "I can't tell you how terrific he is."

"Hey! No need to convince me. The man was willing to bankroll the Hart Line."

"*Is* willing," Amanda amended.

Annie shook her head. "Look, the last thing I want to do is compromise your safety."

A lump formed in Amanda's throat. How nice it felt to have a friend worry about her safety. "Knowing Lionel, he will have examined every angle, and that includes checking with the marshal assigned to our case. Believe me, my father's not going to do anything that would put you or me or himself at risk."

The restaurant was a small country French bistro awash in white-wood furniture and blue-and-white-checkered fabric. Stiff ladder-back chairs with ruffled cushions sat primly around each table like maiden aunts at a church bazaar. Copper pots and pudgy ceramic animals decorated the mantel of an enormous hearth that centered the room. Rough-hewn beams lined the ceiling, lavishly sluiced plaster covered the walls. The effect was that of a large, peasant kitchen shipped lock, stock, and wine-fermenting barrel to New York from a farmhouse in the Dordogne.

Amanda and Annie arrived at precisely seven-thirty. The entrance to the private dining room was through a short, dim hallway, up a flight of stairs; it completely bypassed the main room, precluding the possibility of anyone seeing them. The maître d' offered them a glass of the hearty Bordeaux Lionel had selected. Annie accepted with pleasure. Amanda declined. Even though it was hours away, she didn't like to drink before going on duty.

Half an hour went by. Lionel hadn't shown up. Their waiter brought them a plate of assorted cheeses and patés. Annie had a second glass of wine. Amanda was concerned. It wasn't like Lionel to be late.

By eight-thirty, Amanda was convinced something was wrong.

"I'm going to the town house," she announced, unconsciously patting her gun, making certain it was secure in its holster.

"I'll go with you," Annie said.

"No. You stay here in case he shows up." As Amanda talked, she searched the room for bugs, sliding her hand beneath shelves and chairs and the table, looking in light sockets and on the moldings that framed the doors and windows. "I have an uneasy feeling in the pit of my stomach." She pressed her back against a wall and sneaked a peek out the window, surveying the street for possible enemies. "Which," she said, lifting the seat cushions, "could turn out to be nothing more than hunger." She realized she was making Annie nervous. "I'm probably being my usual paranoid self and making a mountain out of a molehill. He said he was working on some papers. Maybe he simply lost track of time or we got our signals crossed."

"Right," Annie said, feeling the warm effect of the wine disappear and a chill invade the room. "I'm sure it's nothing."

"The room's clean," Amanda said, hoisting her backpack onto her shoulder and heading for the stairs. "I won't be long. Will you be all right?"

"Sure," Annie lied.

The truth was, she was terrified. Standing alone in that room, surrounded by invisible threats, it occurred to her that tonight she had walked through a door into a dangerous world of secrets and camouflaged identities and long-standing vendettas. Amanda knew the rules of this twisted game. She was an experienced player to whom it was second nature to look around corners and over her shoulder and under her bed. She was a policewoman who carried a weapon and wouldn't hesitate to use it. Not only didn't Annie know how to protect herself, but she didn't know what or whom she'd be protecting herself from.

Suddenly, Annie wondered what she had gotten herself into. And how, if ever, she'd be able to get out.

CHAPTER

FOURTEEN

Amanda was beginning to think she had been a cop too long. Dealing with crime and its grim aftermath on a steady basis had programmed her to have a pessimistic response to anything even vaguely out of the ordinary. In her defense, Lionel was annoyingly prompt. There was nothing vague about being more than an hour late. As she turned the corner on Madison and Seventy-seventh and approached the town house, her pace slowed. Her hand reached beneath her jacket and found her gun. She checked it, and returned it to its holster. Every nerve ending and corpuscle was on alert. Her eyes scanned the street on both sides. She looked down into stairwells and up at windows, behind trees and in front of buildings. Not even an elderly couple strolling arm in arm escaped her scrutiny.

She advanced slowly, from the opposite side of the street, checking the windows of the town house. There was a light on in the library and one of the fifth-floor bedrooms. Most of the staff was off on Sundays. Perhaps Thompson, who lived in the house, was spending the evening in his room. Or perhaps it was one of Lionel's bodyguards, resting in the extra staff room. Uncertain as to who was or should be present, she called Lionel's private line from her cell phone. She knew she shouldn't—it would allow a trace—but she was not about to walk into a trap if she could avoid it. The phone rang several times before his machine picked up. Amanda hung up without leaving a message. Quickly, she dialed the main number. If Thompson was home, night off or not, he wouldn't let a call go unanswered. Lionel once said he was sure that if awakened in the middle of the night,

Thompson's first words would be, "Baird residence." After ten rings, she disconnected.

Amanda thought about placing an anonymous call to the police and having the One-Nine check things out, but if she was overreacting and he had simply lost track of time, she'd feel terrible. False alarms wasted time, money, and manpower. She was debating striding up the front steps and ringing the bell when she remembered Lionel telling her about a secret entrance. He explained that the previous owner had a mistress and had created this so they could rendezvous whenever his libido called. Amanda struggled to recall the details. You came into the house on the basement level. A hidden panel in the small foyer outside of the kitchen opened onto a stairway that led to a false wall in the library. At the time, Lionel said he thought Amanda should know about it—just in case.

Well, she thought, this was as good a time as any to try it out.

Peering through the wrought-iron fence that guarded the steps leading to the service entrance, she noted with grateful satisfaction that the kitchen was dark. She readied her key and reached into one of the pockets of her backpack for a pair of latex gloves. When there was a lull in the traffic, she raced across the street, keeping her body low to the ground. Hurriedly, she opened the gate, slipped inside, and closed it behind her. A red light on a small panel to the right of the door told her the alarm was activated. Fortunately, Lionel had given her the code: 1669. It was easy to remember because it was based on her birth date, January 16, 1969. She punched in the numbers, unlocked the door, and swiftly stepped inside, closing the door behind her and reactivating the system.

The foyer was dark, save the residual illumination from a nearby streetlamp. She pressed her back flat against the wall so she could watch the window and see if she had been followed or was being observed. While she monitored the street, she made wide sweeps with her hand, searching for a crack that might indicate an opening. Each time a car passed by and a light pierced her shadowy cover, she held her breath and pressed closer to the wall. Finally, her fingers skirted what felt like a seam.

Carefully, but quickly, she nudged and pressed until the door gave way and opened onto another passageway submerged in a midnight pitch. She rummaged around her backpack for her keys which were attached to a tiny flashlight. Keeping its limited beam pointed at the ground, she groped for the banister and ascended the narrow staircase, one step at a time. Here, too, she hugged the wall.

By the time she reached the top of the stairs, her eyes had adjusted to the darkness. She shined the flashlight in front of her, spotlighting a handle that would push the door into the library. At eye level, she noticed the outline of a small rectangle with a knob at its center. Gingerly, she tugged on the knob. As she suspected, it was a peephole. She pulled it back slowly, in case there was someone on the other side with a howitzer pointed at the heart of this peekaboo. Fortunately, no one was looking back at her. The library was fully illuminated, and from what she could see there appeared to be no movement, but her range of vision was severely limited. She couldn't see the desk or the doorway.

She stuck her flashlight and keys in her pocket, slid her backpack off her shoulder, and stuffed it in the corner of the landing so it wouldn't tumble down the stairs. She drew her gun, balanced herself, pushed the door open with her foot, and burst into the room, arms outstretched, finger on the trigger of her .38. It took only seconds to sweep arms and eyes from left to right, only seconds before her gaze reached the desk. She gasped in horror. Lionel was sitting in his chair. He was leaning back. It looked as if he was napping, but the top of his head was missing. Pieces of bone and gray matter and tissue clung to the ceiling and the shelved wall behind him. Dark patches of blood stained the bindings of his prized first editions and pooled on the Aubusson at his feet. Cast-off spatters sullied the leather top on his Louis XVI desk and stippled his shirt.

Amanda's reactions were so intense they made her dizzy. She stumbled and had to catch herself on a chair so she wouldn't fall. Shaken to her core, she covered her mouth with her hand and swallowed a shriek as she fought for control and some way to comprehend the harrowing sight confronting her. She had seen this hundreds of times before, yet never before, because the woman who had entered this room was not the dispassionate policewoman, but a daughter who couldn't help but keen at the sight of her father's brutalized body.

Trying not to faint, she gulped for air and leaned against the chair until she felt steady enough to walk. Her body was quaking so violently that she locked and holstered her gun, frightened that she might fire it accidentally. Taking deep breaths, swallowing a spate of nausea, she forced her system to calm enough for her to function. All the while, her mind raced, one question leapfrogging over the other. *Should she call the police? An ambulance? Lt. Clarke? Beth? Sam? If she called 911, who would she say she was? Why was she here? How would she explain her connection to Lionel Baird?* Her head swooned from fear and indecision, but her gut told her not to call anyone yet.

Praying she could stand without falling, she advanced toward the desk, her hands automatically clasped behind her back, her vision blurred by tears. When she looked at Lionel, his mouth open and bloodied, his head split and pulverized like an exploded melon, she gripped her sides and sobbed. This man was her father, her elegant, gallant, sartorially splendid father, with his brains spewed around his favorite room, his pants stained with the contents of his bladder and his bowel, his life's blood splashed all over his Italian silk tie and English bespoke shirt.

His chair was drawn so close to the desk that his left arm still rested there, almost normally. His right arm hung down, his beautiful, gold-inlaid pistol dangling from limp, bloodied fingers. One didn't have to be a policewoman to call this a suicide, yet Amanda resisted. Inside, her head was screaming with disbelief, shrieking denials, obliterating any possibility of rational thought.

Why would he do this? Were there signs? Had she missed something? Could she have prevented this? Had she somehow caused this?

No! she responded vehemently. She made him happy. That's what he told her over and over again. That's what he had told her just last night. She brought joy into his life. Not this. Not death.

She reached out to caress her father's cheek, but her eye caught sight of her latex glove and instinct kicked in. She pulled back her hand, not wanting to compromise the scene. Her heart was pounding, but her head was beginning to clear. Lionel wouldn't do this, she insisted. He hated guns. He'd told her so. He was uncomfortable even holding a weapon. How could he put one in his mouth and pull the trigger?

Whether it was the result of years of training and on-the-job experience, or simply because suicide didn't make sense, Amanda willed herself to detach from the emotion of this ordeal and begin viewing it through the eyes of a forensics expert. She breathed deeply, choked back her sorrow, and struggled to collect herself. Wiping tears on her sleeve, she turned her attention to the body—not Lionel, her father, but the body of the victim.

His skin was purplish and waxy. His lips and nails were pale. The body was still warm, and there wasn't much evidence of rigor mortis, only a slight stiffening of the eyelids and neck. All were consistent with death that would have occurred anywhere within the past half hour to two hours. Reverting to type, Amanda went to fetch her camera from her backpack.

She didn't bother with a grid or a notation pad. There was no time. If someone was home, they could wander in. *Although if someone was home, why didn't they hear the gunshot?* Someone might have seen her enter the house surreptitiously and notified the police. For all she knew, there was a silent alarm that could be set to override the general system. Whatever, she held her Nikon up to her eye and followed basic forensic procedure, snapping off shot after shot, roll after roll, taking overalls from every angle, close-ups of the wound, and his hands and the desk and the surrounding area.

She thought it would be easier to look at Lionel through her lens, to see him as a subject and not a person, but the sight of his shattered body wrenched her insides. Nothing could provide enough distance to save her from the tidal wave of grief that threatened to drown her. She could take a thousand pictures with the longest lens and that man would still be her father. And his death would still be her tragedy.

Tears distorted the images in her viewfinder, but for the first time, she empathized with the family members of the victims she photographed. She'd never thought about them when she did her work. She'd never wondered whether any of them vomited or fainted or cried when they came upon loved ones mutilated by death. She'd never thought about how they felt when they were notified or how they felt days or weeks or months after. Now she knew they felt sick and frightened and angry and guilty. That their stomachs lurched and their bodies quaked and their hearts broke and their minds asked a million unanswerable questions. Now she knew what their nightmares looked like.

Habit compelled her to check her watch. She had been here seventeen minutes. She had to leave or risk being discovered. Swiftly, she gathered her equipment and returned it to her knapsack. Then, despite nearly 250 pictures, she scrutinized the room one last time, on the lookout for something that would tell her why Lionel had done this. Or why someone else had done this to him. She concentrated on the area around the desk. Logic dictated that whatever clues might have been left behind would be there.

A newspaper rested beneath Lionel's left hand. Amanda recognized it as that morning's *New York Times*. There was a sheaf of papers near his right hand that appeared to be the incorporation documents for the Hart Line Cosmetic Company. Another paper peeked out from beneath them, but Amanda couldn't see what it was.

She worried that it might be important, but if she moved anything, the CSU team that caught the case would know. She couldn't take the chance. Someone might connect her to Lionel—the maître d' of the bistro where they were supposed to have dinner, for instance—and she'd be asked questions she didn't dare answer. Later, when all the evidence was logged in, she'd check it out.

The locked drawer where Lionel kept his gun was open. *Where was the key?* Amanda scanned the floor around Lionel's body. It wasn't on the rug or on the desk or in either of Lionel's hands. When she looked to see if it had fallen into the drawer, she noticed the camera Lionel had brought to her apartment the night before. Her hands turned clammy beneath her gloves. What if that roll of film was still in the camera? It wasn't. The back of the camera was open and there was no film. Had Lionel taken it to New Jersey to be developed as he had planned? Or had someone else removed it? Either way, Amanda was in trouble. Her picture was on that roll. So was Beth's. Why would Lionel Baird have a roll of film with their pictures on it if they weren't connected to him in some way? If someone other than a Kodak lab had that film, it wouldn't be long before they figured out the truth.

She hated thinking about herself while in the presence of her dead father, but, she thought angrily, life was like that. Especially life in the program where self-preservation was the number one priority. No matter what happened—or to whom—you had to go on pretending to be who you were not so that somewhere out there, the faceless enemy wouldn't discover who you really were.

Her head was pounding, as was her heart, but she knew she had to leave. Lifting her hand to her mouth, she kissed the tip of her index finger and touched it to Lionel's cool, pale lips.

"Good-bye, Daddy," she whispered, wishing she had called him that more often. "I love you."

A fresh spate of tears washed her cheeks as she slipped through the secret door and turned away from the man who had given her life. As she tiptoed down the secret stairway, she continued to speculate about why he might have taken his. It didn't make any sense, she kept telling herself. He was happy. He spoke about the future, about having a son-in-law, grandchildren, the day that they would be free to go public with their relationship. She suspected he envisioned a rapprochement with Beth, maybe even a renewal of their romance. *What put that gun in his hand? What made him pull that trigger?*

She checked the street before letting herself out of the house. It was quiet, and unless someone was peering through the window of a darkened room, she felt safe in assuming her exit went unobserved. Once outside, she raced to the corner of Seventy-seventh and Madison, where there was a telephone booth. With her fingertips still protected by the latex glove, she dialed 911.

"I think something's wrong at 14 East Seventh-seventh," she said, disguising her voice by talking through the sleeve of her sweater. "I heard a shot." She hung up the phone and practically collapsed from nervousness. Not wanting to be anywhere near the town house when the police came screaming up the block, she headed for Lexington Avenue and the bistro where she'd left Annie.

No, she thought. She couldn't go there. Frantically, she called information on her cell phone, got the number of the restaurant, and dialed it up. The maître d' seemed happy to hear from her. He asked if everything was all right.

"Everything's fine," she said, straining to keep her voice even. "Is my friend still there?"

"Mais oui." He asked her to hold on while he went to get her.

It felt like an eternity until Annie picked up. When she did, Amanda could hear fear in her voice.

"What's going on?" she asked, tremulously.

"Meet me across the street."

"Okay. Should I take care of . . ."

"I'm sure Lionel gave them a credit card number. Just leave."

"Okay. I'll be right there."

Amanda waited in the doorway of a pharmacy that was closed for the night. When she saw Annie crossing the street, she stepped out of the shadows, waved briefly, and merged with some people walking by. She turned down toward Third Avenue. Annie followed. When they were out of sight of the bistro, Amanda stopped and waited for Annie to catch up.

"What's wrong?"

"Lionel's dead." Even as she said it, she couldn't believe it. "It looks like suicide."

"What?" Annie was stunned and incredulous. But as Amanda had done, she completely rejected the notion that he had taken his own life. "No way. He wouldn't off himself. Uh-uh."

"The gun was in his hand." Amanda thought it best not to describe the scene in any greater detail. Already, Annie was squirming.

"I don't care," she said. "He didn't do it. He had no reason to do it. Why would anyone who had a life like his snuff it out?"

Why indeed, Amanda thought. She was actually relieved that Annie's reaction was the same as hers had been. It validated her suspicions.

An ambulance screamed by them. The sight of it pushed Amanda to tears. Annie cried as well, as she embraced her friend and tried to comfort her. Both of them knew that comfort was all anyone could offer. There was no way to explain or understand why this had happened.

"Come home with me," Annie said. "You can stay at my place tonight."

Amanda shook her head and looked at her watch. It was a quarter to ten. "I'm going to work."

"Are you crazy? You're a wreck. You need to calm down. You need to take stock." She looked deep into Amanda's eyes and winced from the pain she saw there. "And you have to mourn."

Amanda shook her head and sucked in her breath, trying to stem her tears. "No. The best thing I can do is stick to my usual patterns. Besides, I'll be well protected while I'm on the job."

Annie shivered. She hadn't been in this world very long, but already, she hated it. Suddenly, she thought about what Amanda did. "How will you handle . . ."

"I will," Amanda insisted, seeing Lionel's distorted face, the devastation done to his head. "Because I have to." Her internal vision shifted to the open drawer and the empty camera. "If this wasn't suicide, someone's going to know that Lionel Baird and I know each other. It won't be long before they figure out why."

"Then you have to hide," Annie said, panic underscoring her words.

"I know," Amanda said, "but sometimes, the safest place to hide, is in plain sight."

The first case Amanda and Pete caught was a double homicide on the Lower East Side. Two members of the *Blanca Muerte* had been shot, laid out in a school playground, and sprinkled with so much Propaine they looked like sugared French toast.

"Whatever happened to clean executions?" Pete said as they circled the corpses.

Instead of the usual single shot to the head, these guys had been blasted with an assault weapon, probably an AK-47. Not only were their faces devoid of any discernible features, but their insides were spilled all over the foul line of the school basketball court.

Amanda set about taking her pictures quickly and silently, performing by rote. She focused, snapped, made notations in her book, focused, snapped, made additional notations and so on. Pete noticed she was quieter than usual and behaving like an automaton, but he figured everyone was entitled to a mood. Maybe it was that time of the month.

As he watched her move in slow motion, he recalled that the other night, she and Jake Fowler had been doing some kind of weird mating dance. Doyle's eyes narrowed as he considered the possibility that Jake had done something to hurt her. If he had, he'd better watch his ass. Pete Doyle protected his friends.

Speak of the devil, Pete thought as he saw Jake Fowler get out of a cab and approach the scene.

"What's with you Fowler? Are you color blind?" he shouted, pointing to the yellow crime-scene tape that cordoned off the area.

"I just can't stay away from you, Doyle. It must be that musky cologne you bathe in." Jake lifted the tape and scooted under it, unperturbed by Doyle's killer stare. "Believe it or not, big fella, I'm here on official business."

"Yeah. And I'm Brad Pitt researching a role."

"Doyle, Doyle, Doyle. You have no faith," Jake said, addressing Pete, but watching Amanda. "In case you've forgotten the details of my sterling résumé, I know a thing or two about the way the mob works. I prosecuted them. I reported on them. And as a private dick, I've tracked 'em, trailed 'em, and spied on 'em enough to know who goes to the potty when." He eyed the bodies. "You've got a war going on here, Doyle. The brass is smart enough to know they need every able-bodied soldier they can muster." He grinned at Pete. "And this, in case you don't know the difference," he said, pointing to his highly toned abdomen, while sneering at Pete's quaggy middle, "is an able body."

Pete snorted and went back to work, his watchful eye still trained on Amanda.

"Hey," Jake said. "How're you doing?"

Amanda was afraid to look at him. She had managed to keep her emotions in check, but they were so close to the surface, anything was liable to set her off.

"Fine," she mumbled from behind her camera, begging herself not to cry.

If Jake thought she seemed chilly or remote, he made no comment. "Welcome to another bloody episode of *Family Feud.*" He backed off, giving Amanda room to work, but his eyes remained fixed on the bodies of the two boys who would never be men. "Assault weapons. My, my. The conflict has stepped up a notch, hasn't it?"

Before Amanda could respond, the ME's van arrived, allowing her to busy herself getting the last of her shots before the bodies were removed. She finished, but before Jake could engage her in conversation, Pete approached the two of them, looking disturbed.

"Cleland just called in," he announced. "You know that Wall Street honcho they think's been washing drug money? What's his name, Lionel Baird? He was found dead tonight. Apparent suicide."

Amanda froze.

"Lionel Baird?" Jake was stunned, but as he absorbed the information and watched the latest victims of the drug wars being carted off in body bags, his brain began spitting out news bulletins and headlines. "Wasn't he accused recently of being connected to the Savianos in some way?"

"Yeah," Pete said. "I think he was."

Jake's recollections grew more lucid. "Chisolm accused him of laundering money for some guy named Della Robbia who turned out to be a tool of the Saviano Family. What do you think?" he asked Pete and Amanda, who was struggling valiantly to look as if all this was indeed news to her. "Could his death be tied in to this?" He pointed to the departing van.

The thought of Lionel's death being linked to anything as sordid as a gang war over drugs made Amanda physically ill. She hated to draw attention to herself, but if she didn't sit down, she was going to throw up or pass out. She walked over to the fence and sat on the ground, holding her knees up to her chin and taking deep breaths. Pete and Jake rushed over. Pete was particularly concerned. This wasn't like Max. He had never seen her so much as sway at a scene, no matter how gruesome. Max was always rock-solid, which was why the guys loved working with her. He leaned down and looked into her eyes, assessing her color. He pressed his wrist up against her forehead, checking for fever.

"What's up, Max?" he asked gently. "You okay?"

"I don't know," she said, cupping her head in her hands, squeezing her eyes shut to hold back her tears. "I'm feeling a little queasy. Just give me a minute. I'll be fine."

"What'd you eat tonight?" Pete said, his fingers on her pulse.

Amanda suddenly remembered she hadn't eaten anything. "Nothing," she said. "I wasn't really hungry. I had a big brunch." She knew that would satisfy Jake. Pete was another story. In his mind, only the dead missed a meal.

"Fowler, make yourself useful. Find a convenience store and get my partner something to eat."

"Aye, aye, Captain," Jake said, clicking his heels, but nodding to Pete as if to say, "good call."

He took off in the direction of Houston Street, where he was certain to find a restaurant or a *bodega*. Pete assured himself Amanda was okay and, at her insistence, went back to work. Within a few minutes, she was by his side, bursting with apology.

"Sorry, Doyle. I didn't mean to dog it."

"Don't be sorry, Max. Be grateful." He leered at her, evoking a smile, which was all he really wanted.

Jake returned with a container of minestrone soup, half a loaf of Italian bread, and information that didn't help Amanda's appetite.

"Baird's death is all over the news. Right now it's mostly bare-bones reporting, but they are beginning to speculate that perhaps there was some truth to those stories putting Baird in bed with the drug lords."

"I don't believe that for a minute!" Amanda snapped. "Those articles were gratuitous swipes with no other purpose than free publicity for a desperate politician and national exposure for a hack reporter."

"Down girl!" Pete said, somewhat taken aback. Max's normal demeanor was one of complete equanimity.

Jake also was unnerved by the force of her retort. "Yeah, really. It was simply conjecture at this point, a way of filling airtime. But wait until they pick up on what happened here tonight. Between this retaliation for the hit on Saviano's people and Baird blowing his brains out you've got to wonder if the incidents are related in some way."

"Like how?" she demanded.

"I don't know exactly, but those headlines didn't come out of nowhere. They may not have been one hundred percent accurate, but there must have been enough underlying truth for the *Times* and the other papers to have hopped onto the bandwagon."

That's what Lionel had said. Amanda's heart ached. She tried to get a grip on her emotions, but all she could see was Lionel's face, splashed with blood.

"I guess." She wanted to argue with him, to defend her father's name and reputation, but she didn't have the strength.

Mindful of Doyle's presence and Amanda's penchant for privacy, yet concerned, Jake put his arm around her and asked again if she felt all right. Fortunately, Pete wasn't a complete boor.

"We're just about done here," he said, making a graceful exit. "Why don't I finish up while you sit in the car with Fowler and eat that soup. Frankly, my dear, you don't look so swell."

Amanda smiled, grateful for his friendship and understanding. "I think I will," she said meekly.

For a while, they didn't speak. Amanda ate, Jake watched. When color had returned to her face and she felt steady enough, she thanked him for the soup and for introducing him to her family.

"I really did have a wonderful time."

"I'm glad."

He leaned against the door of the car, twisting his body so he could get a good look at her. She appeared haggard and beaten down. That afternoon when he left her, she was bubbly and beautiful and full of cheer. What had happened between then and now?

"According to Grace, you have an open invitation. Me? I have to apply for a seat at the table. Don't tell anyone I said so, but I'm not sure I have the votes."

Amanda tried to smile. "Oh, I think you've got Barry and Brenda on your side."

"Probably, but I can't bank on Jocelyn and Brad. It could come down to you, you know." That delicious, slow smile appeared. "So what do you say? Would you break the tie in my favor or vote against me?"

"Depends on my mood."

"Spoken just like a woman."

Amanda snuffled. "You've been spending too much time hanging around Pete."

Jake reached for her hand. "I'd much rather spend my time with you."

She pulled her hand away. She couldn't explain it to him, but this was not the time for flirting or advancing a romance. Her father was lying in the morgue with a tag on his toe. She couldn't identify him or claim his body. That would probably fall to that love-starved secretary of his, Fredda MacDougall. A wave of nausea came over her as she pictured Fredda staring at her father's disfigured face. She didn't want anyone to see him that way. She wished she hadn't seen him that way.

Jake wasn't bothered by her withdrawal as much as he was by the look on her face. It was sad and frightened and confused. "If I'm rushing you," he said, "I'm sorry, but I can't help it. You're simply the most spectacular woman I've ever met. You're smart and tough and soft and brave. You're kind to inquisitive, overprotective mothers and nice to adorable, but pesky kids. And, in case you haven't looked in a mirror lately, you're gorgeous, whether you're lying next to me in the altogether or sitting in a police car in your NYPD blues."

Touched to the point of being unable to verbalize a response, Amanda began to weep. Without asking any questions, Jake folded her into his arms and held her.

She tried to stem the torrent of tears that flowed onto Jake's chest, but it was impossible. She was too fragile, too frightened, too unsteady, too ravaged by the battle raging inside of her. For Amanda, it was the familiar clash between instinct and need. Her WITSEC training begged her to get out of the car and go off by herself, to mourn Lionel alone in her apartment, to get away from this man before she told him things she shouldn't. But WITSEC hadn't taught her how to deal with coming upon her father's body, of seeing her father's head blown off, purportedly by his own hand. WITSEC hadn't taught her how to hide grief this overwhelming or to camouflage distress this acute. At that moment, her heart, though shattered and bleeding, held more sway over her than her head, perhaps because the wound to her heart was so deep and so profound. It pleaded with her not to run, but to stay and continue to take comfort in Jake's arms. He was a loving human being. She had experienced that for herself and had witnessed it again this morning with his family. And he was a man who knew how it felt to lose a father.

So while her instincts continued to issue warnings, Amanda nestled against Jake and surrendered to her needs.

Somehow, Amanda managed to pull herself together and finish her shift, despite the protestations of both Jake and Pete. Jake left when Amanda and Pete were called to cover a robbery gone bad. Amanda promised to call him the next day. When they clocked out, Pete insisted on accompanying her home. It was nine o'clock in the morning when he dropped her off at her apartment.

"Don't you dare show up tonight unless you get some sleep. You look like shit, Max."

Amanda kissed his cheek. "Thanks, Doyle," she said, as she got out of the car and furtively checked the area around her building.

"Don't mention it," he called after her. Pete noticed the quick surveillance, scared and nervous-like. He stayed stubbornly parked until she was safely inside the building, then lingered at the end of the block for a few minutes to see if anyone peculiar approached the building.

Once inside her apartment, Amanda ran her usual checks for bugs and unwanted visitors. Everything seemed okay. Nonetheless, Amanda kept her gun at her side. She unzipped her backpack and, from a concealed pouch, retrieved a plastic bag loaded with black film cartridges. The sight of it mesmerized her. How had she managed to take so many pictures of such a horrible sight? Training, shock, curiosity, or perhaps even denial, whatever it was, she knew that these photographs would tell her what had happened to her father. Holding the bag away from her and staring at the cartridges as if they contained a contagion that unleashed, would provoke an epidemic, she headed for her darkroom.

When Amanda moved into this apartment, she had converted an unusually large closet in the living room into a darkroom; deep enough for her to work in with the door closed and wide enough to accommodate a cabinet to house her equipment, it was one of the reasons she had taken this apartment. Before she had a couch or a dresser, she bought and installed a special cabinet fitted with a pull-down table, shelves, storage space, and a special unit to hold her enlarger, which she painted matte black to minimize reflections. The only thing she didn't have was a wet bench to wash her prints, but the kitchen was only steps away. She was tempted to develop the pictures immediately, but knowing what she would see when the images developed, she conceded that she didn't have the strength, either emotional or physical. She closed the door, went down the hall to her linen closet, and stashed the bag in an empty detergent box.

When she returned to the living room, the message light on her answering machine summoned her. Annie had called three times. Beth had called, using one of her aliases. She sounded very upset; Amanda assumed she'd heard about Lionel. Tyler Grayson had called, also sounding rattled. He wanted to see her and asked her to please, please return his call. She would, but later. After she'd had a hot shower, a stiff drink, and some much-needed sleep.

Jake also had a raft of messages on his answering machine. His mother and sister wanted to grill him about Amanda. The district attorney wanted to arrange a meeting so they could continue their conversation about Jake's role in the mayor's new task force. Hallie Brendel wondered why she hadn't heard from him. He wondered why she would even wonder about that after all this time. But the message that intrigued him the most was the urgent call from Pamela Baird demanding to see him ASAP.

C H A P T E R

FIFTEEN

Off in the distance something buzzed, droning like a hungry insect homing in on a delectable patch of skin. Amanda swatted the air, her aim dulled by sleep. The buzzing grew louder, more menacing. Startled into wakefulness, Amanda jerked out of the arms of her slumber and sat upright, grabbing for the Remington that stood guard by the side of her bed. She pumped it and aimed it, fully prepared to blow away whoever or whatever dared to fill the doorway of her bedroom. Her breath came in short, nervous bursts, but her eye stayed steady over the sight. She waited for the intruder to show himself, but the portal remained empty. Amanda fought to clear her head. The noisome screeching grew insistent. Finally recognizing it as the buzzer from downstairs, she allowed herself to exhale. She slipped out of bed and, holding the shotgun by her side, padded to the intercom.

"Who is it?" she demanded.

"Tyler. I need to see you."

"Give me a minute."

"Fine. I'll wait down here if you like."

"Please."

Amanda ran to the bathroom, washed, threw on a light pair of sweatpants and a tee shirt, tucked the Remington under her bed, and let Tyler in. While he climbed the three flights, she made coffee. When she opened the door, his eyes were puffy and his complexion was the color of uncooked dough. He needed coffee as much as she did.

"Did you hear about Lionel Baird?"

He strode past her and into her apartment as if they were in the middle of a conversation instead of at the beginning. He was agitated, wandering about the living room as if selecting a place to sit presented a major dilemma. He eyed the couch and the chairs, assessing, considering, waiting for one of them to make him an offer. Ultimately, he settled on the couch, yet continued to fidget, shifting one throw pillow behind his back, another under his arm, then rearranging them again.

Amanda sympathized with his disquietude. Aside from the shock of hearing that someone you knew killed himself, Lionel *was* Baird, Nathanson & Spelling. The staff had to be reeling with concern about who would be taking over the helm, how that would affect the company, clients, individual jobs, the bottom line. The men in contention for the associate CEO slot had to be practically schizophrenic. Most, like Tyler, had praised Lionel to his face, while spewing all kinds of negatives behind his back. Now he was dead, and they were feeling embarrassed, perhaps even remorseful. At the same time, an enormous opportunity had just presented itself.

"I heard about it last night from the team that caught it," Amanda said, matter-of-factly.

"He shot himself." Tyler's face telegraphed disbelief. "Why would he do that?"

"I have no idea."

"Neither do I," he muttered, looking off track and puzzled.

Amanda excused herself and retreated to her kitchen. This was easier to talk about from a distance. Tyler didn't seem to notice her absence. He was too busy ruminating.

"I once heard that people who commit suicide don't want to die, they simply want to end the pain. What pain do you think Lionel Baird was in?"

Amanda bent over the sink and swallowed hard. She had to get a grip on her emotions. Everyone was going to be talking about Lionel. She had to find a way to control herself in public.

"The man had everything. What'd he have to be depressed about?"

Amanda wished she had an answer. She put the coffee on a tray and brought it into the living room. Tyler leaped to his feet like the gallant that he was, took the tray from her, and set it down on the cocktail table. Amanda poured the steaming black coffee and offered Tyler some seven-grain toast and black cherry jam from Sarabeth's. He declined, but she needed the sustenance.

"Your place is great," Tyler said, making a feeble attempt at polite conversation.

"Thanks." She glanced over her shoulder at the bouquet he'd sent. "Your flowers certainly help to brighten things up."

He nodded and smiled briefly, but his mind continued to drift elsewhere. As did hers. She thought about Tyler's flowers and remembered the pink camellias keeping sweet vigil by her bedside. She looked at Tyler sitting across from her on the couch and saw Lionel drinking wine, teasing her about boyfriends, complimenting her tapenade. Afraid that she might well up and invite unwanted questions, she lowered her eyes and blew on her coffee.

"It's the ultimate act of selfishness," Tyler said. "Bang! You're out of your misery while someone else cleans up the mess you left behind."

Amanda recoiled at his implied criticism. She wanted to defend Lionel against Tyler's charge, but she couldn't find her voice. Then again, she didn't think Tyler was expecting a response. He appeared to be having a conversation with himself.

"He had everything to live for," he went on.

"As far as you know," Amanda said, as if she, too, believed Lionel had taken his own life. Frankly, at that moment, she didn't know what to believe.

"That's true. I only knew him at work. Anything I knew about his personal life came from the gossip columns."

"Not exactly what I would call reliable."

Tyler looked sheepish, as if he had been caught reading a supermarket tabloid.

"Do you think the news about that Della Robbia guy might have pushed him over the edge?" If Amanda had to talk about this, she decided, she might as well get her own questions answered.

"Maybe. Sometimes people kill themselves on impulse." Amanda looked dubious. "Something sets them off, something that threatens to shame or humiliate them. Death looms as the only viable escape, so they take it."

"Was the evidence that incriminating?"

"Only to people who don't understand the business."

"People like me, you mean."

Tyler smiled apologetically. "With all due respect, yes. People like you. Look, we're in a bullish period when investors are taking big risks because they anticipate big rewards. Tons of money's flowing through the Street right now. Who's to say how much of it's being washed."

"Knowingly or unknowingly?"

"Both."

Amanda wondered if Tyler ever got his hands wet.

"Where do you think Hallie Brendel's getting her information?"

Tyler shrugged. "Any number of places. Don't forget, Lionel Baird was not Mr. Congeniality. He made more than a few enemies on his way up the corporate ladder."

Amanda winced. When Lionel was alive, she was better able to handle comments like that. If Tyler noticed her flash of discomfort, he didn't pursue it.

"Who knows? He may have been correct in assuming that the mob leaked that information to Chisolm. It makes sense. They'd much rather have the press yammering about Lionel Baird than whatever Little Ray Saviano is up to."

Amanda envisioned those two boys lying dead in the schoolyard. She could almost see the horror on their mothers' faces when they were told what had happened. Those boys may have been pushers and even murderers, but they were also their mothers' sons.

"Are you all right?" Tyler asked, beginning to worry about the doleful mask that seemed glued to her face.

She kneaded her brow. "Every now and then, my job gets to me." She sighed. "So much of it is about death."

"I didn't mean to depress you," Tyler said. "I was . . . I don't know, rocked by the news. I needed someone to talk to, and I thought of you." He smiled. She made an attempt to smile back. "Actually, I think about you a lot," he confessed. His pale gray eyes fixed on hers. "In case you haven't guessed: I'm falling in love with you all over again, Amanda Maxwell."

Amanda didn't know whether to laugh or cry. She didn't know if this was one of God's jokes, but just as her life was collapsing around her, two incredible men stepped forward to declare their affection.

"I'm touched, Tyler, really I am, but this just isn't a good time. I can't explain it, but I'm . . ."

As she searched for the right words, Tyler jumped to his own conclusions.

"Are you involved with someone else?" He was so crestfallen, she couldn't help but be flattered.

"Not exactly." She prattled because she didn't want to turn Tyler away. She simply wanted to put him on a shelf until this hurricane that was her life dissipated and she could welcome him as a suitor. "For reasons I'd rather not go into, the only person I'm involved with these days is me, and I'm a handful."

"Okay, I won't pursue it, but remember, I don't give up easily."

"I'm counting on that."

He glanced at his watch, probably seeking a graceful way out. "I have to get back to the office. Needless to say, it's bedlam."

"I'll bet." A thought occurred to her. "How's that Frieda Mac-Dougall handling this?" She deliberately mispronounced the name, hoping her question sounded spur of the moment.

"Fredda," he corrected. "And how do you know her?"

"I saw her being interviewed on television the other day. Something about an affair she had with a clerk who committed suicide rather than go to jail."

"Douglas Welch."

"I thought she came off sounding as if Lionel Baird was the love of her life, not Douglas Welch."

"She probably made the whole thing up."

"Really? You think so? Why would she do that?"

"Look at her," Tyler said with clear disgust. "She's a hideous-looking woman. She has to know that. Maybe she wants the world to think that she wasn't always a dreary spinster, that once, she was a desirable woman who carried on a passionate affair. Who can say? Who really cares?" Suddenly, he seemed impatient to leave. "I have to go. I'm sorry if I disturbed you."

Amanda took his face in her hands and brought his mouth to hers, kissing him sweetly. "You didn't disturb me at all, Tyler. I loved having coffee with you."

"It was nice," he said, kissing her back, loath to pull away. She watched him lope down the stairs, bolted the door behind him, cleaned up, and returned to her bedroom. Tired and upset, she lay down on the bed, trying to find solace in her pink-and-white aerie. She turned toward the nightstand where the pink camellias sat, reached out, and caressed the petal of one of the flowers. The velvety feel provoked such powerful memories that her eyes filled with tears.

She struggled to recall Lionel in life, but the image of him in death was too potent. Hard as she tried, she couldn't erase the sight of him lying in that chair, sullied with his own waste, splattered with pieces of his own brain. It was simply too wretched to contemplate, yet her mind refused to block it out or even blur its edges. She thought repression was supposed to shield the psyche from pain, erasing that which was too difficult to bear. Why did her mind insist on pushing those images of Lionel front and center?

Perhaps because despite the preponderance of evidence, she didn't believe he could or would do that to himself. Or to her.

Pamela Baird was grief-stricken. Last night, during an insufferable bout of insomnia, the movie she'd been watching was interrupted with a bulletin. Lionel's picture flashed on the screen, and her heart began jackhammering inside her chest; at that hour, it was doubtful that the bulletin was about one of his business coups. She gripped her bed jacket and hugged it close to her body, as if the chill she felt could be warded off by a marabou-trimmed coverup. When the commentator said, "Lionel Baird's death was the apparent result of a self-inflicted gunshot wound," Pamela heard a shriek. She pressed her hands against her ears, but the shrieking wouldn't stop. It took awhile to realize that she was the one producing the earsplitting squall.

When her hysteria subsided, she telephoned John and relayed the dreadful news. Half an hour later, he was at her apartment, with a doctor who administered a sedative.

"Did we do this to him?" she whispered, her body trembling.

"No, darling." He meant to reassure her, but on some level, he needed to convince himself that they were indeed blameless. He didn't like Lionel, but he'd never wished him dead. Penniless, maybe. "Lionel had a host of demons."

Pamela blubbered in agreement. Everyone knew Lionel was positively tormented over the deaths of his first wife and daughter. Of course, only Pamela knew the extent of that wound. It was huge and omnipresent and intrusive. Even when she and Lionel were in the throes of passion, she could feel the sainted Cynthia Stanton Baird lying next to them.

Though Lionel insisted his feelings were born of grief, Pamela sensed a certain amount of guilt. She reasoned that if she could uncover the genesis of that guilt, assuage it and eliminate it from their marriage, Lionel would finally allow the dear, departed Cynthia to rest in peace and view Pamela as the real, true love of his life. It was with that honorable goal in mind that she had befriended the hapless Ms. MacDougall. Naturally, Fredda was only too happy to fill Pamela in on the details about Lionel's activities back then, seasoning her recollections with the rumors surrounding his possible involvement with her lover, Douglas Welch.

For a long time, Pamela kept that information stored in a compartment labeled: in case of emergency. Threatened and hurt, she had been only too happy to dip into her store and feed those rumors to Hallie Brendel. Which had spawned the series of articles in the *Telegraph*. Which may, in turn, have precipitated Lionel's death. She began to weep, almost convulsively.

"If something we did put that gun in his hand," she sobbed, unable to imagine herself functioning in a world without Lionel, even more incapable of dealing with the realization that she might in some way be culpable, "I'll never be able to forgive myself. Or you."

John bristled. "Lionel did this to himself, Pamela. We had nothing to do with his death, do you understand that?"

Pamela only understood that the man she loved was gone and that the man she was with could not have cared less.

John stayed with her until she fell asleep, then left rather than face the horde of reporters who would surely be camped outside Pamela's building in the morning. Pamela would be upset when she woke up, but he had a campaign to consider. When Lionel was alive, tarring him was a benefit. Now that he was dead, promoting the story became a liability. Well, John reasoned, if you can't say anything nice . . . say as little as possible.

Despite the sedative, Pamela's sleep was fitful. Pleasant dreams mingled with repellent nightmares as her subconscious grappled with the why of Lionel's death. Sleep created a fiction in which she played the heroine, stalking antagonists and slaying villains who sought to harm her hero. Now and then, the villain showed a face; sometimes it was hers. Pamela tossed and turned, trying to escape the imagined criticism and avoid condemnation. Her psyche must have been plumbing the depths to find absolution, because at some point, it dredged up the name, Max, and painted the devil's face on it. Pamela chased the image of this youthful Fury, looking to expunge it from her dreams, but the faceless sorcerer continued to haunt. Who was she? Was it simply her youth that had held Lionel in such thrall? Or was it something else, something far more insidious?

When Pamela finally awoke it was in a bath of triumph, not because she had bested her enemy, but because she had managed to cleanse herself of blame. "It wasn't my fault" became a mantra she repeated over and over again, washing away any and all responsibility, transferring the sin onto the young woman with whom Fredda claimed Lionel had been smitten.

As she sipped her tea, hoping the chamomile would soothe her frazzled nerves, Pamela worked at validating her theory that this vixen bore some responsibility for Lionel's demise. When she reflected on her own encounters with Lionel over the past six months, she admitted that he'd been belligerent, but that wasn't new. Lionel was never an easy man to live with. She attributed some of that ill-mannered behavior to their divorce proceedings: he was being a bully because no matter what he said, she didn't believe he really wanted to dissolve their relationship. She thought he was punishing her for being with someone else. When she'd suffered enough, he'd demand that she break up with John—which she would do in an instant—then he'd invite her back into his life and his bed.

Quite suddenly it seemed, their meetings turned contentious. He stopped returning her phone calls. He was abrupt if they did speak. He grew short with her, snappish, cruel at times, like that night in the gallery when he was so awful she'd had no choice but to chasten him by telling Hallie Brendel what she knew.

Thinking about it now, it seemed obvious. Just about the time *Max* entered his life, he became uncharacteristically mysterious about what he was doing and with whom. For a man who'd never been shy about flaunting the many women in his life, this should have sounded an alarm. Fredda, who knew about his latest strumpet, should have worried about how furtive he'd become. Pamela, who'd been told about Lionel's latest paramour, should have realized that such extreme reticence to gloat was a sign of trouble. Both of them should have paid more attention to Max.

While they were doing nothing but wringing their hands, this woman cast a spell over Lionel, bewitching him in a way that drained him of everything sensible, leaving him exposed and vulnerable. Then she must have pushed him to do things he couldn't live with, pushed him until he hurt people he couldn't live without—like her—pushed him until he had no other choice but to put a gun in his mouth and pull the trigger. It was the only explanation Pamela could come up with: The devil made him do it.

Shaken, Pamela scrambled under her covers, seeking refuge and answers. Finding neither, she allowed her mind to race, becoming a spectator almost, as she vaulted over the hurdles that had littered her recent past and caused her to stumble: precarious finances, insecurity, jealousy, an unrequited love that had pushed her to do terrible things simply for revenge. Anger interrupted her grief and self-flagellation as she blamed Lionel for her descent into commonness. It was his fault that she had turned into a harridan, his fault that she had allied herself with his archenemy, his fault that she had been desperate enough to wash their dirty laundry in public, his fault that their divorce . . .

Pamela sprang up as if someone had set fire to her feet. Her eyes bugged and her breath stalled somewhere between her lungs and her nose. *Their divorce.* Her green eyes narrowed as color returned to her cheeks and her mouth curled into a Cheshire-cat smile. She and Lionel weren't divorced. That made her his widow. And his heir.

She grabbed the phone and dialed her lawyer. He'd heard the news and had anticipated her call. Yes, she and Lionel were still married. According to the law, that entitled her to a sizable portion of Lionel's estate, whether he bequeathed anything to her or not. Yes, Pamela Richardson Baird was going to get what was coming to her.

Then she called Jake Fowler, because she wanted Max to get what was coming to her.

Beth thought she'd go mad. Sam was out of town. Amanda was out of reach. And Lionel was dead. She knew better than to break existing patterns, but she was in no condition to teach a class. She called in sick, because that's what she was.

From the moment she heard about his death, she remained glued to the television, switching channels seeking news or commentary. She listened to anyone and everyone who had anything to say about his suicide. Perhaps someone could tell her why this man would have taken his life. Like everyone else, she was at a loss.

The Lionel Baird she had been married to never would have taken his life; he'd been too egotistical to believe the world could exist without him. The Lionel Baird she knew today was a softer, more contented fellow, a man who was reveling in the second chance life had provided, a man who was looking forward, not some lost soul staring into a dead end.

Amanda didn't know it, but since their reunion in Wisconsin, Lionel had taken to writing Beth—through the Marshals Service, of course. Most of his letters were about Amanda: either telling Beth what an extraordinary young woman their daughter was or asking what kind of child she'd been. Passages glowed with pride over her art and, although grudgingly, about how good she was at "that ghoulish activity she calls a job." He reported on her show at the gallery, sent photographs of the bleakscapes he'd bought and clippings of the reviews. He recounted his meeting with Annie Hart, availing Beth of both his impressions and his reservations. And he kept her abreast of any conversations he and their daughter had about prospective beaux. Weeks before Amanda had that conversation with Beth about bells and chimes, Lionel had delighted her with his version of the men's résumés. He'd made both of them sound too idiosyncratic to be suitable marriage material, but Beth assumed that was because Lionel couldn't bear the thought of Amanda committing herself to any man—other than himself.

He frequently inquired about her, walking that tightrope between prying and asking. Knowing Lionel, Beth appreciated the effort it took for him not to sound proprietary. To his credit, he managed, which was why she answered all of his questions, except the one he left unasked: Could you ever love me again?

Though she would never admit this to anyone, including Amanda, his letters made her feel girlish and giddy. Lionel was a romantic and while he was wooing her between the lines, the sentiment within those spaces was vivid and palpable. So much so that they had become a burr in Sam's ego. He delivered them, so he knew of their existence, but because Beth deemed them personal and private, he knew nothing of their content.

Normal procedure required that she return the letters to the Marshals Service. Beth complied, but bent the rules. She read the letters until she'd memorized every word, then shredded them in front of Sam, rather than provide an opportunity for him to read them. That bothered Sam, and he said so, but his pique didn't persuade Beth to share Lionel's musings with him. Sam didn't push. He knew better. He and his colleagues had taught Beth how to shut off her emotions if the need arose. To quit a situation if it became uncomfortable or appeared menacing. They had trained her to let go without looking back. Which was why if Sam had any objections, he kept them to himself.

All those years underground had been hard on Beth, but they had toughened her. The burdens of extended concealment were heavy. Eventually, anxiety and hardship built up, solidifying into a thick, protective shell almost impossible to penetrate. Like a turtle, Beth poked her head out and crawled slowly through the day-to-day. But when the light was too bright or she sensed danger ahead or she simply didn't want to cope with the charade that was her life, she retreated into that dark and silent place where she could be alone. And be herself.

Lionel's letters became an invitation to slide out from beneath that weighty encumbrance. Free, if only for those few minutes it took to read them, they enabled Beth to fly back to those years when her parents and her brother were alive, when she and Lionel were married, when the biggest problem she had was juggling a briefcase, a baby, and a bag of groceries. Free to wander within the confines of those pages, she allowed herself to dream of living a normal life, of doing the things normal families did, like sharing stories of the past and showing pictures of relatives and being honest with friends.

She loved Sam and doubted that she'd ever leave him for Lionel, but as she told Amanda: Sam was her choice in this life. If that life changed, there might be other choices. She might make other decisions.

But Lionel was dead. Now, she'd never know.

The one-hour photo shop was busy. It was near closing, and the clerk at the counter was tired and hassled. He took customers' tickets, found their pictures, took their money, and moved on to the next, eager to clear out the store so he could go home. One man paid for his pictures and stepped to the side so he could flip through the pack. No one paid any attention, because nothing seemed out of order. Most people rifled through their snapshots before leaving the store. They were anxious to see what had been captured on film.

But this man was not most people. And these were not his pictures.

C H A P T E R
SIXTEEN

New York's criminal population must have taken a sabbatical from wreaking havoc on the city, because it was a slow day at the Crime Scene Unit. When Amanda clocked in that morning, she was told that unless they were needed in the field, she and Pete were scheduled to spend the day in the office. For Amanda, who wanted to find out as much as she could about Lionel's death, that was good news. Being inside, she'd have access to the files and would be able to nose around.

Another bit of good news was that Cleland Jones and Harpo Foley, the team on-site, were also working in-house. And, as she should have expected, this case was all anyone could talk about. When Amanda returned to the office after visiting the coffee wagon, Cleland had already begun regaling his cronies with the details of their celebrated suicide.

The ballistics report indicated that the .38 slug they found plugged into a ceiling molding bore the markings of the revolver in Lionel's hand. The roof of his mouth and the fingers of his right hand had powder burns consistent with near contact firing of a weapon. The path of destruction, as well as the flight of the bullet, were also consistent with a gun leveled at the roof of his mouth. An initial toxicology screen ruled out alcohol, narcotics, and ordinary poisons. Testing for anything more exotic required special orders and the ME had ruled out additional lab time.

The report from the Homicide guys at the Nineteenth Precinct also seemed to substantiate suicide. The entrance to the library was locked. The security system was armed. The victim was the only one in the house. According to the staff, Sunday was an off day for everyone except a bodyguard; on duty that night, Bruno Vitale.

Pete asked, "Was Vitale the one who called in the 911?"

Cleland thumbed through the report. "No. It was a woman. Claimed to be a neighbor, but the canvass hasn't found anyone who admits to the call."

Harpo, a young man whose mop of curly strawberry blond hair earned him his nickname, shrugged. "No surprise there. No one wants to get involved with anything messy, especially in that part of town."

Grateful that no one pursued the matter, Amanda asked, "Was the bodyguard in the house?" She was curious about the light in that upper-floor bedroom.

"Nope. He showed up just after the blues arrived."

"So where exactly was this Hercules-for-hire when Baird was blowing his brains out?" Pete dismissed high-paid strongmen as bar bouncers in fancy suits. He was not alone in that opinion.

"He said the old man planned to spend the night working and asked him to run out and get dinner."

That fit, Amanda, thought. Lionel never brought a bodyguard along when he met her.

Harry Benson, who had strolled in several minutes before, sounded skeptical. "That's fifteen minutes, tops. What'd Baird do? Ask Vitale to pick up a pie, stick the gun in his mouth, and wait to hear the door close before pulling the trigger?"

Cleland held up his hand to silence the comments coming at him. "Vitale went downtown to a restaurant in Little Italy."

"Little Italy?" Pete hooted, his eyebrows raised. "Were all the pizzerias on the Upper East Side closed for vacation? Or was Vitale bucking for a raise?"

Cleland tried to keep a straight face. "He went to get Baird's favorite dish: Il Cortile's sausage and peppers."

"Well, ex-cuuuuse me!"

"Muzzle it, Doyle."

"Who's on the case from the One-Nine?" Amanda asked.

Harpo answered. "Green and Moran."

"Does Vitale's story check out?"

"Seems to."

That meant not every t was crossed.

"Who took the pictures?" Amanda prayed she sounded casual, one professional to another.

"Want to come into my darkroom and admire my talent?" Harpo leered.

Amanda eyed him as if he had just opened a raincoat and flashed her. "You're pitiful."

Being one of the few women on staff, she accepted some off-color comments and lecherous looks as part of the ordinary course of things. She wouldn't tolerate that sort of behavior from everyone, but she knew where these guys stood. Cleland, Harry Benson, Harpo, and especially, Pete, considered her a friend and a respected colleague. There was a difference between teasing and harassing. Amanda knew which was which. So did they.

"Do you have the pictures here or are they at the lab?" Pete was as curious as she was.

Harpo said he got them back that morning.

"For crissakes, Foley, do you need an engraved invitation?"

"Awright, awright." Harpo extracted a thick folder from a pile on his desk, pushed everything else aside, and started to lay out the pictures.

Amanda steeled herself before approaching his desk. Confronting her was Lionel as she first saw him: from a distance, his body limp, his head pulpy, his immediate surroundings spotted with bodily debris. She stood alongside the others, trying not to show any more emotion than she might if they were looking at an anonymous victim. It was almost impossible, but she managed.

Knowing she was too involved to view the situation clearly, she listened carefully to everyone's musings. They were professionals with no preconceived notions or bias. Unfortunately, their conclusion was the same as the Homicide detectives: suicide. No note. No apparent reason. No sign of any witnesses. Even so, Harpo said Caleb Green planned to visit the scene again. He didn't like neat, easy cases, even suicides, especially when victims were high-profile personalities with everything to live for.

"What's Green after?" Pete said. "A shot at second-grade? Baird's reputation was headed for the crapper. The press was onto him like a dog with a bone. If he did do something nasty, and he knew it was about to come out . . . hey! That could be motive enough."

"That Brendel broad accused him of being a longtime laundry-man." Harry Benson, one of the more thoughtful men at the CSU, seemed to be cogitating. "If there was any meat on that, the Feds would've been all over him. And they're not."

"That you know of. Maybe the net was about to close," Pete said.

Benson wasn't convinced. "I don't see Brendel as some Woodward or Bernstein investigative type. She's a wanna-be who's being manipulated by that blowhard, Chisolm."

"Okay, so then why does a guy who has everything off himself?"

Benson rubbed his chin and studied the pictures. "*We* think he had everything. Maybe *he* didn't think so. Remember, the guy lost a wife and daughter twenty years ago in a really ugly explosion. That's enough to give someone major-league guilt. Multiply that by twenty years, and you could have a real nut job." His forehead crinkled as he ruminated about Lionel's life. "I mean, look at his marital record. Two divorces and a third pending. He was not exactly living in Happily-Ever-After-Land."

"Has anyone questioned the soon-to-be-ex-Mrs. Baird?" Pete looked from one to the other. No one seemed to have an answer.

Cleland checked his notes. "According to Moran, Pamela Richardson Baird was going toe-to-toe with the late Lionel. Their divorce proceedings were not exactly amicable."

"Amicable or not, if they weren't divorced, she's his widow."

Amanda was suddenly very curious about Pamela's whereabouts. "By the way, where was she Sunday night?"

Judging by the expressions on their faces, everyone else was wondering the same thing.

"Probably at some fancy-dress ball with a thousand witnesses."

Cleland looked down at his notepad. "Actually, Doyle, she was at home." Dramatic pause. "Alone."

Pete crossed his arms and offered a quick, oh-yeah nod. "Sounds like an airtight alibi to me."

"Anyone visit Mr. Baird's town house that evening?" Amanda wanted to know if a nosy neighbor might have spotted her entering or leaving.

Foley shook his head, causing his curls to bob up and down. "Not according to the canvass or Vitale, but he claims he didn't come on duty until five."

"Caleb's questioning the butler and the other two bodyguards."

Amanda sipped her coffee, trying to remain in the background, which was difficult because she had a thousand questions, the most important of which was: Could Lionel have been murdered? While no one voiced those exact words, they spent the morning dancing around the possibility; if they couldn't justify a suicide, it had to be homicide.

The consensus was that the articles in the *Telegraph* weren't damaging enough to put a gun in the hand of someone as powerful as Lionel Baird. Men like Lionel had the resources to wriggle out of white-collar crime arrests and resurrect even the most savaged reputation. And, as Amanda pointed out, he'd been eviscerated by the press before.

None of them knew enough about his personal life to project whether or not a broken heart would be motive enough to shatter his brain, but they explored that possibility. They wondered why Lionel's latest divorce was so slow in coming and what Pamela Baird had up her sleeve. That led to speculation about mistresses coming forward or other sordid details of Lionel's sex life being fed to the scandal-starved Hallie Brendel. Pete squashed those theories with another of his class-conscious observations: Mistresses and scandal were the norm among the rich and the royal.

Amanda nodded in agreement, but inside, she couldn't stand to hear Lionel discussed this way, as if he was a chapter in a psychology textbook, with stereotypical habits, problems, and solutions. She didn't believe there was anything textbook about his death, which was why she longed to dispel those rumors of mistresses and dismiss any hint of tawdry scandal. But she couldn't. Just as she couldn't mourn her father in public, she couldn't defend him. She couldn't explain that Lionel's heart was full, not broken. That his daughter and his first wife were an integral part of his life, not a painful memory. And that he was very much looking forward to the future, not wallowing in the past.

All she could do was what the others were doing: Stare at the pictures and wonder why?

"This is rather awkward," Pamela said, delicately dabbing the corners of her eyes.

For a woman who professed to be in deep mourning, Jake noticed that her manicure was fresh, as was her dye job. Obviously, certain salons made condolence calls.

"Then again, my circumstances are awkward." She sighed and leaned forward so she could rest her hand on Jake's knee. "Whatever I say to you is in the strictest confidence, isn't it?"

Jake assured her that it was.

"I think my husband was murdered. I want you to find his killer."

Jake was stunned, but he shouldn't have been. She wasn't the only one who found it hard to believe that Lionel Baird took his own life, Jake included.

"The police are fairly certain it was suicide." He had stopped off at the One-Nine and spent a few minutes with Caleb Green before heading over here. Caleb had shared the ME's findings with him. Jake saw no need, however, to share them with Pamela.

"They don't know Lionel as well as I do." She sniffled, but her eyes were hard. "He was too vain to ever allow anyone to find him so, well . . . so, splattered about."

Interesting point. Jake recalled the evening at Lloyd Franks's gallery. Lionel Baird was immaculate, every hair in place, his tie perfectly centered, his skin buffed and well cared for. Also, while Jake had been doing the hand jive with Hallie and Pamela Baird, he'd been eavesdropping on Lionel's conversation with Franks. He was unbelievably precise about where he wanted Amanda's bleakscapes hung, how many inches down from the ceiling and in from the side, when he wanted them delivered, and by whom. A man that anal probably wouldn't have been comfortable being discovered in such a mess. Then again, by the time someone reaches the point where he's willing to take his own life, he's beyond worrying about how he'll look when he's found.

"And," she said, her mouth tight with the shame of rejection, "there's no way he would've let me win."

"I beg your pardon?"

"As you know, we were in the middle of a divorce." Her lips pursed from the sour taste those proceedings left in her mouth.

Jake sought to refresh his memory. "Contentious, yes?"

"Very."

"I'm sorry, I don't recall if you ever told me the major roadblock."

"I signed a prenuptial agreement without benefit of counsel. Lionel insisted it was valid. I vehemently disagreed." Her attention strayed for a moment, visiting a less angry place. "No one agrees with me, but sometimes, I think he was dragging these proceedings out because he didn't really want a divorce."

Her lower lip trembled as she looked at Jake and silently pleaded for confirmation. He felt for her. She looked pathetic: a well-heeled woman of a certain age, surrounded by the accoutrements of status and success, as insecure as any pimply adolescent.

"Forgive me for joining the naysayers, but from what you told me during our other sessions, your divorce had reached a point where it was only about money. The dissolution of the marriage was a foregone conclusion."

She nodded, slowly, sadly. "Once upon a time, Lionel and I had a very passionate relationship." She lowered her eyes and rolled the edges of her handkerchief around in her fingers. "When it faded, my world became a wasteland."

"But then you and Senator Chisolm found each other," Jake prompted. He hated playing Dear Abby, but sometimes the job required it.

She rebounded on cue. "True, but Lionel was as jealous and competitive as he was passionate. He could go and do whatever he wanted with whomever he wanted, and I was not permitted to complain. But when I found sanctuary in the arms of another man, particularly one he considered an arch rival, he was not happy." Her momentary look of triumph was a sight to behold. "If I wanted my freedom, he was going to make me fight for it."

"Did you?"

"Nobly." She lifted her chin and held her pose, waiting for the photographer to capture her regal profile for the cover of *Time*. Her reign as Woman of the Year ended abruptly when she remembered something. "We were scheduled for another round next week."

"To finalize the agreement?"

"I doubt it."

"So, what did you mean before, when you said that Lionel wouldn't let you win?"

"We weren't officially divorced. Lionel's death made me his widow."

"Which," Jake interjected, following her train of thought, "entitles you to two-thirds of his estate."

"Which he knew." She looked rueful as she said, "Believe me, Mr. Fowler, judging by his mood the last few times we encountered each other, Lionel never would have allowed that to happen." She could still feel Lionel's slap of dismissal that night at the gallery. She could hear the frost in his voice and see the disgust in his eyes. "No matter how distraught he was, before he put that gun in his mouth, he would've made damn certain those divorce papers were signed, sealed, and delivered!"

Pamela was wallowing in self-pity and an exaggerated sense of self-importance, but since Lionel's death appeared inexplicable, any element was viable.

"Even if he cut you out of his will," Jake said, thinking out loud, "you could contest it."

"Exactly. The law doesn't care whether or not we were happy." Something tickled her memory. "Since he has no children, I might even be able to claim the remaining third, although that's highly unlikely." Her voice dropped as she wandered off. "Knowing Lionel's mammoth ego, he probably buried most of his money in some irrevocable trust earmarked for a hospital wing or a museum or some other lavish means of memorializing himself."

Jake was certain he heard a calculator whirring, adding and subtracting.

"Other than his vanity and your belief that he wouldn't have left his estate vulnerable," he said diplomatically, "what makes you think this was something other than suicide?"

She stared at him as if he was either innately stupid or had taken momentary leave of his senses. "Because while there were plenty of people with reason to kill him, including me, Lionel had no reason to want to die!"

"Mrs. Baird, Mr. Baird put a gun in his mouth, pulled the trigger, and blew off the top of his head. There was no indication that anyone was in the room with him, but even if there was, he had a loaded gun in his hand. He could've defended himself."

She nodded and waved her hand at him, impatiently. She had considered that and dismissed it as irrelevant. Jake didn't see how. He pressed on, trying to inject some much-needed logic into the conversation.

"Only one bullet was found. According to the coroner, it traveled through Lionel's brain before lodging in the library ceiling. It was fired by the gun in Mr. Baird's hand. Also, it was the only bullet fired from that gun. How do you reconcile those facts with your theory?"

She couldn't, but rather than back down—he guessed she was headed in another, as yet unrevealed, direction—she offered a more esoteric explanation. "There are other ways of murdering a man."

Jake wanted to groan. She was turning cryptic. Jake didn't deal well with cryptic.

"I think someone was pushing Lionel hard up against a wall, making him feel he had no way out."

"Other than you and Senator Chisolm?" He couldn't resist.

The room temperature plummeted. Jake kept his eyes fixed on her face, despite the chill.

"Lionel understood that John's comments were political, not personal."

"Sorry, Mrs. B. I watched that press conference. He took those articles very personally."

She squiggled about on her chair as if something had spilled and wet her skirt.

"And I regret that," she said at last, "but Lionel was accustomed to battling in that testosterone-flooded arena. None of that jousting would have inspired suicide. If anything, it stirred his juices." She shook her head. "In my opinion, he was being pressured about something more important, more potentially devastating, than business."

They were about to get to the point of this visit. "And that would be?"

"His manhood." She arched an eyebrow, hoping Jake caught her drift. He did. "I believe he was being coerced by someone who was dragging him around by his . . . pride."

Jake's expression warned, there'd better be more.

"Lionel was seeing a young woman. A much younger woman."

Jake sighed. Pamela sounded like a helium balloon that kept coming untethered. She'd float off into the distance, he'd pull her back. She'd float off again. He would have to ground her again.

"Do not dismiss this!" she snapped, annoyed by his obvious skepticism. He was on her payroll. He should have been an automatic believer. "I'm telling you there was something strange about their relationship. For one thing, he kept it secret, and Lionel was never secretive about his *affaires de coeur.*" Bitterness painted her lips into a tight line. "He derived too much pleasure out of throwing them in my face. Also, this nymphet was different than his other women. Plainer, with absolutely no chic."

Pamela's jealousy was so obvious it was embarrassing. She must have been mindful of that, because she moved ahead quickly.

"Once he took up with her, it was as if he'd undergone a complete metamorphosis."

The investigator in Jake was willing to bite. "In what way?"

"He changed habits that had been inviolate. He went on trips without having his assistant, Fredda, book them. He flew commercial airlines! He went out without a bodyguard. He took long drives without the benefit of his chauffeur. He stopped frequenting his favorite restaurants. He'd accept invitations to charity functions and dinner parties and then not show up. And over the past several weeks,

Fredda said Lionel was on the phone with his lawyer more often than usual."

"Maybe your hopes were going to be realized."

"That's kind of you to say, Mr. Fowler, but according to my attorney, a reconciliation was not in the works."

In fact, her attorney said, after a brief conversation with Lionel's attorney, his guess was Lionel hadn't left her a dime.

"I know this is unpleasant, but with all due respect, Mrs. Baird, Lionel was good-looking, charming, cultured, and loaded. There's nothing strange about a young woman falling in love with a rich, older guy who wines and dines her."

"Romances require sex, Mr. Fowler." She granted him a nod; she assumed he knew as much. "May-December romances with lusty, young women sometimes push older men beyond their capabilities." Her face was awash with wishful thinking. "Perhaps Lionel wasn't able to perform on that level."

Jake considered pointing out that lusty and young were two qualities known to arouse men who were advancing in years, but he decided the better part of valor was to leave that unsaid.

"Even if he couldn't . . . perform, so what? If she wasn't happy, or satisfied, she could've dumped him."

"She was not of his station," she stated with authority. "Women like that don't dump men like Lionel. She seduced him, discovered his weakness, then tormented him with his inadequacies."

"To what end?"

She shrugged her shoulders helplessly. "To get him to finalize his divorce with me and marry her. To negotiate a hefty payoff. I don't know. That's what I want you to find out."

The desperation in her eyes was unsettling. Whoever this other woman was, she'd better watch her back. Pamela Baird was on the hunt and loaded for bear.

"If either of those two suggestions was accurate, why would she want Lionel dead? From her point of view, it's a win-win. Either she'd be married to a rich man and have unlimited credit on her Amex card, or she'd be making a healthy deposit in her bank account."

"What if neither of those was about to happen," Pamela persisted. "What if he told her he was getting a divorce, but had no intention of marrying her? And no intention of giving her any money. What if he was dumping her? She might have threatened to sell her sordid little bedtime story to the tabloids or write a book, like that loathsome stableboy who squealed about his liaison with Princess Diana." Her eyes watered, but the angry fire in them was not extinguished. "As you so cruelly reminded me, Lionel was already being dragged through the mud. Perhaps he couldn't deal with another humiliation."

That was a possibility. "Okay, but you're describing possible motives for suicide, Mrs. Baird, not murder."

"Some way, somehow, she put that gun in his hand!"

"Metaphorically speaking, of course."

"Whatever!" She was shaking with frustration. "You're supposed to be a detective. As such, you're supposed to look for weapon, motive, and opportunity. The weapon was Lionel's. He kept it in his desk. This woman was his lover. She had access to his home and ample opportunity to put that gun in his hand—metaphorically or actually. And as for motive, you're being much too narrow. You seem unwilling or unable to understand the power money wields over some people."

"Particularly the have-nots," he said dryly.

"Exactly!" Her answer was automatic. When she realized what she'd said, she had the decency to blush, but only slightly. "Greed makes people do terrible things."

Not for the first time, Jake wondered if she was talking about herself.

"Look, Mrs. Baird, Mr. Baird's death was a shock." His voice was soothing. "I sympathize with your loss, because I know that suicides have many victims. I can well understand your need to grasp on to something, to find a reason that this vibrant man would have taken his life, but this is not . . . reasonable."

"You're wrong." Pamela shook her head. "She's involved. She may not have pulled the trigger, but she had something to do with the fact that Lionel Baird is dead. I know it!"

"How do you know?"

"I have a feeling."

Jake had a feeling this was more about a woman scorned than a man killing himself. Then again, when he heard Lionel Baird shot himself, his first reaction was, "No way."

"Okay. I'll check it out," he said, willing to play out her hunch and his curiosity. "Do you know this woman's name? Where she works? Or lives?"

Pamela glared at him as if to say, that' your job. "Lionel called her Max."

*   *   *

"You have a visitor," Grace said as she handed Jake a sheaf of messages. He glanced around the small, well-appointed, but empty reception area. Grace tilted her head in the direction of his private office and sneered. He knew immediately who his guest was.

Sure enough, Hallie Brendel was ensconced in a corner of his couch, her eyes hidden behind dark sunglasses, her face shrouded by a large hat that covered her hair.

"Mata Hari, I presume," he said, as he closed the door behind him.

"Where the hell have you been?"

Jake studied his left hand, walked to his desk, opened the top drawer, and made a show of flipping through the pages of his scheduler. "Gee, no wedding band. No appointment." His face was bland, bored. "No reason to have to account for my whereabouts."

"I've been besieged by death threats." She took off her glasses so he could get the full effect of her dismay. Her eyes were puffed and rimmed with dark circles. "There are people out there who hold me personally responsible for Lionel Baird's suicide."

"Aren't you?" He dropped into his leather swivel chair and began reading his messages.

"Omigod! How can you say that?" Hallie bounded from the couch and practically threw herself on his desk. "Everything I wrote was the truth."

"According to whom?"

"That's not fair, Jake. I checked out whatever Chisolm and Lady Pamela fed me."

"And then blew it out of proportion so it sounded far more criminal than it really was."

"Maybe a little."

"If Chisolm was so hot on eliminating drugs, why wasn't he talking about the gang war going on over distribution rights? Why wasn't he screaming about Propaine and what it's doing to the city's kids? Why wasn't he demanding that the federal government use its muscle to go after the Mexicans who are shipping that shit into the country?" He leaned back in his chair and looked squarely at Hallie. "Why was Chisolm's only complaint Lionel Baird, and some cash washing he may or may not have done, now or twenty years ago?"

Hallie squirmed. She hated when Jake was right.

"If you weren't so blinded by the notion of being a kingmaker, you would've made drugs the issue, not the money made off drugs."

His face registered disgust. "Instead, you beat up on Lionel Baird and gave the Savianos and those scumbag gangs a free ride. Nice going, Brendel."

Hallie discarded her hat and plopped back onto the couch like a rag doll, weary and woebegone.

"I was tracking a story. I had no idea Baird would kill himself because of it."

In an involuntary gesture of respect, both of them lapsed into respectful silence. Lionel Baird was a titan. Unlike ordinary mortals, his death created not only headlines, but a void. And because it was a suicide, controversy.

There are other ways of murdering a man. Pamela Baird might have been viewing this situation through a slightly distorted scope, but she wasn't entirely off base. There were ways of murdering someone without pulling the trigger yourself. Most people thought of suicide solely as the result of internal demons. As much as that eased the consciences of those acquainted with the victim, that wasn't always the case. Often, external demons played a role, agitating the devils within until the walls closed in and death did appear to be the only route to peace. Jake wondered who Lionel's demons were and what pokers they had used to stoke the flames of his distress.

"Who was your primary source of information? Chisolm or Pamela Baird?"

"They both seemed to have major axes to grind. Pamela gave me the stuff on Douglas Welch. Chisolm handed me the lead on Della Robbia."

"Were those axes sharp enough to kill him?"

Hallie sat up and stared at Jake. "Are you asking if Senator Chisolm or Pamela Baird pulled the trigger that killed Lionel?"

Jake shrugged. "There are other ways of murdering a man." He laughed to himself at the idea of quoting Pamela, but if the slogan fit . . . "They might've made stuff up, or hired someone to torment him or maybe one or both threatened to reveal something we can't even imagine."

Hallie rolled that around in her brain, trying to reconcile Jake's conjecture with what she knew of the people in question. "I don't know. Chisolm definitely had a big-time hate going for Baird, but frankly, I think he wanted to secure his Senate seat. Lionel was simply a means to an end."

"And Pamela?"

"Lionel was the love of her life, and he broke her heart. That's enough to make any woman upset." Jake refused to connect the dots. "But she wouldn't kill him. She was still hanging on to the dream that he'd see the error of his ways and come back to her."

"That was never going to happen."

Hallie winced. He was talking about them.

"Why are you asking these kinds of questions?" Her reporter's antennae had just tuned in. "The police say suicide. What do you know that they don't?"

"Nothing. I'm just curious."

"Yeah. And I'm a virgin. What's up, Jake?"

"Nothing." He tapped a pencil on his leather-top desk and stared into space. She waited. "What do you know about Baird's personal life?"

"According to the columns, he was a bon vivant who usually had someone fabulous hanging on his arm. According to Pamela, he was an indiscriminate womanizer."

"You said, usually. Wasn't he seeing anyone the last few months?"

Hallie scanned a mental screen. "Actually, no he wasn't, and the folks who trade in gossip were not happy about it. Lionel Baird was always good copy."

"Maybe he and Pamela were working on a secret reconciliation."

"She was definitely working on it, but I think she knew it was a lost cause."

"If it wasn't, would she have dropped the senator?"

"In a heartbeat."

"Did he know that?" Powerful man didn't like to be cuckolded. Duels were fought over things like that.

"I don't think so. She had the clinging-vine routine down pat."

"So what was Chisolm's problem?"

"Lionel was a pain in Chisolm's butt. It's as simple and as complicated as that."

"A game of one-upmanship?"

"You got it."

Working on Pamela's theory of, as Jake dubbed it, malevolently assisted suicide, Chisolm might have had a motive, depending on who was up in this game, and by how many points. Jake intended to check that out. As for Pamela, she remained a major contender. Heartbreak *and* the possibility of inheriting vast stores of money were historic motives for murder. Despite her disclaimer. And the finger she was pointing at Max.

Max. Jake had walked the twenty blocks from Pamela's apartment to his office. He'd needed the time to sort out all that she'd said, particularly the part about a woman named Max having an affair with Lionel Baird. He closed his eyes and kneaded them with the palms of his hands, seeking to erase the vision of Amanda lying beneath him, naked and loving. She couldn't have given herself to him that way if she'd been involved with someone else. *Unless the someone else was a rich guy she intended to hold up for cash.*

No. Couldn't be, he told himself, feeling her body next to his, seeing her in the car, clinging to him, crying on his shoulder . . . the night Lionel Baird died!

"Jake. What's the matter? You look sick."

Jake looked at Hallie without really seeing her. "I feel sick."

"Do you want me to take you home?"

He shook his head. "No. Thanks. I'll be all right. But, if you don't mind . . ."

"Yeah. Okay." She gathered her belongings, but before she left, she went over to Jake, caressed his cheek, and kissed him softly. "If you need a friend, you know where I am."

He nodded and gifted her with a smile. "Same here."

After Hallie left, Jake dimmed the lights, stretched out on his couch and assumed his thinking posture: arms folded behind his head, eyes closed, feet crossed at the ankles and propped on the arm of the couch. He breathed in and out through his nose the way his yogi had taught him, attempting to rid his mind of everyday clatter so he could think clearly, without superficial distraction.

So many questions: Could the Max he knew and the Max Pamela claimed was involved with Lionel Baird be one and the same? It pained him to say, why not? After all, how well did Jake know Max? Not very. They'd gone out a couple of times. Knew each other through work. Had a few things in common. They'd slept together only once, although it had been a spectacular once. He'd taken her home to meet his family; she liked them, they liked her. He thought that was good, that it meant something. Maybe not.

Then there was the other night, when she clung to him in the car and cried. Jake thought her tears were because she was overtired from the strain of her job, the exuberance of their lovemaking, the stress—and joy—of brunching with the Fowlers. Or that her tears were a chick thing, that she was touched because he was being sweet and they were getting close.

Now he wondered if she was crying because she'd just found out her lover was dead.

★　★　★

Amanda's shift ended at four. By five o'clock, she'd locked herself in her darkroom, intent on immersing herself in the facts and images of Lionel's death. Her telephone rang, but went unanswered. Night fell, but went unnoticed. Her stomach rumbled, but went unfed. Amanda attacked her grim task with rabid compulsion, developing roll after roll, creating dozens of color contact sheets, recording essential exposure data for each negative in a notebook.

When all the pictures she'd taken on that terrible night were printed, she laid the sheets out on her cocktail table. With her S&W holstered at her side, her Remington close at hand, and a pot of fresh coffee at the ready, she separated the photographs into categories: overalls, close-ups, surroundings. Using a magnifying glass, she went through each stack, marking which ones she intended to enlarge, which ones demanded closer study.

The main thing she determined from the overalls was that when the secret door was closed, it was impossible to locate. The seams were that tight. She recalled the night Lionel told her about it. He'd asked her to try and find the opening. She couldn't do it then. She couldn't spot it now. He explained how the carpenter who built the library painstakingly split one of the decoratively grooved pilasters that separated the sections and the moldings that fronted each of the shelves. The evenness of the mahogany stain, the precision of the cuts and the masterful hinging, the invisible fit, it was all so perfectly executed that if she hadn't pushed through from the other side, she never would have known it existed. Judging from the talk at the office, the Homicide guys missed it completely. Since the only way the library door could have been locked was from the inside, that meant if she was right and Lionel was murdered, his killer knew about the secret entrance.

She avoided the close-up views of Lionel's wound. Not only couldn't she bear to look at them, but there was no debate about the cause of death. The physical destruction was blunt, straightforward, and consistent with a gun being fired through the roof of the mouth.

Instead, she devoted a great deal of time to studying the area surrounding the victim. How Lionel sat in the chair, what was near him, on the desk, on the floor, under his hands, in his lap. Amanda scrutinized each picture as if that one would tell her what she wanted to know. None gave her answers, but they raised some interesting questions. In the trash basket, she spied a crumpled note on paper from the scratch pad on Lionel's desk. His stationery and notepads all bore the same engraved insignia: the little red caboose from a Lionel electric train set, the same caboose she had kept with her all those years. *What did that note say?* She jotted a memo to herself to try and find out from Caleb Green, Mickey Moran or, if need be, by poking around in the evidence file.

There was the open drawer and the camera, of course. The matter of the missing film cartridge still disturbed her.

Then there was Lionel's tie. It was tucked inside his shirt, between the second and third buttons. Amanda had never seen him do that, not even when he ate pasta with red sauce. Why would he tuck his tie into his shirt just before he intended to kill himself? It wasn't his habit, so it had to have been a conscious thought, a deliberate action. If not his, someone else's.

Also odd, Lionel's left hand rested on a newspaper headline insinuating that he was guilty of money laundering. His index finger pointed to his name. Was that his suicide note? His way of telling the world why he killed himself?

By ten o'clock, she'd lost perspective. Her eyes were bleary from looking at so many pictures, and she was too tired to think. Whatever she might have absorbed needed time to coalesce. She gathered up the contact sheets, slid them into their envelopes, and hid them, along with the notebook, in a false bottom she'd built in one of her kitchen cabinets.

She was staring into her barren refrigerator wondering how she was going to appease her angry stomach when the buzzer summoned her.

"Who is it?"

"Jake."

Amanda smiled, but habitual caution forced her to ask, "Are you alone?"

"Yes. Are you?"

"Not for long. Come on up."

Quickly, she checked to see if she'd left anything incriminating lying around, then stowed the Remington and the S&W in her bedroom. After a quick glance in her mirror, she combed her hair, smoothed her tee shirt, and waited for Jake to climb the three flights. When she opened the door, he had a pizza box in his hands and a bottle of wine tucked under his arm. Also, he was unshaven and looked exhausted.

"I was hungry and I hate to eat alone," he said as he walked into her apartment, located the kitchen, and relieved himself of his packages. He was almost grumpy.

"Don't mind if you do," she said, laughing as she followed him. "Corkscrew."

He put out his hand like a surgeon awaiting a scalpel. She rummaged through a drawer, found what he requested, and slapped it in his palm.

"Plates," he commanded as he removed the cork from the bottle.

She opened a cabinet, got two plates and, anticipating his next directive, two wineglasses. He split the pie, three pieces each, handed her the wine bottle and glasses, and proceeded to carry the plates into the living room, laying out his feast on the first empty expanse he found, which happened to be the cocktail table.

"Anything else I can get you, sire?" Amanda asked.

He stifled a grin. "No. Not at the moment." He plunked down on the floor, stuck his legs under the table, and leaned back against the couch. "Join me, won't you?"

Amused, Amanda complied. He poured each of them some wine.

"How're you feeling?" he asked with a mouthful of pizza. "I was worried about you the other night."

"I'm much better. Thanks." She swirled a straggly piece of cheese back up and onto her slice, then took a healthy bite. "Ummm. I was starving, and this is my all-time favorite meal! Bless you, Jake Fowler."

Jake smiled. She looked like a little girl with her legs crossed, her hair tumbling loose around her shoulders, and her eyes wide with pleasure. He gulped his wine, hoping its sedative properties would quell the conflict that raged within him. He had debated most of the evening about the wisdom of showing up on Amanda's doorstep. In the end, he had no choice. He had to see her.

"How come you didn't eat dinner? It's late."

"I got lost in my darkroom," she said, hiding behind her wine. She opted to tell him the truth, though not the whole truth. "I was developing the pictures I took at your mother's. Want to see?"

"Sure. Great."

She'd thought he'd be more excited than that. She wriggled out from beneath the table and went to her darkroom. She could feel Jake's eyes on her back. Flipping on a light, she opened the door to the bottom cabinets, pulled out a file drawer, and extracted a large manila envelope. She emptied the pictures and returned the envelope to its slot. Shutting the light and closing up her darkroom, she whispered a silent thank-you to the Powers That Be. She'd developed these pictures by accident. When she emptied her knapsack, she didn't realize this roll had mingled with those she took at the town house. Not only had they provided a much-needed respite earlier, but they gave her a handy diversion now.

She put the one she liked best on top: a close-up of Jake, Barry, and Brenda. They had their heads together and were laughing. Though they were looking at the camera, their emotional connection, one to the other, overwhelmed the portrait. They all looked so sweet, she'd printed one for herself.

"Nice," Jake said, smiling appreciatively as he looked at her work. "Very nice."

"I do weddings and bar mitzvahs."

"I'll have to remember that."

Amanda sipped her wine as he continued to peruse the pictures. Even now, in the abstract, his love for his family was blatant and overpowering. Strangely jealous, she realized that part of his attraction was that protective aura he emitted like a scent, that message he telegraphed so clearly: Nothing was ever going to hurt one of his.

"I made two extra sets," she said, wanting to be one of his. "For Jocelyn and Grace."

"They'll like that. Thanks." He refilled their wineglasses, swigged some of his, and stared at her. "So what's the buzz in the house about the Baird case?"

The subject change was so abrupt, Amanda's breath caught in her throat. She recovered quickly, but not quickly enough. Jake had been watching for a hesitation and spotted it. His eyes clouded.

"It's a suicide. The only buzz is why a guy like that would take his life."

"Why, indeed." He began to tap his finger on the table. "I don't get it. Do you, Max?"

Amanda shook her head, but there was something discordant about the way he called her, Max. "From where I sit, he had everything to live for."

Including you? "Are Green and Moran closing it out, or are they going to poke around some more?"

She shrugged her shoulders, feigning ignorance. She wondered how he knew Green and Moran had caught it. "I wasn't at the precinct."

Suddenly uneasy, she rose and began to clear the dishes. Jake offered to help, but she said she could handle it. He watched her walk into the kitchen, wondering whether she was cleaning up or retreating. Unable to stay put, he followed her. She was at the sink. His eyes scanned her body, alluring and sensuous even in the simplest of garb. The conflict he'd been battling all day returned, pitting what he'd been told against what he wanted to believe. He wished he'd never answered Pamela Baird's call. He wished he'd never gone up there, never heard what she had to say. Quickly, as if mere physical proximity to Amanda was all he needed to expunge his feelings of doubt, he slid his arms around her waist, drew her back up against him, and nuzzled the nape of her neck, losing himself in the lemony scent of her hair and the sweet, clean smell of her skin.

"I feel terrible," he said, desire triumphing over suspicion.

Amanda disagreed.

"I forgot to bring dessert." He nibbled her earlobe and hugged her closer.

"Unfortunately, my nickname is Mother Hubbard."

"That is unfortunate." His lips continued to explore her neckline.

"If you give me a minute to rummage around my cupboards, I might be able to find something."

He released her, but the space between them was minimal. Amanda turned. They were inches apart. He didn't have to move very far to kiss her, so he did. Only their lips touched, but she felt consumed by him.

"Do we have any wine left?"

"Uh-huh." He placed his hands on the sink behind her, caging her within his arms. Again, his mouth brushed hers.

She slid away from him, needing to breathe. "You take care of the wine. I'll see what I can dig up in here."

Reluctantly, he went back into the living room. He replenished their wine, but was too wired to sit. He paced until she joined him, carrying a plate of Oreos.

"It's a far cry from *vin santo* and *biscotti*," she said, eyeing him as he reconnoitered the room, "but this is the best I could do on such short notice."

Without looking at what she'd brought, he said, "It's fine."

She set the plate down on the table and waited for him to complete his tour. When finally he stopped in front of her, she dipped a cookie into her wine and fed it to him. He rewarded her with a smile. If only he knew how those dimples affected her, she thought, he'd smile more often. But his mood had changed. He stared at her, his eyes dark, his forehead knotted as if he was embroiled in a testy debate. Then he swept her in his arms and kissed her, pressing her body against his so tightly he took her breath away.

"That's what I call dessert," she said when they separated.

"Think so?" One hand continued to hold her while the other slipped beneath her tee shirt, gliding up onto her breast, then down again to her waist.

"Know so," she said, excited, but nervous. His blue eyes bored into her, hot with an intensity that wasn't only sexual.

His tongue licked her lower lip as his hand traced the fly on her jeans. Her body melted in his arms. He reached down for a glass and held it to her mouth, as if beseeching her to take part in some private ceremony. Without knowing what he was asking of her beyond the obvious, she agreed. Because she trusted him. She sipped the wine, secretly savoring the glorious sensation of believing in another person. She wished she could call Lionel and tell him how right he was about love and trust and being open to both. But Lionel was gone. A lump formed in her throat and tears gathered in her eyes as she fixed her gaze on Jake.

He took the glass from her, finished the rest of the wine, and kissed her again, deeply, almost desperately.

"Where's your bedroom?" he said, devouring her lips as he undid her jeans. She moaned when his hand slid inside and caressed her.

"Much too far away." Her fingers trembled eagerly as they unbuttoned his shirt and pushed it off him. When they found the buckle on his belt, they became purposeful.

"Take me there." He unhooked her bra and his hands swept across her breasts like flame on a match.

"Take me here." She could barely get the words out.

Within seconds they were naked, on the floor, passion spreading like a spark toward dynamite. These two people craved each other so ravenously that desire didn't rumble deep within, it sizzled on the surface, hot and volcanic. They came together quickly, explosively, as if the carpet had been doused in something highly combustible. Hands, lips, breasts, thighs, wherever they touched their flesh responded as if it was raw, stinging from even the merest contact. Still, like magnets, their bodies seemed unable to separate.

With Jake, Amanda experienced a completeness that made sex new for her. Each one of his caresses came gloved in emotion so strong it not only aroused her body, but also her heart. She didn't know why he had preceded this joining with a ritualistic toast, or why his mood kept swinging from dark to light, but the fullness, the richness, the complete and utter satisfaction resulting from this union described it as a celebration of physical harvest, not an act of penitent sacrifice.

For Amanda, who only an hour before had been steeped in death, this was all about reaffirming life.

For Jake, it was a test. All afternoon, he agonized about what Pamela Baird had told him. *Lionel called her Max.* She'd given him a physical description of the "younger woman who'd claimed Lionel Baird's full and complete attention." There could be more than one, Jake reasoned. This was, after all, a city of over eight million people. And Pamela Baird was one sandwich shy of a picnic.

But his gut said his Max, her Max and Lionel's Max, were the same woman, the one cradled in his arms right now. His heart shouted that in the big picture none of that mattered. Even if she did know Lionel Baird, that didn't mean they were having an affair or that she'd had anything to do with his death. Or that she had been dishonest with Jake.

He stroked her hair, letting it strain through his fingers. Her eyes were closed, but she smiled contentedly. Her lips were still moist from his kiss. Her body was still part of his. He bent down and kissed her again, luxuriating in the feel of her instant response. Why couldn't he trust what was right there in front of him? Why would he allow Pamela Baird's jealous ravings to come between him and this remarkable woman?

Because something nagged at him. Something that made him want to ask: "Were you sleeping with Lionel Baird?" "Were you there the night he died?" "Did you know what he was about to do?" "Could you have stopped it?" "Could you have caused it?" "Did you care?" Most important, he wanted to ask, "Do you care about me?"

But he didn't. He couldn't. Not now. He'd come here because he needed to be convinced that whatever her connection to Lionel Baird might have been, once she'd been with him, no one else mattered.

Tonight, that's what he believed.

Tomorrow was another day.

CHAPTER
SEVENTEEN

Angel Rodriguez, alias Jaime Bastido, sat at the far end of the counter in a seedy coffee shop on Ninth Avenue and Thirty-eighth Street. Located around the corner from the Port Authority Bus Terminal, the place was always packed with people in transit, people who buried their noses in newspapers or stared into their plates. There was little or no conversation. The loudest sounds were cups clinking down on saucers and fat sizzling on the griddle. No one came to The Bus Stop to make friends. Certainly, no one came for the ambience or the food. This was a place where one came to kill time, either coming or going.

Jaime kept an eye on the door as he gnawed on a piece of burnt toast. Thanks to the chin implant, his jaw didn't move as freely as it once did. Annoyed at the inconvenience, he washed the dried bread down with coffee that tasted as if it had been brewed from dirt. He wanted to spit it in the face of the surly cow who'd served it to him, but he refrained. He needed to remain anonymous. Besides, he thought, dumping another packet of sugar into the vile black liquid, he was Colombian. He knew what good coffee was. He couldn't expect that unfortunate peasant to know the difference.

As he nibbled on the slimy fried eggs, greasy sausage, and overdone hash brown potatoes that were billed as a Port Authority Special, a man sat down on the stool next to him and ordered the same breakfast.

"Get the eggs well-done," Jaime advised.

"You heard him," the stranger said to the cow. "Make sure the eggs are well-done."

The large woman glared at Jaime, mumbled an epithet or two

under her breath, then barked something unintelligible to the beleaguered cook sweating in the tiny kitchen behind the counter.

"Would you mind watching my newspaper while I visit the men's
room?"

"No problem," Jaime said. "Take your time."

The man headed for the rest rooms. Several minutes later, when
the cow brought his food, he still hadn't returned.

"Where'd he go?" she demanded of Jaime and the woman on
the other side of the empty stool. Both shrugged their shoulders.
Grumbling about deadbeats, she slammed the plate down. If the guy
did return, it would serve him right if his food was cold. Someone
at the other end of the counter yelled for more coffee. Grumbling
some more, she grabbed a pot and stormed off.

Once she and her tantrum had moved on, Jaime appropriated the
man's newspaper. He slipped his fingers inside the fold and retrieved
an envelope, which he immediately stuffed in his jacket pocket. Having collected his package, he could relax and finish his breakfast. He
raised his cup, coffee dripped onto the front page of the newspaper.
No matter, Jaime thought, his upper lip curling slightly. No one was
coming back to claim it.

After blotting the coffee spills, Jaime looked at the *Telegraph* and
snickered. Three days after his death, Lionel Baird was still the main
event. Stories about him filled the front page. Jaime skimmed a few
of them, interested, but only barely. He was delighted that the man
was dead, but Lionel was not the Baird on his Most Wanted list.

On page ten, however, there was a story that grabbed his attention:
Mexican authorities were holding a member of the notorious
Espinosa family, seeking to draw up drug and other charges against
him after his arrest at a highway checkpoint for illegal possession of
a pistol.

Jaime laughed out loud. That call he made from Denver to the
border patrol had done the trick. Emilio Espinosa, the youngest of
the four brothers, was in custody.

The article went on to say that "it remained unclear whether
Mexico's antidrug agencies had collected sufficient evidence to put
Emilio Espinosa, thirty-two, on trial for his work with his older
brothers' cartel, which a senior American official called 'a trafficking
organization of global proportions,' but they were hopeful." That's
because their Angel had promised to produce all the evidence they
needed to put Emilio and the rest of the Espinosa boys away for
good.

He reached into his pocket and extracted a pencil and a piece of lined paper on which he had scribbled several names. With a bold stroke, he put a line through the name of Emilio Espinosa. As broadly as his tightly stitched jaw would allow, he smiled. One down.

Jaime stuffed the paper and pencil back into his pocket, then retrieved the envelope of photographs the courier had left for him. Holding them so no one else could see, he perused the pictures. There were only fifteen. Obviously, poor Lionel shot himself before he had a chance to shoot the rest of the roll. Jaime chuckled at his own joke, but only for a moment. After riffling through several meaningless pictures of people yukking it up at a fancy party, the smile was wiped right off his face.

Grinning back at him was that bitch, Cynthia Stanton. Her hair was shorter, and she'd aged, but he'd know her anywhere. How could he forget her? For weeks, while his lawyers fought to keep her off the witness stand, his cohorts made threats to her and her family, none of them veiled. When she defied them and showed up in court, Jaime stared at her, daring her to take the stand and testify. But she stared back. She accepted his dare, took the stand, and nailed his ass to the wall!

It had been more than twenty years since they confronted each other in Miami, but time moves slowly in prison. Hostilities fester like untreated sores. If it took another twenty years, he and Cynthia Stanton were going to confront each other again, only this time, Jaime was going to be the one in the catbird seat. He glowered at his nemesis's likeness and gritted his teeth, unmindful of the pain in his jaw. She thought she was safe, relocated in some small town in the middle of nowhere, protected by the mighty Marshals Service. But she wasn't safe. No matter where she was or what it took, he'd find a way to get to her.

Snarling as a rage that had simmered over years began to boil, he flipped through the other pictures, slapping them down on the counter, one after the other. Cynthia on a couch. Cynthia alongside a fireplace. Cynthia enjoying the good life while he struggled to survive each and every day. Cynthia with her arm around some foxy young woman. Cynthia and the same person making silly faces at the camera. Jaime picked one of the pictures up and held it closer. He'd never seen this person before, yet something about her seemed familiar. It took awhile, but suddenly, he was certain he knew exactly who she was.

"My, my," he muttered like a child who'd received an unexpected gift. "It looks like little Erica Baird is all grown-up."

Jake came out of the subway on Lexington Avenue, walked down a block and turned east on Sixty-seventh Street. Midblock on the north side was the Nineteenth Precinct. His step slowed, and he hesitated before going inside. He felt guilty coming here, having spent the night with Amanda. Yet being with her had made him even more determined to prove that whatever Pamela was insinuating was nothing but the twisted suggestion of a woman who needed to justify her jealousy through baseless accusations.

He'd left Amanda's at two o'clock in the morning, tired and as sated as a man obsessed by a woman could be. They'd made love in the living room and then moved into her bedroom, a precious Arcadia that spoke of Amanda's more feminine side, her love of flowers and edenic surroundings, her preference for pink and ruffles and candles that delicately perfumed the air. Lying next to her in that confection of a bed, he wished he could prolong the night and prevent the dawn, remaining there with her in a capsule of suspended time. As always, reality intruded. She had the early shift; with him there, she wouldn't get any sleep. Ever the gallant, he kissed her good night and returned to his apartment, which suddenly felt empty and cold.

He slept, but fitfully. The tape inside his head whirred, first on fast-forward racing to conclusions, then rewinding and going over things again. When he woke, he realized he had lots of rumors, a number of suppositions, a few false starts, but very few facts.

His first stop that morning was Lionel's office. Pamela had called ahead and alerted Fredda, who handed over Xeroxed copies of Lionel's appointment book for the past six months and the next several weeks. Jake asked for, and received, a list of telephone calls—both in and out—and messages for the week preceding his death. Heeding Pamela's warnings, he'd been charming and complimentary and promised the exceedingly cooperative Ms. MacDougall that he would keep her up-to-date on everything he unearthed during the course of his investigation. Naturally, since they were now friends, she felt compelled to share her opinion on the matter of the woman known as Max.

"Mr. Baird never talked about her," Fredda confided. "And I know that Mrs. Baird considers this woman an evil influence, but to tell you the truth, she made Lionel very happy."

"How do you know that?"

She was aghast. Does a mother know her own child? "Other than Mrs. Baird, I was the person closest to Lionel. In fact, I probably knew his moods better than anyone else, including Mrs. Baird. After all, I spent the most time with him."

If this didn't involve a dead man and a woman he was falling in love with, Jake might find this pissing contest between the secretary and the soon-to-be-ex-wife funny.

"When did this relationship begin?" he asked.

She paused, reflecting. "I don't know exactly when Max came into his life, but six months or so ago, he seemed visibly lighter, as if a weight had been lifted off his shoulders. I know that's a cliché, but it's the only way I can describe it. Until Senator Chisolm began attacking him in the press, Lionel was behaving like a Teflon man. Nothing bothered him. Don't tell Mrs. Baird I said so, but I think that was due to the new love in his life."

If Fredda had personal regrets about not being the chosen one, she hid them well. Jake gave her points for that. "Did you ever see her with him?"

"Once. He brought her up here. Said she was an art broker who was helping him add some photographs to his collection. I had no reason to question that, so I didn't." She scrunched her eyebrows together. It wasn't an attractive gesture. "I did think it was strange that she didn't leave a business card and that he refused to give me an address or phone number where she could be reached."

"Did he ask you to make dinner reservations for them?"

"Rarely. That, too, was strange. I usually handled that sort of thing for Mr. Baird."

"But every now and then, you took care of that?"

She nodded, still piqued about being sidestepped. "I suppose you want to know where and when."

"It would help. How about vacations? Weekends in the country? Did you book anything like that?"

She tapped her finger against her chin. Something she'd done without thinking suddenly seemed curious. "Actually, several times he asked me to reserve hotel rooms in the city. The man lives in the most luxurious town house in town. Why would he need a hotel room?"

"Why indeed?" Jake said. Ms. MacDougall was turning out to be a veritable fount of information. "If you don't mind, I'd like those dates and places as well."

She didn't answer. She was still rummaging about in her mental store.

"You know what else is strange? Sometime around the end of March, the beginning of April, he told me he was going away for the weekend, but didn't ask me to book a hotel or rooms for his flight crew. I didn't arrange for a car or theater tickets. Hell! He didn't even tell me where he was going!"

April. Jake recalled playing telephone tag with Amanda sometime around then. He called her apartment several times trying to make a date, but she wasn't around. Frustrated, he called the CSU. Doyle informed him, with obvious glee, that she was out of town. He'd have to check his own phone log to see exactly when that was. But even if it was the same weekend, he cautioned, it might be nothing more than coincidence.

Unfortunately, Jake didn't hold too much stock in coincidence. Which was why he'd come to the Nineteenth.

The sergeant at the precinct desk called upstairs and asked if Detectives Green and Moran were around.

"Detective Green says to go on up."

On his way, Jake waved to several of the uniforms and a couple of the detectives. He worked the area frequently, so he knew most of the guys at this house. They made a show of not wanting to share information with him, but since he helped them whenever he could, despite the show, they returned the favor whenever they could. He was hoping this was one of those times.

"Hey," he said, extending his hand toward Caleb Green. "Thanks for seeing me."

Green lurched backward, as if an alien creature had invaded the house. "Jake Fowler saying thank you before we even sit down? What's wrong with this picture?"

"Your face, for one." Jake delivered his insult and grabbed a chair.

Green sighed. "I feel much better now." He reclaimed his seat behind his desk, shoving the remains of a bagel into his mouth and washing it down with some coffee. "Moran's out grabbing up some skel on a Homicide he worked with Maldonato. What's up, Fowler?"

"I've been retained to look into the Baird suicide."

Green folded his arms behind his head and planted his feet on his desk. He didn't look at all surprised. "By the widow Baird?"

"You guessed it."

"What's there to look into? The guy blew his brains out."

"I think she's trying to get as much ammo as she can before the will goes to probate."

"The guy popped himself. If she's still the legal Mrs., she gets a chunk of his pie. What's the ammo for?"

"Lionel Baird was a smart man. Contesting his will could be tough."

Green was unmoved by the widow's plight. "So she hires another lawyer. Why'd she hire you?"

Jake shrugged. "She's got a bug up her ass. She thinks this was some sort of malevolently assisted suicide."

"You wanna run that by me again?"

"I told her the evidence points to suicide. She insists it's murder. As a compromise, I came up with malevolently assisted suicide. Like Kevorkian without permission."

Caleb thought for a minute before responding, which was why Jake liked him. He was a cop who didn't jump to conclusions even if they seemed to be staring him in the face.

"Malevolently assisted suicide." He tried the phrase on and walked around in it before deciding it fit. "That's a good one, Jake." He flashed a quick, perfunctory smile, then grew somber. "You know officially this case is closed."

"And unofficially?"

"I saw the guy at the scene." Caleb's eyes grew vague, as if his sights had returned to the library where Lionel Baird ended his life. "I know what the forensics say, but I'm having a hard time buying into suicide myself."

"Why?"

"You and I handle guns all the time. This guy didn't drive his own car or pour his own coffee. If he was going to do himself in, why not barbiturates or hanging himself with one of his designer belts?" He looked truly puzzled as he tried to picture the sequence of events. "Can you imagine sticking one of these cannons in your mouth and pulling back on that trigger?" He shuddered. When he was on patrol, Caleb Green had fired his weapon many times. He'd killed someone once. He understood the brute power of firearms.

"No," Jake admitted. "But suicide's tough to figure. I've heard of cases where people are happy as clams one minute and then, without warning, they tip over, go into another room, and do the deed."

Caleb nodded. He'd caught a few of those.

"You and I don't get it because hard-asses like us can't believe there's not another way out or another angle to try." Jake fidgeted with a signet ring Archie had given him for his fourteenth birthday. "They say people who kill themselves, even violently, are in such incredible psychic pain, they're not afraid of a rope or a razor blade or a gun. To them, it spells relief."

"I guess." Green still didn't get it.

"Where does Moran come down on this?"

Caleb laughed. "You know Moran. Rich guy offs himself. Too bad. Next case."

"And you?"

"Believe it or not, Fowler, I'm glad you showed up." Jake's specialty was the case the department closed, but didn't feel locked up tight. "I'll go with forensics: Baird pulled the trigger. But something about this case stinks."

Green sounded just like Pamela. Jake didn't think he'd be pleased with the comparison.

"So what do you want to do about it," he asked.

"I can't pursue this on city time."

"I hear you." Jake lowered his voice. "I'm already on this, Caleb. You give me a heads-up, I'll keep you in the loop."

"Okay, but no poking your nose where it doesn't belong, then mouthing off that I gave you the green light."

"You've got my word." Green nodded. Jake's word was good with him. "What'd you pick up at the scene?" Jake was after a note, a phone call on an answering machine, something that might have terrified—or humiliated—Lionel Baird beyond the point of reason.

"There was no suicide note and there were no messages. He was home and apparently answered whatever calls came in. There were some business documents on his desk. Looked like he might've been going over them." Again, Green grew thoughtful. "There was a copy of the *Telegraph* sitting there, too."

Caleb took a photograph Harpo had taken of the desk area out of a folder and showed it to Jake.

"He'd seen that edition already," Jake said, dismissively.

"I know, but the guy's finger's pointing to the headline like some damn Ouija board."

Jake picked up the picture and looked at it again, more closely this time. The finger pointing to the newspaper was peculiar, but Jake had fixed on a name that appeared on the documents. It struck a bell. Annie Hart was a friend of Amanda's.

"What's up with these papers?" he asked. "Anything that might've put that old S&W in his paw?"

"I doubt it. They're all about bankrolling a start-up cosmetics business headed by this Annie Hart. Unless that was Baird's way of jumping out of the closet and declaring himself a member of the all-boys' choir, it's a nonissue."

Jake scrambled to come up with a visual of Annie Hart. Amanda had provided a description so he could look for her at the gallery. He thought he spotted her, but he'd been into Max's work and his sighting of Annie Hart had been brief.

"Have you questioned her?"

"Yeah. Makeup artist on a soap opera. She was supposed to meet Baird for dinner to sign off on the deal. She waited at the restaurant, but he never showed. Then she got a phone call and left."

"Who called her?"

"The maître d' said it was the woman who'd come to the restaurant with Miss Hart and was supposed to have dinner with her and Lionel Baird." Green tapped a pencil on his desk. Jake's blood slowed in his veins. "When Baird was over an hour late, this other woman left. She never came back."

"Do we know who it was?" Jake held his breath, though he knew the answer.

"Amanda Maxwell. The shooter from the CSU. Remember her?"

Jake forced himself to look surprised. "Max is tough to forget." He swallowed hard. "What was she doing there?" More important, where did Max go when she left the restaurant? Why didn't she come back? And why didn't she mention any of this to him?

"Hart claims they're close friends. Evidently, Max made the intro between Hart and Baird." Judging by the expression on Caleb's face, that intrigued him. "How the hell did she ever hook up with the likes of Baird?"

Jake let that go by. In truth, he didn't know.

"Anyway," Green continued, "since the dinner was supposed to be a celebration, Max was invited to come along."

Jake squirmed uncomfortably. Annie Hart was not only up front about knowing Amanda, but also about Amanda knowing Lionel well enough to bring him a business deal. Obviously, she didn't feel the need to keep her friend's relationship a secret. Pamela knew about Amanda and Lionel. So did Fredda. The only one who didn't know about Amanda's acquaintanceship with the now-dead Lionel Baird was the man who was sleeping with her.

"The maître d' said Baird had asked him to put a bottle of champagne on ice, which seems to confirm the celebration part." He paused, drumming on his desk. "Did you know Max does some kind of art photography on the side?"

Jake wasn't about to tell Caleb the intimate details of his relationship with Amanda, but in case it came out later that they knew each other, he'd lose all credibility if he lied outright. Fudging the facts, however, felt permissible.

"Yeah. I went to an exhibition at a Chelsea gallery that showed some of her stuff. She's good."

Caleb's eyes narrowed slightly. "No kidding." In his mind, art and Homicide didn't mix.

"She does these costume things where she gets done up like someone famous and then snaps herself. It's weird, but interesting."

"Hart claims she did the makeup for Max's photo shoots."

"You sound like you're not too sure about her."

"It's because I am sure, that I'm not sure."

Jake slapped the side of his head, as if his ears were clogged. "Come again."

"Baird had her checked out by the Bureau."

"What?"

"I suppose the guy was being careful because he was about to invest *mucho dinero* in a business."

"I gather you're not talking about the credit bureau."

Caleb chuckled. "I'm talking G-men, Fowler."

"Why run her through the FBI? Does she have a record?"

"Clean as a whistle."

"So what was he looking for?"

"If I knew that, I wouldn't need you, now would I?"

Jake gave Caleb a touché. "Can I get a copy of the report?" Jake thought if he tracked down some of the answers, he'd know the reason for the questions. Caleb said he'd fax it to him. "Why does Moran like suicide?" he asked.

"To him, Baird was all over the lot. First, he plans a soiree with champagne and the works. Then, he asks his bodyguard to go all the way downtown to Little Italy to bring back a dinner he has no intention of eating. Mickey thinks Baird was toying with the idea of suicide for a long time. Yes, no. Yes, no. That sort of thing. When he finally makes up his mind to do it, he gets Vitale out of the house fast, before he loses his nerve."

"Does the muscleman's story check out?"

"Yeah." Caleb looked at his notes. "We've got him at Il Cortile around eight o'clock. Witnesses put him at the bar, where he was loud and obnoxious, coming on to some broad." He flipped a page. "There was a 911 call at nine-oh-six. Our guys arrived at nine-twelve. Vitale walked in at nine-twenty."

"I hate to say this, Caleb, my friend, but Mickey might've called this one."

Green shook his head. "Baird sends his bodyguard away so he can blow his brains out? What difference does it make if Vitale's upstairs or in Little Italy? You stick that gun in your mouth and pull the trigger, there ain't no saving you."

"Suicide is not a rational act."

"Granted. But usually there's some reason for it. We can't come up with one in this case. Baird didn't have any debts. He had no history of depression. I checked with his doctor. He wasn't suffering from a fatal illness or taking Prozac." Caleb threw up his hands. "Other than Brendel and Chisolm slamming him in the press, the guy's life was sweet."

"What about old enemies? Colleagues with a beef? Wasn't he reorganizing Baird, Nathanson & Spelling?"

"Yeah, but the VPs were looking to move up. If any of them was into murder, they'd knock off each other, not Baird."

"What about women? Maybe there was a really scandalous bimbo eruption on the horizon?"

Green shrugged. "Could be." He remembered something. "We found a note in his wastebasket." He rummaged around in the folder until he found a piece of crumpled paper, which had been flattened and saved in a plastic bag. He handed it to Jake.

Send flowers to Beth. Call Bates—find out how.

"What do you make of this?"

"I'm guessing maybe Beth was a lady friend. They had a fight. He was looking to make nice-nice with the flowers."

"Is Bates the butler?"

"Nope. That's Thompson. And he never heard of Beth. Or Bates."

Jake found that interesting. Maybe Pamela and Fredda had it wrong. Beth was the woman who lit up Lionel's life, and he was keeping her under wraps until after his divorce was finalized.

"Could Beth have been squeezing Baird?" he asked, using Pamela's theory, substituting Beth for Max. "Like threatening to go public with something nasty?"

"Why not?" Caleb said. "She wouldn't be the first woman to grab a sugar daddy by his *cojones* and hold him up."

"You checked his address book, phone records, Rolodex, whatever?"

"No Beth. No Bates."

"Did he scribble that memo on the day of the suicide?"

Caleb nodded. "Thompson said the wastebasket had been emptied in the morning."

"What else?"

"One of the desk drawers was open."

"The gun might have been in there."

"Probably. It had a lock, but we didn't find the key."

"Anything else missing that should've been there?"

"Not really. But there was a camera in that same drawer. Open and empty."

"Usually, people take the film out and snap the back shut."

"Unless they're in a hurry."

"Thompson say he took any film in to be developed recently?"

"Nope. He didn't even know Baird owned a camera."

Amanda didn't eat dinner last night because she was locked in her darkroom. It couldn't have taken five hours to develop the pictures she took at Grace's. Again, Jake wondered where Amanda went when she left the restaurant.

"What do you think is on that roll of film, Caleb?"

"I don't know, but the way it looks, it was important enough for someone to steal."

"Before or after Lionel Baird blew his brains out?"

"Good question." Caleb fixed his hazel eyes on Jake. "Go find the answer."

Jake nodded. Slowly, he stood and shook Caleb's hand. His shoulders were hunched, his blue eyes dark and wary.

"You know what frightens me?" he said. "Pamela Baird's looking less and less like a screwball."

Late that night, EMS admitted a patient to Lenox Hill Hospital's emergency room. A gentleman in his midsixties, he'd been severely beaten about the chest and head. Fading in and out of consciousness, he had three broken ribs, internal bleeding that necessitated surgery, and a heartbeat that was perilously rapid and irregular. In addition to the standard array of X-rays taken in battery cases, the attending physician, fearing an attack, ordered an EKG. They were awaiting the results when suddenly, the man they'd identified as Reid Thompson, opened his eyes and tugged at the pants of the nurse standing along-side him.

"Call her," he croaked, desperation giving strength to a voice weakened by an injured larynx.

The nurse bent down close to his mouth so he didn't have to strain. "Call who?" He'd given the EMS crew his name, but no way to contact family members or friends. Considering the extent of his injuries, it would be good to have at least one phone number.

"Max. CSU. Please!" His eyes implored the nurse to pay attention and not dismiss his instructions as the ravings of someone with diminished capacities. "Max. New York Crime Scene Unit. Get her. Please! Need to see her."

"Okay," she said, taking his hand in hers. He looked so frail and frightened. She'd never understand how anyone could inflict this kind of damage on a man his age.

"Please!"

"I will. Don't worry. I'll have her here when you wake up from surgery."

He scanned her face like a minesweeper searching for truth.

"You have my word, Mr. Thompson. Whoever this Max is, I'll find her."

A smile flickered on his swollen lips. A second later, he was uncon-scious.

It was four o'clock in the morning before Thompson was out of surgery, five-thirty by the time he was set up in the ICU. His eyelids fluttered as he seesawed between the conscious and unconscious world. High-pitched blips and beeps provided the background music as a soft hand held his. A voice that sounded vaguely familiar urged him to awaken.

"Thompson," the voice said. "It's me, Max."

He tried to smile, but couldn't. He went to open his eyes, but that, too, was difficult. Gathering his resources, he pushed his eyelids up so that he could see her.

"Welcome back," she said, softly caressing his forehead. It was one of the few places that wasn't obscured by bandages or tubes.

His eyes watered. He was glad to be alive, relieved to see that Max was alive as well. He tried to speak, but his energy store was low. As Max held a straw to his lips and encouraged him to sip the water, a nurse checked his vitals and increased the flow of the glucose drip.

"The doctors say you're going to be fine." When Max asked what happened, all they could tell her was that a heavyweight had used Thompson as a punching bag.

Thompson drifted away for a bit. Amanda continued to hold his hand. It sickened her to see him like this. Judging by the gruesome rundown of contusions, traumas, and multiple wounds provided by the ICU nurse, Max knew whoever worked Thompson over was a pro. His mouth was puffy, his lower lip was split, and there was a bad bruise on his chin. The first punch was meant to disarm and disable. Considering Thompson's age and the ferocity of the punch, Max was certain it did. The bulk of Thompson's injuries were internal. Those blows were delivered after questions went unanswered.

For Max, however, Thompson's attack answered one very important question: Lionel's death had not been a suicide.

"He wanted your name and address."

His voice was so weak, Max didn't hear him at first. She was still mulling the meaning behind the assault. Thompson squeezed her hand.

"He wanted your name. Address." He swallowed hard. His throat was dry. Max fed him more water.

Another important question had been answered: Lionel's murder was related to the case that put her and Beth into WITSEC. Max gritted her teeth. "Who wanted my name, Thompson?"

He rolled his eyes. He had no idea. She hadn't expected he would. The faceless enemy came out of nowhere and resembled no one.

"I didn't tell . . ."

"I know you didn't," she said, astounded at the courage this man had displayed. He was a gentleman's gentleman, a man whose purpose in life was to maintain an atmosphere of regal elegance in a world that had grown increasingly crude and common. She felt guilty, knowing that her past had done this to him.

Forcing herself to focus on the present, she reviewed what Thompson would and would not know about her. Very little, unless Lionel had filled him in without her knowledge. He knew her name, Amanda Maxwell, and that she worked for the CSU; when the ER nurse called, one of the detectives on duty called Max and relayed the pertinent information. Thompson didn't know her home phone number or address; he never picked her up at home. Whenever he drove her to meet Lionel, he met her either outside a large hotel or a busy restaurant, wherever a parked limousine wouldn't draw attention.

She winced at the thought that Thompson endured this kind of pain for no real reason.

He dozed for a while. When he awoke, he seemed stronger. "Who are you?" he asked.

Amanda thought the sedatives were playing tricks on his mind. Patiently, she said, "Max. Amanda Maxwell."

His head lolled from side to side. "I mean really. Who are you?"

Amanda's heart began to race. "I don't know what you mean."

"Yes, you do." He licked his lips. She could see how difficult this was for him. "Why did Mr. Baird keep everything about you so secret?"

He deserved the truth, but to protect him, she withheld it. "It's better if you don't know.' "

"For now," he said, agreeing not to press the issue. "But when I get out of here . . ."

Amanda simply smiled, grateful for his understanding.

He groaned, and the nurse came in to give him a shot. When she left, Amanda pulled her chair up against the bed and once again, took his hand in hers.

"Thompson, I'm so sorry about all this," she said, tears welling. "I wish I could have prevented this."

"I know." His eyes were gentle as they fixed on her. He wasn't accusing, he was asking. "Could you have prevented Mr. Baird's suicide?"

The question hit her hard. Her hand covered her eyes as she wept. It was his turn to soothe her. He patted her hand. She fought to regain control.

"I'm not so sure it was a suicide," she said, eager to see his reaction.

The drugs were taking effect, and he had to struggle to think clearly. "I agree. He seemed fine. Happy." He patted her hand again. "You made him happy."

Max smiled. She could tell by the tone of his voice that Thompson knew she wasn't Lionel's mistress. She was curious as to who he thought she might be, but this was not the time for that conversation.

"Thompson. Is there anything I should know about the day Lionel died?"

"It's hard to remember." It was unsettling to watch him battle through the drugs and the pain.

"I know. Take your time." She waited as he searched through the fog.

"I'm not certain, but the day before, Mr. Baird was supposed to meet with Tyler Grayson. Mr. Grayson couldn't make it. Maybe he stopped by on Sunday. I wasn't there. I don't know."

"Did you tell the police that?"

"No. I just remembered."

Amanda recalled how rattled Tyler had been when he dropped in on her, how focused he was on the causes of suicide. Could he have said something to Lionel? Something that would have made death desirable? Or necessary?

When she looked at Thompson, he'd fallen into deep sleep. She stayed with him until seven. She had to leave so she could report in at eight. She rose. His eyes opened. He looked disoriented, then frightened, as if he didn't want her to leave.

"I'll be back tonight," she said.

"No!" His eyes widened, and his breathing became labored. "It's dangerous."

He was right. They'd be watching. She patted his hand reassuringly. "Okay. But I'm going to call in and find out how you're doing."

He nodded. She thought he smiled, but it was hard to tell. She leaned over, kissed his forehead and tiptoed out of his room. She was happy to see that while she'd been with Thompson, the police had posted a guard. She recognized him as one of the uniforms from the Nineteenth.

Mindful that someone could already be outside the hospital—if there was a plant inside watching Thompson's room there was little she could do—she decided to leave through the emergency room. It was too early for visitors and vendors, so the main lobby would be empty. The ER rarely was. She stuffed her hair up under her New York Yankees hat, stuffed her CSU jacket in her backpack, and took the stairs down to the main floor. She hovered in the background until an EMS crew burst through the doors with the survivors of a rush-hour accident on the East River Drive. In the midst of the hubbub, she slipped out the door and made a beeline for the subway.

As Amanda suspected, there was someone watching the front exit. He missed her. But another man spotted her as he crossed the street on his way to visit Reid Thompson. His eye caught her just as she turned toward Lexington Avenue: tall and willowy with a determined stride, a bulky, black nylon backpack slung over her left shoulder, aviator sunglasses. He would've recognized that silhouette anywhere, but if he had any doubt, the Yankee cap confirmed it. After all, he'd bought it and bent it, just for her.

★ ★ ★

The sun was setting in Los Angeles when Sam walked through the door to Beth's apartment. His post office address was a studio across town, but most of Sam's clothes, and his heart, were here. Since the living room faced west, an orange haze filtered through the window, burnishing the mocha-colored walls and casting a warm glow on the ivory and beige tones of the decor. At first, the silence was so complete he thought the room was empty, but then, his nose picked up her light, patchouli scent. She was in the corner, hidden by shadows, sitting tall in a chair meant for a more relaxed posture. It looked as if she had been in that same position for hours, staring at the door, waiting for him to cross the threshold.

"Where've you been?" Her voice was cold, accusatory.

"I heard about Lionel," Sam said, remaining by the door, taking a pulse.

Beth didn't respond. Clearly, she didn't intend to until he answered her question.

"I was visiting my sister, Gail. She's ill." He winced at the cliché. "She has ovarian cancer. She was operated on a few weeks ago. I wanted to be with her."

Beth nodded. She'd never met Sam's sister. He'd mentioned her perhaps twice in twenty years. Since she never—until today—questioned where Sam went or what he did when he wasn't with her, she had no idea how often he visited Gail, if ever. But Sam never lied to her. His brutal frankness was one of the things she loved and hated about him. If he said his sister was ill, she was.

"Is she going to be all right?" Beth asked.

"I hope so." He crossed the room warily, kneeling at Beth's side. "Are you all right?"

She shook her head and tears dripped down her cheeks. "No, I'm not. I'm terribly, terribly sad."

Sam caressed her cheek. "I'm sorry I wasn't with you when you found out."

"So am I."

He heard the edge and regretted it, but some things couldn't be helped.

"Lionel's butler, Thompson, was roughed up."

Sam hadn't heard that. "Was that on the news?"

"No. Amanda called about an hour ago. Whoever did it wanted to know her name and address." Sam's jaw tightened. "Thompson didn't know her address. He refused to give them her name." Beth sounded weary, as if she, too, had been interrogated by a brute.

"The Service probably wasn't notified because the NYPD doesn't know to call us."

Since Amanda had returned to New York and left the protective aegis of WITSEC, the Marshals Service wouldn't be tracking her movements or the activity of her pursuers. Sam knew that to Beth that was a technicality.

"Don't you think someone should clue them in?" Her eyes were glassy and hard.

"Beth, Lionel committed suicide. NYPD has no reason to connect Thompson's beating to Lionel's death."

"Do you think it's connected?"

"It certainly looks suspicious."

Beth appeared to chew on that before moving on. "Amanda wants you to prevent Lionel's body from being released for burial."

Sam was not happy about this request, and it showed.

"Is that a problem?" The edge had returned.

"Why does she want him held?"

"Until she's certain this death was from Lionel's own hand, she doesn't want him buried. In case they need to redo the autopsy or something."

"What's she up to?"

Beth glared at him. "She's doing what you taught her to do: She's protecting her back!"

Her agitation was real, and it touched Sam, infusing him with guilt. Sometimes he forgot that Beth wasn't simply a good-looking college professor who'd been his lover for a dozen years. She was a protected witness. There was a bounty on her head as well as her daughter's. She had a right to be anxious.

"I'll speak to Amanda, then I'll call the authorities in New York." He answered the question in Beth's eyes. "I'll make sure no one connects the call to Max."

Beth nodded. Then her eyes clouded and she left him. Though her body remained in the chair, her spirit had traveled elsewhere. "It's begun," she said quietly. "I knew it would. I knew Ricki and I would never be free of this."

There was a hint of capitulation in her voice that Sam had never heard before, and that frightened him. He believed Beth had survived her travails because from the beginning she'd adopted a fiercely determined, eyes-front philosophy: You can't change the past, but you can design your future. She also maintained a belief in the system. Her decision to testify was correct, justice was done, and despite the hardships incumbent upon relocation, the Marshals Service would protect her and her daughter so they could live a good and decent life.

Lionel's sudden death removed whatever level of comfort she'd achieved over the years. For Beth, Lionel was more than her first love and her first husband. He represented an anchor to the past, a living symbol of what life had been before, who she had been before. With him gone, there was no one, other than Amanda, to remind Beth that Cynthia Stanton Baird ever existed.

Except those who wanted to kill her.

"Nothing's going to happen to you or Amanda." He needed to remind her that Ricki Baird no longer existed and to reassure her that he was there to protect them.

"Lionel had bodyguards protecting him around the clock. Something happened to him. Why not us?"

She was looking directly at him, but Sam sensed she was still in that other place, that private hell that only she and Amanda appreciated.

"Beth, Lionel's suicide is tragic. I know what a loss it is for you and Max, but please, don't give it a berth wider than it deserves." He saw the anger kindle and sought to douse it immediately. "That sounds cavalier, but I don't mean it that way. I met Lionel. I spoke to him a few times after that. He was a remarkable man, Beth."

The flame died, tears fell onto her cheeks in a sad cascade of surrender.

"You and Lionel reconnected recently. I know that stirred up all kinds of feelings. Obviously, I know the two of you corresponded, but I'll bet those letters had nothing to do with business or his problems with Senator Chisolm or too much else beyond Amanda and how the two of you felt about each other." He wiped her eyes and lifted her chin so she was looking directly at him. "In truth, Beth, you didn't know Lionel very well. For all you know, there were extenuating circumstances. He may have had business reverses or an illness or . . ."

"Lionel didn't commit suicide." Her tone was sharp, definite, intolerant of any argument to the contrary. "He wouldn't do that. Especially now."

Sam wondered if her conviction came from something Lionel wrote in those letters. Or if it was simply the denial of the bereaved.

Whatever its root, Beth needed reassurance. "I'll assign a couple of marshals to Max. And I'll bring you to a safe house."

He expected to see relief bathing her face, and a resurgence of faith in her support system. Instead, he read resignation and hopelessness.

"I told Amanda you'd say that. That the Service would hide us again." Beth looked into Sam's eyes. Her own looked lifeless. "Do you know what she said?"

Sam's heart broke. He'd seen too many of these situations not to know exactly how Beth and Amanda felt.

"She said, 'There's no place left to hide.' "

Beth grasped Sam's hands within hers and drew him so close a whisper sounded like a command. "Tell me the truth. Is she right? Have we run out of places to hide?"

He wanted to say no, that the Service could always move them to the middle of another nowhere and assign another identity. But the reality was that sometimes, despite the Service's best efforts, witnesses became incapable of shedding yet another skin.

"I don't know," he said honestly. "Could be."

CHAPTER

EIGHTEEN

Amanda first met Lupe Vazquez when she was working anticrime out of the Thirty-Second Precinct. Domestic violence was not an uncommon crime in that neighborhood, but Lupe's husband, Jesús, was an animal, a violent man who constantly felt the need to display his machismo by savaging women. Lupe was a small woman who once possessed a lively spirit and a big heart, so said her friends. These days, Lupe was withdrawn and quivered like a twig in the wind, even when the air was still. Before Jesús disfigured her, she was a pretty woman, with dark, snapping eyes, high cheekbones, and a full, expressive mouth that was usually spread in a smile. Thanks to Jesús, she looked like a boxer who had gone one too many rounds.

Amanda's introduction to Lupe was in a fifth-floor apartment on 135th Street. She was cowering in a corner, her nose smashed and bloody, the flesh on her neck and breasts singed from deep cigarette burns, her wrist fractured in three places. A neighbor had heard Lupe's screams and called the police. On the way to the hospital, Amanda gently suggested that Lupe seek help, but the woman was too frightened to listen; Amanda's other suggestion, to bring charges against Jesús, was completely out of the question.

Amanda rescued Lupe three more times before moving out of the precinct into the Crime Scene Unit. Each time, the beating was more severe, Lupe's body more damaged. Still, her determination not to punish the man who was punishing her remained firm. That blind insistence on accepting the unacceptable disturbed Amanda, because it wasn't love or loyalty that was keeping her silent. It was the voice of subjugation, the sense that Lupe had been brutalized so badly and so often, she had surrendered her soul to Jesús' malicious dominance. Amanda wanted Lupe to fight back.

Asking around, Amanda found a battered women's shelter operating out of a church basement in Washington Heights. Run by a couple of experienced social workers and a staff of motivated volunteers, The Bent Wing was a makeshift safe house high on good intentions and low on funds. By reaching out and appealing to the samaritan that still existed within many in the community of man, they found ways to arrange for medical care, psychological counseling, legal advice, temporary housing, and child care. Bound by strong feelings of sisterhood and conscience, the founders of The Bent Wing operated under a mandate that said they would take in any woman who knocked on their door. There were many. Unfortunately, there were more who should have come and didn't.

Since many of the women who visited shelters like The Bent Wing returned to their abusers, Amanda volunteered to teach those who wanted to learn how to document their abuse. She taught them—and often, their children—how to use Polaroid instant cameras to capture the violence on film. Though injuries could be photographed up to five days following an attack, it was best to take the pictures as quickly as possible. If a weapon was used, it should be photographed adjacent to the bruises, then, if possible, directly above the bruise. She explained that documentation by photography was a powerful tool in the investigation and prosecution of domestic violence crimes.

"If the pictures are good enough," she said, moved by the terror that was a constant in these women's eyes, "the State can prosecute successfully without your testimony." For women in fear of their lives, that was important because reprisals by jailed abusers were frequent, usually devastating, sometimes fatal.

Knowing that her lectures meant nothing without equipment, she started a pool that collected money from female members of the NYPD and the NYFD to buy Polaroids and disposable cameras that could be handed out to those in need. She also gave them her telephone number at CSU. If anyone cried for help, she promised she would listen.

The Bent Wing became her cause. Whenever she had a few extra hours she visited the shelter, if not to teach, then to serve food, babysit frightened children, tend to bruises, swab a floor, or simply help comfort a woman in trouble. Over time, Amanda realized why she cared so deeply about this project: She acknowledged a kinship with these women. Like her, they had lost their identity. Isolated from friends and family, alienated from society, unable to share their truth, they became as hidden and as controlled by a code of secrecy as anyone in WITSEC. The difference was that those in WITSEC were protected.

Three years ago, Amanda was at The Bent Wing when Lupe and her son, Manuel, came seeking shelter. Both had been viciously pummeled. Lupe had so many broken bones she could barely move, but she refused to go to the hospital. She was afraid Children's Services would be notified and her son would be taken from her. Not only couldn't she bear the thought of losing Manuel, but she knew she could never convince Jesús that it wasn't her fault. He would surely kill her.

One of the doctors who regularly volunteered at the shelter set Lupe's arm, taped her ribs, and bandaged her left eye, which was livid and swollen shut. He suspected internal damage and begged to hospitalize her. When she said no, he administered painkillers and told the women tending her what to watch for. If they noticed any signs of acute distress, they were to call an ambulance immediately. At that point, he told them, they wouldn't have a problem. Lupe wouldn't be able to argue.

Manuel, who had two broken fingers, three missing teeth, and a dislocated jaw, never left his mother's side. It had been his idea to come to the shelter.

"I heard about this place from a friend," he confided to Max. "His mom came here. He told me my mom would be safe."

Manuel was ten, a dangerously impressionable age when many in his neighborhood were beginning to select role models; some were beginning to compile police records. Often they got caught up in the mystique of gangs, attracted by the concept of safety in numbers and a sense of belonging. When the heads of those family-alternatives demanded criminal acts as initiation rites, the children obeyed; they craved approval and would do whatever was necessary to get it.

It was not a giant leap from there into the heart of the drug culture, which was growing more and more pervasive. Youngsters with a need to please were easily intimidated and experimented with drugs to prove how manly they were. For so many in the Three-Two, adolescence presented life choices that would have been difficult for most adults. Yet every day, these children were being forced to choose between long-term, but vague, rewards and instant gratification.

Amanda spent a lot of time with Manuel at Lupe's bedside. They spoke about his dreams of being an architect and designing big beautiful buildings for families to live in. They spoke about his mother, whom he loved fiercely and felt duty-bound to protect, as well as his father, for whom his feelings were more ambivalent. Jesús was a local celebrity. He was feared, fearless, and always seemed to have pockets stuffed with money, which to many in their community translated into power. Manuel respected that, and admitted he enjoyed being the prince. What he didn't enjoy was his father's violent temper. He wanted to blame it on Jesús' drug habit, but even when his father was straight, he was vicious.

Amanda sensed this was a boy on the brink. He could follow his father into a life of unrepentant crime, or set himself on a path that would lead him out of the barrio. To do the latter required courage. And a mentor. That's when Amanda approached Pete Doyle and asked him to become a big brother to Manuel. She wasn't surprised when Pete agreed. Children were his soft spot.

Pete was perfect for Manuel. He didn't come on all tough and parental. Rather, he was a pal to the boy, someone who didn't lecture or lay down a lot of rules. If they talked, it was while they were engaged in an activity they both liked, like shooting hoops, taking in a movie, or running along the Hudson. Being on the force, Pete had seen dozens of men like Jesús, so he knew to be careful. If Jesús thought some other man was fathering his son, not only would Pete become a target, but Manuel would pay dearly for his betrayal. Each week during the three months the boy and his mother lived at the shelter—and long after they'd left—Manuel called the CSU so that Pete could give him his schedule. If Manuel could get away and Pete wasn't busy, they got together. Often, Pete brought his kids along on his outings with Manuel. He wanted his children to know people from varying circumstances so they could understand how big and complicated the world was. He wanted Manuel to know that even a separated family could be a loving entity.

During Lupe's stay at the shelter, the social workers, aided by Max and Pete, repeatedly advised her to have Jesús arrested.

"He has to know there are consequences," they told her.

A psychiatrist and a lawyer reassured her that pressing charges was the best thing she could do for herself and for son. What these advisors neglected to take into account was that Lupe and Manuel were dependent on Jesús for food and shelter. When they were healed and strong enough to leave The Bent Wing, they didn't have many options so they chose to go home. When Jesús was released from jail he also went home. When his case came to trial, Lupe refused to testify against him.

Over the next several years, while their visits were sporadic and difficult to arrange, Pete continued to mentor Manuel, and Amanda stayed in touch with Lupe. That connection turned into a blessing, when six months ago, Manuel called Pete, frantic, crying, and screaming into the phone, almost unintelligible in his panic. He begged Pete and Max to come quickly.

They found Lupe in an alley. She was near death. Her spleen had burst. Her left eye socket was shattered. Her right knee was fractured. One lung was collapsed. There was vaginal bleeding. And her back was painted with wide purple welts. Manuel said they came from a thick, wooden table leg that Jesús had used in the attack. Manuel showed Pete the trash can where Jesús had tossed it.

Amanda took some pictures at the scene to illustrate how Lupe had been discarded like a piece of trash, but she intended to document this beating fully and completely. Later that night, or as soon as Lupe was able, she intended to bring a Victim's Assistant from the District Attorney's Office to conduct an interview. Then, she would photograph every inch of Lupe's body. She and Pete had decided that if they had to drag Lupe into court, they would.

Amanda strode purposefully into the Manhattan Criminal Court Building, her eyes shaded by sunglasses, her gait brisk and steady, despite her high heels. Checking the cluster of people milling about— since Thompson's beating, she was particularly vigilant—she headed for the elevators, eager to get this day over with. She had been called to testify as an expert witness in the *State v. Jesús Vazquez*. The charge was attempted murder.

Pete was waiting for her in the hallway outside the courtroom. Like Amanda, he was wearing a dark suit and a grim expression.

"I'm glad the DA didn't give this prick a chance to plead out," Pete hissed as they were escorted to their seats by an attorney from the prosecutor's office.

It wasn't unusual for abusers charged with assault and battery to plead guilty in hopes of getting a suspended sentence contingent upon their receiving counseling. When the DA read the doctor's report, he upped Jesús's charges to attempted murder, eliminating any chance of his pleading out and escaping jail time. At the time of the attack, Lupe had been five months pregnant. Jesús Vazquez had killed his child and almost killed his wife. In the opinion of the State, he was beyond counseling.

Manuel and Lupe were not in court, but they were what this trial was all about: the quality of their lives, their physical safety, their ability to move on and pull some smidgen of happiness out of the rotten hand they had been dealt. Since Jesús's arrest, the two of them had been living at an undisclosed sister shelter in Queens. Manuel transferred to another school, where he was registered under another name; Amanda took him aside and spoke to him at great length about how to deal with pretending to be who he was not. During Lupe's recovery, she refreshed her skills as a seamstress, taking in work from several dry cleaners in the neighborhood. Once the trial was over, she hoped to find an apartment, get a job, and start over. Before she and Manuel could do that, however, they had to know that Jesús wouldn't be able to find them. And hurt them.

On the way down the aisle to their seats, Amanda noted that the audience was a sea of white satin: The *Blanca Muerte* was out in full force. It was during her trial preparations with Mike Schwartz, the assistant district attorney trying the case, that she learned Jesús Vazquez was the head of the New York branch of the LA-based gang. Knowing their connection to the Espinosas, her instinct was to beg off, to tell Schwartz she couldn't, or wouldn't, testify. It was simply too déjà vu.

Sam agreed. He felt uneasy about her parading into a courtroom and testifying in a case that was bound to attract the press. And the Espinosas.

"I'll explain the situation to the district attorney," he said. "He'll be discreet."

Amanda was torn between thoughts about her own safety and visions of Lupe's battered body.

"I promised her I'd be there if she stepped up. I promised other women who came to the shelter the same thing. If I don't show, I'm as bad as the men who beat them."

"Absolutely not! You're protecting yourself against a very real threat," Sam said.

"Maybe so, but the message these women will get is that they don't matter. I can't say that to them."

"You'd be putting yourself at risk."

"They're putting themselves at risk by bringing charges against these animals."

After this last barbarous assault, Lupe needed a hysterectomy and weeks in a body cast after surgery to repair damaged vertebrae. Her face was healed, but scarred, as was her soul. Yet she continued to tough it out, crediting Max and the women at The Bent Wing with providing the motivation to get on with her life: to stand up to Jesús and set an example for Manuel.

"If she's brave enough to do that," Amanda agonized, "how can I let her and Manuel down?

"What's brave for one might be foolish for another," Sam warned. "Let Doyle testify. He was there. He can corroborate her charges."

"I took the pictures. And I made the promises. Besides," she said, defending her decision, "the faceless ones don't know my name or what I look like."

That was three months ago. Before Jaime Bastido was released from prison. Before Lionel killed himself. Before someone tried to beat her name and address out of poor Thompson. Before someone got hold of that roll of film.

"What's the matter with you," Pete whispered. "You look like you're having one of those hot flash things. Are you older than I think?"

She laughed and squeezed his hand. "Just a little nervous. Testifying against a gang leader when his soldiers are glaring at you is not exactly my idea of a good time. Know what I mean?"

"I do indeed."

The trial proceeded quickly. Schwartz presented his case as cut-and-dried attempted murder. Jesús Vazquez had a history of violence and abuse that extended over many years. On this particular night, he assaulted his wife with the intention of killing her. He beat her so savagely, he terminated a five-month pregnancy, nearly broke Mrs. Vazquez's back, and inflicted such severe internal bleeding, the only reason she didn't die, was that her son managed to get help in time to save her.

The defense's strategy was simple: Yes, Jesús beat her, but it got out of hand because he suspected that she was pregnant by another man. Never, at any time, did he intend to kill her. In fact, if the court agreed, he'd be happy to go for counseling. He loved his wife and his son and wanted his family back. Schwartz told Pete and Amanda, Vazquez's lawyer had tried to plea-bargain the charge down to assault several times. The DA's office refused. They felt their case was that strong. Also, Judge Meyer carried a reputation of being tough, but fair.

While the attorneys presented their opening arguments to the jury,

Amanda watched Jesús. His eyes roved the courtroom continuously. Amanda wondered if he was looking for Lupe. If so, he was going to be disappointed. The ADA would not be calling her to the stand.

Sybil Whitehall, one of the social workers who founded The Bent Wing, was the first to testify. With Schwartz's guidance, she described her first encounter with Lupe and Manuel, relating both their physical and mental states at that time. She recounted discussions she'd had with Lupe during her three-month stay at the shelter, during which Lupe expressed fear for her life.

"Why didn't she take her son and leave Mr. Vazquez?"

"Because he told her if she ever left, he'd track her down and kill her. But before he did, he said he'd make her watch as he killed Manuel."

"Objection!" Jesús's lawyer bounded to his feet. "Hearsay."

Schwartz walked back to the counsels' table and picked up a piece of paper. "If it please the court, I'd like to enter this into evidence. It's a signed affidavit attesting to Mrs. Vazquez's belief that her life was in constant danger if she stayed with her husband, and especially if she left."

Following Sybil's appearance was a parade of the caretakers who had tended to Lupe's wounds, both mental and physical. Each one painted a dreadful picture of habitual torture. Amanda found these testimonies difficult, but they were not impressing the gallery. Their faces said: Whatever Jesús did to Lupe, she deserved. Of course they were programmed to side with Jesús. Amanda was more interested in the reaction of the jury. So far, their sympathies appeared to be with Lupe. In fact, if Amanda had to hazard a guess, the jeers and growls of Jesús' army weren't helping his case.

When Pete took the stand, Jesús became particularly attentive, which worried Amanda. She and Pete had asked Schwartz not to mention Pete's mentoring of Manuel. The less said about the boy's reaching out to others for the things his father was supposed to provide, the better. Still, someone might have seen them together. Or Jesús could have beaten it out of Manuel.

Schwartz slowed his pace and skillfully elicited a harrowing account of finding Lupe in the alley. Pete's answers, though short and within the bounds of acceptable testimony, were graphic and unsettling. Even some of the *Muerte* girls looked uncomfortable.

On cross-examination, Jorge Ramos, the defense attorney, opted to leapfrog over Lupe's injuries and attack Pete's credibility as a witness.

"Do you have a relationship with Manuel Vazquez?" he asked, loudly and boldly.

"Objection," Schwartz rose. "Relevancy. This case does not involve Manuel Vazquez, Your Honor."

Ramos eyed the judge. "May we approach?"

Meyer invited both attorneys to join him at the bench for a sidebar conversation.

"Detective Doyle has established a friendship with my client's son which we believe prejudices him against Mr. Vazquez," Ramos said.

Schwartz was incredulous. "In what way?"

"We think he wants to take over the fathering of this child. If Mr. Vazquez is convicted and sent away, he stands a better chance."

"Your Honor, that's absurd. Mr. Ramos is bringing this up as a distraction from the main issue, which," Schwartz emphasized, "is the attempted murder of Lupe Vazquez."

The judge agreed. "Objection sustained. Move along, Mr. Ramos."

"No further questions, Your Honor."

Ramos took his seat, satisfied. He'd succeeded in doing two things: creating a diversion that might prevent jurors from ruminating over the gruesome details of Pete's testimony and raising a question that was deemed irrelevant, yet remained unanswered. Jorge only needed one person to find that mysterious enough to raise a reasonable doubt.

When the judge called a lunch recess before beginning with the next witness, Ramos swaggered out of the courtroom, convinced the momentum had shifted and he had the advantage.

Immediately after lunch, Amanda was called to the stand. Whatever advantage Ramos thought he'd gained, was lost. On the counsels' table, Schwartz had a stack of mounted photographs, huge enlargements of nasty wounds, as well as eight-by-tens to pass around the jury box for hands-on, close-up examination. On the stand, he had a young woman with an impressive calm and an impeccable reputation.

After she was sworn in, Schwartz asked her to identify herself.

"Amanda Maxwell, Detective First Grade assigned to the New York City Crime Scene Unit."

"Do you have a specialty, Detective Maxwell?"

"Forensic photography."

"How and when did you meet the victim, Lupe Vazquez?"

Amanda recalled their encounters during her tour with the Thirty-

Second Precinct, succinctly and without editorial. That information was background. It would not convict. To Schwartz's question about what she found when arriving at the alley on the night in question, Amanda responded clinically, yet with an undertone of clear compassion.

"What did you do, Detective, upon finding Ms. Vazquez?"

"While we waited for the ambulance, I took an initial set of photographs."

"For what purpose?"

"To show the extent of the injuries almost immediately after they had been administered. And the callousness with which she had been discarded." She could feel the heat of Jesús's anger. He wanted to leap from his chair and throttle her neck. She kept her eyes on the ADA, who was selecting the first photograph for display and entering it into evidence.

With no other introduction, he placed it on a huge easel for everyone in the courtroom to see: a black-and-blue lump of flesh lying amidst open bags of garbage. Food scrapings, gnawed steak bones, dirty diapers, and other pieces of filth littered Lupe's body, but nothing could obscure the vicious nature of her wounds. Two women on the jury gasped. Several young women in the gallery looked away. Even the young studs in their cockatoo white-satin jackets seemed to lose some of their color.

Aware that Ramos might have diluted Pete's testimony with his side show, Mike Schwartz opted to reexplore that territory. He began this phase of his questioning by getting Max to give an accounting of Lupe's injuries. Once the jury was reminded of the viciousness of the attack, he moved on.

"Did you visit Mrs. Vazquez after she was admitted to the hospital?"

"My partner and I followed the ambulance there. I saw her immediately after the doctors completed their examination."

"After Mrs. Vazquez's surgeries?" Ramos might look to confuse the jury by claiming many of Lupe's bruises were the result of her operations.

"No. In the emergency room. Before any invasive medical treatment was initiated."

"Were you alone with her?"

"No. A nurse and a resident were present throughout."

"Throughout what?"

"I was permitted to bring a Victim's Assistant from the District Attorney's Office in to interview Mrs. Vazquez."

"Did you photograph her at that time?"

"Yes."

Following a preset agenda, Schwartz led Max through her protocol. He placed blowups on the easel; she described what procedures she had followed and why.

Several normal-range photographs of Lupe's head and neck were displayed for identification purposes. Her back and lower region were also shown. Having established that Lupe Vazquez was the victim in the photographs, Mike moved to the close-ups. The first was a shot of Lupe's arm. There was a large prune-colored contusion marring the flesh on the upper arm. A rectangular card tinted gray rested alongside the injured appendage.

"This rectangle," Max said, using a pointer to indicate the card, "is an 18 percent gray scale. I laid it against Mrs. Vazquez's arm so that when the film was developed, the lab could assign the proper skin tones."

"That means the livid color of these bruises is accurate."

"Correct."

Mike displayed several other pictures: close-ups of her right knee and thigh, her other arm, her neck. It was a barbarous parade.

"Would you please tell the court how these were taken."

"I used a single-lens reflex camera with a macro lens. We find that in domestic-violence cases, we need the minimum focusing distance so that we can fill the frame with the wound site without distortion."

Lupe's smashed face stared at the crowd, although it was clear that Lupe couldn't see anything out of her left eye.

"If you look at the left cheek, just below the eye, you can see marks consistent with those found on blunt instruments known as brass knuckles."

Mike introduced a set of brass knuckles collected at the Vazquez home, then laid them against the photograph. They fit perfectly; Max also testified that the blood on the knuckles was determined to be Lupe's. When she described the welts on Lupe's back, Mike entered the bloody table leg into evidence.

"Bruises are transfer patterns," she explained. "If you hold that piece of wood against those wounds"—which Mike did—"the relationship between them becomes clear and irrefutable."

As she made that last statement, Amanda turned toward Jesús

with a glint of triumph in her eyes. His fingerprints were all over that table leg, and they both knew it. It was the only time during the trial that Jesús looked away.

When it was Ramos's turn to cross-examine, he moved out from behind his counsels' table slowly. With a stealth he hoped was menacing, he approached the witness stand. For several minutes, he paced back and forth in front of Amanda, stalking her, assessing her. If he was trying to make her flinch, he failed. Her eyes followed him, diluting his intensity with a look that bordered on amusement. This was a performance Ramos was putting on for the sake of his client and whoever was sitting in the audience that might replace Jesús in the *Muerte* hierarchy in the event that the jury didn't return a not-guilty verdict. Amanda gave his performance a thumbs-down.

Infuriated, Ramos came right at her.

"You're a regular volunteer at The Bent Wing, is that right?"

"Yes."

"One of the things you do there is teach photography to women and children. Correct?"

"Yes."

"Not just any kind of photography. You teach small children how to take pictures of scratches and cuts. Isn't that right, Detective." He was so close to her she could smell the garlic he had for lunch on his breath.

"I teach children who are frightened by the beatings they witness to document the abuse that goes on in their homes."

"But if they don't witness the so-called abuse, Detective Maxwell, do you really think children know the difference between an injury that's caused by accident and one that's deliberate?"

Amanda turned for a moment, redirecting the jury's attention to Lupe's body lying in the alley. "Yes, Mr. Ramos, I do."

He moved to her right, placing his back to the photograph, blocking the jury's view. He faced the twelve, washed all anger from his face, and rested an arm on the ledge framing the witness stand, all chummy-like.

"Your job exposes you to a great deal of violence, wouldn't you say?"

"I would."

"Seeing it day after day must make you angry."

It wasn't a question, so Amanda didn't respond.

"It must make you want to change things, make things right."

Again, Amanda left him hanging.

"On the whole, do you think there's more violence directed at women than men?"

"Yes."

"Does that bother you?"

"Of course."

He nodded as if he had just scored a point.

"You've stated that you got to know Lupe Vazquez over a number of years, is that correct?"

"Yes."

"Would you say you were friends?"

"In a manner of speaking."

"Yes or no, Detective."

She knew he was looking to paint her as prejudicial, but there was little she could do except respond as directed.

"Yes.

"Do you look to help your friends out? Especially your female friends?"

"Objection."

"Sustained. Mr. Ramos, I fail to see where this line of questioning has any relevancy. Either get to the point or move on."

"Yes, Your Honor." Certain that he was about to deliver a crippling blow, he faced Amanda. "Isn't it true, Detective, that using a flash can distort pictures of bruises?"

From their respective seats, Mike Schwartz and Pete smirked. Ramos was known for having a low opinion of women. They had anticipated that he wouldn't give Amanda the respect she deserved.

"That is true, Mr. Ramos, which is why I used available light and a Cokin A.036 correction filter for this series. Also, the room in which these photographs were taken had fluorescent lighting, which also tends to distort color. This particular filter corrects all that. The photographs you have before you are completely accurate. The bruises are as devastating as they appear."

The courtroom buzzed. Ramos flushed and glowered at Amanda. Undaunted, she returned his hostility. Bested, Ramos retreated to his table and riffled through some notes, buying time. Amanda glanced over at her colleagues. Pete gave her a quick, unobtrusive thumbs-up. Mike awarded her a quick nod. She had destroyed Ramos's cross and practically assured a conviction. A smile started to form, then stopped.

Little Ray Saviano was seated in the back of the courtroom. A shiver trilled up her spine. When did he walk in? Gulping down a rush of alarm, she watched one of Jesús's henchmen lean forward and poke him. Jesús turned in his seat. He made eye contact with Little Ray. It was obvious immediately there was no love lost between these two men. They were in the middle of a vicious turf war. To their respective organizations, this battle was being waged over control of Propaine distribution. To them, it was about ego and pride and dominance.

Jesús sneered and tossed his head dismissively as he faced the court. Little Ray slouched in his seat, spread his arms on the ledge running behind the row, and laughed. His merriment displeased the men and women in white satin. Almost as one, they turned and glared at him. Little Ray laughed harder and louder. The judge rapped his gavel and called for order. The *Muerte* gang obeyed.

Amanda noticed how quickly the smile on Little Ray's face faded. Serious now, he looked to the opposite corner of the gallery where an older Hispanic gentleman sat. Amanda hadn't noticed him before either. He had an odd expression on his face, pinched, as if his jaw was wired. The two spoke via head bobs and hand signals. For an instant, she was certain the Hispanic man's head bobbed in her direction. Who was he? And what connection did he have to Little Ray?

Amanda felt as if she'd been transported into the middle of a nightmare. Twenty years before, her mother sat on a witness stand in a courtroom and testified against members of the mob and the Espinosa cartel. Her life and Amanda's were changed forever. Now Amanda was in a courtroom, face-to-face with the second generation of those her mother convicted. Amanda prayed this confluence of descendants was a coincidence, that Little Ray was doing his cock-of-the-walk routine and was there to taunt the *Muerte* gang, not to scope her out. It would be just like him to gloat over his ability to hit the *Muerte*'s two runners and walk free, while Jesús knocked his woman around and was facing the real possibility of jail time. Amanda prayed that all of them being in the same courtroom at the same time was a fluke and not history repeating itself.

"I have no further questions," Ramos said, admitting defeat.

Amanda didn't move. She was transfixed.

"Detective Maxwell," Judge Meyer said sharply, snapping Amanda out of her fog. "You're dismissed."

"Yes. Thank you, Your Honor." She willed herself to stand and walk to her seat without falling.

Pete whispered congratulations to her and patted her hand, but she heard and felt nothing. She was numbed by the knowledge that the monster which lived deep within her had broken free of its restraints. Big and horrible, the monster had been born a long time ago. Dependent on fear for its existence, it was fed and nurtured by years of running and hiding and looking over her shoulder. Over the past several years, however, Amanda had grown complacent, even a bit lax, because she'd convinced herself that the monster lay dormant. She'd even begun to believe it had died.

Then Lionel killed himself. Thompson was brutalized. An incriminating roll of film disappeared. And now, the evil specter of Big Ray Saviano and Raoul Espinosa had reared its ugly head.

The monster was alive. And out to get her.

CHAPTER

NINETEEN

It took the jury less than an hour to return a guilty verdict. Jesús Vazquez was remanded to Rikers Island to await sentencing. The *Blanca Muerte* reacted predictably. They booed and hissed, shook their fists at the jury, and muttered threats, as if the twelve men and women who'd heard the case had mistaken those satin jackets for a fashion trend. As Jesús was escorted out, he also leveled threats, only his were aimed directly at Amanda and Pete.

Mike Schwartz sought to reassure his two witnesses. "Don't worry about Jesús. He's going away for a long time. As for his minions, those clowns have bigger fish to fry than the two of you. No disrespect intended."

"None taken," Pete said, watching the subject of their conversation being led out of the courtroom. He and Amanda had testified in hundreds of cases. They knew what to expect. "I don't worry about skels like Vazquez and the *Muertes*. If I did, I couldn't do my job. Right, Max?"

She agreed, but she was listening with only half an ear. Her thoughts were focused on Little Ray Saviano, who'd left quickly so as to avoid tangling with Jesús's supporters, the people behind Vazquez, and the man with the stiff jaw who also seemed to have disappeared. Her internal radar said he was trouble.

"I know it's early, but how 'bout some dinner?" Pete asked as they rode down in the elevator.

"I'm beat."

"Me too, but you've gotta eat." He wrapped an arm around her shoulder, gave her an affectionate squeeze, and whispered in her ear. "I promise not to hit on you."

Amanda pouted. "How will I ever get through the evening?"

"Well, if you insist . . ."

"Forget it!" she said laughing as they walked out of the courthouse into the cool air of evening. She could always count on Pete to shake away the cobwebs.

As Pete debated whether to go to Chinatown or Little Italy, Max's radar system beeped. Off to the side, that odd man was huddled with Little Ray.

"Who's that guy talking to Saviano?" she asked, directing Pete's attention to their right.

"I don't know." Pete eyed the pair carefully. "I've never seen him before."

"He was in the courtroom. When I was on the stand, I saw the two of them signaling to each other."

Pete took her elbow and steered her across the street. "Maybe he came from LA to take over from Vazquez."

"Possible, but I thought the Savianos and the *Blanca Muerte* were at war. These guys look chummy."

Pete remembered the two youngsters they scraped up off that basketball court. "He could be an Espinosa lieutenant up from Mexico for a lookee-see." Pete chuckled. "I can't imagine the four enchiladas were too happy to hear about our boy Jesús being charged with attempted murder. They don't give a shit if he beats his wife senseless, but they're dealing dope by the truckload. They don't want the law anywhere near them."

"You think Little Ray's trying to cut a deal with the Espinosas?"

"Could be. He needs to do something."

"What do you mean?"

"According to our man on the mayor's task force," he said, referring to Jake, "Little Ray's a colossal fuck-up. If he's not strutting around like a peacock looking to get his mug on TV, he's crushing skulls."

"I thought that's what Mafia dons did best."

"True, but all that cock-of-the-walk crap is only impressive if you've got money in the bank. Word is, the little man's let business slide so badly, the family's practically broke. If he blows this drug deal, the Savianos could be history."

"Big Ray must be furious." Amanda hoped he was. He had destroyed her family. She wouldn't weep if someone destroyed his.

"That's putting it mildly." Pete hailed a cab and directed the driver to take them to Mott Street. All this talk about the Mafioso had killed his taste for Italian food. "Who knows. If things get really bad, Big Ray might start calling the shots from the Big House."

Amanda had considered that, then dismissed it. Perhaps she shouldn't have. "He's been away a long time and he's never getting out. Why would anyone listen to him?"

The taxi stopped in front of Hunan Garden. Pete paid the cabby and steered her toward the door. "Because Big Ray Saviano was the Don of dons, Max. He could be doing time in an igloo up at the North Pole, it wouldn't matter. Someone's always going to listen to him."

Jake got off the Merritt Parkway, turned right, and headed toward Banksville. Throughout the ride from the city, he reviewed the facts he'd gleaned so far, then tried to rewrite them. The first weekend in April, Lionel flew via Northwest Airlines to Madison, Wisconsin, via Detroit. He rented a car and stayed in a suite at the Edgewater Hotel. As far as anyone could recall, he was alone. On that same weekend, Amanda Maxwell took America West into Chicago's Midway Airport, en route to Madison, Wisconsin. There was no record of her registering in any of that city's lodgings.

Several times over the past six months, Fredda told Jake she'd reserved rooms at the Pierre, the Plaza, and the Waldorf. The management at each of those hotels confirmed the reservations, but said no one actually stayed in those rooms.

"Could it be that Mr. Baird only wanted them for an hour or so?" It was a feeble attempt at subtlety, but it was the most Jake could manage.

To a one, they informed him that nothing in the rooms was touched, not the bed or anything in the bathroom. At the Plaza, one of the clerks at the reception desk did recall that a young woman fitting Max's description picked up a key to a room reserved for Lionel Baird. It was dropped in the return-key slot the next morning, but no one saw who turned the key in, and housekeeping was certain no one used the room. Jake wondered why a reception clerk at a busy hotel would remember something so minor.

"I was getting off at the time," he explained. "I handed this young woman the key and watched as she went to the elevator across from the desk. She was the only one in the car. I don't know why I watched the floor indicator, but I did. It showed that the car stopped at the second floor. The room key I'd handed her was for fifteen-eleven. Not more than five minutes later, I left the desk and went for my break. Just as I was passing the elevator bank, she stepped out in front of me and walked around to the Fifth Avenue exit. I was curious, so I watched her. She ran down the steps and got into a waiting limousine."

"Was anyone in the car?"

"It was dark. I couldn't tell. But after taking a key, then not going up to the room, I guess I paid attention because it struck me as strange."

Indeed. Was Lionel having an affair? Or had he set up an elaborate ruse to make someone think that he was? And who was the someone: Pamela? Why bother? And why use Max? Jake tried to fill in a few blanks with Thompson, but struck out. Thompson may have been sedated, but he wasn't too drugged to tell Jake that he had nothing to say to Pamela or her representative. The only thing that seemed certain was that the one constant in Lionel's life over the past six months was a women who could have been Amanda's double. Or Amanda herself.

At La Crémaillère, Robert offered Jake a seat at the bar and a refreshment. It was late afternoon, and the dining rooms were being set for the dinner crowd.

While Jake reiterated the purpose of his visit, a waiter set down a ramekin of warm apple-and-brioche bread pudding topped with crème fraîche, then poured steaming black coffee into an expensive-looking china cup. The aroma was strong, describing a freshly ground blend heavily laden with dark, French-roasted beans. Jake tasted both and swooned.

"I was told Mr. Baird was a regular here. I can see why."

Robert seemed pleased, yet anxious. "I'm proud to say that he was both a longtime patron and a friend." Robert's posture straightened, his gregarious nature muted for a moment by honest grief.

"Did he dine here often?"

"For a man who lived in the city, yes." It was clear that Robert enjoyed their relationship. "Whenever he needed to escape to the country, he came here."

Jake had no quarrel with that. La Crémaillère was the quintessential country inn: bucolic setting, low ceilings, a large fireplace, small rooms, lots of antiques, and slanted stone floors that attested to its longevity. Its chic came from the food, the French accents of the wait staff, and, Jake assumed, its clientele.

"Did he join a group of people from the area? Or did he come with a guest?"

Robert's smile indicated an anthology of tales he could tell. "Mr. Baird never dined alone, or at large tables."

"Over the past several months, was his dinner companion a younger woman? Tall, about five-nine, auburn hair, bordering on gorgeous? She goes by the name of Max."

Recognition flashed in Robert's eyes, but he wasn't ready to acknowledge the acquaintance. "Why are you asking?"

"I've been retained by Mr. Baird's widow to look into the circumstances surrounding his death."

"Widow? I thought the Bairds were divorced."

Pamela must have irked the hell out of Robert, because an involuntary sneer insinuated itself on his lips.

"They were in the process, but it wasn't finalized, so technically, she's his widow." Jake shrugged. "It's a long story. Let's just say, those who cared about him are trying to understand why he might have taken his life."

Robert didn't chime in the way Jake had hoped.

"I just want to ask this other woman a few questions. That's all."

Robert acquiesced, but reluctantly. He confirmed that Max and Lionel dined there at least five times over six months. They always arrived separately, but left together. They had a favorite table, held hands occasionally, but never pawed or fawned over each other. Robert had no idea what Max's last name was, where she lived, what, if anything, she did for a living, and whether or not Lionel's intentions were honorable or dishonorable.

"He seemed completely delighted with her, as well he should have been."

Jake finished the last of the bread pudding. "I take it you liked her."

"Very much." Robert looked around, as if someone, maybe Pamela, was lurking in the background and might overhear. "She didn't have any airs. That's rather unusual, you know. Especially for women who consort with men like Lionel Baird."

Jake wanted to say, "Yes, I know," but the words froze on his lips. He was beginning to realize there was an awful lot about Amanda Maxwell he didn't know.

After dinner, Amanda declined Pete's invitation to drop her off at her apartment, and headed instead to Annie's. They hadn't seen each other since the night Lionel died, and Amanda was worried about her friend.

"I've been frantic," Annie said as she pulled Amanda into the loft and bolted the door behind her. They hugged, holding each other tight. "Are you all right? Tell me what's happening!"

"In a minute." Amanda moved swiftly and stealthily through the loft, peering out each window, making certain she hadn't been followed.

"I don't know how you live like this," Annie said, rushing to uncork a bottle of wine. "I'm a wreck!"

"I am too, I just hide it better." Amanda hated the fact that Annie was tangled in this nasty web. At the same time, she thought guiltily, it felt wonderful to have a confidante.

They bivouacked on the couch and Amanda filled Annie in about what she'd heard around the house as well as what she and Pete discussed over dinner.

Annie's eyes grew so wide they looked like a cartoonist had drawn them. "This makes my soap sound like the adventures of Peter Cottontail."

Amanda tsked. "Don't romanticize this stuff, Annie. These villains use real guns, and their victims wind up real dead."

Chastised, Annie retreated into her wineglass, but only for a moment. "I can't believe Little Ray Saviano was in the audience when you testified. Ugh! Talk About your major greasers." She looked positively repulsed. "Was he there because of you?"

"I don't think so. He seemed more interested in this weird-looking Hispanic guy."

Max described the man with the tight jaw.

"He either had a chin implant, his jaw wired, or some other heavy-duty plastic surgery," Annie said with authority.

The color drained from Max's cheeks. "Plastic surgery?"

"Absolutely! Why? What's up? Who do you think he is?"

Amanda didn't have to think. She knew who it was. "Jaime Bastido."

"He's one of the guys your mom put away." Amanda was surprised Annie recognized the name so quickly. She explained. "When I was certain you were who I thought you were, I spent an afternoon in the library reacquainting myself with the details of Operation Laundry Day. I didn't want to say the wrong thing to the wrong person and risk having anything happen to you."

"I love you," Amanda said, tears peeking out from her eyes.

"You don't have much of a choice. I'm the only friend you've got!"

"Isn't that the truth!"

They laughed. For Annie, it was a miraculous moment, because it was familiar. She and Ricki Baird used to laugh like this all the time; Amanda Maxwell wasn't quite as loose. As their laughter faded, Annie looked closely at the courageous, but tightly wound woman seated across from her and, as she often did, wondered what kind of woman Ricki Baird would have been.

"Okay, so what's the story with Jaime Bastido?" she asked, shooing those thoughts away.

Amanda's mood turned cold sober. "He's been out of prison for a couple of months. They thought he went to Mexico, and maybe he did, but if what you say is true, he's alive and well and living in New York." She was on her feet, pacing, thinking aloud. "I felt something was up. He and Little Ray were signaling each other. And then again outside, they were in a huddle."

"So what?" Annie asked. "They don't know what your new name is or what you look like."

Amanda stopped dead in her tracks. "The film. What if he saw the pictures?"

"What film?" Annie asked, her heart racing. "What pictures?"

Amanda told her about the camera in Lionel's drawer, the pictures Lionel had insisted on taking of her and Beth, and finally, about the missing film cartridge.

"If the man in the courtroom was Bastido, and he saw those pictures . . ." Amanda left the thought hanging, but within seconds, it gathered strength and whirled through the room like a Texas dust storm, scattering grisly possibilities in its wake.

"Then he knows what you look like and can connect a name with a face."

"Exactly." Amanda's stride was getting longer, her pace more frantic. "And he knows what my mother looks like."

Annie shivered. Her hands were ice-cold as one awful image linked up with another. "He doesn't know her name or where she lives, does he?" Max had never told her where Cynthia was or what her new name was.

"I don't see how he could." She thought about what was lying on Lionel's desk when she found him. She saw nothing that compromised Beth. But she didn't know what the note in the trash said or what might have been taken along with the film.

"Is he stalking you?"

"Not yet." Amanda was annoyed with herself for not committing his face to memory. "My partner thinks Bastido came to court to hook up with Saviano or introduce himself to Vazquez's people." For a moment, she stood in the center of Annie's living room, helpless and forlorn, waiting for tragedy to strike. "If Bastido saw those pictures, my being there must have seemed like a bonus." She was so angry, she practically growled.

"How did he get his hands on those pictures?"

"I wish I knew."

An evil notion suddenly filled the room, daring one of them to acknowledge it. Annie picked up the gauntlet. "Could Bastido have killed Lionel?"

Amanda nodded. Her head was clanging from fear colliding with fact. "Maybe."

"How?" Annie hated where this was going. Depressing as it was to think of Lionel killing himself, murder opened a lot of doors, all of them leading to a very dark place. "You said it was suicide. Cut-and-dried. No question about it, suicide."

Amanda shrugged her shoulders. "I know. That's what I saw. That's what the CSU and Homicide saw."

"But you don't believe it."

Amanda heard the skepticism in Annie's voice. "In here," she said, tapping her hand against her heart, "I don't believe my father would schedule a dinner with us and kill himself instead of showing up."

"Could grief be coloring your thinking?" Annie asked, tiptoeing.

"Possibly." Amanda admitted, pacing again. "I'm not saying the pieces fit, but there are enough of them floating around to warrant a second look."

"Where exactly are you looking?"

"I took hundreds of pictures at the scene. Somewhere in there, there's a clue. I just have to find it."

Annie couldn't bear seeing her friend in such pain. Suddenly, she had a thought. "What about asking Jake for help? He's a private eye, isn't he?"

"A very good one."

"And you trust him, don't you?"

Annie had no idea what a loaded question that was. Like most people, she probably viewed trust as a one-size-fits-all investment. In fact, trust was a many-layered thing. Without thinking about it, people apportioned trust according to need: who they trusted with their phone number, their car, their hairdresser's name, their money, their husbands, their wives, their children. Amanda had two responses to the question, "Who do you trust?" No one and the few she trusted with her life. For a protected witness, there was no in between.

"I do, but I'm not sure I want to involve him in all this."

"If he loves you, he's already involved," Annie said, stating what she considered to be the obvious.

"I don't know that he does," Amanda said, her face turning pink.

"What does he say?" Annie probed. "How does he act when he's around you?"

The blush intensified. "We can't seem to keep our hands off each other."

Annie laughed at the sight of the cool, calm detective shuffling her feet like a nine-year-old at her first dance class. "Okay, we've established a serious lust factor. Lust is good."

"And he did say he thinks he's falling for me."

"Duh!" Annie shook her head and groaned. "How dense can you be? Call him. Speak to him. Once he hears Lionel was your father . . ."

"No!" It was as if a buzzer sounded, signaling a time's up for the warm and fuzzy recess. Whatever softness had decorated Amanda's face was gone. "No one else can know about my relationship to Lionel!"

"You're right. I'm sorry." Annie held up her hands. "I just want so desperately to help you."

"I know." Amanda said, somewhat distracted. Looking over Annie's head, she spied the long table with the wigs and the makeup. "And I think I've figured out exactly how you can do that."

She grabbed Annie's hand and practically dragged her to the other side of the room.

"Whoever stole those pictures knows what I look like, right?"

"Yeah."

"So, I can't look like me."

Annie had tuned in and was totally turned on. "Welcome to Miss Annie's Funny Face Farm," she chuckled, inviting Max to take a seat. "Make yourself comfortable while we conjure up a new look, or two, or three, or seven."

For the next several hours, Annie taught Amanda how to fit wigs, use stage makeup, and apply pieces of soft rubber to alter her facial features. They figured out what she needed to carry with her so she could accomplish quick changes at work or if she suspected she was being followed. Along with the makeup and wigs, she'd need a change of clothes and shoes. Annie found a reversible jacket and a squishy hat they thought could be useful, plus a pair of slacks and an old polyester dress that could be folded up and stashed in a backpack.

By the time Amanda left, wearing a short blond wig, a longer nose, rounder chin, louder makeup, and a short black leather skirt and boots that marked her as a downtown denizen, her own mother wouldn't have recognized her.

Which was a good thing, because it wasn't her mother who was waiting outside Annie's apartment. Amanda had no way of knowing that the homeless man crumpled in a doorway she passed on her way to the subway was Jaime Bastido.

Even Itzhak Perlman's violin couldn't soothe Jake's growing sense of dread. The more he looked into Lionel Baird's death, the more curious it became. Aside from everything he'd learned during the course of his day about Amanda's relationship with the late Mr. Baird, Caleb had left a message on his machine to call him. In April, Lionel put millions of dollars into a trust fund that listed East Gorham Associates as its nominee. Caleb had no idea who or what East Gorham Associates was, but he thought it was worth looking into.

Also, he'd faxed the FBI report on Annie Hart. Basically, it was unremarkable. She had no arrest record, no financial debts, no suspicious family history, no reason to even come to the attention of the FBI. Annie Hart was not her real name, but that didn't raise a flag for Jake. She'd been married once, briefly, and decided to retain her erstwhile husband's name. Her parents still lived in a modest home in a community north of Miami. The Colons were of Cuban extraction and elderly. Aña, as Annie was named, was adopted. For an instant, Jake wondered if Lionel might be the biological father, but Aña was the child of a Cuban immigrant who died en route to America.

"So why would Lionel's due diligence on a start-up include a dossier put together by the FBI?" Jake asked himself, shuffling papers as if by moving them about they'd magically form a picture that makes sense. "What, if anything, does Annie Hart's background have to do with Lionel's death? Who the hell is East Gorham Associates? And," he grumbled, trying to push Max's image out of his mind, "why should I care about any of this?"

★ ★ ★

It was eleven o'clock by the time Amanda got home. The message light on her answering machine was blinking. She was hoping it was Jake. Instead it was Carl Steinmetz. He said she could call him up to midnight.

"Your hours are as bad as mine," she said when they connected.

"That's because we're the good guys. The bad guys have been in bed since ten."

Amanda laughed. Uncle Sam liked Carl Steinmetz. She could see why. "So, what's up?" After the day she'd had, she hoped it was good news, although in the case of Jake's father, she wasn't certain what would be considered good news.

"I've got the information you asked for."

"You work fast."

"I'd like to take a big bow and impress the hell out of you, but it was easy. I knew where to go."

"Okay, give it up."

"Archie Fowler is dead."

Amanda winced. "Did he die in 1977 or recently?"

"Seventy-seven. He was the man they found in the trunk of that Dodge Dart."

"Why couldn't they verify it then?"

"I got all this from a Mafia snitch who's in the program," Carl explained. "He was the driver the night Vito Albanese executed the hit on Fowler. According to him, after Vito shot Archie, they burned his fingertips with acid to remove his prints. Another guy drove the car to Hoboken, where it was dumped off, flattened, and put on the scrap heap."

"Are you sure about this?"

"As sure as you can be when you get your information from a professional criminal." He paused, letting Max process what he'd told her. "My source was one of the guys caught in the sweep that netted Big Ray Saviano. I was on the team that entered him into WITSEC. I remembered he was questioned about the Dodge Dart murder, but at the time he wouldn't rat out Albanese."

"Saviano was the bigger fish," Amanda said.

"Exactly. Giving up Albanese might have gained him a reduced sentence, but snitching on Big Ray got him into the program."

Amanda hated that she and her mother were lumped with murderers, drug peddlers, porn merchants, pimps, and the like.

"Thanks for looking into this, Carl. I hope it wasn't a problem."

"Not at all."

"I hear the pause," she said. "Out with it! Say whatever it is you want to say."

"You wanted this information for a friend, right?"

"I thought he might want to know the truth."

"A word of advice: Sometimes telling someone the truth means dashing their hopes. Not everyone views that as a friendly gesture."

"I hear you." She knew when she called Carl this would be difficult. Now that she knew Archie was dead, she'd have to figure out when, how and, she supposed, if she was going to tell Jake. "By the way, is Sam back?"

"Strolled in a few days ago."

"Do me a favor?"

"Name it."

"Ask him to call me. Tell him it's important."

CHAPTER

TWENTY

"The conviction of Jesús Vazquez takes a violent man off the streets, but that doesn't mean our children are safe."

John Chisolm's elegant visage filled the screen. His green eyes were aflame with indignation, his chin elevated with noble purpose.

"The *Blanca Muerte,* which Vazquez headed, is a vicious gang bent on distributing dangerous drugs throughout this city." He faced the camera and stared directly into the lens. "They want to hook our children on Propaine, a drug that kills like a machine gun—quickly, indiscriminately, and in large numbers."

The senator was holding forth on an evening-news roundtable. Normally, Hallie Brendel wouldn't have been part of this forum of national correspondents, but John Chisolm had made it a condition of his appearance. She broke the story of his antidrug crusade and continued to trumpet it despite intense criticism. He owed her.

At first, Hallie stayed in the background, intimidated into a respectful silence by the lofty status of her colleagues. The longer she listened, however, the less impressed—and more irritated—she became. Not only were they blatantly dismissing her as an unworthy associate, but their questions were blandly esoteric, more about the history of the government's battle against drugs and the philosophies behind the various strategies than the effects of the drugs on American society. Hallie was bored. The audience had to be comatose.

"Senator Chisolm." Her sharp tone drew everyone's attention. Two stared as if they'd just realized she was part of the panel. "In recent months, you've been very outspoken about Wall Street's role in America's chronic drug problem."

"That's correct," Chisolm responded, clearly pleased to be given an opening. He was about to reel off several paragraphs from his stump speech when Hallie continued.

"Your message seems to be that it's not the junkie's need that's accelerating the use of drugs. It's corporate greed."

Chisolm's eyes—and his opening—narrowed. "Corporate greed plays a role in this, but individuals are responsible for their own addictions."

"I agree, but isn't the government responsible for stopping the flow of drugs across our border?"

Chisolm glared at her. Defending customs agents and border patrols was not going to win him votes. "Total interdiction is an admirable, but unrealistic goal."

"Perhaps, but considering the constant flow of rhetoric out of Washington about how much better off we'd be if America were drug-free, shouldn't we expect the government to do more about the constant flow of drugs into this country?"

"Often, government action is restricted by the influence of special-interest groups," he said, a don't-blame-me-I-tried-as-hard-as-I-could expression on his face.

"Such as the financial community's powerful lobby?"

Chisolm bristled. He'd expected that Hallie, a member of his team, would drop this line of questioning and move on. Hallie had decided it was every man for himself.

"No one likes to admit it, but yes, the financial industry would certainly be affected by the loss of drug dollars."

"So let me get this straight. While school-age kids are dying, bankers and brokers are getting rich." Hallie's face displayed honest disgust. "I guess it's true: Corruption begins at the top."

Chisolm had to regain the high ground and fast. "I believe it's incumbent upon those of us in Washington and on Wall Street to set an example, which is why I've made the eradication of corporate profit from drugs the centerpiece of my Senate campaign."

Hallie allowed him his moment, then struck again. "Over the past several months, you pointed a constant finger at Lionel Baird, claiming he was the personification of corporate corruption." She ignored the warning look on the senator's face. "Do you feel at all responsible for Mr. Baird's suicide?"

There was a collective gasp as Chisolm flushed with fury. "Absolutely not!"

Before the others could chime in and steal her spotlight, Hallie barreled ahead. "Do you think his suicide was an admission of guilt? Was he laundering drug money? Was your committee about to go public with proof of his complicity?"

Chisolm's face was so red, he appeared seconds away from a stroke. "Suicide is particularly unsettling," he hissed through gritted teeth, "because it rarely answers the question: why?"

"According to the American Suicide Foundation, shame is a common cause, Senator." Hallie met his murderous stare head-on. "You publicly humiliated Mr. Baird. Don't you think that might've contributed to his death?"

Chisolm leaned forward, menacingly. "I think you're looking to aggrandize yourself by humiliating me, Ms. Brendel."

"Not at all, Senator. I'm simply waiting for you to respond to my questions. Did you have proof that Lionel Baird was laundering drug money? Or were your accusations suppositions fed to the media in order to gain political advantage?"

"We have a serious drug problem in this country," Chisolm said, regrouping yet again. "A problem that is exacerbated by the fact that many of our major financial institutions profit off the sale of these heinous chemicals."

He turned away from Hallie toward the camera and spoke earnestly to the audience that mattered: the invisible electorate. "The day America's banks stop laundering these ill-gotten gains, is the day the importation of drugs into this country will cease. No profit, no product. It's as simple as that."

"Nothing about drugs is simple, Senator," Hallie interjected, stomping on his sound bite. "Twenty years ago, the Colombian cartel run by the Espinosa family was America's single largest supplier of narcotics. Lionel Baird's wife, Cynthia Stanton Baird, blew the whistle on them as well as on the Saviano crime family. She died for her efforts.

"Today, the Espinosas and the Savianos are still dealing dope, still laundering money. And now Lionel Baird is found dead. How can you say there's no connection between the past and the present?"

Chisolm squirmed uncomfortably. If he could have wrung her neck right there on camera, he would.

"It's an unfortunate coincidence," he said, determined to smother her innuendo with an avalanche of facts, "but the differences are greater than the similarities. Raoul Espinosa was an omnipotent drug czar able to control the market with a single, iron fist. Today there are more drugs, more users and more competition than there were in the seventies. Also, the base of supply has moved from Colombia to Mexico, which makes sneaking it across our borders a lot easier.

"Raoul Espinosa's sons followed the money to Juarez. While they control a great deal of the current supply, in order to meet the demand, they partnered with local distributors. They're the bankroll behind the *Blanca Muerte* gang in Los Angeles and the suppliers for the Saviano crime family here in New York.

"The *Blanca Muerte* is only one of many gangs siphoning members from the discontented youth of our inner cities. How long this particular one lasts and how high they rise in that bloody firmament remains to be seen.

"The Savianos are Mafiosi, well-known within their community and to the police. According to the press, they're currently engaged in a turf war over the distribution of Propaine. I disagree. The real reason New York City's crime families are at war is that their influence, and their bankrolls, are waning. Like the *Blanca Muerte* gang and the Espinosas, the Savianos are fighting for survival.

"As for the Bairds, Cynthia Stanton Baird was murdered by criminals seeking vengeance. Lionel Baird took his own life for his own reasons."

Quickly, almost imperceptibly, he bowed his head, as if in mournful respect. Then, convinced he had cleansed himself of whatever mud Hallie had thrown, he gazed again into the friendly eye of the camera.

"What we as a nation have to do is dedicate ourselves to waging an all-out war against the Espinosas, the Savianos, the *Blanca Muertes,* and anyone who supports these purveyors of evil. And, ladies and gentlemen, we have to let Lionel Baird rest in peace."

Jake wondered if that was possible. He clicked off the television and glanced over at his dining-room table. It was covered with hastily scribbled notes and official-looking documents which, when combined, raised enough questions to effectively deny Lionel Baird the peace John Chisolm was so eager to grant him. Making matters worse, minutes before the roundtable began, Caleb had called to tell Jake the coroner had received a request to hold Lionel Baird's body, no explanation given.

"Who issued the order?"

"Someone from the Justice Department."

"Justice?" Jake was baffled.

"That's what the man said." Clearly, Caleb shared Jake's confusion.

"Could this have any connection to the FBI background check on Annie Hart that was found on Baird's desk?"

He could almost see Caleb shrug his shoulders. "I can't see how."

"Maybe the FBI didn't want to make the call themselves."

"Because?"

"They didn't want to interfere with NYPD business."

Caleb snorted. "Yeah! Like all of a sudden they're afraid of stepping on our toes."

Jake chuckled. The rivalry between the two law-enforcement groups was legendary. "For all you know they've added sensitivity training to their indoctrination program."

"Right. And John Chisolm is running for office because he cares so deeply about the man on the street!"

"Speaking of Chisolm," Jake said, still thinking out loud. "He's head of the Senate Banking Committee."

"Yeah. And?"

"He's been making an awful lot of noise about investigating money laundering on the Street. Maybe his crew turned up some nasty evidence on Baird and turned it over to the boys at Justice."

"Okay, but why hold the body?" Caleb asked. "To try him in absentia?"

"Good point," Jake conceded, and moved on. Usually, he enjoyed brainstorming with Caleb because more often than not, the process led them somewhere fruitful. So far, every path they'd taken had led to a dead end. "Did the coroner run a tox screen?"

"Yep."

Aside from testing for alcohol, street drugs, sedatives, and household poisons, coroners used standard toxicology tests to determine dosage; in suicides, it assisted in distinguishing been accident and self-administration.

"Anything show up?"

"Nope."

"Did he check for injection sites?" During an autopsy, the pathologist normally inspected all skin surfaces for any type of break in the skin.

"Where are you going with this? You think Lionel got high before he blew himself away? That's a bit of a reach, my friend."

"Granted, but all the buzz surrounding this case has to do with drugs. Drug money. Drug dealers. Drug wars. Who knows? Maybe there's a connection."

"If anyone in the Coroner's Office is following that train," Caleb said, "they'll run a GC-MS." A gas chromatography–mass spectrometry was a method used by crime labs for identification of drugs and toxins that went beyond the standard screen. "I'll keep tabs on it."

"Thanks. I realize this sounds like it's coming out of left field, but everything about this case seems too pat, which makes me think it's a bit off."

Caleb laughed. "I'm beginning to think we're a bit off. The coroner, Moran, and most of my Homicide squad, say flat out: This is a suicide. All the evidence seems to bolster that conclusion, yet you and I are busting our humps to prove it's a murder. What's wrong with this picture?"

"For one thing," Jake said, his frustration evident, "why the hell would the Feds care if Lionel Baird rots in the morgue or in the ground?"

Immediately after Jake hung up with Caleb, Pamela Baird called, wondering the same thing.

"They won't let me bury him," she said in a voice bordering on the hysterical.

Though she went on and on about how the city was conspiring to prolong her grief, Jake suspected her anxiety had more to do with probating Lionel's will than laying his body to rest.

"Maybe *she* told them not to release his body to me," she whined.

"Not possible." Jake wished to deflect her attention from Max. Unfortunately, that was not possible.

"Have you found her? Do you know where she lives so we can have her arrested?"

For the time being, Jake felt the smarter move was to keep Max's identity under wraps. He told himself that when he had more facts, and if they indicated that Max was involved in any way in Lionel's death, he would provide Pamela with a full report. For now, the less she knew, the better.

"We have no basis on which to arrest anyone, Mrs. Baird. For that, we need . . ."

"Probable cause."

"No. We need evidence to support probable cause."

"We've got plenty of that," she insisted.

"No. What you have is wishful thinking. The police don't issue arrest warrants based on wishful thinking."

"Then get me facts, Mr. Fowler."

"I'm working on it, Mrs. Baird."

He'd said good-bye and turned on his TV, hoping to find a light distraction. Instead, he found himself watching a political Punch-and-Judy show. Once Hallie and Senator Chisolm had completed their blood match, he turned off his television and resorted to pacing his living room.

As he perambulated, he wondered how those various facts he promised to deliver to Pamela Baird would lay out and what they would tell him. Facts were funny things: on their own, they were like bits of clay, sometimes interesting to ponder, most often insignificant little lumps. When put together, however, they could be shaped a number of different ways, depending on the whim of the sculptor. If he wanted to arrange things to look as if Lionel Baird did indeed commit suicide, he was certain he could find whatever he needed to substantiate that conclusion. If, on the other hand, he wanted the outcome to point to murder, he could probably arrange that as well. The difficulty was in gathering the bits, putting them together into a cohesive whole, and having the ability to discern—and accept—the truth.

Jake continued his circuit, staring at the scraps of paper littering his table. It would be nice, he thought, if all he had to do was wish and have everything come together into a neat, coherent picture. But wishing never accomplished anything. Jake had learned that when he was fourteen.

Motivated by a sudden burst of purpose, he sat down at the table, pushed the unruly stack of papers aside, and constructed a list of things to do: find out who was behind East Gorham Associates, who Bates and Beth were and what their relationship was to Lionel, why someone would want to rough up Lionel Baird's butler, exactly where Max was and what she was up to the night of Lionel's death.

And why she'd never discussed any of this with him.

That was the most difficult fact to swallow. Jake had to struggle against interpreting her silence as a sign of self-incrimination. He told himself there could be a dozen reasons why Max hadn't shared her familiarity with Lionel Baird, but he was hard-pressed to find one that he bought easily. If she was nothing more than an art advisor, why not admit she knew him after the news broke that he killed himself? It was the number one topic of conversation on everyone's lips—except hers.

Even if Pamela was correct and Max was Lionel Baird's mistress,

Jake found it dillicult to explain her silence. He was dead. Why not acknowledge the relationship? Why not vent her confusion or grief or anger? Why not seek someone else's opinion about why this man might have taken his life?

"Because, you asshole, it's not polite to discuss the death of one lover in the embrace of another," Jake sputtered, unable to skim the bitterness from his voice.

He poured himself a glass of wine. Anguished by conflict, he began to craft more appealing analyses, theories that didn't compromise his ego or challenge the emotion that filled his heart.

If their affair was over, she might not have wanted to draw attention to herself. Judging by the voracious news coverage, who could blame her?

Perhaps their relationship was never sexual and she feared that since it was kept so private people might think it was. Pamela did. He did.

Perhaps Lionel was mentoring her photography career. Jake saw him at the Lloyd Franks show. Lionel bought several pieces of her work. He'd noticed another bleakscape in Lionel's office when he visited Fredda. It wouldn't be the first time Lionel Baird had acted as an artist's patron.

Perhaps it started as patronage and developed into a purely platonic, mutually satisfying friendship. It was known to happen. They had common interests; that much was established. Lionel was between wives and mistresses. Max was a delightful companion. As Jake had told Pamela, Lionel was sophisticated, good-looking, and had money to burn. Max might've been charmed by his attention. She was an NYPD detective, after all. On her salary, she wasn't dining at Le Cirque or La Côte Basque, nor was she readily eschewing the subway in favor of limousines.

When she heard about Lionel's death, she might've been too embarrassed to admit being starry-eyed over his wealth and position. Jake had witnessed her hair-trigger sense of pride and independence up close. Maybe some part of her felt she'd sold out a little and didn't want to explain herself to anyone, least of all, him.

He plunked himself down on the couch and sipped his Shiraz, aware that he was working awfully hard to mold a pile of disagreeable bits into an agreeable form. But, he told himself, like facts gathered but not yet joined by the adhesive of logic, clay left on its own grew hard and brittle. With gentle kneading, however, it became pliable enough to sculpt disparate pieces into something meaningful.

Jake drank his wine and continued to knead the facts at hand. He thought about what he'd learned from the clerk at the Plaza and Robert at La Crémaillère. He reviewed Fredda's observations, Pamela's suspicions, and his own unease.

He'd always prided himself on his ability to detach himself from his work, to bring to his investigations a clean and objective vision that didn't get distorted by rose-colored glasses or lenses ground to fit one particular prescription. Yet try as he might, he couldn't void himself of the love he felt for Max. It influenced every question he asked and every answer he received. It blocked avenues of thought that should have remained open and allowed rationalizations to push through doors that should have remained closed.

With near desperation, Jake put his glass down, shook his head, and took a deep, cleansing breath, exhorting himself to get back on track.

"Let the facts lead you," he chanted like a mantra. "The truth is out there. All you have to do is track it down."

Like a coach rallying his team, Jake pumped himself up, chiding himself for emotional laziness. He recalled his conversation with Pamela Baird earlier that evening and gave himself the same warning he'd given her: "Don't get hung up on words like probable cause or wishful thinking. Think evidence! Solid, irrefutable, if-you-don't-have-it-you'll-look-like-a-moron-in-court, evidence!"

His eyes rested on the darkened TV screen and suddenly, a thought surfaced. A very intriguing thought. During their verbal slugfest, Hallie had posed an interesting question. Was Lionel's death brought on by current public humiliation? Or was it the final act in a twenty-year-old tragedy? Chisolm's reluctance even to address the issue made it something to consider. Maybe the ghosts of a twenty-year-old trial had come back to haunt Lionel Baird. And had put that .38 in his hand.

Or maybe, Jake thought shamefacedly, he was grasping at straws again, looking to blame anyone—including ghosts—for the death of Lionel Baird.

Anyone except Amanda Maxwell.

Telephoning his father was as much a part of Little Ray Saviano's Sunday as having dinner with his mother. Both activities were sacrosanct, but even if they'd been erased from the list of filial obligations, Little Ray wouldn't miss dinner with his mother. She fed him and cooed over him and massaged his ego, maintaining an unshakable belief in his inherent goodness, no matter what the press and the police said about him. His father was a much tougher gig.

Every Sunday at precisely seven o'clock, Little Ray dialed a special pay phone at Joliet. After the preliminary how-are-you's and the encapsulated updates on various family members, Little Ray was expected to provide a rundown of the Family's business activities. Since they had every reason to believe their calls were monitored, they spoke in code, a circumstance that made it even more difficult for the verbally challenged Little Ray. Most times, it was a struggle to find something that wouldn't precipitate a dressing-down. Nothing he did met with the old man's approval. Big Ray was forever touting the way things used to be. Little Ray tried to educate him about how things were, but Saviano senior was rarely receptive to his son's explanations. Admittedly, a few more successes might strengthen Little Ray's argument, but, as he reminded his father each week, he was the one on the street. He was the one leading the day-to-day battles. He was the one carrying the Saviano banner.

And, his father reminded him each week, he was the one in danger of losing the family franchise.

This time, however, there was good news.

"That stupid spic is goin' away," Little Ray said, pumping his fist and gloating. "Man! He beat the crap outta his wife. You should've seen the pictures."

"Jesús Vazquez is an animal. He deserves to be punished."

Big Ray had little patience for men who didn't respect the mothers of their children. He had even less respect for those who got caught and were forced to parade their domestic problems in front of their enemies.

"The judge pretty much said the same thing." He chortled. "Called that dickhead a savage beast. I got off on it, but man, his homies were pissed."

"Why do you think this is good news for us? LA will replace Vazquez and we have to do the dance all over again."

"They have replaced Vazquez, but I met with the guy already," Little Ray reported, pleased for once to tell his father something he didn't know. "Angel Rodriguez. An older dude the Espinosas sent up from Mexico. We talked outside the courthouse."

"And?"

"And we're cool. He understands that it's better to work with us than against us."

Big Ray nodded, a slow smile tickling the edges of his mouth. "Good. So, how's business?"

"I gotta hand it you, Padre," Little Ray said with more humility and respect than the older Saviano had heard in a long while, "you were right. Operating underneath the radar screen is the way to go. Already, we've taken over from two of the other Families."

"So you've put an end to the turf wars?"

"Not exactly," Little Ray confessed, "but we're doing what you said. We're being more careful, dumping the bodies where they ain't gonna be found so quick instead of leaving them around to be discovered by the cops."

"And reported by the press."

"Yeah." To Little Ray, giving up his press coverage was a major sacrifice. "Actually, it don't matter what we do. Right now, they're so caught up in that Wall Streeter's suicide, they wouldn't give a shit if we was all killed and laid head to toe down Fifth Avenue."

"Lucky for us," Big Ray said.

"Yeah." Little Ray agreed, but without conviction. "Real lucky."

CHAPTER
TWENTY-ONE

Amanda was on the phone with Thompson when her beeper said to call Beth. Assured that Thompson was on the mend and that after his release from the hospital he intended to continue his recovery at Lionel's estate in the Hamptons—accompanied by a police guard—Amanda hung up and dialed the number Beth had left. It was a phone booth at the Beverly Wilshire Hotel.

"I'm coming to New York," she announced abruptly.

"You're not supposed to do that." Returning to a designated Danger Zone violated the conditions of the Memorandum of Understanding.

"Jaime Bastido is not supposed to be missing. And Lionel is not supposed to be dead."

Amanda wasn't about to tell her mother she was ninety percent certain that Jaime Bastido was no longer missing, but alive and well and trolling around New York City in a surgical disguise.

Instead, she said quietly, "I'm looking into Dad's death."

Beth was taken aback by Amanda's referring to Lionel as "Dad." It sounded strange and wonderful and sad, all at the same time. "I didn't know you'd started calling him Dad."

"Every now and then. When we were alone."

"I'll bet he loved it."

A sob threatened. Amanda swallowed hard. "He did."

There was a heavy silence, during which both women indulged their grief.

"I'm so glad I came to New York and reunited with him. My only regret is that I waited so long."

"Don't do that to yourself," Beth admonished. "Cherish the time you had. Don't diminish it with regret."

"I came to love him all over again," Amanda whispered as intimate scenes between father and daughter flashed before her: sharing a pizza at Rudy's, the time he gave her the gold watch, listening to him marvel about her photographs and complain about her job, that last dinner at her apartment. She looked at the small vase that held the pink camellias he'd brought her that night. They, too, were dead.

"He was awfully good to me," she said, suddenly laughing as she wiped tears from her eyes. "He was trying so hard to make up for lost time, if he could have, I think he would've taken me to Disney World."

Beth smiled. "Probably. He loved you, sweetheart. He would've given you whatever or taken you wherever you wanted."

"He tried, but as you know, I don't care about expensive things or fancy places, and that drove him crazy." She chuckled again, but her voice wobbled. "All I wanted was to spend time with him. I didn't care if it was take-out Chinese or a gourmet meal. He was my dad. And I miss him."

"I miss him, too." Beth rarely held anything back from Amanda, but she decided not to mention how much time she'd been spending in the land of what-might-have-been. "Which is why I'm coming to New York. You and I need to reconnect and talk, face-to-face."

Beth's upbeat tone didn't fool Amanda. Beth's antennae were finally tuned. She was scared. "What does Uncle Sam think about this trip?"

"I didn't tell him."

"Why not?" An alarm was ringing inside Max's head.

"For one thing, he'd disapprove. For another, he's out of town again. Probably visiting his sister."

When Amanda spoke to Sam about contacting the coroner, he had told her about Gail's illness. He went to great lengths to assure her that his being away didn't compromise Beth's safety, but he needn't have bothered. Amanda knew that under circumstances like these, protection was automatic. WITSEC protection was guaranteed for life—assuming none of the rules were broken.

"Even with Sam out of town, the Service will know." One of the ongoing aspects of the protection program encompassed the strict monitoring of a witness's telephone calls and mail.

"I'm not calling you from home. And your phone isn't monitored."

"Still, coming to New York might be a big mistake." Amanda was determined not to alarm her mother, but if she was being stalked, and she believed she was, the worst thing they could do is provide their enemies a chance of hitting two birds with one shot. "We shouldn't be in the same place at the same time."

"I'm tired of all the shoulds," Beth said wearily. "I need to see you. I need to hold you and assure myself that you're all right. That we're both all right."

Amanda wrestled with her heart and her head, both of which were giving her conflicting advice.

"Okay," she said finally. "Book a flight into Newark Airport. I'll meet you in a room at the Marriot. We'll spend a few hours together, then I'll put you on a plane back to California. How's that?"

"Great." She paused, smiling into the phone. "Because I already have a ticket on this afternoon's two-thirty flight. I change planes in Dallas and arrive in Newark at twelve-thirty in the morning."

For the next several hours, Amanda occupied herself with some basic detective work. She studied the photographs she took at Lionel's town house for the umpteenth time. As always, something nagged at her, the sense that what she wanted to know was staring back at her, but for some reason, she was blinded to it. She felt as if she'd picked up a book that told a story she'd read before, but this time, it was written in a language she didn't understand. Annoyed and frustrated, she returned the photos to their hiding place.

As a detective and forensic specialist, Amanda accepted the value of patience, even though she wasn't always adept in the art of it. It would be nice if each piece of physical evidence collected at a scene was a solid clue that would not only nab a suspect, but also stand up in court. More often than not, much of what was gathered turned out to be superficial and irrelevant. That didn't allow for shortcuts, however. Raising questions, reviewing answers, cataloging clues, examining possibilities, creating plausible theories while maintaining a tightly linked chain of evidence—it was all part of the gumshoe process. Thankfully, modern technology made it possible to do much of the legwork at home on a computer.

Logging on to the NYPD database, tapping into a file Lionel kept for his personnel records and searching through some other relevant Web sites available to those in law enforcement, she ran checks on Lionel's household employees. As expected, his domestic staff, hired and vetted by Thompson, came up clean. Even the extra waiters and waitresses Thompson brought in for special parties had been with Lionel for years and boasted spotless résumés.

Al Heflin, the newest member of the security team, was a former policeman whom Lionel had described as a tough guy with a big heart. He was on the force for ten years, assigned to one of the rougher precincts in Queens. He did undercover work for the Narcotics Division, but after losing his second partner to the city's mean streets, he quit. After leaving the NYPD, Heflin worked as a chauffeur/bodyguard for an oft-divorced corporate titan for three years, then for a family. He would have stayed with them, but apparently, Lionel made him an offer he couldn't refuse. Aside from an extremely generous compensation package, Lionel promised to donate an amount equivalent to half of Heflin's yearly salary to the fund that took care of families of fallen police officers.

Tony Calandra was the oldest member of the team. Forty, remarkably fit, and a weapons expert, he'd spent twenty years in the army. When he retired, he decided to supplement his pension with security work. He applied for a job at Baird, Nathanson & Spelling and within two years had reorganized the fifty-man staff that secured the building into an efficient, effective team. Once he'd established a protocol and trained his personnel in "aggressive vigilance," Lionel appropriated him for his personal use.

Amanda remembered him referring to Tony as "Schwarzenegger without the accent."

Bruno Vitale was also an ex-military man, but his service had been much shorter than Calandra's. He'd enlisted in the Marines fresh out of high school and completed two tours before mustering out. Amanda tried to find whether his discharge had been honorable, but she couldn't seem to access that information. Lionel's file showed that Vitale had a succession of jobs after leaving the military: bouncer, limo driver, hospital orderly, EMT technician, construction worker. Eventually, he found his niche and worked several jobs as a bodyguard before entering Lionel's employ. Of the three, Lionel had felt most comfortable when Bruno was watching his back.

"He's a thug," Lionel had said, "but he's fearless, follows orders without asking questions, and is as loyal as they come."

Having satisfied herself that there was nothing in any of the backgrounds of Lionel's staff that aroused suspicion, Amanda pondered other possible avenues of inquiry. Two things came to mind: Thompson's mention of an appointment with Tyler Grayson and something Lionel had told her—he taped all of his meetings.

Did he have recording devices in the town house or only at the office? She scratched her head, as if that would jog her memory. They were voice-activated, of that she was certain. If people didn't know they were being recorded, Lionel reasoned, they said what they wanted, rather than what they thought would sound good in the playback. When he showed her the setup in his offiee, he explained that the microphone fed into his computer as well as onto an ordinary tape deck. If the meeting was of no lasting importance, Lionel erased the tape and deleted the file from his computer. If, however, he felt he might want to refer to it at another time, the interview was stored in a secret file on his computer and the tape was erased.

"Great!" Amanda grumbled, pounding her fist with frustration. "I don't know the password. Hell! I don't even know if there is a recording device in the town house." And if there was, it was of no value if she couldn't unlock the file.

Suddenly, her eyes brightened. There was no computer in the town house library. If there was a recording device, it taped onto a reel.

Was there a tape in the police evidence file? She didn't recall seeing one. *That didn't mean there wasn't one.* If the recorder was as well hidden as the door, the police might not have been able to find it.

She had to get back into Lionel's library and search for that tape. If someone killed him, his or her voice would be on it. If Lionel killed himself, maybe he said something that would explain why.

"This is risky business, girl," she warned at the same time as her mind plotted when and how of a possible break-in.

Another to-do was a visit to the library. She loathed Hallie Brendel, but last night on that news program with Chisolm, she reiterated something that was becoming an anthem for her: the past had killed Lionel Baird.

Since Amanda also suspected the involvement of ghosts, she decided that, much as she dreaded the prospect, it might be wise to take, a good, hard look into the past.

Before it killed her.

Amanda never made it to the library. Just as she was about to leave her apartment, Tyler Grayson called and asked if he could take her to dinner.

The restaurant, March, was an elegant town house on the East Side, small and intimate. Tyler asked to be seated in the back, overlooking the garden. When they were settled, he ordered a bottle of wine.

"To what do I owe this unexpected pleasure?" Amanda asked, noting how handsome and prosperous he looked in his finely tailored midnight navy suit, baby blue pin-stripe shirt and iridescent royal blue tie. Tyler was the quintessential picture of success. Only the shadows clouding his eyes revealed him as a man not totally sure of who he was and where he stood.

"The last time I saw you, I was a jerk. I wanted to dispel that image before it became permanent."

She smiled because she was honestly flattered and still had a romantic soft spot for him, but a finger of guilt poked at her back. Moments before he'd called, she'd declared pumping him a priority. She didn't know whether this was a coincidence, a sign or merely affirmation of the saying: Timing is everything.

"Declaring your feelings doesn't make you a jerk, Tyler. Quite the contrary. Compared to commitment cowards like myself, you come off looking like an emotional Hercules." He smiled at the compliment. "Besides," she said, smoothly segueing to the matter uppermost on her mind, "if I remember correctly, you were upset about the tragic death of your boss."

Before Tyler could respond, the waiter arrived with the wine and menus. Amanda cursed the interruption, but Tyler was oblivious to her distress. He was absorbed in the ritual of the dedicated oenophile: swirling, sniffing, tasting, swallowing, sighing. At last, he nodded his approval of the sauvignon blanc. The waiter poured some into Amanda's glass, added to Tyler's portion, and exited discreetly.

"To Lionel Baird," he said, raising his glass. "May he rest in peace."

Amanda commanded her feelings not to display themselves. "That was nice, Tyler," she said as she sipped her wine.

He shrugged and furrowed his brow. "I still can't get over it. His death seems so unnecessary." He swirled the pale liquid in the glass, watching it as if it had the power to explain the inexplicable. "But I guess that's how all suicides seem. Especially when there's no note."

How did he know there was no note?

"You two were pretty close," Amanda ventured. "Did you get the impression that he was depressed?"

"What do you mean?" His tone was gruff, almost embarrassed, as if she'd walked in on him during a private moment.

"I don't mean anything really. It's just you and he worked so closely, I can't imagine not being able to see the kind of dark mood I assume precedes a suicide."

"We only spoke about business. I'd have no idea if something in his personal life was bothering him."

True. "I take it he wasn't the type to confide in his associates."

"No. And I doubt if he had a lot of friends."

It bothered Amanda to admit that Tyler was correct, but to the best of her knowledge Lionel didn't have an address book bursting with names. Most of his relationships were business or, she supposed, sexual.

"Even so, business on the Street is booming. He should've been happy about that."

"He would've been if not for the threat of consolidation." Amanda looked puzzled. "One or two of the larger banks had bought brokerage houses. Lionel was concerned this was a trend. That if Baird, Nathanson & Spelling wasn't careful, it would be gobbled up by a banking behemoth."

Amanda recalled having this conversation with Lionel. He was concerned about a hostile takeover. Had he heard something that day or the day before? Was a takeover imminent? If so, would that have been provocation for suicide? And was Tyler the bearer of those bad things?

"In fact," Tyler continued, as if he too was trying to decide what really happened to Lionel, "he and Senator Chisolm had at it over all this."

"Really?" Amanda's heart was pounding.

"Lionel and the heads of most of the other large brokerage houses wanted Chisolm to support a bill that would prevent this sort of conglomeration. Chisolm agreed to sponsor it, but then, a couple of months ago, Lionel said Chisolm did a one-eighty and put the legislation on hold."

"Because of his reelection campaign?"

"I don't think so. First of all, Chisolm had friends in the financial community. He came from the Street. He knew how disastrous that kind of corporate consolidation could be. He also knew that despite the bombastic rhetoric, most of those in his former stomping ground weren't at all bothered by his preaching about the immorality of laundering drug money. The reality was that nothing would be done. They knew it. And he knew it." He shook his head, as if confounded by the hypocrisy inherent in the affiliation between politics and business. "I have to agree with Lionel on this one: Chisolm's change of heart was strictly personal."

Amanda's jaw tightened. *Pamela Baird.* "That could be. Wasn't Senator Chisolm engaged to the soon-to-be-ex-Mrs. Baird?"

"Indeed, only now, she's the widow Baird."

Whenever Amanda thought of Pamela parading around in her designer widow's weeds, she cringed. Not only had she fed misleading information to Hallie Brendel, but clearly, she was the inspiration behind this attempt to interfere with the conduct of Baird, Nathanson & Spelling. No wonder Lionel was so bitter.

"When you think about it," she continued, pushing aside her enmity toward Pamela, "Chisolm's Senate campaign seemed like a carefully calculated smear job. Every time he opened his mouth he was slamming Mr. Baird. He may have thought it won him political points. I thought he came off sounding petty and vindictive."

"Totally." Tyler emptied his glass. He seemed anxious. He summoned the waiter to pour more wine and take their dinner orders. Amanda declined the wine. She wanted to keep a clear head.

When they were alone, Amanda reopened their discussion.

"I would've thought that in the wake of the suicide, Chisolm might have backed off bad-mouthing Mr. Baird. Out of respect, if nothing else."

Tyler snorted. "No way! Men like John Chisolm only have respect for their poll numbers. If he thinks kicking Lionel Baird grabs him extra votes, he'll drag that man's dead body up onto the stage of his rallies and have at him. Chisolm's a pig!"

"Well, that reporter, Hallie Brendel, isn't much better. Just the other night on some news program, she said Baird's past sins had caught up to him. That sounds a little out there to me. What do you think? Could that Laundry Day thing have been the reason he killed himself?"

She paused, giving him a chance to jump in, but he passed. Their food had arrived, and his attention shifted to his red snapper. She played with her food for a minute or two, then tried again.

"Was the negative press affecting Baird, Nathanson & Spelling's bottom line?"

"A little, yes, but with the market, it's hard to tell whether a downturn is the result of a general trend or something more specific."

"But a downturn is probably just what Chisolm wanted."

"Meaning?" Tyler's eyes widened slightly. He set his glass down on the table.

"They're rivals. To men whose power is based on money, the Achilles' heel has to be the bank balance. Putting a major dent in Baird's bottom line is a big score. What Baird had to do was fight back."

"He answered Chisolm's charges."

It fascinated Amanda to note that as often as Tyler railed against Lionel, he revealed his admiration for the man by taking his side.

"No," she corrected. "He defended himself against Chisolm's charges. He should've staged a counterattack. He should've demanded to know *why* Chisolm wasn't going forward on that legislation. Bring his behind-the-scenes maneuvering public. Put Chisolm on the defensive."

"You're absolutely right!" Tyler exclaimed, shedding his cloak of reticence. "I told him that when I went to the town house that afternoon."

Bingo! "What afternoon?"

Tyler flushed, struck by the realization that he'd said something he shouldn't and there was no taking it back. He eyed Amanda carefully, assessed her reliability as a confidant. When he finally spoke, his voice was so low, Amanda had to lean closer just to hear him.

"I met with Lionel a few hours before the suicide."

"You did?" She sounded appropriately surprised, but she kept her voice calm. "You were there? At the town house?"

He nodded, his gray eyes dark and haunted.

"What did you talk about?"

"Business. It was always business with us."

Uh-uh, she thought. *The look on your face says that this time, things got personal.* "Was there news of a takeover? Had Lionel asked you to help plan a strategy to stave it off?"

He shook his head then sought refuge in the crystal goblet, mesmerized by whatever images he saw reflected in the glass.

"Was it the vice chairman position? Oh, Tyler! Were you the winner?" She was groping, but if one button didn't work, press another. "Did he invite you to the town house to tell you the good news before he told the others?"

When he looked up his jaw was rigid, his eyes as black and hard as granite. "No, Amanda, I was the loser. He invited me into his lair to tell me there was to be no vice chairman. He had changed his mind. He had decided not to retire. Not now nor any time in the immediate future." His mouth lifted in an asymmetrical, ironic smile. "He felt renewed and reenergized."

Amanda's head was swimming. It took all her training to maintain a sympathetic façade.

"Did he fire or demote you?" she asked gingerly, almost fearful of the answer. She desperately wanted the truth, but she didn't want that truth to involve Tyler.

"No. He dismissed me. He behaved as if my aspirations and the aspirations of my colleagues were our problem. As if we invented this contest and had only ourselves to blame for our thwarted ambitions. He was happy. That was all that mattered." He glowered into his goblet. "As always, Lionel Baird was completely disconnected and disinterested. He was not to blame for our inconveniences or insecurities. He didn't care about conflicts or consequences. He was the reigning monarch, and he didn't have to answer to anyone for anything."

Amanda's stomach tightened. She wished she'd never started this conversation, never came here tonight. With each sentence, Tyler confirmed her suspicions that Lionel's death was far from accidental. Worse, he seemed to be implicating himself. His hostility presented a motive. His presence in the town house hours before the suicide provided opportunity—if during his visit he ascertained how to get in and out of the library without being discovered, he could have come back later. The only remaining question was means. Knowing where Lionel kept his gun was one thing; getting him to put it in his own hand and pull the trigger was something else again.

"Did you tell him how you felt?"

His color faded. "Yes."

"Did he get upset?"

Tyler pursed his lips and tugged at his beard. "Very." His eyes seemed vacant, as if he had returned to the town house and was reliving that last visit. "We argued. I said some things I shouldn't have."

"Like what?"

It was as if she'd snapped her fingers and awakened him from an hypnotic trance. His eyes cleared. His color returned, and his mouth formed a deliberate smile.

"It doesn't matter." He cut into his fish and resumed eating.

"It does matter, Tyler. Shortly after you left, Lionel Baird killed himself."

He put his fork down and leaned forward. "Believe me, Amanda, nothing I said prompted that suicide. I didn't mean enough to him for my anger to upset his stomach, let alone motivate a fatal response."

"How do you know?"

"Because he said as much. Now, please, your dinner's getting cold."

Tyler dropped her off at her apartment at eleven o'clock. Fortunately, he didn't ask to accompany her upstairs. When she called the airport, she was told Beth's flight was on time. Quickly, she stripped off her dress, threw on slacks and a sweater, packed a bag with another change of clothes, a wig, and her new disguise kit, hailed a cab, and set out for Newark Airport.

She got out on the Departure level, walked into the United terminal and headed for the escalators that led to the gate area. When she was certain she wasn't being followed, she did an about-face, took the escalator down another floor, and exited on the Arrivals level. She flagged another taxi and asked to be taken to the Marriott where she checked into a room reserved under the name Jane Roberts. Half an hour later, Beth knocked on the door.

Their reunion was emotional. Mother and daughter clung to each other as if physical contact was all they needed to assure their safety. Neither believed it was that simple, which was why they moved quickly to the practical. Beth reported on her journey: no one lingering behind her or appearing and then reappearing where he or she shouldn't, no taxicabs tailing hers, no passengers insisting upon striking up senseless conversations, no faceless stranger bumping into her or hovering too closely. Amanda followed with her own recitation.

This detailed examination of the seemingly picayune was part of a routine Amanda and Beth had established as a way of cross-checking their observation skills and protecting against possible slip-ups. One of the first things they learned when they joined WITSEC was that being alert to what went on around them was vital to their survival. Death wasn't going to come in a face-to-face confrontation. Rather it would sneak around a corner or crash through a window or blow up in their faces. Seeing through what's visible to that which is invisible was difficult, but possible if one's senses were keen. And, if one remained constantly on guard and consistently suspicious.

Being able to relax honestly with only one other human being was unnatural, but as with most negatives, there was a positive. Their forced isolation allowed for a unique sense of equality. While Amanda showed her mother proper filial respect and Beth's guiding principle was always the protection of her child, from the day they fled Miami, both understood that in one very vital respect, they were peers: Their risk was the same.

Over the years, Amanda and Beth sought to minimize that risk by testing each other, exchanging methods and ideas. Beth taught her nine-year-old-child to pay attention to details, to look carefully at someone's face, rather than quickly, to memorize one distinguishing feature, to notice colors or tics or physical habits, like tilting the head to one side, or rubbing one's hands together, or nibbling on a lip. Amanda taught her mother to take stock surreptitiously of her environment: simply stop now and then, hold her breath, and listen to sounds that seemed out of place and sense movement when there should have been stillness.

There was stillness now as they faced each other and thought about the tragedy that brought them to this place. They joined hands and talked about Lionel, cried over his sudden passing, and allowed themselves a rare moment of feeling sorry for themselves.

"How sick does this sound?" Beth asked. "I want to mourn. I want to wear a black dress and a black veil, sit in a chapel and listen to people eulogize a man whose name I used to bear. I don't want to pretend that I don't know him or don't care that he left this earth prematurely. I knew him. I loved him. I do care that he's gone. And I don't want to have to hide my grief the way I did when my parents died."

Beth rose from her chair and walked to the window. Habit compelled her to peek out the side of the curtains and scan the street below.

"But I can't mourn openly," she said, studying the movement of shadows on the ground. "If I do, I could be next. And," she said, facing her daughter, "then you would have to find a way to mourn me."

Amanda refused to discuss the possibility of losing her mother, so she changed the subject.

"Did Sam do what I asked? Did he arrange for Lionel's body to be held?"

Beth returned to her chair. "Yes. He had a Justice Department official make the call. That way, the NYPD wouldn't know which agency made the request. More than likely, they'll assume it was the FBI."

"Mom, was there a Grayson involved in any of the Laundry Day trials?"

It took Beth awhile to thumb through names and places. It had been a long time. "I don't think so."

"No one from the bank in Florida?" Beth shook her head. "Maybe someone connected to the Savianos?" Again, she said no.

"Why do you ask?"

"Remember that guy I was seeing? The one I met in Italy?"

Beth nodded cautiously. "The bells?"

Amanda smiled, remembering Lionel's advice to ignore Beth's advice. "Right. Well, his name is Tyler Grayson. He and Lionel actively disliked each other."

"So?"

"Tonight, Tyler told me he and Lionel argued on the day of the suicide." She repeated the conversation, trying not to leave anything out. "I began to think that maybe Tyler had a connection to the past."

"If he does, I don't know where the link is. To the best of my recollection, no one named Grayson was a defendant in either of the trials." Beth folded her arms across her chest and stared at the carpet. "Why not go into the newspaper morgue or see if you can get hold of the Prosecutor's Office files. Maybe Grayson was a relative of a defendant."

"Probably not," Amanda said, disheartened. Logic proclaimed this another dead end. "Other than the bank officers from Hudson National, most of the defendants had Spanish or Italian names. Grayson isn't quite ethnic enough."

"What else do you know that I don't?" Beth said. Ever since their phone call, she'd harbored the feeling that Amanda knew more than she was letting on.

"I know that you and Sam are having problems."

Beth smiled. "Really. And how do you know that?"

"Because whenever I ask you about him, you sound distanced and disinterested. And when I ask him about you, he sounds nervous and defensive. What's up?"

Beth sighed. Some things were too complicated to dilute into a few words. She tried for the simplest of explanations. "I'm upset about Lionel. He's upset about his sister. And the fact that I'm upset about Lionel."

"Okay." Amanda accepted that. Lionel's death had complicated her emotional life as well.

"What else are you holding back?" Amanda feigned confusion. Beth wasn't buying. "Out with it."

"I think Bastido is in New York."

If she expected Beth to gulp, swoon, or look frightened, she was disappointed. Her mother simply nodded and pursed her lips.

"I figured he'd show up here."

"I'm not a hundred percent sure." She told Beth about the odd man at the Vazquez trial and about Annie's certitude that he'd had plastic surgery. "Other than that painfully pinched smile, I didn't get a close look at him. At the time, I didn't realize who I was looking at." She was angry with herself, and it showed.

"Don't beat yourself up. It's a waste of energy," said Beth, the mathematical, practical one. She believed people had a finite amount of emotional energy and that it was better not to squander it on what-ifs. There would be enough occasions when that energy was necessary. "What are you doing to protect yourself? Other than arming yourself with every weapon you own?"

"I'm playing dress up," Amanda said mischievously.

"I beg your pardon?"

Amanda went for her bag and took out the cosmetics kit she and Annie had put together.

"She showed me how to apply spirit gum and this thin rubber stuff to alter my features. She gave me a dozen different wigs and body pads and whatever else I'd need. I can become a fat, old woman, a buxom blonde, a pregnant brunette, even a pimply-faced teenage boy at will." Her mother looked amused, but skeptical. "I know it's not a solution. It's a stopgap, but until I can figure out what happened, I need to be able to roam the city freely. I can't always be looking over my shoulder."

"Yes, you can." Beth's tone was stern. "And you should."

"You're right. And I do. I just meant that . . ."

"I know what you meant, but this isn't a school play," she snapped, up and pacing again. "Makeup and padding and costumes aren't going to fool Bastido or his minions for very long."

"Right again, but I don't know what else to do. If I go to the police, I have to tell them who I am, and I can't do that. With all the press surrounding Lionel's death, I'd become the focus of a media manhunt and an even bigger target than I already am."

"Supposedly, the FBI is on the case, as are the marshals." Beth's expression telegraphed a been-there-done-that attitude. "Not that it's going to do us much good."

"Why do you say that?" Amanda asked, bothered by the cynicism coloring Beth's tone. "Don't you think these guys want to catch

Bastido? If what I saw outside that courthouse means anything, that dirtbag is back working for the Espinosas, dealing drugs and doing deals with the Savianos. The way I see it, it's in the interest of the FBI and the DEA to nail his sorry ass to the wall."

"And how are they going to do that? By tossing us out there as bait?"

"Maybe," Amanda retorted, her jaw tight, her temper crackling. "But I'd rather be out there doing something to end this nightmare we've been living, than running and hiding and denying myself a life while I wait like a good little girl for them to come get me!"

Beth and Amanda found themselves squared off in the center of the room, snarling at each ether. Beth stared at her irate daughter for a long moment. Then, her eyes softened. Gently, she caressed Amanda's cheek.

"I'm delighted to hear that," she said, smiling.

"What?" Amanda was completely confused.

"Obviously, you've finally found someone with whom you think you could have a life. My guess is that he's the chimes. What was his name? Jake something."

"Fowler." Amanda blushed, but confessed. "I don't know if we'd wind up making a life with each other, but I can't even try until this evil, carnivorous monkey is off my back."

"Have you told him who you are?"

Amanda shook her head. "I can't. Not yet."

"Why not?"

She looked deep into Beth's eyes and spoke frankly. "Because I don't want him hurt. Jake and I can't have a future, Mom, until I close the door to our past."

"Easier said than done," Beth warned.

"No," Amanda replied, exhausted, yet focused. "Nothing could be harder than living this lie you and I call a life."

Beth's eyes pooled. "I agree," she whispered. She gave herself a moment, then wiped her tears and gave Amanda her full attention. "So where do we go and what do we do?"

Amanda took her mother's hands in hers and squeezed them. "We're going to take a quick nap. I'm going to put you on a plane back to LA. And I'm going to figure out who killed my father." Her chin wobbled, but she remained strong. "When we know that, we can go to the police. Until then, we're on our own."

"We've been on our own for twenty years, sweetheart, and despite the best efforts of the Espinosas and the Savianos and whoever else wishes us dead, we're still here." Beth hugged her daughter. "We'll make it through this. I know we will."

"We'll do better than that," Amanda pledged. "Not only will we survive, but we're going find a way to slam the door on our past and lock it forever!"

Beth touched her finger to Amanda's lips, then kissed it herself and held it skyward. "Amen to that."

After Amanda dropped Beth at her gate, she went to work. She was dragging, but she'd worked double shifts before. She could handle a single on two hours' sleep. If she was lucky, they wouldn't have a heavy load, and the coffee from the cart would be hot and fresh. Thankfully, the latter was true. She grabbed a large container, a bagel, and an apple and made her way upstairs.

When she clocked in, she found a stack of manila envelopes in her mailbox from the photo lab downtown—processed film from cases she'd caught. She dropped them on her desk, pushed them aside, and devoted herself to her coffee. The caffeine barely had time to enter her veins when Pete started yelling at her.

"Get the lead out, Detective. We've got a multiple in Hell's Kitchen."

Over the next seven hours, Amanda and Pete documented the butchered remains of a family—four children, a grandmother, and a mother—on Tenth Avenue, a stabbing in Washington Heights, and three kids under the age of eighteen in an abandoned building on Avenue B, who'd overdosed on Propaine. By the time they returned to CSU headquarters, they were exhausted. Pete fell into a chair and proceeded to plot out his idea of an enchanted evening: beer, pizza and a remote-control medley of sporting events.

"Care to join me?" He winked and twirled an imaginary handlebar mustache.

"It would take a court order," she said, seeking sanctuary behind her desk. As she emptied the first of the manila envelopes and began to study the contact sheets, Pete groaned.

"You can't possibly have the energy to go through those now."

She didn't, but she wanted him to leave before she headed for the ladies' room to disguise herself for the trip home.

"It won't take long. You go on ahead." She offered him an encouraging smile.

He dragged his body toward the door. "Sure you don't want to change your mind? I could throw in some tiramisu, if that would make the evening more appealing."

"Thanks, but no thanks."

He shook his head. "There's no accounting for taste."

He blew her a kiss and left. She went through the other envelopes one at a time, quickly scanning them. In the morning, when she was fresher, she'd give them all a closer look.

The last envelope looked odd. She didn't remember it being part of the stack she'd received that morning. This one was flatter than the others and addressed to Detective Amanda Maxwell, but it hadn't been sent through the post office or processed through NYPD channels. Amanda eyed it cautiously. It was thin, minus alarming bulges that might indicate a letter bomb. She palpated it anyway. Assured that it wouldn't blow up in her face, she opened the envelope and slipped its contents onto her desk, thereby preserving any possible fingerprints.

Amanda was stunned by the hideousness of what lay before her. She stared at the visual venom with gaping eyes, too terrified to move or breathe or scream. Beth's face and her own, enlarged to a big, bold eleven by fourteen inches, stared up at her. It was one of the photographs Lionel had taken in Wisconsin: a close-up, mother and daughter with their arms draped around each other's shoulders, heads together, laughing at the camera.

But this photograph had been dramatically altered. Dead in the middle of each woman's forehead was a real bullet hole made by a real gun.

Amanda ran to the ladies' room, her entire body convulsed with fear. Once inside, she crammed herself and her duffel inside the tiny stall, balanced the large bag on the toilet, and hugged herself, trying to suppress the tremors that had overwhelmed her. Frightened that someone might hear her, she pressed her hands to her mouth and muffled the sobs that refused to stay at bay.

Her cries rebounded off the cold tile walls, echoing the pitiful sound of a fragile world collapsing. How foolish she had been to believe that she could live a normal life: being a daughter, having friends, loving a man, dreaming of a future. How stupid of her to think she could function like other women who went to work, came home, and went to bed with every expectation of waking up in the morning. With trembling fingers, she dug the mutilated photograph out of her duffel and stared again at what was clearly a portent of brutality. Seeing her own face punctured by the searing force of a bullet was unnerving. The sight of her mother with a deadly wound was more than she could bear.

She went over every minute of her visit with Beth, torturing herself to visualize and examine each step she'd taken. She was almost certain no one had followed her to the airport. If they had, she'd lost them by the time she reached the hotel. Or so she believed.

Beth had assured her that to the best of her knowledge, her trip to New York had been free of a tail. But what about the trip back? She and Beth had worked out a plan in which Beth would fly to San Francisco, stay there overnight, drive to Sacramento, and fly from there into Los Angeles.

But could there have been something in Lionel's library that might have given away where Beth was living? He couldn't have a phone number or an address; her mother never would have given either of them to Lionel, no matter how close their former ties. Amanda had never even hinted at Beth's whereabouts. It was something neither of them could bring themselves to do. Their conditioning was that complete.

Did Lionel have a phone number for Sam? Knowing Sam, he must have worked out some way for Lionel to contact him in case of an emergency, but would Lionel have left something so potentially dangerous lying around?

Amanda rubbed her temples. She tried to think, but clarity was impossible. Doubts mushroomed into dark impediments, clouding all attempts at reason and deduction. Suddenly, Amanda wasn't certain of anything. What Lionel might have thought or done. What instructions Sam might have given. What was known about her or Beth or Lionel. Whether they were followed or not. What was suicide and what was murder. The only bankable certainties were that Amanda was on a hit list and her assassins knew where she worked. If they didn't know where she lived, they were lurking outside, waiting for her to lead them there.

Suddenly, she felt claustrophobic. Gasping for air, she opened the door and checked to see if she was alone. Assured that she was, she ran to the sink and splashed her face with cold water. Slowly, she raised her head and looked around, half-expecting, to see Jaime Bastido standing over her. Instead, she was confronted with a silence so fraught with the promise of barbarism, it was equally terrifying.

The bathroom was small and old, with gray tiles that seemed dirty seconds after being scrubbed. Next to the sink where she stood was a small window that overlooked an adjacent parking lot. It was barred, but just then, fettered by this mood of desperation, bars felt appropriate.

For most of her life, Max felt as if she was a captive of circumstance, locked into an existence that was not of her making. More than once, she'd resented her mother for placing them inside the jail that was their life. But her resentment quickly faded because it only made things worse. She and Beth were isolated enough. Being estranged, even for an hour, produced an emptiness so overpowering that nothing was as important as ending their alienation.

That was how Amanda felt now, isolated, separated from her mother, alienated from everything that symbolized safety and connection.

She splashed her face again, recoiling from the smack of the cold water against her skin. Another spasm of dread gripped her. Her hands closed around the sides of the sink. She closed her eyes and willed the avalanche of horrid thoughts away. When she opened her eyes, she was greeted by a stranger: a young woman with colorless skin, straggly hair and eyes that looked like they were recovering from a well-placed punch.

She leaned into the mirror. Something about the stranger was disturbingly familiar. Amanda shuddered.

The face in the mirror was Erica Baird when she had seen her house explode on a television screen.

Molly Taylor when she had to tell her mother she had told her class she'd lived in a place where it never snowed.

Julie Stark confessing she'd slipped and used the name, Erica.

Laura Cooper confiding that she used to have a dog.

The face in the mirror was a young girl with a dozen other names who fought hard to remember who she was no matter who she was pretending to be. A young girl who found it hard to lie, but understood that the truth could be a killer.

The face in the mirror was Amanda Maxwell, a grown woman who, as a young girl, had slipped up so many times that in her heart she believed if anything terrible happened to anyone she loved, it was her fault.

C H A P T E R

TWENTY-TWO

Jaime Bastido reached into the coin box at the side of the cart and handed change to the customer who had just bought a salted pretzel. The man counted the coins, which annoyed Jaime. He'd borrowed this pushcart for the afternoon, so he didn't care whether he gave this man more or less than he deserved, but the man was standing in Jaime's line of sight. How was he going to spot his prey if idiots like this insisted on blocking his view.

"I think you owe me a nickel," the man said.

Jaime didn't apologize for the oversight or challenge the man's math. He reached into the box, extracted a nickel, and handed it over. In exchange for such willing compliance, he expected the fellow to move on. When he wasn't quick about it, Jaime glared.

"This piece of sidewalk isn't for rent, *mi amigo*. I'm trying to sell pretzels here."

The man glowered at Jaime, but walked away, spewing a string of unkind words. Jaime's eyes were trained on the door.

Her shift ended at four. It was almost five-fifteen. Even if she'd lingered to study his artwork, she should've been out by now. He was certain he hadn't seen her, and he knew she was in the building. He'd watched as Amanda and her partner, Doyle, returned from their day on the streets. Doyle left a little after four.

Where the hell is she? His foot rat-a-tatted like a jackhammer. His eyes kept a cold and steady vigil.

A young woman pushed through the door. Young. Hispanic. Great body. Too short.

Four men. Three women. All black.

A couple of civil-servant types. Jaime sneered.

Ten minutes later, two other women exited the building. One—old and fat, her shoulders hunched from the weight of two large, sloppy shopping bags—looked like a Polish cleaning lady. The second was as thin and nervous as a Chihuahua.

Jaime was growing impatient. By five-thirty, the crowd on the street was larger, but fewer and fewer people were going in and out of the building. The shift change had been completed long ago. Office hours were over. Here and there, a cluster of workers came out, but Amanda was not among them. Somehow, he'd missed her.

His expression turned dark and nasty. He was thisclose to getting revenge for all those years he'd spent in prison, living in a box, being abused by men who were bigger and needier than he was. His body practically shuddered with rage.

But, he reminded himself, prison wasn't a totally wasted experience. He'd learned to control that rage. He'd learned to spot his enemies faster and keep a friend longer. Most important, he'd learned how to survive.

And how to wait.

An elderly woman hobbled through the door of The Bent Wing and headed straight for Sybil Whitehall's office. She knocked lightly and entered when invited, closing the door behind her.

"I need your help," she stated bluntly. "I'm being stalked by an assassin."

Sybil thought she recognized the voice, but the body from which it emanated was completely unfamiliar.

"Please sit down," she said, certain her mind was playing tricks.

The woman dropped her shopping bags on the floor and took the seat opposite Sybil's desk. Before Sybil could say a word, the wizened old woman removed a gray wig, wire-rim glasses, and blobs of latex that had made her look forty years older than she was. She untied scuffed oxfords, then peeled off woolen stockings, followed by leg pads that had widened her own slender legs by inches.

Amazed, amused, frightened, Sybil simply stared as a friend emerged from the body of this lumpy stranger. "Max! What the hell's going on?"

Amanda had struggled with the decision to come here. In the end, she felt she had no choice. This was a shelter, and that was precisely what she needed. More than that, she needed someone she could trust. She'd seen Sybil go to the mat for women she'd never seen before and knew she'd never see again. Sybil wouldn't betray her.

"I'm being stalked. I can't go home. This is the only place I could think of where I stood a chance of being safe."

Sybil's complexion turned ashen. "You can stay for as long as you want." She walked around from behind her desk and hugged Amanda, holding her close, offering her a personal harbor. "You can stay at my house if that makes you more comfortable."

"No!" Amanda pushed Sybil away and stepped back, as if she was afraid of infecting the other woman with a fatal virus. Her response was automatic and, she realized, a bit harsh. "Thank you, but no. I couldn't do that to you."

Sybil was stunned at how raw and vulnerable Amanda seemed. Detective Max, as she was known at the shelter, was always calm and in control, suffused with an aura of quiet proficieney. Over the years, Sybil had admired the compassion Max displayed when counseling the women and teaching them how to record their most private and painful moments. Somehow, she seemed to connect with them, to communicate sympathy void of pity. It was as if she related to their shame, their penchant for keeping their abuse secret, and their belief that whatever horror befell them was their own fault.

She steered Amanda to the couch, and said, gently, "Can you tell me what this is about?"

Amanda worried a fold in her jacket. "I can tell you some of it."

Sybil held her hand. "As much as you wish."

Haltingly at first, Amanda told Sybil the story of her life, in abbreviated form, of course. Without revealing her true identity, she confessed to being a former participant in WITSEC. She said the case which put her into the program involved drugs, but she never mentioned Operation Laundry Day, Beth, her uncle Ken or, Lionel. She never revealed where she'd come from, any of the cities in which she'd lived, or any of her aliases. She did feel she owed it to her friend to tell her about Bastido. She described him as best she could.

Sybil rose from the couch and walked to the other side of her office, creating a neutral space in which she could digest what she'd been told. She was undeniably rattled by Amanda's story. All Sybil really knew about the Witness Security Program was what she read in the papers or saw on a screen: It was a haven for criminals, a plot in a story about the mob, or a footnote in a magazine article about the Marshals Service or the Justice Department or the war on drugs and organized crime.

Suddenly, a woman claiming to be a protected witness was seated in her office, seeking sanctuary. This woman admitted she had a fake name, fake credentials, and an invented history. Sybil didn't need a great deal of time to decide what to do. Her gut told her that name and background forgeries aside, Amanda Maxwell was the same person Sybil had liked and admired yesterday. Amanda wasn't a criminal, nor was she a Mafia princess. She'd entered this program as a child—an innocent child. Yet despite her innocence, despite all those years she'd spent paying unwarranted penance, she was being stalked by well-trained, well-paid killers.

Being punished for doing the right thing, spending your life in hiding while crooks and drug dealers roamed free—it was wrong and it made Sybil angry.

She closed her eyes and clenched her fists as her own history asserted itself. She'd watched her alcoholic father beat her mother night after night until the poor woman died. That was wrong, and Sybil knew it, so she turned her father in to the police. She was ten years old. She thought she had done the right thing. But instead of being rewarded with a good and caring home with relatives, she was thrown into the foster-care system, moving from one awful situation to another. She was sixteen before she found the Whitehalls. If she hadn't, she'd be dead.

Meg and Stan Whitehall nursed Sybil back to mental health by giving her large doses of love, unremitting nurturing, guidance, and by setting a fine example. Stan Whitehall showed her that men can be gentle and caring and respectful. He taught her to act, rather than simply react, to reach up, not down, and never to simply accept what's put on her plate.

"If you don't like what's served to you, get up and make your own," he told her.

Meg focused on rebuilding Sybil's fragile ego, insisting that the young woman view herself as a valuable addition to the world, not as the awful burden she'd come to believe she was. Instead of hand-me-downs and a quick chop with a sewing scissors, she bought Sybil her own clothes and took her to a local beauty salon for haircuts. She gave Sybil a ton of books and took her to the movies, teaching her how to laugh again, how to cry and be sentimental without fear of being taunted for being wimpy.

And when things looked gray and Sybil felt alone with no one to listen to her woes, Meg told her to think about her mother in heaven.

"She's the angel with the bent wing," Meg assured the emotionally battered girl. "And she's looking out for you. Because that's what mothers are supposed to do."

Sybil swallowed the lump that had formed in her throat. She was supposed to protect the women who sought shelter at The Bent Wing. She couldn't compromise their safety, but neither was she willing to throw Amanda to whatever wolves were lurking the darkness outside these doors.

"You're more than welcome here, Max. I hope you know that."

Amanda nodded and wiped her eyes with her sleeve. She didn't trust herself to speak.

"I think we could both use a pot of tea."

Sybil went to the kitchen. When she returned, Amanda's weepy spell had subsided.

"I didn't know where else to turn," she said, as she sipped the hot, orange spice brew.

"That's why we're here," Sybil reminded her. "Besides, you've been a big part of our success. We owe you."

Amanda shook her head and rubbed her eyes. She was exhausted, running on three hours' sleep and little else. "Somewhere in the back of my mind, I probably knew that sooner or later it would come to this, but consciously, I don't think I ever believed I'd be too frightened to go home."

"No one does."

Amanda didn't tell Sybil that her current apartment was the only residence she'd ever called home. Every other place had been the house in Nowhereland, a temporary refuge during what she'd hoped was a temporary phase of her life. She didn't tell Sybil that she thought her apartment signaled a sea change, that she'd found a man she trusted, a job she liked, a father she could rely on, a life in which she could be productive and protected and, possibly, one day, happy. She didn't tell Sybil any of this, because when she looked at those mutilated photographs, she knew her apartment, Jake, the job and happily ever after was nothing more than a childish dream. Reality was Lionel sitting in his library with his head blown open. And Jaime Bastido lying in wait for a chance to kill her.

Her hands shook as she raised the teacup to her lips.

Sybil noticed the tremors and fretted. She'd never seen Amanda so threadbare. "Do you plan to go to the police?"

"I can't. At least not right now."

Sybil wished she could ask why. "What about work?" she asked instead.

"That's probably the only place I feel safe." Though, after receiving that package she wondered just how safe the station house was.

"How will you get in and out without being seen?"

"I can go in as I am. On the job, I'm surrounded by too many guns for the odds to favor Bastido and his henchmen. When I leave, I'll disguise myself and take circuitous routes in and around the city to make sure I never show up here with a tail." She leaned forward, rested her arms on her thighs, and fixed her gaze on Sybil. "If I have to, I'll sleep somewhere else. I'd never put you or the women in this shelter at risk. I hope you know that."

"I do," Sybil said. "But stalkers look for patterns."

"I thought I'd stagger my off hours by bunking in with another friend now and then. Plus, my schedule is erratic. And, I don't plan on making this a forever thing."

"For your sake, as much as ours, I hope this is over quickly. Maybe then, you can come out of hiding."

Amanda responded with a nod and a smile, but in her head, she was nine years old, asking Samuel Bates, United States Marshal, if she'd have to hide forever. He said she would.

She wondered then the same thing she wondered now: How long is forever?

Jake didn't have lots of friends in high places, but, as he was fond of saying, he did have friends who were well placed. He was about to leave the office when two of those prize contacts called—the first was a woman who worked at the telephone company. She was older, married, and bored enough to think that doing an occasional favor for a private detective was exceedingly cool.

Jake had asked her to check calls to and from Lionel's town house on the night of the suicide. According to the phone company records, there were calls from the town house to Annie Hart and Max during the early afternoon, a call from Max's apartment to the town house late afternoon.

The next interesting nugget of information came from an officer at a small but top-drawer bank known for its trust and estate work. Naturally, whatever he was about to tell Jake had to stay off the record.

"East Gorham Associates oversees two very large trust funds," the man said. "Each is worth many millions of dollars. The nominee for both is a man named Samuel Bates."

Bates! "Do you know who this Bates guy is?" he asked.

"No, but he withdrew sixty thousand dollars a couple of weeks ago. In cash."

"Really?"

"Really."

"Did Baird know?"

"Absolutely. His instructions were that he was to be notificd about any and all withdrawals."

"What was his reaction?"

"Nuclear."

"No kidding."

"Lionel Baird never kidded about his money."

"Is this Bates character a relative or a business associate?"

"Neither, as far as I know."

"So who the hell is he?" *Who is Beth? And who were they to Lionel?*

"The guy's probably a front for the real beneficiaries. He gets paid a hefty fee for his name being on the papers, but at the end of the day, the trusts aren't his. He's just a baby-sitter for a whole lot of cash. It's done all the time."

"Why?"

"Because people like Baird don't want people like you and me to know who's going to get his fortune."

He certainly didn't want Pamela Baird to know, Jake thought, as he thanked his friend and hung up the phone. But give credit where credit was due: Pamela said Lionel probably buried the bulk of his estate in irrevocable trusts. Apparently, she was correct. But who were the beneficiaries? Pamela believed Lionel might have been planning to gift Max with money. Was East Gorham Associates the wrapping for that gift? If so, who was the intended recipient of the second trust? Beth?

He unlocked the drawer of his desk and took out the file on Lionel's death, more specifically, the note the CSU team found in the wastebasket.

Send Beth flowers. Call Bates—find out how.

Jake placed the plastic bag containing the note on his desk and stared at it. Bates was more than a front, he was sure of it.

He threw his feet up on his desk and laid the plastic bag on his thighs as if it were a talisman with telepathic powers. If he kept it close, it would open the door to the land of second sight and allow him to see what, so far, had eluded him. Then he leaned back, clasped his hands behind his head, and stared into space as he meditated on possibilities.

Lionel was notified about the withdrawal and hit the roof. He called Bates, chewed him out. Bates came to see Lionel. They argued about the money. Bates turned on Lionel and threatened him, either physically or verbally. If it was physical, and Bates actually killed Lionel, how did he do it? If it was verbal, what could he have threatened that would have been horrible enough for Lionel to think death was preferable?

It all came down to secrets. What were Lionel's secrets? What would happen or who would be hurt if they were revealed? And who else knew what they were?

Returning to the present, Jake's gaze reverted to the note. Almost casually, he focused on the stationery, rather than the words. Neatly engraved, top center, was a little red caboose, reminiscent of the standard Lionel electric trains. *Clever logo*, Jake thought, running his finger across the raised insignia. He'd always thought of Lionel Baird as a clever, incisive businessman, but he'd never thought of him as someone who'd have such an idiosyncratic seal. It was unique, distinctive.

The bemused smile on Jake's lips disappeared as he remembered seeing a caboose exactly like this one lovingly displayed—on a night table next to Max's bed.

"How dare you!" Pamela Baird's anger reached through the phone and slapped Hallie across the face. She flushed from the heat. "You're supposed to be advancing the senator's cause. Instead, you manhandled him!"

"I did no such thing," Hallie replied, thankful they were not in the same room. "I asked him reasonable questions and expected reasonable answers. If he came off sounding like Gene Kelly, that's his problem. He's the one who chose to tap-dance around the issues."

"Lionel Baird is not an issue in this campaign."

"Speaking of tap dancing," Hallie snorted. "Really, Pamela! You were the one who insinuated your late husband into this so-called process. You were the one who fed me all that stuff about Operation Laundry Day, suggesting that if he washed money then, we should assume he's washing it now."

The silence on the other end was deadly. Hallie was certain that if she pressed the receiver closer to her ear, she'd hear a bomb ticking. If she continued mouthing off, she'd probably lose Pamela as a source—if she hadn't lost her already—and could add the influential

Mrs. Baird to an ever-expanding list of enemies, but she didn't care. There was a limit to Hallie's appetite for crow.

"When did you become so sensitive about hurting Lionel's feelings?" she continued. "Was it before or after he blew his brains out?"

Pamela didn't respond as much as she detonated. "You little whore! You used us to advance your pitiful career. You toyed with us, and then, when you decided you'd given us our money's worth, sold us out."

"If that's how you see it, Pamela, there's not much I can say to change your mind, but the fact is, you contacted me. You and the senator laid out an agenda you wanted me to pursue. You personally handed me a dossier on Lionel Baird and instructed me to make him the living, breathing symbol of Wall Street's deadly greed. I did what you asked. Now Lionel's dead, and you feel guilty."

"You're the one who should feel guilty!" the woman ranted. "You're nothing but a hack! Instead of making a credible case, you tarred and feathered him in that rag you call a newspaper!"

"Maybe so, but don't forget who supplied the tar and the feathers."

"Don't say that!" she shrieked. "It's your fault my husband is dead." Pamela's nerves were frayed. Her voice was shrill. "It was you and those sleazy articles that put the gun in Lionel's hand. You're going to pay for what you did, Hallie Brendel. And dearly!"

The phone slammed in her ear. Hallie returned the receiver to its cradle, but instead of being frightened or disturbed or even slightly dismayed, she started to laugh. If Pamela thought hers was the last word, she was in for a big surprise.

It had been years since Jake was on a stakeout; usually, he sent someone from his office, or a freelancer. Since he'd kept this particular file close to his vest, he couldn't do either of those things without a lot of questions he wasn't prepared, or willing, to answer. Only Caleb Green knew his plans, and even Caleb couldn't foresee anything coming from this camping expedition that would make or break their case. Nonetheless, Jake said he had an itch to watch the town house. Caleb told him to "go ahead and scratch."

Jake had forgotten how tedious and boring and lonely surveillance could be. Accompanied by a thermos of coffee, a bag of bagels, a wide-mouthed jar for answering nature's call, a cassette player so he could pass the time listening to a book on tape, and nightscope binoculars, he parked his car across the street from Lionel's town house and settled in for what promised to be a long night.

He checked his watch: eight o'clock. The town house was dark. He'd walked by earlier and noted that the security system was armed. Caleb said Tony Calandra checked the premises every day, but at present, no one was actually living there. Jake opened a notebook to jot down the time when he remembered Hallie was appearing on *Newsline* tonight. Now! Jake had promised to watch, but forgot to set his VCR.

No problem, he told himself. Hallie would have a tape. Or two. Or three dozen!

From what she said, she got the call immediately after her confrontational—and controversial—appearance on the roundtable. The booker for *Newsline* invited her to appear on the highly rated, three-times-a-week news magazine as the in-studio interview. They were doing a story on Lionel that attempted to answer the question everyone was asking: Why would a titan of Lionel Baird's magnitude take his own life? Trey Gallagher, one of the hosts of the show, was impressed with the way Hallie took Senator Chisolm on and curious about her belief that Operation Laundry Day somehow impacted on Lionel's tragic decision.

Jake smiled. Hallie was ecstatic, certain that this was her big break. Jake presumed this was the kind of opportunity she'd expected when she teamed up with Pamela Baird and John Chisolm. Unfortunately, that joint venture had yielded little. Despite a series of forceful, attention-grabbing articles, Hallie was still known as "that reporter from the *Telegraph.*" She probably believed tonight's performance would change all that.

For her sake, Jake hoped things turned out the way she wanted, but he remained skeptical. So far, nothing associated with the death of Lionel Baird seemed to be giving people what they wanted.

The *Newsline* staff put together the background with a mix of dramatic reenactments and file footage documenting the two trials, Cynthia Stanton Baird's dramatic testimony and the fiery conclusion of that tragic tale. They followed up with a recap of the rumors and accusations that had dogged Lionel in the weeks and months preceding his death—many of them having their genesis in columns penned by Hallie. During the next segment, she was to be interviewed live, in the studio, by the host, Trey Gallagher.

She took her seat and allowed a production assistant to snake the small black microphone up the back of her suit jacket and attach it to the lapel. She had dressed smartly—navy blue suit, cream silk blouse, gold pin and earrings—but made certain her blond hair was silky smooth and her makeup made the most of her eyes and lips. Also, that her skirt was short enough to show off her legs, but not so short that it became a challenge to her credibility. Gallagher was one of *People* magazine's fifty sexiest men, but took his job very seriously. Hallie was determined to come off as an equal, matching him beauty for beauty, brains for brains.

Trey joined her on the set, complimented her on the way she looked, wished her good luck, then looked beyond her into the eye of camera one. When the red light blinked, he began.

"Several weeks ago, one of the most powerful men in the country, Lionel Baird, killed himself amid a flurry of rumors and accusations that his company was laundering money for major drug cartels. Hallie Brendel, one of the people advancing those rumors, is a reporter for the *Telegraph*, a New York daily newspaper."

He turned to Hallie and moved on, taking away her chance to rebut his subtle tag of rumormonger.

"Recently, you said you believe there's a connection between this shocking suicide and Operation Laundry Day, an interagency government task force that broke up a major money-laundering scheme in south Florida during the late seventies. What makes you think that a twenty-year-old case would have anything to do with the recent death of Lionel Baird?"

Hallie's expression telegraphed the perfect blend of heartfelt concern and journalistic acumen; she'd practiced it for over an hour.

"Because the government's key witness in that famous case was the love of Lionel Baird's life: his first wife, Cynthia Stanton Baird." She furrowed her brows slightly, as if this story was actually painful to tell. Inside, she was grinning, imagining Pamela's face fuchsia with jealous rage.

"Cynthia Baird was that rare commodity: the noble whistleblower who came forward simply because it was the right thing to do. She testifed in Miami against the powerful Colombian cartel run by the legendary Raoul Espinosa and again in New York against members of the vicious Saviano crime family.

"On the day the Espinosa operatives were sentenced, her house in North Miami exploded." Hallie paused dramatically. "To the world, Cynthia and her daughter, Erica, were dead."

Trey Gallagher caught the prompt and leaned forward expectantly. "Are you suggesting they didn't die in that explosion?"

She'd better have something substantial to back this up, Trey thought, or the next thing to go up in flames would be his career. Knowing the camera was on her, he felt free to glower. She was unfazed.

"I'm suggesting that WITSEC, the Justice Department's Witness Security Program, was created for people like Cynthia and Erica Baird."

Trey's face was exquisite: shock, followed by a begrudging acceptance of plausibility. It was as if she'd rehearsed him.

"It's entirely possible that the government staged that explosion," she continued, laying out her case. "Colombian cartels are known for exacting revenge. So is the Mafia. Perhaps the only way to protect the Bairds was to eliminate them."

Trey's color paled, even beneath his ably applied pancake makeup. "Do you think Lionel Baird knew the truth?"

She shrugged her shoulders delicately. "What is the truth?" Her entire mien was one of compassion. "There are those who think the truth is that Lionel Baird's wife and daughter were blown to smithereens and twenty years later he was still laundering drug money, still committing the very crime that got them killed." She shook her head. "Looking at the film of that explosion, knowing how much he loved them, I can't imagine that."

"You wrote a series of articles implying just that," Trey said pointedly. "In fact, you were quite savage in your allegations. Are you saying that those charges were false?"

"I'm saying, I didn't level those charges," she said, splitting hairs and hoping to get away with it. "I was reporting on a political campaign."

"Senator Chisolm's reelection campaign," Trey informed his national audience.

"Correct." Hallie nodded. At this point, Pamela had to be apoplectic. "But in addition to what Senator Chisolm was saying, there were a number of similar stories circulating in the financial community, including the one on Lionel Baird. I reported on those that seemed relevant."

"What about the Della Robbia commodities scandal?" Trey paused just long enough to make Hallie nervous. "And what about Lionel Baird's assertion that your insinuation that he sanctioned and encouraged money laundering for drug traffickers was, and I quote,"—he looked down at his notes—"brazen, misguided, and self-serving."

"I'm a journalist. My job is to report the news, whether it pleases the subject or not, whether it advances my career or not." Hallie attempted to sound confident, but this was shaky ground. "As for being misguided, the government launched a large-scale investigation into the matter, based, in part, on my reports."

"Any results?"

"At the time of his death, the accusations against Lionel Baird remained simply that, accusations."

"Did his death put an end to the investigation?"

"No. Because it didn't put an end to the drug trafficking, the money laundering, or the turf wars that are leaving dead bodies all over the streets of New York."

"So why not continue to pursue those stories? Why speculate about whether Lionel Baird's wife and child died in that explosion twenty years ago? What's the point?"

Trey hated going down blind alleys, but Wall Street stories and mob wars were old. This other, more personal, angle was fraught with risk, but this was what they'd advertised. This was what his programming chief believed would play with the female demographic. Besides, if Brendel had anything solid, it might spawn a follow-up.

"Lionel Baird's death raised a number of questions," Hallie stated, hoping she didn't sound as defensive as she felt.

"How about answers? Have you unearthed anything to back up your assertion?"

Hallie was sweating, despite the chill emanating from her companion. "The Marshals Service isn't exactly forthcoming about who's living under the protection of WITSEC."

Obviously, she scored, because Trey didn't come back at her. A large screen behind them suddenly filled with Lionel's image.

"During that press conference we mentioned a moment ago," Trey said, "Mr. Baird exhibited great passion when he spoke about his former wife and daughter. Take a look."

They replayed a portion of Lionel's press conference. In it, Lionel spoke movingly of the courage it took for Cynthia to testify. Hallie stiffened as she watched Lionel focus on the spot where she'd been sitting. His expression was poisonous. She shuddered, knowing what was coming.

"She did it because drug traffickers had murdered her brother. In the end, they murdered her and my nine-year-old daughter."

The red light on camera two was illuminated. Hallie didn't know if it was trained on her because she was fixed on Trey, who was clearly moved by what he'd just seen.

"Even after twenty years, Lionel Baird's emotions seem so raw," he said, his tone quiet and respectful, yet curious.

This was her chance. Hallie jumped in before it could slip away. "And current. Doesn't it make you wonder whether they're alive?"

"I suppose . . ."

"Think about it: if they're alive, and if Lionel knew where they were, he was also a target." She paused dramatically. "Cynthia Baird was responsible for a number of people going to jail for a very long time. She was also responsible for shutting down the Espinosa cartel, as well as putting a major dent in the Saviano's drug-distribution business."

"That was then," Trey said, unhappy with the path this interview was taking. "Raoul Espinosa is dead and Big Ray Saviano is a permanent resident of Joliet. It's hard to carry out a grudge from the grave."

"But their descendants are alive and well and living among us," Hallie shot back. "The Espinosa brothers moved to Mexico. Little Ray Saviano is running the family business here in New York. And both groups are making a fortune pumping Propaine into our kids."

"Then why would Lionel Baird matter to them? Why would they want to harm him? Especially if he was laundering their profits."

"Because the Espinosas and the Savianos are murderers with long memories and a big score to settle," Hallie insisted, knowing she had to stand her ground or look like a fool. "I believe Lionel Baird killed himself rather than reveal the whereabouts of his wife and his daughter. That he died to keep them safe."

If Hallie expected applause or any show of support, she was disappointed. Trey's response was patronizing at best. "That's a rather heroic theory," he said, "but without any facts to back it up, Miss Brendel, I'm afraid it sounds like fiction. And it doesn't put to rest the other, more popular theory which, I might point out, you helped initiate—that Mr. Baird killed himself rather than suffer through the humiliation of a trial."

"The only way to know which theory is correct," Hallie said, going for broke, "is if Cynthia or Erica Baird comes forward." Ignoring the horrified look on Trey's face, she turned to the camera. "Wherever you are, please, call me. I'll maintain your privacy. Just tell me the truth. Let me clear Lionel Baird's name so he can rest in peace. And you can live in peace."

Trey signaled to the director to cut her off. The light on her camera shut off as did her microphone. Trey hastily began his wrap-up.

"As always, the truth is elusive. We may never know what really happened to Lionel Baird, or his wife and daughter. What we do know is that America is engaged in a mighty war against drugs, a war some believe we cannot win. Maybe so, but twenty years ago, Cynthia Stanton Baird was drafted into service and proved herself a heroine. Exhibiting inordinate courage, she put herself on the front lines. And paid a price few of us would be willing to pay. On behalf of a grateful nation, we thank her."

The lights dimmed. When the director shouted, "It's a wrap!" Trey Gallagher and the entire *Newsline* crew stared at Hallie in dumbfounded silence.

"Are you crazy? Or just plain stupid?" Trey asked, clearly disgusted. "Do you realize you just put a price on the heads of Cynthia Baird and her daughter Erica?"

"And how did I do that?" *Did I do that?* She was unnerved by the disapproving stares of those around her.

"You implied that they were definitely, positively, absolutely alive. Hell! You did everything except publish their damn address!"

"No, I didn't. I simply put forth a theory. One that fit the theme you'd set for your show, and one, for a nanosecond, you seemed to think was quite plausible."

"This was live," Trey said, knowing he was partly culpable. "And foolish me, I actually thought you'd based this cockamamie theory on something substantial."

"Your staff didn't ask for evidence. I didn't offer any. Nor did I state on the air that it was an absolute certainty that either of those women is alive. I simply said what others have to be thinking." She looked around, practically begging them to see her point. "I mean, really. WITSEC isn't exactly new or top secret."

Trey backed off, but only slightly. "Okay, while I don't buy the notion that Lionel Baird killed himself to safeguard them, they could be protected witnesses."

Hallie said nothing.

"Still, if by some miracle they are alive, you just dared a bunch of drug lords and Mafia hit men to go out and grab their pound of flesh. If either one of these women turns up dead, I'm going to hate myself for giving you a forum. But," he said, bringing his face inches from hers, "I'm going to hate you more."

As she left the studio and headed for home, she realized Trey's diatribe marked the second time in one night that she was blamed for someone's death. Suddenly, she was nervous. For Cynthia and Erica Baird, if in fact, they were alive.

And for herself.

Amanda and Sybil, relaxing in Sybil's office, turned the TV on by chance. Less than a minute into the *Newsline* piece, Sybil knew, by the abject terror on her face, who Amanda really was. Before she had a chance to reassure Amanda of her silence, Amanda was out of the office and out of the shelter. Sybil couldn't imagine where she'd gone. But she prayed to everything that was holy, she'd come back.

The first thing Amanda did was find a phone booth to call Annie. It was late, but she needed clothes and the photographs she'd taken the night of Lionel's death. Figuring they needed someplace public, but not overly busy, they arranged to meet in the ladies' room in the subway at 175th Street.

By the time Annie arrived, it was after midnight. There were few, if any, passengers on the platform, no one in the bathroom. From home, Annie had brought a few things Amanda needed to get her through the night and the morning. Amanda gave Annie the key to her apartment and told her where the photographs were hidden. The plan was for Annie to go up sometime the following day. She was not to go alone and not to go without being fully disguised.

"You're making me nervous," Annie admitted.

Amanda took hold of Annie's arms and looked her squarely in the eye. "I want you to be nervous," she said. "I want you to look left and right and over your shoulder every single minute of the day. You're my friend, Annie, and much as I hate it, that puts you in danger. Please, take this seriously."

Annie nodded. "I do." She pulled Amanda to her, but her embrace couldn't loosen the tightness she felt in Amanda's body. She was rigid with fear and determination. "Did Brendel's performance make things worse?"

"You bet! It's as if she put out an APB on us." Amanda's jaw was tight, her eyes blazing with anger. "I'd like to strangle that woman."

"Not if I get to her first." Annie was equally enraged, but her first concern was Amanda. Hallie Brendel would get hers later.

A woman walked into the bathroom and went into a stall. Amanda turned on the water and washed her hands. Annie fussed with her face. Neither one spoke. When the woman left, Annie turned to Amanda.

"Tell me where you're staying. What you're doing. How I can reach you."

Amanda shook her head. "It's better if you don't know where I am. Besides, I won't be in the same place for too long. I need to find out who killed Lionel,"

Unspoken, but understood by both Amanda and Annie: "Before they kill me and my mother."

Working quickly, Annie changed disguises, reworked Amanda's face so she was unrecognizable, and left. Amanda remained in the ladies' room for another half hour, perched on the rim of a toilet seat so anyone using the facilities or peeking in would think the room was empty. When enough time had passed to discourage anyone who might have followed her, she took out her cell phone and dialed Uncle Sam's number. Instead of leaving a message and a phone number the way she was supposed to, she demanded that if he was there, he come on the line. He did.

"You've got to get to Mom," she said, unwilling to listen to a recitation of procedure and protocol. She explained about Beth's clandestine trip to New York, the stolen film cartridge, Bastido, and Hallie Brendel's appearance on *Newsline*. "Mom was going to lay over for a couple of hours in San Francisco just in case and then fly home. I'm not comfortable with her being alone and unguarded. Bastido may not know exactly where she lives, but he knows what she looks like. And just in case someone tailed me to that hotel . . ." She couldn't bear to finish the thought. Instead, she gave him the flight number. "Please, Uncle Sam, meet that plane."

He assured her that he would and that he would get back to her. Swallowing her fear, Amanda slipped out of the ladies' room and onto a train headed downtown.

She exited at Seventy-seventh and Lexington and walked uptown a couple of blocks, then west toward Fifth. Seventy-ninth Street was busy, providing her with some cover. Remaining fully alert, she listened for footstep patterns and watched for consistent shadows. She stopped to look in a shop window, then continued, still watching and listening. Content that, for now, she was minus a tail, she turned onto Fifth, walked down two blocks, and turned left onto Lionel's block. Trying to blend into the shadows, she proceeded slowly, looking into lighted windows and darkened doorways for eyes that might be able to see what she didn't want to be seen.

Believing she was unobserved, she slipped on a pair of latex gloves and opened the wrought-iron gate. Moving quickly, she punched in the security code and unlocked the door, closed it behind her, and reactivated the system. Cupping the beam of her flashlight so nothing would show through the window, she found the secret door and climbed up to the library.

For a long time, she stood on the landing outside the room where her father died. She reached for the knob that would allow her entrance, then pulled back, overcome with a flood of emotion. She bowed her head and cried, frozen, unable to move. It was irrational, she knew that, but she honestly feared she'd open that door and find his body still in that chair, rotting and decomposed, reduced to shreds of flesh clinging to sinew and bone. The image was so horrifying and so real that she swooned, catching herself on the banister. Summoning whatever reservoir of strength remained within her, she breathed deeply, pushed the door aside, and entered.

The room was dark and musty. Secondary light from a streetlamp peered inside, cutting the blackness somewhat, but an insistent gray pall remained. It was cold, yet death continued to scent the air, lingering like cheap perfume that refused to dissipate. When her eyes got accustomed to the light, she noticed that most of the furniture was in its place. Only the desk and the chair behind it had been moved out of position. Both were covered with brown bloodstains and splotches of black powder used to dust for fingerprints.

Unable to look at them, she shifted her attention to the right and aimed her flashlight so it shined down a row of bookshelves. On the train, she had forced herself to go over the pictures she'd taken that awful night with her mind's eye. If there was a recorder in that room, it had to be hidden behind a group of books, probably on the same side of the room as the telephone wires. Once a passageway was created for one set of wires, snaking another series through was easy.

She ran her hand along the first row of books, pushing at them one by one to see if indeed, they were separate entities. When that row yielded nothing, she tried the second row and then the third. Midway, her fingers finally met with resistance. She focused the flashlight on what appeared to be a collection of poems by Robert Browning, Elizabeth Barrett Browning, Byron, and Keats. Again, she nudged at individual volumes. When they didn't budge, she tucked the flashlight under her arm and tried to ease the well-camou-flaged container out.

It was a tight fit, but, eventually, she was able to extract the box. Inside, she found the recorder. But no cassette. Shining a light on the spools, she found a tiny piece of tape lying flat where the cassette had been. Whoever removed the cassette had been in a hurry and ripped it out of the machine. He wasn't looking to preserve the tape, but to destroy it. She reached into her pocket for a plastic bag and tweezers. Gently, she deposited the scrap of tape into the bag, closed it, tucked it into her pocket, and hastened to return the box to its place.

She had found what she was looking for. Now she had to get out before anyone found her.

Jake almost missed it. He'd been staring at the town house for so long, his eyes had grown bleary. Also, the spot of light had come and gone so quickly, it would've been easy to dismiss it as fatigue. Then he saw it again. Someone was definitely inside the house. More to the point, in Lionel's library.

Jake sank down in his seat, obscuring his silhouette. He planted his binoculars on the dashboard next to the steering wheel and peered through them, making certain he had a clear view of the town house and the street.

His heart pounded as he waited. It seemed like forever, but his watch said it was less than ten minutes before someone emerged from the lower level of the town house.

The intruder was tall and rangy, but dressed in black, making it difficult to distinguish gender or specific features. Jake zoomed closer to the face. Round, slightly doughy, perhaps an alcoholic or someone whose weight seesawed, thereby slackening the flesh. Yet the body was trim, the stride firm of foot. He made out a leather jacket, what looked like black jeans, probably a sweater, and a newsboy cap. He was unable to get any details. Whoever it was was moving too fast for that.

He allowed the trespasser to get almost to the corner before bounding out of his car. He left the door ajar rather than attract attention by slamming it and took off after his prey. But he hadn't been quick enough. The sidewalks up and down Fifth Avenue were clear. Jake's suspect must have scurried into Central Park. He was too late.

Disgruntled and disappointed, he returned to his car, but debated about leaving. Maybe the intruder forgot something and would come back. Maybe the perpetrator had been tailed, and the tail would also decide to check out the premises. Maybe . . .

His cell phone interrupted his woolgathering.

"Jake. Where are you?"

His heart pumped inside his chest. It was Amanda. Her voice was shaky.

"I was out picking up some milk. Why," he asked. "What's up?"

"I need to see you. Can I come to your place?"

"Sure. Fifteen minutes?"

The phone went dead.

Jake wished he could make his brain as silent. And his heart as still.

CHAPTER
TWENTY-THREE

Leaving Lionel's, Amanda sought sanctuary in Central Park, disappearing into the darkness that existed beyond the sidewalks and bike paths and roadways that snaked their way through the city's public patch of green. She didn't panic often, but certain now that someone had killed her father, knowing that a roll of film containing their present images was missing, that a tape containing damning evidence was also gone, she could no longer deny that the forces of evil were closing in on her and Beth. She needed time to figure out where her next safe haven might be.

Running north from Seventy-ninth Street where she entered, yet steering clear of the heavily trafficked East Drive, she headed for the area around Belvedere Lake. This time of night, the entire area should be quiet and isolated. Most joggers avoided the interiors after dark and kept to the lighted paths. Fortunately, it was spring, and the foliage was lush, providing a buffet of camouflage opportunities. Finding a stand of trees, she faced away from the lake and toward the Obelisk, pressing her body against the trunk of an old oak.

Close by, she heard the clump-clump-clump of rapid footfalls on grass. She gulped a lungful of air and held her breath. People were racing toward her. She listened carefully. Two, maybe three, but not in a runner's rhythm. She pressed closer to the tree trunk, trying to become one with it, praying that no one broke from the group to go exploring. The trotting grew nearer. Soon, it was on top of her. Her hand was on her gun. Her fingers gripped the trigger.

As they ran past, she heard the laughter of kids, probably racing home from somewhere, trying to make a curfew. Amanda closed her eyes and exhaled, limp with relief. Unfortunately, she had no time to savor the moment. Beth's plane should have landed by now. With fingers trembling from fear and an excess of adrenaline, she turned on her cell phone and dialed her mother's apartment. When no one responded, she called Uncle Sam. When again, no one picked up, she called Carl Steinmetz and asked if he'd heard anything about her mother. He hesitated. Amanda's eyes closed. Her heart thumped inside her chest.

"Your mother was gunned down outside LAX," Steinmetz said, knowing there was no way to soften news like that.

She gasped and slid down the trunk of the tree onto the ground, her legs too weak to hold her. "Is she alive?"

"Yes. She's at Cedars-Sinai. In surgery." By his tone, she knew Beth's life was hanging on a very slim thread.

"Where was Sam?"

"The plane was early. Sam and several other inspectors got to the airport just as Beth was leaving the terminal. Before he could get to her, a car raced by and . . ."

"How many shooters?"

"One."

"How badly was she hit?"

"She's critical, Max. They're doing everything they can."

She was too tired and too heartsick to smother her sobs. Her entire body quaked as she reacted to the unthinkable possibility that her mother might die. And the equally horrid knowledge that it was her fault. She never should have allowed Beth to come to New York. She knew better. She was a police officer. She'd seen Bastido. And she knew he'd seen her. How could she have agreed to something so stupid? How could she believe that she hadn't been tailed to that hotel? That the tail hadn't attached himself to Beth?

"Don't blame yourself, Max," Steinmetz cautioned, knowing she couldn't do anything else. "It's a waste of valuable time and energy. Listen to me. It's not going to help your mom, and it could hurt you. What you have to do now is get yourself to our office in New York. You know where it is. Go there. Let us protect you. Please!"

"I'll call in to find out how my mother is. Don't try and call me."

She hung up, unwilling to listen to the party line. The only point she was willing to concede was that she needed to get off the street. And she needed help.

That's when she called Jake.

★ ★ ★

Before heading over to his place, she found a public bathroom where she could wash up, change from the jacket into a sweater, and collect her wits. Some tasks were easier than others. When she arrived at Jake's apartment, stripped of her disguise and her defenses, she appeared like an apparition, ghostly white, with dead eyes and a body completely void of spirit. Her hair hung in limp strands around her face. Her lips were dry and cracked. She was so wrecked, she could barely lift her backpack off her shoulders.

"Cripes!" Jake said, removing the bulky sack and helping her inside. "What the hell happened to you?"

Stunned by what he saw, he closed the door and led her to the couch, certain that any second she would collapse. Automatically, he scanned her body for wounds or bloodstains. She looked that bad.

Once he had settled her on the couch, he pressed his fingers against her pulse, which was racing. He poured her a brandy, but she couldn't manage it. Her hands were trembling. He raised the glass to her lips and practically poured the liquor into her mouth. When she seemed steadier, he put water on for tea. Whatever thoughts or suspicions he'd been entertaining got shunted aside. For the moment, all Jake cared about was what was right in front of him.

He sat down next to her and nestled her in his arms, stroking her hair and holding her until the tremors lessened. When she was calm, he brought her tea and a slice of bread. She said nothing until she'd finished her tea. She couldn't eat the bread.

"Thanks," she whispered.

He caressed her cheek and smiled. "Don't mention it."

"I have a lot to tell you," she said. Her eyes were haunted. Her voice sounded hollow. "Including some things I should've told you a while ago."

Her plan was to reveal everything—WITSEC, her relationship to Lionel, her belief that he was murdered and that whoever did it had gotten to Beth and was looking for her—but before she did, she needed to tell him what she'd learned from Carl Steinmetz. Not only because she knew that any news about Archie was of tantamount importance to Jake, but selfishly—with an eye toward her own defense at being secretive and untruthful—because she hoped he'd view it as a quid pro quo: She helped him find out the truth about his father, he'd help her find out the truth about hers.

"A few weeks ago, I called a friend of mine and asked him to check out the story about your father."

Of all the things he might have expected her to say—and he had a lengthy list—that never entered his mind. He pulled back and eyed her warily. Had she spotted him outside the town house? Was this a scam to cover herself? And if this was all she had to say, why did she look as messed up as she did?

"Archie's dead, Jake. It was his body in the trunk of that car."

"And you know this, how?"

His posture stiffened. She could almost hear his defense mechanisms clicking in. He knew what was coming, he'd known for years. Still, he wasn't prepared.

"My friend's source was the guy who drove Vito Albanese the night he killed your father." She reached for his hand. He retracted it.

"Forensics never positively ID'd the body."

"This guy was there, Jake. He said the man in the trunk was definitely Archie Fowler. That the murder was payback. That Big Ray Saviano ordered the hit when he found out Archie was skimming."

Jake shook his head, slowly, but emphatically. "I don't believe you."

Amanda wished she had the words to make this easier for him. She combed her hair off her face with her fingers, frustrated and annoyed at her inability to salve Jake's pain.

Jake stared at her. Not only couldn't he believe what he'd just heard, he couldn't believe what he just saw: right on the hairline, a paper-thin piece of latex clung to her skin. His blood froze in his veins.

"I know how devastating this is," Amanda said softly.

"Don't patronize me."

"I'm not." *Why is he looking at me that way?* "I guess I'm not saying this very well. But, Jake. It's true."

"Why should I believe you?"

"Because my source has no reason to lie. Neither do I."

He was glaring at her, his anger rising like the mercury in a thermometer, ascending quickly to the point of boiling rage. "You've lied to me since the day I met you."

"About what?" His reaction was so furious and out of character, it frightened her.

"About everything!" He rose from the couch and went for her backpack, practically ripping it open. He pulled out the leather jacket

Annie had lent her and held it up, waving it as if it was incontrovertible proof of a crime. "Where were you tonight?"

Her heart sank to her shoes. She closed her eyes and rubbed them disconsolately. When she opened them, instead of seeing the man she loved and had come to for help, she saw a stranger.

"I asked you a question, Max. Where the hell were you?" He threw the jacket on the floor. He couldn't stand to hold onto it a moment longer.

"Why do you want to know?"

"Were you at Lionel Baird's town house?" He wasn't asking. He was demanding.

"Were you following me?"

"No. But I saw you. I recognized you, despite your disguise."

Her hand went to her face. Her fingers found the stray piece of latex.

"You sneaked into that house and I want to know why. Did you need to get something? Something you left there, perhaps on another visit?"

His blue eyes were dark and thunderous. The dimples she loved were nowhere to be seen. In their place was a tightly clenched jaw. Slowly, menacingly, he began to stalk the couch, circling her, making her feel like an animal in a trap. Obviously, he knew more than she'd imagined. But what? Since she had no idea what he actually knew and what he thought he knew, she didn't know what to confess, what to hold back.

"Why would you think that? And what were you doing staked out in front of Baird's town house?" she asked, evading his questions by drilling him with some of her own.

His pace slowed, but the hounding continued. "Pamela Baird thinks you had something to do with Lionel's death."

"Really?" Thrown slightly off-balance by that comment, it took a minute for her to sort out her thoughts. On the upside, he didn't know her true relationship with Lionel, he was fishing. Then it dawned on her: Pamela Baird had hired Jake to investigate her. "How about you?" She wondered what his snooping had turned up. And why he'd taken the case. "What do you think?"

He leaned down, bringing his face close to hers. His voice was cold. "I think you knew Lionel Baird a lot better than you've let on."

"That's true." The time had come to tell him. "I did."

Even though he'd been pressing for a confession, when it came,

Jake's face registered a panoply of emotion ranging from disgust to heartbreak. He stopped pacing and stared at her.

"Lionel was . . .

The phone rang, startling both of them. Amanda stopped, expecting Jake to pick it up. He didn't move. Amanda started again, but the jangling of the telephone was so loud, so unnerving. Jake's stare was so intense, so accusing. She lowered her eyes and rolled the edge of her sweater in her fingers.

"Lionel and I were . . . it's hard to explain. We were . . .

The telephone was becoming insistent. Annoyed, Jake picked it up. "What!"

"And a good evening to you!" Hallie's voice was so chirpy it seemed crass and out of place, like laughter at a funeral. "Did you catch the show? Was I fabulous or what?"

"I was busy." His eyes never left Amanda. He dared her to look at him. She did but not easily.

"Did you tape it at least?"

"No. I forgot."

"Really, Jake. The one time I ask you to do something." She giggled. "Well, maybe not the one time, but how could you miss it? It was incredible!"

"I'm sure."

"Your excitement is underwhelming to say the least, but I forgive you. I've got a tape. Actually, I've got a couple of tapes. In case you want one for your own personal library. And a bottle of champagne. Want to come over and watch it with me?" She giggled again.

Without bothering to reply, he hung up and demanded that Amanda complete the sentence she had begun before the interruption.

"You and Lionel were, what?" When she hesitated, he went at her. "I don't see why you're having such trouble spitting this out. You didn't have a problem telling me my father was dead. How come you can't say, 'Lionel was my lover'!"

"*What?*"

"You and Lionel Baird. Lovers. Paramours. Sweethearts. Bedmates. How many different ways do you want me to spell it? You were lovers!"

"We weren't! You don't know what you're saying."

"I know exactly what I'm saying. You left a trail of restaurant reservations and hotel rooms."

Amanda groaned. She'd set herself up.

"You even keep a little red caboose by your bed. A Lionel train. How precious!" He was beyond the point of reason. "Did that remind you of him while you were making love with me?"

"No! Oh, Jake, you are so wrong."

She left the couch and started for him, but he backed away and held up his hand, warding her off. She respected his request for distance, but refused to be silent. Unfortunately, she had so much to explain that it all came out in an incomprehensible tumble.

"Lionel and I couldn't be lovers. Whatever you found was a cover. It wasn't real. It wasn't what you think. That's why I came over here tonight. To tell you . . ."

"I know. That my father's dead. You did that already." He opened a closet and grabbed a coat.

"Jake!" she cried, trying desperately to figure out a way to get through to him. "You have to know how I feel."

"How about caught?"

He opened the front door. She ran for him and grabbed his arm. "Jake, I . . ."

He shook her off like a nettlesome flea and snarled. "Whatever it is, I don't want to hear it! And I don't want to find you here when I get back."

He stormed out and slammed the door, leaving Amanda alone. And lost.

"Jake," she whispered to the emptiness around her, "I love you."

He shouldn't have gone there, but he found himself drawn to Hallie's door.

"Hi," she said, surprised and delighted at first to see him, her pleasure dissipating seconds later when he marched past her into the living room, threw off his coat, and helped himself to a drink, scotch, no rocks. He tossed it back and poured another.

"So, Jake. Nice of you to stop by. Have a drink, why don't you? Don't mind if I do. And by the way, Hallie, I'm sorry I hung up on you. No problem, Jake. I love being dissed. So, Hallie, how are you really? Oh, and how did your appearance on *Newsline* go? Fabulously well? I'm so happy to hear that."

She stood with her arms akimbo, prattling on, tapping her foot. Jake took a hefty swig of his second scotch before facing her. She was dressed in a short, white-satin nightgown, topped by an equally short robe. He didn't know whether she was expecting him or not.

Suddenly, he noticed a bottle of champagne floating in a bucket of melted ice.

"Sorry about that," he said, nodding toward the unopened bottle. "If it's all right with you, I prefer this." He held up his scotch, then finished it. "You look fabulous, by the way."

He plopped down on her sofa, a plump love seat with fat, rolled arms, a high back, and thickly braided fringe that looked like cheese straws, except it was white, like everything else in her apartment. Carpet, furniture, curtains, drapes, flowers, throw pillows, candles— the place was a veritable alphabet of whites: alabaster, chalk, cream, eggshell, fleece, ivory, lily, milk, oyster, paper, pearl, snow, swan, zinc. Needless to say, Hallie couldn't help but stand out against such a pristine backdrop, even in her white nightie.

"Thanks," she said, eyeing him carefully. "I wish I could say the same for you."

She poured herself a glass of wine—white, of course—and perched on a tufted and fringed ottoman.

"I'm sorry I didn't get to watch your interview," he said. "How'd it go?"

The words were right, but the tone was wrong—rote, disengaged, as if he was reading off cue cards.

"Very well, thank you."

"I'm sure you were great!"

He punctuated his compliment with a quick bow of his head, then went to the bar again. When he'd poured yet another scotch, he embarked on a tour of the room. He was walking something off, or drinking it away, that much was clear. As much as Hallie wanted to know what had set him off, that's how much she didn't want to know. Whatever it was, he'd come here to work it out, which, at that moment, was all that mattered to her.

"I have a tape, if you're interested."

"Absolutely!" he muttered, not looking at her, not stopping his perambulation. "I can't wait to see it."

"Yeah, sure."

She was amused, but curious. And cautious. Instead of pressing him, she sipped her wine and watched him prowl. His movements were long and loping, the stretch of his legs pulling his trousers tight across his thighs and buttocks. He gulped his scotch and set the glass down on the bar, his fingers balling into fists as he resumed his pilgrimage. His eyes were growing cloudy with drink, but a fire raged in them nonetheless.

"Do you want to watch it now?" she asked, leaving her seat and walking toward him. When he didn't respond, she stepped directly in his path, forcing him to look at her. What she saw unnerved her. His anguish was overwhelming.

She put her hands on his arms, holding him gently. "Do you want to tell me what's bothering you?"

When she called him earlier, it was because she was bothered. She'd needed a friend and reached out to Jake because she knew he'd be honest with her. He'd tell her whether she put someone in harm's way or simply said what no one else had thought to say. But that was then. Now, Jake was the one in need.

"Is there anything I can do to help?"

He didn't answer her, but he didn't walk away.

"We can talk." He responded by removing her hands from his arms and pouring himself yet another refill. "Or not," she said, sighing.

In spite of his fog, he heard the dejection in her voice. "I don't have anything to talk about," he said simply.

"Perhaps there's something else you'd rather do?"

He turned and looked at her, uncertain about what she was suggesting. To make it clearer, she untied her robe, shook it off and let it fall into a satin puddle on the floor. His gaze followed the drifting fabric, then traveled leisurely up the length of her body, bare feet to bare shoulders, and everything in between. He eyed her hungrily.

She closed her mind to the fact that he was drunk, obviously perturbed, and responding more to physical instinct than desire. She preferred to believe that he could have stayed home or gone to a bar or to someone else's apartment. He was here because he wanted to be with her.

She approached him slowly, giving him a chance to change his mind. He didn't say a word. He simply stared at her, his lips curled in an appreciative smile. She reached up and kissed him. His tongue tasted like scotch.

"Finish your drink," she said in a husky voice as she headed down the hall to her bedroom. "Then if you want to, come join me."

Jake stood in the middle of Hallie's snow-white palace and chugged his drink. His head was swimming. He knew he was getting tanked, but he was helpless to stop. He was trying to blind himself to the sight of Max showing up on his doorstep so bedraggled and vulnerable. He was trying to deafen himself to the sound of her voice telling him that Archie was dead, that all his boyhood hopes were dead, that his dreams of a father-son reconciliation were dead. But most of all, he was trying to numb himself to the pain of hearing her admit that she and Lionel were more than patron and artist, that they meant a great deal more to each other than anyone, especially Jake, had imagined.

On some level where his brain was still functioning, he knew that to go inside to Hallie was wrong, but his flesh was weak. And his need was strong.

He set his glass down and proceeded down the hall. What greeted him was an orgy of candlelight. Wherever he looked, clusters of white columns glowed soft yellow. The air wafted with a familiar scent, but his nose was incapable of distinguishing freesia from tuberose or vanilla. He paused in the doorway, moved by the beauty of the vignette, but overcome by conscience and indecision.

"It's okay. After all, it's not like we've never done this before."

Hallie's voice drifted across the room as if it had hitched a ride on a perfumed breeze. She was sitting in her bed, resting against a pile of pillows that from where Jake stood, looked like marshmallows. She was naked, but in an odd gesture of modesty, was holding a sheet against her.

Jake tried to focus, but his vision was fuzzy. He stepped forward, but the scent of the candles, as well as the bunches of flowers that enlivened the various tabletops, proved overpowering. He grabbed on to the door to steady himself.

Hallie slid out of bed. Her eyes locked on his and held him in her sway as she went to him, sylphlike. Without allowing her gaze to drift, she took his hands in hers and touched them to her flesh. She ran them down her breasts, holding them against her, making them feel her, using his hands to excite her. He went to kiss her, but she resisted, dragging his hands across her skin, moving them lower, making him touch her and experience the heat that he had created. Still holding his hands, she had him caress himself until he was as hot as she was.

Silently, she led him back to her bed. She sat down on the edge and drew his mouth down onto hers. As they kissed, she undid his shirt and his pants. He did the rest, shedding his clothes and his inhibitions. He pushed her down on the bed and straddled her, barely managing to protect himself before entering her.

Hallie reveled in the familiarity of their coupling, the smell of him, the feel of him, the joy of being intimate with this man who could excite her with a look, ravage her with a kiss. For her, it was just like it used to be, raw and voluptuous, wild and inventive, a glorious, rhapsodic ride rife with unbridled passion and unadorned sex.

And just like it used to be, when it was over, she was the only one in love.

A beige panel truck pulled up in front of a modest brownstone on Eighty-ninth Street, just off Columbus Avenue. Maneuvering into a nearby spot vacant because of a NO PARKING sign, the driver put an emergency sign in the front window to stave off any overzealous meter maids who might wander by. A big burly guy with a well-pumped physique, he hoisted a huge toolbox out of the back, slammed the door, and locked it. His associate was smaller but nimble, judging by the way he bounded up the stairs, two at a time. According to the logo emblazoned on the backs of their beige overalls, they were employees of Big City Plumbing.

Across the street, from behind a wall fronting another, larger brownstone, a man watched the plumbers wait, then open the door to the lobby. He assumed they'd been called to fix a leaky pipe or a stopped-up toilet and were buzzed in. Since the door from the small entry into the lobby was curtained, he couldn't see whether they stayed on the ground floor or went up the stairs. As far as he was concerned, it didn't matter. He was looking for a trim woman about five-seven with auburn hair. Neither plumber fit that description.

Bored and annoyed at being stuck here for another couple of hours, he unzipped his pants, relieved himself, and headed off to the corner for a doughnut and coffee. Nothing was going to happen here. Bastido said the broad he was looking for was a cop. What cop would be stupid enough to come back to her own place? As far as he was concerned, this job was a big fat waste of time.

On the third floor, Annie Hart let herself into Amanda's apartment. Her friend, Jimbo, one of the cameramen on her soap—and an avid bodybuilder—guarded her back. She flicked on a light and almost fainted. The place had been ransacked. Furniture was turned over, drawers and cupboards had been emptied. Amanda's darkroom was destroyed, deliberately and viciously. Cabinet doors were pulled off their hinges. Her enlarger was smashed, as was the rest of her equipment. Photographs were strewn over the floor like autumn leaves.

Annie tiptoed down the hall, terrified as to what she might find. Amanda's bedroom, her beautiful, private little garden, had also been savaged. Her comforter had been slashed, her sheets ripped from the bed, her pillows eviscerated. Every stitch of clothing she owned had been tossed out of closets and dressers and scattered about like the remnants of a close-out sale.

Annie stood in the middle of the destruction, paralyzed with fear. She looked at Jimbo, who was as stunned as she was. Making matters worse was the sensation that they hadn't seen it all. Amanda had asked her to get some clothes, the photographs taken at Lionel's town house, and her shotgun, which was supposed to be in a rack under her bed. After a quick, whispered conference, they decided Jimbo should retrieve the weapon, just in case.

He lay flat on the floor and reached under the bed skirt, feeling the underbelly of the box spring.

"It's here," he mouthed, sliding the gun out of its holder, slowly and very carefully. Amanda had warned Annie it was loaded.

Armed with a weapon they prayed they wouldn't have to use, Jimbo and Annie walked back into the hall, alert for anything that might indicate they weren't alone. Jimbo nodded at the closed door on their left—the bathroom. Annie bit her lower lip and closed her eyes, knowing that something horrific lay behind that door. Jimbo leveled the shotgun at the center of the door. Standing on the side, Annie reached over and with a shaky hand, turned the doorknob, and pushed open the door. As she did, she flattened her back against the wall, expecting a firestorm. Instead, they were greeted with a deadly silence and a putrid smell. Jimbo turned away, which probably frightened Annie more than anything.

"It's not Amanda," she told herself, trying to build up the courage to look. She closed her eyes and prayed for strength. Then she took a deep breath, literally counted to three, and spun into the doorway. "Oh, God!"

Floating in the bathtub was a dog, a black-and-white cocker spaniel. Stuck in its belly like a sail on a mast, was a note attached to some kind of stake: CHECKMATE.

Annie started to cry hysterically. Jimbo took her out of the bathroom, leading her into the living room. He uprighted the couch and made her sit down. He checked the door, making certain it was locked, and rechecked the shotgun.

He realized now why had Annie asked him to help her. Jimbo was a good old boy from the back hills of Kentucky. He knew his way around guns, which for this gig was key. He'd met Annie in a bar several years back. She befriended him and helped him get a job. He owed her. Although, after today, he figured his debt was paid.

"We've got to get out of here," she said, wringing her hands. "And we've got to take that poor animal with us."

"Can't we call someone?"

Annie shook her head. Amanda was very specific about that. No police.

"Okay," the big guy said. "I'll get the dog. You get whatever else we came here for."

Grateful beyond words, Annie stood up and kissed his cheek. "I never dreamed . . ."

"It's okay, babe. I'm sure your friend never dreamed we'd walk into something like this either."

Actually, Annie thought, *I'm sure Amanda's dreams are just like this.*

Jimbo rummaged through the junk in the kitchen until he found several large garbage bags. He went off to the bathroom to complete his grim task. Annie went into the kitchen to do what she'd come to do.

Her heart pounded as she bent down and looked into the cabinet next to the sink. Everything in it had been tossed, but that wasn't her concern. She was worried that after this particular cabinet had been cleaned out, someone might have looked inside and noticed that the floor was slightly higher than in the others.

"Thank you, thank you, thank you," she muttered to the Almighty.

Nothing had been disturbed. Following Amanda's directions, she stretched her hand toward the back and groped around until she found a small hole. Sticking her index finger inside, she lifted up a panel that folded back. Quickly, she emptied the makeshift vault, congratulating her friend on her ingenuity, as well as her carpentry skills.

Slipping the files into the empty toolbox they'd carried in, she went toward the bedroom, closing her eyes as she passed the bathroom where Jimbo was cleaning up. Once inside Amanda's special bower, Annie forced herself to clear her head of the ugliness around her and do her job. Rummaging through the mess, she found underwear, a couple of tee shirts, a pair of jeans, an all-purpose black sweater, and, just because it was sitting in front of her, one of Amanda's little black dresses. She bundled them all into a package, stuffed them into the toolbox, and looked around for anything else Amanda might need. She'd already been to the store to pick up a new cell phone; Amanda was certain Bastido had tapped into the one she usually carried.

"You ready?" Jimbo said, calling from the front hall.

"More than ready."

Taking one last look around, wondering how she was going to tell Amanda what she'd seen, she grabbed the toolbox and walked out the door. Jimbo followed, toting his sad parcel. He'd put the note in a small plastic bag which Annie now carried in the pocket of her jumpsuit. As for the shotgun, when they reached the ground floor, he unloaded it, slipped it inside his jumpsuit, secured it with a belt, and walked quickly to the truck.

Two minutes later, they pulled into the street, barely missing a guy crossing the street holding a cup of coffee in one hand, a doughnut in the other.

The brrrring of the telephone jolted Hallie out of her sleep. Her hand slid across the sheet toward Jake, but he was gone. *Long gone,* probably, she thought, as she redirected her hand and grabbed the phone.

"I saw you on *Newsline,*" a man said after she picked up. He didn't give his name. He had an accent, Spanish, she thought. "That guy made you look bad. I got somethin' make you look real good. You want it?"

Hallie was just about to slam the phone down when the caller told her what he had.

"You bet. I want it!"

Suddenly she was wide-awake. And Jake was a pleasant memory.

Jake was banking on coffee to soothe his hangover. Knowing that one trip to the kitchen was all he was capable of, he took the pot and a double-sized mug into his bedroom. Before returning to his bed, he stuck Hallie's tape into his VCR. He figured the least he could do was watch her interview. He felt like a cad running out on her, and helping himself to a tape on the way, but the thought of waking up next to her and dealing with the aftermath of their *nuit d'amour* was more painful than his headache.

He sipped the hot mocha-java carefully, concentrating as if that would hasten the cure. After one huge cup, he poured himself another and pressed the PLAY button, confident that now, he was able to watch and understand.

He barely paid any attention to the background piece; he'd heard it all before. On the periphery of his consciousness, he did note how nice-looking Cynthia Stanton Baird was and how sweet Lionel's daughter, Erica was.

She looks like him, he thought, glugging more coffee, chasing it with three Tylenol.

He fast-fowarded past the commercial, restarting the tape when Trey introduced Hallie. She looked good, like a grown-up, serious journalist, not a tabloid sex kitten. His head pounded, probably as payback for thinking something as cheesy as that. He didn't seem to mind the sex-kitten side of her last night, he admitted with no small amount of guilt.

Forcing himself to pay closer attention, he listened to her defend her attacks on Lionel Baird. Hearing the man's name made Jake sick. He almost turned the tape off. Then, he heard Hallie imply that the mother and daughter didn't die in the explosion. Trey pressed her on it. And why not? It was a spotlight grab. He knew it. Trey knew it. He was certain Hallie knew it. Jake sipped his coffee, assuming she'd sidestep and Trey would move on to something else. Then he heard Hallie say she thought Lionel Baird killed himself to protect the whereabouts of his wife and daughter.

An alarm inside Jake's alcohol-fried brain went off.

He rewound the tape, listening again to Hallie wonder aloud if Cynthia and Erica Baird had died in that explosion. He listened again to Hallie conjecture about Lionel taking his life to protect the lives of his wife and daughter. He closed his eyes and listened again to Max trying to explain her relationship with Lionel.

Lionel and I couldn't be lovers. It's not what you think. It's hard to explain.

He saw the anguish on her face. He recalled how terrified she'd been when she showed up at his door. *And where did she get the information about Archie? What friend did she have who would know Vito Albanese's driver?* A United States Marshal would know! An inspector attached to WITSEC could find something like that out. Albanese's driver had testified against Saviano and was never heard from again. *Because he's in the program.* Just like Erica Baird. Alias Amanda Maxwell.

Jake bolted out of bed and grabbed for the phone. The tape was still running. He listened with half an ear as he punched in Max's number and prayed she'd pick up. Three rings. Four rings. Seven rings. Nothing. Not even an answering machine. He called her cell phone. No answer. His head was throbbing, but the pain was nothing compared to the pain in his heart. She'd come to him for help, he realized that now. And instead of giving it to her, he walked out and left her alone.

He caught the look on Trey Gallagher's face when Hallie called for Cynthia and Erica Baird to come forward.

He saw the fear in Max's eyes when she walked into this apartment. And no wonder: She was Erica Baird, Lionel was her father. Which meant, if someone had murdered Lionel, Max was on a hit list.

Frantic now, he called the CSU.

"Detective Maxwell isn't in," the receptionist said when he asked for her.

"Pete Doyle, then."

"Just a minute."

"Doyle."

"Pete. It's Jake Fowler. Is Max in?"

Normally, Pete would take advantage of an opening like that and come back with a wisecrack, but something in Jake's voice told him not to joke. "No. She's out sick. What's up?"

"Do you know where she is?"

"At home, would be my guess."

"I called there."

"Maybe she's sleeping. Or maybe, she doesn't want to talk to you."

"That could be," Jake said woefully.

"What'd you do to her, Fowler? I swear, I'll break your fucking neck if you hurt her."

"Do me a favor, Doyle. Go over to her place and check on her. Now."

"You're making me nervous, Jake."

"I'm making me nervous. Pete, please, do as I ask. Don't tell anyone where you're going or why, but go. I'll meet you there in half an hour."

"Jesus! What the hell happened here?" Pete tiptoed around the debris, his hands clasped behind his back.

"I don't know, but I'm glad Mr. Ziegler's bursitis was acting up."

When Pete knocked on Aaron Ziegler's door and asked for the key to Max's apartment, the super grilled the two of them. Pete showed his badge and explained that Max was a colleague; Jake was Pete's partner. Max was out of town on a case and had left some important photographs at home. Pete was there to pick them up and mail them to her. He offered to have Mr. Ziegler escort them upstairs, but the elderly man declined. He extracted a promise that they wouldn't disturb anything and would return the key when they were finished. Pete agreed to both conditions.

"Did you expect this?" he asked Jake as he righted a table, his tone a mix of bewilderment and accusation.

"I suppose I did."

He hadn't told Pete about Max's real identity; he wasn't one hundred percent certain of that himself. What he did tell him was an abridged version of the truth: she came to his apartment last night looking terribly distressed. She said she had things to tell him. She started off by telling him his father was dead, they got into a fight, he stormed out, when he got back, she was gone.

When he said he thought she'd been behaving strangely, Pete told him about how nervous she'd been at the Jesús Vazquez trial, how rattled she'd been by some pinched-face Latino who'd been jaw-boning with Little Ray Saviano. Pete wondered if anyone from the *Blanca Muerte* gang had threatened her. Jake said he wouldn't discount the Savianos.

"With Vazquez going away, the boys had to take a little time to reorganize. Time is money. And if what I've heard about their finances are correct, Little Ray's got no time to waste!"

The two men proceeded with extreme caution. Not only were they nervous about what they might find, but habit dictated that they protect a crime scene. Guns drawn, they moved down the hall in tandem. Pete stopped outside the bathroom.

"Check the bedroom."

The hairs on the back of Jake's neck prickled at Pete's tone, but he did as he was told. When he came upon the wreckage, he recoiled. Max loved this room. He remembered how pleased she was that he wasn't uncomfortable surrounded by all the feminine fuss. Then, again, he'd been lying in her arms when she asked if the flowers bothered him. At that moment, a bed of cactus wouldn't have bothered him.

He went to tell Pete what he saw—and didn't see—but his relief at not finding a body was short-lived. Pete was leaning over the bathtub collecting samples. Using an eyedropper, he sucked up the water that had settled around the drain, then squeezed it into a small bottle. He labeled it and set it aside. Using a scraper, he removed some of the scum that had formed a gray rim around the inside of the tub. That, too, went into a container and received a label.

"What'd you find?" Jake asked, dreading the answer.

Pete's face was pinched and colorless. "There's blood in this water. Judging by the smell of this place, whoever was in this tub, is dead. The question is: Who was it? And where's the body?"

CHAPTER
TWENTY-FOUR

After spending a fitful night in a hotel near the Port Authority Bus Terminal, Amanda arranged to meet Annie at a diner on Twelfth Avenue across from the Hudson River piers. With no major cruise ships in port, they had the place pretty much to themselves. They sat in the back, in view of, but not next to a window overlooking the street. Over scrambled eggs and toast, Annie told her about the morning she and Jimbo spent. Amanda wasn't surprised that her apartment had been trashed, but her stomach revolted at Annie's revelation about the dog.

"What did you do with it?" she asked, pushing her eggs away, wondering if she'd ever be able to live in that apartment again.

Annie gulped. "We stashed it in a Dumpster down in the meat district. I saved the note, though, in case there were fingerprints."

"Good." Amanda nodded approvingly, though she doubted a dusting would turn anything up. Anyone clever enough to get into her building and break into her apartment without arousing suspicion was clever enough not to leave prints.

"I brought you some clothes." Annie winced. "I wanted to put everything away, but, well, after we . . ."

"Don't worry about it." Amanda forced a smile and patted her friend's hand. "Besides, it won't take much to replace my wardrobe. They weren't exactly designer duds, you know."

She expected a laugh or a sarcastic comment about her limited selection and lack of taste. None of those was forthcoming.

"What's going on, Max?" Annie's voice was a harsh whisper born of fear. "I'm worried about you." She thought for a moment, then amended her statement. "Worried and yes, if the truth be known, scared shitless!"

"With good reason." Amanda lowered her eyes and played with the napkin in her lap. Without looking up, she said, "They shot my mother."

"What!" Annie's hand flew to her mouth to stop a shriek. Nothing could stop the tears from welling.

"It was a drive-by. She's out of surgery now, but it's still touch-and-go."

"Where was that guy you call Uncle Sam?"

That was a good question.

"I thought he was supposed to protect her."

"Me too."

One of the last calls Amanda made on her cell phone before ditching it, was to Dan Connor. After apologizing for not discouraging Beth's breach of security, she asked what kind of security had been placed in the hospital, what, if anything, was being done to find and arrest Jaime Bastido, and why she hadn't been able to reach Sam. Dan assured her a squad of inspectors was at Cedars-Sinai and that both the Marshals Service and the FBI were on the case; the LAPD already had two suspects under arrest for Beth's shooting. Not surprisingly, they were members of the *Blanca Muerte*. As for Sam, the Service put him on report for negligence. Amanda asked if Sam's recent absences had contributed to the charge, but Dan wouldn't comment. He did reiterate Carl's plea for Amanda to allow the Service to protect her until Bastido was captured. She gave him the same answer she gave Steinmetz.

"It's time to get help!" Amanda still hadn't raised her head. Annie could feel a wall going up, brick by brick. "You're on the police force, for crissakes. Those guys are your buds. Tell them what's going on." No response. "At least tell Pete." Still nothing. "Or Jake."

Slowly, Amanda looked at Annie. She wasn't crying, but her being was enveloped by such ineffable sadness that tears would have been redundant.

"Jake doesn't want anything to do with me," she said simply.

Annie doubted that, and said so, but she could tell by the tone of Amanda's voice that something awful had gone down between them, something that to Amanda, at least, seemed incontrovertible.

"I don't want you calling him," Amanda warned. "And if he calls you, you haven't seen or spoken to me." Annie was busy picking the dough out of the center of her bagel. "I need you to promise you won't say anything." Annie continued to excavate. Amanda took the bagel away, so her friend would pay attention. "Annie, there's no match to make. He was investigating me."

"No!"

"On behalf of Pamela Baird."

"What a scumbag!" Annie screwed her face into a portrait of disgust.

Amanda knew that wasn't so, but it served her purposes to let Annie believe the worst of Jake.

"So what now?" Annie asked, mentally shoving Jake into the same Dumpster as the dog.

"I'm going to go over the photographs you brought me, change my clothes and . . ."

"Speaking of changing clothes," Annie interrupted, "Jimbo told me to give you these." She handed Amanda a set of keys. "He thought you might need a place to crash. He's got a studio on Eighty-sixth and First."

Amanda took the keys, swallowing the lump that had formed in her throat. She didn't even know this guy. "That's sweet. Where's he going to stay?"

Annie flushed. "With me." She took one look at Amanda and hastened to correct an obvious misinterpretation. "No. We are not an item. It's just, well, I was a little unnerved this morning. He thought maybe I'd feel a little more secure having a bruiser like him bunk in with me."

Amanda smiled. "I don't know about you, but I feel better knowing you've got a bodyguard." The minute she said it, her smile faded. Lionel had had a bodyguard. It didn't save his life.

"Yeah. He's a nice guy. So, what's next on your agenda?"

"I'm going to the library."

Annie leaned back, scratched her chin and nodded, her face registering utter incredulity. "Sure. I can see that. People are trashing your apartment, leaving dead dogs in your bathtub, investigating your every move, and instead of going to the police, you're going to the library." She nodded sarcastically. "Oh, yeah! That's a real good plan. Wish I'd thought of it."

Amanda laughed. It felt good.

"I'm going to the library to find whatever I can on Operation Laundry Day," she explained. "If the past is catching up with me,

I'd better find out everything I can about the past. Maybe then," she said with a shrug, "I'll be able to outwit it."

Hallie spent the day agonizing about what to do. By some quirk of fate, she'd come into the possession of something stupendous, but if it wasn't handled correctly, she'd never get the bounce out of it she wanted, or deserved. Her caller, "an interested party," claimed to have vital information on the recent arrests of the remaning three Espinosa brothers. According to her source, the Mexican authorities arrested them two days before for the murder of Jorge Velez, a plastic surgeon in Acapulco.

A story about the roundup of the infamous Espinosa brothers was sensational enough—Hallie wondered why she hadn't seen anything about it on the wires—but the reason she'd been called, was that Velez was the surgeon who had changed the appearance of Jaime Bastido, the primary money launderer for Raoul Espinosa, and one of the men Cynthia Baird sent to prison in 1978. After being released, Bastido disappeared. He turned up in Juarez for a while, then disappeared again. American authorities from the DEA to the CIA were on the lookout for him. Hallie's caller claimed to have something they needed: Bastido's before-and-after photographs.

The reason he contacted her was that he'd watched her on *Newsline* and agreed with what she'd said: WITSEC was created for people like Cynthia and Erica Baird. Not only did he believe it was possible that they were alive, but if they were, he was certain Jaime Bastido was out to kill them. They, and the authorities, needed to know what he looked like.

Hallie needed to know who the caller was. He sounded young and frightened, which she understood, but as she explained, no matter how exciting this lead was, she couldn't run with this story unless she could back it up. While he wouldn't give her his name, he answered enough background questions to assure credibility. He told her he met Jaime at the Espinosa compound; he was a bookkeeper.

"In Juarez, drugs are the business. You either work for them, or you don't work."

He was a local, but he was smart, particularly good in math, which was why he was assigned to Jaime. It didn't take long to realize how disenchanted the older man was, how dishonored he felt by the sons of his old friend, Raoul, how tired he was of toiling in the trenches with little chance of attaining a place of prominence within the cartel. One night, after too many tequilas, Jaime confessed he wanted to leave Mexico. He hinted at an agenda that might bring him back one day in a different capacity. He spoke of friends he'd met in prison and associates he'd made. But they were in the States. Before he could get there and inaugurate his plan, he needed to find a plastic surgeon.

"My girlfriend worked for Dr. Velez."

Even Hallie had heard of Jorge Velez. Young, handsome, and ambitious on a global scale, he was known in celebrity circles for improving the images of Hollywood stars and, it was whispered, underworld villains.

"I was drunk and made the mistake of offering to introduce Jaime to Dr. Velez. Three weeks later, when he left Juarez, I went with him."

If he hadn't, he explained, the Espinosas would have killed him. He knew Jaime was out for revenge. If something happened to one of the brothers or a shipment was stolen or the authorities were tipped off or the business was harmed in any way, the Espinosas would never believe he didn't know where Bastido had gone or that he wasn't in on whatever he had planned.

"When the first of the brothers was arrested," he told Hallie, "Amalita and I came to the States."

"Why did Amalita take the pictures?"

"For insurance."

"Against whom?"

"The Espinosas. And Jaime."

"Where are the pictures now?" If she didn't get them soon, there was a chance someone else would break the story.

"They'll be delivered to your office by courier fifteen minutes after we hang up."

And they were. For Hallie, what followed was the angst over how to get the most mileage out of this. Naturally, the *Telegraph* would break the story in print, but there was her national profile to consider. And a little matter of back-at-ya'.

The first two times she called Trey Gallagher, his secretary did the he's-in-a-meeting-he'll-get-back-to-you dance. The third time, Hallie refused to rhumba.

"Either he gets on the phone, or he can watch me on the competition!"

Beth's eyelids fluttered as she began to regain consciousness. An ICU nurse hovered over her, checking the stability of all the various tubes and needles going in and out of her body. Machines monitoring everything from her breathing to her fluid output blipped and beeped in macabre accompaniment to the oscillating lines and spiking dots dancing about on a variety of screens. It was the intensive-care sound-and-light show, an electronic reminder of the intricacy of the functioning human anatomy and the fragility of human existence.

Sam Bates stood next to Beth's bed and held her hand. Wedged in between a heart monitor and a respirator, he had no place to sit or move about, but he refused to leave her side. He'd been with her in the ambulance, through her seven hours of surgery and an almost equal amount of time in the recovery room. Even when Dan Connor had flown in and insisted on having a private meeting with him, Sam refused to leave the lounge outside the ICU.

That hour with Dan should have been devastating. Juxtaposed with the thought of losing Beth, having his badge lifted seemed like a small price to pay for his sins. When Dan asked why, of late, Sam seemed so distracted, Sam told him about Gail's illness. He probably could have stopped there—Dan was sympathetic—but his soul was in need of a thorough cleansing, so he confessed to helping himself to sixty thousand dollars from trust funds Lionel had set up for Beth and Amanda.

He didn't attempt to sugarcoat his actions because he couldn't. Borrowing from the trust was a shameless thing to do on several counts. Not only was he acting on privileged information, but he was taking advantage of the faith witnesses in his charge, and worse, people he cared deeply about, had placed in him. At the time, he felt like he had no other choice.

"I intend to pay back every dime," he told Dan, through personal loans and by turning back whatever fees he was entitled to as nominee of the trusts.

When Dan asked, "Do you think Lionel knew?" Sam shrugged, his shoulders sagging from the weight of his guilt.

"He asked if he could help me out with a loan." The irony was devastating. "I told him I'd taken care of it already."

"How about Beth? Does she know?"

Sam shook his head then, and now, as he stared at her heavily bandaged body and wondered how he would bring himself to tell her—and Max—what he'd done. And how he could make it up to them.

The nurse asked him to step out of the room so she could check whether Beth was capable of breathing on her own. If she was, the doctors would remove the breathing tube and detach her from the respirator. Reluctantly, Sam withdrew to the lounge.

Alone in the room, Sam took a seat on a couch. He hadn't realized how tired he was until he sat down. He'd been on his feet for hours, pacing, standing alongside Beth, wandering the halls during her surgery. He couldn't remember the last time anything other than vending-machine coffee had passed his lips. The television was on, the sound muted. He wasn't particularly interested in anything that was going on outside of this building, so while he stared at the screen, the images went by in a blur. When he felt himself dozing off, he found the remote and deactivated the muting to prevent him from falling into a deep sleep.

Suddenly, he heard the name, Jaime Bastido. He jolted upright, fully awake. On screen was an attractive young woman identified as Hallie Brendel. Sam recognized the name: To Beth, she was Public Enemy Number One. Quickly, he amplified the sound just as Brendel's image dissolved into a split screen. He recognized the man on the left immediately: the elusive Jaime Bastido. The man on the right, according to Ms. Brendel was also Bastido—new and surgically improved.

Before he could say or do anything, three fellow inspectors descended on the lounge. One of them was speaking on a cell phone. Sam heard him address the party on the other end of the line as Chief Connor. He handed the phone to Sam.

"Chief," Sam said, his eyes still glued to the screen, "are you watching?"

"I am. Sam," Dan said in a tone that demanded Sam's full attention.

"Yes, sir."

"You are not to leave that hospital."

"I understand, sir." He didn't, but Dan Connor was his superior, and Sam was in no position to question his authority. Dan had been gracious enough simply to put him on report; after what he did, he should have been terminated.

"I've got Steinmetz flying to New York. He seems to have some sort of relationship with Max. I'm hoping he can bring her in."

"That would be good, sir." Sam cringed at the thought of having to tell an incapacitated Beth that something horrendous had happened to her daughter.

"What's the name of that PI you said she was involved with?"

"Fowler. Jake Fowler."

"And her partner at the CSU?"

"Pete Doyle."

"Have you checked them out?"

"Thoroughly. They'll cooperate. I'd also contact Annie Hart."

"We've tried. She's not answering her phone, either at work or at home. We're sending someone to visit her. Perhaps a personal interview will be more productive." Dan paused. He regretted the harsh tone of their talk and the suspension. Sam was like a son to him, but if children disobeyed, they had to be disciplined. "You take care of Beth," he said. "We'll take care of Max."

Sam signed off, but he knew, just as Dan and every inspector in the Service knew, that until someone took care of Bastido, Beth and Max remained targets.

Jake hunkered over the bar and sipped his coffee. While his brain craved the sedative properties of scotch, his head and his body had argued more convincingly in favor of coffee. He was waiting for Pete, who'd rushed his samples to the police lab and had promised not to leave until he had an answer.

All day, Jake tried to reach Max, albeit unsuccessfully. Every time he thought of how he'd left her, his heart ached. Realistically, he accepted the fact that there was no way he could have, or should have, known who she really was. But now that he believed he did, so many things fell into place.

The call from the Justice Department requesting that Lionel's body not be released. WITSEC was an agency under the aegis of the Justice Department. Maybe Max made the request. Or her mother. Maybe they wanted to figure out a way to bury him the way they wanted, as opposed to leaving that painful chore to the likes of Pamela Baird.

All the convoluted reservations at various hotels around the city, the unused rooms, the out-of-town restaurants, the seemingly ridiculous travel plans to, of all places, Madison, Wisconsin. They were what she said they were—a cover.

As for the note in Lionel's trash basket, Jake thought he'd figured that out as well. Beth was probably Max's mother. If Lionel needed to ask how to send her flowers Jake's guess was that Bates was the WITSEC inspector who acted as liaison between the parties.

Annie Hart. She was another piece of the puzzle that finally fit. That FBI report sitting on Lionel's desk had her family living in the same north Miami community as Cynthia and Erica Baird. She and

Max must have been childhood chums. Did Max know that before the FBI report? Did she know it now?

Then there was her aloofness at work. She kept everyone, including Pete, at arm's length. Even Jake had heard some behind-her-back banter about how she consistently refused to join her compadres at any after-hours get-togethers and never let anyone know anything about her personal life.

Too, there was the absence of photographs in her apartment. She was a photographer, after all. One would expect tons of albums and framed remembrances. Yet there were none. Even when she took pictures, she declined to be in them. Or, if she was, he thought, recalling her show at the gallery, she was thoroughly disguised. It made sense when he realized that she was a woman in hiding, a woman whose life depended on not allowing anyone to see too much or get too close. A woman whose best photographs, the bleakscapes, were the most disturbing because they were the most personal.

He closed his eyes and squeezed them shut, vainly attempting to block the psychic pain that assaulted him whenever he thought about her and how much it must have taken to bring him into her home and into her heart. He couldn't imagine the hell she'd gone through before showing up at his door the other night. Yes, she wanted to tell him about Archie—something he hadn't completely dealt with yet. But more than that, she'd wanted to tell him all about her relationship to Lionel and, if her nervousness and her squalid appearance were any indication, to ask him for help. She also might have explained what she was doing sneaking into Lionel's library—if he'd given her the chance.

"It wasn't her."

Jake's head snapped in the direction of Pete's voice. Doyle dragged his body onto the barstool and barked for a whiskey. He was whipped.

"Lab tests indicate an animal, probably a dog. I don't really give a shit. As long as the blood in that tub wasn't human." He poured the whiskey down his throat, his eyes tearing from the sting. He chased it with a gulp of water and turned to Jake. "It wasn't Max, and that's all I care about."

Jake nodded. He could barely get the words out of his mouth. "Me too."

"So where is she?"

"I wish I knew."

For the umpteenth time that day, Jake toyed with the idea of telling Pete what he suspected. It wasn't that he thought Doyle was a closet subversive or anything other than who he seemed to be, and certainly, it wasn't that he doubted Pete's affection for and loyalty to his partner, but an inner voice warned him to respect Max's judgment. If she'd wanted Pete to know, she would have taken him into her confidence. Jake couldn't be certain she would've told him anything if Lionel hadn't died and she didn't feel threatened in some way. Maybe when he knew where the threat was coming from, he'd feel free to . . .

"Turn that up!" Pete poked Jake in the side and pointed toward the television set hanging over the bar in the corner. "It's that Brendel dame."

The two of them watched in rapt silence as Hallie laid out the story of the capture of the Espinosa brothers. She'd barely finished when Trey Gallagher introduced his colleague from Los Angeles, who outlined the connection between the *Blanca Muerte* gang and the Espinosas.

The Espinosas were the largest exporter of the killer drug, Propaine. They processed it outside of Juarez and in several other locations scattered throughout Mexico, employing an army of mules to smuggle the drugs over the border into Texas and California. The *Muerte* gang distributed the Propaine in Los Angeles, their subsidiary did the same in New York. In an effort to maximize their profits, the reporter said, the Espinosas also supplied the powerful Saviano family, which pushed the drug in New York, Chicago, and Boston.

Gallagher tried to insinuate himself into the story by ticking off a list of gangland-style murders believed to be part of the battle for distribution rights, but Hallie stopped him by announcing that the Espinosa arrests were not due to their alleged dealings in drugs.

"They were arrested and charged with the murder of a prominent Acapulco plastic surgeon, Dr. Jorge Velez."

Trey, ceding the spotlight, asked the obvious question: "Why would a group of drug kingpins murder a plastic surgeon?"

"To pay him back for aiding and abetting the escape of a man who had turned in their brother, Emilio, and who, they suspected, planned to wrest control of their cartel—Jaime Bastido. In case that name sounds familiar, it should. Jaime Bastido was the infamous money launderer sent to prison by the testimony of Cynthia Stanton Baird."

Jake ordered a scotch. Pete called for coffee.

"According to my source, Bastido submitted to extensive plastic surgery so he could reenter the United States and roam freely about our cities. While his specific plans are not known, on more than one occasion he was overheard saying he had scores to settle. These photographs might help level the playing field."

"That's the guy who made Max so squirrely outside the court-house," Pete hissed, pointing to the after-shot of Bastido. "She spotted him schmoozing with Little Ray Saviano and it freaked her out."

Jake studied the picture of Jaime Bastido, memorizing every strange feature on his reconstructed face, just in case, but Pete's description of Max's behavior disturbed him. Max's mother put Bastido and a bunch of Big Ray's lieutenants away, but she wouldn't freak just seeing them together. She was too cool for that. Unless she believed that one, or both, recognized her. *The camera in Lionel's drawer.* There must have been a roll of film in there that showed what she, and possibly her mother, looked like now. *No wonder she looked so petrified.* Her cover had been blown.

"Bastido could be the one who brought the wrecking ball to Max's place," Pete said.

"I don't think so." Jake shook his head. "What was he looking for?"

"How about Max?"

"Nope. Whoever trashed her place knew she wasn't there. He came to look for something, and, if he didn't find it, to leave that dog as a warning."

"Talk about sick!" Pete gulped his coffee, then checked his watch. "Shit! I've got to get to the job. I'm pulling a double so no one squeezes my shoes about missing my shift this morning."

"You're not working on a lot of sleep, pal."

"Won't be the first time." He eased himself off the stool and slapped Jake on the back. "Listen. Call me if you hear anything. I'll do the same."

Jake said he would, but his voice contained little hope.

"Hey, Fowler," Pete said, grinning over his shoulder. "I don't know if it makes things any easier, but she's got a real case for you."

Jake smiled as the big man left, but having Pete confirm Max's feelings for him only made him feel worse, knowing she was out there, alone, believing that he didn't love her, running and hiding from heaven knows what. He slapped some bills on the bar and headed out into the night. He wasn't sure where he was going, but he couldn't just sit there and do nothing. He had to find Max. And if Hallie's report was accurate, he had to find her soon.

★ ★ ★

Amanda had been sitting in the library for hours, secluded in a basement carrel searching acres of microfiche for everything relating to Operation Laundry Day. This wasn't the first time she'd read these files. As a student at John Jay, she'd availed herself of their library, going through police reports, analyses by professors at the school, as well as many of the same newspaper articles she was scrolling through now. Ever since she first looked through the pictures she'd taken at the town house, something had been nibbling at the edges of her consciousness, the sense that she had seen it all before.

That nagging sense of déjà vu was why she'd sequestered herself in the library today. Once and for all, she intended to find out what in those pictures had convinced her she had come upon a homicide and not a suicide.

Unsuccessful with the news accounts, she went back to the card catalogue, opting to attack the matter from a different angle. Dozens of books had been written on Operation Laundry Day and other, similar, government stings. Several focused on money laundering, tracing the methods used in that investigation to methods currently being practiced. Several others slanted the material so they could take advantage of the public's fascination with organized crime. Two of the attorneys who prosecuted the case—one in Miami, the other from New York—had penned their versions of how the trials were handled, how the evidence was presented, and what the effective prosecution of the various parties meant to society as a whole.

Someday, Amanda thought, *when I have a year or two, I'll read these.* Right now, however, she needed something less pedantic, more specific. Forcing herself to step back for a moment and think, it dawned on her that the bulk of material at John Jay was related to police procedure. If some picayune nugget of information was lodged in a crevice of her brain, the only way to dislodge it was to narrow the area, then pick it clean.

Quickly, almost feverishly, she started to cross-reference Operation Laundry Day, riffling through every possible category from gangster to rinse cycle to government task forces. Suddenly, she came upon a compilation of photographs taken during the trial.

That's it! She practically screamed with delight. That's where the answer lay. She could feel it. She raced up the stairs, through the stacks, anxious to get her hands on this book before the library closed. When she found it, she hastened back to the privacy of her carrel.

Giving herself a moment to catch her breath and rid herself of cumbersome emotional blocks, she placed the book on the desk and turned it over, opening the back cover to where the withdrawal card was. Being a forensic photographer, she admitted to a natural curiosity about how often a book like this was taken out of the library. Not very, was the answer: 1986, 1989, 1993, 1995 and April of this year. She found that more than a little intriguing.

Turning the book right side up, she began her journey. She turned each page slowly, perusing the photographs carefully, waiting for that inner switch to click. The one she was looking for was near the end, but when she found it her heart stopped. It was a picture taken by a forensic photographer of Douglas Welch, one of several taken at the scene of his suicide. He was sitting in a chair behind a desk, the arm holding the gun dangling at his side. His other hand was on the desk, next to a newspaper. Amanda's heart went from comalike-stillness to thumping-so-rapidly, she thought it was going to break through her chest. His index finger was pointing to a picture of himself beneath the headline: GUILTY!

But that wasn't the worst of it. Douglas Welch's tie was tucked neatly, almost obsessively, into his shirt, between the second and third buttons.

She laid her head on the book and pounded her hand against the desk, weeping, railing against whoever had done this to her father. Nearly spent, she raised her head and looked at the photograph again. From the first, she'd suspected that particular contrivance was a sick, cryptic bit of shorthand meant to deliver a message, but now she knew for certain: Lionel's death was someone's revenge. But whose? Someone who'd carried a grudge over a lot of years. Someone who'd managed to establish a relationship that allowed access to Lionel's library. Someone whom Lionel called, friend. Or colleague.

Racing against time, she went back to the microfiche and searched for Douglas Welch's obituary. She needed names, family members, a brother, an uncle, a nephew. Someone who might have blamed Lionel for Welch's death. When it came up on the screen, it took Amanda's breath away. She closed her eyes, hoping that when she opened them, her first sighting was wrong. But no, there it was: "Welch, Douglas . . . survived hy his wife, Emma Grayson Welch, and his son, Tyler."

Tyler Grayson!

She scrolled back to a newspaper article that had appeared that same day, detailing the tragic end to the story of the backroom clerk who'd stolen stock certificates to pay off his gambling debts to the mob. Down a paragraph. One more. There—". . . the body was found by Welch's teenage son, Tyler."

Suddenly, the carrel was too small. There wasn't enough air. Amanda couldn't breathe. She stumbled out of the confined space, held on to the wall and took huge gulps of air. Oxygen. That's what she needed. She'd been in this hole in the wall too long. Her brain was playing tricks on her. *Tyler!* It wasn't possible. Tyler couldn't have . . .

"No!" She whispered, unable to stop her body from shaking or to get her mind to wrap around what seemed obvious and conclusive. "No!" She refused to believe it.

Leaving everything on the desk, she ran, desperate to escape a truth too horrible, too offensive to comprehend. She had made love with this man. He told her he was falling in love with her. He wouldn't kill her father. The Tyler Grayson she knew couldn't kill anyone! *But his father killed himself. Lionel's killer duplicated Douglas Welch's suicide scene.* She raced out of the library, grabbed a cab, and headed to Jimbo's apartment. She needed to be alone. To sort all this out. To think.

All the way uptown, her mind shuttled between vague possibility and absolute denial, between one remembrance that substantiated the incredible likelihood that Tyler was connected to Lionel's death and another that negated even the remotest chance of him having been involved. By the time she unlocked the door to the small studio, her body was convulsing as if consumed with fever. With trembling fingers, she clicked on a light, locked the door, tilted a chair under the doorknob, slid her gun out of its holster, and visually surveyed the room. Carefully, she checked the bathroom and all the closets. Certain there was no one lurking, she holstered her gun and allowed herself to collapse on the daybed.

On the table in front of her was a bouquet of flowers with a note from Annie: "Just remember, we got each other!"

Amanda smiled, her emotions spilling over onto her cheeks. When they were kids, she and Annie performed in a school play. Dressed as hobos, they sang a song that became their personal anthem, a song of friendship between "two lost souls." As only children, one adopted, one the child of divorce, that was often how they felt. That was how Amanda felt now—lost and alone, except for Annie. She wiped her eyes. The smile was gone.

Bitterly, she fingered a rose, recalling that Tyler had sent her flowers. They were there when Lionel came for dinner. And when

Tyler came to see her after Lionel's supposed suicide. He'd been so distressed that morning, so rattled by the news. Was his concern genuine, or an incredible job of acting? Couldn't his strange behavior simply be attributed to the natural discomfort of relating one suicide to another? Finding his father had to be traumatic; she could attest to that. It must be a nightmare that never dissipates, never completely disappears.

But Lionel's body was placed in the same pose as Douglas Welch. His tie was tucked into his shirt, à la Douglas Welch. And Tyler had visited Lionel at the town house. That day. Only hours before his death.

The other night at dinner he confessed he and Lionel had words. But he wouldn't say about what. On other occasions, Tyler grumbled that Lionel refused to be accountable, that he escaped punishment and censure while others suffered for his sins. More than once, he said Lionel should take responsibility for what he'd done. Welch had confessed to the theft. Was Tyler angry that Lionel didn't stand up for Welch or defend him in some way? Had Tyler decided to mete out his own form of justice?

Even if he did—and she still couldn't declare that an unequivocal reality—how had he managed to get Lionel to stick a gun in his mouth and pull the trigger?

Jake was on his way downtown when his cell phone rang. Before his hopes could escalate, Doyle's voice dashed them.

"We caught something I thought you should know about." From the background noises, Jake guessed Pete was calling from a pay phone. "Gangland execution. Male. Two bullets to the back of the head. Hands and feet bound. Throat slit. Body dumped along the East River, up by the Willis Avenue Bridge. Tentative ID pegs the stiff as Jaime Bastido."

Jake whistled in astonishment. "How long's he been lying there?"

"I don't think he got to see his mug on national TV, if that's what you mean"

"Was he around for the recent dog-and-pony show?" Jake hated playing word games, but it was easy to tap into cell phones. If he and Pete had a third party on the line, he didn't want to spell everything out.

"I think he was otherwise engaged at the time."

"I don't know if that's good news or bad news."

"Speaking of news . . ."

"Nothing."

"I'll be in touch. Keep the faith."

"Yeah. You too."

Frankly, Jake was low on faith just then. He'd been all over the city looking for Max. He drove by the town house, checked at her apartment, and finally, recalling the Lupe Vazquez case, visited The Bent Wing.

It took a lot of convincing to get Sybil Whitehall to even speak to him, let alone to tell him anything about Amanda. In the end, Jake's powers of persuasion, and fear for her friend's safety, overcame Sybil's reticence. She told Jake how Amanda reacted to the story on *Newsline,* but she couldn't tell him where Amanda had gone.

Having run out of alternatives, he decided to confront the one person he was certain had some idea where he might find Max.

He paid the cabby, got out at West Houston and Broadway, and walked the five or six blocks to Annie Hart's building. She was refusing to answer her phone, but Jake's gut said she was home. One way or the other, she was going to speak to him.

He buzzed up. She didn't answer, but he didn't care; he intended to hang on that buzzer until either he drove her insane or she relented.

"What!" It was a man's voice, loud and vexed.

"I need to see Annie," Jake replied, wondering whether he was speaking to friend or foe.

"We're busy. You know what I mean?"

"Yeah, well, aren't you lucky. I still need to see Annie. Tell her it's about her long-lost childhood friend."

The lock clicked, the door opened. Jake stepped into the elevator and rode up to the third floor. When the elevator doors opened, his gun was drawn. Annie's friend was huge, but unarmed.

"Jake Fowler," he said, holstering his gun as he introduced himself.

"It's okay, Jimbo, I know him." She stepped aside, grudgingly.

Jimbo thought about it before allowing Jake to come inside.

"What do you want?"

Annie's tone was unexpectedly harsh. Max must've told her about his horrible behavior the previous evening, which, on the good side, confirmed his belief they'd seen each other—recently. Suddenly, he eyed Jimbo. Someone had carried that poor dog out of Max's apartment. This guy could've hauled a horse down three flights of stairs without breaking a sweat.

"I need to find Max," he said, deciding honesty was the best policy.

"I thought you said you had news about her."

"I lied." So much for honesty. "But I've been calling you all day. I figured the only way you'd see me was if I said I knew something."

Her arms were folded across her chest, her foot was keeping time to a military march. If looks could kill, he'd be in a box with a bouquet of lilies on his chest.

"Okay," he said, opting again for honesty, peppered this time with humility. "I'm guessing you heard about last night. I admit, I wasn't exactly Mr. Nice Guy. I'm not proud of my behavior, but being a jackass has nothing to do with not loving her. And I do love her!"

Annie snorted with disbelief. To his credit, Jimbo was standing against a wall, out of the way, but on guard in case Jake did something he shouldn't.

"She told me something I didn't want to hear." He paused, wondering whether the quietude he was feeling inside was resignation or closure. "I got so angry I didn't hear what she wanted to tell me."

Annie's foot tapping slowed. She eyed him cautiously.

"It's complicated, and I'd like to explain what happened, but there's no time. Max is in trouble. If I can find her, I can help her."

"Help her do what?" Annie's posture had softened, but barely.

"Look," Jake said bluntly, "you both know what happened at her apartment."

Annie tried to hide it, but her breath snagged in her throat.

"You were there," Jake insisted. "Max's landlord said two *plumbers* had been to her apartment." He let that sink in. "Although there was a problem with the bathtub."

Jimbo moved off the wall, ready, willing, and able to crush Jake like a walnut.

"I think you carted an unwanted visitor out of Max's apartment," he said, pointing a finger at a noticeably nervous Jimbo. The guy was in over his head, and Jake knew it. "That was real chivalrous of you, and, for Max's sake, I thank you, but the police might see it as evidence tampering."

He turned back to Annie, letting Jimbo stew. "I have an unconfirmed report that Jaime Bastido is dead."

Annie gasped. "Seriously?"

"Murder is always serious, Annie."

"We just saw a news report . . ." Jimbo started to say.

"Which is now irrelevant. By the way, no offense, but do you have a name other than Jimbo? I'm not a nickname kind of fella."

"Don't say any . . ."

"Beauford."

Annie's protest was too late. Jake got what he wanted.

"Relax," he said to Annie. "I'm not turning Jim, or you, in to the police." Annie's eyes grew wide. She'd never even considered that. "But if you know where Max is, I suggest you tell me."

"I don't."

"You're sure."

"Yes."

Strike three. He took out a notepad, jotted his cell-phone number down, and handed it to a defiant Annie Hart. "Just in case this temporary amnesia fades."

"Nice meeting you," she said as she opened the doors to the elevator. "Don't come again."

The guard approached Big Ray's cell. "You've got a call."

Ray looked at his watch. Being allowed out of his cell for any reason at this time of night meant someone died or was arrested. It turned out to be both.

The call was from Dan Crocetti, the Savianos' attorney: Little Ray had been arrested for extortion and as an accessory to the murder of Jaime Bastido. He was denied bond, but Crocetti expected to have him released within a day or two. The extortion claim was iffy and could be bargained. The accessory charge was more difficult. There was an eyewitness.

"The Espinosas put out a hit on Bastido," Crocetti said. "And framed us by squeezing one of Ray's boys until he rolled over."

Crocetti also reported that the Feds seized a notebook containing the names of Family friends—those who'd benefited from the Family's largesse at one time or another and could be depended upon to return the favor.

"That could be trouble," the Saviano mouthpiece warned.

"It won't be if you do your job."

Crocetti bristled. He was well aware of his job description, but Little Ray Saviano's congenital stupidity and unremitting arrogance made it difficult to protect him and his minions.

"We've entered a plea of not guilty and arranged for bail day after tomorrow." If it was up to Crocetti, he'd leave the younger Saviano to rot in jail. "When he calls you, and he will, I'd appreciate a word of support, Ray. This Bastido thing could get messy."

"He didn't listen," Big Ray muttered, slamming down the phone, his face purple with rage. "I told him to watch his back, but he didn't listen."

Crocetti was left to wonder who didn't listen—Little Ray or Jaime Bastido.

Jake walked out of Annie's building and headed for the first phone booth he could find. It was late, but he couldn't afford good manners. He dialed the home number of his friend at the telephone company and prayed she was home.

"Hey!" he said, rushing to apologize in case he woke her or interrupted her evening. She said she was watching an old movie. No big deal. "I need the phone number and the address for Jim Beauford." One. Two. Three. "This one's an emergency, darlin'."

"Okay. But you owe me, Jake."

"Fine with me. Nothing I like better than paying off my debts to beautiful women."

"Liar."

She had to call a cohort at the phone company. He gave her the number of the pay phone, and said he'd wait. It was the longest ten minutes of his life. When he hung up, he ran to the corner to catch a cab uptown.

He was a man on a mission, which was why he never noticed the man parked outside Annie's apartment. Or the car that followed him to Jimbo's apartment.

C H A P T E R
TWENTY-FIVE

Amanda showered, washed her hair, threw on a sweat suit Annie had retrieved for her, and fixed a bowl of pasta. She wasn't hungry, but her energy was sapped and she needed refueling. Twice, she called California to check on Beth's condition. The first time, she spoke to an ICU nurse. Beth was still listed as critical, but she was improving. The second time Amanda called, Uncle Sam came on the line.

"She's going to be all right, but she's concerned," he said. "We're both very concerned. Dan says you refuse to let the Service protect you."

"Don't talk to me about protection, Sam."

"I was there, Amanda. I left as soon as you alerted me to the situation, but the plane came in early." There was plenty she could fault him for, and this was not the time for reprimands, but certain truths remained. "And she never should have gone to New York. You both know better."

She responded with a stony silence.

"Where are you?"

"I'd rather not say."

He wanted to press her, but she was on a cell phone. "Have you been anywhere near a television?"

"No."

He told her about Hallie Brendel's appearance on *Newsline* and the pictures of Bastido. "You need to take extra care, Amanda. With his face plastered all over the news, he could panic."

That'll make us even, she thought.

"Carl Steinmetz is flying to New York. In fact, he's probably there by now. Please call in." He rubbed his eyes, but it wasn't fatigue that was causing them to water. It was knowing that he'd let both Beth and Amanda down. "I know you think you can't trust me, but please, don't be foolish. Let Carl help you. Let someone help you, Max. For your mother's sake."

Amanda hung up the phone. A few minutes later, she picked it up again for her father's sake. She didn't know whether Pete was on or off shift, but she decided to take a chance. When she heard his voice, she welled up with emotion.

"I need you to do something for me," she said, hoping to override the lump in her throat by speaking quickly.

"First you do something for me," he said, lowering his voice to a near growl. "Tell me where the hell you are!"

"I can't do that." She expected him to make a stink, but she could hear other voices nearby. He wasn't about to give her away. She loved him for that.

"Awright. What's up?"

She swallowed hard. She never trusted easily. Lately, it was getting harder and harder. But necessity was the mother of exceptions. "I want you to call the coroner."

"And?"

"Have him check for puncture marks in Lionel Baird's scalp or along the hairline. Also, ask him to run a GC-MS."

"What're you looking for?"

"A neuromuscular blocking agent."

In the shower, she realized the only way a gun was going into Lionel's mouth was if someone subdued him so he couldn't fight back. Curare, succinylcholine, or some other drug used to immobilize muscles for surgery were a distinct possibility. They would do more than subdue him, they would paralyze him.

"I wouldn't ask you to do this if it wasn't important, Pete."

"I know that." A long silence followed as Pete tried to figure out why she was suddenly interested in Lionel Baird's corpse. "By the way, Fowler and I buddied up the other day."

"Really."

"Yeah. We went to visit a friend. We probably should've called first, though."

"And why is that?"

"Because her place was a mess. Clothes all over. Stuff hanging out of drawers. A really nasty ring around the bathtub." He pressed the phone against his ear and waited for her to say something.

"Make that call for me, will you?" she asked, unable to speak without sniffling.

"How do I reach you?"

"I'll get back to you." She was about to hang up when Pete lowered his voice again.

"Jake's crazed, babe. He's been looking all over town for you. He's real upset."

"Aren't we all," she snapped as she ended the call.

The ring of the phone startled Jake. He pulled the electronic gizmo from his pocket, flipped it open and put it to his ear.

"Fowler."

"Doyle."

"Anything?" Jake leaned back and pressed into the corner, bracing himself against potentially bad news.

Pete relayed Amanda's call, clearly puzzled by her request. Again, Jake was tempted to fill him in, but even if he wanted to, now was not the time, and this cab was not the place.

"Don't you make the call," he said, realizing that coming from Pete, this could raise damaging questions. "I'll get Green to authorize it." He had to fill Caleb in anyway. "What's her mood'?"

"Ornery."

Jake smiled. No surprise there. "I'm glad she reached out to you, Doyle."

"A blip on the screen. She reaches out, then true to form, pulls back. She's got a trust problem."

That's because people like me keep betraying her, Jake thought as he reached Eighty-sixth Street. Before going into Jimbo's building, he called Caleb Green. Then he roused one of his associates out of bed.

"I need everything you can find on Jaime Bastido and Operation Laundry Day. And I need it first thing in the morning."

That done, he rushed into the building, prepared to deliver whatever tale of woe would allow him to weasel his way up to the apartment. No need to bother. There was no doorman, only a tired elevator operator who couldn't wait for his shift to end. A little working-man-to-working-man commiseration and Jake was chauffeured up to the eighth floor.

"That one. End of the hall on the left."

Jake laid a five-dollar bill in the man's hand and bade him good night. It would be nice if Max proved to be as accommodating, but he doubted it. Instead of laying on the buzzer, he knocked lightly. When there was no response, he knocked again, a little harder.

"It's me, Jake," he said, loud enough for her to hear, not loud enough to invite an audience. "I know you're there. Come on." He rapped his knuckles against the metal door. "I'm here to deliver a major-league, chest-beating, bent-knee, *mea culpa* apology. The only way you're going to get to see this once-in-a-lifetime phenomenon is if you let me in."

He heard her undoing the locks, four of them. Good for Jimbo. He was big, but not careless. When she opened the door, his stomach lurched. Pale, tense, exceptionally guarded, she held a gun on him as he walked inside. After checking the hallway, she closed the door and bolted the locks. She thought for a minute before holstering her gun. That hurt.

"What do you want?" She had granted him two square feet of space, no more.

"To apologize for being such a jerk. I never should've stormed out that way. It's just . . ."

"Apology accepted. Now, please leave." Her eyes were like black ice, cold and dark.

"No can do. You see, whether you like it or not, I happen to be in love with you." He grinned and splayed his hands as if to say, so there you have it! "And," he continued, unnerved by her refusal to give even an inch, "I don't intend to let anything happen to you."

"Nothing's going to happen to me, but thank you for your concern."

"Brrrrrrr!" He shivered, displaying his response to the cold shoulder she was throwing at him. "Where's that global warming when you need it?"

"It's late. Why don't you find someone who appreciates this lounge act."

"Like Hallie Brendel?"

She flinched. He didn't know whether it was because she suspected that he'd gone to Hallie's after leaving her, or because Hallie was blabbing her life story all over the airwaves. Probably a little bit of both.

"I take it you saw the story about the Espinosa brothers being arrested?" No verbal response, but she did raise an eyebrow. "They were accused of murdering the plastic surgeon who redid this guy, Jaime Bastido's, face."

Not even a flicker of recognition. Maybe he'd jumped to the wrong conclusions. Maybe she wasn't who he thought.

"Bastido was Raoul Espinosa's main money man in Miami. You remember, Raoul Espinosa? Big drug dealer in the seventies. The Feds busted his organization, thanks to a really courageous witness, and sent Bastido off to jail."

Her expression didn't change, but she shifted her weight from one foot to another. Encouraging.

"When he got out, he went to Mexico and worked for the brothers, but it seems Jaime was a greedy little bugger. He wanted to take over. They said no. Jaime felt he had to play hide-and-seek, so he bought himself a redo. Judging by the photographs, I wouldn't recommend this Velez. The after-shots weren't pretty. Pinched lips. Tight chin. Eyes that looked like they couldn't blink."

He wished her eyes would blink, but, he supposed, this blank screen was the product of a lifetime of hiding her emotions.

"But none of that matters anymore." He paused dramatically. "Jaime Bastido's dead."

That got a reaction, but not the one he expected. "So?"

"So the man is history." Skepticism stared back at him. "Doyle caught the case last night. Two shots to the head and a slit throat. If you don't believe me, call him."

"Oh, I don't have to call anyone for verification. I believe *you.*" Her voice dripped with sarcasm.

"I deserve that. I was awful to you. Cruel, actually. But, I . . ."

"You know what, Jake. I don't want to hear it. I said what I had to say."

"You had more to say. I walked out before you could finish."

She shook her head. "No. I'm finished. You're finished here." She started for the door. "And we're finished."

"Look, Max. I figured it out. Hallie was on the news talking about the possibility of Cynthia and Erica Baird being in WITSEC. She said maybe Lionel killed himself to protect his wife and his daughter. I put two and two together . . ."

"And got five. Now, if you don't mind. I'm expecting someone."

"No, you're not!" He threw up his hands in frustration. "You're not home because someone trashed your place and left a dead pooch in your bathtub. This apartment belongs to a hulk who jockeys a camera on Annie's soap. For crissakes, Max. I know you have no reason to trust me, but I wish you would. Pete and I are trying to help you. Can't you break that wall down just a little?"

"Good night, Jake." She stood by the door, an iceberg in a sweat suit.

Dejected and guilt-ridden, but recognizing that, at the moment, there was nothing more he could say or do, he agreed to leave. But he had no intention of leaving her alone.

Neither did the man in the car.

Grace Fowler ambled into her kitchen and headed for the refrigerator. When she opened the door, she got a quite a start. Jake was sitting at the table, staring out the window.

"The coffee's fresh," he said, casually pointing to the automatic drip machine on the counter, as if his presence at this hour was usual. "I made it a couple of minutes ago."

Grace looked at the clock—6:00 A.M.—then at her son. His face was shadowed by unshaved stubble, but it was the gray circles beneath his eyes that troubled her. If she didn't know better, she'd say this tough guy had been sitting here crying in the dark. Wordlessly, she poured herself some coffee and joined him at the table. For a while, they sat in companionable silence.

When Grace felt more awake, and she thought Jake had spent enough time wallowing, she asked, "To what do I owe this rare pleasure?"

"Archie's dead."

"I know that, dear."

"Yeah, well, now I know it, too," he said, his voice catching.

He rubbed his eyes and lowered his head, grieving for a father who'd died years before, grieving, too, for a dream that died only hours before.

Grace combed his hair with her fingers, the same way she used to when he was a boy.

"What happened?" she asked. "Why have you suddenly decided to accept the truth?"

"I had no choice. Someone I trusted laid it out for me in no uncertain terms. But," he said, with a self-deprecating chuckle, "as I'm sure you can imagine, I didn't accept it easily."

Grace smiled. "No, I'm sure you didn't." She caressed his cheek. She wanted to soothe him, but his pain was the kind that went beyond the healing power of a mother's kiss. "What were you told and by whom?"

He relayed the information Max had provided. Grace wasn't upset because she wasn't surprised. She was upset, however, by the look on Jake's face when he mentioned Amanda's name. Lovesick was one thing, fear was another.

"How did she get this information? And why do you look so miserable?"

He told her about Steinmetz and how badly he'd reacted. He confessed to a temper tantrum and storming out, but omitted the part about him seeking solace in the arms of Hallie Brendel. When he told her about his belief that Amanda Maxwell was in reality, Erica Baird, Grace was dumbstruck. He went through everything he knew, everything he suspected, what he and Pete had found in her apartment, what he and Caleb were working on and every wrong move he made.

"I blew it." he said, clearly at a loss as to how that had happened and what he could do to rectify it. "I tracked her down. I told her I loved her. I apologized." He forced a grin. "I offered myself up as a savior. And was tossed out on my butt. Can you imagine that?"

Grace laughed because he wanted her to, not because she found anything he was saying even remotely amusing.

"Now, not only doesn't she want me as a lover, but she's determined to fight these bad guys by herself." His eyes darkened. "And you know what, Mom? She's not paranoid. There are bad guys out there gunning for her. Literally."

"Why not enlist the aid of the police?" Grace asked. "Caleb already believes Lionel Baird was murdered. Even if it's not absolutely one hundred percent certain that Max is Erica Baird, her apartment being trashed should be enough to warrant police protection."

Jake didn't disagree. But for most of the night he'd been trying to understand why Amanda hadn't brought in the police, why she hadn't sounded the signal for the FBI or the U.S. Marshals Service. Why was she keeping this so close to the vest?

"I think Max views this as a hydraheaded situation," he said. "Chop off one head, another one takes its place. My guess is she wants to find the trunk, the base from which all this murderous hostility stems, and destroy it. If she does, she can get on with her life. If she doesn't, she'll never be free."

"And you'll never be together," Grace said, divining the root of his heartache.

"Probably not."

"Then help her. Do whatever it takes." Grace took her son's hands in hers and looked deep into his eyes. "She's worth it."

Jake nodded and kissed his mother's hand, grateful, as always, for her love and her support. "I agree. Now I just have to figure out what to do and how to get it done."

"You will. I have confidence in you," Grace said as she rose from her chair and went to the refrigerator again. "But before you do anything, you're going to have breakfast!"

Amanda was exhausted. Jake's visit had left her roiling in an emotional whirlpool—one minute things were clear, the next minute they were tangled up with so many other thoughts and feelings that everything became a blur. Aside from the stunning news he'd delivered about Bastido, which she was still trying to digest, she had to deal with his declaration of love and the strong intimation that he knew who she was—and didn't care. Alone and hunted, the temptation to confess and team up with him was strong, but she resisted. Once she thought she could trust Jake completely. Now, she was so besieged by doubt, she didn't trust anyone, including herself. After all, she had trusted Tyler Grayson.

After Jake had gone and she'd had herself a good cry, she turned on the television flipping channels until she found an all-night news station. Hallie's interviews—both of them—were being regurgitated over and over, back-to-back. It was more of Hallie Brendel than Amanda could stand, but after watching the first interview, she could see where Jake might have put things Hallie conjectured together with things he knew and come up with Erica Baird. Any other time, she might have been unnerved wondering who else he might've told, who else might have figured out who she was, but now, who she was didn't matter. Who murdered Lionel did.

Early the next morning, after checking on Beth—who was steadily improving—she left Jimbo's armed with a plan. If she'd been able to close her eyes for more than twenty minutes at a stretch, she might've been more alert, but her head was so clogged with possible do's and definite don'ts, she never noticed the ubiquitous beige car parked across the street from the building or the man inside, sipping coffee and munching on a bagel, his face hidden by mirrored aviator sunglasses.

Since her plan still needed some fine-tuning, she opted to take a bus instead of the subway. At the corner of Second Avenue, she grabbed a Number 15, grateful to find a vacant seat in the back. Had she looked out the rear window, she might have noticed the beidge car pull in behind the bus, but she was too focused on what was ahead of her.

At Forty-second Street, she got off and headed west. Her destination was the *Telegraph* building, specifically, Hallie Brendel's office. Amanda marched into the lobby and found herself confronted by a large desk and several security guards who looked as if they took their jobs very seriously.

"I'm here to see Hallie Brendel," she said.

"Do you have an appointment?"

"No, but it's important that I see her."

"We'll have to call upstairs and see if she's available."

The man behind the desk punched a few keys and waited for someone upstairs to answer. He was about to tell Amanda to go away when she asked him to give her the phone.

"Please." She turned her back to the guard and brought the receiver close to her mouth. "This is Erica Baird," she said flatly.

A thunderous silence pounded in her ear as Hallie responded to Amanda's announcement.

"How do I know you are who you say you are?"

"You don't. You're going to have to take me at my word. The same way you expect the public to take you at your word."

"Come upstairs where we can talk. I'm on the twenty-seventh floor."

"I'm in the lobby. We can talk in a coffee shop." She handed the phone back to the guard and smiled pleasantly. "Thanks."

She walked to a corner, faced the elevator banks, and waited. It wouldn't take long. Within minutes, Hallie bolted into the lobby, her eyes locking on every woman they saw. It took a minute to fix on Amanda. When she did, her face registered shock and then, recognition.

"I saw you . . ."

"On the stairwell in Jake Fowler's brownstone." Amanda was quick to eliminate the preliminaries "I'm not here to discuss Mr. Fowler."

"I understand."

"I'm here because you seem quite determined to drag my mother and me out of our carefully maintained anonymity. Almost as determined as you were to ruin my father." Her tone was harsh.

Hallie flushed in the face of Amanda's justified anger. She attempted to explain. "I was simply trying to make sense of a tragedy."

Amanda raised her hand like a stop sign. "Don't insult me by flinging your do-gooder bullshit, Miss Brendel. The only thing you were trying to do was further your career." She made no secret of her disdain. "Well, this must be your lucky day because I'm here to offer you a major coup: an interview with the formerly deceased Erica Baird."

"However you want to . . ."

"I want to go to a very busy coffee shop where I can't be shanghaied by one of your cameramen or taped by a secret microphone. Until I'm ready to go public, we do this my way or not at all."

"Agreed!"

The two women walked out of the building onto Forty-second Street. A little after nine, traffic was screaming at a rush-hour pace. The nearest coffee shop was on Forty-first, just off Second Avenue. They walked briskly to the end of the block, turned right, went down one more block, and turned the corner. The entrance was about ten yards in.

Suddenly, Amanda heard the piercing screech of tires. She glanced over her shoulder just as a beige car wheeled around the corner, cutting onto the curb and heading straight for them. She reached out and grabbed Hallie, trying to tug her toward the building, but Hallie panicked and pulled away just as the car veered right. Amanda watched in horror as tons of metal slammed into Hallie's body, tossing her into the air like a rag doll. Amanda was thrown to the ground by the impact, twisting an ankle and smacking her head against the sidewalk. The car raced up the street and disappeared before she could get a plate number.

People on the avenue heard the noise and began to gather. Ignoring the pain in her ankle, Amanda made her way over to where Hallie lay, leaned down, pressed her fingers against Hallie's neck and felt for a pulse; it was thready. Her body appeared contorted, as if it had sustained serious bone breakage. Her color was poor, and she was unconscious. Amanda worried that she might slip into a coma, or worse.

She looked up to ask someone to call 911 when two blue-and-whites pulled up. She stood and stepped back, hurriedly camouflaging herself in the horde of onlookers. One of the officers asked what happened. Five people spoke at once, relieving her of the obligation. When the ambulance arrived and she knew Hallie was in good hands, Amanda took advantage of the confusion and took off. Much as she hated leaving a scene, she couldn't afford to be questioned.

Grand Central Station was only a few blocks away. Trying not to attract attention, she kept pace with the crowd, moving as briskly up

Forty-second Street as her ankle would allow, crossing at Vanderbilt, pushing her way through the entrance doors. She held her breath as she made her way down the stairs. This being New York, she was being bumped and elbowed by commuters and travelers eager to get to wherever they were going. An assassin could plunge a knife through her ribs and escape before anyone noticed.

When she reached the main floor, her eyes scanned the vast underground cavern that was Grand Central Station, assessing the man drinking coffee over there, wondering about the woman buying a newspaper over here. Logic warned of the fruitlessness of searching for a chimera. But recent occurrences contradicted that advice. The faceless enemies who'd been tracking her all her life suddenly had faces. And names.

After pinpointing exits, stairwells, and subway entrances, she stopped at a food stall, bought a liter of bottled water, and asked for a large glass of ice. She bought Advil at a sundry shop and from a souvenir stand, two scarves printed with scenes of New York: a woolen square and a long silky muffler. Then, she found a ladies' room.

Ducking into a corner stall, she removed her footwear and wrapped her ankle as tightly as she could, hoping to contain the swelling. Then, she dumped some ice into the woolen square and tied it into a sack. Finding a way to ice down her ankle in such cramped quarters was complicated, but with nowhere else to go, she had to be inventive. Perched on the toilet, she elevated her injured leg by propping it up against the wall and rested the makeshift ice pack on the injured area. She swallowed several Advil, used the rest of the water to clean the dirt out of her badly scraped palms, and tried to quiet her nerves. It was a nearly impossible task. She was rattled and upset and angry. First Lionel. Then Beth. Now Hallie Brendel. Even Jaime Bastido. Joined like links on a lethal chain. When would her turn come, she wondered as she examined her wound. And how? Would they run her down? Would they shoot her? Would they poison her? Or would they simply scare her to death?

"No!" she hissed to whatever demons had affixed themselves to her soul. "No!"

Desperate to revitalize her inner strength, she closed her eyes, blocked out the sounds and chatter of other women coming and going, and demanded that she stop dwelling on death and reacquaint herself with life.

Find a pretty picture, she said, forcing her brain to repaint the present with images from the past. Snapshots of brief moments slid by, flickers of happy times, but the one that lingered was that night in Wisconsin, when Beth and Lionel and she were together around a dinner table, when everything had seemed so idyllic and so ordinary, when they'd been a family.

She breathed deep, branding that image onto her consciousness, making it the banner she intended to carry into battle, because surely, that was where she was headed. Somewhere out there her name was on a list of people who someone decided deserved to be punished. Her name had been on that list since she was nine years old.

Slowly, fueled by an ancient rage, Amanda opened her eyes. She waited for the tears to dry and the fire to return. With it came the clear outline of a plan and the determination to see it through to the end.

They took her father. They tried to take her mother. This morning, they tried to take her. But she was not going to go easily. And she wasn't going alone.

She emerged from the subway and found an ATM machine. As she waited to collect her money she cringed. Her bank balance was so low it was almost negligible. She had to go back to work or she was going to lose her job. Soon, she told herself as she walked into the building that housed Baird, Nathanson & Spelling. Soon, it would be over.

When she got off the elevator on the executive floor, she was greeted by a guard who demanded to know who she was, whom she was going to see, and why. Amanda knew this was against regulations, but she displayed her badge nonetheless.

"I'm here to see Miss MacDougall on a matter related to the death of Mr. Lionel Baird." That much was true. And, she rationalized, she didn't say she was there on official business.

"I'll let her know you're here," the guard said, starting for the phone.

"I'd rather you didn't." Amanda needed to take Fredda by surprise. She didn't want her alerting Pamela Baird or the police. "I'd prefer that her responses be spontaneous," she said, law enforcer to law enforcer. He thought about it, then said, okay. Amanda gave him a quick salute. "I know where her office is."

She strode down the hall, keeping her eyes front, avoiding contact with anyone who might remember she'd been there before. When she reached Lionel's suite, she paused, making certain Fredda wasn't entertaining anyone. She was on the phone. Amanda waited until the call was completed, then presented herself.

"We have to talk," she said in a no-nonsense tone of voice.

Fredda was flabbergasted. And nervous. "What're you doing here?"

She reached for the phone. Amanda took the receiver from her and clamped it down. When Fredda looked as if she might scream, Amanda pulled her jacket to the side, revealing her gun.

"Don't do anything stupid," Amanda warned. Fredda nodded dumbly. "Now let's go into Lionel's office and have a chat."

Fredda pushed away from her desk, rose, and walked slowly to the door. Amanda stayed right behind her. The instant they were inside, Amanda closed the door and locked it.

"Have a seat, Fredda." Her proprietary tone visibly aggravated the older woman. Clearly, she considered Lionel's office her domain and Amanda a trespasser.

"Is this visit upsetting you?"

"Yes."

"Why?"

"Because you're not supposed to be here."

"By whose orders? Pamela Baird's?"

"She is Mr. Baird's widow, you know."

"As opposed to his mistress?"

"Well, yes!"

"You were Douglas Welch's mistress. Does that make us equals?"

Fredda flushed beet red. Her hands were clenched into fists. "What do you want?" she demanded.

"I want to ask you some questions."

"What if I don't want to answer them?"

"Look, Fredda. Let's cut to the chase. You were correct if you suspected that Lionel's story about me being an art dealer was a sham." She looked smug. Amanda almost felt sorry for her. Obviously, being right was her claim to fame. "I'm a detective with the New York City Police Department." Again, Amanda flashed her badge.

Fredda's balloon of self-congratulation deflated. Nervousness returned.

"I'm here because Lionel didn't commit suicide. He was murdered."

Pete had indeed confirmed the presence of succinylcholine and a puncture wound in the back of the neck, just below the hairline.

"What! That's ridiculous! That's . . ." Suddenly, she couldn't catch her breath. Her hand flew to her chest. She gasped until her lungs filled with oxygen. "You don't think that I had . . ."

"No, I don't." Amanda was quick to reassure her that she was not under a cloud or about to be arrested. "But I do need your help finding out who did."

"What if I refuse?"

Interesting, Amanda thought. *Who is she protecting?* The woman who claimed to be Lionel's widow and Fredda's benefactor? Or the son of her former lover?

"You're not going to do that, Fredda, and do you know why? Because you loved Lionel. And you miss him. And you can't understand why he would kill himself."

Amanda had struck a chord. Fredda's eyes filled with tears. She did love Lionel, and she missed him terribly, but she wasn't about to expose her grief to Amanda. To her, the younger woman was an interloper and had given her no reason to believe otherwise.

"You have no right to be here!" she sputtered, dabbing at her eyes and glaring.

"Oh, but I do." Amanda leaned against the door and folded her arms across her chest. "I'm Lionel's daughter, Erica."

For a moment, it looked as if Fredda would have a heart attack, her face turned that blue. Amanda prayed she wouldn't have to summon an ambulance for the second time in one day. However, Fredda's normal pallor returned within seconds. So did her antagonism.

"Prove it," she said, declaring herself the final arbiter of what was true, what was false.

Amanda wasn't at all perturbed. Fredda shouldn't accept a statement like that without demanding some sort of evidence to back it up.

"My dog's name was Checkers. My father called me Ricki. My birthday is January 16 and every year on that date, you sent an arrangement of pink roses to the cemetery for my grave and Lionel had you put a bouquet of pink camellias on his desk as a remembrance. My mother's birthday is November 14. He sent her lilies of the valley."

"Oh, my God!" Again, Fredda's complexion imitated a color wheel. She was stunned, aghast, and then, suddenly, almost hysterical. "I knew it!" she exclaimed. "I told Pamela there was something about you that made Lionel deliriously happy. She hated hearing it, but from the minute you came into his life he changed. I knew it!"

She bolted up from her chair and embraced Amanda like a long-lost aunt. Then, just as suddenly, she backed away.

"You really think someone killed Lionel? I mean, your father." She blushed, unsure about how to act and what to say.

"Lionel's fine. And yes, I do."

"What can I do to help?"

Amanda smiled gratefully. "First, you can answer a personal question for me." Fredda blushed even redder. Amanda gathered the woman was about to confess her love for Lionel. She prevented the disclosure by asking, "Did you ever meet Douglas Welch's son?"

Fredda regrouped. "No," she said. "The boy never came to the office, and, well, I wasn't welcome at the funeral."

Interesting, Amanda thought. Judging by Fredda's response, she had no idea who Tyler Grayson was. Obviously, he was as adept at hiding his true identity as Amanda. Did Lionel know?

"Why do you ask?"

"If he thought Lionel should've defended his father or prevented his arrest in any way, he might've harbored a lot of hostility over the years." Fredda lowered her eyes and bobbed her head. "Should Lionel have defended Douglas Welch?"

"He did believe Lionel knew there was money laundering going on."

Possible, Amanda thought.

"He said Lionel didn't care because he was looking to make partner. The bigger his bottom line, the better his chances."

Amanda recalled that Tyler had said almost the same thing about his quest for greater status.

"Lionel told me he had an obsession with security," she said, moving on.

Fredda's body language told how pleased she was that the subject had changed. "He became paranoid after you and your mother were . . . when he thought you were killed." She still had trouble grasping the fact that Erica Baird was standing before her.

Amanda didn't have time to nurse her stupification. "He said his office and his library at the town house were wired so he could tape his meetings."

"That's true."

"Where's the recording device in here?"

"Actually, the computer contains the recorder." Fredda walked over to Lionel's desk and grinned mischievously. "The microphone is in here," she said, pointing to one of the pens mounted on an Alfred Dunhill twin pen set.

Amanda smiled. "Clever."

"He thought so."

Suddenly, Amanda had a thought. "If he had a meeting at the town house, was that recorder hooked up to this computer?"

"Yes." Fredda realized what Amanda was thinking.

"Then you have the password for those files."

Fredda's face fell. "No. Whenever Lionel wanted something transcribed from one of those meetings, he brought me the tape from the recorder at home and I worked from that."

"Fredda, I need you to do me a favor."

"Anything."

"I need you to keep everyone, and I mean everyone, out of this office while I try and break into that file."

"You think those tapes can tell us what happened to Lionel, don't you?"

"The killer may be on those tapes, Fredda," she said as she sat down in Lionel's chair and turned on the computer. "By the end of the day, I swear, we're going to know exactly who he is."

"As usual, Fowler, you're breaking every rule in the book," Caleb grumbled as he settled on the couch in Jake's office. "Whatever you have to say, you should be saying it at headquarters. And I shouldn't be here."

"My office is prettier than yours. There are too many busybodies at the station. And Grace makes better coffee than Moran."

The door opened and Pete strolled in. He looked around and whistled. "Nice digs. I guess PI work pays better than mopping up after the depraved." He took the coffee Jake handed him and shook Caleb's hand. "Ah, another partner in crime. Jake sure knows how to throw a party, doesn't he?"

He joined Caleb on the couch, both of them waiting for Jake to begin. Neither one understood Jake's insistence on secrecy until he dropped his bomb.

"Our mutual friend, Amanda Maxwell, is Erica Baird."

It took him fifteen minutes to go through all that he knew and whatever he suspected, but he had decided it was time to bring these two men up to speed. Pete was particularly unsettled by this revelation. He granted Max the right to keep her identity to herself.

He couldn't bear the thought of her being stalked by assassins. But her being in WITSEC did answer an awful lot of questions.

It also raised an awful lot of questions, the main one being why Jake didn't want to enlarge their little operation.

"Too many cops spoil the broth." He believed it would take too long for the NYPD, the FBI, and the Marshals Service to coordinate personnel and plans. "Max doesn't have a minute to spare."

"Bastido met his Maker before Fido met his," Pete said, siding with Jake. "Which means that someone else is out there with a bead on our girl."

"Exactly."

"Okay," Caleb said, throwing in with them, "who do you think that someone else is?"

"I'm not sure, but I think I have a lead."

"Are we sharing?" Caleb asked, prompted by past experience. "Or are we running off half-cocked?"

"Hey! I'm a man of the nineties. We're sharing." Jake flashed a brief smile, then got down to business. "When Jaime Bastido was convicted in 1978, he was sent to a federal penitentiary in northern Florida. A couple of his business associates were sent there in the mideighties and caused trouble for Jaime, so he was transferred." He looked at his cohorts. "To Joliet, where, according to my sources, he befriended none other than Big Ray Saviano."

"I thought the Big Man was in solitary," Pete said.

"This was before he got the shit kicked out of him and had to be isolated. When I heard this, I called a fairly reliable snitch who did time at Joliet. He told me everyone knew about the friendship between Ray and Jaime. Ray talked a lot about his son being a screwup. Jaime offered him some advice, who knows what. Anyway, they bonded. The fact that they both hated Cynthia Baird probably served as another glob of glue."

He mulled all that over, then continued.

"It can't be a coincidence that Bastido and Little Ray were having a confab. Maybe Big Ray sent Bastido to New York to shape the kid up. He might've promised Bastido that if he made the Savianos flush, they'd make him the Man."

Caleb leaned forward, resting his arms on this thighs as he put this news together with some of his own. "Little Ray was picked up the other day. One of the charges levied against him was conspiracy in the murder of the aforementioned Señor Bastido."

Pete shrugged. "I can't imagine Little Ray being happy about some stranger taking over his crown. I can imagine him eliminating the competition."

Caleb agreed with Pete in theory, "but the preliminary evidence is screaming setup."

"I don't care about their ego battle. It has nothing to do with Max or Lionel Baird," Jake reminded his friends.

"On the surface, maybe," Pete said, "but you've two thugs in bed together with a common enemy."

"I can see why Bastido and Saviano might be out to get Maxwell," Caleb said, thinking aloud, "but why kill Lionel Baird?"

"I'm not sure. Maybe Baird meant what he said. Maybe he refused to do any laundering. The boys don't like that."

"Also," Pete interjected, "Baird's suicide stole the front pages from the bloody war that's going on over the distribution of that Propaine shit. A rich man blowing his brains out is more interesting than poor drug addicts getting their guts spilled in the streets by greedy dealers and strung-out junkies."

"Maybe it's both." Jake shrugged his shoulders impatiently. "That doesn't matter right now. With all due respect, Lionel Baird's dead. My concern is keeping his daughter alive."

Pete heard the catch in Jake's voice. He caught his eye and nodded as if to signal: No matter what it took, they would keep her safe.

"When the guys in Brooklyn picked up Little Ray, they confiscated a Golden Rule list." They could tell by Caleb's voice that he was betraying a confidence, but he had started Jake on this outside path. It wouldn't be right to abandon him now.

"Okay, I'll play dumb," Pete said. "Explain."

"Do unto others as you would have them do unto you." Caleb considered organized crime a plague on society. Lists like this were part of the reason why. "This list carries the names of ordinary people who've gotten into a jam, people for whom the mob has done special favors. The implication is, they expect favors in return."

"Can you snag a copy of that list?" Jake asked.

Caleb produced one from his suit jacket pocket and handed it to Jake. "What else did you come up with?"

"One of my associates spent the morning in the library going over everything he could find on Operation Laundry Day. By matching up the names of the various principals with databases we have here, he discovered that Douglas Welch's son was one of Lionel Baird's VP's: Tyler Grayson."

Pete and Caleb's curiosity was piqued.

"He ran back to the library to get everything he could on Welch and came up with a book of police photographs." The young man told Jake the librarian was annoyed because the book had been left in a carrel, along with a stack of other books on the same subject. Jake knew it was Max. "Take a look at this."

He opened the book to the picture of Welch. Both men noticed the similarity between his position and the way Lionel Baird had been found. Both men wondered aloud about Tyler Grayson.

"Some of my sources said they heard Baird was the one who fingered Welch," Caleb said, finally finding a place to put that piece of news. "Also, when I questioned Thompson, the butler, after he was released from the hospital, he said Grayson was at the town house the afternoon of the suicide. This guy should be brought in, Jake."

"I agree, but if you arrest him, he's going to get out on bail, and if he is the one who killed Lionel, he's going to hunt Max down like a dog. How about putting a tail on him?"

Caleb shook his head. He was too much of a cop to let a prime homicide suspect roam free.

"Twenty-four hours," Jake begged. "Give us twenty-four hours and then, if we haven't brought him or whoever in, grab him up."

"What makes you so sure this case is ready to break?"

Jake's pain was palpable. "Because Max is ready to break. She's sick of running and hiding and watching her back."

"What do you think she's going to do?" Pete was as nervous as Jake.

"The only thing she can do. She's going to make herself a target."

CHAPTER
TWENTY-SIX

Amanda had been at it for more than two hours with no success. She tried family names, places, words associated with Lionel's penchant for golf, skiing, art, and fine wine, as well as odd appellations that might have been prompted by ego, such as the names of English kings and the truly historic American presidents, like Jefferson, Lincoln, and Roosevelt. She was hampered by the lost years, during which an event or person might have impressed Lionel in such a way as to become a private password. They had reminisced often, filling each other in on the more important occurrences, but passwords came from small, meaningful specifics, not generalities like adolescent rites of passage or corporate mergers.

Fredda made a dutiful Cerberus, guarding Lionel's office with a heightened sense of purpose. Now and then, she brought Amanda coffee or a sandwich, using the occasion to peek over her shoulder and offer advice. Once, when Amanda was expressing her frustration, Fredda patted her shoulder maternally.

"He didn't speak of you often, but anyone who listened knew that your . . . passing was the single most traumatic moment in his life. He never got over the loss. Ever."

That got Amanda thinking. Maybe she was the password. Reinvigorated, she typed in, ERICA. Nothing. RICKI. Nothing. RED CABOOSE. PINK CAMELLIA. BABYGIRL. CHECKERS. Each time, the words, INAPPROPRIATE PASSWORD, TRY AGAIN appeared, taunting her as if her credibility was on the line, as if this was a test of what kind of daughter she was. She got up to stretch her legs, and her memory.

The blood rushed to her feet, and her ankle began to throb. She'd kept that foot elevated and, thanks to her new best friend, well iced, but it was still sore, a reminder that time was of the essence. As she limped to the door to ask Fredda about getting a real ice pack, she heard a familiar voice.

"I need to get into Lionel's computer," Tyler was saying. "There's a meeting of all the vice presidents tomorrow. Lionel kept files of some of our bigger clients on his computer. There may be valuable information in those files that would assure our ability to keep these Goliaths in house. I need them for this meeting."

"I'm sorry, Tyler, but you can't go in there."

"Fredda, this is not a mausoleum. It's an office."

His tone reeked of condescension, as if he were punishing Fredda for her involvement with his father. Still, Amanda wondered why he never told her who he was. At the very least, he might've gained an ally, someone else who'd loved Douglas Welch and spoke of him with respect. At best, he might've found a friend.

"I'm sorry Lionel is dead," he said, "but Baird, Nathanson & Spelling is not. It's a business, and if we're going to keep it going, I need to get those files!"

Amanda felt a slight thump. Fredda must have moved up against the door to block Tyler's entrance.

"The police have said no one is to go in there. That includes you."

"Rather than waste time arguing with you, I'll respect your wishes, for now. But I intend to come back, Fredda. And when I do, I'm going into that office and into Lionel's computer."

"Not unless you have a note from a judge or an official of the police department."

No wonder Lionel kept her in his employ for so many years, Amanda thought as she hobbled back to the desk. Her ankle would have to heal itself. Hearing the edge in Tyler's voice had increased her sense of urgency. She was fighting against the notion that he had anything to do with Lionel's death, but one way or another, she had to know. She started the process again.

ERICABAIRD. RBAIRD. ESB. ACIRE.

She remembered something. Lionel called her Ricki. When she was first learning to speak, she tried to imitate him, but couldn't pronounce her r's. She referred to herself as Icki. For years, Lionel teased her about that. Even recently.

She typed it in and held her breath. ICKI. Suddenly, the screen dissolved into a long list of files, each one with a date and time. She moved the cursor to the day of the suicide and clicked the PLAY icon. The first voice she heard was Bruno's.

"Mr. Grayson is here to see you."

"Fine. Send him in."

"Are you going to need me this evening, sir?"

"No. Thanks, Bruno. I'm dining out."

The machine clicked off, then on again when Tyler came in.

For the next half hour, Amanda listened with rapt attention to the conversation between Tyler and her father. He had come to speak to Lionel about the promotion. Lionel explained he wasn't promoting anyone because he wasn't retiring anytime soon.

Tyler had told her as much over dinner. Maybe her imagination was working overtime. She had, after all, considered other possibilities. Maybe she was making a murderer out of a coincidence.

The discussion escalated when Tyler said he deserved to be named associate CEO whether Lionel was retiring or not.

"And why is that?" Lionel didn't sound angry. In fact, he seemed almost amused. But not for long.

"Because you owe me."

"Again, I say, and why is that?"

"I'm Douglas Welch's son. Isn't that reason enough?"

Lionel didn't answer at first. Amanda wished she could see his face, read his mind. Had he known already?

"No, Tyler, your parentage is not a reason to become associate CEO of Baird, Nathanson & Spelling."

"You knew, didn't you?" Tyler said.

"Knew what?"

"Who I am."

"How would I know if you didn't tell me?"

Exactly what Amanda was thinking.

"When I first came to Baird, Nathanson & Spelling, I got a call from Big Ray Saviano. Direct from Joliet. He wanted me to launder money for the family. I refused."

How angry did that make Big Ray, she wondered. *Did he threaten to expose Tyler? Or punish him some other way?*

"That was the right thing to do. Good for you."

Amanda could tell Lionel wasn't pleased by Tyler's association with the senior Saviano, no matter how short-lived.

"I did it so no one could say, like father like son." There was a pause. Amanda felt sorry for Tyler. She knew what it was to have the sins of a parent visited on a child. "No matter what he did, you should've stood up for my father, Lionel. Because you didn't, he killed himself."

"Your father was an addicted gambler, Grayson. He killed himself because he couldn't bear the shame of what he'd done. I'm sorry about that, and I'm sorry that you lost your father, but I'm not to blame for his gambling or his death."

"You knew the pressure the mob was placing on him. And you knew all about the money laundering that was going on at Nathanson & Spelling. But you didn't care, as long as those profits went to your bottom line."

"And your point is?"

Amanda cringed at Lionel's veiled admission.

"You got to be a name partner at Nathanson & Spelling by stepping on the backs of people like my father! That's the point."

Tyler's anguish had turned to rage. Amanda was certain that Lionel's aristocratic sangfroid was only making things worse.

"Your father was convicted for stealing hundreds of thousands of dollars of blank stock certificates."

"You looked away."

"I wasn't his guardian, Tyler. I wasn't even his immediate superior. It wasn't my job to watch his every move. I know this hurts, but the man was a thief."

The argument continued in the same vein for several minutes more. Tyler's voice grew louder and more vehement as he insisted that Lionel bring everything full circle.

"I'm giving you a chance to make reparations," he said, sounding desperate.

Lionel was silent for a bit. When he spoke, Amanda could tell he was reining his anger so as not to incite Tyler any further.

"If it makes you feel any better, before I decided not to appoint an associate at the present time, you were one of two I was considering."

"Don't throw me any bones, Lionel," Tyler ranted.

"I assure you, that's not what I'm doing. I'm telling you the truth. You're a talented man, Tyler. Bright and incisive. You don't need threats to get ahead. But I must warn you that if they continue, your future at Baird, Nathanson & Spelling will come to an unpleasant end."

Tyler railed awhile longer until Lionel buzzed for Bruno to escort him out.

Amanda sat at the computer, drained and upset. If Tyler was

capable of murder, and there were those who believed everyone could be pushed to that ignoble brink, Lionel had just handed him a motive.

It was with a heavy heart that she scrolled down to the last entry in this file, a recording made only two hours later. She clicked PLAY and steeled herself to listen to the last moments of her father's life.

An hour later, Amanda left Lionel's office. She'd listened to the tape several times, verifying what she'd heard, planning what she had to do. She made a duplicate for evidence, closed the file, and watched Fredda put the tape in Lionel's safe.

"Don't you want to know the combination?"

"No." It was safer that way. "Is there somewhere you can go, Fredda, until this is over?"

"I do have some vacation time coming," she said with a brave smile.

"Be spontaneous," Amanda said, accompanying her suggestion with an enthusiastic flourish. "Go somewhere exotic!"

Fredda hugged the younger woman. "Stay safe," she said.

Amanda returned her embrace. "I'm going to try."

After going over some last-minute things with Fredda, Amanda headed for the elevators. She was too focused on her next move to notice Tyler Grayson lurking in the corner.

Grace Fowler kept a small television in a cabinet alongside her desk. She was a news junkie and never liked to be out of the loop. Usually, the sound was muted. She knew if there was a bulletin, her eye would catch it. The networks weren't exactly subtle.

Around four-thirty, the twelve-inch screen turned blue. The words, BREAKING NEWS pulsed red, demanding her attention. She turned up the volume.

"We interrupt your regularly scheduled broadcast for this late-breaking news.

"Good afternoon ladies and gentlemen. This is Trey Gallagher, speaking to you from our newsroom in New York. Early this morning, Hallie Brendel, a reporter for the *Telegraph,* was seriously injured by a hit-and-run driver. According to doctors at New York Hospital, she came out of surgery a short while ago. Her condition is listed as critical.

"A few nights ago, I interviewed Ms. Brendel on the matter of the late Lionel Baird. During that interview, she suggested that perhaps Mr. Baird's first wife and daughter were not killed in the explosion that destroyed their home, but instead, had become protected witnesses. Frankly, I disagreed. But it appears as if Ms. Brendel was correct."

Grace buzzed Jake over the intercom. "Get out here! There's news about Max!" He and the rest of the staff rushed to the reception area. Suddenly everyone was watching Grace's tiny TV.

"In the studio with me is Erica Baird. She was with Ms. Brendel at the time of the accident."

The camera shifted to Amanda. Jake thought she looked pale, but remarkably self-assured. Looking more closely, he smiled. She must've refused to let the makeup artist smear her with pancake. She was clean-faced, except for her favorite brown-pink lipstick, a swipe of eyeliner, and a touch of mascara. Next to her, Gallagher looked orange.

"Is it true, Ms. Baird, that you and your mother were protected witnesses?"

"When I came to New York," Amanda said, deliberately ignoring the part about her mother, "I forfeited the right to federal protection."

"Why are you coming forward now?"

There were a hundred questions Trey wanted to ask, but Amanda had told him if he veered away from her script, she'd walk out and sue him—and the station—for endangerment.

"My father, Lionel Baird, did not commit suicide. He was murdered. I believe the same person is responsible for Hallie Brendel's near-fatal accident. I also believe he was aiming for me."

"That's quite an allegation, Ms. Baird. Do you have proof that your father was murdered?"

"Yes."

"Do you have any idea who might've done this?"

"Yes."

"Have you given his or her name to the police?"

"I'm in the process of obtaining conclusive evidence. When I have it in my possession, and I will shortly, I'll go to the police."

Jake called the Nineteenth Precinct immediately. Caleb confirmed Jake's worst fears.

"I don't know what she's talking about! I don't know who she's after or what she's after." Caleb was upset. Jake knew he was feeling guilty about going the rogue route. "You were on the money, Fowler. She painted a big red target on her chest and dared a killer to come get her."

"I know," Jake said, automatically securing his gun in his holster. "Which means we'd better find her before he does."

Amanda had taped the interview at three-thirty and left the studio at four, half an hour before it aired. The delay was part of her arrangement with Gallagher, so she could get home before the story broke.

She wasn't sure why she went back to her apartment. Probably because she felt that no matter what condition it was in, it was hers. It was something she could see and touch and feel connected to. And just then, connection was what she needed most.

Before walking in, she thought she was prepared for the avalanche. She wasn't. Seeing her furniture upended and her belongings thrown about saddened and infuriated her. Aside from the material devastation, she felt personally plundered. This was yet another insult in a long line of affronts. As she went around, picking up and setting things right, she vowed this would be the last.

She'd been denied her name, her family, her friends, the right to form new friendships or have relationships, the right to an identity. Well, this afternoon she changed that. She stood up and announced, "This is who I am!" The last time she had made a declaration like that—identifying herself as Erica Baird, daughter of Lionel Baird— she was in the fourth grade.

Standing alone in her living room, she said it again. "I'm Erica Baird, Lionel Baird's daughter."

She'd read so many articles and seen so many interviews in which women bemoaned the fact that their identity was always tied up with someone else, that they were someone's wife, or daughter, or mother, rather than an individual. Amanda understood that, but her life had been the exact opposite. She was known only by her name, her profession, and her accomplishments. No one judged her on her genetic or marital affiliations because they either didn't exist or remained unknown. Other women had a wardrobe of hats from which to choose. For someone like Amanda, whose only hat was being Beth's daughter, having another one available felt wonderful!

Before going to the studio, she had called Beth. It was the first time they'd spoken since the shooting. Amanda wanted to prepare her mother for what she was about to do, and whatever fallout resulted. Beth listened carefully to Amanda's recitation of all that had happened and why she felt she had to take this risk.

"If I don't, we'll have to go through this again," she said. "And I couldn't bear it."

Beth was physically weak, but her spirit was as strong as ever. "Do what you have to do," she told her daughter. "But be smart and be careful."

"I will," Amanda promised. Both of them knew promises were easy, guarantees were impossible.

Amanda walked into her bedroom and found that it had been tidied up. Her bed was made, her clothes were back in their drawers and closets, and the bouquet from Jimbo's apartment had found its way to her dresser. At first, that made her nervous, but there was a note attached.

"We didn't have time to do it all, but hey! We also returned your toys. XXXX"

Amanda bent down and felt under her bed. Her Remington was back where it belonged. She was tempted to take it with her, but its bulk would be conspicuous and, possibly, inhibiting. Instead, she went to the closet shelf where she stored her ammunition. She slipped a full magazine into her Glock 9mm, cocked it, locked it, and holstered it on her belt. She riffled through a drawer to find her ankle holster and loaded the Chief. She intended to be prepared.

Her phone rang. She hurried to the living room. This was another reason she'd come home—to hear the response to her little psycho-drama. She had no intention of actually speaking to anyone, but she wanted to hear who called and what messages they left. She didn't expect any crank calls. As a means of control, she refused to allow Gallagher to refer to her as Amanda Maxwell. Anyone who called already knew who she was, where she lived, and her phone number.

Jake was first. "You're out of your mind. Now I'm out of my mind worrying about you. But I love you. And I'm going to find you. We'll deal with it all. Later."

"I love you, too," she whispered.

Two minutes later, Pamela Baird called. That was a shock. "I'm positively astounded! I had no idea Lionel's daughter was alive. How absolutely wonderful!"

What utter crap, Amanda thought, chuckling as she listened to Pamela lie outright.

"Where did you ever come from? And why didn't I know? Is your mother alive as well? We really must get together and talk. About Lionel, of course."

And his will, of course.

John Chisolm called to express his amazement and his sympathy. He, too, thought it would be delightful to get to know Lionel's only offspring.

And to find out whatever secrets Lionel told me about him.

"You get out of this alive and you're going to have to buy a slew of little black dresses," Amanda said as she returned to her bedroom, slipped into a black turtleneck, and pulled her hair into a ponytail. "You're going to be a regular social butterfly."

She donned a pair of black jeans and eased her feet into lug-soled loafers. She would've preferred sneakers, but they came up too high, and her ankle was badly bruised. The only other accommodation she made to her impairment was to replace the very fetching Empire State Building tourniquet she'd been wearing all day with a boring, but effective, Ace bandage.

Uncle Sam called. She thought about speaking to him, but changed her mind when she realized that he probably had three government agencies armed and ready to come to her rescue. It wasn't that she couldn't use the backup. She couldn't afford a screwup. She would be near a telephone. When she had things under control, she'd call for the troops.

"Have you forgotten everything I taught you about staying out of sight?" he said, his voice betraying exasperation and concern. "I don't know what you're about to do, but my gut says it's risky and probably foolish. Please, honey, call in. Let us help you. We'll get whoever it is. I promise."

Another promise with no guarantee.

The machine clicked off. The ensuing silence screamed at her in reproach, mimicking Sam's plea for sanity, demanding that she reassess her plan and reexamine her motivation. Was she looking to be a heroine or to capture a killer? If it was the latter, her access to qualified assistance was limitless. So why was she refusing to allow anyone in on her collar? Pride? When she was on the street, she'd never been so conceited or cocksure that she didn't call for backup. Why break pattern now? Was it her need for revenge against the man who killed her father? Or was it her symbolic battle for independence against the faceless enemy that had stalked her all her life?

She tried to shake off Sam's criticism, but no matter where she went in the apartment, no matter how she tried to distract herself, it clung to her like the strands of a spider's web. Again, she considered calling the marshals, calling Caleb Green, Pete. Or Jake. She thought about what she'd heard on that tape. And again, she chided herself.

She should have known. All along, her gut had been whispering to her, warning her of the disaster to come. She had cautioned Lionel, but he didn't listen. And now, Lionel was dead. She hadn't listened to her inner voice when Beth wanted to come to New York, and now Beth was in intensive care. She would not ignore her instincts again.

Rather than fill the next couple of hours torturing herself, she attacked the mess. By six-thirty, she'd straightened out her living room, reorganized her kitchen, put her darkroom back together, packed a bag with everything she'd need, and was ready to go. It was time. The sun was receding behind the somber gray of dusk. Without any light, unfriendly shadows invaded her apartment, turning familiar objects into strangers, comfortable surroundings into an ominous enclosure. As she strapped on her ankle holster and slipped the Chief into place, she wondered why she still hadn't heard fron Tyler.

The phone rang. She froze, barely breathing, almost as if she was afraid the caller could see and hear her. Another ring; the machine clicked on.

"Hey. It's me. I'm not here right now, but if you let me know who you are and where you are, I'll get back to you."

The machine clicked off. No message. Amanda smiled. Just as she thought: He was checking to see if she was home. She was betting he'd call back later, just to be sure. To increase her odds, she took her phone off the hook. When he called back, he'd get a busy signal and assume she was home.

When he showed up at the town house, he'd get a surprise.

The last time Jake checked in with Caleb, Grayson was drowning his sorrows in a bar on Second Avenue and Seventy-third. The tail was sticking close, in case Mr. Wing Tips was downing a pint of liquid-courage in preparation for another hit. Pete was at the Crime Lab reworking the forensics in Lionel's case, hoping to pick up something new, something definitive beyond the fact that someone had injected Lionel with a paralytic drug, then shoved a gun in his mouth and used the victim's finger to pull the trigger.

Jake wasn't as eager as most to jump on the Grayson bandwagon. The evidence was compelling, but pat. Jake didn't like coincidence. And he didn't like pat. On paper, the case was solved. He should've been able to relax. Grayson had a tail pinned on him. Nothing was going to go down without the police being all over this guy.

But Amanda had gone on national television to declare herself a target. She could've called Grayson on the phone, invited him over for a drink, and greeted him along with the entire Nineteenth Precinct, guns drawn. Or she could've gone to his place, also accompanied by a regiment. She didn't, because Grayson wasn't the perp.

Knowing the clock was ticking, Jake closeted himself in his office with his computer and the Golden Rule list that Caleb had faxed him. Jake wasn't about to eliminate Grayson—those police photographs of Douglas Welch said Grayson was involved—but Amanda's behavior urged him to look elsewhere. His personal antipathy for the Savianos said, look there first.

He typed the names on the Saviano list into his computer, cross-checking them against his own files on organized-crime figures, which was extensive, and a list of names of those who orbited around Lionel. Since it seemed entirely possible that Big Ray had orchestrated this hit, Jake concentrated on his compadres, the old soldiers who had been killed in battle or sent away. Then he searched his files for their sons or grandsons or nephews, checking on their current whereabouts, running down their rap sheets, cross-referencing them against Baird, Nathanson & Spelling employment rolls.

"Come on!" he urged his computer, egging his megahertz to go faster. "Let's go! Let's go!"

Someone on these lists had to have a major grudge against Lionel. Or a really good reason to do whatever Big Ray asked.

Name. Check. Golden Rule List. Cross-check. BNS. New name. New file.

He was typing and pacing, unable to believe that he couldn't find anything. Then he did. It wasn't perfect, it was mostly circumstantial, so they'd need tangible evidence to convict, but to Jake, it was logical enough to be lethal.

The question now was where Max planned to rendezvous with her father's killer. Jake had to figure it out. And soon.

It was nine-thirty when he entered the town house. With his back to a wall and his gun drawn, he turned on the hall light, quickly tracing a half circle through the air with the long, black barrel of his .45. He climbed the staircase cautiously, his firing arm in constant motion, looking ahead of him, then behind. He didn't expect anyone, but after Amanda's performance, he wasn't discounting the possibility of a visit by the police. It didn't matter. He had dozens of plausible explanations for his presence.

The truth was, if she hadn't unnerved him with what she said about having proof, he'd never come back here. That night was a horror. He had no desire to relive it. But what could she have? What else was she looking for?

He reached the top floor and stopped. The doorway to the bathroom was blocked by yellow police tape. He'd washed down the shower after he finished, just as he'd wiped clean any stains on the stairway carpet, but blood might have dried on the grouting or mixed with water lingering near the drain. Worried, he clutched the doorknob and pushed open the door.

Panic coursed through his body like an air bubble, flying through his veins, making his head throb and his heart thump. Throughout the room, there were splotches and stipples glowing in the dark like variegated specters coming back to haunt him. He remembered running up here, sick to his stomach and disgusted. In his haste to get into the shower, he'd ripped off his clothes, almost violently, desperate to rid himself of the evidence of his sins. He'd washed these walls, removing whatever stains he could see, but he'd forgotten about Luminol, a chemical capable of seeing what he forgot to erase.

Frantic, he turned his back on the iridescent nightmare and stumbled down the stairs. He had to get to the library. As he made his way through the house, he wondered, again, how she knew and what she had. He'd worn gloves. There couldn't have been any fingerprints. He'd stolen the tape. *Was there a video camera in the library? Or in the secret hallway?*

Yellow tape blocked the door to the library as well. He thought about using the secret entrance, but decided against it. If by some chance he was interrupted by the police, he didn't want to have to explain how he got in. He removed thc tape, opened the door, and walked in. As he'd done that night, he closed the door behind him and locked it.

He turned on the light and stared. Here, there was no need for Luminol. The blood that had spurted from Lionel Baird's head was visible, manifesting itself in nasty dark brown stains. In the weeks since, he tried to think of what occurred here as a ritual, a rite of passage that took him from one world into another. But standing here, all he could see was a scene of slaughter.

He remembered walking in, hands behind his back, a needle already filled with succinylcholine. Lionel never knew what hit him. He grabbed Lionel's head and held it against his body as he jabbed the needle into Lionel's flesh. Lionel had flailed at him and sputtered, stunned and frightened. Within minutes, he was paralyzed, unable to move, but perfectly able to see his own gun being shoved into his mouth. It was ghoulish, almost unspeakable. Lionel's eyes had stared at him until the last, wondering why, watching in horror as the trigger was pulled and his life was blown away.

He closed his eyes and heaved, sickened by the memory and the knowledge of what he'd done.

"Are you remembering how you felt when you killed him, Bruno?"

Surprised, he spun around, momentarily thrown off-balance. Amanda had watched through the peephole, waiting until he moved past the secret door so she could sneak in behind him. Her gun was aimed directly at his heart.

"He trusted you. He believed in you. More than once I warned him he couldn't trust anyone. That everyone had a price. What was your price, Bruno?"

He started to reach for his gun.

"I'll kill you," she said calmly. "You make a move, and I'll blow you away without a second thought. Just like you did to my father."

He stood statue-still, but she wasn't fooled. Like an animal, he was waiting to pounce.

"Big Ray's not going to be able to get you out of this one," she said, taunting him. "You're on tape, Bruno. That rich baritone voice of yours comes across loud and clear."

"You're lying!" He shouted, starting for her. "I didn't say anything."

"You did now."

He rushed her, grabbing her arm, forcing the gun out of her hand. In the process, he shoved her. Her ankle gave way, and she tumbled to the floor. He reached for her gun. As he bent down she hinged her good leg back and launched it into his stomach. He doubled over. She sprang to her feet and, ignoring the waves of pain, came at him, feet flying, hands chopping like cleavers.

She hammered him with powerful side-kicks and precisely aimed short-arm blows, pummeling him with deadly swipes at his face and body. But Bruno was a big man, able to withstand her attacks. Suddenly, his fist crashed into her jaw, propelling her across the floor. He chased after her. She stuck her foot out and tripped him. As he bent against the wall, his hand slapped against the knob that controlled the lights, plunging the room into shadows. The only illumination came from a streetlamp.

Amanda scrambled to her feet, desperate to get to her other gun.

Before she could find it, he was on her. She scratched at him and butted her elbow into his face. Furious, his hands clasped her neck, but as he rose above her and tightened his grip, she kneed him in the groin. He recoiled, screaming in pain. She rebounded, once again rising to her feet, preparing for another onslaught, summoning whatever inner strength she'd need to repel him.

He came at her like a grizzly in the wild, hands raised, fngers curled like vicious claws. With no time for anything else, she surrendered to instinct. Forgetting about her ankle, she leaned, raised her leg, leaped into the air, and gunned her foot into his shoulder. He shrieked in outraged agony. She slammed to the ground. She'd hit him with such driving force, she broke her ankle. Writhing in pain, she patted the floor, searching for her .38. Her fingertips felt the cold metal of the barrel, but he was faster than she was. He wrested away control of the gun.

Suddenly, there was a loud crash and the door to the library fell to the floor. Bruno turned. Amanda gritted her teeth, sucked in some air, loosened the gun from his hand, and pinned his arm to the floor. She didn't have to do much else. Jake was on Bruno like a blanket, beating him with such force the larger man was immobilized within seconds.

As Jake hunkered over his quarry, a gun pressed against Bruno's neck for insurance, he looked over at Amanda. In the dusky light, it was hard to know how badly she was injured.

"Are you all right?"

"What took you so long?" She was in such pain, she could barely speak.

"You didn't leave enough bread crumbs, Gretel. It was hard finding my way through the forest."

A weak smile flickered across Amanda's lips. "Next time, Hansel, I'll leave a map."

The lights snapped on.

"For crissakes, Max." It took Pete three long strides to get to her side. He looked at her ankle and groused. "You did a hell of a job, Wonder Woman. You're going to be in a cast for weeks."

"Sorry, Pete."

"Yeah. Sure. Anything to make my life difficult." His hand swept lightly across her cheek. She caught it and squeezed.

Within seconds, the room was filled with police and EMTs. Moran read Bruno his rights, cuffed him, and took him into custody. Caleb kneeled down next to Amanda.

"You didn't have to do this solo," he said softly. "We would've backed you up."

"I know." She shuddered as a paramedic lifted her leg and rested her ankle on a pillow, tying it with cravats to stabilize it. It took a minute for the searing pain to subside before she could continue. "But I needed him to confess on tape."

"Okay, that's it, gentlemen," the lead EMT said. "This lady needs to get to a hospital. Visiting hours are twelve to two, six to eight. See you then."

They lifted her onto a gurney and carried her out of the town house, down the steps to where the ambulance awaited. As they slid the gurney into the wagon, Jake jumped in and planted himself alongside her. The driver was about to object, when Jake stared him down.

"Don't even think about asking me to leave," he said.

"How'd you know where I was?" Max asked, grimacing, as the ambulance pulled away from the curb and took off for the hospital.

Jake held her hand, gazed down at her, and grinned. "Brilliant detective work."

She rewarded him with the briefest of smiles. The intensity of her discomfort was obvious. He swept a strand of hair off her face, mindful of her jaw, which was already turning purple.

"And," he said, quietly, seriously, "I was motivated by a desperate desire to make sure nothing happened to you. Because, in case you weren't paying attention the last time, I love you."

"Me too you."

Overcome by fatigue and relief and pain, she closed her eyes. Only then did Jake allow his mask to drop and a tear to fall.

When she opened her eyes again, it was late morning, the next day. She'd undergone surgery for her ankle, now in a thick cast and elevated by a sling, and been given a healthy dose of sedatives. After a sponge bath, a nurse helped her into a fresh gown and called down to the kitchen for coffee and toast. Along with her breakfast came several colorful bouquets.

Amanda smiled at the flowers and the balloons, but she didn't feel like eating.

"You're going to need your strength," the nurse said. "The waiting room is filled with people eager to see you."

To take my statement, Amanda thought. She relented, nibbling on the toast and drinking the full cup of coffee. She'd need a clear head to answer the questions that were going to be put to her.

When she was feeling up to it, the swarm descended. Jake stood on the far side of her bed, resuming the position her nurse said he'd occupied throughout the night. Pete had also participated in the bedside vigil. He walked in front of Green and Moran and, in front of his colleagues, kissed her hello.

"Wally and the guys will be here later," he said.

"Annie's in the lounge. With my mother," Jake added with a sly smile. "Sam Bates is on his way. His plane lands in about an hour. And I spoke to your mother. I assured her you were going to be fine."

Amanda's lips quivered as she realized what all these people had gone through on her behalf. She wasn't used to this kind of attention or affection.

Caleb approached the bed. His tone was friendly, but he had his official face on. "I hate to do this, but are you up for a few questions?"

"Fire away."

He smiled. "I remember when Moran and I caught this case, we didn't see a need to spray that upstairs bathroom with Luminol. And I don't recall taping the doorways. May I assume that was your handiwork?"

"I needed to spook him into believing that either you or I had gone back there and found something tangible."

"We would've gone back if we believed it was a homicide," Moran said, following her train of thought.

"And if you were looking to nail someone for the crime. When I announced I was Lionel's daughter, that gave me access to the town house and a reason to rip the place apart looking for clues."

"Muscle Man thought he was home free," Moran said, chuckling. "Your TV appearance must've rattled his cage big-time!"

"As you knew it would," Jake added, still amazed that she set herself up that way. Amanda neither disagreed nor apologized.

Caleb looked at his notebook, wanting to follow up on a couple of things. "Last night, you said you lured Vitale to the town house because you needed to get a confession on tape."

"I needed the confession to ensure conviction."

Jake smiled. Bottom line, she was a great cop. If you're going to make the collar, make it good.

"We spoke to Fredda Macdougall," Caleb continued. "She said you spent the afternoon in Mr. Baird's office listening to a tape made the day of the murder. She was under the impression you were certain of the killer's identity when you left."

"I was, but not because his voice was on the tape. Bruno knew Lionel's recorder was voice-activated. He remained silent the entire time he was in the library."

"Then why were you certain it was Vitale and not Tyler Grayson?" Moran asked.

"The only thing on the tape was Lionel saying, 'What are you doing back here?' "

"That could've been Grayson."

"True, but earlier, Lionel told Bruno he was going out for dinner and that he could have the night off. That's not what Bruno told the police. Also, when I was at the library, I noticed that someone had checked out a book of police photographs."

Jake told her they'd seen the book and the shots of Douglas Welch.

"Tyler Grayson didn't need a book to tell him what his father looked like. He discovered the body. You don't forget something like that. Ever!"

"So why pose Baird . . . Mr. Baird to imitate Welch?" Now that Pete knew Max was Baird's daughter, he felt the need to be more respectful.

"To frame Tyler for my father's murder."

It was the first time she had said that aloud. It pained her to think she ever entertained the notion that Tyler could do such a dastardly thing. She couldn't imagine how he was going to feel when the details of this were made public.

"Big Ray Saviano asked Tyler to launder money for the organization. Tyler refused. My guess is that Saviano pressured Tyler by threatening to tell Lionel who Tyler was. When Tyler continued to resist the pressure, Saviano put him on the enemies list."

"Speaking of lists," Jake said, "it was Little Ray's Golden Rule sheet that fingered Vitale. His father, Carlo, was one of Saviano's lieutenants. He was killed during an attempt on the Don's life. He threw himself in front of Saviano and caught the barrage of bullets meant for his boss.

"Being the generous soul that he is, Big Ray's been taking care of Carlo's family ever since. He sends the widow money every month, paid for the daughter's wedding, schooling for two of the brothers, and just generally wiped up after them. In Bruno's case that included a bad-conduct discharge from the army, which is given to someone convicted repeatedly of minor offenses. Bruno's minor offenses always involved his fists."

Amanda smiled. "Lionel called him a thug."

"To put it mildly," Moran said. "I pulled his sheet. He's been pulled in half a dozen times for some form of assault."

Jake concurred. "It looks as if he tried to straighten himself out by using his army training as a medic to get jobs in the medical field, but there, too, he was mustered out."

No one could look at Amanda. Clearly, it was Bruno's medical training that inspired the use of a paralytic.

"Was it Big Ray's idea for him to work for my father, do you think?"

"No," Caleb said. "We questioned Vitale about that. Evidently, it was an unfortunate coincidence. He took the job because it was respectable. He said he thought his mother would like that."

"Then one day, Big Ray called," Pete said grimly.

Tyler called that afternoon. He was distraught and stunned and besides himself that she might have believed he had a hand in Lionel's murder. When Caleb brought him in for questioning and he realized why she'd been in Lionel's office, he was ashamed of what he'd said on that fatal day and how he'd comported himself. He admitted that when he thought it was a suicide, he was concerned about the effect of their argument. Now, his fear was that she believed he had had no feelings for Lionel whatsoever. His feelings were confused, but admiration and respect were part of the mix. Most of all, he was worried about her. He inquired about the state of her health and asked for her forgiveness. She gave him that, along with an invitation to visit her and the promise of her continued friendship. He gladly said yes to both.

Later that evening, after everyone had gone, Jake returned. Amanda had dozed off. When she woke, he was putting some flowers in a vase—pink camellias.

"I know these have a special meaning for you. I brought them because you're special to me." He bent down and kissed her forehead. Her jaw was puffy and badly discolored. "How're you feeling?"

"Loved," she said, marveling at the feeling. "And not just by you."

"I think I'm jealous." He feigned distress.

"Don't be. You're way up there on my list of favorites."

"I don't do second," he said, shaking his head.

"I'm aware," she said, stifling a smile. "When your mother was here, she said she would've had you after Jocelyn, but you insisted on being her firstborn."

"I've been meaning to talk to Grace about what she reveals and to whom."

"She's a terrific lady, your mom."

"Speaking of moms, yours has invited me to come to California to meet her." Shy was not a word usually associated with Jake Fowler. Amanda couldn't help but take note of the moment. "I thought we'd go together. After you're healed and everything."

"Sounds like a plan."

"Speaking of plans, what're you going to do about your name? Are you going to keep Amanda Maxwell? Or resume being Erica Baird?"

Amanda had been thinking about that for longer than Jake might imagine. Almost from the day she reunited with Lionel.

"I can't be Erica Baird. She's dead. But I've spent a very long time creating and building and being Amanda Maxwell. I like who she is. I like what she does and where she lives. I like her colleagues and her friends. And I'm crazy about the guy who's crazy about her."

Jake actually blushed. "In that case, how would you feel about changing your address? And maybe, one day," he said, flashing those incredible dimples, "your name?"

She had thought about that, too, also for longer than he might imagine. "I've changed my name too many times." His face fell. "How would you feel about changing yours?"

He was totally confused, afraid to open his mouth and say the wrong thing. She was completely amused.

"Okay, how about compromising with a hyphen?"

"As in Fowler-Maxwell?"

"Or Maxwell-Fowler. I'm willing to negotiate the point."

"Well, I should hope so!" Jake smiled.

They both knew she didn't have to negotiate. Anyway she wanted it was fine with him.

"And what about your address?" he asked. "How would you feel about getting a new one?"

Her eyes welled. For so long, she had feared this was beyond her reach.

"Here. There. Somewhere. Anywhere would be wonderful with you!"

She laughed at the thought of it. It felt so good to be free of the past and talking about a future.

"As long as we're not stuck in the middle of nowhere," she said quietly. "I've spent enough time there already."